To Sally,

from [signature]

2007

MARK

THE TIME QUARTET

To Alex
from Mama
with love

2016

BY MADELEINE L'ENGLE

THE L'ENGLE

THOSE WHO CROSS AND CONNECT
CHRONOS * * AND *KAIROS* *

Canon Tallis
The Arm of the Starfish, The Young Unicorns,
A Circle of Quiet, The Summer of the Great-grandmother,
Dragons in the Waters, The Irrational Season, Walking on Water

Adam Eddington
(Starfish, Light)

Mr. Theotocopoulous
(Unicorns, Dragons)

Katherine Forrester = Justin Michel Vigneras
(A Severed Wasp, The Small Rain)

Felix Bodeway
(Wasp, Rain)

Zachary Gray
(Lotus, Moon, Light, Acceptable)

Virginia Bowen Porcher
(A Winter's Love, Lotus)

Frank Rowan
(Camilla, Lotus)

Emily Gregory
(Wasp, Unicorns)

Philippa Hunter
(Wasp, And Both Were Young)

Theron Renier = Stella
(The Other Side of the Sun)

Leonis Phair (Dragons)	**Simon Renier** (Dragons)	**Mimi Renier** **Oppenheimer** (Wasp)
	Queron Renier **"Renny"** (Lotus)	

*Kairos is real time, pure numbers with no measurement.
**Chronos is ordinary, wrist-watch, alarm-clock time.

FAMILY TREE

THE MURRY-O'KEEFES, *KAIROS* *

A Wrinkle in Time, A Wind in the Door, A Swiftly Tilting Planet, Many Waters, An Acceptable Time

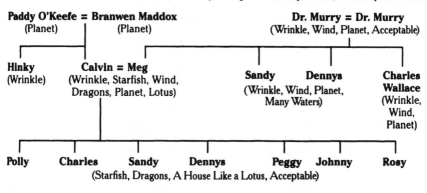

Paddy O'Keefe = Branwen Maddox
(Planet)   (Planet)

Dr. Murry = Dr. Murry
(Wrinkle, Wind, Planet, Acceptable)

Hinky
(Wrinkle)

Calvin = Meg
(Wrinkle, Starfish, Wind, Dragons, Planet, Lotus)

Sandy   Dennys
(Wrinkle, Wind, Planet, Many Waters)

Charles Wallace
(Wrinkle, Wind, Planet)

Polly   Charles   Sandy   Dennys   Peggy   Johnny   Rosy
(Starfish, Dragons, A House Like a Lotus, Acceptable)

THE AUSTINS, *CHRONOS* * *

Meet the Austins, The Moon by Night, The Twenty-four Days before Christmas, The Young Unicorns, A Ring of Endless Light, The Anti-Muffins

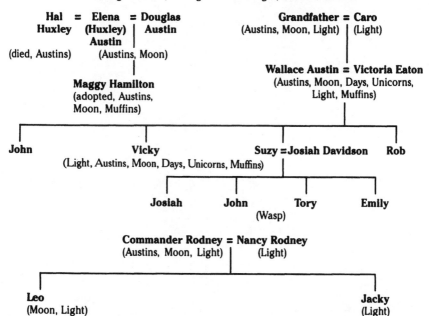

Hal = Elena = Douglas
Huxley   (Huxley)   Austin
    Austin
(died, Austins)   (Austins, Moon)

Grandfather = Caro
(Austins, Moon, Light) | (Light)

Maggy Hamilton
(adopted, Austins, Moon, Muffins)

Wallace Austin = Victoria Eaton
(Austins, Moon, Days, Unicorns, Light, Muffins)

John   Vicky   Suzy = Josiah Davidson   Rob
(Light, Austins, Moon, Days, Unicorns, Muffins)

Josiah   John   Tory   Emily
(Wasp)

Commander Rodney = Nancy Rodney
(Austins, Moon, Light)   (Light)

Leo
(Moon, Light)

Jacky
(Light)

THE
TIME QUARTET

A WRINKLE IN TIME
A WIND IN THE DOOR
A SWIFTLY TILTING PLANET
MANY WATERS

Madeleine L'Engle

50 YEARS SFBC SCIENCE FICTION

First SFBC Science Fiction Printing: September 2003

Published by arrangement with:
Farrar, Straus & Giroux
19 Union Square West
New York, NY 10003

Visit us online at http://www.sfbc.com

ISBN # 0-7394-3970-7

Printed in the United States of America.

CONTENTS

A WRINKLE IN TIME

For
Charles Wadsworth Camp
and
Wallace Collin Franklin

Contents

1 Mrs Whatsit

It was a dark and stormy night.

In her attic bedroom Margaret Murry, wrapped in an old patchwork quilt, sat on the foot of her bed and watched the trees tossing in the frenzied lashing of the wind. Behind the trees clouds scudded frantically across the sky. Every few moments the moon ripped through them, creating wraithlike shadows that raced along the ground.

The house shook.

Wrapped in her quilt, Meg shook.

She wasn't usually afraid of weather.—It's not just the weather, she thought.—It's the weather on top of everything else. On top of me. On top of Meg Murry doing everything wrong.

School. School was all wrong. She'd been dropped down to the lowest section in her grade. That morning one of her teachers had said crossly, "Really, Meg, I don't understand how a child with parents as brilliant as yours are supposed to be can be such a poor student. If you don't manage to do a little better you'll have to stay back next year."

During lunch she'd roughhoused a little to try to make herself feel better, and one of the girls said scornfully, "After all, Meg, we aren't grade-school kids any more. Why do you always act like such a baby?"

And on the way home from school, as she walked up the road with her arms full of books, one of the boys had said something about her "dumb baby brother." At this she'd thrown the books on the side of the road and tackled him with every ounce of strength she had, and arrived home with her blouse torn and a big bruise under one eye.

Sandy and Dennys, her ten-year-old twin brothers, who got home from school an hour earlier than she did, were disgusted. "Let *us* do the fighting when it's necessary," they told her.

—A delinquent, that's what I am, she thought grimly.—That's what they'll be saying next. Not Mother. But Them. Everybody Else. I wish Father—

But it was still not possible to think about her father without the danger of tears. Only her mother could talk about him in a natural way, saying, "When your father gets back—"

Gets back from where? And when? Surely her mother must know what people were saying, must be aware of the smugly vicious gossip. Surely it must hurt her as it did Meg. But if it did she gave no outward sign. Nothing ruffled the serenity of her expression.

—Why can't I hide it, too? Meg thought. Why do I always have to *show* everything?

The window rattled madly in the wind, and she pulled the quilt close about her. Curled up on one of her pillows, a gray fluff of kitten yawned, showing its pink tongue, tucked its head under again, and went back to sleep.

Everybody was asleep. Everybody except Meg. Even Charles Wallace, the "dumb baby brother," who had an uncanny way of knowing when she was awake and unhappy, and who would come, so many nights, tiptoeing up the attic stairs to her—even Charles Wallace was asleep.

How could they sleep? All day on the radio there had been hurricane warnings. How could they leave her up in the attic in the rickety brass bed, knowing that the roof might be blown right off the house and she tossed out into the wild night sky to land who knows where?

Her shivering grew uncontrollable.

—You asked to have the attic bedroom, she told herself savagely.— Mother let you have it because you're the oldest. It's a privilege, not a punishment.

"Not during a hurricane, it isn't a privilege," she said aloud. She tossed the quilt down on the foot of the bed, and stood up. The kitten stretched luxuriously, and looked up at her with huge, innocent eyes.

"Go back to sleep," Meg said. "Just be glad you're a kitten and not a monster like me." She looked at herself in the wardrobe mirror and made a horrible face, baring a mouthful of teeth covered with braces. Automatically she pushed her glasses into position, ran her fingers through her mouse-brown hair, so that it stood wildly on end, and let out a sigh almost as noisy as the wind.

The wide wooden floorboards were cold against her feet. Wind blew in the crevices about the window frame, in spite of the protection the storm sash was supposed to offer. She could hear wind howling in the chimneys. From all the way downstairs she could hear Fortinbras, the big black dog, starting to bark. He must be frightened, too. What was he barking at? Fortinbras never barked without reason.

Suddenly she remembered that when she had gone to the post office to pick up the mail she'd heard about a tramp who was supposed to have stolen twelve sheets from Mrs. Buncombe, the constable's wife. They hadn't caught him, and maybe he was heading for the Murrys' house right now, isolated on a back road as it was; and this time maybe he'd be after more than sheets. Meg hadn't paid much attention to the talk about the tramp at the time, because the postmistress, with a sugary smile, had asked if she'd heard from her father lately.

She left her little room and made her way through the shadows of the main attic, bumping against the ping-pong table.—Now I'll have a bruise on my hip on top of everything else, she thought.

Next she walked into her old dolls' house, Charles Wallace's rocking horse, the twins' electric trains. "Why must everything happen to me?" she demanded of a large teddy bear.

At the foot of the attic stairs she stood still and listened. Not a sound from Charles Wallace's room on the right. On the left, in her parents' room, not a rustle from her mother sleeping alone in the great double bed. She tiptoed down the hall and into the twins' room, pushing again at her glasses as though they could help her to see better in the dark. Dennys was snoring. Sandy murmured something about baseball and subsided. The twins didn't have any problems. They weren't great students, but they weren't bad ones, either. They were perfectly content with a succession of B's and an occasional A or C. They were strong and fast runners and good at games, and when cracks were made about anybody in the Murry family, they weren't made about Sandy and Dennys.

She left the twins' room and went on downstairs, avoiding the creaking seventh step. Fortinbras had stopped barking. It wasn't the tramp this time, then. Fort would go on barking if anybody was around.

—But suppose the tramp *does* come? Suppose he has a knife? Nobody lives near enough to hear if we screamed and screamed and screamed. Nobody'd care, anyhow.

—I'll make myself some cocoa, she decided.—That'll cheer me up, and if the roof blows off, at least I won't go off with it.

In the kitchen a light was already on, and Charles Wallace was sitting at the table drinking milk and eating bread and jam. He looked very small and vulnerable sitting there alone in the big old-fashioned kitchen, a blond little boy in faded blue Dr. Dentons, his feet swinging a good six inches above the floor.

"Hi," he said cheerfully. "I've been waiting for you."

From under the table where he was lying at Charles Wallace's feet, hoping for a crumb or two, Fortinbras raised his slender dark head in greeting to Meg, and his tail thumped against the floor. Fortinbras had arrived on their doorstep, a half-grown puppy, scrawny and abandoned, one winter night. He was, Meg's father had decided, part Llewellyn setter and part greyhound, and he had a slender, dark beauty that was all his own.

"Why didn't you come up to the attic?" Meg asked her brother, speaking as though he were at least her own age. "I've been scared stiff."

"Too windy up in that attic of yours," the little boy said. "I knew you'd be down. I put some milk on the stove for you. It ought to be hot by now."

How did Charles Wallace always know about her? How could he always tell? He never knew—or seemed to care—what Dennys or Sandy were thinking. It was his mother's mind, and Meg's, that he probed with frightening accuracy.

Was it because people were a little afraid of him that they whispered about the Murrys' youngest child, who was rumored to be not quite bright? "I've heard that clever people often have subnormal children," Meg had once overheard. "The two boys seem to be nice, regular children, but that unattractive girl and the baby boy certainly aren't all there."

It was true that Charles Wallace seldom spoke when anybody was around, so that many people thought he'd never learned to talk. And it was true that he hadn't talked at all until he was almost four. Meg would turn white with fury when people looked at him and clucked, shaking their heads sadly.

"Don't worry about Charles Wallace, Meg," her father had once told her. Meg remembered it very clearly because it was shortly before he went away. "There's nothing the matter with his mind. He just does things in his own way and in his own time."

"I don't want him to grow up to be dumb like me," Meg had said.

"Oh, my darling, you're not dumb," her father answered. "You're like Charles Wallace. Your development has to go at its own pace. It just doesn't happen to be the usual pace."

"How do you *know*?" Meg had demanded. "How do you *know* I'm not dumb? Isn't it just because you love me?"

"I love you, but that's not what tells me. Mother and I've given you a number of tests, you know."

Yes, that was true. Meg had realized that some of the "games" her parents played with her were tests of some kind, and that there had been more for her and Charles Wallace than for the twins. "IQ tests, you mean?"

"Yes, some of them."

"Is my IQ okay?"

"More than okay."

"What is it?"

"That I'm not going to tell you. But it assures me that both you and Charles Wallace will be able to do pretty much whatever you like when you grow up to yourselves. You just wait till Charles Wallace starts to talk. You'll see."

How right he had been about that, though he himself had left before Charles Wallace began to speak, suddenly, with none of the usual baby preliminaries, using entire sentences. How proud he would have been!

"You'd better check the milk," Charles Wallace said to Meg now, his diction clearer and cleaner than that of most five-year-olds. "You know you don't like it when it gets a skin on top."

"You put in more than twice enough milk." Meg peered into the saucepan.

Charles Wallace nodded serenely. "I thought Mother might like some."

"I might like what?" a voice said, and there was their mother standing in the doorway.

"Cocoa," Charles Wallace said. "Would you like a liverwurst-and-cream-cheese sandwich? I'll be happy to make you one."

"That would be lovely," Mrs. Murry said, "but I can make it myself if you're busy."

"No trouble at all." Charles Wallace slid down from his chair and trotted over to the refrigerator, his pajamaed feet padding softly as a kitten's. "How about you, Meg?" he asked. "Sandwich?"

"Yes, please," she said. "But not liverwurst. Do we have any tomatoes?"

Charles Wallace peered into the crisper. "One. All right if I use it on Meg, Mother?"

"To what better use could it be put?" Mrs. Murry smiled. "But not so loud, please, Charles. That is, unless you want the twins downstairs, too."

"Let's be exclusive," Charles Wallace said. "That's my new word for the day. Impressive, isn't it?"

"Prodigious," Mrs. Murry said. "Meg, come let me look at that bruise."

Meg knelt at her mother's feet. The warmth and light of the kitchen had relaxed her so that her attic fears were gone. The cocoa steamed fragrantly in the saucepan; geraniums bloomed on the windowsills and there was a bouquet of tiny yellow chrysanthemums in the center of the table. The curtains, red, with a blue-and-green geometrical pattern, were drawn, and seemed to reflect their cheerfulness throughout the room. The furnace purred like a great, sleepy animal; the lights glowed with steady radiance; outside, alone in the dark, the wind still battered against the house, but the angry power that had frightened Meg while she was alone in the attic was subdued by the familiar comfort of the kitchen. Underneath Mrs. Murry's chair Fortinbras let out a contented sigh.

Mrs. Murry gently touched Meg's bruised cheek. Meg looked up at her mother, half in loving admiration, half in sullen resentment. It was not an advantage to have a mother who was a scientist and a beauty as well. Mrs. Murry's flaming red hair, creamy skin, and violet eyes with long dark lashes seemed even more spectacular in comparison with Meg's outrageous plainness. Meg's hair had been passable as long as she wore it tidily in braids. When she went into high school it was cut, and now she and her mother struggled with putting it up, but one side would come out curly and the other straight, so that she looked even plainer than before.

"You don't know the meaning of moderation, do you, my darling?" Mrs. Murry asked. "A happy medium is something I wonder if you'll ever learn. That's a nasty bruise the Henderson boy gave you. By the way, shortly after you'd gone to bed his mother called up to complain about how badly you'd hurt him. I told her that since he's a year older and at least twenty-five pounds heavier than you are, I thought I was the one who ought to be doing the complaining. But she seemed to think it was all your fault."

"I suppose that depends on how you look at it," Meg said. "Usually, no matter what happens, people think it's my fault, even if I have nothing to do with it at all. But I'm sorry I tried to fight him. It's just been an awful week. And I'm full of bad feeling."

Mrs. Murry stroked Meg's shaggy head. "Do you know why?"

"I *hate* being an oddball," Meg said. "It's hard on Sandy and Dennys, too. I don't know if they're really like everybody else, or if they're just able to pretend they are. I try to pretend, but it isn't any help."

"You're much too straightforward to be able to pretend to be what you aren't," Mrs. Murry said. "I'm sorry, Meglet. Maybe if Father were here he could help you, but I don't think I can do anything till you've managed to plow through some more time. Then things will be easier for you. But that isn't much help right now, is it?"

"Maybe if I weren't so repulsive-looking—maybe if I were pretty like you—"

"Mother's not a bit pretty; she's beautiful," Charles Wallace announced, slicing liverwurst. "Therefore I bet she was awful at your age."

"How right you are," Mrs. Murry said. "Just give yourself time, Meg."

"Lettuce on your sandwich, Mother?" Charles Wallace asked.

"No, thanks."

He cut the sandwich into sections, put it on a plate, and set it in front of his mother. "Yours'll be along in just a minute, Meg. I think I'll talk to Mrs Whatsit about you."

"Who's Mrs Whatsit?" Meg asked.

"I think I want to be exclusive about her for a while," Charles Wallace said. "Onion salt?"

"Yes, please."

"What's Mrs Whatsit stand for?" Mrs. Murry asked.

"That's her name," Charles Wallace answered. "You know the old shingled house back in the woods that the kids won't go near because they say it's haunted? That's where they live."

"They?"

"Mrs Whatsit and her two friends. I was out with Fortinbras a couple of days ago—you and the twins were at school, Meg. We like to walk in the woods, and suddenly he took off after a squirrel and I took off after him and we ended up by the haunted house, so I met them by accident, as you might say."

"But nobody lives there," Meg said.

"Mrs Whatsit and her friends do. They're very enjoyable."

"Why didn't you tell me about it before?" Mrs. Murry asked. "And you know you're not supposed to go off our property without permission, Charles."

"I know," Charles said. "That's one reason I didn't tell you. I just rushed off after Fortinbras without thinking. And then I decided, well, I'd better save them for an emergency, anyhow."

A fresh gust of wind took the house and shook it, and suddenly the rain began to lash against the windows.

"I don't think I like this wind," Meg said nervously.

"We'll lose some shingles off the roof, that's certain," Mrs. Murry said. "But this house has stood for almost two hundred years and I think it will last a little longer, Meg. There's been many a high wind up on this hill."

"But this is a hurricane!" Meg wailed. "The radio kept saying it was a hurricane!"

"It's October," Mrs. Murry told her. "There've been storms in October before."

As Charles Wallace gave Meg her sandwich Fortinbras came out from under the table. He gave a long, low growl, and they could see the dark fur slowly rising on his back. Meg felt her own skin prickle. "What's wrong?" she asked anxiously.

Fortinbras stared at the door that opened into Mrs. Murry's laboratory, which was in the old stone dairy right off the kitchen. Beyond the lab a pantry led outdoors, though Mrs. Murry had done her best to train the family to come into the house through the garage door or the front door and not through her lab. But it was the lab door and not the garage door toward which Fortinbras was growling.

"You didn't leave any nasty-smelling chemicals cooking over a Bunsen burner, did you, Mother?" Charles Wallace asked.

Mrs. Murry stood up. "No. But I think I'd better go see what's upsetting Fort, anyhow."

"It's the tramp, I'm sure it's the tramp," Meg said nervously.

"What tramp?" Charles Wallace asked.

"They were saying at the post office this afternoon that a tramp stole all Mrs. Buncombe's sheets."

"We'd better sit on the pillowcases, then," Mrs. Murry said lightly. "I don't think even a tramp would be out on a night like this, Meg."

"But that's probably why he *is* out," Meg wailed, "trying to find a place *not* to be out."

"In which case I'll offer him the barn till morning." Mrs. Murry went briskly to the door.

"I'll go with you." Meg's voice was shrill.

"No, Meg, you stay with Charles and eat your sandwich."

"Eat!" Meg exclaimed as Mrs. Murry went out through the lab. "How does she expect me to eat?"

"Mother can take care of herself," Charles said. "Physically, that is." But he sat in his father's chair at the table and his legs kicked at the rungs; and Charles Wallace, unlike most small children, had the ability to sit still.

After a few moments that seemed like forever to Meg, Mrs. Murry came back in, holding the door open for—was it the tramp? It seemed small for Meg's idea of a tramp. The age or sex was impossible to tell, for it was completely bundled up in clothes. Several scarves of assorted colors were tied about the head, and a man's felt hat perched atop. A shocking-pink stole was knotted about a rough overcoat, and black rubber boots covered the feet.

"Mrs Whatsit," Charles said suspiciously, "what are you doing here? And at this time of night, too?"

"Now, don't you be worried, my honey." A voice emerged from

among turned-up coat collar, stole, scarves, and hat, a voice like an unoiled gate, but somehow not unpleasant.

"Mrs—uh—Whatsit—says she lost her way," Mrs. Murry said. "Would you care for some hot chocolate, Mrs Whatsit?"

"Charmed, I'm sure," Mrs Whatsit answered, taking off the hat and the stole. "It isn't so much that I lost my way as that I got blown off course. And when I realized that I was at little Charles Wallace's house I thought I'd just come in and rest a bit before proceeding on my way."

"How did you know this was Charles Wallace's house?" Meg asked.

"By the smell." Mrs Whatsit untied a blue-and-green paisley scarf, a red-and-yellow flowered print, a gold Liberty print, a red-and-black bandanna. Under all this a sparse quantity of grayish hair was tied in a small but tidy knot on top of her head. Her eyes were bright, her nose a round, soft blob, her mouth puckered like an autumn apple. "My, but it's lovely and warm in here," she said.

"Do sit down." Mrs. Murry indicated a chair. "Would you like a sandwich, Mrs Whatsit? I've had liverwurst and cream cheese; Charles has had bread and jam; and Meg, lettuce and tomato."

"Now, let me see," Mrs Whatsit pondered. "I'm passionately fond of Russian caviar."

"You peeked!" Charles cried indignantly. "We're saving that for Mother's birthday and you can't have any!"

Mrs Whatsit gave a deep and pathetic sigh.

"*No*," Charles said. "Now, you mustn't give in to her, Mother, or I shall be very angry. How about tuna-fish salad?"

"All right," Mrs Whatsit said meekly.

"I'll fix it," Meg offered, going to the pantry for a can of tuna fish.

—For crying out loud, she thought,—this old woman comes barging in on us in the middle of the night and Mother takes it as though there weren't anything peculiar about it at all. I'll bet she *is* the tramp. I'll bet she *did* steal those sheets. And she's certainly no one Charles Wallace ought to be friends with, especially when he won't even talk to ordinary people.

"I've only been in the neighborhood a short time," Mrs Whatsit was saying as Meg switched off the pantry light and came back into the kitchen with the tuna fish, "and I didn't think I was going to like the neighbors at all until dear little Charles came over with his dog."

"Mrs Whatsit," Charles Wallace demanded severely, "why did you take Mrs. Buncombe's sheets?"

"Well, I *needed* them, Charles dear."

"You must return them at once."

"But, Charles, dear, I *can't*. I've *used* them."

"It was very wrong of you," Charles Wallace scolded. "If you needed sheets that badly, you should have asked me."

Mrs Whatsit shook her head and clucked. "You can't spare any sheets. Mrs. Buncombe can."

Meg cut up some celery and mixed it in with the tuna. After a moment's hesitation she opened the refrigerator door and brought out a jar of little sweet pickles.—Though why I'm doing it for her I don't know, she thought, as she cut them up.—I don't trust her one bit.

"Tell your sister I'm all right," Mrs Whatsit said to Charles. "Tell her my intentions are good."

"The road to hell is paved with good intentions," Charles intoned.

"My, but isn't he cunning." Mrs Whatsit beamed at him fondly. "It's lucky he has someone to understand him."

"But I'm afraid he doesn't," Mrs. Murry said. "None of us is quite up to Charles."

"But at least you aren't trying to squash him down." Mrs Whatsit nodded her head vigorously. "You're letting him be himself."

"Here's your sandwich," Meg said, bringing it to Mrs Whatsit.

"Do you mind if I take off my boots before I eat?" Mrs Whatsit asked, picking up the sandwich nevertheless. "Listen." She moved her feet up and down in her boots, and they could hear water squelching. "My toes are ever so damp. The trouble is that these boots are a mite too tight for me, and I never can take them off by myself."

"I'll help you," Charles offered.

"Not you. You're not strong enough."

"I'll help." Mrs. Murry squatted at Mrs Whatsit's feet, yanking on one slick boot. When the boot came off, it came suddenly. Mrs. Murry sat down with a thump. Mrs Whatsit went tumbling backward with the chair onto the floor, sandwich held high in one old claw. Water poured out of the boot and ran over the floor and the big braided rug.

"Oh, dearie me," Mrs Whatsit said, lying on her back in the over-turned chair, her feet in the air, one in a red-and-white striped sock, the other still booted.

Mrs. Murry got to her feet. "Are you all right, Mrs Whatsit?"

"If you have some liniment I'll put it on my dignity," Mrs Whatsit said, still supine. "I think it's sprained. A little oil of cloves mixed well with garlic is rather good." And she took a large bite of sandwich.

"Do please get up," Charles said. "I don't like to see you lying there that way. You're carrying things too far."

"Have you ever tried to get to your feet with a sprained dignity?" But Mrs Whatsit scrambled up, righted the chair, and then sat back down on the floor, the booted foot stuck out in front of her, and took another bite. She moved with great agility for such an old woman. At least Meg was reasonably sure that she was an old woman, and a very old woman at that.

Mrs Whatsit, her mouth full, ordered Mrs. Murry, "Now pull while I'm already down."

Quite calmly, as though this old woman and her boots were nothing out of the ordinary, Mrs. Murry pulled until the second boot relinquished the foot. This foot was covered with a blue-and-gray Argyle sock, and Mrs Whatsit sat there, wriggling her toes, contentedly finishing her sandwich before scrambling to her feet. "Ah," she said, "that's ever so much better," and took both boots and shook them out over the sink. "My stomach is full and I'm warm inside and out and it's time I went home."

"Don't you think you'd better stay till morning?" Mrs. Murry asked.

"Oh, thank you, dearie, but there's *so* much to do I just can't waste time sitting around frivoling."

"It's much too wild a night to travel in."

"Wild nights are my glory," Mrs Whatsit said. "I just got caught in a downdraft and blown off course."

"Well, at least till your socks are dry—"

"Wet socks don't bother me. I just didn't like the water squishing around in my boots. Now, don't worry about me, lamb." ("Lamb" was not a word one would ordinarily think of calling Mrs. Murry.) "I shall just sit down for a moment and pop on my boots and then I'll be on my way. Speaking of ways, pet, by the way, there *is* such a thing as a tesseract."

Mrs. Murry went very white and with one hand reached backward and clutched at a chair for support. Her voice trembled. "What did you say?"

Mrs Whatsit tugged at her second boot. "I said," she grunted, shoving her foot down in, "that there is"—shove—"such a thing"—shove—"as a tesseract." Her foot went down into the boot, and grabbing shawls, scarves, and hat, she hustled out the door. Mrs. Murry stayed very still, making no move to help the old woman. As the door opened, Fortinbras streaked in, panting, wet and shiny as a seal. He looked at Mrs. Murry and whined.

The door slammed.

"Mother, what's the matter!" Meg cried. "What did she say? What is it?"

"The tesseract—" Mrs. Murry whispered. "What did she mean? How could she have known?"

2 Mrs Who

When Meg woke to the jangling of her alarm clock the wind was still blowing but the sun was shining; the worst of the storm was over. She sat up in bed, shaking her head to clear it.

It must have been a dream. She'd been frightened by the storm and worried about the tramp, so she'd just dreamed about going down to the kitchen and seeing Mrs Whatsit and having her mother get all frightened and upset by that word—what was it? Tess—tess something.

She dressed hurriedly, picked up the kitten still curled up on the bed, and dumped it unceremoniously on the floor. The kitten yawned, stretched, gave a piteous miaow, trotted out of the attic and down the stairs. Meg made her bed and hurried after it. In the kitchen her mother was making French toast and the twins were already at the table. The kitten was lapping milk out of a saucer.

"Where's Charles?" Meg asked.

"Still asleep. We had rather an interrupted night, if you remember."

"I hoped it was a dream," Meg said.

Her mother carefully turned over four slices of French toast, then said in a steady voice, "No, Meg. Don't hope it was a dream. I don't understand it any more than you do, but one thing I've learned is that you don't have to understand things for them to *be*. I'm sorry I showed you I was upset. Your father and I used to have a joke about tesseract."

"What *is* a tesseract?" Meg asked.

"It's a concept." Mrs. Murry handed the twins the syrup. "I'll try to explain it to you later. There isn't time before school."

"I don't see why you didn't wake us up," Dennys said. "It's a gyp we missed out on all the fun."

"You'll be a lot more awake in school today than I will." Meg took her French toast to the table.

"Who cares," Sandy said. "If you're going to let old tramps come into the house in the middle of the night, Mother, you ought to have Den and me around to protect you."

"After all, Father would expect us to," Dennys added.

"We know you have a great mind and all, Mother," Sandy said, "but you don't have much sense. And certainly Meg and Charles don't."

"I know. We're morons." Meg was bitter.

"I wish you wouldn't be such a dope, Meg. Syrup, please." Sandy reached across the table. "You don't have to take everything so personally. Use a happy medium, for heaven's sake. You just goof around in school and look out the window and don't pay any attention."

"You just make things harder for yourself," Dennys said. "And Charles Wallace is going to have an awful time next year when he starts school. We know he's bright, but he's so funny when he's around other people, and they're so used to thinking he's dumb, I don't know what's going to happen to him. Sandy and I'll sock anybody who picks on him, but that's about all we can do."

"Let's not worry about next year till we get through this one," Mrs. Murry said. "More French toast, boys?"

At school Meg was tired and her eyelids sagged and her mind wandered. In social studies she was asked to name the principal imports and exports of Nicaragua, and though she had looked them up dutifully the evening before, now she could remember none of them. The teacher was sarcastic, the rest of the class laughed, and she flung herself down in her seat in a fury. "Who cares about the imports and exports of Nicaragua, anyhow?" she muttered.

"If you're going to be rude, Margaret, you may leave the room," the teacher said.

"Okay, I will." Meg flounced out.

During study hall the principal sent for her. "What seems to be the problem now, Meg?" he asked, pleasantly enough.

Meg looked sulkily down at the floor. "Nothing, Mr. Jenkins."

"Miss Porter tells me you were inexcusably rude."

Meg shrugged.

"Don't you realize that you just make everything harder for yourself by your attitude?" the principal asked. "Now, Meg, I'm convinced that you can do the work and keep up with your grade if you will apply yourself, but some of your teachers are not. You're going to have to do something about yourself. Nobody can do it for you." Meg was silent.

"Well? What about it, Meg?"

"I don't know what to do," Meg said.

"You could do your homework, for one thing. Wouldn't your mother help you?"

"If I asked her to."

"Meg, is something troubling you? Are you unhappy at home?" Mr. Jenkins asked.

At last Meg looked at him, pushing at her glasses in a characteristic gesture. "Everything's *fine* at home."

"I'm glad to hear it. But I know it must be hard on you to have your father away."

Meg eyed the principal warily, and ran her tongue over the barbed line of her braces.

"Have you had any news from him lately?"

Meg was sure it was not only imagination that made her feel that behind Mr. Jenkins's surface concern was a gleam of avid curiosity. Wouldn't he like to know! she thought. And if I knew anything he's the last person I'd tell. Well, one of the last.

The postmistress must know that it was almost a year now since the last letter, and heaven knows how many people *she'd* told, or what unkind guesses she'd made about the reason for the long silence.

Mr. Jenkins waited for an answer, but Meg only shrugged.

"Just what was your father's line of business?" Mr. Jenkins asked. "Some kind of scientist, wasn't he?"

"He *is* a physicist." Meg bared her teeth to reveal the two ferocious lines of braces.

"Meg, don't you think you'd make a better adjustment to life if you faced facts?"

"I do face facts," Meg said. "They're lots easier to face than people, I can tell you."

"Then why don't you face facts about your father?"

"You leave my father out of it!" Meg shouted.

"Stop bellowing," Mr. Jenkins said sharply. "Do you want the entire school to hear you?"

"So what?" Meg demanded. "I'm not ashamed of anything I'm saying. Are you?"

Mr. Jenkins sighed. "Do you enjoy being the most belligerent, uncooperative child in school?"

Meg ignored this. She leaned over the desk toward the principal. "Mr. Jenkins, you've met my mother, haven't you? You can't accuse her of not facing facts, can you? She's a scientist. She has doctor's degrees in both biology and bacteriology. Her *business* is facts. When she tells me that my father isn't coming home, I'll believe it. As long as she says Father *is* coming home, then I'll believe that."

Mr. Jenkins sighed again. "No doubt your mother wants to believe that your father is coming home, Meg. Very well, I can't do anything else with you. Go on back to study hall. Try to be a little less antagonistic. Maybe your work would improve if your general attitude were more tractable."

When Meg got home from school her mother was in the lab, the twins were at Little League, and Charles Wallace, the kitten, and Fortinbras were waiting for her. Fortinbras jumped up, put his front paws on her shoulders, and gave her a kiss, and the kitten rushed to his empty saucer and mewed loudly.

"Come on," Charles Wallace said. "Let's go."

"Where?" Meg asked. "I'm hungry, Charles. I don't want to go anywhere till I've had something to eat." She was still sore from the interview with Mr. Jenkins, and her voice sounded cross. Charles Wallace looked at her thoughtfully as she went to the refrigerator and gave the kitten some milk, then drank a mugful herself.

He handed her a paper bag. "Here's a sandwich and some cookies and an apple. I thought we'd better go see Mrs Whatsit."

"Oh, golly," Meg said. "*Why*, Charles?"

"You're still uneasy about her, aren't you?" Charles asked.

"Well, yes."

"Don't be. She's all right. I promise you. She's on our side."

"How do you know?"

"*Meg*," he said impatiently. "I *know*."

"But why should we go see her now?"

"I want to find out more about that tesseract thing. Didn't you see how it upset Mother? You know when Mother can't control the way she feels, when she lets us see she's upset, then it's something big."

Meg thought for a moment. "Okay, let's go. But let's take Fortinbras with us."

"Well, of course. He needs the exercise."

They set off, Fortinbras rushing ahead, then doubling back to the two children, then leaping off again. The Murrys lived about four miles out of the village. Behind the house was a pine woods and it was through this that Charles Wallace took Meg.

"Charles, you know she's going to get in awful trouble—Mrs Whatsit, I mean—if they find out she's broken into the haunted house. And taking Mrs. Buncombe's sheets and everything. They could send her to jail."

"One of the reasons I want to go over this afternoon is to warn them."

"Them?"

"I told you she was there with her two friends. I'm not even sure it was Mrs Whatsit herself who took the sheets, though I wouldn't put it past her."

"But what would she want all those sheets for?"

"I intend to ask her," Charles Wallace said, "and to tell them they'd better be more careful. I don't really think they'll let anybody find them, but I just thought we ought to mention the possibility. Sometimes during vacations some of the boys go out there looking for thrills, but I don't think anybody's apt to right now, what with basketball and everything."

They walked in silence for a moment through the fragrant woods, the rusty pine needles gentle under their feet. Up above them the wind made music in the branches. Charles Wallace slipped his hand confidingly in Meg's, and the sweet, little-boy gesture warmed her so that she felt the tense knot inside her begin to loosen. *Charles* loves me at any rate, she thought.

"School awful again today?" he asked after a while.

"Yes. I got sent to Mr. Jenkins. He made snide remarks about Father."

Charles Wallace nodded sagely. "I know."

"*How* do you know?"

Charles Wallace shook his head. "I can't quite explain. You tell me, that's all."

"But I never say anything. You just seem to know."

"Everything about you tells me," Charles said.

"How about the twins?" Meg asked. "Do you know about them, too?"

"I suppose I could if I wanted to. If they needed me. But it's sort of tiring, so I just concentrate on you and Mother."

"You mean you read our minds?"

Charles Wallace looked troubled. "I don't think it's that. It's being able to understand a sort of language, like sometimes if I concentrate very hard I can understand the wind talking with the trees. You tell me, you see, sort of inad—inadvertently. That's a good word, isn't it? I got Mother to look it up in the dictionary for me this morning. I really must learn to read, except I'm afraid it will make it awfully hard for me in school next year if I already know things. I think it will be better if people go on thinking I'm not very bright. They won't hate me quite so much."

Ahead of them Fortinbras started barking loudly, the warning bay that usually told them that a car was coming up the road or that someone was at the door.

"Somebody's here," Charles Wallace said sharply. "Somebody's hanging around the house. Come *on*." He started to run, his short legs straining. At the edge of the woods Fortinbras stood in front of a boy, barking furiously.

As they came panting up the boy said, "For crying out loud, call off your dog."

"Who is he?" Charles Wallace asked Meg.

"Calvin O'Keefe. He's in Regional, but he's older than I am. He's a big bug."

"It's all right, fella. I'm not going to hurt you," the boy said to Fortinbras.

"Sit, Fort," Charles Wallace commanded, and Fortinbras dropped to his haunches in front of the boy, a low growl still pulsing in his dark throat.

"Okay." Charles Wallace put his hands on his hips. "Now tell us what you're doing here."

"I might ask the same of you," the boy said with some indignation. "Aren't you two of the Murry kids? This isn't your property, is it?" He started to move, but Fortinbras's growl grew louder and he stopped.

"Tell me about him, Meg," Charles Wallace demanded.

"What would I know about him?" Meg asked. "He's a couple of grades above me, and he's on the basketball team."

"Just because I'm tall." Calvin sounded a little embarrassed. Tall he certainly was, and skinny. His bony wrists stuck out of the sleeves of his blue sweater; his worn corduroy trousers were three inches too short. He had orange hair that needed cutting and the appropriate freckles to go with it. His eyes were an oddly bright blue.

"Tell us what you're doing here," Charles Wallace said.

"What *is* this? The third degree? Aren't you the one who's supposed to be the moron?"

Meg flushed with rage, but Charles Wallace answered placidly, "That's right. If you want me to call my dog off you'd better give."

"Most peculiar moron I've ever met," Calvin said. "I just came to get away from my family."

Charles Wallace nodded. "What kind of family?"

"They all have runny noses. I'm third from the top of eleven kids. I'm a sport."

At that Charles Wallace grinned widely. "So'm I."

"I don't mean like in baseball," Calvin said.

"Neither do I."

"I mean like in biology," Calvin said suspiciously.

"*A change in gene,*" Charles Wallace quoted, "*resulting in the appearance in the offspring of a character which is not present in the parents but which is potentially transmissible to their offspring.*"

"What gives around here?" Calvin asked. "I was told you couldn't talk."

"Thinking I'm a moron gives people something to feel smug about," Charles Wallace said. "Why should I disillusion them? How old are you, Cal?"

"Fourteen."

"What grade?"

"Junior. Eleventh. I'm bright. Listen, did anybody ask you to come here this afternoon?"

Charles Wallace, holding Fort by the collar, looked at Calvin suspiciously. "What do you mean, *ask?*"

Calvin shrugged. "You still don't trust me, do you?"

"I don't *dis*trust you," Charles Wallace said.

"Do you want to tell me why you're here, then?"

"Fort and Meg and I decided to go for a walk. We often do in the afternoon."

Calvin dug his hands down in his pockets. "You're holding out on me."

"So're you," Charles Wallace said.

"Okay, old sport," Calvin said, "I'll tell you this much. Sometimes I get a feeling about things. You might call it a compulsion. Do you know what compulsion means?"

"*Constraint. Obligation. Because one is compelled.* Not a very good definition, but it's the Concise Oxford."

"Okay, okay," Calvin sighed. "I must remember I'm preconditioned in my concept of your mentality."

Meg sat down on the coarse grass at the edge of the woods. Fort gently twisted his collar out of Charles Wallace's hands and came over to Meg, lying down beside her and putting his head in her lap.

Calvin tried now politely to direct his words toward Meg as well as Charles Wallace. "When I get this feeling, this compulsion, I always do what it tells me. I can't explain where it comes from or how I get it, and it doesn't happen very often. But I obey it. And this afternoon I had a feeling that I must come over to the haunted house. That's all I know, kid. I'm not holding anything back. Maybe it's because I'm supposed to meet you. You tell *me*."

Charles Wallace looked at Calvin probingly for a moment; then an almost glazed look came into his eyes, and he seemed to be thinking at him. Calvin stood very still, and waited.

At last Charles Wallace said, "Okay. I believe you. But I can't tell you. I think I'd like to trust you. Maybe you'd better come home with us and have dinner."

"Well, sure, but—what would your mother say to that?" Calvin asked.

"She'd be delighted. Mother's all right. She's not one of us. But she's all right."

"What about Meg?"

"Meg has it tough," Charles Wallace said. "She's not really one thing or the other."

"What do you mean, *one of us*?" Meg demanded. "What do you mean I'm not one thing or the other?"

"Not now, Meg," Charles Wallace said. "Slowly. I'll tell you about it later." He looked at Calvin, then seemed to make a quick decision. "Okay, let's take him to meet Mrs Whatsit. If he's not okay she'll know." He started off on his short legs toward the dilapidated old house.

The haunted house was half in the shadows of the clump of elms in which it stood. The elms were almost bare now, and the ground around the house was yellow with damp leaves. The late afternoon light had a greenish cast which the blank windows reflected in a sinister way. An unhinged shutter thumped. Something else creaked. Meg did not wonder that the house had a reputation for being haunted.

A board was nailed across the front door, but Charles Wallace led the way around to the back. The door there appeared to be nailed shut, too, but Charles Wallace knocked and the door swung slowly outward, creaking on rusty hinges. Up in one of the elms an old black crow gave its raucous cry, and a woodpecker went into a wild rat-a-tat-tat. A large gray rat scuttled around the corner of the house and Meg let out a stifled shriek.

"They get a lot of fun out of using all the typical props," Charles Wallace said in a reassuring voice. "Come on. Follow me."

Calvin put a strong hand to Meg's elbow, and Fort pressed against her leg. Happiness at their concern was so strong in her that her panic fled, and she followed Charles Wallace into the dark recesses of the house without fear.

They entered into a sort of kitchen. There was a huge fireplace with a big black pot hanging over a merry fire. Why had there been no smoke visible from the chimney? Something in the pot was bubbling, and it smelled more like one of Mrs. Murry's chemical messes than something to eat. In a dilapidated Boston rocker sat a plump little woman. She wasn't Mrs Whatsit, so she must, Meg decided, be one of Mrs Whatsit's two friends. She wore enormous spectacles, twice as thick and twice as large as Meg's, and she was sewing busily, with rapid jabbing stitches, on a sheet. Several other sheets lay on the dusty floor.

Charles Wallace went up to her. "I really don't think you ought to have taken Mrs. Buncombe's sheets without consulting me," he said, as cross and bossy as only a very small boy can be. "What on earth do you want them for?"

The plump little woman beamed at him. "Why, Charlsie, my pet! *Le coeur a ses raisons que la raison ne connaît point.* French. Pascal. *The heart has its reasons, whereof reason knows nothing.*"

"But that's not appropriate at all," Charles said crossly.

"Your mother would find it so." A smile seemed to gleam through the roundness of spectacles.

"I'm not talking about my mother's feelings about my father," Charles Wallace scolded. "I'm talking about Mrs. Buncombe's sheets."

The little woman sighed. The enormous glasses caught the light again and shone like an owl's eyes. "In case we need ghosts, of course," she said. "I should think you'd have guessed. If we have to frighten anybody away, Whatsit thought we ought to do it appropriately. That's why it's so much fun to stay in a haunted house. But we really didn't mean you to know about the sheets. *Auf frischer Tat ertappt.* German. *In flagrante delicto.* Latin. *Caught in the act.* English. As I was saying—"

But Charles Wallace held up his hand in a peremptory gesture. "Mrs Who, do you know this boy?"

Calvin bowed. "Good afternoon, ma'am. I didn't quite catch your name."

"Mrs Who will do," the woman said. "He wasn't my idea, Charlsie, but I think he's a good one."

"Where's Mrs Whatsit?" Charles asked.

"She's busy. It's getting near time, Charlsie, getting near time. *Ab honesto virum bonum nihil deterret.* Seneca. *Nothing deters a good man from doing what is honorable.* And he's a very good man, Charlsie, darling, but right now he needs our help."

"Who?" Meg demanded.

"And little Megsie! Lovely to meet you, sweetheart. Your father, of course. Now go home, loves. The time is not yet ripe. Don't worry, we won't go without you. Get plenty of food and rest. Feed Calvin up.

Now, off with you! *Justitiae soror fides.* Latin again, of course. *Faith is the sister of justice.* Trust in us! Now shoo!" And she fluttered up from her chair and pushed them out the door with surprising power.

"Charles," Meg said. "I don't understand."

Charles took her by the hand and dragged her away from the house. Fortinbras ran on ahead, and Calvin was close behind them. "No," he said, "I don't either, yet. Not quite. I'll tell you what I know as soon as I can. But you saw Fort, didn't you? Not a growl. Not a quiver. Just as though there weren't anything strange about it. So you know it's okay. Look, do me a favor, both of you. Let's not talk about it till we've had something to eat. I need fuel so I can sort things out and assimilate them properly."

"Lead on, moron," Calvin cried gaily. "I've never even seen your house, and I have the funniest feeling that for the first time in my life I'm going home!"

3 Mrs Which

In the forest, evening was already beginning to fall, and they walked in silence. Charles and Fortinbras gamboled on ahead. Calvin walked with Meg, his fingers barely touching her arm in a protective gesture.

This has been the most impossible, the most confusing afternoon of my life, she thought, yet I don't feel confused or upset anymore; I only feel happy. Why?

"Maybe we weren't meant to meet before this," Calvin said. "I mean, I knew who you were in school and everything, but I didn't know you. But I'm glad we've met now, Meg. We're going to be friends, you know."

"I'm glad, too," Meg whispered, and they were silent again.

When they got back to the house Mrs. Murry was still in the lab. She was watching a pale blue fluid move slowly through a tube from a beaker to a retort. Over a Bunsen burner bubbled a big, earthenware dish of stew. "Don't tell Sandy and Dennys I'm cooking out here," she said. "They're always suspicious that a few chemicals may get in with the meat, but I had an experiment I wanted to stay with."

"This is Calvin O'Keefe, Mother," Meg said. "Is there enough for him, too? It smells super."

"Hello, Calvin." Mrs. Murry shook hands with him. "Nice to meet you. We aren't having anything but stew tonight, but it's a good thick one."

"Sounds wonderful to me," Calvin said. "May I use your phone, so my mother'll know where I am?"

"Of course. Show him where it is, will you, please, Meg? I won't ask you to use the one out here, if you don't mind. I'd like to finish up this experiment."

Meg led the way into the house. Charles Wallace and Fortinbras had gone off. Outdoors she could hear Sandy and Dennys hammering at the fort they were building up in one of the maples. "This way." Meg went through the kitchen and into the living room.

"I don't know why I call her when I don't come home," Calvin said, his voice bitter. "She wouldn't notice." He sighed and dialed. "Ma?" he said. "Oh, Hinky. Tell Ma I won't be home till late. Now, don't forget. I don't want to be locked out again." He hung up, looked at Meg. "Do you know how lucky you are?"

She smiled rather wryly. "Not most of the time."

"A mother like that! A house like this! Gee, your mother's gorgeous! You should see my mother. She had all her upper teeth out and Pop got her a plate but she won't wear it, and most days she doesn't even comb her hair. Not that it makes much difference when she does." He clenched his fists. "But I love her. That's the funny part of it. I love them all, and they don't give a hoot about me. Maybe that's why I call when I'm not going to be home. Because I care. Nobody else does. You don't know how lucky you are to be loved."

Meg said in a startled way, "I guess I never thought of that. I guess I just took it for granted."

Calvin looked somber; then his enormous smile lit up his face again. "Things are going to happen, Meg! Good things! I feel it!" He began wandering, still slowly, around the pleasant, if shabby, living room. He stopped before a picture on the piano of a small group of men standing together on a beach. "Who's this?"

"Oh, a bunch of scientists."

"Where?"

Meg went over to the picture. "Cape Canaveral. This one's Father."

"Which?"

"Here."

"The one with glasses?"

"Yup. The one who needs a haircut." Meg giggled, forgetting her worries in her pleasure at showing Calvin the picture. "His hair's sort of the same color as mine, and he keeps forgetting to have it cut. Mother usually ends up doing it for him—she bought clippers and stuff—because he won't take the time to go to the barber."

Calvin studied the picture. "I like him," he announced judiciously. "Looks kind of like Charles Wallace, doesn't he?"

Meg laughed again. "When Charles was a baby he looked *exactly* like Father. It was really funny."

Calvin continued to look at the picture. "He's not handsome or anything. But I like him."

Meg was indignant. "He is, too, handsome."

Calvin shook his head. "Nah. He's tall and skinny like me."

"Well, I think you're handsome," Meg said. "Father's eyes are kind of like yours, too. You know. Really blue. Only you don't notice his as much because of the glasses."

"Where is he now?"

Meg stiffened. But she didn't have to answer because the door from lab to kitchen slammed and Mrs. Murry came in, carrying a dish of stew. "Now," she called, "I'll finish this up properly on the stove. Have you done your homework, Meg?"

"Not quite," Meg said, going back into the kitchen.

"Then I'm sure Calvin won't mind if you finish before dinner."

"Sure, go ahead." Calvin fished in his pocket and pulled out a wad of folded paper. "As a matter of fact, I have some junk of mine to finish up. Math. That's one thing I have a hard time keeping up in. I'm okay on anything to do with words, but I don't do as well with numbers."

Mrs. Murry smiled. "Why don't you get Meg to help you?"

"But, see, I'm several grades above Meg."

"Try asking her to help you with your math, anyhow," Mrs. Murry suggested.

"Well, sure," Calvin said. "Here. But it's pretty complicated."

Meg smoothed out the paper and studied it. "Do they care *how* you do it?" she asked. "I mean, can you work it out your own way?"

"Well, sure, as long as I understand and get the answers right."

"Well, *we* have to do it *their* way. Now look, Calvin, don't you see how much easier it would be if you did it *this* way?" Her pencil flew over the paper.

"Hey!" Calvin said. "Hey! I think I get it. Show me once more on another one."

Again Meg's pencil was busy. "All you have to remember is that every ordinary fraction can be converted into an infinite periodic decimal fraction. See? So ³⁄₇ is 0.428571."

"This is the craziest family." Calvin grinned at her. "I suppose I should stop being surprised by now, but you're supposed to be dumb in school, always being called up on the carpet."

"Oh, I am."

"The trouble with Meg and math," Mrs. Murry said briskly, "is that Meg and her father used to play with numbers and Meg learned far too many short cuts. So when they want her to do problems the long way around at school she gets sullen and stubborn and sets up a fine mental block for herself."

"Are there any more morons like Meg and Charles around?" Calvin asked. "If so, I should meet more of them."

"It might also help if Meg's handwriting were legible," Mrs. Murry said. "With a good deal of difficulty I can usually decipher it, but I doubt very much if her teachers can, or are willing to take the time. I'm planning on giving her a typewriter for Christmas. That may be a help."

"If I get anything right, nobody'll believe it's me," Meg said.

"What's a megaparsec?" Calvin asked.

"One of Father's nicknames for me," Meg said. "It's also 3.26 million light-years."

"What's $E = mc^2$?"

"Einstein's equation."

"What's E stand for?"

"Energy."

"m?"

"Mass."

"c^2?"

"The square of the velocity of light in centimeters per second."

"By what countries is Peru bounded?"

"I haven't the faintest idea. I think it's in South America somewhere."

"What's the capital of New York?"

"Well, New York City, of course!"

"Who wrote Boswell's *Life of Johnson*?"

"Oh, Calvin, I'm not any good at English."

Calvin groaned and turned to Mrs. Murry. "I see what you mean. Her I wouldn't want to teach."

"She's a little one-sided, I grant you," Mrs. Murry said, "though I blame her father and myself for that. She still enjoys playing with her dolls' house, though."

"Mother!" Meg shrieked in agony.

"Oh, darling, I'm sorry," Mrs. Murry said swiftly. "But I'm sure Calvin understands what I mean."

With a sudden enthusiastic gesture Calvin flung his arms out wide, as though he were embracing Meg and her mother, the whole house. "How did all this happen? Isn't it wonderful? I feel as though I were just being born! I'm not alone any more! Do you realize what that means to me?"

"But you're good at basketball and things," Meg protested. "You're good in school. Everybody likes you."

"For all the most unimportant reasons," Calvin said. "There hasn't been anybody, anybody in the world I could talk to. Sure, I can function on the same level as everybody else, I can hold myself down, but it isn't me."

Meg took a batch of forks from the drawer and turned them over and over, looking at them. "I'm all confused again."

"Oh, so'm I," Calvin said gaily. "But now at least I know we're going somewhere."

Meg was pleased and a little surprised when the twins were excited at having Calvin for supper. They knew more about his athletic record and were far more impressed by it than she. Calvin ate five bowls of stew, three saucers of Jell-O, and a dozen cookies, and then Charles Wallace insisted that Calvin take him up to bed and read to him. The twins, who had finished their homework, were allowed to watch half an hour of TV. Meg helped her mother with the dishes and then sat at the table and struggled with her homework. But she could not concentrate.

"Mother, are you upset?" she asked suddenly.

Mrs. Murry looked up from a copy of an English scientific magazine through which she was leafing. For a moment she did not speak. Then, "Yes."

"Why?"

Again Mrs. Murry paused. She held her hands out and looked at them. They were long and strong and beautiful. She touched with the fingers of her right hand the broad gold band on the third finger of her left hand. "I'm still quite a young woman, you know," she said finally, "though I realize that that's difficult for you children to conceive. And I'm still very much in love with your father. I miss him quite dreadfully."

"And you think all this has something to do with Father?"

"I think it must have."

"But what?"

"That I don't know. But it seems the only explanation."

"Do you think things always have an explanation?"

"Yes. I believe that they do. But I think that with our human limitations we're not always able to understand the explanations. But you see, Meg, just because we don't understand doesn't mean that the explanation doesn't exist."

"I like to understand things," Meg said.

"We all do. But it isn't always possible."

"Charles Wallace understands more than the rest of us, doesn't he?"

"Yes."

"Why?"

"I suppose because he's—well, because he's different, Meg."

"Different how?"

"I'm not quite sure. You know yourself he's not like anybody else."

"No. And I wouldn't want him to be," Meg said defensively.

"Wanting doesn't have anything to do with it. Charles Wallace is what he is. Different. New."

"New?"

"Yes. That's what your father and I feel."

Meg twisted her pencil so hard that it broke. She laughed. "I'm sorry. I'm really not being destructive. I'm just trying to get things straight."

"I know."

"But Charles Wallace doesn't *look* different from anybody else."

"No, Meg, but people are more than just the way they look. Charles Wallace's difference isn't physical. It's in essence."

Meg sighed heavily, took off her glasses and twirled them, put them back on again. "Well, I know Charles Wallace is different, and I know he's something *more*. I guess I'll just have to accept it without understanding it."

Mrs. Murry smiled at her. "Maybe that's really the point I was trying to put across."

"Yah," Meg said dubiously.

Her mother smiled again. "Maybe that's why our visitor last night didn't surprise me. Maybe that's why I'm able to have a—a willing suspension of disbelief. Because of Charles Wallace."

"Are *you* like Charles?" Meg asked.

"I? Heavens no. I'm blessed with more brains and opportunities than many people, but there's nothing about me that breaks out of the ordinary mold."

"Your looks do," Meg said.

Mrs. Murry laughed. "You just haven't had enough basis for comparison, Meg. I'm very ordinary, really."

Calvin O'Keefe, coming in then, said, "Ha ha."

"Charles all settled?" Mrs. Murry asked.

"Yes."

"What did you read to him?"

"Genesis. His choice. By the way, what kind of an experiment were you working on this afternoon, Mrs. Murry?"

"Oh, something my husband and I were cooking up together. I don't want to be *too* far behind him when he gets back."

"Mother," Meg pursued. "Charles says I'm not one thing or the other, not flesh nor fowl nor good red herring."

"Oh, for crying out loud," Calvin said, "you're *Meg*, aren't you? Come on and let's go for a walk."

But Meg was still not satisfied. "And what do you make of Calvin?" she demanded of her mother.

Mrs. Murry laughed. "I don't want to make anything of Calvin. I like him very much, and I'm delighted he's found his way here."

"Mother, you were going to tell me about a tesseract."

"Yes." A troubled look came into Mrs. Murry's eyes. "But not now, Meg. Not now. Go on out for that walk with Calvin. I'm going up to kiss Charles and then I have to see that the twins get to bed."

Outdoors the grass was wet with dew. The moon was halfway up and dimmed the stars for a great arc. Calvin reached out and took Meg's hand with a gesture as simple and friendly as Charles Wallace's. "Were you upsetting your mother?" he asked gently.

"I don't think *I* was. But she's upset."

"What about?"

"Father."

Calvin led Meg across the lawn. The shadows of the trees were long and twisted and there was a heavy, sweet, autumnal smell to the air. Meg stumbled as the land sloped suddenly downhill, but Calvin's strong hand steadied her. They walked carefully across the twins' vegetable garden, picking their way through rows of cabbages, beets, broccoli, pumpkins. Looming on their left were the tall stalks of corn. Ahead of them was a small apple orchard bounded by a stone wall, and beyond this the woods through which they had walked that afternoon. Calvin led the way to the wall, and then sat there, his red hair shining silver in the moonlight, his body dappled with patterns from the tangle of branches. He reached up, pulled an apple off a gnarled limb, and handed it to Meg, then picked one for himself. "Tell me about your father."

"He's a physicist."

"Sure, we all know that. And he's supposed to have left your mother and gone off with some dame."

Meg jerked up from the stone on which she was perched, but Calvin grabbed her by the wrist and pulled her back down. "Hold it, kid. I didn't say anything you hadn't heard already, did I?"

"No," Meg said, but continued to pull away. "Let me go."

"Come on, calm down. *You* know it isn't true, *I* know it isn't true. And how *any*body after one look at your mother could believe any man would leave her for another woman just shows how far jealousy will make people go. Right?"

"I guess so," Meg said, but her happiness had fled and she was back in a morass of anger and resentment.

"Look, dope." Calvin shook her gently. "I just want to get things straight, sort of sort out the fact from fiction. Your father's a physicist. That's a fact, yes?"

"Yes."

"He's a Ph.D. several times over."

"Yes."

"Most of the time he works alone but some of the time he was at the Institute for Higher Learning in Princeton. Correct?"

"Yes."

"Then he did some work for the government, didn't he?"

"Yes."

"You take it from there. That's all I know."

"That's about all I know, too," Meg said. "Maybe Mother knows more. I don't know. What he did was—well, it was what they call Classified."

"Top Secret, you mean?"

"That's right."

"And you don't even have any idea what it was about?"

Meg shook her head. "No. Not really. Just an idea because of where he was."

"Well, where?"

"Out in New Mexico for a while; we were with him there; and then he was in Florida at Cape Canaveral, and we were with him there, too. And then he was going to be traveling a lot, so we came here."

"You'd always had this house?"

"Yes. But we used to live in it just in the summer."

"And you don't know where your father was sent?"

"No. At first we got lots of letters. Mother and Father always wrote each other every day. I think Mother still writes him every night. Every once in a while the postmistress makes some kind of a crack about all her letters."

"I suppose they think she's pursuing him or something," Calvin said, rather bitterly. "They can't understand plain, ordinary love when they see it. Well, go on. What happened next?"

"Nothing happened," Meg said. "That's the trouble."

"Well, what about your father's letters?"

"They just stopped coming."

"You haven't heard anything at all?"

"No," Meg said. "Nothing." Her voice was heavy with misery.

Silence fell between them, as tangible as the dark tree shadows that fell across their laps and that now seemed to rest upon them as heavily as though they possessed a measurable weight of their own.

At last Calvin spoke in a dry, unemotional voice, not looking at Meg. "Do you think he could be dead?"

Again Meg leaped up, and again Calvin pulled her down. "No!

They'd have told us if he was dead! There's always a telegram or something. They always tell you!"

"What *do* they tell you?"

Meg choked down a sob, managed to speak over it. "Oh, Calvin,
Mother's tried and tried to find out. She's been down to Washington
and everything. And all they'll say is that he's on a secret and dangerous
mission, and she can be very proud of him, but he won't be able to—
to communicate with us for a while. And they'll give us news as soon
as they have it."

"Meg, don't get mad, but do you think maybe *they* don't know?"

A slow tear trickled down Meg's cheek. "That's what I'm
afraid of."

"Why don't you cry?" Calvin asked gently. "You're just crazy about
your father, aren't you? Go ahead and cry. It'll do you good."

Meg's voice came out trembling over tears. "I cry much too much.
I should be like Mother. I should be able to control myself."

"Your mother's a completely different person and she's a lot older
than you are."

"I wish I were a different person," Meg said shakily. "I hate myself."

Calvin reached over and took off her glasses. Then he pulled a
handkerchief out of his pocket and wiped her tears. This gesture of
tenderness undid her completely, and she put her head down on her
knees and sobbed. Calvin sat quietly beside her, every once in a while
patting her head.

"I'm sorry," she sobbed finally. "I'm terribly sorry. Now you'll hate
me."

"Oh, Meg, you *are* a moron," Calvin said. "Don't you know you're
the nicest thing that's happened to me in a long time?"

Meg raised her head, and moonlight shone on her tear-stained face;
without the glasses her eyes were unexpectedly beautiful. "If Charles
Wallace is a sport, I think I'm a biological mistake." Moonlight flashed
against her braces as she spoke.

Now she was waiting to be contradicted. But Calvin said, "Do you
know that this is the first time I've seen you without your glasses?"

"I'm blind as a bat without them. I'm nearsighted, like Father."

"Well, you know what, you've got dreamboat eyes," Calvin said.
"Listen, you go right on wearing your glasses. I don't think I want
anybody else to see what gorgeous eyes you have."

Meg smiled with pleasure. She could feel herself blushing and she
wondered if the blush would be visible in the moonlight.

"Okay, hold it, you two," came a voice out of the shadows. Charles

Wallace stepped into the moonlight. "I wasn't spying on you," he said quickly, "and I hate to break things up, but this is it, kids, this is it!" His voice quivered with excitement.

"This is what?" Calvin asked.

"We're going."

"Going? Where?" Meg reached out and instinctively grabbed for Calvin's hand.

"I don't know exactly," Charles Wallace said. "But I think it's to find Father."

Suddenly two eyes seemed to spring at them out of the darkness; it was the moonlight striking on Mrs Who's glasses. She was standing next to Charles Wallace, and how she had managed to appear where a moment ago there had been nothing but flickering shadows in the moonlight Meg had no idea. She heard a sound behind her and turned around. There was Mrs Whatsit scrambling over the wall.

"My, but I wish there were no wind," Mrs Whatsit said plaintively. "It's so *difficult* with all these clothes." She wore her outfit of the night before, rubber boots and all, with the addition of one of Mrs. Buncombe's sheets, which she had draped over her. As she slid off the wall the sheet caught in a low branch and came off. The felt hat slipped over both eyes, and another branch plucked at the pink stole. "Oh, *dear*," she sighed. "I shall *never* learn to manage."

Mrs Who wafted over to her, tiny feet scarcely seeming to touch the ground, the lenses of her glasses glittering. "*Come t'è picciol fallo amaro morso!* Dante. *What grievous pain a little fault doth give thee!*" With a clawlike hand she pushed the hat up on Mrs Whatsit's forehead, untangled the stole from the tree, and with a deft gesture took the sheet and folded it.

"Oh, *thank* you," Mrs Whatsit said. "You're *so* clever!"

"*Un asno viejo sabe más que un potro.* A. Pérez. *An old ass knows more than a young colt.*"

"Just because you're a paltry few billion years—" Mrs Whatsit was starting indignantly, when a sharp, strange voice cut in.

"Alll rrightt, girrllss. Thiss iss nno ttime forr bbickkering."

"It's Mrs Which," Charles Wallace said.

There was a faint gust of wind, the leaves shivered in it, the patterns of moonlight shifted, and in a circle of silver something shimmered, quivered, and the voice said, "I ddo nott thinkk I willl matterrialize commpletely. I ffindd itt verry ttirinngg, andd wee hhave mmuch ttoo ddoo."

4 The Black Thing

The trees were lashed into a violent frenzy. Meg screamed and clutched at Calvin, and Mrs Which's authoritative voice called out, "Qquiett, chilldd!"

Did a shadow fall across the moon, or did the moon simply go out, extinguished as abruptly and completely as a candle? There was still the sound of leaves, a terrified, terrifying rushing. All light was gone. Darkness was complete. Suddenly the wind was gone, and all sound. Meg felt that Calvin was being torn from her. When she reached for him her fingers touched nothing.

She screamed out, "Charles!" and whether it was to help him or for him to help her, she did not know. The word was flung back down her throat and she choked on it.

She was completely alone.

She had lost the protection of Calvin's hand. Charles was nowhere, either to save or to turn to. She was alone in a fragment of nothingness. No light, no sound, no feeling. Where was her body? She tried to move in her panic, but there was nothing to move. Just as light and sound had vanished, she was gone, too. The corporeal Meg simply was not.

Then she felt her limbs again. Her legs and arms were tingling faintly, as though they had been asleep. She blinked her eyes rapidly, but though she herself was somehow back, nothing else was. It was not as simple as darkness, or absence of light. Darkness has a tangible quality; it can be moved through and felt; in darkness you can bark your shins; the world of things still exists around you. She was lost in a horrifying void.

It was the same way with the silence. This was more than silence. A deaf person can feel vibrations. Here there was nothing to feel.

Suddenly she was aware of her heart beating rapidly within the cage of her ribs. Had it stopped before? What had made it start again? The tingling in her arms and legs grew stronger, and suddenly she felt movement. This movement, she felt, must be the turning of the earth, rotating on its axis, traveling its elliptic course about the sun. And this feeling of moving with the earth was somewhat like the feeling of being in the ocean, out in the ocean beyond this rising and falling of the breakers, lying on the moving water, pulsing gently with the swells, and feeling the gentle, inexorable tug of the moon.

I am asleep; I am dreaming, she thought. I'm having a nightmare. I want to wake up. Let me wake up.

"Well!" Charles Wallace's voice said. "That was quite a trip! I do think you might have warned us."

Light began to pulse and quiver. Meg blinked and shoved shakily at her glasses and there was Charles Wallace standing indignantly in front of her, his hands on his hips. "Meg!" he shouted. "Calvin! Where are you?"

She saw Charles, she heard him, but she could not go to him. She could not shove through the strange, trembling light to meet him.

Calvin's voice came as though it were pushing through a cloud. "Well, just give me time, will you? I'm older than you are."

Meg gasped. It wasn't that Calvin wasn't there and then that he was. It wasn't that part of him came first and then the rest of him followed, like a hand and then an arm, an eye and then a nose. It was a sort of shimmering, a looking at Calvin through water, through smoke, through fire, and then there he was, solid and reassuring.

"Meg!" Charles Wallace's voice came. "Meg! Calvin, where's Meg?"

"I'm right here," she tried to say, but her voice seemed to be caught at its source.

"Meg!" Calvin cried, and he turned around, looking about wildly.

"Mrs Which, you haven't left Meg be*hind*, have you?" Charles Wallace shouted.

"If you've hurt Meg, any of you—" Calvin started, but suddenly Meg felt a violent push and a shattering, as though she had been thrust through a wall of glass.

"Oh, *there* you are!" Charles Wallace said, and rushed over to her and hugged her.

"But *where* am I?" Meg asked breathlessly, relieved to hear that her voice was now coming out of her in more or less a normal way.

She looked around rather wildly. They were standing in a sunlit field, and the air about them was moving with the delicious fragrance that comes only on the rarest of spring days when the sun's touch is gentle and the apple blossoms are just beginning to unfold. She pushed her glasses up on her nose to reassure herself that what she was seeing was real.

They had left the silver glint of a biting autumn evening; and now around them everything was golden with light. The grasses of the field were a tender new green, and scattered about were tiny multicolored flowers. Meg turned slowly to face a mountain reaching so high into the sky that its peak was lost in a crown of puffy white clouds. From the trees at the base of the mountain came a sudden singing of birds. There was an air of such ineffable peace and joy all around her that her heart's wild thumping slowed.

"When shall we three meet again,
In thunder, lightning, or in rain,"

came Mrs Who's voice. Suddenly the three of them were there, Mrs Whatsit with her pink stole askew; Mrs Who with her spectacles gleaming; and Mrs Which still little more than a shimmer. Delicate multicolored butterflies were fluttering around them, as though in greeting.

Mrs Whatsit and Mrs Who began to giggle, and they giggled until it seemed that, whatever their private joke was, they would fall down with the wild fun of it. The shimmer seemed to be laughing, too. It became vaguely darker and more solid; and then there appeared a figure in a black robe and a black peaked hat, beady eyes, a beaked nose, and long gray hair; one bony claw clutched a broomstick.

"Wwell, jusstt ttoo kkeepp yyou girrlls happpy," the strange voice said, and Mrs Whatsit and Mrs Who fell into each other's arms in gales of laughter.

"If you ladies have had your fun, I think you should tell Calvin and Meg a little more about all this," Charles Wallace said coldly. "You scared Meg half out of her wits, whisking her off this way without any warning."

"Finxerunt animi, raro et perpauca loquentis," Mrs Who intoned. "Horace. *To action little, less to words inclined."*

"Mrs Who, I wish you'd stop quoting!" Charles Wallace sounded very annoyed.

Mrs Whatsit adjusted her stole. "But she finds it so difficult to verbalize, Charles dear. It helps her if she can quote instead of working out words on her own."

"Anndd wee mussttn'tt looose ourr sensses of hummorr," Mrs

Which said. "Thee onnlly wway ttoo ccope withh ssometthingg ddeadly sseriouss iss ttoo ttry ttoo trreatt itt a llittlle lligghtly."

"But that's going to be hard for Meg," Mrs Whatsit said. "It's going to be hard for her to realize that we *are* serious."

"What about me?" Calvin asked.

"The life of your father isn't at stake," Mrs Whatsit told him.

"What about Charles Wallace, then?"

Mrs Whatsit's unoiled-door-hinge voice was warm with affection and pride. "Charles Wallace knows. Charles Wallace knows that it's far more than just the life of his father. Charles Wallace knows what's at stake."

"But remember," Mrs Who said, "Αεηπου οὐδὲυ, πὰυτα δ' εηπὶζειυ χρεωτ. Euripedes. *Nothing is hopeless; we must hope for everything.*"

"Where are we now, and how did we get here?" Calvin asked.

"Uriel, the third planet of the star Malak in the spiral nebula Messier 101."

"This I'm supposed to believe?" Calvin asked indignantly.

"Aas yyou llike," Mrs Which said coldly.

For some reason Meg felt that Mrs Which, despite her looks and ephemeral broomstick, was someone in whom one could put complete trust. "It doesn't seem any more peculiar than anything else that's happened."

"Well, then, someone just tell me how we got here!" Calvin's voice was still angry and his freckles seemed to stand out on his face. "Even traveling at the speed of light, it would take us years and years to get here."

"Oh, we don't travel at the speed of *anything*," Mrs Whatsit explained earnestly. "We *tesser*. Or you might say, we *wrinkle*."

"Clear as mud," Calvin said.

Tesser, Meg thought. Could that have anything to do with Mother's tesseract?

She was about to ask when Mrs Which started to speak, and one did not interrupt when Mrs Which was speaking. "Mrs Whatsit iss yyoungg andd nnaïve."

"She keeps thinking she can explain things in *words*," Mrs Who said. "*Qui plus sait, plus se tait*. French, you know. *The more a man knows, the less he talks.*"

"But she has to use words for Meg and Calvin," Charles reminded Mrs Who. "If you brought them along, they have a right to know what's going on."

Meg went up to Mrs Which. In the intensity of her question she had forgotten all about the tesseract. "Is my father here?"

Mrs Which shook her head. "Nnott heeere, Megg. Llett Mrs Whatsitt expllainn. Shee isss yyoungg annd thee llanguage of worrds iss eeasierr fforr hherr thann itt iss fforr Mrs Whoo andd mee."

"We stopped here," Mrs Whatsit explained, "more or less to catch our breaths. And to give you a chance to know what you're up against."

"But what about Father?" Meg asked. "Is he all right?"

"For the moment, love, yes. He's one of the reasons we're here. But, you see, he's only one."

"Well, where is he? Please take me to him!"

"We can't, not yet," Charles said. "You have to be patient, Meg."

"But I'm *not* patient!" Meg cried passionately. "I've never been patient!"

Mrs Who's glasses shone at her gently. "If you want to help your father, then you must learn patience. *Vitam impendere vero. To stake one's life for the truth.* That is what we must do."

"That is what your father is doing." Mrs Whatsit nodded, her voice, like Mrs Who's, very serious, very solemn. Then she smiled her radiant smile. "Now! Why don't you three children wander around and Charles can explain things a little. You're perfectly safe on Uriel. That's why we stopped here to rest."

"But aren't you coming with us?" Meg asked fearfully.

There was silence for a moment. Then Mrs Which raised her authoritative hand. "Sshoww themm," she said to Mrs Whatsit, and at something in her voice Meg felt prickles of apprehension.

"Now?" Mrs Whatsit asked, her creaky voice rising to a squeak. Whatever it was Mrs Which wanted them to see, it was something that made Mrs Whatsit uncomfortable, too.

"Nnoww," Mrs Which said. "Tthey mmay aas welll knoww."

"Should—should I *change?*" Mrs Whatsit asked.

"Bbetter."

"I hope it won't upset the children too much," Mrs Whatsit murmured, as though to herself.

"Should I change, too?" Mrs Who asked. "Oh, but I've had *fun* in these clothes. But I'll have to admit Mrs Whatsit is the best at it. *Das Werk lobt den Meister.* German. *The work proves the craftsman.* Shall I transform now, too?"

Mrs Which shook her head. "Nnott yett. Nnott heere. Yyou mmay wwaitt."

"Now, don't be frightened, loves," Mrs Whatsit said. Her plump little body began to shimmer, to quiver, to shift. The wild colors of her clothes became muted, whitened. The pudding-bag shape stretched, lengthened, merged. And suddenly before the children was a creature more beautiful than any Meg had even imagined, and the beauty lay in far more than the outward description. Outwardly Mrs Whatsit was surely no longer a Mrs Whatsit. She was a marble-white body with powerful flanks, something like a horse but at the same time completely unlike a horse, for from the magnificently modeled back sprang a nobly formed torso, arms, and a head resembling a man's, but a man with a perfection of dignity and virtue, an exaltation of joy such as Meg had never before seen. No, she thought, it's not like a Greek centaur. Not in the least.

From the shoulders slowly a pair of wings unfolded, wings made of rainbows, of light upon water, of poetry.

Calvin fell to his knees.

"No," Mrs Whatsit said, though her voice was not Mrs Whatsit's voice. "Not to me, Calvin. Never to me. Stand up."

"Ccarrry themm," Mrs Which commanded.

With a gesture both delicate and strong Mrs Whatsit knelt in front of the children, stretching her wings wide and holding them steady, but quivering. "Onto my back, now," the new voice said.

The children took hesitant steps toward the beautiful creature.

"But what do we call you now?" Calvin asked.

"Oh, my dears," came the new voice, a rich voice with the warmth of a woodwind, the clarity of a trumpet, the mystery of an English horn. "You can't go on changing my name each time I metamorphose. And I've had such pleasure being Mrs Whatsit I think you'd better keep to that." She? he? it? smiled at them, and the radiance of the smile was as tangible as a soft breeze, as directly warming as the rays of the sun.

"Come." Charles Wallace clambered up.

Meg and Calvin followed him, Meg sitting between the two boys. A tremor went through the great wings and then Mrs Whatsit lifted and they were moving through the air.

Meg soon found that there was no need to cling to Charles Wallace or Calvin. The great creature's flight was serenely smooth. The boys were eagerly looking around the landscape.

"Look." Charles Wallace pointed. "The mountains are so tall that you can't see where they end."

Meg looked upwards and indeed the mountains seemed to be reaching into infinity.

They left the fertile fields and flew across a great plateau of granite-like rock shaped into enormous monoliths. These had a definite, rhythmic form, but they were not statues; they were like nothing Meg had ever seen before, and she wondered if they had been made by wind and weather, by the formation of this earth, or if they were a creation of beings like the one on which she rode.

They left the great granite plain and flew over a garden even more beautiful than anything in a dream. In it were gathered many creatures like the one Mrs Whatsit had become, some lying among the flowers, some swimming in a broad, crystal river that flowed through the garden, some flying in what Meg was sure must be a kind of dance, moving in and out above the trees. They were making music, music that came not only from their throats but from the movement of their great wings as well.

"What are they singing?" Meg asked excitedly.

Mrs Whatsit shook her beautiful head. "It won't go into your words. I can't possibly transfer it to your words. Are you getting any of it, Charles?"

Charles Wallace sat very still on the broad back, on his face an intently listening look, the look he had when he delved into Meg or his mother. "A little. Just a very little. But I think I could get more in time."

"Yes. You could learn it, Charles. But there isn't time. We can only stay here long enough to rest up and make a few preparations."

Meg hardly listened to her. "I want to know what they're saying! I want to know what it means."

"Try, Charles," Mrs Whatsit urged. "Try to translate. You can let yourself go, now. You don't have to hold back."

"But I can't!" Charles Wallace cried in an anguished voice. "I don't know enough! Not yet!"

"Then try to work with me and I'll see if I can't verbalize it a little for them."

Charles Wallace got his look of probing, of listening.

I know that look! Meg thought suddenly. Now I think I know what it means! Because I've had it myself, sometimes, doing math with Father, when a problem is just about to come clear—

Mrs Whatsit seemed to be listening to Charles's thoughts. "Well, yes, that's an idea. I can try. Too bad you don't really know it so you can give it to me direct, Charles. It's so much more work this way."

"Don't be lazy," Charles said.

Mrs Whatsit did not take offense. She explained, "Oh, it's my favorite kind of work, Charles. That's why they chose me to go along, even though I'm so much younger. It's my one real talent. But it takes a tremendous amount of energy, and we're going to need every ounce of energy for what's ahead of us. But I'll try. For Calvin and Meg I'll try." She was silent; the great wings almost stopped moving; only a delicate stirring seemed to keep them aloft. "Listen, then," Mrs Whatsit said. The resonant voice rose and the words seemed to be all around them so that Meg felt that she could almost reach out and touch them: *"Sing unto the Lord a new song, and his praise from the end of the earth, ye that go down to the sea, and all that is therein; the isles, and the inhabitants thereof. Let the wilderness and the cities thereof lift their voice; let the inhabitants of the rock sing, let them shout from the top of the mountains. Let them give glory unto the Lord!"*

Throughout her entire body Meg felt a pulse of joy such as she had never known before. Calvin's hand reached out; he did not clasp her hand in his; he moved his fingers so that they were barely touching hers, but joy flowed through them, back and forth between them, around them and about them and inside them.

When Mrs Whatsit sighed, it seemed completely incomprehensible that through this bliss could come the faintest whisper of doubt.

"We must go now, children." Mrs Whatsit's voice was deep with sadness, and Meg could not understand. Raising her head, Mrs Whatsit gave a call that seemed to be a command, and one of the creatures flying above the trees nearest them raised its head to listen, and then flew off and picked three flowers from a tree growing near the river and brought them over. "Each of you take one," Mrs Whatsit said. "I'll tell you how to use them later."

As Meg took her flower she realized that it was not a single blossom but hundreds of tiny flowerets forming a kind of hollow bell.

"Where are we going?" Calvin asked.

"Up."

The wings moved steadily, swiftly. The garden was left behind, the stretch of granite, the mighty shapes, and then Mrs Whatsit was flying upward, climbing steadily up, up. Below them the trees of the mountain dwindled, became sparse, were replaced by bushes and then small, dry grasses, and then vegetation ceased entirely and there were only rocks, points and peaks of rock, sharp and dangerous. "Hold on tight," Mrs Whatsit said. "Don't slip."

Meg felt Calvin's arm circle her waist in a secure hold.

Still they moved upward.

Now they were in clouds. They could see nothing but drifting whiteness, and the moisture clung to them and condensed in icy droplets. As Meg shivered, Calvin's grip tightened. In front of her Charles Wallace sat quietly. Once he turned just long enough to give her a swift glance of tenderness and concern. But Meg felt as each moment passed that he was growing farther and farther away, that he was becoming less and less her adored baby brother and more and more one with whatever kind of being Mrs Whatsit, Mrs Who, and Mrs Which in actuality were.

Abruptly they burst out of the clouds into a shaft of light. Below them there were still rocks; above them the rocks continued to reach up into the sky, but now, though it seemed miles upward, Meg could see where the mountain at last came to an end.

Mrs Whatsit continued to climb, her wings straining a little. Meg felt her heart racing; cold sweat began to gather on her face and her lips felt as though they were turning blue. She began to gasp.

"All right, children, use your flowers now," Mrs Whatsit said. "The atmosphere will continue to get thinner from now on. Hold the flowers up to your face and breathe through them and they will give you enough oxygen. It won't be as much as you're used to, but it will be enough."

Meg had almost forgotten the flowers, and was grateful to realize that she was still clasping them, that she hadn't let them fall from her fingers. She pressed her face into the blossoms and breathed deeply.

Calvin still held her with one arm, but he, too, held the flowers to his face.

Charles Wallace moved the hand with the flowers slowly, almost as though he were in a dream.

Mrs Whatsit's wings strained against the thinness of the atmosphere. The summit was only a little way above them, and then they were there. Mrs Whatsit came to rest on a small plateau of smooth silvery rock. There ahead of them was a great white disk.

"One of Uriel's moons," Mrs Whatsit told them, her mighty voice faintly breathless.

"Oh, it's beautiful!" Meg cried. "It's beautiful!"

The silver light from the enormous moon poured over them, blending with the golden quality of the day, flowing over the children, over Mrs Whatsit, over the mountain peak.

"Now we will turn around," Mrs Whatsit said, and at the quality of her voice, Meg was afraid again.

But when they turned she saw nothing. Ahead of them was the thin clear blue of sky; below them the rocks thrusting out of the shifting sea of white clouds.

"Now we will wait," Mrs Whatsit said, "for sunset and moonset."

Almost as she spoke the light began to deepen, to darken.

"I want to watch the moon set," Charles Wallace said.

"No, child. Do not turn around, any of you. Face out toward the dark. What I have to show you will be more visible then. Look ahead, straight ahead, as far as you can possibly look."

Meg's eyes ached from the strain of looking and seeing nothing.

Then, above the clouds which encircled the mountain, she seemed to see a shadow, a faint thing of darkness so far off that she was scarcely sure she was really seeing it.

Charles Wallace said, "What's that?"

"That sort of shadow out there," Calvin gestured. "What is it? I don't like it."

"Watch," Mrs Whatsit commanded.

It was a shadow, nothing but a shadow. It was not even as tangible as a cloud. Was it cast by something? Or was it a Thing in itself?

The sky darkened. The gold left the light and they were surrounded by blue, blue deepening until where there had been nothing but the evening sky there was now a faint pulse of star, and then another and another and another. There were more stars than Meg had ever seen before.

"The atmosphere is so thin here," Mrs Whatsit said as though in answer to her unasked question, "that it does not obscure your vision as it would at home. Now look. Look straight ahead."

Meg looked. The dark shadow was still there. It had not lessened or dispersed with the coming of night. And where the shadow was, the stars were not visible.

What could there be about a shadow that was so terrible that she knew there had never been before or ever would be again anything that would chill her with a fear that was beyond shuddering, beyond crying or screaming, beyond the possibility of comfort?

Meg's hand holding the blossoms slowly dropped and it seemed as though a knife gashed through her lungs. She gasped, but there was no air for her to breathe. Darkness glazed her eyes and mind, but as she started to fall into unconsciousness her head dropped down into the flowers, which she was still clutching; and as she inhaled the fragrance of their purity her mind and body revived, and she sat up again.

The shadow was still there, dark and dreadful.

Calvin held her hand strongly in his, but she felt neither strength nor reassurance in his touch. Beside her a tremor went through Charles Wallace, but he sat very still.

He shouldn't be seeing this, Meg thought. This is too much for so little a boy, no matter how different and extraordinary a little boy.

Calvin turned, rejecting the dark Thing that blotted out the light of the stars. "Make it go away, Mrs Whatsit," he whispered. "Make it go away. It's evil."

Slowly the great creature turned around so that the shadow was behind them, so that they saw only the stars unobscured, the soft throb of starlight on the mountain, the descending circle of the great moon swiftly slipping over the horizon. Then, without a word from Mrs What-sit, they were traveling downward, down, down. When they reached the corona of clouds Mrs Whatsit said, "You can breathe without the flowers now, my children."

Silence again. Not a word. It was as though the shadow had some-how reached out with its dark power and touched them so that they were incapable of speech. When they got back to the flowery field, bathed now in starlight, and moonlight from another, smaller, yellower rising moon, a little of the tenseness went out of their bodies, and they realized that the body of the beautiful creature on which they rode had been as rigid as theirs.

With a graceful gesture it dropped to the ground and folded its great wings. Charles Wallace was the first to slide off. "Mrs Who! Mrs Which!" he called, and there was an immediate quivering in the air. Mrs Who's familiar glasses gleamed at them. Mrs Which appeared, too; but, as she had told the children, it was difficult for her to materialize completely, and though there was the robe and peaked hat, Meg could look through them to mountain and stars. She slid off Mrs Whatsit's back and walked, rather unsteadily after the long ride, over to Mrs Which.

"That dark Thing we saw," she said. "Is that what my father is fighting?"

5 The Tesseract

"Yes," Mrs Which said. "Hhee iss beehindd thee ddarrkness, sso thatt eevenn wee cannott seee hhimm."

Meg began to cry, to sob aloud. Through her tears she could see Charles Wallace standing there, very small, very white. Calvin put his arms around her, but she shuddered and broke away, sobbing wildly. Then she was enfolded in the great wings of Mrs Whatsit and she felt comfort and strength pouring through her. Mrs Whatsit was not speaking aloud, and yet through the wings Meg understood words.

"My child, do not despair. Do you think we would have brought you here if there were no hope? We are asking you to do a difficult thing, but we are confident that you can do it. Your father needs help, he needs courage, and for his children he may be able to do what he cannot do for himself."

"Nnow," Mrs Which said. "Arre wee rreaddy?"

"Where are we going?" Calvin asked.

Again Meg felt an actual physical tingling of fear as Mrs Which spoke.

"Wwee musstt ggo bbehindd thee sshaddow."

"But we will not do it all at once," Mrs Whatsit comforted them. "We will do it in short stages." She looked at Meg. "Now we will tesser, we will wrinkle again. Do you understand?"

"No," Meg said flatly.

Mrs Whatsit sighed. "Explanations are not easy when they are about things for which your civilization still has no words. Calvin talked about traveling at the speed of light. You understand that, little Meg?"

"Yes," Meg nodded.

"That, of course, is the impractical, long way around. We have learned to take short cuts wherever possible."

"Sort of like in math?" Meg asked.

"Like in math." Mrs Whatsit looked over at Mrs Who. "Take your skirt and show them."

"*La experiencia es la madre de la ciencia.* Spanish, my dears. Cervantes. *Experience is the mother of knowledge.*" Mrs Who took a portion of her white robe in her hands and held it tight.

"You see," Mrs Whatsit said, "if a very small insect were to move from the section of skirt in Mrs Who's right hand to that in her left, it would be quite a long walk for him if he had to walk straight across."

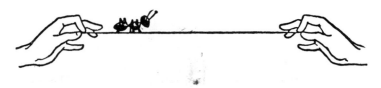

Swiftly Mrs Who brought her hands, still holding the skirt, together.

"Now, you see," Mrs Whatsit said, "he would *be* there, without that long trip. That is how we travel."

Charles Wallace accepted the explanation serenely. Even Calvin did not seem perturbed. "Oh, *dear*," Meg sighed. "I guess I *am* a moron. I just don't get it."

"That is because you think of space only in three dimensions," Mrs Whatsit told her. "We travel in the fifth dimension. This is something you can understand, Meg. Don't be afraid to try. Was your mother able to explain a tesseract to you?"

"Well, she never did," Meg said. "She got so upset about it. Why, Mrs Whatsit? She said it had something to do with her and Father."

"It was a concept they were playing with," Mrs Whatsit said, "going beyond the fourth dimension to the fifth. Did your mother explain it to you, Charles?"

"Well, yes." Charles looked a little embarrassed. "Please don't be hurt, Meg. I just kept at her while you were at school till I got it out of her."

Meg sighed. "Just explain it to me."

"Okay," Charles said. "What is the first dimension?"

"Well—a line: ————————"

"Okay. And the second dimension?"

"Well, you'd square the line. A flat square would be in the second dimension."

"And the third?"

"Well, you'd square the second dimension. Then the square wouldn't be flat any more. It would have a bottom, and sides, and a top."

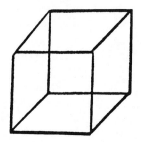

"And the fourth?"

"Well, I guess if you want to put it into mathematical terms you'd square the square. But you can't take a pencil and draw it the way you can the first three. I know it's got something to do with Einstein and time. I guess maybe you could call the fourth dimension Time."

"That's right," Charles said. "Good girl. Okay, then, for the fifth dimension you'd square the fourth, wouldn't you?"

"I guess so."

"Well, the fifth dimension's a tesseract. You add that to the other four dimensions and you can travel through space without having to go the long way around. In other words, to put it into Euclid, or old-fashioned plane geometry, a straight line is *not* the shortest distance between two points."

For a brief, illuminating second Meg's face had the listening, probing expression that was so often seen on Charles's. "I see!" she cried. "I got it! For just a moment I got it! I can't possibly explain it now, but there for a second I saw it!" She turned excitedly to Calvin. "Did you get it?"

He nodded. "Enough. I don't understand it the way Charles Wallace does, but enough to get the idea."

"Sso nnow wee ggo," Mrs Which said. "Tthere iss nott all thee ttime inn tthe worrlld."

"Could we hold hands?" Meg asked.

Calvin took her hand and held it tightly in his.

"You can try," Mrs Whatsit said, "though I'm not sure how it will work. You see, though we travel together, we travel alone. We will go first and take you afterward in the backwash. That may be easier for you." As she spoke the great white body began to waver, the wings to dissolve into mist. Mrs Who seemed to evaporate until there was nothing but the glasses, and then the glasses, too, disappeared. It reminded Meg of the Cheshire Cat.

—I've often seen a face without glasses, she thought;—but glasses without a face! I wonder if I go that way, too. First me and then my glasses?

She looked over at Mrs Which. Mrs Which was there and then she wasn't.

There was a gust of wind and a great thrust and a sharp shattering as she was shoved through—what? Then darkness; silence; nothingness. If Calvin was still holding her hand she could not feel it. But this time she was prepared for the sudden and complete dissolution of her body. When she felt the tingling coming back to her fingertips she knew that this journey was almost over and she could feel again the pressure of Calvin's hand about hers.

Without warning, coming as a complete and unexpected shock, she felt a pressure she had never imagined, as though she were being completely flattened out by an enormous steamroller. This was far worse than the nothingness had been; while she was nothing there was no need to breathe, but now her lungs were squeezed together so that although she was dying for want of air there was no way for her lungs to expand and contract, to take in the air that she must have to stay alive. This was completely different from the thinning of atmosphere when they flew up the mountain and she had had to put the flowers to her face to breathe. She tried to gasp, but a paper doll can't gasp. She thought she was trying to think, but her flattened-out mind was as unable to function as her lungs; her thoughts were squashed along with the rest of her. Her heart tried to beat; it gave a knifelike, sidewise movement, but it could not expand.

But then she seemed to hear a voice, or if not a voice, at least words, words flattened out like printed words on paper: "Oh, no! We can't stop here! This is a *two*-dimensional planet and the children can't manage here!"

She was whizzed into nothingness again, and nothingness was wonderful. She did not mind that she could not feel Calvin's hand, that she could not see or feel or be. The relief from the intolerable pressure was all she needed.

Then the tingling began to come back to her fingers, her toes; she could feel Calvin holding her tightly. Her heart beat regularly; blood coursed through her veins. Whatever had happened, whatever mistake had been made, it was over now. She thought she heard Charles Wallace saying, his words round and full as spoken words ought to be, "*Really*, Mrs Which, you might have killed us!"

This time she was pushed out of the frightening fifth dimension with a sudden, immediate jerk. There she was, herself again, standing with Calvin beside her, holding on to her hand for dear life, and Charles Wallace in front of her, looking indignant. Mrs Whatsit, Mrs Who, and Mrs Which were not visible, but she knew that they were there; the fact of their presence was strong about her.

"Cchilldrenn, I appolloggize," came Mrs Which's voice.

"Now, Charles, calm down," Mrs Whatsit said, appearing not as the great and beautiful beast she had been when they last saw her, but in her familiar wild garb of shawls and scarves and the old tramp's coat and hat. "You know how difficult it is for her to materialize. If you are not substantial yourself, it's *very* difficult to realize how limiting protoplasm is."

"I *ammm* ssorry," Mrs Which's voice came again; but there was more than a hint of amusement in it.

"It is *not* funny." Charles Wallace gave a childish stamp of his foot.

Mrs Who's glasses shone out, and the rest of her appeared more slowly behind them. *"We are such stuff as dreams are made on."* She smiled broadly. "Prospero in *The Tempest*. I *do* like that play."

"You didn't do it on *purpose?*" Charles demanded.

"Oh, my darling, of course not," Mrs Whatsit said quickly. "It was just a very understandable mistake. It's very difficult for Mrs Which to think in a corporeal way. She wouldn't hurt you deliberately; you know that. And it's really a very pleasant little planet, and rather amusing to be flat. We always enjoy our visits there."

"Where are we now, then?" Charles Wallace demanded. "And why?"

"In Orion's belt. We have a friend here, and we want you to have a look at your own planet."

"When are we going home?" Meg asked anxiously. "What about Mother? What about the twins? They'll be terribly worried about us. When we didn't come in at bedtime—well, Mother must be frantic by now. She and the twins and Fort will have been looking and looking for us, and of course we aren't there to be found!"

"Now, don't worry, my pet," Mrs Whatsit said cheerfully. "We took care of that before we left. Your mother has had enough to worry her with you and Charles to cope with, and not knowing about your father, without our adding to her anxieties. We took a time wrinkle as well as a space wrinkle. It's very easy to do if you just know how."

"What do you mean?" Meg asked plaintively. "Please, Mrs Whatsit, it's all so confusing."

"Just relax and don't worry over things that needn't trouble you," Mrs Whatsit said. "We made a nice, tidy little time tesser, and unless something goes terribly wrong we'll have you back about five minutes before you left, so there'll be time to spare and nobody'll ever need to know you were gone at all, though of course you'll be telling your mother, dear lamb that she is. And if something goes terribly wrong it won't matter whether we ever get back at all."

"Ddon'tt ffrrightenn themm," Mrs Which's voice came. "Aare yyou llosingg ffaith?"

"Oh, no. No, I'm not."

But Meg thought her voice sounded a little faint.

"I hope *this* is a nice planet," Calvin said. "We can't *see* much of it. Does it ever clear up?"

Meg looked around her, realizing that she had been so breathless from the journey and the stop on the two-dimensional planet that she had not noticed her surroundings. And perhaps this was not very surprising, for the main thing about the surroundings was exactly that they *were* unnoticeable. They seemed to be standing on some kind of nondescript, flat surface. The air around them was gray. It was not exactly fog, but she could see nothing through it. Visibility was limited to the nicely definite bodies of Charles Wallace and Calvin, the rather unbelievable bodies of Mrs Whatsit and Mrs Who, and a faint occasional glimmer that was Mrs Which.

"Come, children," Mrs Whatsit said. "We don't have far to go, and we might as well walk. It will do you good to stretch your legs a little."

As they moved through the grayness Meg caught an occasional glimpse of slaglike rocks, but there were no traces of trees or bushes, nothing but flat ground under their feet, no sign of any vegetation at all.

Finally, ahead of them there loomed what seemed to be a hill of stone. As they approached it Meg could see that there was an entrance that led into a deep, dark cavern. "Are we going in there?" she asked nervously.

"Don't be afraid," Mrs Whatsit said. "It's easier for the Happy Medium to work within. Oh, you'll like her, children. She's very jolly. If ever I saw her looking unhappy I would be very depressed myself. As long as she can laugh I'm sure everything is going to come out right in the end."

"Mmrs Whattsitt," came Mrs Which's voice severely, "jusstt because yyou arre verry youngg iss nno exxcuse forr tallkingg tooo muchh."

Mrs Whatsit looked hurt, but she subsided.

"Just how old *are* you?" Calvin asked her.

"Just a moment," Mrs Whatsit murmured, and appeared to calculate rapidly upon her fingers. She nodded triumphantly. "Exactly 2,379,152,497 years, 8 months, and 3 days. That is according to *your* calendar, of course, which even you know isn't very accurate." She leaned closer to Meg and Calvin and whispered, "It was really a *very* great honor for me to be chosen for this mission. It's just because of my verbalizing and materializing so well, you know. But of course we can't take any credit for our talents. It's how we use them that counts. And I make far too many mistakes. That's why Mrs Who and I enjoyed seeing Mrs Which make a mistake when she tried to land you on a two-dimensional planet. It was *that* we were laughing at, not at you. She was laughing at herself, you see. She's really terribly nice to us younger ones."

Meg was listening with such interest to what Mrs Whatsit was saying that she hardly noticed when they went into the cave; the transition from the grayness of outside to the grayness of inside was almost unnoticeable. She saw a flickering light ahead of them, ahead and down, and it was toward this that they went. As they drew closer she realized that it was a fire.

"It gets very cold in here," Mrs Whatsit said, "so we asked her to have a good bonfire going for you."

As they approached the fire they could see a dark shadow against it, and as they went closer still, they could see that the shadow was a woman. She wore a turban of beautiful pale mauve silk, and a long, flowing, purple satin gown. In her hands was a crystal ball into which she was gazing raptly. She did not appear to see the children, Mrs Whatsit, Mrs Who, and Mrs Which, but continued to stare into the crystal ball; and as she stared she began to laugh; and she laughed and laughed at whatever it was that she was seeing.

Mrs Which's voice rang out clear and strong, echoing against the walls of the cavern, and the words fell with a sonorous clang.

"WWEE ARRE HHERRE!"

The woman looked up from the ball, and when she saw them she got up and curtsied deeply. Mrs Whatsit and Mrs Who dropped small curtsies in return, and the shimmer seemed to bow slightly.

"Oh, Medium, dear," Mrs Whatsit said, "these are the children. Charles Wallace Murry." Charles Wallace bowed. "Margaret Murry." Meg felt that if Mrs Whatsit and Mrs Who had curtsied, she ought to, also; so she did, rather awkwardly. "And Calvin O'Keefe." Calvin bobbed his head. "We want them to see their home planet," Mrs Whatsit said.

The Medium lost the delighted smile she had worn till then. "Oh, *why* must you make me look at unpleasant things when there are so many delightful ones to see?"

Again Mrs Which's voice reverberated through the cave. "Therre willl nno llonggerr bee sso manyy pplleasanntt thinggss too llookk att iff rressponssible ppeoplle ddo nnott ddoo ssomethingg abboutt thee unnppleassanntt oness."

The Medium sighed and held the ball high.

"Look, children," Mrs Whatsit said. "Look into it well."

"*Que la terre est petite à qui la voit des cieux!* Delille. *How small is the earth to him who looks from heaven,*" Mrs Who intoned musically.

Meg looked into the crystal ball, at first with caution, then with increasing eagerness, as she seemed to see an enormous sweep of dark and empty space, and then galaxies swinging across it. Finally they seemed to move in closer on one of the galaxies.

"Your own Milky Way," Mrs Whatsit whispered to Meg.

They were headed directly toward the center of the galaxy; then they moved off to one side; stars seemed to be rushing at them. Meg flung her arm up over her face as though to ward off the blow.

"Llookk!" Mrs Which commanded.

Meg dropped her arm. They seemed to be moving in toward a planet. She thought she could make out polar ice caps. Everything seemed sparkling clear.

"No, no, Medium dear, that's Mars," Mrs Whatsit reproved gently.

"Do I *have* to?" the Medium asked.

"Nnoww!" Mrs Which commanded.

The bright planet moved out of their vision. For a moment there was the darkness of space; then another planet. The outlines of this planet were not clean and clear. It seemed to be covered with a smoky haze. Through the haze Meg thought she could make out the familiar outlines of continents like pictures in her Social Studies books.

"Is it because of our atmosphere that we can't see properly?" she asked anxiously.

"Nno, Mmegg, yyou knnoww thatt itt iss nnott tthee attmossphee-ere," Mrs Which said. "Yyou mmusstt bee brrave."

"It's the Thing!" Charles Wallace cried. "It's the Dark Thing we saw from the mountain peak on Uriel when we were riding on Mrs Whatsit's back!"

"Did it just come?" Meg asked in agony, unable to take her eyes from the sickness of the shadow which darkened the beauty of the earth. "Did it just come while we've been gone?"

Mrs Which's voice seemed very tired. "Ttell herr," she said to Mrs Whatsit.

Mrs Whatsit sighed. "No, Meg. It hasn't just come. It has been there for a great many years. That is why your planet is such a troubled one."

"But why—" Calvin started to ask, his voice croaking hoarsely.

Mrs Whatsit raised her hand to silence him. "We showed you the Dark Thing on Uriel first—oh, for many reasons. First, because the atmosphere on the mountain peaks there is so clear and thin you could see it for what it is. And we thought it would be easier for you to understand it if you saw it—well, someplace *else* first, not your own earth."

"I hate it!" Charles Wallace cried passionately. "I hate the Dark Thing!"

Mrs Whatsit nodded. "Yes, Charles dear. We all do. That's another reason we wanted to prepare you on Uriel. We thought it would be too frightening for you to see it first of all about your own, beloved world."

"But what is it?" Calvin demanded. "We know that it's evil, but what is it?"

"Yyouu hhave ssaidd itt!" Mrs Which's voice rang out. "Itt iss Eevill. Itt iss thee Ppowers of Ddarrkknesss!"

"But what's going to happen?" Meg's voice trembled. "Oh, please, Mrs Which, tell us what's going to happen!"

"Wee wwill cconnttinnue tto ffightt!"

Something in Mrs Which's voice made all three of the children stand straighter, throwing back their shoulders with determination, looking at the glimmer that was Mrs Which with pride and confidence.

"And we're not alone, you know, children," came Mrs Whatsit, the comforter. "All through the universe it's being fought, all through the cosmos, and my, but it's a grand and exciting battle. I know it's hard for you to understand about size, how there's very little difference in the size of the tiniest microbe and the greatest galaxy. You think about that, and maybe it won't seem strange to you that some of our very best fighters have come right from your own planet, and it's a *little* planet, dears, out on the edge of a little galaxy. You can be proud that it's done so well."

"Who have our fighters been?" Calvin asked.

"Oh, *you* must know them, dear," Mrs Whatsit said.

Mrs Who's spectacles shone out at them triumphantly. "*And the light shineth in darkness; and the darkness comprehended it not.*"

"Jesus!" Charles Wallace said. "Why, of course, Jesus!"

"Of course!" Mrs Whatsit said. "Go on, Charles, love. There were others. All your great artists. They've been lights for us to see by."

"Leonardo da Vinci?" Calvin suggested tentatively. "And Michelangelo?"

"And Shakespeare," Charles Wallace called out, "and Bach! And Pasteur and Madame Curie and Einstein!"

Now Calvin's voice rang with confidence. "And Schweitzer and Gandhi and Buddha and Beethoven and Rembrandt and St. Francis!"

"Now you, Meg," Mrs Whatsit ordered.

"Oh, Euclid, I suppose." Meg was in such an agony of impatience that her voice grated irritably. "And Copernicus. But what about Father? Please, what about Father?"

"Wee aarre ggoingg tto yourr ffatherr," Mrs Which said.

"But where is he?" Meg went over to Mrs Which and stamped as though she were as young as Charles Wallace.

Mrs Whatsit answered in a voice that was low but quite firm. "On a planet that has given in. So you must prepare to be very strong."

All traces of cheer had left the Happy Medium's face. She sat holding the great ball, looking down at the shadowed earth, and a slow tear coursed down her cheek. "I can't stand it any longer," she sobbed. "Watch now, children, watch!"

6 The Happy Medium

Again they focused their eyes on the crystal ball. The earth with its fearful covering of dark shadow swam out of view and they moved rapidly through the Milky Way. And there was the Thing again.

"Watch!" the Medium told them.

The Darkness seemed to seethe and writhe. Was this meant to *comfort* them?

Suddenly there was a great burst of light through the Darkness. The light spread out and where it touched the Darkness the Darkness disappeared. The light spread until the patch of Dark Thing had vanished, and there was only a gentle shining, and through the shining came the stars, clear and pure. Then, slowly, the shining dwindled until it, too, was gone, and there was nothing but stars and starlight. No shadows. No fear. Only the stars and the clear darkness of space, quite different from the fearful darkness of the Thing.

"You see!" the Medium cried, smiling happily. "It can be overcome! It is being overcome all the time!"

Mrs Whatsit sighed, a sigh so sad that Meg wanted to put her arms around her and comfort her.

"Tell us exactly what happened, then, please," Charles Wallace said in a small voice.

"It was a star," Mrs Whatsit said sadly. "A star giving up its life in battle with the Thing. It won, oh, yes, my children, it won. But it lost its life in the winning."

Mrs Which spoke again. Her voice sounded tired, and they knew that speaking was a tremendous effort for her. "Itt wass nnott sso llongg aggo fforr yyou, wwass itt?" she asked gently.

Mrs Whatsit shook her head.

Charles Wallace went up to Mrs Whatsit. "I see. Now I understand. You were a star once, weren't you?"

Mrs Whatsit covered her face with her hands as though she were embarrassed, and nodded.

"And you did—you did what that star just did?"

With her face still covered, Mrs Whatsit nodded again.

Charles Wallace looked at her, very solemnly. "I should like to kiss you."

Mrs Whatsit took her hands down from her face and pulled Charles Wallace to her in a quick embrace. He put his arms about her neck, pressed his cheek against hers, and then kissed her.

Meg felt that she would have liked to kiss Mrs Whatsit, too, but that after Charles Wallace, anything that she or Calvin did or said would be anticlimax. She contented herself with looking at Mrs Whatsit. Even though she was used to Mrs Whatsit's odd getup (and the very oddness of it was what made her seem so comforting), she realized with a fresh shock that it was not Mrs Whatsit herself that she was seeing at all. The complete, the true Mrs Whatsit, Meg realized, was beyond human understanding. What she saw was only the game Mrs Whatsit was playing; it was an amusing and charming game, a game full of both laughter and comfort, but it was only the tiniest facet of all the things Mrs Whatsit *could* be.

"I didn't mean to tell you," Mrs Whatsit faltered. "I didn't mean ever to let you know. But, oh, my dears, I did so love being a star!"

"Yyouu arre sstill verry yyoungg," Mrs Which said, her voice faintly chiding.

The Medium sat looking happily at the star-filled sky in her ball, smiling and nodding and chuckling gently. But Meg noticed that her eyes were drooping, and suddenly her head fell forward and she gave a faint snore.

"Poor thing," Mrs Whatsit said, "we've worn her out. It's very hard work for her."

"Please, Mrs Whatsit," Meg asked, "what happens now? Why are we here? What do we do next? Where is Father? When are we going to him?" She clasped her hands pleadingly.

"One thing at a time, love!" Mrs Whatsit said.

Mrs Who cut in. "*As paredes tem ouvidos.* That's Portuguese. *Walls have ears.*"

"Yes, let us go outside," Mrs Whatsit said. "Come, we'll let her sleep."

But as they turned to go, the Medium jerked her head up and smiled at them radiantly. "You weren't going to go without saying goodbye to me, were you?" she asked.

"We thought we'd just let you sleep, dear." Mrs Whatsit patted the Medium's shoulder. "We worked you terribly hard and we know you must be very tired."

"But I was going to give you some ambrosia or nectar or at least some tea—"

At this Meg realized that she was hungry. How much time had passed since they had had their bowls of stew? she wondered.

But Mrs Whatsit said, "Oh, thank you, dear, but I think we'd better be going."

"*They* don't need to eat, you know," Charles Wallace whispered to Meg. "At least not food, the way we do. Eating's just a game with them. As soon as we get organized again I'd better remind them that they'll have to feed us sooner or later."

The Medium smiled and nodded. "It does seem as though I should be able to do something *nice* for you, after having had to show those poor children such horrid things. Would they like to see their mother before they go?"

"Could we see Father?" Meg asked eagerly.

"Nno," Mrs Which said. "Wwee aare ggoingg tto yourr ffatherr, Mmegg. Doo nnott bbee immpatientt."

"But she *could* see her mother, couldn't she?" the Medium wheedled.

"Oh, why not," Mrs Whatsit put in. "It won't take long and it can't do any harm."

"And Calvin, too?" Meg asked. "Could he see his mother, too?"

Calvin touched Meg in a quick gesture, and whether it was of thanks or apprehension she was not sure.

"I tthinkk itt iss a misstake." Mrs Which was disapproving. "Bbutt ssince yyou hhave menttionedd itt I ssupposse yyouu musstt ggo aheadd."

"I hate it when she gets cross," Mrs Whatsit said, glancing over at Mrs Which, "and the trouble is, she always seems to be right. But I really don't see how it could hurt, and it might make you all feel better. Go on, Medium dear."

The Medium, smiling and humming softly, turned the crystal ball a little between her hands. Stars, comets, planets flashed across the sky, and then the earth came into view again, the darkened earth, closer, closer, till it filled the globe, and they had somehow gone through the darkness until the soft white of clouds and the gentle outline of continents shone clearly.

"Calvin's mother first," Meg whispered to the Medium.

The globe became hazy, cloudy, then shadows began to solidify, to clarify, and they were looking into an untidy kitchen with a sink full of unwashed dishes. In front of the sink stood an unkempt woman with gray hair stringing about her face. Her mouth was open and Meg could see the toothless gums and it seemed that she could almost hear her screaming at two small children who were standing by her. Then she grabbed a long wooden spoon from the sink and began whacking one of the children.

"Oh, dear—" the Medium murmured, and the picture began to dissolve. "I didn't really—"

"It's all right," Calvin said in a low voice. "I think I'd rather you knew."

Now, instead of reaching out to Calvin for safety, Meg took his hand in hers, not saying anything in words but trying to tell him by the pressure of her fingers what she felt. If anyone had told her only the day before that she, Meg, the snaggle-toothed, the myopic, the clumsy, would be taking a boy's hand to offer him comfort and strength, particularly a popular and important boy like Calvin, the idea would have been beyond her comprehension. But now it seemed as natural to want to help and protect Calvin as it did Charles Wallace.

The shadows were swirling in the crystal again, and as they cleared, Meg began to recognize her mother's lab at home. Mrs. Murry was sitting perched on her high stool, writing away at a sheet of paper on a clipboard on her lap. She's writing Father, Meg thought. The way she always does. Every night.

The tears that she could never learn to control swam to her eyes as she watched. Mrs. Murry looked up from her letter, almost as though she were looking toward the children, and then her head drooped and she put it down on the paper, and sat there, huddled up, letting herself relax into an unhappiness that she never allowed her children to see.

And now the desire for tears left Meg. The hot, protective anger she had felt for Calvin when she looked into his home she now felt turned toward her mother.

"Let's go!" she cried harshly. "Let's *do* something!"

"She's always so right," Mrs Whatsit murmured, looking toward Mrs Which. "Sometimes I wish she'd just say I told you so and have done with it."

"I only meant to help—" the Medium wailed.

"Oh, Medium, dear, *don't* feel badly," Mrs Whatsit said swiftly. "Look at something cheerful, do. I can't bear to have you distressed!"

"It's all right," Meg assured the Medium earnestly. "Truly it is, Mrs. Medium, and we thank you very much."

"Are you sure?" the Medium asked, brightening.

"Of course! It really helped ever so much because it made me mad, and when I'm mad I don't have room to be scared."

"Well, kiss me goodbye for good luck, then," the Medium said.

Meg went over to her and gave her a quick kiss, and so did Charles Wallace. The Medium looked smilingly at Calvin, and winked. "I want the young man to kiss me, too. I always did love red hair. And it'll give you good luck, laddie-me-love."

Calvin bent down, blushing, and awkwardly kissed her cheek.

The Medium tweaked his nose. "You've got a lot to learn, my boy," she told him.

"Now, goodbye, Medium dear, and many thanks," Mrs Whatsit said. "I dare say we'll see you in an eon or two."

"Where are you going, in case I want to tune in?" the Medium asked.

"Camazotz," Mrs Whatsit told her. (Where and what was Camazotz? Meg did not like the sound of the word or the way in which Mrs Whatsit pronounced it.) "But please don't distress yourself on our behalf. You know you don't like looking in on the dark planets, and it's very upsetting to us when you aren't happy."

"But I must know what happens to the children," the Medium said. "It's my worst trouble, getting fond. If I didn't get fond I could be happy all the time. *Oh*, well, *ho* hum, I manage to keep pretty jolly, and a little snooze will do wonders for me right now. Goodbye, everyb—" and her word got lost in the general b-b-bz-z of a snore.

"Ccome," Mrs Which ordered, and they followed her out of the darkness of the cave to the impersonal grayness of the Medium's planet.

"Nnoww, cchilldrenn, yyouu musstt nott bee frrightennedd att whatt iss ggoingg tto hhappenn," Mrs Which warned.

"Stay angry, little Meg," Mrs Whatsit whispered. "You will need all your anger now."

Without warning Meg was swept into nothingness again. This time the nothingness was interrupted by a feeling of clammy coldness such as she had never felt before. The coldness deepened and swirled all about her and through her, and was filled with a new and strange kind of darkness that was a completely tangible thing, a thing that wanted to eat and digest her like some enormous malignant beast of prey.

Then the darkness was gone. Had it been the shadow, the Black Thing? Had they had to travel through it to get to her father?

There was the by-now-familiar tingling in her hands and feet and the push through hardness, and she was on her feet, breathless but unharmed, standing beside Calvin and Charles Wallace.

"Is this Camazotz?" Charles Wallace asked as Mrs Whatsit materialized in front of him.

"Yes," she answered. "Now let us just stand and get our breath and look around."

They were standing on a hill and as Meg looked about her she felt that it could easily be a hill on earth. There were the familiar trees she knew so well at home: birches, pines, maples. And though it was warmer than it had been when they so precipitously left the apple orchard, there was a faintly autumnal touch to the air; near them were several small trees with reddened leaves very like sumac, and a big patch of goldenrod-like flowers. As she looked down the hill she could see the smokestacks of a town, and it might have been one of any number of familiar towns. There seemed to be nothing strange, or different, or frightening, in the landscape.

But Mrs Whatsit came to her and put an arm around her comfortingly. "I can't stay with you here, you know, love," she said. "You three children will be on your own. We will be near you; we will be watching you. But you will not be able to see us or to ask us for help, and we will not be able to come to you."

"But is Father here?" Meg asked tremblingly.

"Yes."

"But where? When will we see him?" She was poised for running, as though she were going to sprint off, immediately, to wherever her father was.

"That I cannot tell you. You will just have to wait until the propitious moment."

Charles Wallace looked steadily at Mrs Whatsit. "Are you afraid for us?"

"A little."

"But if you weren't afraid to do what you did when you were a star, why should you be afraid for us now?"

"But I was afraid," Mrs Whatsit said gently. She looked steadily at each of the three children in turn. "You will need help," she told them, "but all I am allowed to give you is a little talisman. Calvin, your great gift is your ability to communicate, to communicate with all kinds of people. So, for you, I will strengthen this gift. Meg, I give you your faults."

"My faults!" Meg cried.

"Your faults."

"But I'm always trying to get rid of my faults!"

"Yes," Mrs Whatsit said. "However, I think you'll find they'll come in very handy on Camazotz. Charles Wallace, to you I can give only the resilience of your childhood."

From somewhere Mrs Who's glasses glimmered and they heard her voice. "Calvin," she said, "a hint. For you a hint. Listen well:

> *... For that he was a spirit too delicate*
> *To act their earthy and abhorr'd commands,*
> *Refusing their grand hests, they did confine him*
> *By help of their most potent ministers,*
> *And in their most unmitigable rage,*
> *Into a cloven pine; within which rift*
> *Imprisoned, he didst painfully remain ...*

Shakespeare. *The Tempest.*"

"Where are you, Mrs Who?" Charles Wallace asked. "Where is Mrs Which?"

"We cannot come to you now." Mrs Who's voice blew to them like the wind. "*Allwissend bin ich nicht; doch viel ist mir bewusst.* Goethe. *I do not know everything; still many things I understand.* That is for you, Charles. Remember that you do not know everything." Then the voice was directed to Meg. "To you I leave my glasses, little blind-as-a-bat. But do not use them except as a last resort. Save them for the final moment of peril." As she spoke there was another shimmer of spectacles, and then it was gone, and the voice faded out with it. The spectacles were in Meg's hand. She put them carefully into the breast pocket of her jacket, and the knowledge that they were there somehow made her a little less afraid.

"Tto alll tthreee off yyou I ggive mmy ccommandd," Mrs Which said. "Ggo ddownn inttoo tthee ttownn. Ggo ttogetherr. Ddoo nnott llett tthemm ssepparate yyou. Bbee sstrongg." There was a flicker and then it vanished. Meg shivered.

Mrs Whatsit must have seen the shiver, for she patted Meg on the shoulder. Then she turned to Calvin. "Take care of Meg."

"I can take care of Meg," Charles Wallace said rather sharply. "I always have."

Mrs Whatsit looked at Charles Wallace, and the creaky voice seemed somehow both to soften and to deepen at the same time. "Charles Wallace, the danger here is greatest for you."

"Why?"

"Because of what you are. Just exactly because of what you are you will be by far the most vulnerable. You *must* stay with Meg and Calvin.

You must *not* go off on your own. Beware of pride and arrogance, Charles, for they may betray you."

At the tone of Mrs Whatsit's voice, both warning and frightening, Meg shivered again. And Charles Wallace butted up against Mrs Whatsit in the way he often did with his mother, whispering, "Now I think I know what you meant about being afraid."

"Only a fool is not afraid," Mrs Whatsit told him. "Now go." And where she had been, there was only sky and grasses and a small rock.

"Come *on*," Meg said impatiently. "Come on, let's *go!*" She was completely unaware that her voice was trembling like an aspen leaf. She took Charles Wallace and Calvin each by the hand and started down the hill.

Below them the town was laid out in harsh angular patterns. The houses in the outskirts were all exactly alike, small square boxes painted gray. Each had a small, rectangular plot of lawn in front, with a straight line of dull-looking flowers edging the path to the door. Meg had a feeling that if she could count the flowers there would be exactly the same number for each house. In front of all the houses children were playing. Some were skipping rope, some were bouncing balls. Meg felt vaguely that something was wrong with their play. It seemed exactly like children playing around any housing development at home, and yet there was something different about it. She looked at Calvin, and saw that he, too, was puzzled.

"Look!" Charles Wallace said suddenly. "They're skipping and bouncing in rhythm! Everyone's doing it at exactly the same moment."

This was so. As the skipping rope hit the pavement, so did the ball. As the rope curved over the head of the jumping child, the child with the ball caught the ball. Down came the ropes. Down came the balls. Over and over again. Up. Down. All in rhythm. All identical. Like the houses. Like the paths. Like the flowers.

Then the doors of all the houses opened simultaneously, and out came women like a row of paper dolls. The print of their dresses was different, but they all gave the appearance of being the same. Each woman stood on the steps of her house. Each clapped. Each child with the ball caught the ball. Each child with the skipping rope folded the rope. Each child turned and walked into the house. The doors clicked shut behind them.

"How can they do it?" Meg asked wonderingly. "We couldn't do it that way if we tried. What does it mean?"

"Let's go back." Calvin's voice was urgent.

"Back?" Charles Wallace asked. "Where?"

"I don't know. Anywhere. Back to the hill. Back to Mrs Whatsit and Mrs Who and Mrs Which. I don't like this."

"But they aren't there. Do you think they'd come to us if we turned back now?"

"I don't like it," Calvin said again.

"Come *on*." Impatience made Meg squeak. "You *know* we can't go back. Mrs Whatsit *said* to go into the town." She started on down the street, and the two boys followed her. The houses, all identical, continued, as far as the eye could reach.

Then, all at once, they saw the same thing, and stopped to watch. In front of one of the houses stood a little boy with a ball, and he was bouncing it. But he bounced it rather badly and with no particular rhythm, sometimes dropping it and running after it with awkward, furtive leaps, sometimes throwing it up into the air and trying to catch it. The door of his house opened and out ran one of the mother figures. She looked wildly up and down the street, saw the children and put her hand to her mouth as though to stifle a scream, grabbed the little boy and rushed indoors with him. The ball dropped from his fingers and rolled out into the street.

Charles Wallace ran after it and picked it up, holding it out for Meg and Calvin to see. It seemed like a perfectly ordinary, brown rubber ball.

"Let's take it in to him and see what happens," Charles Wallace suggested.

Meg pulled at him. "Mrs Whatsit said for us to go on into the town."

"Well, we *are* in the town, aren't we? The outskirts, anyhow. I want to know more about this. I have a hunch it may help us later. You go on if you don't want to come with me."

"No," Calvin said firmly. "We're going to stay together. Mrs Whatsit said we weren't to let them separate us. But I'm with you on this. Let's knock and see what happens."

They went up the path to the house, Meg reluctant, eager to get on into the town. "Let's hurry," she begged, "*please!* Don't you want to find Father?"

"Yes," Charles Wallace said, "but not blindly. How can we help him if we don't know what we're up against? And it's obvious we've been brought here to help him, not just to find him." He walked briskly up the steps and knocked at the door. They waited. Nothing happened. Then Charles Wallace saw a bell, and this he rang. They could hear the bell buzzing in the house, and the sound of it echoed down the street. After a moment the mother figure opened the door. All up and down the street other doors opened, but only a crack, and eyes peered toward the three children and the woman looking fearfully out the door at them.

"What do you want?" she asked. "It isn't paper time yet; we've had milk time; we've had this month's Puller Prush Person; and I've given my Decency Donations regularly. All my papers are in order."

"I think your little boy dropped his ball," Charles Wallace said, holding it out.

The woman pushed the ball away. "Oh, no! The children in our section *never* drop balls! They're all perfectly trained. We haven't had an Aberration for three years."

All up and down the block, heads nodded in agreement.

Charles Wallace moved closer to the woman and looked past her into the house. Behind her in the shadows he could see the little boy, who must have been about his own age.

"You can't come in," the woman said. "You haven't shown me any papers. I don't have to let you in if you haven't any papers."

Charles Wallace held the ball out beyond the woman so that the little boy could see it. Quick as a flash the boy leaped forward and grabbed the ball from Charles Wallace's hand, then darted back into the shadows. The woman went very white, opened her mouth as though to say something, then slammed the door in their faces instead. All up and down the street, doors slammed.

"What are they afraid of?" Charles Wallace asked. "What's the matter with them?"

"Don't *you* know?" Meg asked him. "Don't you know what all this is about, Charles?"

"Not yet," Charles Wallace said. "Not even an inkling. And I'm trying. But I didn't get through anywhere. Not even a chink. Let's go." He stumped down the steps.

After several blocks the houses gave way to apartment buildings; at least Meg felt sure that that was what they must be. They were fairly tall, rectangular buildings, absolutely plain, each window, each entrance exactly like every other. Then, coming toward them down the street, was a boy about Calvin's age riding a machine that was something like a combination of a bicycle and a motorcycle. It had the slimness and lightness of a bicycle, and yet as the foot pedals turned they seemed to generate an unseen source of power, so that the boy could pedal very slowly and yet move along the street quite swiftly. As he reached each entrance he thrust one hand into a bag he wore slung over his shoulder, pulled out a roll of papers, and tossed it into the entrance. It might have been Dennys or Sandy or any one of hundreds of boys with a newspaper route in any one of hundreds of towns back home, and yet, as with the children playing ball and jumping rope, there was something wrong about it. The rhythm of the gesture never varied. The paper flew in identically the same arc at each doorway, landed in identically the same spot. It was impossible for anybody to throw with such consistent perfection.

Calvin whistled. "I wonder if they play baseball here?"

As the boy saw them he slowed down on his machine and stopped, his hand arrested as it was about to plunge into the paper bag. "What are you kids doing out on the street?" he demanded. "Only route boys are allowed out now, you know that."

"No, we don't know it," Charles Wallace said. "We're strangers here. How about telling us something about this place?"

"You mean you've had your entrance papers processed and everything?" the boy asked. "You must have if you're here," he answered himself. "And what are you doing here if you don't know about us?"

"You tell me," Charles Wallace said.

"Are you examiners?" the boy asked a little anxiously. "Everybody knows our city has the best Central Intelligence Center on the planet. Our production levels are the highest. Our factories never close; our machines never stop rolling. Added to this, we have five poets, one musician, three artists, and six sculptors, all perfectly channeled."

"What are you quoting from?" Charles Wallace asked.

"The Manual, of course," the boy said. "We are the most oriented city on the planet. There has been no trouble of any kind for centuries. All Camazotz knows our record. That is why we are the capital city of Camazotz. That is why CENTRAL Central Intelligence is located here. That is why IT makes ITs home here." There was something about the way he said "IT" that made a shiver run up and down Meg's spine.

But Charles Wallace asked briskly, "Where is this Central Intelligence Center of yours?"

"CENTRAL Central," the boy corrected. "Just keep going and you can't miss it. You *are* strangers, aren't you! What are you doing here?"

"Are you supposed to ask questions?" Charles Wallace demanded severely.

The boy went white, just as the woman had. "I humbly beg your pardon. I must continue my route now or I will have to talk my timing into the explainer." And he shot off down the street on his machine.

Charles Wallace stared after him. "What is it?" he asked Meg and Calvin. "There was something funny about the way he talked, as though—well, as though he weren't really doing the talking. Know what I mean?"

Calvin nodded, thoughtfully. "Funny is right. Funny peculiar. Not only the way he talked, either. The whole thing smells."

"Come *on*." Meg pulled at them. How many times was it she had urged them on? "Let's go find Father. He'll be able to explain it all to us."

They walked on. After several more blocks they began to see other people, grown-up people, not children, walking up and down and across the streets. These people ignored the children entirely, seeming to be completely intent on their own business. Some of them went into the apartment buildings. Most of them were heading in the same direction as the children. As these people came to the main street from the side streets, they would swing around the corners with an odd, automatic stride, as though they were so deep in their own problems and the route was so familiar that they didn't have to pay any attention to where they were going.

After a while the apartment buildings gave way to what must have been office buildings, great stern structures with enormous entrances. Men and women with briefcases poured in and out.

Charles Wallace went up to one of the women, saying politely, "Excuse me, but could you please tell me—" But she hardly glanced at him as she continued on her way.

"Look." Meg pointed. Ahead of them, across a square, was the largest building they had ever seen, higher than the Empire State Building, and almost as long as it was high.

"This must be it," Charles Wallace said, "their CENTRAL Central Intelligence or whatever it is. Let's go in."

"But if Father's in some kind of trouble with this planet," Meg objected, "isn't that exactly where we *shouldn't* go?"

"Well, how do you propose finding him?" Charles Wallace demanded.

"I certainly wouldn't ask *there!*"

"I didn't say anything about asking. But we aren't going to have the faintest idea where or how to begin to look for him until we find out something more about this place, and I have a hunch that that's the place to start. If you have a better idea, Meg, why of course just say so."

"Oh, get down off your high horse," Meg said crossly. "Let's go to your old CENTRAL Central Intelligence and get it over with."

"I think we ought to have passports or something," Calvin suggested. "This is much more than leaving America to go to Europe. And that boy and the woman both seemed to care so much about having things in proper order. We certainly haven't got any papers in proper order."

"If we needed passports or papers Mrs Whatsit would have told us so," Charles Wallace said.

Calvin put his hands on his hips and looked down at Charles Wallace. "Now look here, old sport. I love those three old girls just as much as you do, but I'm not sure they know *everything*."

"They know a lot more than we do."

"Granted. But you know Mrs Whatsit talked about having been a star. I wouldn't think that being a star would give her much practice in knowing about people. When she tried to be a person she came pretty close to goofing it up. There was never anybody on land or sea like Mrs Whatsit the way she got herself up."

"She was just having fun," Charles said. "If she'd wanted to look like you or Meg, I'm sure she could have."

Calvin shook his head. "I'm not so sure. And these people seem to be *people*, if you know what I mean. They aren't like us, I grant you that, there's something very offbeat about them. But they're lots more like ordinary people than the ones on Uriel."

"Do you suppose they're robots?" Meg suggested.

Charles Wallace shook his head. "No. That boy who dropped the ball wasn't any robot. And I don't think the rest of them are, either. Let me listen for a minute."

They stood very still, side by side, in the shadow of one of the big office buildings. Six large doors kept swinging open, shut, open, shut, as people went in and out, in and out, looking straight ahead, straight ahead, paying no attention to the children whatsoever, whatsoever. Charles wore his listening, probing look. "They're not robots," he said suddenly and definitely. "I'm not sure *what* they are, but they're not robots. I can feel minds there. I can't get at them at all, but I can feel them sort of pulsing. Let me try a minute more."

The three of them stood there very quietly. The doors kept opening and shutting, opening and shutting, and the stiff people hurried in and out, in and out, walking jerkily like figures in an old silent movie. Then, abruptly, the stream of movement thinned. There were only a few people and these moved more rapidly, as if the film had been speeded up. One white-faced man in a dark suit looked directly at the children, said, "Oh, dear, I shall be late," and flickered into the building.

"He's like the white rabbit." Meg giggled nervously.

"I'm scared," Charles said. "I can't reach them at all. I'm completely shut out."

"We have to find Father—" Meg started again.

"Meg—" Charles Wallace's eyes were wide and frightened. "I'm not sure I'll even know Father. It's been so long, and I was only a baby—"

Meg's reassurance came quickly. "You'll know him! Of course you'll know him! The way you'd know me even without looking, because I'm always there for you, you can always reach in—"

"Yes." Charles punched one small fist into an open palm with a gesture of great decision. "Let's go to CENTRAL Central Intelligence."

Calvin reached out and caught both Charles and Meg by the arm. "You remember when we met, you asked me why I was there? And I told you it was because I had a compulsion, a feeling I just had to come to that particular place at that particular moment?"

"Yes, sure."

"I've got another feeling. Not the same kind, a different one, a feeling that if we go into that building we're going into terrible danger."

7 The Man with Red Eyes

"We knew we were going to be in danger," Charles Wallace said. "Mrs Whatsit told us that."

"Yes, and she told us that it was going to be worse for you than for Meg and me, and that you must be careful. You stay right here with Meg, old sport, and let me go in and case the joint and then report to you."

"No," Charles Wallace said firmly. "She told us to stay together. She told us not to go off by ourselves."

"She told *you* not to go off by yourself. I'm the oldest and I should go in first."

"No." Meg's voice was flat. "Charles is right, Cal. We have to stay together. Suppose you didn't come out and we had to go in after you? Unh-unh. Come on. But let's hold hands if you don't mind."

Holding hands, they crossed the square. The huge CENTRAL Central Intelligence Building had only one door, but it was an enormous one, at least two stories high and wider than a room, made of a dull, bronzelike material.

"Do we just knock?" Meg giggled.

Calvin studied the door. "There isn't any handle or knob or latch or anything. Maybe there's another way to get in."

"Let's try knocking, anyhow," Charles said. He raised his hand, but before he touched the door it slid up from the top and to each side, splitting into three sections that had been completely invisible a moment before. The startled children looked into a great entrance hall of dull, greeny marble. Marble benches lined three of the walls. People were sitting there like statues. The green of the marble reflecting on their faces made them look bilious. They turned their heads as the door opened, saw the children, looked away again.

"Come on," Charles said, and still holding hands, they stepped in. As they crossed the threshold the door shut silently behind them. Meg looked at Calvin and Charles and they, like the waiting people, were a sickly green.

The children went up to the blank fourth wall. It seemed unsubstantial, as though one might almost be able to walk through it. Charles put out his hand. "It's solid, and icy cold."

Calvin touched it, too. "Ugh."

Meg's left hand was held by Charles, her right by Calvin, and she had no desire to let go either of them to touch the wall.

"Let's ask somebody something." Charles led them over to one of the benches. "Er, could you tell us what's the procedure around here?" he asked one of the men. The men all wore nondescript business suits, and though their features were as different one from the other as the features of men on earth, there was also a sameness to them.

—Like the sameness of people riding in a subway, Meg thought.— Only, on a subway, every once in a while there's somebody different, and here there isn't.

The man looked at the children warily. "The procedure for what?"

"How do we see whoever's in authority?" Charles asked.

"You present your papers to the A machine. You ought to know that," the man said severely.

"Where is the A machine?" Calvin asked.

The man pointed to the blank wall.

"But there isn't a door or anything," Calvin said. "How do we get in?"

"You put your S papers in the B slot," the man said. "Why are you asking me these stupid questions? Do you think I don't know the answers? You'd better not play any games around here or you'll have to go through the Process machine again and you don't want to do *that*."

"We're strangers here," Calvin said. "That's why we don't know about things. Please tell us, sir, who you are and what you do."

"I run a number-one spelling machine on the second-grade level."

"But what are you doing here now?" Charles Wallace asked.

"I am here to report that one of my letters is jamming, and until it can be properly oiled by an F grade oiler, there is danger of jammed minds."

"Strawberry jam or raspberry?" Charles Wallace murmured. Calvin looked down at Charles and shook his head warningly. Meg gave the little boy's hand a slight, understanding pressure. Charles Wallace, she was quite sure, was not trying to be rude or funny; it was his way of whistling in the dark.

The man looked at Charles sharply. "I think I shall have to report you. I'm fond of children, due to the nature of my work, and I don't like to get them in trouble, but rather than run the risk myself of re-processing, I must report you."

"Maybe that's a good idea," Charles said. "Who do you report us to?"

"To *whom* do I report you."

"Well, to whom, then. I'm not on the second-grade level yet."

—I wish he wouldn't act so sure of himself, Meg thought, looking anxiously at Charles and holding his hand more and more tightly until he wriggled his fingers in protest. That's what Mrs Whatsit said he had to watch, being proud.—Don't, please don't, she thought hard at Charles Wallace. She wondered if Calvin realized that a lot of the arrogance was bravado.

The man stood up, moving jerkily as though he had been sitting for a long time. "I hope he isn't too hard on you," he murmured as he led the children toward the empty fourth wall. "But I've been reprocessed once and that was more than enough. And I don't want to get sent to IT. I've never been sent to IT and I can't risk having that happen."

There was IT again. What was this IT?

The man took from his pocket a folder filled with papers of every color. He shuffled through them carefully, finally withdrawing one. "I've had several reports to make lately. I shall have to ask for a requisition for more A-21 cards." He took the card and put it against the wall. It slid through the marble, as though it were being sucked in, and disappeared. "You may be detained for a few days," the man said, "but I'm sure they won't be too hard on you because of your youth. Just relax and don't fight and it will all be much easier for you." He went back to his seat, leaving the children standing and staring at the blank wall.

And suddenly the wall was no longer there and they were looking into an enormous room lined with machines. They were not unlike the great computing machines Meg had seen in her science books and that she knew her father sometimes worked with. Some did not seem to be in use; in others lights were flickering on and off. In one machine a long tape was being eaten; in another a series of dot-dashes were being punched. Several white-robed attendants were moving about, tending the machines. If they saw the children they gave no sign.

Calvin muttered something.

"What?" Meg asked him.

"There is nothing to fear except fear itself," Calvin said. "I'm quoting. Like Mrs Who. Meg, I'm scared stiff."

"So'm I." Meg held his hand more tightly. "Come on."

They stepped into the room with the machines. In spite of the enormous width of the room, it was even longer than it was wide. Perspective made the long rows of machines seem almost to meet. The children walked down the center of the room, keeping as far from the machines as possible.

"Though I don't suppose they're radioactive or anything," Charles Wallace said, "or that they're going to reach out and grab us and chew us up."

After they had walked for what seemed like miles, they could see that the enormous room did have an end, and that at the end there was something.

Charles Wallace said suddenly, and his voice held panic, "Don't let go my hands! Hold me tight! He's trying to get at me!"

"Who?" Meg squeaked.

"I don't know. But he's trying to get in at me! I can feel him!"

"Let's go back." Calvin started to pull away.

"No," Charles Wallace said. "I have to go on. We have to make decisions, and we can't make them if they're based on fear." His voice sounded old and strange and remote. Meg, clasping his small hand tightly, could feel it sweating in hers.

As they approached the end of the room their steps slowed. Before them was a platform. On the platform was a chair, and on the chair was a man.

What was there about him that seemed to contain all the coldness and darkness they had felt as they plunged through the Black Thing on their way to this planet?

"I have been waiting for you, my dears," the man said. His voice was kind and gentle, not at all the cold and frightening voice Meg had expected. It took her a moment to realize that, though the voice came from the man, he had not opened his mouth or moved his lips at all, that no real words had been spoken to fall upon her ears, that he had somehow communicated directly into their brains.

"But how does it happen that there are three of you?" the man asked.

Charles Wallace spoke with harsh boldness, but Meg could feel him trembling. "Oh, Calvin just came along for the ride."

"Oh, he did, did he?" For a moment there was a sharpness to the voice that spoke inside their minds. Then it relaxed and became soothing again. "I hope that it has been a pleasant one so far."

"Very educational," Charles Wallace said.

"Let Calvin speak for himself," the man ordered.

Calvin growled, his lips tight, his body rigid. "I have nothing to say."

Meg stared at the man in horrified fascination. His eyes were bright and had a reddish glow. Above his head was a light, and it glowed in the same manner as the eyes, pulsing, throbbing, in steady rhythm.

Charles Wallace shut his eyes tightly. "Close your eyes," he said to Meg and Calvin. "Don't look at the light. Don't look at his eyes. He'll hypnotize you."

"Clever, aren't you? Focusing your eyes would, of course, help," the soothing voice went on, "but there are other ways, my little man. Oh, yes, there are other ways."

"If you try it on me I shall kick you!" Charles Wallace said. It was the first time Meg had ever heard Charles Wallace suggesting violence.

"Oh, will you, indeed, my little man?" The thought was tolerant, amused, but four men in dark smocks appeared and flanked the children.

"Now, my dears," the words continued, "I shall of course have no need of recourse to violence, but I thought perhaps it would save you pain if I showed you at once that it would do you no good to try to oppose me. You see, what you will soon realize is that there is no need to fight me. Not only is there no need, but you will not have the slightest desire to do so. For why should you wish to fight someone who is here only to save you pain and trouble? For you, as well as for the rest of all the happy, useful people on this planet, *I*, in my own strength, am willing to assume all the pain, all the responsibility, all the burdens of thought and decision."

"We will make our own decisions, thank you," Charles Wallace said.

"But of *course*. And our decisions will be one, yours and mine. Don't you see how much better, how much *easier* for you that is? Let me show you. Let us say the multiplication table together."

"No," Charles Wallace said.

"Once one is one. Once two is two. Once three is three."

"Mary had a little lamb!" Charles Wallace shouted. "Its fleece was white as snow!"

"Once four is four. Once five is five. Once six is six."

"And everywhere that Mary went, the lamb was sure to go!"

"Once seven is seven. Once eight is eight. Once nine is nine."

"Peter, Peter, pumpkin eater, had a wife and couldn't keep her—"

"Once ten is ten. Once eleven is eleven. Once twelve is twelve."

The number words pounded insistently against Meg's brain. They seemed to be boring their way into her skull.

"Twice one is two. Twice two is four. Twice three is six."

Calvin's voice came out in an angry shout. "Fourscore and seven years ago our fathers brought forth on this continent a new nation, conceived in liberty, and dedicated to the proposition that all men are created equal."

"Twice four is eight. Twice five is ten. Twice six is twelve."

"Father!" Meg screamed. "Father!" The scream, half involuntary, jerked her mind back out of darkness.

The words of the multiplication table seemed to break up into laughter. "Splendid! Splendid! You have passed your preliminary tests with flying colors."

"You didn't think we were as easy as all that, falling for that old stuff, did you?" Charles Wallace demanded.

"Ah, I hoped not. I most sincerely hoped not. But, after all, you are very young and very impressionable, and the younger the better, my little man. The younger the better."

Meg looked up at the fiery eyes, at the light pulsing above them, and then away. She tried looking at the mouth, at the thin, almost colorless lips, and this was more possible, even though she had to look obliquely, so that she was not sure exactly what the face really looked like, whether it was young or old, cruel or kind, human or alien.

"If you please," she said, trying to sound calm and brave. "The only reason we are here is because we think our father is here. Can you tell us where to find him?"

"Ah, your father!" There seemed to be a great chortling of delight. "Ah, yes, your father! It is not *can* I, you know, young lady, but *will* I?"

"Will you, then?"

"That depends on a number of things. Why do you want your father?"

"Didn't you ever have a father yourself?" Meg demanded. "You don't want him for a *reason*. You want him because he's your *father*."

"Ah, but he hasn't been *acting* very like a father lately, has he? Abandoning his wife and his four little children to go gallivanting off on wild adventures of his own."

"He was working for the government. He'd never have left us otherwise. And we want to see him, please. Right now."

"My, but the little miss is impatient! Patience, patience, young lady."

Meg did not tell the man on the chair that patience was not one of her virtues.

"And by the way, my children," he continued blandly, "you don't need to vocalize verbally with me, you know. I can understand you quite as well as you can understand me."

Charles Wallace put his hands on his hips defiantly. "The spoken word is one of the triumphs of man," he proclaimed, "and I intend to continue using it, particularly with people I don't trust." But his voice was shaking. Charles Wallace, who even as an infant had seldom cried, was near tears.

"And you don't trust me?"

"What reason have you given us to trust you?"

"What cause have I given you for *dis*trust?" The thin lips curled slightly.

Suddenly Charles Wallace darted forward and hit the man as hard as he could, which was fairly hard, as he had had a good deal of coaching from the twins.

"Charles!" Meg screamed.

The men in dark smocks moved smoothly but with swiftness to Charles. The man in the chair casually raised one finger, and the men dropped back.

"Hold it—" Calvin whispered, and together he and Meg darted forward and grabbed Charles Wallace, pulling him back from the platform.

The man gave a wince and the thought of his voice was a little breathless, as though Charles Wallace's punch had succeeded in winding him. "May I ask why you did that?"

"Because you aren't you," Charles Wallace said. "I'm not sure what you are, but you"—he pointed to the man on the chair—"aren't what's talking to us. I'm sorry if I hurt you. I didn't think you were real. I thought perhaps you were a robot, because I don't feel anything coming directly from you. I'm not sure where it's coming from, but it's coming *through* you. It isn't you."

"Pretty smart, aren't you?" the thought asked, and Meg had an uncomfortable feeling that she detected a snarl.

"It's not that I'm smart," Charles Wallace said, and again Meg could feel the palm of his hand sweating inside hers.

"Try to find out who I am, then," the thought probed.

"I have been trying," Charles Wallace said, his voice high and troubled.

"Look into my eyes. Look deep within them and I will tell you."

Charles Wallace looked quickly at Meg and Calvin, then said, as though to himself, "I have to," and focused his clear blue eyes on the red ones of the man in the chair. Meg looked not at the man but at her brother. After a moment it seemed that his eyes were no longer focusing. The pupils grew smaller and smaller, as though he were looking into an intensely bright light, until they seemed to close entirely, until his eyes were nothing but an opaque blue. He slipped his hands out of Meg's and Calvin's and started walking slowly toward the man on the chair.

"No!" Meg screamed. "No!"

But Charles Wallace continued his slow walk forward, and she knew that he had not heard her.

"No!" she screamed again, and ran after him. With her inefficient flying tackle she landed on him. She was so much larger than he that he fell sprawling, hitting his head with a sharp crack against the marble floor. She knelt by him, sobbing. After a moment of lying there as though he had been knocked out by the blow, he opened his eyes, shook his head, and sat up. Slowly the pupils of his eyes dilated until they were back to normal, and the blood came back to his white cheeks.

The man on the chair spoke directly into Meg's mind, and now there was a distinct menace to the words. "I am not pleased," he said to her. "I could very easily lose patience with you, and that, for your information, young lady, would not be good for your father. If you have the slightest desire to see your father again, you had better cooperate."

Meg reacted as she sometimes reacted to Mr. Jenkins at school. She scowled down at the ground in sullen fury. "It might help if you gave us something to eat," she complained. "We're all starved. If you're going to be horrible to us, you might as well give us full stomachs first."

Again the thoughts coming at her broke into laughter. "Isn't she the funny girl, though! It's lucky for you that you amuse me, my dear, or I shouldn't be so easy on you. The boys I find not nearly so diverting. Ah, well. Now tell me, young lady, if I feed you, will you stop interfering with me?"

"No," Meg said.

"Starvation does work wonders, of course," the man told her. "I hate to use such primitive methods on you, but of course you realize that you force them on me."

"I wouldn't eat your old food, anyhow." Meg was still all churned up and angry, as though she were in Mr. Jenkins's office. "I wouldn't trust it."

"Of course our food, being synthetic, is not superior to your messes of beans and bacon and so forth, but I assure you that it's far more nourishing, and though it has no taste of its own, a slight conditioning is all that is necessary to give you the illusion that you are eating a roast turkey dinner."

"If I ate now I'd throw up, anyhow," Meg said.

Still holding Meg's and Calvin's hands, Charles Wallace stepped forward. "Okay, what next?" he asked the man on the chair. "We've had enough of these preliminaries. Let's get on with it."

"That's exactly what we were doing," the man said, "until your sister interfered by practically giving you a brain concussion. Shall we try again?"

"No!" Meg cried. "No, Charles. *Please*. Let me do it. Or Calvin."

"But it is only the little boy whose neurological system is complex enough. If you tried to conduct the necessary neurons your brains would explode."

"And Charles's wouldn't?"

"I think not."

"But there's a possibility?"

"There's always a possibility."

"Then he mustn't do it."

"I think you will have to grant him the right to make his own decisions."

But Meg, with the dogged tenacity that had so often caused her trouble, continued. "You mean Calvin and I can't know who you really are?"

"Oh, no, I didn't say that. You can't know it in the same way, nor is it as important to me to have you know. Ah, here we are!" From somewhere in the shadows appeared four more men in dark smocks carrying a table. It was covered with a white cloth, like the tables used by Room Service in hotels, and held a metal hot box containing something that smelled delicious, something that smelled like a turkey dinner.

There's something phony in the whole setup, Meg thought. There is definitely something rotten in the state of Camazotz.

Again the thoughts seemed to break into laughter. "Of course it doesn't *really* smell, but isn't it as good as though it really did?"

"I don't smell anything," Charles Wallace said.

"I know, young man, and think how much you're missing. This will all taste to you as though you were eating sand. But I suggest that you force it down. I would rather not have your decisions come from the weakness of an empty stomach."

The table was set up in front of them, and the dark-smocked men heaped their plates with turkey and dressing and mashed potatoes and gravy and little green peas with big yellow blobs of butter melting in them and cranberries and sweet potatoes topped with gooey browned marshmallows and olives and celery and rosebud radishes and—

Meg felt her stomach rumbling loudly. The saliva came to her mouth.

"Oh, Jeeminy—" Calvin mumbled.

Chairs appeared and the four men who had provided the feast slid back into the shadows.

Charles Wallace freed his hands from Meg and Calvin and plunked himself down on one of the chairs.

"Come on," he said. "If it's poisoned it's poisoned, but I don't think it is."

Calvin sat down. Meg continued to stand indecisively.

Calvin took a bite. He chewed. He swallowed. He looked at Meg. "If this isn't real, it's the best imitation you'll ever get."

Charles Wallace took a bite, made a face, and spit out his mouthful. "It's unfair!" he shouted at the man.

Laughter again. "Go on, little fellow. Eat."

Meg sighed and sat. "I don't think we should eat this stuff, but if you're going to, I'd better, too." She took a mouthful. "It tastes all right. Try some of mine, Charles." She held out a forkful of turkey.

Charles Wallace took it, made another face, but managed to swallow. "Still tastes like sand," he said. He looked at the man. "Why?"

"You know perfectly well why. You've shut your mind entirely to me. The other two can't. I can get in through the chinks. Not all the way in, but enough to give them a turkey dinner. You see, I'm really just a kind, jolly old gentleman."

"Ha," Charles Wallace said.

The man lifted his lips into a smile, and his smile was the most horrible thing Meg had ever seen. "Why don't you trust me, Charles? Why don't you trust me enough to come in and find out what I am? I am peace and utter rest. I am freedom from all responsibility. To come in to me is the last difficult decision you need ever make."

"If I come in, can I get out again?" Charles Wallace asked.

"But of course, if you want to. But I don't think you will want to."

"If I come—not to stay, you understand—just to find out about you, will you tell us where Father is?"

"Yes. That is a promise. And I don't make promises lightly."

"Can I speak to Meg and Calvin alone, without your listening in?"

"No."

Charles shrugged. "Listen," he said to Meg and Calvin. "I have to find out what he really is. You know that. I'm going to try to hold back.

I'm going to try to keep part of myself out. You mustn't stop me this time, Meg."

"But you won't be able to, Charles! He's stronger than you are! You know that!"

"I have to try."

"But Mrs Whatsit warned you!"

"I have to try. For Father, Meg. Please. I want—I want to know my father—" For a moment his lips trembled. Then he was back in control. "But it isn't only Father, Meg. You know that, now. It's the Black Thing. We have to do what Mrs Which sent us to do."

"Calvin—" Meg begged.

But Calvin shook his head. "He's right, Meg. And we'll be with him, no matter what happens."

"But what's going to happen?" Meg cried.

Charles Wallace looked up at the man. "Okay," he said. "Let's go."

Now the red eyes and the light above seemed to bore into Charles, and again the pupils of the little boy's eyes contracted. When the final point of black was lost in blue he turned away from the red eyes, looked at Meg, and smiled sweetly, but the smile was not Charles Wallace's smile.

"Come on, Meg, eat this delicious food that has been prepared for us," he said.

Meg snatched Charles Wallace's plate and threw it on the floor, so that the dinner splashed about and the plate broke into fragments. "No!" she cried, her voice rising shrilly. "No! No! No!"

From the shadows came one of the dark-smocked men and put another plate in front of Charles Wallace, and he began to eat eagerly. "What's wrong, Meg?" Charles Wallace asked. "Why are you being so belligerent and uncooperative?" The voice was Charles Wallace's voice, and yet it was different, too, somehow flattened out, almost as a voice might have sounded on the two-dimensional planet.

Meg grabbed wildly at Calvin, shrieking, "That isn't Charles! Charles is gone!"

8 The Transparent Column

Charles Wallace sat there tucking away turkey and dressing as though it were the most delicious thing he had ever tasted. He was dressed like Charles Wallace; he looked like Charles Wallace; he had the same sandy brown hair, the same face that had not yet lost its baby roundness. Only the eyes were different, for the black was still swallowed up in blue. But it was far more than this that made Meg feel that Charles Wallace was gone, that the little boy in his place was only a copy of Charles Wallace, only a doll.

She fought down a sob. "Where is he?" she demanded of the man with red eyes. "What have you done with him? Where is Charles Wallace?"

"But, my dear child, you are hysterical," the man thought at her. "He is right there, before you, well and happy. Completely well and happy for the first time in his life. And he is finishing his dinner, which you also would be wise to do."

"You know it isn't Charles!" Meg shouted. "You've got him somehow."

"Hush, Meg. There's no use trying to talk to him," Calvin said, speaking in a low voice into her ear. "What we have to do is hold Charles Wallace tight. He's there, somewhere, underneath, and we mustn't let them take him away from us. Help me hold him, Meg. Don't lose control of yourself. Not now. You've got to help me hold Charles!" He took the little boy firmly by one arm.

Fighting down her hysteria, Meg took Charles's other arm and held it tightly.

"You're hurting me, Meg!" Charles said sharply. "Let me go!"

"No," Meg said grimly.

"We've been all wrong." Charles Wallace's voice, Meg thought, might have been a recording. There was a canned quality to it. "He isn't an enemy at all. He's our friend."

"Nuts," Calvin said rudely.

"You don't understand, Calvin," Charles Wallace said. "Mrs Whatsit, Mrs Who, and Mrs Which have confused us. They're the ones who are really our enemies. We never should have trusted them for a minute." He spoke in his calmest, most reasonable voice, the voice which infuriated the twins. He seemed to be looking directly at Calvin as he spoke, and yet Meg was sure that the bland blue eyes could not see, and that someone, something else was looking at Calvin through Charles.

Now the cold, strange eyes turned to her. "Meg, let go. I will explain it all to you, but you must let go."

"No." Meg gritted her teeth. She did not release her grasp, and Charles Wallace began to pull away with a power that was not his own, and her own spindly strength was no match against it. "Calvin!" she gasped as Charles Wallace wrenched his arm from her and stood up.

Calvin the athlete, Calvin the boy who split firewood and brought it in for his mother, whose muscles were strong and controlled, let go Charles Wallace's wrist and tackled him as though he were a football. Meg, in her panic and rage, darted at the man on the chair, intending to hit him as Charles Wallace had done, but the black-smocked men were too quick for her, and one of them held her with her arms pinioned behind her back.

"Calvin, I advise you to let me go," came Charles Wallace's voice from under Calvin.

Calvin, his face screwed up with grim determination, did not relax his hold. The man with red eyes nodded and three of the men moved in on Calvin (at least it took three of them), pried him loose, and held him as Meg was being held.

"Mrs Whatsit!" Meg called despairingly. "Oh, Mrs Whatsit!"

But Mrs Whatsit did not come.

"Meg," Charles Wallace said. "Meg, just listen to me."

"Okay, I'm listening."

"We've been all wrong, I told you; we haven't understood. We've been fighting our friend, and Father's friend."

"If Father tells me he's our friend, maybe I'll believe it. Maybe. Unless he's got Father—under—under a spell, or whatever it is, like you."

"This isn't a fairy tale. Spells, indeed," Charles Wallace said. "Meg, you've got to stop fighting and relax. Relax and be happy. Oh, Meg, if you'd just relax you'd realize that all our troubles are over. You don't understand what a wonderful place we've come to. You see, on this planet everything is in perfect order because everybody has learned to relax, to give in, to submit. All you have to do is look quietly and steadily into the eyes of our good friend here, for he is our friend, dear sister, and he will take you in as he has taken me."

"Taken you in is right!" Meg said. "You know you're not you. You know you've never in your life called me *dear sister*."

"Shut up a minute, Meg," Calvin whispered to her. He looked up at the man with red eyes. "Okay, have your henchmen let us go and stop talking to us through Charles. We know it's you talking, or whatever's talking through you. Anyhow, we know you have Charles hypnotized."

"A most primitive way of putting it," the man with red eyes murmured. He gestured slightly with one finger, and Meg and Calvin were released.

"Thanks," Calvin said wryly. "Now, if you are our friend, will you tell us who—or what—you are?"

"It is not necessary for you to know who I am. I am the Prime Coordinator, that is all you need to know."

"But you're being spoken through, aren't you, just like Charles Wallace? Are you hypnotized, too?"

"I told you that was too primitive a word, without the correct connotations."

"Is it you who is going to take us to Mr. Murry?"

"No. It is not necessary, nor is it possible, for me to leave here. Charles Wallace will conduct you."

"Charles Wallace?"

"Yes."

"When?"

"Now." The man with red eyes made the frightening grimace that passed for his smile. "Yes, I think it might as well be now."

Charles Wallace gave a slight jerk of his head, saying, "Come," and started to walk in a strange, gliding, mechanical manner. Calvin followed him. Meg hesitated, looking from the man with red eyes to Charles and Calvin. She wanted to reach out and grab Calvin's hand, but it seemed that ever since they had begun their journeyings she had been looking for a hand to hold, so she stuffed her fists into her pockets and walked along behind the two boys.—I've got to be brave, she said to herself.—I *will* be.

They moved down a long, white, and seemingly endless corridor.

Charles Wallace continued the jerky rhythm of his walk and did not once look back to see if they were with him.

Suddenly Meg broke into a run and caught up with Calvin. "Cal," she said, "listen. Quick. Remember Mrs Whatsit said your gift was communication and that was what she was giving you. We've been trying to fight Charles physically, and that isn't any good. Can't you try to communicate with him? Can't you try to get in to him?"

"Golly day, you're right." Calvin's face lit up with hope, and his eyes, which had been somber, regained their usual sparkle. "I've been in such a swivet—It may not do any good, but at least I can try." They quickened their pace until they were level with Charles Wallace. Calvin reached out for his arm, but Charles flung it off.

"Leave me alone," he snarled.

"I'm not going to hurt you, old sport," Calvin said. "I'm just trying to be friendly. Let's make it up, hunh?"

"You mean you're coming around?" Charles Wallace asked.

"Sure." Calvin's voice was coaxing. "We're reasonable people, after all. Just look at me for a minute, Charlibus."

Charles Wallace stopped and turned slowly to look at Calvin with his cold, vacant eyes. Calvin looked back, and Meg could feel the intensity of his concentration. An enormous shudder shook Charles Wallace. For a brief flash his eyes seemed to see. Then his whole body twirled wildly, and went rigid. He started his marionette's walk again. "I should have known better," he said. "If you want to see Murry you'd better come with me and not try any more hanky-panky."

"Is that what you call your father—Murry?" Calvin asked. Meg could see that he was angry and upset at his near-success.

"Father? What is a father?" Charles Wallace intoned. "Merely another misconception. If you feel the need of a father, then I would suggest that you turn to IT."

IT again.

"Who's this IT?" Meg asked.

"All in good time," Charles Wallace said. "You're not ready for IT yet. First of all, I will tell you something about this beautiful, enlightened planet of Camazotz." His voice took on the dry, pedantic tones of Mr. Jenkins. "Perhaps you do not realize that on Camazotz we have conquered all illness, all deformity—"

"We?" Calvin interrupted.

Charles continued as though he had not heard. And of course he hadn't, Meg thought. "We let no one suffer. It is so much kinder simply to annihilate anyone who is ill. Nobody has weeks and weeks of runny noses and sore throats. Rather than endure such discomfort, they are simply put to sleep."

"You mean they're put to sleep while they have a cold, or that they're murdered?" Calvin demanded.

"Murder is a most primitive word," Charles Wallace said. "There is no such thing as murder on Camazotz. IT takes care of all such things." He moved jerkily to the wall of the corridor, stood still for a moment, then raised his hand. The wall flickered, quivered, grew transparent. Charles Wallace walked through it, beckoned to Meg and Calvin, and they followed. They were in a small, square room from which radiated a dull, sulphurous light. There was something ominous to Meg in the very compactness of the room, as though the walls, the ceiling, the floor might move together and crush anybody rash enough to enter.

"How did you do that?" Calvin asked Charles.

"Do what?"

"Make the wall—open—like that."

"I merely rearranged the atoms," Charles Wallace said loftily. "You've studied atoms in school, haven't you?"

"Sure, but—"

"Then you know enough to know that matter isn't solid, don't you? That you, Calvin, consist mostly of empty space? That if all the matter in you came together you'd be the size of the head of a pin? That's plain scientific fact, isn't it?"

"Yes, but—"

"So I simply pushed the atoms aside and we walked through the space between them."

Meg's stomach seemed to drop, and she realized that the square box in which they stood must be an elevator and that they had started to move upward with great speed. The yellow light lit up their faces, and the pale blue of Charles's eyes absorbed the yellow and turned green.

Calvin licked his lips. "Where are we going?"

"Up." Charles continued his lecture. "On Camazotz we are all happy because we are all alike. Differences create problems. You know that, don't you, dear sister?"

"No," Meg said.

"Oh, yes, you do. You've seen at home how true it is. You know that's the reason you're not happy at school. Because you're different."

"*I'm* different, and I'm happy," Calvin said.

"But you pretend that you *aren't* different."

"I'm different, and I like being different." Calvin's voice was unnaturally loud.

"Maybe I don't like being different," Meg said, "but I don't want to be like everybody else, either."

Charles Wallace raised his hand and the motion of the square box ceased and one of the walls seemed to disappear. Charles stepped out, Meg and Calvin following him, Calvin just barely making it before the wall came into being again and they could no longer see where the opening had been.

"You wanted Calvin to get left behind, didn't you?" Meg said.

"I am merely trying to teach you to stay on your toes. I warn you, if I have any more trouble from either of you, I shall have to take you to IT."

As the word IT fell from Charles's lips, again Meg felt as though she had been touched by something slimy and horrible. "So what is this IT?" she asked.

"You might call IT the Boss." Then Charles Wallace giggled, a giggle that was the most sinister sound Meg had ever heard. "IT sometimes calls ITself the Happiest Sadist."

Meg spoke coldly, to cover her fear. "I don't know what you're talking about."

"That's s-a-d-i-s-t, not s-a-d-d-e-s-t, you know," Charles Wallace said, and giggled again. "Lots of people don't pronounce it correctly."

"Well, I don't care," Meg said defiantly. "I don't ever want to see IT, and that's that."

Charles Wallace's strange, monotonous voice ground against her ears. "Meg, you're supposed to have *some* mind. Why do you think we have wars at home? Why do you think people get confused and unhappy? Because they all live their own, separate, individual lives. I've been trying to explain to you in the simplest possible way that on Camazotz individuals have been done away with. Camazotz is ONE mind. It's IT. And that's why everybody's so happy and efficient. That's what old witches like Mrs Whatsit don't want to have happen at home."

"She's not a witch," Meg interrupted.

"No?"

"No," Calvin said. "You know she's not. You know that's just their game. Their way, maybe, of laughing in the dark."

"In the dark is correct," Charles continued. "They want us to go on being confused instead of properly organized."

Meg shook her head violently. "No!" she shouted. "I know our world isn't perfect, Charles, but it's better than this. This isn't the only alternative! It can't be!"

"Nobody suffers here," Charles intoned. "Nobody is ever unhappy."

"But nobody's ever happy, either," Meg said earnestly. "Maybe if you aren't unhappy sometimes, you don't know how to be happy. Calvin, I want to go home."

"We can't leave Charles," Calvin told her, "and we can't go before we've found your father. You know that. But you're right, Meg, and Mrs Which is right. This is Evil."

Charles Wallace shook his head, and scorn and disapproval seemed to emanate from him. "Come. We're wasting time." He moved rapidly down the corridor, but continued to speak. "How dreadful it is to be low, individual organisms. Tch-tch-tch." His pace quickened from step to step, his short legs flashing, so that Meg and Calvin almost had to run to keep up with him. "Now see this," he said. He raised his hand and suddenly they could see through one of the walls into a small room. In the room a little boy was bouncing a ball. He was bouncing it in rhythm, and the walls of his little cell seemed to pulse with the rhythm of the ball. And each time the ball bounced he screamed as though he were in pain.

"That's the little boy we saw this afternoon," Calvin said sharply, "the little boy who wasn't bouncing the ball like the others."

Charles Wallace giggled again. "Yes. Every once in a while there's a little trouble with cooperation, but it's easily taken care of. After today he'll never desire to deviate again. Ah, here we are."

He moved rapidly down the corridor and again held up his hand to make the wall transparent. They looked into another small room or cell. In the center of it was a large, round, transparent column, and inside this column was a man.

"FATHER!" Meg screamed.

9 IT

Meg rushed at the man imprisoned in the column, but as she reached what seemed to be the open door she was hurled back as though she had crashed into a brick wall.

Calvin caught her. "It's just transparent like glass this time," he told her. "We can't go through it."

Meg was so sick and dizzy from the impact that she could not answer. For a moment she was afraid that she would throw up or faint. Charles Wallace laughed again, the laugh that was not his own, and it was this that saved her, for once more anger overcame her pain and fear. Charles Wallace, her own real, dear Charles Wallace, never laughed at her when she hurt herself. Instead, his arms would go quickly around her neck and he would press his soft cheek against hers in loving comfort. But the demon Charles Wallace snickered. She turned away from him and looked again at the man in the column.

"Oh, Father—" she whispered longingly, but the man in the column did not move to look at her. The horn-rimmed glasses, which always seemed so much a part of him, were gone, and the expression of his eyes was turned inward, as though he were deep in thought. He had grown a beard, and the silky brown was shot with gray. His hair, too, had not been cut. It wasn't just the overlong hair of the man in the snapshot at Cape Canaveral; it was pushed back from his high forehead and fell softly almost to his shoulders, so that he looked like someone in another century, or a shipwrecked sailor. But there was no question, despite the change in him, that he was her father, her own beloved father.

"My, he looks a mess, doesn't he?" Charles Wallace said, and sniggered.

Meg swung on him with sick rage. "Charles, that's Father! Father!"
"So what?"

Meg turned away from him and held out her arms to the man in the column.

"He doesn't see us, Meg," Calvin said gently.

"Why? Why?"

"I think it's sort of like those little peepholes they have in apartments, in the front doors," Calvin explained. "You know. From inside you can look through and see everything. And from outside you can't see anything at all. We can see him, but he can't see us."

"Charles!" Meg pleaded. "Let me in to Father!"

"Why?" Charles asked placidly.

Meg remembered that when they were in the room with the man with red eyes she had knocked Charles Wallace back into himself when she tackled him and his head cracked the floor; so she hurled herself at him. But before she could reach him his fist shot out and punched her hard in the stomach. She gasped for breath. Sickly, she turned away from her brother, back to the transparent wall. There was the cell, there was the column with her father inside. Although she could see him, although she was almost close enough to touch him, he seemed farther away than he had been when she had pointed him out to Calvin in the picture on the piano. He stood there quietly as though frozen in a column of ice, an expression of suffering and endurance on his face that pierced into her heart like an arrow.

"You say you want to help Father?" Charles Wallace's voice came from behind her, with no emotion whatsoever.

"Yes. Don't you?" Meg demanded, swinging around and glaring at him.

"But of course. That is why we are here."

"Then what do we *do*?" Meg tried to keep the franticness out of her voice, trying to sound as drained of feeling as Charles, but nevertheless ending on a squeak.

"You must do as I have done, and go in to IT," Charles said.

"No."

"I can see you don't really want to save Father."

"How will my being a zombie save Father?"

"You will just have to take my word for it, Margaret," came the cold, flat voice from Charles Wallace. "IT wants you and IT will get you. Don't forget that I, too, am part of IT, now. You know I wouldn't have done IT if IT weren't the right thing to do."

"Calvin," Meg asked in agony, "will it really save Father?"

But Calvin was paying no attention to her. He seemed to be concentrating with all his power on Charles Wallace. He stared into the pale blue that was all that was left of Charles Wallace's eyes. *"And, for thou wast a spirit too delicate/To act her earthy and abhorr'd commands . . . /she did confine thee . . . into a cloven pine—"* he whispered, and Meg recognized Mrs Who's words to him.

For a moment Charles Wallace seemed to listen. Then he shrugged and turned away. Calvin followed him, trying to keep his eyes focused on Charles's. "If you want a witch, Charles," he said, "IT's the witch. Not our ladies. Good thing I had *The Tempest* at school this year, isn't it, Charles? It was the witch who put Ariel in the cloven pine, wasn't it?"

Charles Wallace's voice seemed to come from a great distance. "Stop staring at me."

Breathing quickly with excitement, Calvin continued to pin Charles Wallace with his stare. "You're like Ariel in the cloven pine, Charles. And I can let you out. Look at me, Charles. Come back to us."

Again the shudder went through Charles Wallace.

Calvin's intense voice hit at him. "Come back, Charles. Come back to us."

Again Charles shuddered. And then it was as though an invisible hand had smacked against his chest and knocked him to the ground, and the stare with which Calvin had held him was broken. Charles sat there on the floor of the corridor whimpering, not a small boy's sound, but a fearful, animal noise.

"Calvin." Meg turned on him, clasping her hands intensely. "Try to get to Father."

Calvin shook his head. "Charles almost came out. I almost did it. He almost came back to us."

"Try Father," Meg said again.

"How?"

"Your cloven-pine thing. Isn't Father imprisoned in a cloven pine even more than Charles? Look at him, in that column there. Get him out, Calvin."

Calvin spoke in an exhausted way. "Meg. I don't know what to do. I don't know how to get in. Meg, they're asking too much of us."

"Mrs Who's spectacles!" Meg said suddenly. Mrs Who had told her to use them only as a last resort, and surely that was now. She reached into her pocket and the spectacles were there, cool and light and comforting. With trembling fingers she pulled them out.

"Give me those spectacles!" Charles Wallace's voice came in a harsh command, and he scrambled up off the floor and ran at her.

She barely had time to snatch off her own glasses and put on Mrs

Who's, and, as it was, one earpiece dropped down her cheek and they barely stayed on her nose. As Charles Wallace lunged at her she flung herself against the transparent door and she was through it. She was in the cell with the imprisoning column that held her father. With trembling fingers she straightened Mrs Who's glasses and put her own in her pocket.

"Give them to me," came Charles Wallace's menacing voice, and he was in the cell with her, with Calvin on the outside pounding frantically to get in.

Meg kicked at Charles Wallace and ran at the column. She felt as though she were going through something dark and cold. But she was through. "Father!" she cried. And she was in his arms.

This was the moment for which she had been waiting, not only since Mrs Which whisked them off on their journeys, but during the long months and years before, when the letters had stopped coming, when people made remarks about Charles Wallace, when Mrs. Murry showed a rare flash of loneliness or grief. This was the moment that meant that now and forever everything would be all right.

As she pressed against her father, all was forgotten except joy. There was only the peace and comfort of leaning against him, the wonder of the protecting circle of his arms, the feeling of complete reassurance and safety that his presence always gave her.

Her voice broke on a happy sob. "Oh, Father! Oh, Father!"

"Meg!" he cried in glad surprise. "Meg, what are you doing here? Where's your mother? Where are the boys?"

She looked out of the column, and there was Charles Wallace in the cell, an alien expression distorting his face. She turned back to her father. There was no more time for greeting, for joy, for explanations. "We have to go to Charles Wallace," she said, her words tense. "Quickly."

Her father's hands were moving gropingly over her face, and as she felt the touch of his strong, gentle fingers, she realized with a flooding of horror that she could see him, that she could see Charles in the cell and Calvin in the corridor, but her father could not see them, could not see her. She looked at him in panic, but his eyes were the same steady blue that she remembered. She moved her hand brusquely across his line of vision, but he did not blink.

"Father!" she cried. "Father! Can't you see me?"

His arms went around her again in a comforting, reassuring gesture. "No, Meg."

"But, Father, I can see you—" Her voice trailed off. Suddenly she shoved Mrs Who's glasses down her nose and peered over them, and immediately she was in complete and utter darkness. She snatched them off her face and thrust them at her father. "Here."

His fingers closed about the spectacles. "Darling," he said, "I'm afraid your glasses won't help."

"But they're Mrs Who's, they aren't mine," she explained, not realizing that her words would sound like gibberish to him. "Please try them, Father. Please!" She waited while she felt him fumbling in the dark. "Can you see now?" she asked. "Can you see now, Father?"

"Yes," he said. "Yes. The wall is transparent, now. How extraordinary! I could almost see the atoms rearranging!" His voice had its old familiar sound of excitement and discovery. It was the way he sounded sometimes when he came home from his laboratory after a good day and began to tell his wife about his work. Then he cried out, "Charles! Charles Wallace!" And then, "Meg, what's happened to him? What's wrong? That *is* Charles, isn't it?"

"IT has him, Father," she explained tensely. "He's gone into IT. Father, we have to help him."

For a long moment Mr. Murry was silent. The silence was filled with the words he was thinking and would not speak out loud to his daughter. Then he said, "Meg, I'm in prison here. I have been for—"

"Father, these walls. You can go through them. I came through the column to get in to you. It was Mrs Who's glasses."

Mr. Murry did not stop to ask who Mrs Who was. He slapped his hand against the translucent column. "It seems solid enough."

"But I got in," Meg repeated. "I'm here. Maybe the glasses help the atoms rearrange. Try it, Father."

She waited, breathlessly, and after a moment she realized that she was alone in the column. She put out her hands in the darkness and felt its smooth surface curving about her on all sides. She seemed utterly alone, the silence and darkness impenetrable forever. She fought down panic until she heard her father's voice coming to her very faintly.

"I'm coming back in for you, Meg."

It was almost a tangible feeling as the atoms of the strange material seemed to part to let him through to her. In their beach house at Cape Canaveral there had been a curtain between dining and living room made of long strands of rice. It looked like a solid curtain, but you could walk right through it. At first Meg had flinched each time she came up to the curtain; but gradually Meg got used to it and would go running right through, leaving the long strands of rice swinging behind her. Perhaps the atoms of these walls were arranged in somewhat the same fashion.

"Put your arms around my neck, Meg," Mr. Murry said. "Hold on to me tightly. Close your eyes and don't be afraid." He picked her up and she wrapped her long legs around his waist and clung to his neck. With Mrs Who's spectacles on, she had felt only a faint darkness and coldness as she moved through the column. Without the glasses, she felt the same awful clamminess she had felt when they tessered through the outer darkness of Camazotz. Whatever the Black Thing was to which Camazotz had submitted, it was within as well as without the planet. For a moment it seemed that the chill darkness would tear her from her father's arms. She tried to scream, but within that icy horror no sound was possible. Her father's arms tightened about her, and she clung to his neck in a stranglehold, but she was no longer lost in panic. She knew that if her father could not get her through the wall he would stay with her rather than leave her; she knew that she was safe as long as she was in his arms.

Then they were outside. The column rose up in the middle of the room, crystal-clear and empty.

Meg blinked at the blurred figures of Charles and her father, and wondered why they did not clear. Then she grabbed her own glasses out of her pocket and put them on, and her myopic eyes were able to focus.

Charles Wallace was tapping one foot impatiently against the floor. "IT is not pleased," he said. "IT is not pleased at all."

Mr. Murry released Meg and knelt in front of the little boy. "Charles." His voice was tender. "Charles Wallace."

"What do you want?"

"I'm your father, Charles. Look at me."

The pale blue eyes seemed to focus on Mr. Murry's face. "Hi, Pop," came an insolent voice.

"That isn't Charles!" Meg cried. "Oh, Father, Charles isn't like that. IT has him."

"Yes." Mr. Murry sounded tired. "I see." He held his arms out. "Charles. Come here."

Father will make it all right, Meg thought. Everything will be all right now.

Charles did not move toward the outstretched arms. He stood a few feet away from his father, and he did not look at him.

"Look at me," Mr. Murry commanded.

"No."

Mr. Murry's voice became harsh. "When you speak to me you will say 'No, Father,' or 'No, sir.' "

"Come off it, Pop," came the cold voice from Charles Wallace—

Charles Wallace who, outside Camazotz, had been strange, had been different, but never rude. "You're not the boss around here."

Meg could see Calvin pounding again on the glass wall. "Calvin!" she called.

"He can't hear you," Charles said. He made a horrible face at Calvin, and then he thumbed his nose.

"Who's Calvin?" Mr. Murry asked.

"He's—" Meg started, but Charles Wallace cut her short.

"You'll have to defer your explanations. Let's go."

"Go where?"

"To IT."

"No," Mr. Murry said. "You can't take Meg there."

"Oh, can't I!"

"No, you cannot. You're my son, Charles, and I'm afraid you will have to do as I say."

"But he *isn't* Charles!" Meg cried in anguish. Why didn't her father understand? "Charles is nothing like that, Father! You know he's nothing like that!"

"He was only a baby when I left," Mr. Murry said heavily.

"Father, it's IT talking through Charles. IT isn't Charles. He's— he's bewitched."

"Fairy tales again," Charles said.

"You know IT, Father?" Meg asked.

"Yes."

"Have you seen IT?"

"Yes, Meg." Again his voice sounded exhausted. "Yes. I have." He turned to Charles. "You know she wouldn't be able to hold out."

"Exactly," Charles said.

"Father, you can't talk to him as though he were Charles! Ask Calvin! Calvin will tell you."

"Come along," Charles Wallace said. "We must go." He held up his hand carelessly and walked out of the cell, and there was nothing for Meg and Mr. Murry to do but to follow.

As they stepped into the corridor Meg caught at her father's sleeve. "Calvin, here's Father!"

Calvin turned anxiously toward them. His freckles and his hair stood out brilliantly against his white face.

"Make your introductions later," Charles Wallace said. "IT does not like to be kept waiting." He walked down the corridor, his gait seeming to get more jerky with each step. The others followed, walking rapidly to keep up.

"Does your father know about the Mrs W's?" Calvin asked Meg.

"There hasn't been time for anything. Everything's awful." Despair settled like a stone in the pit of Meg's stomach. She had been so certain that the moment she found her father everything would be all right. Everything would be settled. All the problems would be taken out of her hands. She would no longer be responsible for anything.

And instead of this happy and expected outcome, they seemed to be encountering all kinds of new troubles.

"He doesn't understand about Charles," she whispered to Calvin, looking unhappily at her father's back as he walked behind the little boy.

"Where are we going?" Calvin asked.

"To IT. Calvin, I don't want to go! I can't!" She stopped, but Charles continued his jerky pace.

"We can't leave Charles," Calvin said. "They wouldn't like it."

"Who wouldn't?"

"Mrs Whatsit & Co."

"But they've betrayed us! They brought us here to this terrible place and abandoned us!"

Calvin looked at her in surprise. "You sit down and give up if you like," he said. "I'm sticking with Charles." He ran to keep up with Charles Wallace and Mr. Murry.

"I didn't mean—" Meg started, and pounded after them.

Just as she caught up with them Charles Wallace stopped and raised his hand, and there was the elevator again, its yellow light sinister. Meg felt her stomach jerk as the swift descent began. They were silent until the motion stopped, silent as they followed Charles Wallace through long corridors and out into the street. The CENTRAL Central Intelligence Building loomed up, stark and angular, behind them.

—Do something, Meg implored her father silently.—Do something. Help. Save us.

They turned a corner, and at the end of the street was a strange, domelike building. Its walls glowed with a flicker of violet flame. Its silvery roof pulsed with ominous light. The light was neither warm nor cold, but it seemed to reach out and touch them. This, Meg was sure, must be where IT was waiting for them.

They moved down the street, more slowly now, and as they came closer to the domed building the violet flickering seemed to reach out, to envelop them, to suck them in: they were inside.

Meg could feel a rhythmical pulsing. It was a pulsing not only about her but in her as well, as though the rhythm of her heart and lungs was no longer her own but was being worked by some outside force. The closest she had come to the feeling before was when she had been practicing artificial respiration with the Girl Scouts, and the leader, an immensely powerful woman, had been working on Meg, intoning OUT goes the bad air, IN comes the good! while her heavy hands pressed, released, pressed, released.

Meg gasped, trying to breathe at her own normal rate, but the inexorable beat within and without continued. For a moment she could neither move nor look around to see what was happening to the others. She simply had to stand there, trying to balance herself into the artificial rhythm of her heart and lungs. Her eyes seemed to swim in a sea of red.

Then things began to clear, and she could breathe without gasping like a beached fish, and she could look about the great, circular, domed building. It was completely empty except for the pulse, which seemed a tangible thing, and a round dais exactly in the center. On the dais lay—what? Meg could not tell, and yet she knew that it was from this that the rhythm came. She stepped forward tentatively. She felt that she was beyond fear now. Charles Wallace was no longer Charles Wallace. Her father had been found but he had not made everything all right. Instead, everything was worse than ever, and her adored father was bearded and thin and white and not omnipotent, after all. No matter what happened next, things could be no more terrible or frightening than they already were.

Oh, couldn't they?

As she continued to step slowly forward, at last she realized what the Thing on the dais was.

IT was a brain.

A disembodied brain. An oversized brain, just enough larger than normal to be completely revolting and terrifying. A living brain. A brain that pulsed and quivered, that seized and commanded. No wonder the brain was called IT. IT was the most horrible, the most repellent thing she had ever seen, far more nauseating than anything she had ever imagined with her conscious mind, or that had ever tormented her in her most terrible nightmares.

But as she had felt she was beyond fear, so now she was beyond screaming.

She looked at Charles Wallace, and he stood there, turned toward IT, his jaw hanging slightly loose; and his vacant blue eyes slowly twirled.

Oh, yes, things could always be worse. These twirling eyes within Charles Wallace's soft round face made Meg icy cold inside and out.

She looked away from Charles Wallace and at her father. Her father stood there with Mrs Who's glasses still perched on his nose—did he remember that he had them on?—and he shouted to Calvin, "Don't give in!"

"I won't! Help Meg!" Calvin yelled back. It was absolutely silent within the dome, and yet Meg realized that the only way to speak was to shout with all the power possible. For everywhere she looked, everywhere she turned, was the rhythm, and as it continued to control the systole and diastole of her heart, the intake and outlet of her breath, the red miasma began to creep before her eyes again, and she was afraid that she was going to lose consciousness, and if she did that, she would be completely in the power of IT.

Mrs Whatsit had said, "Meg, I give you your faults."

What were her greatest faults? Anger, impatience, stubbornness. Yes, it was to her faults that she turned to save herself now.

With an immense effort she tried to breathe against the rhythm of IT. But ITs power was too strong. Each time she managed to take a breath out of rhythm, an iron hand seemed to squeeze her heart and lungs.

Then she remembered that when they had been standing before the man with red eyes, and the man with red eyes had been intoning the multiplication table at them, Charles Wallace had fought against his power by shouting out nursery rhymes, and Calvin the Gettysburg Address.

"*Georgie, porgie, pudding and pie,*" she yelled. "*Kissed the girls and made them cry.*"

That was no good. It was too easy for nursery rhymes to fall into the rhythm of IT.

She didn't know the Gettysburg Address. How did the Declaration of Independence begin? She had memorized it only that winter, not because she was required to at school, but simply because she liked it.

"We hold these truths to be self-evident!" she shouted, "that all men are created equal, that they are endowed by their creator with certain unalienable rights, that among these are life, liberty, and the pursuit of happiness."

As she cried out the words she felt a mind moving in on her own, felt IT seizing, squeezing her brain. Then she realized that Charles Wallace was speaking, or being spoken through by IT.

"But that's exactly what we have on Camazotz. Complete equality. Everybody exactly alike."

For a moment her brain reeled with confusion. Then came a moment of blazing truth. "No!" she cried triumphantly. "*Like* and *equal* are not the same thing at all!"

"Good girl, Meg!" her father shouted at her.

But Charles Wallace continued as though there had been no interruption. "In Camazotz all are equal. In Camazotz everybody is the same as everybody else," but he gave her no argument, provided no answer, and she held on to her moment of revelation.

Like and equal are two entirely different things.

For the moment she had escaped from the power of IT.

But how?

She knew that her own puny little brain was no match for this great, bodiless, pulsing, writhing mass on the round dais. She shuddered as she looked at IT. In the lab at school there was a human brain preserved in formaldehyde, and the seniors preparing for college had to take it out and look at it and study it. Meg had felt that when that day came she would never be able to endure it. But now she thought that if only she had a dissecting knife she would slash at IT, cutting ruthlessly through cerebrum, cerebellum.

Words spoke within her, directly this time, not through Charles. "Don't you realize that if you destroy me, you also destroy your little brother?"

If that great brain were cut, were crushed, would every mind under ITs control on Camazotz die, too? Charles Wallace and the man with red eyes and the man who ran the number-one spelling machine on the second-grade level and all the children playing ball and skipping rope and all the mothers and all the men and women going in and out of the buildings? Was their life completely dependent on IT? Were they beyond all possibility of salvation?

She felt the brain reaching at her again as she let her stubborn control slip. Red fog glazed her eyes.

Faintly she heard her father's voice, though she knew he was shouting at the top of his lungs. "The periodic table of elements, Meg! Say it!"

A picture flashed into her mind of winter evenings spent sitting before the open fire and studying with her father. "Hydrogen. Helium," she started obediently. Keep them in their proper atomic order. What next. She knew it. Yes. "Lithium. Beryllium. Boron. Carbon. Nitrogen. Oxygen. Fluorine." She shouted the words at her father, turned away from IT. "Neon. Sodium. Magnesium. Aluminum. Silicon. Phosphorus."

"Too rhythmical," her father shouted. "What's the square root of five?"

For a moment she was able to concentrate. Rack your brains yourself, Meg. Don't let IT rack them. "The square root of 5 is 2.236," she cried triumphantly, "because 2.236 times 2.236 equals 5!"

"What's the square root of 7?"

"The square root of 7 is—" She broke off. She wasn't holding out. IT was getting at her, and she couldn't concentrate, not even on math, and soon she, too, would be absorbed in IT, she would *be* an IT.

"Tesser, sir!" she heard Calvin's voice through the red darkness. "Tesser!"

She felt her father grab her by the wrist, there was a terrible jerk that seemed to break every bone in her body, then the dark nothing of tessering.

If tessering with Mrs Whatsit, Mrs Who, and Mrs Which had been a strange and fearful experience, it was nothing like tessering with her father. After all, Mrs Which was experienced at it, and Mr. Murry— how did he know anything about it at all? Meg felt that she was being torn apart by a whirlwind. She was lost in an agony of pain that finally dissolved into the darkness of complete unconsciousness.

10 Absolute Zero

The first sign of returning consciousness was cold. Then sound. She was aware of voices that seemed to be traveling through her across an arctic waste. Slowly the icy sounds cleared and she realized that the voices belonged to her father and Calvin. She did not hear Charles Wallace. She tried to open her eyes, but the lids would not move. She tried to sit up, but she could not stir. She struggled to turn over, to move her hands, her feet, but nothing happened. She knew that she had a body, but it was as lifeless as marble.

She heard Calvin's frozen voice: "Her heart is beating so slowly—"

Her father's voice: "But it's beating. She's alive."

"Barely."

"We couldn't find a heartbeat at all at first. We thought she was dead."

"Yes."

"And then we could feel her heart, very faintly, the beats very far apart. And then it got stronger. So all we have to do is wait." Her father's words sounded brittle in her ears, as though they were being chipped out of ice.

Calvin: "Yes. You're right, sir."

She wanted to call out to them. "I'm alive! I'm very much alive! Only I've been turned to stone."

But she could not call out, any more than she could move.

Calvin's voice again. "Anyhow, you got her away from IT. You got us both away and we couldn't have gone on holding out. IT's so much more powerful and strong than—How *did* we stay out, sir? How did we manage as long as we did?"

Her father: "Because IT's completely unused to being refused.

That's the only reason I could keep from being absorbed, too. No mind has tried to hold out against IT for so many thousands of centuries that certain centers have become soft and atrophied through lack of use. If you hadn't come to me when you did, I'm not sure how much longer I would have lasted. I was on the point of giving in."

Calvin: "Oh, no, sir—"

Her father: "Yes. Nothing seemed important any more but rest, and of course IT offered me complete rest. I had almost come to the conclusion that I was wrong to fight, that IT was right after all, and everything I believed in most passionately was nothing but a madman's dream. But then you and Meg came in to me, broke through my prison, and hope and faith returned."

Calvin: "Sir, why were you on Camazotz at all? Was there a particular reason for going there?"

Her father, with a frigid laugh: "Going to Camazotz was a complete accident. I never intended even to leave our own solar system. I was heading for Mars. Tessering is even more complicated than we had expected."

Calvin: "Sir, how was IT able to get Charles Wallace before it got Meg and me?"

Her father: "From what you've told me, it's because Charles Wallace thought he could deliberately go into IT and return. He trusted too much to his own strength—listen!—I think the heartbeat is getting stronger!"

His words no longer sounded to her quite as frozen. Was it his words that were ice, or her ears? Why did she hear only her father and Calvin? Why didn't Charles Wallace speak?

Silence. A long silence. Then Calvin's voice again: "Can't we do anything? Can't we look for help? Do we just have to go on waiting?"

Her father: "We can't leave her. And we must stay together. We must *not* be afraid to take time."

Calvin: "You mean we were? We rushed into things on Camazotz too fast, and Charles Wallace rushed in too fast, and that's why he got caught?"

"Maybe. I'm not sure. I don't know enough yet. Time is different on Camazotz, anyhow. Our time, inadequate though it is, at least is straightforward. It may not be even fully one-dimensional, because it can't move back and forth on its line, only ahead; but at least it's consistent in its direction. Time on Camazotz seems to be inverted, turned in on itself. So I have no idea whether I was imprisoned in that column for centuries or only for minutes." Silence for a moment. Then her father's voice again: "I think I feel a pulse in her wrist now."

Meg could not feel his fingers against her wrist. She could not feel her wrist at all. Her body was still stone, but her mind was beginning to be capable of movement. She tried desperately to make some kind of a sound, a signal to them, but nothing happened.

Their voices started again. Calvin: "About your project, sir. Were you on it alone?"

Her father: "Oh, no. There were half a dozen of us working on it and I daresay a number of others we don't know about. Certainly we weren't the only nation to investigate along that line. It's not really a new idea. But we did try very hard not to let it be known abroad that we were trying to make it practicable."

"Did you come to Camazotz alone? Or were there others with you?"

"I came alone. You see, Calvin, there was no way to try it out ahead with rats or monkeys or dogs. And we had no idea whether it would really work or whether it would be complete bodily disintegration. Playing with time and space is a dangerous game."

"But why you, sir?"

"I wasn't the first. We drew straws, and I was second."

"What happened to the first man?"

"We don't—Look! Did her eyelids move?" Silence. Then: "No. It was only a shadow."

But I *did* blink, Meg tried to tell them. I'm sure I did. And I can hear you! *Do* something!

But there was only another long silence, during which perhaps they were looking at her, watching for another shadow, another flicker. Then she heard her father's voice again, quiet, a little warmer, more like his own voice. "We drew straws, and I was second. We know Hank went. We saw him go. We saw him vanish right in front of the rest of us. He was there and then he wasn't. We were to wait a year for his return or for some message. We waited. Nothing."

Calvin, his voice cracking: "Jeepers, sir. You must have been in sort of a flap."

Her father: "Yes. It's a frightening as well as an exciting thing to discover that matter and energy *are* the same thing, that size is an illusion, and that time is a material substance. We can know this, but it's far more than we can understand with our puny little brains. I think you will be able to comprehend far more than I. And Charles Wallace even more than you."

"Yes, but what happened, please, sir, after the first man?"

Meg could hear her father sigh. "Then it was my turn. I went. And here I am. A wiser and a humbler man. I'm sure I haven't been gone two years. Now that you've come I have some hope that I may be able to return in time. One thing I have to tell the others is that we know nothing."

Calvin: "What do you mean, sir?"

Her father: "Just what I say. We're children playing with dynamite. In our mad rush we've plunged into this before—"

With a desperate effort Meg made a sound. It wasn't a very loud sound, but it was a sound. Mr. Murry stopped. "Hush. Listen."

Meg made a strange, croaking noise. She found that she could pull open her eyelids. They felt heavier than marble but she managed to raise them. Her father and Calvin were hovering over her. She did not see Charles Wallace. Where was he?

She was lying in an open field of what looked like rusty, stubby grass. She blinked, slowly, and with difficulty.

"Meg," her father said. "Meg. Are you all right?"

Her tongue felt like a stone tongue in her mouth, but she managed to croak, "I can't move."

"Try," Calvin urged. He sounded now as though he were very angry with her. "Wiggle your toes. Wiggle your fingers."

"I can't. Where's Charles Wallace?" Her words were blunted by the stone tongue. Perhaps they could not understand her, for there was no answer.

"We were knocked out for a minute, too," Calvin was saying. "You'll be all right, Meg. Don't get panicky." He was crouched over her, and though his voice continued to sound cross, he was peering at her with anxious eyes. She knew that she must still have her glasses on, because she could see him clearly, his freckles, his stubby black lashes, the bright blue of his eyes.

Her father was kneeling on her other side. The round lenses of Mrs Who's glasses still blurred his eyes. He took one of her hands and rubbed it between his. "Can you feel my fingers?" He sounded quite calm, as though there were nothing extraordinary in having her completely paralyzed. At the quiet of his voice she felt calmer. Then she saw that there were great drops of sweat standing out on his forehead, and she noticed vaguely that the gentle breeze that touched her cheeks was cool. At first his words had been frozen and now the wind was mild: was it icy cold here or warm? "Can you feel my fingers?" he asked again.

Yes, now she could feel a pressure against her wrist, but she could not nod. "Where's Charles Wallace?" Her words were a little less blurred. Her tongue, her lips were beginning to feel cold and numb, as though she had been given a massive dose of Novocaine at the dentist's. She realized with a start that her body and limbs were cold, that not only was she not warm, she was frozen from head to toe, and it was this that had made her father's words seem like ice, that had paralyzed her.

"I'm frozen—" she said faintly. Camazotz hadn't been this cold, a cold that cut deeper than the wind on the bitterest of winter days at home. She was away from IT, but this unexplained iciness was almost as bad. Her father had not saved her.

Now she was able to look around a little, and everything she could see was rusty and gray. There were trees edging the field in which she lay, and their leaves were the same brown as the grass. There were plants that might have been flowers, except that they were dull and gray. In contrast to the drabness of color, to the cold that numbed her, the air was filled with a delicate, springlike fragrance, almost imperceptible as it blew softly against her face. She looked at her father and Calvin. They were both in their shirtsleeves and they looked perfectly comfortable. It was she, wrapped in their clothes, who was frozen too solid even to shiver.

"Why am I so cold?" she asked. "Where's Charles Wallace?" They did not answer. "Father, where are we?"

Mr. Murry looked at her soberly. "I don't know, Meg. I don't tesser very well. I must have overshot, somehow. We're not on Camazotz. I don't know where we are. I think you're so cold because we went through the Black Thing, and I thought for a moment it was going to tear you away from me."

"Is this a dark planet?" Slowly her tongue was beginning to thaw; her words were less blurred.

"I don't think so," Mr. Murry said, "but I know so little about anything that I can't be sure."

"You shouldn't have tried to tesser, then." She had never spoken to her father in this way before. The words seemed hardly to be hers.

Calvin looked at her, shaking his head. "It was the only thing to do. At least it got us off Camazotz."

"Why did we go without Charles Wallace? Did we just leave him there?" The words that were not really hers came out cold and accusing.

"We didn't 'just leave him,' " her father said. "Remember that the human brain is a very delicate organism, and it can be easily damaged."

"See, Meg"—Calvin crouched over her, tense and worried—"if your father had tried to yank Charles away when he tessered us, and if IT had kept grabbing hold of Charles, it might have been too much for him, and we'd have lost him forever. And we had to do something right then."

"Why?"

"IT was taking us. You and I were slipping, and if your father had gone on trying to help us, he wouldn't have been able to hold out much longer, either."

"*You* told him to tesser," Meg charged Calvin.

"There isn't any question of blame," Mr. Murry cut in severely. "Can you move yet?"

All Meg's faults were uppermost in her now, and they were no longer helping her. "No! And you'd better take me back to Camazotz and Charles Wallace quickly. You're supposed to be able to help!" Disappointment was as dark and corrosive in her as the Black Thing. The ugly words tumbled from her cold lips even as she herself could not believe that it was her father, her beloved, longed-for father, that she was talking to in this way. If her tears had not still been frozen, they would have gushed from her eyes.

She had found her father and he had not made everything all right. Everything kept getting worse and worse. If the long search for her father was ended, and he wasn't able to overcome all their difficulties, there was nothing to guarantee that it would all come out right in the end. There was nothing left to hope for. She was frozen, and Charles Wallace was being devoured by IT, and her omnipotent father was doing nothing. She teetered on the seesaw of love and hate, and the Black Thing pushed her down into hate. "You don't even know where we are!" she cried out at her father. "We'll never see Mother or the twins again! We don't know where Earth is! Or even where Camazotz is! We're lost out in space! What are you going to *do*!" She did not realize that she was as much in the power of the Black Thing as Charles Wallace.

Mr. Murry bent over her, massaging her cold fingers. She could not see his face. "My daughter, I am not a Mrs Whatsit, a Mrs Who, or a Mrs Which. Yes, Calvin has told me everything he could. I am a human being, and a very fallible one. But I agree with Calvin. We were sent here for something. And we know that all things work together for good to them that love God, to them who are the called according to His purpose."

"The Black Thing!" Meg cried out at him. "Why did you let it almost get me?"

"You've never tessered as well as the rest of us," Calvin reminded her. "It never bothered Charles and me as much as it did you."

"He shouldn't have taken me, then," Meg said, "until he learned to do it better."

Neither her father nor Calvin spoke. Her father continued his gentle massage. Her fingers came back to life with tingling pain. "You're hurt-ing me!"

"Then you're feeling again," her father said quietly. "I'm afraid it *is* going to hurt, Meg."

The piercing pain moved slowly up her arms, began in her toes and legs. She started to cry out against her father when Calvin exclaimed, "Look!"

Coming toward them, moving in silence across the brown grass, were three figures.

What were they?

On Uriel there had been the magnificent creatures. On Camazotz the inhabitants had at least resembled people. What were these three strange things approaching?

They were the same dull gray color as the flowers. If they hadn't walked upright they would have seemed like animals. They moved di-rectly toward the three human beings. They had four arms and far more than five fingers to each hand, and the fingers were not fingers but long waving tentacles. They had heads, and they had faces. But where the faces of the creatures on Uriel had seemed far more than human faces, these seemed far less. Where the features would normally be, there were several indentations, and in place of ears and hair were more tentacles. They were tall, Meg realized as they came closer, far taller than any man. They had no eyes. Just soft indentations.

Meg's rigid, frozen body tried to shudder with terror, but instead of the shudder all that came was pain. She moaned.

The Things stood over them. They appeared to be looking down at them, except that they had no eyes with which to see. Mr. Murry con-tinued to kneel by Meg, massaging her.

—He's killed us, bringing us here, Meg thought.—I'll never see Charles Wallace again, or Mother, or the twins . . .

Calvin rose to his feet. He bowed to the beasts as though they could see him. He said, "How do you do, sir—ma'am—?"

"Who are you?" the tallest of the beasts said. His voice was neither hostile nor welcoming, and it came not from the mouthlike indentation in the furry face but from the waving tentacles.

—They'll eat us, Meg thought wildly.—They're making me hurt. My toes—my fingers—I hurt . . .

Calvin answered the beast's question. "We're—we're from earth. I'm not sure how we got here. We've had an accident. Meg—this girl—is—is paralyzed. She can't move. She's terribly cold. We think that's why she can't move."

One of them came up to Meg and squatted down on its huge

haunches beside her, and she felt utter loathing and revulsion as it reached out a tentacle to touch her face.

But with the tentacle came the same delicate fragrance that moved across her with the breeze, and she felt a soft, tingling warmth go all through her that momentarily assuaged her pain. She felt suddenly sleepy.

I must look as strange to it as it looks to me, she thought drowsily, and then realized with a shock that of course the beast couldn't see her at all. Nevertheless, a reassuring sense of safety flowed through her with the warmth which continued to seep deep into her as the beast touched her. Then it picked her up, cradling her in two of its four arms.

Mr. Murry stood up quickly. "What are you doing?"

"Taking the child."

11 Aunt Beast

"No!" Mr. Murry said sharply. "Please put her down." A sense of amusement seemed to emanate from the beasts. The tallest, who seemed to be the spokesman, said, "We frighten you?"

"What are you going to do with us?" Mr. Murry asked.

The beast said, "I'm sorry, we communicate better with the other one." He turned toward Calvin. "Who are you?"

"I'm Calvin O'Keefe."

"What's that?"

"I'm a boy. A—a young man."

"You, too, are afraid?"

"I'm—not sure."

"Tell me," the beast said. "What do you suppose you'd do if three of *us* suddenly arrived on your home planet?"

"Shoot you, I guess," Calvin admitted.

"Then isn't that what we should do with you?"

Calvin's freckles seemed to deepen, but he answered quietly. "I'd really rather you didn't. I mean, the earth's my home, and I'd rather be there than anywhere in the world—I mean, the universe—and I can't wait to get back, but we make some awful bloopers there."

The smallest beast, the one holding Meg, said, "And perhaps they aren't used to visitors from other planets."

"Used to it!" Calvin exclaimed. "We've never had any, as far as I know."

"Why?"

"I don't know."

The middle beast, a tremor of trepidation in his words, said, "You aren't from a dark planet, are you?"

"No." Calvin shook his head firmly, though the beast couldn't see him. "We're—we're shadowed. But we're fighting the shadow."

The beast holding Meg questioned, "You three are fighting?"

"Yes," Calvin answered. "Now that we know about it."

The tall one turned back to Mr. Murry, speaking sternly. "You. The oldest. Man. From where have you come? Now."

Mr. Murry answered steadily. "From a planet called Camazotz." There was a mutter from the three beasts. "We do not belong there," Mr. Murry said, slowly and distinctly. "We were strangers there as we are here. I was a prisoner there, and these children rescued me. My youngest son, my baby, is still there, trapped in the dark mind of IT."

Meg tried to twist around in the beast's arms to glare at her father and Calvin. Why were they being so frank? Weren't they aware of the danger? But again her anger dissolved as the gentle warmth from the tentacles flowed through her. She realized that she could move her fingers and toes with comparative freedom, and the pain was no longer so acute.

"We must take this child back with us," the beast holding her said.

Meg shouted at her father: "Don't leave me the way you left Charles!" With this burst of terror, a spasm of pain wracked her body and she gasped.

"Stop fighting," the beast told her. "You make it worse. Relax."

"That's what IT said," Meg cried. "Father! Calvin! Help!"

The beast turned toward Calvin and Mr. Murry. "This child is in danger. You must trust us."

"We have no alternative," Mr. Murry said. "Can you save her?"

"I think so."

"May I stay with her?"

"No. But you will not be far away. We feel that you are hungry, tired, that you would like to bathe and rest. And this little—what is the word?" The beast cocked its tentacles at Calvin.

"Girl," Calvin said.

"This little girl needs prompt and special care. The coldness of the—what is it you call it?"

"The Black Thing?"

"The Black Thing. Yes. The Black Thing burns unless it is coun- teracted properly." The three beasts stood around Meg, and it seemed that they were feeling into her with their softly waving tentacles. The movement of the tentacles was as rhythmic and flowing as the dance of an undersea plant, and lying there, cradled in the four strange arms, Meg, despite herself, felt a sense of security that was deeper than any- thing she had known since the days when she lay in her mother's arms in the old rocking chair and was sung to sleep. With her father's help she had been able to resist IT. Now she could hold out no longer. She leaned her head against the beast's chest, and realized that the gray body was covered with the softest, most delicate fur imaginable, and the fur had the same beautiful odor as the air.

I hope I don't smell awful to it, she thought. But then she knew with a deep sense of comfort that even if she did smell awful the beasts would forgive her. As the tall figure cradled her she could feel the frigid stiffness of her body relaxing against it. This bliss could not come to her from a thing like IT. IT could only give pain, never relieve it. The beasts must be good. They had to be good. She sighed deeply, like a very small child, and suddenly she was asleep.

When she came to herself again, there was in the back of her mind a memory of pain, of agonizing pain. But the pain was over now and her body was lapped in comfort. She was lying on something wonderfully soft in an enclosed chamber. It was dark. All she could see were occasional tall moving shadows which she realized were beasts walking about. She had been stripped of her clothes, and something warm and pungent was gently being rubbed into her body. She sighed and stretched and discovered that she *could* stretch. She could move again, she was no longer paralyzed, and her body was bathed in waves of warmth. Her father had not saved her; the beasts had.

"So you are awake, little one?" The words came gently to her ears. "What a funny little tadpole you are! Is the pain gone now?"

"All gone."

"Are you warm and alive again?"

"Yes, I'm fine." She struggled to sit up.

"No, lie still, small one. You must not exert yourself as yet. We will have a fur garment for you in a moment, and then we will feed you. You must not even try to feed yourself. You must be as an infant again. The Black Thing does not relinquish its victims willingly."

"Where are Father and Calvin? Have they gone back for Charles Wallace?"

"They are eating and resting," the beast said, "and we are trying to learn about each other and see what is best to help you. We feel now that you are not dangerous, and that we will be allowed to help you."

"Why is it so dark in here?" Meg asked. She tried to look around, but all she could see was shadows. Nevertheless, there was a sense of openness, a feel of a gentle breeze moving lightly about, that kept the darkness from being oppressive.

Perplexity came to her from the beast. "What is this dark? What is this light? We do not understand. Your father and the boy, Calvin, have asked this, too. They say that it is night now on our planet, and that they cannot see. They have told us that our atmosphere is what they call opaque, so that the stars are not visible, and then they were surprised that we know stars, that we know their music and the movements of their dance far better than beings like you who spend hours studying them through what you call telescopes. We do not understand what this means, *to see*."

"Well, it's what things look like," Meg said helplessly.

"We do not know what things *look* like, as you say," the beast said. "We know what things *are* like. It must be a very limiting thing, this seeing."

"Oh, no!" Meg cried. "It's—it's the most wonderful thing in the world!"

"What a very strange world yours must be!" the beast said, "that such a peculiar-seeming thing should be of such importance. Try to tell me, what is this thing called *light* that you are able to do so little without?"

"Well, we can't see without it," Meg said, realizing that she was completely unable to explain vision and light and dark. How can you explain sight on a world where no one has ever seen and where there is no need of eyes? "Well, on this planet," she fumbled, "you have a sun, don't you?"

"A most wonderful sun, from which comes our warmth, and the rays which give us our flowers, our food, our music, and all the things which make life and growth."

"Well," Meg said, "when we are turned toward the sun—our earth, our planet, I mean, toward our sun—we receive its light. And when we're turned away from it, it is night. And if we want to see we have to use artificial lights."

"Artificial lights," the beast sighed. "How very complicated life on your planet must be. Later on, you must try to explain some more to me."

"All right," Meg promised, and yet she knew that to try to explain anything that could be seen with the eyes would be impossible, because the beasts in some way saw, knew, understood, far more completely than she, or her parents, or Calvin, or even Charles Wallace.

"Charles Wallace!" she cried. "What are they doing about Charles Wallace? We don't know what IT's doing to him or making him do. Please, oh, please, help us!"

"Yes, yes, little one, of course we will help you. A meeting is in session right now to study what is best to do. We have never before been able to talk to anyone who has managed to escape from a dark planet, so although your father is blaming himself for everything that has happened, we feel that he must be quite an extraordinary person to get out of Camazotz with you at all. But the little boy, and I understand that he is a very special, a very important little boy—ah, my child, you must accept that this will not be easy. To go *back* through the Black Thing, *back* to Camazotz—I don't know. I don't know."

"But Father left him!" Meg said. "He's got to bring him back! He can't just abandon Charles Wallace!"

The beast's communication suddenly became crisp. "Nobody said anything about abandoning anybody. That is not our way. But we know that just because we want something does not mean that we will get what we want, and we still do not know *what* to do. And we cannot allow you, in your present state, to do anything that would jeopardize us all. I can see that you wish your father to go rushing back to Camazotz, and you could probably make him do this, and then where would we be? No. No. You must wait until you are more calm. Now, my darling, here is a robe for you to keep you warm and comfortable." Meg felt herself being lifted again, and a soft, light garment was slipped about her. "Don't worry about your little brother." The tentacles' musical words were soft against her. "We would *never* leave him behind the shadow. But for now you must relax, you must be happy, you must get well."

The gentle words, the feeling that this beast would be able to love her no matter what she said or did, lapped Meg in warmth and peace. She felt a delicate touch of tentacle to her cheek, as tender as her mother's kiss.

"It is so long since my own small ones were grown and gone," the beast said. "You are so tiny and vulnerable. Now I will feed you. You must eat slowly and quietly. I know that you are half starved, that you have been without food far too long, but you must not rush things or you will not get well."

Something completely and indescribably and incredibly delicious was put to Meg's lips, and she swallowed gratefully. With each swallow she felt strength returning to her body, and she realized that she had had nothing to eat since the horrible fake turkey dinner on Camazotz which she had barely tasted. How long ago was her mother's stew? Time no longer had any meaning.

"How long does night last here?" she murmured sleepily. "It will be day again, won't it?"

"Hush," the beast said. "Eat, small one. During the coolness, which is now, we sleep. And, when you waken, there will be warmth again

and many things to do. You must eat now, and sleep, and I will stay
with you."

"What should I call you, please?" Meg asked.

"Well, now. First, try not to say any words for just a moment. Think
within your own mind. Think of all the things you call people, different
kinds of people."

While Meg thought, the beast murmured to her gently. "No, *mother*
is a special, a one-name; and a father you have here. Not just friend,
nor teacher, nor brother, nor sister. What is *acquaintance*? What a
funny, hard word. Aunt. Maybe. Yes, perhaps that will do. And you
think of such odd words about me. *Thing*, and *monster! Monster*, what
a horrid sort of word. I really do not think I am a monster. *Beast*. That
will do. *Aunt Beast*."

"Aunt Beast," Meg murmured sleepily, and laughed.

"Have I said something funny?" Aunt Beast asked in surprise. "Isn't
Aunt Beast all right?"

"Aunt Beast is lovely," Meg said. "Please sing to me, Aunt Beast."

If it was impossible to describe sight to Aunt Beast, it would be
even more impossible to describe the singing of Aunt Beast to a human
being. It was a music even more glorious than the music of the singing
creatures on Uriel. It was a music more tangible than form or sight. It
had essence and structure. It supported Meg more firmly than the arms
of Aunt Beast. It seemed to travel with her, to sweep her aloft in the
power of song, so that she was moving in glory among the stars, and
for a moment she, too, felt that the words *darkness* and *light* had no
meaning, and only this melody was real.

Meg did not know when she fell asleep within the body of the
music. When she wakened, Aunt Beast was asleep, too, the softness of
her furry, faceless head drooping. Night had gone and a dull gray light
filled the room. But she realized now that here on this planet there was
no need for color, that the grays and browns merging into each other
were not what the beasts knew, and that what she, herself, saw was only
the smallest fraction of what the planet was really like. It was she who
was limited by her senses, not the blind beasts, for they must have
senses of which she could not even dream.

She stirred slightly, and Aunt Beast bent over her immediately.
"What a lovely sleep, my darling. Do you feel all right?"

"I feel wonderful," Meg said. "Aunt Beast, what is this planet
called?"

"Oh, dear," Aunt Beast sighed. "I find it not easy at all to put things
the way your mind shapes them. You call where you came from Camazotz?"

"Well, it's where we came from, but it's not our planet."

"You can call us Ixchel, I guess," Aunt Beast told her. "We share the same sun as lost Camazotz, but that, give thanks, is all we share."

"Are you fighting the Black Thing?" Meg asked.

"Oh, yes," Aunt Beast replied. "In doing that, we can never relax. We are the called according to His purpose, and whom He calls, them He also justifies. Of course we have help, and without help it would be much more difficult."

"Who helps you?" Meg asked.

"Oh, dear, it is so difficult to explain things to you, small one. And I know now that it is not just because you are a child. The other two are as hard to reach into as you are. What can I tell you that will mean anything to you? Good helps us, the stars helps us, perhaps what you would call *light* helps us, love helps us. Oh, my child, I cannot explain! This is something you just have to know or not know."

"But—"

"We look not at the things which are what you would call seen, but at the things which are not seen. For the things which are seen are temporal. But the things which are not seen are eternal."

"Aunt Beast, do you know Mrs Whatsit?" Meg asked with a sudden flooding of hope.

"Mrs Whatsit?" Aunt Beast was puzzled. "Oh, child, your language is so utterly simple and limited that it has the effect of extreme complication." Her four arms, tentacles waving, were outflung in a gesture of helplessness. "Would you like me to take you to your father and your Calvin?"

"Oh, yes, please!"

"Let us go, then. They are waiting for you to make plans. And we thought you would enjoy eating—what is it you call it? oh, yes, breakfast—together. You will be too warm in that heavy fur, now. I will dress you in something lighter, and then we will go."

As though Meg were a baby, Aunt Beast bathed and dressed her, and this new garment, though it was made of a pale fur, was lighter than the lightest summer clothes on earth. Aunt Beast put one tentacled arm about Meg's waist and led her through long, dim corridors in which she could see only shadows, and shadows of shadows, until they reached a large, columned chamber. Shafts of light came in from an open skylight and converged about a huge, round, stone table. Here were seated several of the great beasts, and Calvin and Mr. Murry, on a stone bench that circled the table. Because the beasts were so tall, even Mr. Murry's feet did not touch the ground, and lanky Calvin's long legs dangled as though he were Charles Wallace. The hall was partially enclosed by vaulted arches leading to long, paved walks. There were no empty walls, no covering roofs, so that although the light was dull in comparison to earth's sunlight, Meg had no feeling of dark or of chill. As Aunt Beast led Meg in, Mr. Murry slid down from the bench and hurried to her, putting his arms about her tenderly.

"They promised us you were all right," he said.

While she had been in Aunt Beast's arms Meg had felt safe and secure. Now her worries about Charles Wallace and her disappointment in her father's human fallibility rose like gorge in her throat.

"I'm fine," she muttered, looking not at Calvin or her father but at the beasts, for it was to them she turned now for help. It seemed to her that neither her father nor Calvin was properly concerned about Charles Wallace.

"Meg!" Calvin said gaily. "You've never tasted such food in your life! Come and eat!"

Aunt Beast lifted Meg up onto the bench and sat down beside her, then heaped a plate with food, strange fruits and breads that tasted unlike anything Meg had ever eaten. Everything was dull and colorless and unappetizing to look at, and at first, even remembering the meal Aunt Beast had fed her the night before, Meg hesitated to taste, but once she had managed the first bite she ate eagerly; it seemed that she would never have her fill again.

The others waited until she slowed down. Then Mr. Murry said gravely, "We were trying to work out a plan to rescue Charles Wallace. Since I made such a mistake in tessering away from IT, we feel that it would not be wise for me to try to get back to Camazotz, even alone. If I missed the mark again I could easily get lost and wander forever from galaxy to galaxy, and that would be small help to anyone, least of all to Charles Wallace."

Such a wave of despondency came over Meg that she was no longer able to eat.

"Our friends here," he continued, "feel that it was only the fact that I still wore the glasses your Mrs Who gave you that kept me within this solar system. Here are the glasses, Meg. But I am afraid that the virtue has gone from them and now they are only glass. Perhaps they were meant to help only once and only on Camazotz. Perhaps it was going through the Black Thing that did it." He pushed the glasses across the table at her.

"These people know about tessering"—Calvin gestured at the circle of great beasts—"but they can't do it onto a dark planet."

"Have you tried to call Mrs Whatsit?" Meg asked.

"Not yet," her father answered.

"But if you haven't thought of anything else, it's the *only* thing to do! Father, don't you care about Charles at all!"

At that, Aunt Beast stood up, saying, "Child," in a reproving way. Mr. Murry said nothing, and Meg could see that she had wounded him deeply. She reacted as she would have reacted to Mr. Jenkins. She scowled down at the table, saying, "We've *got* to ask them for help now. You're just stupid if you think we don't."

Aunt Beast spoke to the others. "The child is distraught. Don't judge her harshly. She was almost taken by the Black Thing. Sometimes we can't know what spiritual damage it leaves even when physical recovery is complete."

Meg looked angrily around the table. The beasts sat there, silent, motionless. She felt that she was being measured and found wanting.

Calvin swung away from her and hunched himself up. "Hasn't it occurred to you that we've been trying to tell them about our ladies? What do you think we've been up to all this time? Just stuffing our faces? Okay, you have a shot at it."

"Yes. Try, child." Aunt Beast seated herself again, and pulled Meg up beside her. "But I do not understand this feeling of anger I sense in you. What is it about? There is blame going on, and guilt. Why?"

"Aunt Beast, don't you know?"

"No," Aunt Beast said. "But this is not telling me about—whoever they are you want us to know. Try."

Meg tried. Blunderingly. Fumblingly. At first she described Mrs Whatsit and her man's coat and multicolored shawls and scarves, Mrs Who and her white robes and shimmering spectacles, Mrs Which in her peaked cap and black gown quivering in and out of body. Then she realized that this was absurd. She was describing them only to herself. This wasn't Mrs Whatsit or Mrs Who or Mrs Which. She might as well have described Mrs Whatsit as she was when she took on the form of a flying creature of Uriel.

"Don't try to use words," Aunt Beast said soothingly. "You're just fighting yourself and me. Think about what they *are*. This *look* doesn't help us at all."

Meg tried again, but she could not get a visual concept out of her mind. She tried to think of Mrs Whatsit explaining tessering. She tried to think of them in terms of mathematics. Every once in a while she thought she felt a flicker of understanding from Aunt Beast or one of the others, but most of the time all that emanated from them was gentle puzzlement.

"Angels!" Calvin shouted suddenly from across the table. "Guardian angels!" There was a moment's silence, and he shouted again, his face tense with concentration, "Messengers! Messengers of God!"

"I thought for a moment—" Aunt Beast started, then subsided, sighing. "No. It's not clear enough."

"How strange it is that they can't tell us what they themselves seem to know," a tall, thin beast murmured.

One of Aunt Beast's tentacled arms went around Meg's waist again. "They are very young. And on their earth, as they call it, they never communicate with other planets. They revolve about all alone in space."

"Oh," the thin beast said. "Aren't they *lonely?*"

Suddenly a thundering voice reverberated throughout the great hall: "WWEEE ARRE HHERRE!"

12 The Foolish and the Weak

Meg could see nothing, but she felt her heart pounding with hope. With one accord all the beasts rose to their feet, turned toward one of the arched openings, and bowed their heads and tentacles in greeting. Mrs Whatsit appeared, standing between two columns. Beside her came Mrs Who, behind them a quivering of light. The three of them were somehow not quite the same as they had been when Meg had first seen them. Their outlines seemed blurred; colors ran together as in a wet watercolor painting. But they were there; they were recognizable; they were themselves.

Meg pulled herself away from Aunt Beast, jumped to the floor, and rushed at Mrs Whatsit. But Mrs Whatsit held up a warning hand and Meg realized that she was not completely materialized, that she was light and not substance, and embracing her now would have been like trying to hug a sunbeam.

"We had to hurry, so there wasn't quite time . . . You wanted us?" Mrs Whatsit asked.

The tallest of the beasts bowed again and took a step away from the table and toward Mrs Whatsit. "It is a question of the little boy."

"Father left him!" Meg cried. "He left him on Camazotz!"

Appallingly, Mrs Whatsit's voice was cold. "And what do you expect us to do?"

Meg pressed her knuckles against her teeth, so that her braces cut her skin. Then she flung out her arms pleadingly. "But it's Charles Wallace! IT has him, Mrs Whatsit! Save him, please save him!"

"You know that we can do nothing on Camazotz," Mrs Whatsit said, her voice still cold.

"You mean you'll let Charles be caught by IT forever?" Meg's voice rose shrilly.

"Did I say that?"

"But we can't do anything! You know we can't! We tried! Mrs Whatsit, you have to save him!"

"Meg, this is not our way," Mrs Whatsit said sadly. "I thought you would know that this is not our way."

Mr. Murry took a step forward and bowed, and to Meg's amazement the three ladies bowed back to him. "I don't believe we've been introduced," Mrs Whatsit said.

"It's Father, you know it's Father." Meg's angry impatience grew. "Father—Mrs Whatsit, Mrs Who, and Mrs Which."

"I'm very glad to—" Mr. Murry mumbled, then went on, "I'm sorry, my glasses are broken, and I can't see you very well."

"It's not necessary to see us," Mrs Whatsit said.

"If you could teach me enough more about the tesseract so that I could get back to Camazotz—"

"Wwhatt tthenn?" came Mrs Which's surprising voice.

"I will try to take my child away from IT."

"Annd yyou kknoww tthatt yyou wwill nnott ssucceeedd?"

"There's nothing left except to try."

Mrs Whatsit spoke gently. "I'm sorry. We cannot allow you to go."

"Then let me," Calvin suggested. "I almost got him away before."

Mrs Whatsit shook her head. "No, Calvin. Charles has gone even deeper into IT. You will not be permitted to throw yourself in with him, for that, you must realize, is what would happen."

There was a long silence. All the soft rays filtering into the great hall seemed to concentrate on Mrs Whatsit, Mrs Who, and the faint light that must be Mrs Which. No one spoke. One of the beasts moved a tendril slowly back and forth across the stone tabletop. At last Meg could stand it no longer and she cried out despairingly, "Then what are you going to do? Are you just going to throw Charles away?"

Mrs Which's voice rolled formidably across the hall. "Ssilencce, cchilldd!"

But Meg could not be silent. She pressed closely against Aunt Beast, but Aunt Beast did not put the protecting tentacles around her. "*I* can't go!" Meg cried. "I can't! You know I can't!"

"Ddidd annybbodyy asskk yyou ttoo?" The grim voice made Meg's skin prickle into gooseflesh.

She burst into tears. She started beating at Aunt Beast like a small child having a tantrum. Her tears rained down her face and spattered Aunt Beast's fur. Aunt Beast stood quietly against the assault.

"All right, I'll go!" Meg sobbed. "I know you want me to go!"

"We want nothing from you that you do without grace," Mrs Whatsit said, "or that you do without understanding."

Meg's tears stopped as abruptly as they had started. "But I do understand." She felt tired and unexpectedly peaceful. Now the coldness that, under Aunt Beast's ministrations, had left her body had also left her mind. She looked toward her father and her confused anger was gone and she felt only love and pride. She smiled at him, asking forgiveness, and then pressed up against Aunt Beast. This time Aunt Beast's arm went around her.

Mrs Which's voice was grave. "Wwhatt ddoo yyou unndderrsstanndd?"

"That it has to be me. It can't be anyone else. I don't understand Charles, but he understands me. I'm the one who's closest to him. Father's been away for so long, since Charles Wallace was a baby. They don't know each other. And Calvin's only known Charles for such a little time. If it had been longer, then he would have been the one, but— oh, I see, I see, I understand, it has to be me. There isn't anyone else."

Mr. Murry, who had been sitting, his elbows on his knees, his chin on his fists, rose. "I will not allow it!"

"Wwhyy?" Mrs Which demanded.

"Look, I don't know what or who you are, and at this point I don't care. I will not allow my daughter to go alone into this danger."

"Wwhyy?"

"You know what the outcome will probably be! And she's weak now, weaker than she was before. She was almost killed by the Black Thing. I fail to understand how you can even consider such a thing."

Calvin jumped down. "Maybe IT's right about you! Or maybe you're in league with IT. I'm the one to go if anybody goes! Why did you bring me along at all? To take care of Meg! You said so yourself!"

"But you have done that," Mrs Whatsit assured him.

"I haven't done anything!" Calvin shouted. "You can't send Meg! I won't allow it! I'll put my foot down! I won't permit it!"

"Don't you see that you're making something that is already hard for Meg even harder?" Mrs Whatsit asked him.

Aunt Beast turned tentacles toward Mrs Whatsit. "Is she strong enough to tesser again? You know what she has been through."

"If Which takes her she can manage," Mrs Whatsit said.

"If it will help I could go too, and hold her." Aunt Beast's arm around Meg tightened.

"Oh, Aunt Beast—" Meg started.

But Mrs Whatsit cut her off. "No."

"I was afraid not," Aunt Beast said humbly. "I just wanted you to know that I *would*."

"Mrs—uh—Whatsit." Mr. Murry frowned and pushed his hair back from his face. Then he shoved with his middle finger at his nose as though he were trying to get spectacles closer to his eyes. "Are you remembering that she is only a child?"

"And she's backward," Calvin bellowed.

"I resent that," Meg said hotly, hoping that indignation would control her trembling. "I'm better than you at math and you know it."

"Do you have the courage to go alone?" Mrs Whatsit asked her.

Meg's voice was flat. "No. But it doesn't matter." She turned to her father and Calvin. "You know it's the only thing to do. You know they'd never send me alone if—"

"How do we know they're not in league with IT?" Mr. Murry demanded.

"Father!"

"No, Meg," Mrs Whatsit said. "I do not blame your father for being angry and suspicious and frightened. And I cannot pretend that we are doing anything but sending you into the gravest kind of danger. I have to acknowledge quite openly that it may be a fatal danger. I know this. But I do not believe it. And the Happy Medium doesn't believe it, either."

"Can't she see what's going to happen?" Calvin asked.

"Oh, not in this kind of thing." Mrs Whatsit sounded surprised at his question. "If we knew ahead of time what was going to happen we'd be—we'd be like the people on Camazotz, with no lives of our own, with everything all planned and done for us. How can I explain it to you? Oh, I know. In your language you have a form of poetry called the sonnet."

"Yes, yes," Calvin said impatiently. "What's that got to do with the Happy Medium?"

"Kindly pay me the courtesy of listening to me." Mrs Whatsit's voice was stern, and for a moment Calvin stopped pawing the ground like a nervous colt. "It is a very strict form of poetry, is it not?"

"Yes."

"There are fourteen lines, I believe, all in iambic pentameter. That's a very strict rhythm or meter, yes?"

"Yes." Calvin nodded.

"And each line has to end with a rigid rhyme pattern. And if the poet does not do it exactly this way, it is not a sonnet, is it?"

"No."

"But within this strict form the poet has complete freedom to say whatever he wants, doesn't he?"

"Yes." Calvin nodded again.

"So," Mrs Whatsit said.

"So what?"

"Oh, do not be stupid, boy!" Mrs Whatsit scolded. "You know perfectly well what I am driving at!"

"You mean you're comparing our lives to a sonnet? A strict form, but freedom within it?"

"Yes," Mrs Whatsit said. "You're given the form, but you have to write the sonnet yourself. What you say is completely up to you."

"Please," Meg said. "Please. If I've got to go I want to go and get it over with. Each minute you put it off makes it harder."

"Sshee iss rrightt," boomed Mrs Which's voice. "Itt iss ttime."

"You may say goodbye." Mrs Whatsit was giving her not permission but a command.

Meg curtsied clumsily to the beasts. "Thank you all. Very much. I know you saved my life." She did not add what she could not help thinking: Saved it for what? So that IT could get me?

She put her arms about Aunt Beast, pressed up against the soft, fragrant fur. "Thank you," she whispered. "I love you."

"And I you, little one." Aunt Beast pressed gentle tendrils against Meg's face.

"Cal—" Meg said, holding out her hand.

Calvin came to her and took her hand, then drew her roughly to him and kissed her. He didn't say anything, and he turned away before he had a chance to see the surprised happiness that brightened Meg's eyes.

At last she turned to her father. "I'm—I'm sorry, Father."

He took both her hands in his, bent down to her with his short-sighted eyes. "Sorry for what, Megatron?"

Tears almost came to her eyes at the gentle use of the old nickname. "I wanted you to do it all for me. I wanted everything to be all easy and simple . . . So I tried to pretend that it was all your fault . . . because I was scared, and I didn't want to have to do anything myself—"

"But I wanted to do it for you," Mr. Murry said. "That's what every parent wants." He looked into her dark, frightened eyes. "I won't let you go, Meg. I am going."

"No." Mrs Whatsit's voice was sterner than Meg had ever heard it. "You are going to allow Meg the privilege of accepting this danger. You are a wise man, Mr. Murry. You are going to let her go."

Mr. Murry sighed. He drew Meg close to him. "Little Megaparsec.

Don't be afraid to be afraid. We will try to have courage for you. That
is all we can do. Your mother—"

"Mother was always shoving me out in the world," Meg said.
"She'd want me to do this. You know she would. Tell her—" she
started, choked, then held up her head and said, "No. Never mind. I'll
tell her myself."

"Good girl. Of course you will."

Now Meg walked slowly around the great table to where Mrs Whatsit was still poised between the columns. "Are you going with me?"

"No. Only Mrs Which."

"The Black Thing—" Fear made her voice tremble. "When Father
tessered me through it, it almost got me."

"Your father is singularly inexperienced," Mrs Whatsit said,
"though a fine man, and worth teaching. At the moment he still treats
tessering as though he were working with a machine. We will not let
the Black Thing get you. I don't think."

This was not exactly comforting.

The momentary vision and faith that had come to Meg dwindled.
"But suppose I can't get Charles Wallace away from IT—"

"Stop." Mrs Whatsit held up her hand. "We gave you gifts the last
time we took you to Camazotz. We will not let you go empty-handed
this time. But what we can give you now is nothing you can touch with
your hands. I give you my love, Meg. Never forget that. My love always."

Mrs Who, eyes shining behind spectacles, beamed at Meg. Meg
handed back the spectacles she had used on Camazotz.

"Your father is right." Mrs Who took the spectacles and hid them
somewhere in the folds of her robes. "The virtue is gone from them.
And what I have to give you this time you must try to understand not
word by word but in a flash, as you understand the tesseract. Listen,
Meg. Listen well. *The foolishness of God is wiser than men; and the
weakness of God is stronger than men. For ye see your calling, brethren, how that not many wise men after the flesh, not many mighty, not
many noble, are called, but God hath chosen the foolish things of the
world to confound the wise; and God hath chosen the weak things of
the world to confound the things which are mighty. And base things of
the world, and things which are despised, hath God chosen, yea, and
things which are not, to bring to nought things that are.*" She paused,
and then she said, "May the right prevail." Her spectacles seemed to
flicker. Behind her, through her, one of the columns became visible.
There was a final gleam from the glasses, and she was gone. Meg looked

nervously to where Mrs Whatsit had been standing before Mrs Who spoke. But Mrs Whatsit was no longer there.

"No!" Mr. Murry cried, and stepped toward Meg.

Mrs Which's voice came through her shimmer. "I ccannott hholldd yyourr hanndd, chilldd."

Immediately Meg was swept into darkness, into nothingness, and then into the icy devouring cold of the Black Thing. Mrs Which won't let it get me, she thought over and over while the cold of the Black Thing seemed to crunch at her bones.

Then they were through it, and she was standing breathlessly on her feet on the same hill on which they had first landed on Camazotz. She was cold and a little numb, but no worse than she had often been in the winter in the country when she had spent an afternoon skating on the pond. She looked around. She was completely alone. Her heart began to pound.

Then, seeming to echo from all around her, came Mrs Which's unforgettable voice. "I hhave nnott ggivenn yyou mmyy ggifftt. *Yyou hhave ssomethinngg thatt ITT hhass nnott.* Thiss ssomethinngg iss yyourr onlly wweapponn. Bbutt yyou mmusstt ffinndd itt fforr yyourrssellff." Then the voice ceased, and Meg knew that she was alone.

She walked slowly down the hill, her heart thumping painfully against her ribs. There below her was the same row of identical houses they had seen before, and beyond these the linear buildings of the city. She walked along the quiet street. It was dark and the street was deserted. No children playing ball or skipping rope. No mother figures at the doors. No father figures returning from work. In the same window of each house was a light, and as Meg walked down the street all the lights were extinguished simultaneously. Was it because of her presence, or was it simply that it was time for lights-out?

She felt numb, beyond rage or disappointment or even fear. She put one foot ahead of the other with precise regularity, not allowing her pace to lag. She was not thinking; she was not planning; she was simply walking slowly but steadily toward the city and the domed building where IT lay.

Now she approached the outlying buildings of the city. In each of them was a vertical line of light, but it was a dim, eerie light, not the warm light of stairways in cities at home. And there were no isolated brightly lit windows where someone was working late, or an office was being cleaned. Out of each building came one man, perhaps a watchman, and each man started walking the width of the building. They appeared not to see her. At any rate, they paid no attention to her whatsoever, and she went on past them.

What have I got that IT hasn't got? she thought suddenly. What have I possibly got?

Now she was walking by the tallest of the business buildings. More dim vertical lines of light. The walls glowed slightly to give a faint illumination to the streets. CENTRAL Central Intelligence was ahead of her. Was the man with red eyes still sitting there? Or was he allowed to go to bed? But this was not where she must go, though the man with red eyes seemed the kind old gentleman he claimed to be when compared with IT. But he was no longer of any consequence in the search for Charles Wallace. She must go directly to IT.

IT isn't used to being resisted. Father said that's how he managed, and how Calvin and I managed as long as we did. Father saved me then. There's nobody here to save me now. I have to do it myself. I have to resist IT by myself. Is that what I have that IT hasn't got? No, I'm sure IT can resist. IT just isn't used to having *other* people resist.

CENTRAL Central Intelligence blocked with its huge rectangle the end of the square. She turned to walk around it, and almost imperceptibly her steps slowed.

It was not far to the great dome which housed IT.

I'm going to Charles Wallace. That's what's important. That's what I have to think of. I wish I could feel numb again the way I did at first. Suppose IT has him somewhere else? Suppose he isn't there?

I have to go there first, anyhow. That's the only way I can find out.

Her steps got slower and slower as she passed the great bronzed doors, the huge slabs of the CENTRAL Central Intelligence building, as she finally saw ahead of her the strange, light, pulsing dome of IT.

Father said it was all right for me to be afraid. He said to go ahead and be afraid. And Mrs Who said—I don't understand what she said but I think it was meant to make me not hate being only me, and me being the way I am. And Mrs Whatsit said to remember that she loves me. That's what I have to think about. Not about being afraid. Or not as smart as IT. Mrs Whatsit loves me. That's quite something, to be loved by someone like Mrs Whatsit.

She was there.

No matter how slowly her feet had taken her at the end, they had taken her there.

Directly ahead of her was the circular building, its walls glowing with violet flame, its silvery roof pulsing with a light that seemed to Meg to be insane. Again she could feel the light, neither warm nor cold, but reaching out to touch her, pulling her toward IT.

There was a sudden sucking, and she was within.

It was as though the wind had been knocked out of her. She gasped for breath, for breath in her own rhythm, not the permeating pulsing of IT. She could feel the inexorable beat within her body, controlling her heart, her lungs.

But not herself. Not Meg. It did not quite have her.

She blinked her eyes rapidly and against the rhythm until the redness before them cleared and she could see. There was the brain, there was IT, lying pulsing and quivering on the dais, soft and exposed and nauseating. Charles Wallace was crouched beside IT, his eyes still slowly twirling, his jaw still slack, as she had seen him before, with a tic in his forehead reiterating the revolting rhythm of IT.

As she saw him, it was again as though she had been punched in the stomach, for she had to realize afresh that she was seeing Charles, and yet it was not Charles at all. Where was Charles Wallace, her own beloved Charles Wallace?

What is it I have got that IT hasn't got?

"You have nothing that IT hasn't got," Charles Wallace said coldly. "How nice to have you back, dear sister. We have been waiting for you. We knew that Mrs Whatsit would send you. She is our friend, you know."

For an appalling moment Meg believed, and in that moment she felt her brain being gathered up into IT.

"No!" she screamed at the top of her lungs. "No! You lie!"

For a moment she was free from ITs clutches again.

As long as I can stay angry enough, IT can't get me.

Is that what I have that IT doesn't have?

"Nonsense," Charles Wallace said. "You have nothing that it doesn't have."

"You're lying," she replied, and she felt only anger toward this boy who was not Charles Wallace at all. No, it was not anger, it was loathing; it was hatred, sheer and unadulterated, and as she became lost in hatred she also began to be lost in IT. The red miasma swam before her eyes; her stomach churned in ITs rhythm. Her body trembled with the strength of her hatred and the strength of IT.

With the last vestige of consciousness she jerked her mind and body. Hate was nothing that IT didn't have. IT knew all about hate.

"You are lying about that, and you were lying about Mrs Whatsit!" she screamed.

"Mrs Whatsit hates you," Charles Wallace said.

And that was where IT made ITs fatal mistake, for as Meg said, automatically, "Mrs Whatsit loves me; that's what she told me, that she loves me," suddenly she knew.

She knew!

Love.

That was what she had that IT did not have.

She had Mrs Whatsit's love, and her father's, and her mother's, and the real Charles Wallace's love, and the twins', and Aunt Beast's.

And she had her love for them.

But how could she use it? What was she meant to do?

If she could give love to IT perhaps it would shrivel up and die, for she was sure that IT could not withstand love. But she, in all her weakness and foolishness and baseness and nothingness, was incapable of loving IT. Perhaps it was not too much to ask of her, but she could not do it.

But she could love Charles Wallace.

She could stand there and she could love Charles Wallace.

Her own Charles Wallace, the real Charles Wallace, the child for whom she had come back to Camazotz, to IT, the baby who was so much more than she was, and who was yet so utterly vulnerable.

She could love Charles Wallace.

Charles. Charles, I love you. My baby brother who always takes care of me. Come back to me, Charles Wallace, come away from IT, come back, come home. I love you, Charles. Oh, Charles Wallace, I love you.

Tears were streaming down her cheeks, but she was unaware of them.

Now she was even able to look at him, at this animated thing that was not her own Charles Wallace at all. She was able to look and love.

I love you. Charles Wallace, you are my darling and my dear and the light of my life and the treasure of my heart. I love you. I love you. I love you.

Slowly his mouth closed. Slowly his eyes stopped their twirling. The tic in the forehead ceased its revolting twitch. Slowly he advanced toward her.

"I love you!" she cried. "I love you, Charles! I love you!"

Then suddenly he was running, pelting, he was in her arms, he was shrieking with sobs. "Meg! Meg! Meg!"

"I love you, Charles!" she cried again, her sobs almost as loud as his, her tears mingling with his. "I love you! I love you! I love you!"

A whirl of darkness. An icy cold blast. An angry, resentful howl that seemed to tear through her. Darkness again. Through the darkness to save her came a sense of Mrs Whatsit's presence, so that she knew it could not be IT who now had her in its clutches.

And then the feel of earth beneath her, of something in her arms, and she was rolling over on the sweet-smelling autumnal earth, and Charles Wallace was crying out, "Meg! Oh, Meg!"

Now she was hugging him close to her, and his little arms were clasped tightly about her neck. "Meg, you saved me! You saved me!" he said over and over.

"Meg!" came a call, and there were her father and Calvin hurrying through the darkness toward them.

Still holding Charles, she struggled to stand up and look around. "Father! Cal! Where are we?"

Charles Wallace, holding her hand tightly, was looking around, too, and suddenly he laughed, his own, sweet, contagious laugh. "In the twins' vegetable garden! And we landed in the broccoli!"

Meg began to laugh, too, at the same time that she was trying to hug her father, to hug Calvin, and not to let go of Charles Wallace for one second.

"Meg, you did it!" Calvin shouted. "You saved Charles!"

"I'm very proud of you, my daughter." Mr. Murry kissed her gravely, then turned toward the house. "Now I must go in to Mother." Meg could tell that he was trying to control his anxiety and eagerness.

"Look!" She pointed to the house, and there were the twins and Mrs. Murry walking toward them through the long, wet grass.

"First thing tomorrow I must get some new glasses," Mr. Murry said, squinting in the moonlight, and then starting to run toward his wife.

Dennys's voice came crossly over the lawn. "Hey, Meg, it's bed-time."

Sandy suddenly yelled, "Father!"

Mr. Murry was running across the lawn, Mrs. Murry running toward him, and they were in each other's arms, and then there was a tremendous happy jumble of arms and legs and hugging, the older Murrys and Meg and Charles Wallace and the twins, and Calvin grinning by them until Meg reached out and pulled him in and Mrs. Murry gave him a special hug all of his own. They were talking and laughing all at once, when they were startled by a crash, and Fortinbras, who could bear being left out of the happiness not one second longer, catapulted his sleek black body right through the screened door to the kitchen. He dashed across the lawn to join in the joy, and almost knocked them all over with the exuberance of his greeting.

Meg knew all at once that Mrs Whatsit, Mrs Who, and Mrs Which must be near, because all through her she felt a flooding of joy and of love that was even greater and deeper than the joy and love which were already there.

She stopped laughing and listened, and Charles listened, too. "Hush."

Then there was a whirring, and Mrs Whatsit, Mrs Who, and Mrs Which were standing in front of them, and the joy and love were so tangible that Meg felt that if she only knew where to reach she could touch it with her bare hands.

Mrs Whatsit said breathlessly, "Oh, my darlings, I'm sorry we don't have time to say goodbye to you properly. You see, we have to—"

But they never learned what it was that Mrs Whatsit, Mrs Who, and Mrs Which had to do, for there was a gust of wind, and they were gone.

A WIND IN THE DOOR

For Pat

Contents

"What, nephew," said the king,
"is the wind in that door?"
SIR THOMAS MALORY
Le Morte d'Arthur

1 Charles Wallace's Dragons

"There are dragons in the twins' vegetable garden."

Meg Murry took her head out of the refrigerator where she had been foraging for an after-school snack, and looked at her six-year-old brother. "What?"

"There are dragons in the twins' vegetable garden. Or there were. They've moved to the north pasture now."

Meg, not replying—it did not do to answer Charles Wallace too quickly when he said something odd—returned to the refrigerator. "I suppose I'll have lettuce and tomato as usual. I was looking for something new and different and exciting."

"Meg, did you hear me?"

"Yes, I heard you. I think I'll have liverwurst and cream cheese." She took her sandwich materials and a bottle of milk and set them out on the kitchen table. Charles Wallace waited patiently. She looked at him, scowling with an anxiety she did not like to admit to herself, at the fresh rips in the knees of his blue jeans, the streaks of dirt grained deep in his shirt, a darkening bruise on the cheekbone under his left eye. "Okay, did the big boys jump you in the schoolyard this time, or when you got off the bus?"

"Meg, you aren't listening to me."

"I happen to care that you've been in school for two months now and not a single week has gone by that you haven't been roughed up. If you've been talking about dragons in the garden or wherever they are, I suppose that explains it."

"I haven't. Don't underestimate me. I didn't see them till I got home."

Whenever Meg was deeply worried she got angry. Now she scowled at her sandwich. "I wish Mother'd get the spreadable kind of cream cheese. This stuff keeps going right through the bread. Where is she?"

"In the lab, doing an experiment. She said to tell you she wouldn't be long."

"Where's Father?"

"He got a call from L.A., and he's gone to Washington for a couple of days."

Like the dragons in the garden, their father's visits to the White House were something best not talked about at school. Unlike the dragons, these visits were real.

Charles Wallace picked up Meg's doubting. "But I saw them, Meg, the dragons. Eat your sandwich and come see."

"Where're Sandy and Dennys?"

"Soccer practice. I haven't told anybody but you." Suddenly sounding forlorn, younger than his six years, he said, "I wish the high-school bus got home earlier. I've been waiting and waiting for you."

Meg returned to the refrigerator to get lettuce. This was a cover for some rapid thinking, although she couldn't count on Charles Wallace not picking up her thoughts, as he had picked up her doubts about the dragons. What he had actually seen she could not begin to guess. That he had seen something, something unusual, she was positive.

Charles Wallace silently watched her finish making the sandwich, carefully aligning the slices of bread and cutting it in precise sections. "I wonder if Mr. Jenkins has ever seen a dragon?"

Mr. Jenkins was the principal of the village school, and Meg had had her own troubles with him. She had small hope that Mr. Jenkins would care what happened to Charles Wallace, or that he would be willing to interfere in what he called 'the normal procedures of democracy.' "Mr. Jenkins believes in the law of the jungle." She spoke through a mouthful. "Aren't there dragons in the jungle?"

Charles Wallace finished his glass of milk. "No wonder you always flunk social studies. Eat your sandwich and stop stalling. Let's go and see if they're still there."

They crossed the lawn, followed by Fortinbras, the large, black, almost-Labrador dog, happily sniffing and snuffling at the rusty autumnal remains of the rhubarb patch. Meg tripped over a wire hoop from the croquet set, and made an annoyed grunt, mostly at herself, because she had put the wickets and mallets away after the last game, and forgotten this one. A low wall of barberry separated the croquet lawn from Sandy's and Dennys's vegetable garden. Fortinbras leaped over the barberry, and Meg called automatically, "Not in the garden, Fort," and the big dog backed out, between rows of cabbage and broccoli. The twins were justly proud of their organic produce, which they sold around the village for pocket money.

"A dragon could make a real mess of this garden," Charles Wallace said, and led Meg through rows of vegetables. "I think he realized that, because suddenly he sort of wasn't there."

"What do you mean, he sort of wasn't there? Either he was there, or he wasn't."

"He was there, and then when I went to look closer, he wasn't there, and I followed him—not really him, because he was much faster than I, and I only followed where he'd been. And he went to the big glacial rocks in the north pasture."

Meg looked scowlingly at the garden. Never before had Charles Wallace sounded as implausible as this.

He said, "Come on," and moved past the tall sheaves of corn, which had only a few scraggly ears left. Beyond the corn the sunflowers caught the slanting rays of the afternoon sun, their golden faces reflecting brilliance.

"Charles, are you all right?" Meg asked. It was not like Charles to lose touch with reality. Then she noticed that he was breathing heavily, as if he had been running, though they had not been walking rapidly. His face was pale, his forehead beaded with perspiration, as though from overexertion.

She did not like the way he looked, and she turned her mind back to the unlikely tale of dragons, picking her way around the luxuriant pumpkin vines. "Charles, when did you see these—dragons?"

"A dollop of dragons, a drove of dragons, a drive of dragons," Charles Wallace panted. "After I got home from school. Mother was all upset because I looked such a mess. My nose was still very bloody."

"I get upset, too."

"Meg, Mother thinks it's more than the bigger kids punching me."

"What's more?"

Charles Wallace scrambled with unusual clumsiness and difficulty over the low stone wall which edged the orchard. "I get out of breath."

Meg said sharply, "Why? What did Mother say?"

Charles walked slowly through the high grass in the orchard. "She hasn't *said*. But it's sort of like radar blipping at me."

Meg walked beside him. She was tall for her age, and Charles Wallace small for his. "There are times when I wish you didn't pick up radar signals quite so well."

"I can't help it, Meg. I don't try to. It just happens. Mother thinks something is wrong with me."

"But what?" she almost shouted.

Charles Wallace spoke very quietly. "I don't know. Something bad enough so her worry blips loud and clear. And I know there's something wrong. Just to walk across the orchard like this is an effort, and it shouldn't be. It never has been before."

"When did this start?" she asked sharply. "You were all right last weekend when we went walking in the woods."

"I know. I've been sort of tired all autumn, but it's been worse this week, and much worse today than it was yesterday. Hey, Meg! Stop blaming yourself because you didn't notice."

She had been doing precisely that. Her hands felt cold with panic. She tried to push her fear away, because Charles Wallace could read his sister even more easily than he could their mother. He picked up a windfall apple, looked it over for worms, and bit into it. His end-of-summer tan could not disguise his extreme pallor, nor his shadowed eyes; why hadn't she noticed this? Because she hadn't wanted to. It was easier to blame Charles Wallace's paleness and lethargy on his problems at school.

"Why doesn't Mother have a doctor look at you, then? I mean a real doctor?"

"She has."

"When?"

"Today."

"Why didn't you tell me before?"

"I was more interested in dragons."

"Charles!"

"It was before you got home from school. Dr. Louise came to have lunch with Mother—she does, quite often, anyhow—"

"I know. Go on."

"So when I got home from school she went over me, from top to toe."

"What did she say?"

"Nothing much. I can't read her the way I can read Mother. She's like a little bird, twittering away, and all the time you know that sharp mind of hers is thinking along on another level. She's very good at blocking me. All I could gather was that she thought Mother might be right about—about whatever it is. And she'd keep in touch."

They had finished crossing the orchard and Charles Wallace climbed up onto the wall again and stood there, looking across an unused pasture where there were two large out-croppings of glacial rock. "They're gone," he said. "My dragons are gone."

Meg stood on the wall beside him. There was nothing to see except the wind blowing through the sun-bleached grasses, and the two tall rocks, turning purple in the autumn evening light. "Are you sure it wasn't just the rocks or shadows or something?"

"Do rocks or shadows look like dragons?"

"No, but—"

"Meg, they were right by the rocks, all sort of clustered together, wings, it looked like hundreds of wings, and eyes opening and shutting between the wings, and some smoke and little spurts of fire, and I warned them not to set the pasture on fire."

"How did you warn them?"

"I spoke to them. In a loud voice. And the flames stopped."

"Did you go close?"

"It didn't seem wise. I stayed here on the wall and watched for a long time. They kept folding and unfolding wings and sort of winking all those eyes at me, and then they all seemed to huddle together and go to sleep, so I went home to wait for you. Meg! You don't believe me."

She asked, flatly, "Well, where have they gone?"

"You've never not believed me before."

She said, carefully, "It's not that I don't believe you." In a strange way she did believe him. Not, perhaps, that he had seen actual dragons—but Charles Wallace had never before tended to mix fact and fancy. Never before had he separated reality and illusion in such a marked way. She looked at him, saw that he had a sweatshirt on over his grubby shirt. She held her arms about herself, shivered, and said— although she was quite warm enough—"I think I'll go back to the house and get a cardigan. Wait here. I won't be long. If the dragons come back—"

"I think they will come back."

"Then keep them here for me. I'll be as fast as I can."

Charles Wallace looked at her levelly. "I don't think Mother wants to be interrupted right now."

"I'm not going to interrupt her. I'm just going to get my cardigan."

"Okay, Meg," he sighed.

She left him sitting on the wall, looking at the two great glacial deposits, waiting for dragons, or whatever it was he thought he'd seen. All right, he knew that she was going back to the house to talk to their mother, but as long as she didn't admit it out loud she felt that she managed to keep at least a little of her worry from him.

She burst into the laboratory.

Her mother was sitting on a tall lab stool, not looking into the microscope in front of her, not writing on the clipboard which rested on her knee, just sitting thoughtfully. "What is it, Meg?"

She started to blurt out Charles Wallace's talk of dragons, and that he had never had delusions before, but since Charles Wallace himself had not mentioned them to their mother, it seemed like a betrayal for her to do so, though his silence about the dragons may have been because of the presence of Dr. Louise.

Her mother repeated, a little impatiently, "What is it, Meg?"

"What's wrong with Charles Wallace?"

Mrs. Murry put the clipboard down on the lab counter beside the microscope. "He had some trouble with the bigger boys again in school today."

"That's not what I mean."

"What do you mean, Meg?"

"He said you had Dr. Colubra here for him."

"Louise was here for lunch, so I thought she might as well have a look at him."

"And?"

"And what, Meg?"

"What's the matter with him?"

"We don't know, Meg. Not yet, at any rate."

"Charles says you're worried about him."

"I am. Aren't you?"

"Yes. But I thought it was all school. And now I don't think it is. He got out of breath just walking across the orchard. And he's too pale. And he imagines things. And he looks—I don't like the way he looks."

"Neither do I."

"What is it? What's wrong? Is it a virus or something?"

Mrs. Murry hesitated. "I'm not sure."

"Mother, please, if there's anything really wrong with Charles I'm old enough to know."

"I don't know whether there is or not. Neither does Louise. When we find out anything definite, I'll tell you. I promise you that."

"You're not hiding anything?"

"Meg, there's no use talking about something I'm not sure of. I should know in a few days."

Meg twisted her hands together nervously. "You really are worried."

Mrs. Murry smiled. "Mothers tend to be. Where is he now?"

"Oh—I left him on the stone wall—I said I was coming in for a cardigan. I've got to run back or he'll think—" Without finishing she rushed out of the lab, grabbed a cardigan from one of the hooks in the pantry, and ran across the lawn.

When she reached Charles Wallace he was sitting on the wall, just as she had left him. There was no sign of dragons.

She had not really expected that there would be. Nevertheless, she was disappointed, her anxiety about Charles subtly deepened.

"What did Mother say?" he asked.

"Nothing."

His large, deep-seeing blue eyes focused on her. "She didn't mention mitochondria? Or farandolae?"

"Hunh? Why should she?"

Charles Wallace kicked the rubber heels of his sneakers against the wall, looked at Meg, did not answer.

Meg persisted, "Why should Mother mention mitochondria? Isn't that—talking about them—what got you into trouble your very first day in school?"

"I am extremely interested in them. And in dragons. I'm sorry they haven't come back yet." He was very definitely changing the subject. "Let's wait a while longer for them. I'd rather face a few dragons any day than the kids in the schoolyard. Thank you for going to see Mr. Jenkins on my behalf, Meg."

That was supposed to be a deep, dark secret. "How did you know?"

"I knew."

Meg hunched her shoulders. "Not that it did any good." She had not really had much hope that it would. Mr. Jenkins had been, for several years, the principal of the large regional high school. When he was moved, just that September, to the small grade school in the village, the official story was that the school needed upgrading, and Mr. Jenkins was the only man to do the job. The rumor was that he hadn't been able to handle the wilder element over at Regional. Meg had her doubts whether or not he could handle anybody, anywhere. And she was completely convinced that he would neither understand nor like Charles Wallace.

The morning that Charles Wallace set off for first grade, Meg was far more nervous than he was. She could not concentrate during her last classes, and when school was finally over and she climbed the hill to the house and found him with a puffed and bleeding upper lip and a scrape across his cheek, she had a sinking feeling of inevitability combined with a burning rage. Charles Wallace had always been thought of by the villagers as peculiar, and probably not quite all there. Meg, picking up mail at the post office, or eggs at the store, overheard snatches of conversations: 'That littlest Murry kid is a weird one.' 'I hear clever people often have dumb kids.' 'They say he can't even talk.'

It would have been easier if Charles Wallace had actually been stupid. But he wasn't, and he wasn't very good at pretending that he didn't know more than the other six-year-olds in his class. His vocabulary itself was against him; he had, in fact, not started talking until late, but then it was in complete sentences, with none of the baby preliminaries. In front of strangers he still seldom spoke at all—one of the reasons he was thought dumb; and suddenly there he was in first grade and talking like—like his parents, or his sister. Sandy and Dennys got along with everybody. It wasn't surprising that Charles was resented; everybody expected him to be backward, and he talked like a dictionary.

"Now, children"—the first-grade teacher smiled brightly at the gaggle of new first-graders staring at her that first morning—"I want each one of you to tell me something about yourselves." She looked at her list. "Let's start with Mary Agnes. Which one is Mary Agnes?"

A small girl with one missing front tooth, and straw-colored hair pulled tightly into pigtails, announced that she lived on a farm and that she had her own chickens; that morning there had been seventeen eggs.

"Very *good*, Mary Agnes. Now, let's see, how about you, Richard— are you called Dicky?"

A fat little boy stood up, bobbing and grinning.

"What have *you* got to tell us?"

"Boys ain't like girls," Dicky said. "Boys is made different, see, like—"

"That's *fine*, Dicky, just fine. We'll learn more about that later. Now, Albertina, suppose you tell us something."

Albertina was repeating first grade. She stood up, almost a head taller than the others, and announced proudly, "Our bodies are made up of bones and skinses and muskle and blood cells and stuff like that."

"Very *good*, Albertina. Isn't that good, class? I can see we're going to have a group of real scientists this year. Let's all clap for Albertina, shall we? Now, uh"—she looked down at her list again—"Charles Wallace. Are you called Charlie?"

"No," he said. "Charles Wallace, please."

"Your parents are scientists, aren't they?" She did not wait for an answer. "Let's see what *you* have to tell us."

Charles Wallace ('You should have known better!' Meg scolded him that night) stood and said, "What I'm interested in right now are the farandolae and the mitochondria."

"What was that, Charles? The mighty what?"

"Mitochondria. They and the farandolae come from the prokaryocytes—"

"The *what?*"

"Well, billions of years ago they probably swam into what eventually became our eukaryotic cells and they've just stayed there. They have their own DNA and RNA, which means they're quite separate from us. They have a symbiotic relationship with us, and the amazing thing is that we're completely dependent on them for our oxygen."

"Now, Charles, suppose you stop making silly things up, and the next time I call on you, don't try to show off. Now, George, you tell the class something . . ."

At the end of the second week of school, Charles Wallace paid Meg an evening visit in her attic bedroom.

"Charles," she said, "can't you just not say anything at all?"

Charles Wallace, in yellow footed pajamas, his fresh wounds band-aided, his small nose looking puffy and red, lay on the foot of Meg's big brass bed, his head pillowed on the shiny black bulk of the dog, Fortinbras. He sounded weary, and lethargic, although she hadn't noticed this at the time. "It doesn't work. Nothing works. If I don't talk, I'm sulking. If I talk I say something wrong. I've finished the work-book—the teacher said you must've helped me—and I know the reader by heart."

Meg, circling her knees with her arms, looked down at boy and dog; Fortinbras was strictly not allowed on beds, but this rule was ignored in the attic. "Why don't they move you up to second grade?"

"That would be even worse. They're that much bigger than I."

Yes. She knew that was true.

So she decided to go see Mr. Jenkins. She boarded the high-school bus as usual at seven o'clock, in the grey, uninviting light of an early morning brewing a nor'easter. The grade-school bus, which had not nearly so far to go, left an hour later. When the high-school bus made its first stop in the village she slipped off, and then walked the two miles to the grade school. It was an old, inadequate building, painted the traditional red, overcrowded and understaffed. It certainly did need upgrading, and taxes were being raised for a new school.

She slipped through the side door which the custodian opened early. She could hear the buzz of his electric floor polisher in the front hall by the still-locked entrance doors, and under cover of its busy sound she ran across the hall and darted into a small broom closet and leaned, too noisily for comfort, against the hanging brooms and dry mops. The closet smelled musty and dusty and she hoped she could keep from sneezing until Mr. Jenkins was in his office and his secretary had brought him his ritual mug of coffee. She shifted position and leaned against the corner, where she could see the glass top of the door to Mr. Jenkins's office through the narrow crack.

She was stuffy-nosed and cramp-legged when the light in the office finally went on. Then she waited for what seemed all day but was more like half an hour, while she listened to the click of the secretary's heels on the polished tile floor, then the roar of children entering the school as the doors were unlocked. She thought of Charles Wallace being pushed along by the great wave of children, mostly much bigger than he was.

—It's like the mob after Julius Caesar, she thought,—only Charles isn't much like Caesar. But I'll bet life was simpler when all Gaul was divided in three parts.

The bell screamed for the beginning of classes. The secretary clicked along the corridor again. That would be with Mr. Jenkins's coffee. The high heels receded. Meg waited for what she calculated was five minutes, then emerged, pressing her forefinger against her upper lip to stifle a sneeze. She crossed the corridor and knocked on Mr. Jenkins's door, just as the sneeze burst out anyhow.

He seemed surprised to see her, as well he might, and not at all pleased, though his actual words were, "May I ask to what I owe this pleasure?"

"I need to see you, please, Mr. Jenkins."

"Why aren't you in school?"

"I am. This school."

"Kindly don't be rude, Meg. I see you haven't changed any over the summer. I had hoped you would not be one of my problems this year. Have you informed anybody of your whereabouts?" The early morning light glinted off his spectacles, veiling his eyes. Meg pushed her own spectacles up her nose, but could not read his expression; as usual, she thought, he looked as though he smelled something unpleasant.

He sniffed. "I will have my secretary drive you to school. That will mean the loss of her services for a full half day."

"I'll hitchhike, thanks."

"Compounding one misdemeanor with another? In this state, hitchhiking happens to be against the law."

"Mr. Jenkins, I didn't come to talk to you about hitchhiking, I came to talk to you about Charles Wallace."

"I don't appreciate your interference, Margaret."

"The bigger boys are bullying him. They'll really hurt him if you don't stop them."

"If anybody is dissatisfied with my handling of the situation and wishes to discuss it with me, I think it should be your parents."

Meg tried to control herself, but her voice rose with frustrated anger.

"Maybe they're cleverer than I am and know it won't do any good. Oh, please, please, Mr. Jenkins, I know people have thought Charles Wallace isn't very bright, but he's really—"

He cut across her words. "We've run IQ tests on all the first-graders. Your little brother's IQ is quite satisfactory."

"You know it's more than that, Mr. Jenkins. My parents have run tests on him, too, all kinds of tests. His IQ is so high it's untestable by normal standards."

"His performance gives no indication of this."

"Don't you understand, he's trying to hold back so the boys won't beat him up? He doesn't understand them, and they don't understand him. How many first-graders know about farandolae?"

"I don't know what you're talking about, Margaret. I do know that Charles Wallace does not seem to me to be very strong."

"He's perfectly all right!"

"He is extremely pale, and there are dark circles under his eyes."

"How would *you* look if people punched you in the nose and kept giving you black eyes just because you know more than they do?"

"If he's so bright"—Mr. Jenkins looked coldly at her through the magnifying lenses of his spectacles—"I wonder your parents bother to send him to school at all?"

"If there weren't a law about it, they probably wouldn't."

Now, standing by Charles Wallace on the stone wall, looking at the two glacial rocks where no dragons lurked, Meg recalled Mr. Jenkins's words about Charles Wallace's pallor, and shivered.

Charles asked, "Why do people always mistrust people who are different? Am I really that different?"

Meg, moving the tip of her tongue over her teeth which had only recently lost their braces, looked at him affectionately and sadly. "Oh, Charles, I don't know. I'm your sister. I've known you ever since you were born. I'm too close to you to know." She sat on the stone wall, first carefully checking the rocks: a large, gentle, and completely harmless black snake lived in the stone wall. She was a special pet of the twins, and they had watched her grow from a small snakelet to her present flourishing size. She was named Louise, after Dr. Louise Colubra, because the twins had learned just enough Latin to pounce on the odd last name.

"Dr. Snake," Dennys had said. "Weirdo."

"It's a nice name," Sandy said. "We'll name our snake after her. Louise the Larger."

"Why the Larger?"

"Why not?"

"Does she have to be larger than anything?"

"She is."

"She certainly isn't larger than Dr. Louise."

Dennys bristled. "Louise the Larger is very large for a snake who lives in a garden wall, and Dr. Louise is a very small doctor—I mean, she's a tiny person. I suppose as a doctor she's pretty mammoth."

"Well, doctors don't have to be any size. But you're right, Den, she is tiny. And our snake is big." The twins seldom disagreed about anything for long.

"The only trouble is, she's more like a bird than a snake."

"Didn't snakes and birds, way back in evolution, didn't they evolve originally from the same phylum, or whatever you call it? Anyhow, Louise is a very good name for our snake."

Dr. Louise, fortunately, was highly amused. Snakes were misunderstood creatures, she told the twins, and she was honored to have such a handsome one named after her. And snakes, she added, were on the caduceus, which is the emblem for doctors, so it was all most appropriate.

Louise the Larger had grown considerably since her baptism, and Meg, though not actively afraid of her, was always careful to look for Louise before she sat. Louise, at this moment, was nowhere to be seen, so Meg relaxed and turned her thoughts again to Charles Wallace. "You're a lot brighter than the twins, but the twins are far from dumb. How do *they* manage?"

Charles Wallace said, "I wish they'd tell me."

"They don't talk at school the way they do at home, for one thing."

"I thought if I was interested in mitochondria and farandolae, other people would be, too."

"You were wrong."

"I really *am* interested in them. Why is that so peculiar?"

"I don't suppose it *is* so peculiar for the son of a physicist and a biologist."

"Most people aren't. Interested, I mean."

"They aren't children of two scientists, either. Our parents provide us with all kinds of disadvantages. I'll never be as beautiful as Mother."

Charles Wallace was tired of reassuring Meg. "And the incredible thing about farandolae is their size."

Meg was thinking about her hair, the ordinary straight brown of a field mouse, as against her mother's auburn waves. "What about it?"

"They're so small that all anyone can do is postulate them; even the most powerful micro-electron microscope can't show them. But they're important to us—we'd die if we didn't have farandolae. But nobody at school is remotely interested. Our teacher has the mind of a grasshopper. As you were saying, it's not an advantage having famous parents."

"If they weren't famous—you bet everybody knows when L.A. calls, or Father makes a trip to the White House—they'd be in for it too. We're all different, our family. Except the twins. They do all right. Maybe because they're normal. Or know how to act it. But then I wonder what normal is, anyhow, or isn't? Why are you so interested in farandolae?"

"Mother's working on them."

"She's worked on lots of things and you haven't been this interested."

"If she really proves their existence, she'll probably get the Nobel Prize."

"So? That's not what's bugging you about them."

"Meg, if something happens to our farandolae—well, it would be disastrous."

"Why?" Meg shivered, suddenly cold, and buttoned her cardigan. Clouds were scudding across the sky, and with them a rising wind.

"I mentioned mitochondria, didn't I?"

"You did. What about them?"

"Mitochondria are tiny little organisms living in our cells. That gives you an idea of how tiny they are, doesn't it?"

"Enough."

"A human being is a whole world to a mitochondrion, just the way our planet is to us. But we're much more dependent on our mitochondria than the earth is on us. The earth could get along perfectly well without people, but if anything happened to our mitochondria, we'd die."

"Why should anything happen to them?"

Charles Wallace gave a small shrug. In the darkening light he looked very pale. "Accidents happen to people. Or diseases. Things can happen to anything. But what I've sort of picked up from Mother is that quite a lot of mitochondria are in some kind of trouble because of their farandolae."

"Has Mother actually told you all this?"

"Some of it. The rest I've just—gathered."

Charles Wallace did gather things out of his mother's mind, out of Meg's mind, as another child might gather daisies in a field. "What are farandolae, then?" She shifted position on the hard rocks of the wall.

"Farandolae live in a mitochondrion sort of the same way a mitochondrion lives in a human cell. They're genetically independent of their mitochondria, just as mitochondria are of us. And if anything happens to the farandolae in a mitochondrion, the mitochondrion gets—gets sick. And probably dies."

A dry leaf separated from its stem and drifted past Meg's cheek. "Why should anything happen to them?" she repeated.

Charles Wallace repeated, too, "Accidents happen to people, don't they? And disease. And people killing each other in wars."

"Yes, but that's people. Why are you going on so about mitochondria and farandolae?"

"Meg, Mother's been working in her lab, night and day, almost literally, for several weeks now. You've noticed that."

"She often does when she's on to something."

"She's on to farandolae. She thinks she's proved their existence by studying some mitochondria, mitochondria which are dying."

"You're not talking about all this stuff at school, are you?"

"I do learn some things, Meg. You aren't really listening to me."

"I'm worried about you."

"Then *listen*. The reason Mother's been in her lab so much trying to find the effect of farandolae on mitochondria is that she thinks there's something wrong with my mitochondria."

"What?" Meg jumped down from the stone wall and swung around to face her brother.

He spoke very quietly, so that she had to bend down to hear. "If my mitochondria get sick, then so do I."

All the fear which Meg had been trying to hold back threatened to break loose. "How serious is it? Can Mother give you something for it?"

"I don't know. She won't talk to me. I'm only guessing. She's trying to shut me out till she knows more, and I can only get in through the chinks. Maybe it's not really serious. Maybe it's all just school; I really do get punched or knocked down almost every day. It's enough to make me feel—Hey—look at Louise!"

Meg turned, following his gaze. Louise the Larger was slithering along the stones of the wall towards them, moving rapidly, sinuously, her black curves shimmering purple and silver in the autumn light. Meg cried, "Charles! Quick!"

He did not move. "She won't hurt us."

"Charles, run! She's going to attack!"

But Louise stopped her advance, just a few feet from Charles Wallace, and raised herself up, uncoiling until she stood, barely on the last few inches of her length, rearing up and looking around expectantly.

Charles Wallace said, "There's someone near. Someone Louise knows."

"The—the dragons?"

"I don't know. I can't see anything. Hush, let me feel." He closed his eyes, not to shut out Louise, not to shut out Meg, but in order to see with his inner eye. "The dragons—I think—and a man, but more than a man—very tall and—" He opened his eyes, and pointed into the shadows where the trees crowded thickly together. "Look!"

Meg thought she saw a dim giant shape moving towards them, but before she could be sure, Fortinbras came galloping across the orchard, barking wildly. It was not his angry bark, but the loud announcing bark with which he greeted either of the Murry parents when they had been away. Then, with his heavy black tail lifted straight out behind him, his nose pointing and quivering, he stalked the length of the orchard, jumped the wall to the north pasture, and ran, still sniffing, to one of the big glacial rocks.

Charles Wallace, panting with effort, followed him. "He's going to where my dragons were! Come on, Meg, maybe he's found fewmets!"

She hurried after boy and dog. "How would you know a dragon dropping? Fewmets probably look like bigger and better cow pies."

Charles Wallace was down on his hands and knees. "Look."

On the moss around the rock was a small drift of feathers. They did not look like bird feathers. They were extraordinarily soft and sparkling at the same time; and between the feathers were bits of glinting silver-gold, leaf-shaped scales which, Meg thought, might well belong to dragons.

"You see, Meg! They were here! My dragons were here!"

2 A Rip in the Galaxy

When Meg and Charles Wallace returned to the house, silently, each holding strange and new thoughts, evening was moving in with the wind. The twins were waiting for them, and wanted Charles Wallace to go out in the last of the light to play catch.

"It's too dark already," Charles Wallace said.

"We've got a few minutes. Come on, Charles. You may be bright, but you're slow at playing ball. I could pitch when I was six, and you can't even catch without fumbling."

Dennys patted Charles, a pat more like a whack. "He's improving. Come on, we've only got a few minutes."

Charles Wallace shook his head. He did not mention that he did not feel well; he just said, firmly, "Not tonight."

Meg left the twins still arguing with him, and went into the kitchen. Mrs. Murry was just coming in from the laboratory, and her mind was still on her work. She peered vaguely into the refrigerator.

Meg confronted her, "Mother, Charles Wallace thinks something is wrong with his mitochondria or farandolae or something."

Mrs. Murry shut the refrigerator door. "Sometimes Charles Wallace thinks too much."

"What does Dr. Colubra think? About this mitochondria bit?"

"That it's a possibility. Louise thinks the bad flu strain this autumn, which has caused a lot of deaths, may not be flu at all, but mitochondritis."

"And that's what Charles maybe has?"

"I don't know, Meg. I'm trying to find out. When I know something, I will tell you. I've already said that. Meanwhile, let me alone."

Meg took a step backwards, sat down on one of the dining chairs.

Her mother never talked in that cold, shutting-out way to her children. It must mean that she was very worried indeed.

Mrs. Murry turned towards Meg with an apologetic smile. "Sorry, Megatron. I didn't mean to be sharp. I'm in the difficult position of knowing more about the possible ailments of mitochondria than almost anybody else today. I didn't expect to be confronted with the results of my work quite so soon. And I still don't know enough to tell you—or Louise—anything definite. Meanwhile, there's no point in our getting all worried unless we know there's a real reason. Right now we'd better concentrate on Charles Wallace's problems at school."

"Is he well enough to go to school?"

"I think so. For now. I don't want to take him out until I have to."

"Why not?"

"He'd just have to go back eventually, Meg, and then things would be harder than ever. If he can just get through these first weeks—"

"Mother, nobody around here has ever known a six-year-old boy like Charles."

"He's extremely intelligent. But there was a day when it wasn't unusual for a twelve- or thirteen-year-old to graduate from Harvard, or Oxford or Cambridge."

"It's unusual today. And you and Father can hardly send him to Harvard at six. Anyhow, it isn't just that he's intelligent. How does he know what we're thinking and feeling? I don't know how much you've told him, but he knows an awful lot about mitochondria and farandolae."

"I've told him a reasonable amount."

"He knows more than a reasonable amount. And he knows you're worried about him."

Mrs. Murry perched on one of the high stools by the kitchen counter which divided the work area from the rest of the bright, rambly dining and studying room. She sighed, "You're right, Meg. Charles Wallace not only has a good mind, he has extraordinary powers of intuition. If he can learn to discipline and channel them when he grows up—if he—" She broke off. "I have to think about getting dinner."

Meg knew when to stop pushing her mother. "I'll help. What're we having?" She did not mention Charles Wallace's dragons. She did not mention Louise the Larger's strange behavior, nor the shadow of whatever it was they had not quite seen.

"Oh, spaghetti's easy"—Mrs. Murry pushed a curl of dark red hair back from her forehead—"and good on an autumn night."

"And we've got all the tomatoes and peppers and stuff from the twins' garden. Mother, I love the twins even when they get in my hair, but Charles—"

"I know, Meg. You and Charles have always had a very special relationship."

"Mother, I can't stand what's happening to him at school."

"Neither can I, Meg."

"Then what are you doing about it?"

"We're trying to do nothing. It would be easy—for now—to take Charles out of school. We thought about that immediately, even before he—But Charles Wallace is going to have to live in a world made up of people who don't think at all in any of the ways that he does, and the sooner he starts learning to get along with them, the better. Neither you nor Charles has the ability to adapt that the twins do."

"Charles is a lot brighter than the twins."

"A life form which can't adapt doesn't last very long."

"I still don't like it."

"Neither do your father and I, Meg. Bear with us. Remember, you do have a tendency to rush in when the best thing to do is wait and be patient for a while."

"I'm not in the *least* patient."

"Is that for my information?" Mrs. Murry took tomatoes, onions, green and red peppers, garlic and leeks, out of the vegetable bin. Then, starting to slice onions into a large, black iron pot, she said thoughtfully, "You know, Meg, you went through a pretty rough time at school yourself."

"Not as bad as Charles. And I'm not as bright as Charles—except maybe in math."

"Possibly you're not—though you do tend to underestimate your own particular capacities. What I'm getting at is that you do seem, this year, to be finding school moderately bearable."

"Mr. Jenkins isn't there any more. And Calvin O'Keefe is. Calvin's important. He's the basketball star and president of the senior class and everything. Anybody Calvin likes is sort of protected by his—his aura."

"Why do you suppose Calvin likes you?"

"Not because of my beauty, that's for sure."

"But he does like you, doesn't he, Meg?"

"Well, yes, I guess so, but Calvin likes lots of people. And he could have any girl in school if he wanted to."

"But he chose you, didn't he?"

Meg could feel herself flushing. She put her hands up to her cheeks. "Well. Yes. But it's different. It's because of some of the things we've been through together. And we're friend-friends—I mean, we're not like most of the other kids."

"I'm glad you're friend-friends. I've become very fond of that skinny, carrot-headed young man."

Meg laughed. "I think Calvin confuses you with Pallas Athene. You're his absolute ideal. And he likes all of us. His own family's certainly a mess. I really think he likes me only because of our family."

Mrs. Murry sighed. "Stop being self-deprecating, Meg."

"Maybe at least I can learn to cook as well as you do. Did you know it was one of Calvin's brothers who beat Charles Wallace up today? I bet he's upset—I don't mean Whippy, he couldn't care less—Calvin. Somebody's bound to have told him."

"Do you want to call him?"

"Not me. Not Calvin. I just have to wait. Maybe he'll come over or something." She sighed. "I wish life didn't have to be so complicated. Do you suppose I'll ever be a double Ph.D. like you, Mother?"

Mrs. Murry looked up from slicing peppers, and laughed. "It's really not the answer to all problems. There are other solutions. At this point I'm more interested in knowing whether or not I've put too many red peppers in the spaghetti sauce; I've lost count."

They had just sat down to dinner when Mr. Murry phoned to tell them that he was going directly from Washington to Brookhaven for a week. Such trips were not unusual for either of their parents, but right now anything that took either her father or mother away struck Meg as sinister. Without much conviction she said, "I hope he has fun. He likes lots of the people there." But she felt a panicky dependence on having both her parents home at night. It wasn't only because of her fears for Charles Wallace; it was that suddenly the whole world was unsafe and uncertain. Several houses nearby had been broken into that autumn, and while nothing of great value had been taken, drawers had been emptied with casual maliciousness, food dumped on living-room floors, upholstery slashed. Even their safe little village was revealing itself to be unpredictable and irrational and precarious, and while Meg had already begun to understand this with her mind, she had never before felt it with the whole of herself. Now a cold awareness of the uncertainty of all life, no matter how careful the planning, hollowed emptily in the pit of her stomach. She swallowed.

Charles Wallace looked at her and said, unsmilingly, "The best laid plans of mice and men . . ."

"Gang aft agley," Sandy finished.

"Man proposes, God disposes," Dennys added, not to be outdone.

The twins held out their plates for more spaghetti, neither one ever having been known to lose his appetite. "Why does Father have to stay a whole week?" Sandy asked.

"It's his work, after all," Dennys said. "Mother, I think you could have put more hot peppers in the sauce."

"He's been away a lot this autumn. He ought to stay home with his family at least some of the time. I think the sauce is okay."

"Of course it's okay. I just like it a little hotter."

Meg was not thinking about spaghetti, although she was sprinkling Parmesan over hers. She wondered what their mother would say if Charles Wallace told her about his dragons. If there really were dragons, or a reasonable facsimile thereof, in the north pasture, oughtn't their parents to know?

Sandy said, "When I grow up I'm going to be a banker and make money. Someone in this family has to stay in the real world."

"Not that we don't think science is the real world, Mother," Dennys said, "but you and Father aren't practical scientists, you're theoretical scientists."

Mrs. Murry demurred, "I'm not wholly impractical, you know, Sandy, and neither is your father."

"Spending hours and hours peering into your microelectron microscope, and listening to that micro-sonar whatsit isn't practical," Sandy announced.

"You just look at things nobody else can see," Dennys added, "and listen to things nobody else can hear, and think about them."

Meg defended her mother. "It would be a good idea if more people knew how to think. After Mother thinks about something long enough, then she puts it into practice. Or someone else does."

Charles Wallace cocked his head with a pleased look. "Does *practical* mean that something works out in practice?"

His mother nodded.

"So it doesn't matter if Mother sits and thinks. Or if Father spends weeks over one equation. Even if he writes it on the tablecloth. His equations are practical if someone else makes them work out in practice." He reached in his pocket, as though in answer to Meg's thoughts about the dragons, and drew out a feather, not a bird feather, but a strange glitter catching the light. "All right, my practical brothers, what is this?"

Sandy, sitting next to Charles Wallace, bent over the dragon feather. "A feather."

Dennys got up and went around the table so that he could see. "Let me—"

Charles Wallace held the feather between them. "What kind is it?"

"Hey, this is most peculiar!" Sandy touched the base of the feather. "I don't think it's from a bird."

"Why not?" Charles Wallace asked.

"The rachis isn't right."

"The what?" Meg asked.

"The rachis. Sort of part of the quill. The rachis should be hollow, and this is solid, and seems to be metallic. Hey, Charles, where'd you get this thing?"

Charles Wallace handed the feather to his mother. She looked at it carefully. "Sandy's right. The rachis isn't like a bird's."

Dennys said, "Then what—"

Charles Wallace retrieved the feather and put it back in his pocket. "It was on the ground by the big rocks in the north pasture. Not just this one feather. Quite a few others."

Meg suppressed a slightly hysterical giggle. "Charles and I think it may be fewmets."

Sandy turned to her with injured dignity. "Fewmets are dragon droppings."

Dennys said, "Don't be silly." Then, "Do you know what it is, Mother?"

She shook her head. "What do you think it is, Charles?"

Charles Wallace, as he occasionally did, retreated into himself. When Meg had decided he wasn't going to answer at all, he said, "It's something that's not in Sandy's and Dennys's practical world. When I find out more, I'll tell you." He sounded very like their mother.

"Okay, then." Dennys had lost interest. He returned to his chair. "Did Father tell you why he has to go rushing off to Brookhaven, or is it another of those top-secret classified things?"

Mrs. Murry looked down at the checked tablecloth, and at the remains of an equation which had not come out in the wash; doodling equations on anything available was a habit of which she could not break her husband. "It's not really secret. There've been several bits about it in the papers recently."

"About what?" Sandy asked.

"There's been an unexplainable phenomenon, not in our part of the galaxy, but far across it, and in several other galaxies—well, the easiest way to explain it is that our new supersensitive sonic instruments have been picking up strange sounds, sounds which aren't on any normal register, but much higher. After such a sound—a cosmic scream, the *Times* rather sensationally called it—there appears to be a small rip in the galaxy."

"What does that mean?" Dennys asked.

"It seems to mean that several stars have vanished."

"Vanished where?"

"That's the odd part. Vanished. Completely. Where the stars were there is, as far as our instruments can detect, nothing. Your father was out in California several weeks ago, you remember, at Mount Palomar."

"But things can't just vanish," Sandy said. "We had it in school—the balance of matter."

Their mother added, very quietly, "It seems to be getting unbalanced."

"You mean like the ecology?"

"No. I mean that matter actually seems to be being annihilated."

Dennys said flatly, "But that's impossible."

"E = MC^2," Sandy said. "Matter can be converted into energy, and energy into matter. You have to have one or the other."

Mrs. Murry said, "Thus far, Einstein's law has never been disproved. But it's coming into question."

"Nothingness—" Dennys said. "That's impossible."

"One would hope so."

"And that's what Father's going off about?"

"Yes, to consult with several other scientists, Shasti from India, Shen Shu from China—you've heard of them."

Outside the dining-room windows came a sudden brilliant flash of light, followed by a loud clap of thunder. The windows rattled. The kitchen door burst open. Everybody jumped.

Meg sprang up, crying nervously, "Oh, Mother—"

"Sit down, Meg. You've heard thunder before."

"You're sure it's not one of those cosmic things?"

Sandy shut the door.

Mrs. Murry was calmly reassuring. "Positive. They're completely inaudible to human ears." Lightning flashed again. Thunder boomed. "As a matter of fact, there are only two instruments in the world delicate enough to pick up the sound, which is incredibly high-pitched. It's perfectly possible that it's been going on for billennia, and only now are our instruments capable of recording it."

"Birds can hear sounds way above our normal pitch," Sandy said, "I mean, way up the scale, that we can't hear at all."

"Birds can't hear this."

Dennys said, "I wonder if snakes can hear as high a pitch as birds?"

"Snakes don't have ears," Sandy contradicted.

"So? They feel vibrations and sound waves. I think Louise hears all kinds of things out of human range. What's for dessert?"

Meg's voice was still tense. "We don't usually have thunderstorms in October."

"Please calm down, Meg." Mrs. Murry started clearing the table.

"If you'll stop and think, you'll remember that we've had an unseasonable storm for every month in the year."

Sandy said, "Why does Meg always exaggerate everything? Why does she have to be so cosmic? What's for dessert?"

"I don't—" Meg started defensively, then jumped as the rain began to pelt against the windows.

"There's some ice cream in the freezer," Mrs. Murry said. "Sorry, I haven't been thinking about desserts."

"Meg's supposed to make desserts," Dennys said. "Not that we expect pies or anything, Meg, but even you can't go too wrong with Jello."

Charles Wallace caught Meg's eye, and she closed her mouth. He put his hand in the pocket of his robe again, though this time he did not produce the feather, and gave her a small, private smile. He may have been thinking about his dragons, but he had also been listening carefully, both to the conversation and to the storm, his fair head tilted slightly to one side. "This ripping in the galaxy, Mother—does it have any effect on our own solar system?"

"That," Mrs. Murry replied, "is what we would all like to know."

Sandy brushed this aside impatiently. "It's all much too complicated for me. I'm sure banking is a lot simpler."

"And more lucrative," Dennys added.

The windows shook in the wind. The twins looked through the darkness at the slashing rain.

"It's a good thing we brought in so much stuff from the garden before dinner."

"This is almost hail."

Meg asked nervously, "Is it dangerous, this—this ripping in the sky, or whatever it is?"

"Meg, we really know nothing about it. It may have been going on all along, and we only now have the instruments to record it."

"Like farandolae," Charles Wallace said. "We tend to think things are new because we've just discovered them."

"But is it dangerous?" Meg repeated.

"Meg, we don't know enough about it yet. That's why it's important that your father and some of the other physicists get together at once."

"But it could be dangerous?"

"Anything can be dangerous."

Meg looked down at the remains of her dinner. Dragons and rips in the sky. Louise and Fortinbras greeting something large and strange. Charles Wallace pale and listless. She did not like any of it. "I'll do the dishes," she told her mother.

They cleaned up the kitchen in silence. Mrs. Murry had sent the reluctant twins to practice for the school orchestra, Dennys on the flute, which he played well, accompanied by Sandy, less skillfully, on the piano. But it was a pleasant, familiar noise, and Meg relaxed into it. When the dishwasher was humming, the pots and pans polished and hung on their hooks, she went up to her attic bedroom to do her homework. This room was supposed to be her own, private place, and it would have been perfect except for the fact that it was seldom really private: the twins kept their electric trains in the big, open section of the attic; the ping-pong table was there, and anything anybody didn't want around downstairs but didn't want to throw away. Although Meg's room was at the far end of the attic, it was easily available to the twins when they needed help with their math homework. And Charles Wallace always knew, without being told, when she was troubled, and would come up to the attic to sit on the foot of her bed. The only time she didn't want Charles Wallace was when he himself was what was troubling her. She did not want him now.

Rain was still spattering against her window, but with diminishing force. The wind was swinging around from the south to the west; the storm was passing and the temperature falling. Her room was cold, but she did not plug in the little electric heater her parents had given her to supplement the inadequate heat which came up the attic stairs. Instead, she shoved her books aside and tiptoed back downstairs, stepping carefully over the seventh stair, which not only creaked but sometimes gave off a report like a shot.

The twins were still practicing. Her mother was in the living room, in front of the fire, reading to Charles Wallace, not from books about trains, or animals, which the twins had liked at that age, but from a scientific magazine, an article called "The Polarizabilities and Hyperpolarizabilities of Small Molecules," by the theoretical chemist, Peter Liebmann.

—Ouch, Meg thought ruefully.—This kind of thing is Charles Wallace's bedtime reading and our parents expect him to go to first grade and not get into trouble?

Charles Wallace lay on the floor in front of the fire, staring into the flames, half listening, half brooding, his head as usual pillowed on Fortinbras's comfortable bulk. Meg would have liked to take Fort with her, but that would mean letting the family know she was going out. She hurried as quickly and silently as possible through the kitchen and out into the pantry. As she pulled the kitchen door closed behind her, slowly, carefully, so nobody would hear, the pantry door flew open with a bang, and the door to her mother's lab, on the left, slammed shut in a gust of wind.

She stopped, listened, waited for one of the twins to open the kitchen door and see what was going on. But nothing happened except that the wind blew wildly through the pantry. She shivered, and grabbed the first rain clothes that came to hand, a big black rubber poncho that belonged to the twins and had done double duty as a ground cloth for a tent; and Charles Wallace's yellow sou'wester. Then she took the big flashlight from the hook, shut the pantry door firmly behind her, and ran across the lawn, tripping over the croquet wicket. Limping, she crossed the patch of dandelion, burdock, and milkweed that was growing up in the opening the twins had cut in the barberry fence. Once she was in the vegetable garden she hoped that she would be invisible to anybody chancing to look out a window. She could imagine Sandy's or Dennys's reaction if they asked her where she was going and she told them she was looking for dragons.

Why, in fact, had she come out? And what was she looking for? Was it dragons? Fortinbras and Louise both had seen—and not been afraid of—something, something which had left the feathers and scales. And that something—or somethings—was likely to be uncomfortable in the wet pasture. If it—or they—came to seek shelter in the house, she wanted to be prepared.

Not only for dragons, in which she did not quite believe, despite her faith in Charles Wallace and the feather with the peculiar rachis, but also for Louise the Larger. The twins insisted that Louise was an unusual snake, but this afternoon was the first time Meg had seen any signs that Louise was anything more than a contented, common garden-variety snake.

Meg checked the shadows on the wall, but there was no sign of Louise, so she lingered, not at all anxious to cross the apple orchard and go into the north pasture to the two glacial rocks. For a few minutes she would stay in the homely garden, and gather her courage, and be safe from discovery: the twins were hardly likely to come out after dark in the cold and wet, to admire the last few cabbages, or the vine which had borne their prize cucumber, the size of a vegetable marrow.

The garden was bordered on the east by two rows of sunflowers which stood with their heavy, fringed heads bowed over so that they looked like a huddle of witches; Meg glanced at them nervously; raindrops dripped from their faces with melancholy unconcern, but no longer from the sky. There was a hint of light from the full moon behind the thinning clouds, turning all the vegetables into beings strange and unreal. The gaping rows where once beans had stood, and lettuce, and peas, had a forlorn look; there was an air of sadness and confusion about the carefully planned pattern.

"Like everything else"—Meg spoke to the few remaining cauliflower heads—"it's falling apart. It's not right in the United States of America that a little kid shouldn't be safe in school."

She moved slowly along the orchard wall. The cidery smell of fallen apples was cut by the wind which had completely changed course and was now streaming across the garden from the northwest, sharp and glittery with frost. She saw a shadow move on the wall and jumped back: Louise the Larger, it must be Louise, and Meg could not climb that wall or cross the orchard to the north pasture until she was sure that neither Louise nor the not-quite-seen shape was lurking there waiting to pounce on her. Her legs felt watery, so she sat on a large, squat pumpkin to wait. The cold wind brushed her cheek; corn tassels hished like ocean waves. She looked warily about. She was seeing, she realized, through lenses streaked and spattered by raindrops blowing from sunflowers and corn, so she took off her spectacles, felt under the poncho for her kilt, and wiped them. Better, though the world was still a little wavery, as though seen under water.

She listened; listened. In the orchard she heard the soft plomp of falling apples; wind shaking the trees; branches rustling. She peered through the darkness. Something was moving, coming closer—

Snakes never come out in the cold and dark, she knew that. Nevertheless—

Louise—

Yes, it was the big snake. She emerged from the rocks of the stone wall, slowly, warily, watchfully. Meg's heart was thumping, although Louise was not threatening. At least, Louise was not threatening *her*. But Louise was waiting, and this time there was no welcome in the waiting. Meg looked in fascination as the head of the snake slowly weaved back and forth, then quivered in recognition.

Behind Meg a voice came. "Margaret."

She whirled around.

It was Mr. Jenkins. She looked at him in complete bewilderment.

He said, "Your little brother thought I might find you here, Margaret."

Yes, Charles would guess, would know where she was. But why would Mr. Jenkins have been speaking to Charles Wallace? The principal had never been to the Murrys' house, or any parents', for that matter. All confrontations were in the safe anonymity of his office. Why would he come through the wet grass and the still-dripping garden to look for her instead of sending one of the twins?

He said, "I wanted to come find you myself, Margaret, because I feel that I owe you an apology for my sharpness with you last week when you came to see me." He held out a hand, pale in the moonlight wavering behind the clouds.

In utter confusion she reached out to take his hand, and as she did so, Louise rose up on the wall behind her, hissing and making a strange, warning clacking. Meg turned to see the snake, looking as large and hooded as a cobra, hissing angrily at Mr. Jenkins, raising her large dark coils to strike.

Mr. Jenkins screamed, in a way that she had never known a man could scream, a high, piercing screech.

Then he rose up into the night like a great, flapping bird, flew, screaming across the sky, became a rent, an emptiness, a slash of nothingness—

Meg found that she, too, was screaming.

It could not have happened.

There was no one, no thing there.

She thought she saw Louise slithering back through a dark recess in the stone wall, disappearing—

It was impossible.

Her mind had snapped. It was some kind of hallucination caused by the weather, by her anxiety, by the state of the world—

A thick, ugly smell, like spoiled cabbage, like flower stalks left too long in water, rose like a miasma from the place where Mr. Jenkins had been—

But he could not have been there—

She screamed again, in uncontrollable panic, as a tall shape hurtled towards her.

Calvin. Calvin O'Keefe.

She burst into hysterical tears of relief.

He vaulted over the wall to her, his strong, thin arms tight around her, holding her. "Meg. Meg, what is it?"

She could not control her terrified sobbing.

"Meg, what's the matter? What's happened?" He shook her, urgently.

Gasping, she tried to tell him. "I know it sounds incredible—" she finished. She was still trembling violently, her heart racing. When he did not speak, but continued soothingly to pat her back, she said, through a few final, hiccuping sobs, "Oh, Calvin, I wish I *had* imagined it. Do you think—do you think maybe I did?"

"I don't know," Calvin said flatly. He continued to hold her strongly, comfortingly.

Now that Calvin was here, would take over, she was able to manage a slightly hysterical giggle. "Mr. Jenkins always said I have too much imagination—but it's never been *that* kind of imagination. I've never hallucinated or anything, have I?"

"No," he replied firmly. "You have not. What's that awful stench?"

"I don't know. It's not nearly as bad now as it was just before you came."

"It makes silage smell like roses. Yukh."

"Calvin—Louise the Larger—it's not the first time today Louise has done something peculiar."

"What?"

She told him about Louise that afternoon. "But she wasn't attacking or anything then, she was still friendly. She's always been a friendly snake." She let her breath out in a long, quavering sigh. "Cal, let me have your handkerchief, please. My glasses are filthy and I can't see a thing, and right now I'd like to be able to see what's going on."

"My handkerchief is filthy." But Calvin fished in his pockets.

"It's better than a kilt." Meg spat on her glasses and wiped them. Without their aid she could see no more of the older boy than a vague blur, so she made bold to say, "Oh, Cal, I was hoping you might come over tonight anyhow."

"I'm surprised you're even willing to speak to me. I came over to apologize for what my brother did to Charles Wallace."

Meg adjusted her spectacles with her usual rough shove up the nose, just as a shaft of moonlight broke through the clouds and illuminated Calvin's troubled expression. She returned his handkerchief. "It wasn't your fault." Then—"I must have had a mental aberration or something, about Louise and Mr. Jenkins, mustn't I?"

"I don't know, Meg. You've never had a mental aberration before, have you?"

"Not that I know of."

"Fewmets to Mr. Jenkins, anyhow."

She almost shouted, "What did you say!"

"Fewmets to Mr. Jenkins. Fewmets is my new swear word. I'm tired of all the old ones. Fewmets are dragon droppings, and—"

"I know fewmets are dragon droppings! What I want to know is why you picked on fewmets, of all things?"

"It seemed quite a reasonable choice to me."

Suddenly she was shaking again. "Calvin—please—don't—it's too serious."

He dropped his bantering tone. "Okay, Meg, what's up about fewmets?"

"Oh, Cal, I was so sort of shook about the Mr. Jenkins thing I almost forgot about the dragons."

"The what?"

She told him, all about Charles Wallace and his dragons, "and he's never hallucinated before, either." She told him again about Louise greeting the shadow of something they had not quite seen, "but it certainly wasn't Mr. Jenkins. Louise wasn't in the least friendly about Mr. Jenkins."

"It's wild," Calvin said, "absolutely wild."

"But we did see fewmets, Calvin—or something, more like feathers, really, but not like real feathers. Charles Wallace took one home—there was a whole pile of them—these sort of feathers, and dragon scales, by the biggest rock in the north pasture."

Calvin sprang to his feet. "Let's go, then! Bring your flashlight."

It was possible now for her to cross the orchard and go into the pasture with Calvin to take the lead. Uppermost in Meg's mind, superseding fear, was the need to prove that she and Charles Wallace weren't just making something up, that the wild tales she had told Calvin were real—not Mr. Jenkins turning into a flying emptiness in the sky, she did not want that to be real, but the dragons. For if nothing that had happened touched on reality, then she was going out of her mind.

When they reached the pasture, Calvin took the light from her. "I'll go ahead a bit."

But Meg followed close on his heels. She thought she could sense disbelief as he swept the arc of light around the base of the rock. The beam came to rest in a small circle, and in the center of the circle shone something gold and glittering.

"Phew—" Calvin said.

Meg giggled with relief and tension. "Don't you mean fewmets? Has anybody ever seen a fewmet?"

Calvin was down on hands and knees, running his fingers through the little pile of feathers and scales. "Okay, okay, this is most peculiar. But what left it? After all, a gang of dragons just doesn't disappear."

"A drive of dragons," Meg corrected, automatically. "Do you really think it's dragons?"

Calvin did not answer. He asked, "Did you tell your mother?"

"Charles Wallace showed the feather to the twins during dinner, and Mother saw it, too. The twins said it wasn't a bird's feather because the rachis isn't right, and then the conversation got shifted. I think Charles shifted it on purpose."

"How is he?" Calvin asked. "How badly did Whippy hurt him?"

"He's been hurt worse. Mother put compresses on his eye, and it's turning black and blue. But that's about all." She was not ready, yet, to mention his pallor, or shortness of wind. "You'd think we lived in the roughest section of an inner city or something, instead of way out in the peaceful country. There isn't a day he doesn't get shoved around by one of the bigger kids—it's not only Whippy. Cal, why is it that my parents know all about physics and biology and stuff, and nothing about keeping their son from being mugged?"

Calvin pulled himself up onto the smaller of the two stones. "If it's any consolation to you, Meg, I doubt if my parents know the difference between physics and biology. Maybe Charles would be better off in a city school, where there're lots of different kinds of kids, white, black, yellow, Spanish-speaking, rich, poor. Maybe he wouldn't stand out as being so different if there were other different people, too. Here—well, everybody's sort of alike. People're kind of proud of having your parents live here, and pally with the President and all, but you Murrys certainly aren't like anybody else."

"You've managed."

"Same way the twins have. Playing by the laws of the jungle. You know that. Anyhow, my parents and grandparents were born right here in the village, and so were my great-grandparents. The O'Keefes may be shiftless, but at least they're not newcomers." His voice deepened with an old sadness.

"Oh, Cal—"

He shrugged his dark mood aside. "I think maybe we'd better go talk to your mother."

"Not yet." Charles Wallace's voice came from behind them. "She's got enough worries. Let's wait till the dragons come back."

Meg jumped. "Charles! Why aren't you in bed? Does Mother know you're out?"

"I was in bed. Mother doesn't know I'm out. Obviously."

Meg was near tears of exhaustion. "Nothing is obvious any more." Then, in her big-sister tone of voice: "You shouldn't be out this late."

"What happened?"

"What do you mean?"

"Meg, I came out because something frightened you." He sighed, a strangely tired and ancient sigh from so small a boy. "I was almost asleep and I felt you screaming."

"I don't want to tell you about it. I don't want it to have happened: Where's Fortinbras?"

"I left him at home and told him not to let on that I wasn't sound asleep in bed. I didn't want him tangling with dragons. Meg, what happened? You've got to tell me."

Meg said, "Okay, Charles, I don't doubt your dragons any more. No dragons could be more incredible than Mr. Jenkins coming to look for me in the garden, and then turning into a—a great shrieking bird of nothingness." She spoke quickly, because what she was saying sounded so absurd.

Charles Wallace did not laugh. He opened his mouth to speak, then swung around. "Who's here?"

"Nobody," Calvin said. "Meg and me. You." But he jumped down from the rock.

"There's somebody else. Near."

Meg moved closer to Calvin. Her heart, it seemed, stopped beating.

"Hush," Charles Wallace said, though they had not spoken. He listened with lifted head, like Fortinbras catching a scent.

To the right of the pasture was a woods, a small forest of oak, maple, beech, stripped of all but a few brittle leaves, backed by the dark winter richness of assorted spruce and pine. The ground, which the moonlight did not reach, was covered with fallen damp leaves and pine needles which would silence footsteps. Then they heard the sharp crack of a breaking twig.

Meg and Calvin, straining to peer through the trees, saw nothing.

Then Charles Wallace cried, "My dragons!"

They turned around, and they saw, there by the great rock—

wings, it seemed like hundreds of wings, spreading, folding, stretching—

and eyes

how many eyes can a drive of dragons have?

and small jets of flame

Suddenly a voice called to them from the direction of the woods, "Do not be afraid!"

3 The Man in the Night

A huge dark form strode swiftly through the woods and into the pasture; it reached them in a few strides, and then stood very still, so that the folds of the long robe seemed chiseled out of granite.

"Do not be afraid," he repeated. "He won't hurt you."

He?

Yes. Charles Wallace's drive of dragons was a single creature, although Meg was not at all surprised that Charles Wallace had confused this fierce, wild being with dragons. She had the feeling that she never saw all of it at once, and which of all the eyes could she meet? merry eyes, wise eyes, ferocious eyes, kitten eyes, dragon eyes, opening and closing, looking at her, looking at Charles Wallace and Calvin and the strange tall man. And wings, wings in constant motion, covering and uncovering the eyes. When the wings were spread out they had a span of at least ten feet, and when they were all folded in, the creature resembled a misty, feathery sphere. Little spurts of flame and smoke spouted up between the wings; it could certainly start a grass fire if it weren't careful. Meg did not wonder that Charles Wallace had not approached it.

Again the tall stranger reassured them. "He won't hurt you." The stranger was dark, dark as night and tall as a tree, and there was something in the repose of his body, the quiet of his voice, which drove away fear.

Charles Wallace stepped towards him. "Who are you?"

"A Teacher."

Charles Wallace's sigh was longing. "I wish you were *my* teacher."

"I am." The cello-like voice was calm, slightly amused.

Charles Wallace advanced another step. "And my dragons?"

The tall man—the Teacher—held out his hand in the direction of the wild creature, which seemed to gather itself together, to rise up, to give a great, courteous bow to all of them.

The Teacher said, "His name is Proginoskes."

Charles Wallace said, "He?"

"Yes."

"He's not dragons?"

"He is a cherubim."

"What!?"

"A cherubim."

Flame spurted skywards in indignation at the doubt in the atmosphere. Great wings raised and spread and the children were looked at by a great many eyes. When the wild thing spoke, it was not in vocal words, but directly into their minds.

"I suppose you think I ought to be a golden-haired baby-face with no body and two useless little wings?"

Charles Wallace stared at the great creature. "It might be simpler if you were."

Meg pulled her poncho closer about her, for protection in case the cherubim spouted fire in her direction.

"It is a constant amazement to me," the cherubim thought at them, "that so many earthling artists paint cherubim to resemble baby pigs."

Calvin made a sound which, if he had been less astonished, would have been a laugh. "But cherubim is plural."

The fire-spouting beast returned, "I am practically plural. The little boy thought I was a drive of dragons, didn't he? I am certainly not a cherub. I am a singular cherubim."

"What are you doing here?" Charles Wallace asked.

"I was sent."

"Sent?"

"To be in your class. I don't know what I've done to be assigned to a class with such immature earthlings. I have a hard enough job as it is. I really don't fancy coming back to school at all at my age."

"How old are you?" Meg held her poncho out wide, ready to use it as a shield.

"Age, for cherubim, is immaterial. It's only for time-bound creatures that age even exists. I am, in cherubic terms, still a child, and that is all you need to know. It's very rude to ask questions about age." Two of the wings crossed and uncrossed. The message had been rueful, rather than annoyed.

Charles Wallace spoke to the tall man. "You are my teacher, and his teacher, too?"

"I am."

Charles Wallace looked up at the strange dark face which was stern and gentle at the same time. "It's too good to be true. I think I must be having a dream. I wish I'd just go on dreaming and not wake up."

"What is real?" The Teacher stretched out an arm, and gently touched the bruise on Charles Wallace's cheek, the puffed and discolored flesh under his eye. "You are awake."

"Or if you're asleep," Meg said, "we're all having the same dream. Aren't we, Calvin?"

"The thing that makes me think we're awake is that if I were to dream about a cherubim, it wouldn't look like that—that—"

Several very blue, long-lashed eyes looked directly at Calvin. "Proginoskes, as the Teacher told you. Proginoskes. And don't get any ideas about calling me Cherry, or Cheery, or Bimmy."

"It would be easier," Charles Wallace said.

But the creature repeated firmly, "Proginoskes."

Out of the dark form of the Teacher came a deep, gentle rumbling of amusement, a rumbling which expanded and rose and bubbled into a great laugh. "All right, then, my children. Are you ready to start—we will call it, for want of a better word in your language, school—are you ready to start school?"

Charles Wallace, a small and rather ludicrous figure in the yellow slicker he had pulled on over his pajamas, looked up at the oak-tree height and strength of the Teacher. "The sooner the better. Time's running out."

"Hey, wait a minute," Calvin objected. "What are you going to do with Charles? You and the—the cherubim can't take him off without consulting his parents."

"What makes you think I'm planning to?" The Teacher gave an easy little jump, and there he was, comfortably sitting on the tallest of the glacial rocks as though it were a stool, his arms loosely about his knees, the folds of his robe blending with the moonlit stone. "And I came not only to call Charles Wallace. I came to call all three of you."

Meg looked startled. "All of us? But—"

"You may address me as Blajeny," the Teacher said.

Charles Wallace asked, "Mr. Blajeny? Dr. Blajeny? Sir Blajeny?"

"Blajeny is enough. That is all of my name you need to know. Are you ready?"

Meg still looked astonished. "Calvin and me, too?"

"Yes."

"But—" As always when she felt unsure, Meg was argumentative. "Calvin doesn't need—he's the best student in school, and the best athlete, he's important and everything. And I'm getting along, now. It's Charles who's the trouble—you can see for yourself. School, ordinary school, is just not going to work out for him."

Blajeny's voice was cool. "That is hardly my problem."

"Then why are you here?" That Blajeny might have been sent solely to help her brother did not seem at all astonishing to Meg.

Again came the rumble that bubbled up into a laugh. "My dears, you must not take yourselves so seriously. Why should school be easy for Charles Wallace?"

"It shouldn't be *this* bad. This is the United States of America. They'll hurt him if somebody doesn't do something."

"He will have to learn to defend himself."

Charles Wallace, looking very small and defenseless, spoke quietly. "The Teacher is right. It's a question of learning to adapt, and nobody can do that for me. If everybody will leave me alone, and stop trying to help me, I'll learn, eventually, how not to be conspicuous. I can assure you I haven't mentioned mitochondria and farandolae lately."

The Teacher nodded grave approval.

Charles Wallace moved closer to him. "I'm very glad you haven't come because I'm making such a mess of school. But—Blajeny—if you haven't come because of that, then why are you here?"

"I have come not so much to offer you my help as to ask for yours."

"Ours?" Meg asked.

Charles Wallace looked up at the Teacher. "I'm not much of a help to anybody right now. It isn't just that I'm not getting along at school—"

"Yes," Blajeny said. "I know of the other problem. Nevertheless you are called, and anybody who is invited to study with one of the Teachers is called because he is needed. You have talents we cannot afford to lose."

"Then—"

"We must find out what is making you ill and, if possible, make you well again."

"If possible?" Meg asked anxiously.

Calvin asked sharply, "Charles? Ill? What's wrong? What's the matter with Charles?"

"Look at him," Meg said in a low voice. "Look how pale he is. And he has trouble breathing. He got out of breath just walking across the orchard." She turned to the Teacher. "Oh, please, please, Blajeny, can you help?"

Blajeny looked down at her, darkly, quietly. "I think, my child, that it is you who must help."

"Me?"

"Yes."

"You know I'd do anything in the world to help Charles."

Calvin looked questioningly at the Teacher.

"Yes, Calvin, you too."

"How? How can we help?"

"You will learn as the lessons progress."

Calvin asked, "Where are we going to have these lessons, then? Where's your school?"

Blajeny jumped lightly down from the rock. Despite his height and girth he moved, Meg thought, as though he were used to a heavier gravity than earth's. He strode lightly halfway across the pasture to where there was a large, flat rock where the children often went with their parents to watch the stars. He dropped down onto the rock and lay stretched out on his back, gesturing to the others to join him. Meg lay beside him, with Calvin on her other side, so that she felt protected, not only from the cold night wind but from the cherubim, who had reached the rock with the beat of a wing and assorted himself into an assemblage of wings and eyes and puffs of smoke at a discreet distance from Charles Wallace, who was on Blajeny's other side.

"It's all right, dragons," Charles Wallace said. "I'm not afraid of you."

The cherubim rearranged his wings. "Proginoskes, please."

Blajeny looked up at the sky, raised his arm, and made a wide, embracing gesture. The clouds had almost dispersed; only a few rapidly flying streamers veiled the stars, which blazed with the fierce brilliance of the rapidly plummeting mercury. The Teacher's sweeping motion indicated the entire sparkling stretch of sky. Then he sat up and folded his arms across his chest, and his strange luminous eyes turned inwards, so that he was looking not at the stars nor at the children but into some deep, dark place far within himself, and then further. He sat there, moving in, in, deeper and deeper, for time out of time. Then the focus of his eyes returned to the children, and he gave his radiant smile and answered Calvin's question as though not a moment had passed.

"Where is my school? Here, there, everywhere. In the schoolyard during first-grade recess. With the cherubim and seraphim. Among the farandolae."

Charles Wallace exclaimed, "My mother's isolated the farandolae!"

"So she has."

"Blajeny, do you know if something's wrong with my farandolae and mitochondria?"

Blajeny replied quietly, "Your mother and Dr. Colubra are trying to find that out."

"Well, then, what do we do now?"

"Go home to bed."

"But school—"

"You will all go to school as usual in the morning."

It was total anticlimax. "But *your* school—" Meg cried in disappointment. She had hoped that Charles Wallace would never have to enter the old red school building again, that Blajeny would take over, make everything all right . . .

"My children," Blajeny said gravely, "my school building is the entire cosmos. Before your time with me is over, I may have to take you great distances, and to very strange places."

"Are we your whole class?" Calvin asked. "Meg and Charles Wallace and me?"

Proginoskes let out a puff of huffy smoke.

"Sorry—and the cherubim."

Blajeny said, "Wait. You will know when the time comes."

"And why on earth is one of our classmates a cherubim?" Meg said. "Sorry, Proginoskes, but it does seem very insulting to *you* to have to be with mortals like us."

Proginoskes batted several eyes in apology. "I didn't mean what I said about immature earthlings. If we have been sent to the same Teacher, then we have things to learn from each other. A cherubim is not a *higher* order than earthlings, you know, just different."

Blajeny nodded. "Yes. You have much to learn from each other. Meanwhile, I will give each of you assignments. Charles Wallace, can you guess what yours is?"

"To learn to adapt."

"I don't want you to change!" Meg cried.

"Neither do I," Blajeny replied. "Charles Wallace's problem is to learn to adapt while remaining wholly himself."

"What's my assignment, Blajeny?" Meg asked.

The Teacher frowned briefly, in thought. Then, "I am trying to put it into earth terms, terms which you will understand. You must pass three tests, or trials. You must start immediately on the first one."

"What is it?"

"Part of the trial is that you must discover for yourself what it is."

"But how?"

"That I cannot tell you. But you will not be alone. Proginoskes is to work with you. You will be what I think you would call partners. Together you must pass the three tests."

"But suppose we fail?"

Proginoskes flung several wings over his eyes in horror at the thought.

Blajeny said quietly, "It is a possibility, but I would prefer you not to suppose any such thing. Remember that these three trials will be nothing you could imagine or expect right now."

"But Blajeny—I can hardly take a cherubim to school with me!"

Blajeny looked affectionately at the great creature, whose wings were still folded protectingly about himself. "That is for the two of you to decide. He is not always visible, you know. Myself, I find him a little simpler when he's just a wind or a flame, but he was convinced he'd be more reassuring to earthlings if he enfleshed himself."

Charles Wallace reached out and slipped his hand into the Teacher's. "If I could take him, just this way, looking like a drive of dragons, into the schoolyard with me, I bet I wouldn't have any trouble."

Meg said, "Didn't you tell me you were supposed to bring a pet to school tomorrow?"

Charles Wallace laughed. "We *may* bring a small pet tomorrow to share with the class."

Proginoskes peered under one wing. "I am not a joking matter."

"Oh, Progo," Meg assured him. "It's only whistling in the dark."

Charles Wallace, still holding the Teacher's hand, asked him, "Will you come home with us now and meet my mother?"

"Not tonight, Charles, it is very late for you to be up, and who knows what tomorrow will bring?"

"Don't *you* know?"

"I am only a Teacher, and I would not arrange the future ahead of time if I could. Come, I will walk part of the way back to the house with you."

Meg asked, "What about Progo—Proginoskes?"

The cherubim replied, "If it is not the time for Blajeny to meet your family, it is hardly the time for me. I am quite comfortable here. Perhaps you could come meet me early tomorrow morning, and we can compare our night thoughts."

"Well—okay. I guess that's best. Good night, then."

"Good night, Megling." He waved a wing at her, then folded himself up into a great puff. No eyes showed, no flame, no smoke.

Meg shivered.

Blajeny asked, "Are you cold?"

She shivered again. "That thunderstorm before dinner—I suppose it was caused by a cold front meeting a warm front, but it did seem awfully cosmic. I never expected to meet a cherubim . . ."

"Blajeny," Calvin said, "you haven't given me an assignment."

"No, my son. There is work for you, difficult work, and dangerous, but I cannot tell you yet what it is. Your assignment is to wait, without question. Please come to the Murrys' house after school tomorrow— you are free to do that?"

"Oh, sure," Calvin said. "I can skip my after-school stuff for once."

"Good. Until then. Now, let us go."

Charles Wallace led the way, with Meg and Calvin close behind. The wind was blowing out of the northwest, colder, it seemed, with each gust. When they reached the stone wall to the apple orchard, the moon was shining clearly, with that extraordinary brightness which makes light and dark acute and separate. Some apples still clung to their branches; a few as dark as Blajeny, others shining with a silvery light, almost as though they were illuminated from within.

On top of the pale stones of the wall lay a dark shadow, which was moving slowly, sinuously. It rose up, carefully uncoiling, seeming to spread a hood as it loomed over them. Its forked tongue flickered, catching the light, and a hissing issued from its mouth.

Louise.

But this was not the threatening Louise who had hissed and clacked at the impossible Mr. Jenkins; this was the Louise Meg and Charles Wallace had seen that afternoon, the Louise who had been waiting to greet the unknown shadow—the shadow who, Meg suddenly understood, must have been Blajeny.

Nevertheless, she pressed closer to Calvin; she had never felt very secure around Louise, and the snake's strange behavior that afternoon and evening made her seem even more alien than when she was only the twins' pet.

Now Louise was weaving slowly back and forth in a gentle rhythm, almost as though she were making a serpentine version of a deep curtsy; and the sibilant sound was a gentle, treble fluting.

Blajeny bowed to the snake.

Louise most definitely returned the bow.

Blajeny explained gravely, "She is a colleague of mine."

"But—but—hey, now," Calvin sputtered, "wait a minute—"

"She is a Teacher. That is why she is so fond of the two boys— Sandy and Dennys. One day they will be Teachers, too."

Meg said, "They're going to be successful businessmen and support the rest of us in the way to which we are not accustomed."

Blajeny waved this aside. "They will be Teachers. It is a High Calling, and you must not be distressed that it is not yours. You, too, have a Work."

Louise, with a last burst of her tiny, strange melody, dropped back to the wall and disappeared among the stones.

"Perhaps we're dreaming after all," Calvin said, wonderingly.

"What is real?" the Teacher asked again. "I will say good night to you now."

Charles Wallace was reluctant to leave. "We won't wake up in the morning and find it all never happened? We won't wake up and find we dreamed everything?"

"If only one of us does," Meg said, "and nobody else remembers any of it, then it's a dream. But if we all wake up remembering, then it really happened."

"Wait until tomorrow to find what tomorrow holds," Blajeny advised. "Good night, my children."

They did not ask him where he was going to spend the night—though Meg wondered—because it was the kind of presumptuous question one could not possibly ask Blajeny. They left him standing and watching after them, the folds of his robes chiseled like granite, his dark face catching and refracting the moonlight like fused glass.

They crossed the orchard and garden and entered the house, as usual, by the back way, through the pantry. The door to the lab was open, and the lights on. Mrs. Murry was bent over her microscope, and Dr. Colubra was curled up in an old red leather chair, reading. The lab was a long, narrow room with great slabs of stone for the floor. It had originally been used to keep milk and butter and other perishables, long before the days of refrigerators, and it was still difficult to heat in winter. The long work counter with the stone sink at one end was ideal for Mrs. Murry's lab equipment. In one corner were two comfortable chairs and a reading lamp, which softened the clinical glare of the lights over the counter. But Meg could not think of a time when she had seen her mother relaxing in one of those chairs; she inevitably perched on one of the lab stools.

She looked up from the strange convolutions of the micro-electron microscope. "Charles! What are you doing out of bed?"

"I woke up," Charles Wallace said blandly. "I knew Meg and Calvin were outside, so I went to get them."

Mrs. Murry glanced sharply at her son, then greeted Calvin warmly.

Charles Wallace asked, "Is it okay if we make some cocoa?"

"It's very late for you to be up, Charles, and tomorrow's a school day."

"It'll help me get back to sleep."

Mrs. Murry seemed about to refuse, but Dr. Colubra closed her book, saying, "Why not, for once? Let Charles have a nap when he gets home in the afternoon. I'd like some cocoa myself. Let's make it out here while your mother goes on with her work. I'll do it."

"I'll get the milk and stuff from the kitchen," Meg said.

With Dr. Louise present they were not, she felt, free to talk to their mother about the events of the evening. The children were all fond of Dr. Louise, and trusted her completely as a physician, but they were not quite sure that she had their parents' capacity to accept the extraordinary. Almost sure, but not quite. Dr. Colubra had a good deal in common with their parents; she, too, had given up work which paid extremely well in both money and prestige, to come live in this small rural village. ('Too many of my colleagues have forgotten that they are supposed to practice the *art* of healing. If I don't have the gift of healing in my hands, then all my expensive training isn't worth very much.') She, too, had turned her back on the glitter of worldly success. Meg knew that her parents, despite the fact that they were consulted by the President of the United States, had given up much when they moved to the country in order to devote their lives to pure research. Their discoveries, many of them made in this stone laboratory, had made the Murrys more, rather than less, open to the strange, to the mysterious, to the unexplainable. Dr. Colubra's work was perforce more straightforward, and Meg was not sure how she would respond to talk of a strange dark Teacher, eight or nine feet tall, and even less sure how she would react to their description of a cherubim. She'd probably insist they were suffering from mass psychosis and that they all should see a psychiatrist at once.

—Or is it just that I'm afraid to talk about it, even to Mother? Meg wondered, as she took sugar, cocoa, milk, and a saucepan from the kitchen and returned to the pantry.

Dr. Colubra was saying, "That stuff about cosmic screams and rips in distant galaxies offends every bit of the rational part of me."

Mrs. Murry leaned against the counter. "You didn't believe in farandolae, either, until I proved them to you."

"You haven't proven them to me," Dr. Louise said. "Yet." She looked slightly ruffled, like a little grey bird. Her short, curly hair was grey; her eyes were grey above a small beak of a nose; she wore a grey flannel suit. "The main reason I think you may be right is that you go to that idiot machine—" she pointed at the micro-electron microscope— "the way my husband used to go to his violin. It was always like a lovers' meeting."

Mrs. Murry turned away from her 'idiot machine.' "I think I wish I'd never heard of farandolae, much less come to the conclusions—" She stopped abruptly, then said, "By the way, kids, I was rather surprised, just before you all barged into the lab, to have Mr. Jenkins call to suggest that we give Charles Wallace lessons in self-defense."

Mr. Jenkins? Meg wondered. Aloud she said, "But Mr. Jenkins never calls parents. Parents have to go to him." She almost asked, 'Are you *sure* it was Mr. Jenkins?' And stopped herself as she remembered that she had not told Blajeny about the horrible Mr. Jenkins-not-Mr. Jenkins who had turned into a bird of nothingness, the Mr. Jenkins Louise had resented so fiercely. She should have told Blajeny; she would tell him first thing in the morning.

Charles Wallace climbed up onto one of the lab stools and perched close to his mother. "What I really need are lessons in adaptation. I've been reading Darwin, but he hasn't helped me much."

"See what we mean?" Calvin asked Dr. Louise. "That's hardly what one expects from a six-year-old."

"He really does read Darwin," Meg assured the doctor.

"And I still haven't learned how to adapt," Charles Wallace added.

Dr. Louise was making a paste of cocoa, sugar, and a little hot water from one of Mrs. Murry's retorts. "This *is* just water, isn't it?" she asked.

"From our artesian well. The very best water."

Dr. Louise added milk, little by little. "You kids are too young to remember, and your mother is a good ten years younger than I am, but I'll never forget, a great many years ago, when the first astronauts went to the moon, and I sat up all night to watch them."

"I remember it all right," Mrs. Murry said. "I wasn't that young."

Dr. Louise stirred the cocoa which was heating over a Bunsen burner. "Do you remember those first steps on the moon, so tentative to begin with, on that strange, airless, alien terrain? And then, in a short time, Armstrong and Aldrin were striding about confidently, and the commentator remarked on this as an extraordinary example of man's remarkable ability to adapt."

"But all they had to adapt to was the moon's surface!" Meg objected. "It wasn't inhabited. I'll bet when our astronauts reach some place with inhabitants it won't be so easy. It's a lot simpler to adapt to low gravity, or no atmosphere, or even sandstorms, than it is to hostile inhabitants."

Fortinbras, who had an uncanine fondness for cocoa, came padding out to the lab, his nose twitching in anticipation. He stood on his hind legs and put his front paws on Charles Wallace's shoulders.

Dr. Colubra asked Meg, "Do you think the first-graders in the village school are hostile inhabitants, then?"

"Of course! Charles isn't like them, and so they're hostile towards him. People are always hostile to anybody who's different."

"Until they get used to him," the doctor said.

"They're not getting used to Charles."

Charles Wallace, fondling the big dog, said, "Don't forget to give Fort a saucer—he likes cocoa."

"You have the strangest pets," Dr. Louise said, but she poured a small dish of cocoa for Fortinbras. "I'll let it cool a bit before I put it on the floor. Meg, we need mugs."

"Okay." Meg hurried off to the kitchen, collected a stack of mugs, and returned to the laboratory.

Dr. Louise lined them up and poured the cocoa. "Speaking of pets, how's my namesake?"

Meg nearly spilled the cocoa she was handing to her mother. She looked closely at Dr. Louise, but though the question had seemed pointed, the little bird face showed nothing more than amused interest; as Charles Wallace said, Dr. Louise was very good at talking on one level and thinking on another.

Charles Wallace answered the question. "Louise the Larger is a magnificent snake. I wonder if she'd like some cocoa? Snakes like milk, don't they?"

Mrs. Murry said firmly, "You are not going back out tonight to find if the snake, magnificent though she be, likes cocoa. Save your experimental zeal for daylight. Louise is undoubtedly sound asleep."

Dr. Louise carefully poured out the last of the cocoa into her own mug. "Some snakes are very sociable at night. Many years ago when I was working in a hospital in the Philippines I had a boa constrictor for a pet; we had a problem with rats in the ward, and my boa constrictor did a thorough job of keeping the rodent population down. He also liked cream-of-mushroom soup, though I never tried him on cocoa, and he was a delightful companion in the evenings, affectionate and cuddly."

Meg did not think that she would enjoy cuddling with a snake, even Louise.

"He also had impeccable judgment about human nature. He was naturally a friendly creature, and if he showed me that he disliked or distrusted somebody, I took him seriously. We had a man brought to the men's ward who seemed to have nothing more seriously wrong with him than a slightly inflamed appendix, but my boa constrictor took a dislike to him the moment he was admitted. That night he tried to kill the man in the next bed—fortunately we got to him in time. But the snake knew. After that, I listened to his warnings immediately."

"Fortinbras has the same instinct about people," Mrs. Murry said. "Too bad we human beings have lost it."

Meg wanted to say, "So does Louise the Larger," but her mother or the doctor would have asked her on what experience she based such a remark; it would have sounded more likely coming from the twins.

Charles Wallace regarded Dr. Colubra, who had returned to the red leather chair and was sipping cocoa, her legs tucked under her like a child; as a matter of fact, she was considerably smaller than Meg. Charles said, "We take Louise very seriously, Dr. Louise. Very seriously."

Dr. Louise nodded. Her voice was light and high. "That was what I had in mind."

Calvin finished his cocoa. "Thank you very much. I'd better get on home now. See you in school tomorrow, Meg. Thanks again, Mrs. Murry and Dr. Colubra. Good night."

When he had gone, Mrs. Murry said, "All right, Charles. The twins have been in bed for an hour. Meg, it's time for you, too. Charles, I'll come check on you in a few minutes."

As they left the lab, Meg could see her mother turning back to the micro-electron microscope.

Meg undressed slowly, standing by her attic window, wondering if Dr. Louise's talk about snakes had been entirely casual chat over a cup of cocoa; perhaps it was only the strange events of the evening which caused her to look for meanings under the surface of what might well be unimportant conversation. She turned out the lights and looked out the window. She could see across the vegetable garden to the orchard, but the trees still held enough leaves so that she could not see into the north pasture.

Was there really a cherubim waiting at the star-watching rock, curled up into a great feathery ball, all those eyes closed in sleep?

Was he real?

What is real?

4 Proginoskes

Meg woke up before dawn, suddenly and completely, as though something had jerked her out of sleep. She listened: only the usual noises of the sleeping house. She turned on the light and looked at her clock; she had set the alarm for six, as usual. It was now five. She had another whole hour in which she could curl up under the covers, and luxuriate in warmth and comfort, and doze—

Then she remembered.

She tried to reassure herself that she was remembering a dream, although it was not the way that a dream is remembered. It must have been a dream, obviously it must have been a dream—

The only way to prove that it was nothing but a dream, without waking Charles Wallace and asking him, was to get dressed and go out to the star-watching rock and make sure that there was no cherubim there. And—if by some slim chance it had not been a dream, she had promised the cherubim that she would come to him before breakfast.

Had it not been for the horrible moments with Mr. Jenkins screeching across the sky, she would not have wanted it to be a dream. She desperately wanted Blajeny to be real, to take care of everything. But the unreality of Mr. Jenkins, who had always been disagreeably predictable, was far more difficult for her to accept than the Teacher, or even a cherubim who looked like a drive of dragons.

She dressed hurriedly, putting on her kilt and a clean blouse. She tiptoed downstairs as quietly and carefully as she had the night before, through the kitchen and into the pantry, where she put on her heaviest jacket, and a multi-colored knitted tam o'shanter, one of her mother's rare successful ventures into domesticity.

This time no wind blew, no doors slammed. She turned on the

flashlight to guide her. It was a still, chill pre-dawn. The grass was white with spider-web tracings of dew and light frost. A thin vapor moved delicately across the lawn. The mountains were curtained by ground fog, although in the sky she could see stars. She ran across the garden, looking warily about her. But there was no Mr. Jenkins, of course there was no Mr. Jenkins. At the stone wall she looked carefully for Louise, but there was no sign of the big snake. She crossed the orchard, climbed the wall again—still no Louise, it was much too early and much too cold for snakes, anyhow—and ran across the north pasture, past the two glacial rocks, and to the star-watching rock.

There was nothing there except the mist whirling gently in the faint breeze.

So it had all been a dream.

Then the mist seemed to solidify, to become moving wings, eyes opening and shutting, tiny flickers of fire, small puffs of misty smoke . . .

"You're real," she said loudly. "You're not something I dreamed after all."

Proginoskes delicately stretched one huge wing skywards, then folded it. "I have been told that human beings seldom dream about cherubim. Thank you for being prompt. It is in the nature of cherubim to dislike tardiness."

Meg sighed, in resignation, in fear, and, surprisingly, in relief. "Okay, Progo, I guess you're not a figment of my imagination. What do we do now? I've got just about an hour before breakfast."

"Are you hungry?"

"No, I'm much too excited to be hungry, but if I don't turn up on time, it won't go down very well if I explain that I was late because I was talking with a cherubim. My mother doesn't like tardiness, either."

Proginoskes said, "Much can be accomplished in an hour. We have to find out what our first ordeal is."

"Don't you know?"

"Why would I know?"

"You're a cherubim."

"Even a cherubim has limits. When three ordeals are planned, then nobody knows ahead of time what they are; even the Teacher may not know."

"Then what do we do? How do we find out?"

Proginoskes waved several wings slowly back and forth in thought, which would have felt very pleasant on a hot day, but which, on a cold morning, made Meg turn up the collar of her jacket. The cherubim did not notice; he continued waving and thinking. Then she could feel his words moving slowly, tentatively, within her mind. "If you've been assigned to me, I suppose you must be some kind of a Namer, too, even if a primitive one."

"A what?"

"A Namer. For instance, the last time I was with a Teacher—or at school, as you call it—my assignment was to memorize the names of the stars."

"Which stars?"

"All of them."

"You mean *all* the stars, in *all* the galaxies?"

"Yes. If he calls for one of them, someone has to know which one he means. Anyhow, they like it; there aren't many who know them all by name, and if your name isn't known, then it's a very lonely feeling."

"Am I supposed to learn the names of all the stars, too?" It was an appalling thought.

"Good galaxy, no!"

"Then what *am* I supposed to do?"

Proginoskes waved several wings, which, Meg was learning, was more or less his way of expressing "I haven't the faintest idea."

"Well, then, if I'm a Namer, what does that mean? What does a Namer do?"

The wings drew together, the eyes closed, singly, and in groups, until all were shut. Small puffs of mist-like smoke rose, swirled about him. "When I was memorizing the names of the stars, part of the purpose was to help them each to be more particularly the particular star each one was supposed to be. That's basically a Namer's job. Maybe you're supposed to make earthlings feel more human."

"What's that supposed to mean?" She sat down on the rock beside him; she was somehow no longer afraid of his wildness, his size, his spurts of fire.

He asked, "How do I make you feel?"

She hesitated, not wanting to be rude, forgetting that the cherubim, far more than Charles Wallace, did not need her outward words to know what was being said within. But she answered truthfully, "Confused."

Several puffs of smoke went up. "Well, we don't know each other very well yet. Who makes you least confused?"

"Calvin." There was no hesitation here. "When I'm with Calvin, I don't mind being me."

"You mean he makes you *more* you, don't you?"

"I guess you could put it that way."

"Who makes you feel the least you?"

"Mr. Jenkins."

Proginoskes probed sharply, "Why are you suddenly upset and frightened?"

"He's the principal of the grade school in the village this year. But he was in my school last year, and I was always getting sent to his office. He never understands anything, and everything I do is automatically wrong. Charles Wallace would probably be better off if he weren't my brother. That's enough to finish him with Mr. Jenkins."

"Is that all?"

"What do you mean?"

"When you say *Mr. Jenkins*, I feel such a cold wave of terror wash over you that I feel chilly myself."

"Progo—something happened last night—before we met you and Blajeny—when I was all alone in the garden—" Her voice tailed off.

"*What* happened, earthling? Tell me. I have a feeling this may be important."

Why should it be difficult to tell Proginoskes? The cherubim himself was just as unbelievable. But the cherubim was himself, was Proginoskes, while Mr. Jenkins had not been Mr. Jenkins.

As she tried to explain to Proginoskes she could sense him pulling away, and suddenly he flung all his wings about himself in a frantic reflex of self-preservation. Then two eyes looked out at her under one wing. "Echthroi." It was an ugly word. As Proginoskes uttered it the morning seemed colder.

"What did you say?" Meg asked.

"Your Mr. Jenkins—the real one—could he do anything like the one you just told me about? Could he fly into a nothingness in the sky? This is not a thing that human beings can do, is it?"

"No."

"You say he was like a dark bird, but a bird that was nothingness, and that he tore the sky?"

"Well—that's how I remember it. It was all quick and unexpected and I was terrified and I couldn't really believe that it had happened."

"It sounds like the Echthroi." He covered his eyes again.

"The what?"

Slowly, as though with a great effort, he uncovered several eyes. "The Echthroi. Oh, earthling, if you do not know Echthroi—"

"I don't want to. Not if they're like what I saw last night."

Proginoskes agitated his wings. "I think we must go see this Mr. Jenkins, the one you say is at your little brother's school."

"Why?"

Proginoskes withdrew into all his wings again. Meg could feel him thinking grumpily,—They told me it was going to be difficult . . . Why couldn't they have sent me off some place *quiet* to recite the stars again? . . . Or I'm even willing to memorize farandolae . . . I've never been to Earth before, I'm too young, I'm scared of the shadowed planets, what kind of a star has this planet got, anyhow?

Then he emerged, slowly, one pair of eyes at a time. "Megling, I think you have seen an Echthros. If we are dealing with Echthroi, then— I just know with every feather on my wings (and you might try counting my feathers, sometime) that we have to go see this Mr. Jenkins. It must be part of the trial."

"Mr. Jenkins? Part of our first test? But that's—it doesn't make sense."

"It does to me."

"Progo," she objected, "it's impossible. I can slip off my school bus and then walk to the grade school the way I did when I went to talk to Mr. Jenkins about Charles Wallace—and a fat lot of good *that* did—"

"If you have seen an Echthros, everything is different," Proginoskes said.

"Okay, I can get to the grade school all right, but I can't possibly take you with me. You're so big you wouldn't even fit into the school bus. Anyhow, you'd terrify everybody." At the thought she smiled, but Proginoskes was not in a laughing mood.

"Not everybody is able to see me," he told her. "I'm real, and most earthlings can bear very little reality. But if it will relieve your mind, I'll dematerialize." He waved a few wings gracefully. "It's really more comfortable for me not to be burdened with matter, but I thought it would be easier for you if you could converse with someone you could see."

The cherubim was there in front of her, covering most of the star-watching rock, and then he was not there. She thought she saw a faint shimmer in the air, but it might have been the approach of dawn. She could feel him, however, moving within her mind. "Are you feeling extremely brave, Megling?"

"No." A faint light defined the eastern horizon. The stars were dim, almost extinguished.

"I think we're going to have to be brave, earth child, but it will be easier because we're together. I wonder if the Teacher knows."

"Knows what?"

"That you've seen an Echthros."

"Progo, I don't understand. What is an Echthros?"

Abruptly, Proginoskes materialized, raised several wings, and gathered her in. "Come, littleling. I'll take you some place yesterday and show you."

"How can you take me yesterday?"

"I can't possibly take you today, silly. It's time for you to go in to breakfast and your mother dislikes tardiness. And who knows what we may have to do or where we may have to go before tomorrow? Come." He drew her further in to him.

She found herself looking directly into one of his eyes, a great, amber cat's eye, the dark mandala of the pupil, opening, compelling, beckoning.

She was drawn towards the oval, was pulled into it, was through it. Into the ultimate night on the other side.

Then she felt a great, flaming wind, and knew that somehow she herself was part of that wind.

Then she felt a great shove, and she was standing on a bare stone mountain top, and Proginoskes was blinking and winking at her. She thought she saw the oval, mandala-eye through which she had come, but she was not sure.

The cherubim raised a great wing to sketch the slow curve of sky above them. The warm rose and lavender of sunset faded, dimmed, was extinguished. The sky was drenched with green at the horizon, muting upwards into a deep, purply blue through which stars began to appear in totally unfamiliar constellations.

Meg asked, "Where are we?"

"Never mind where. Watch."

She stood beside him, looking at the brilliance of the stars. Then came a sound, a sound which was above sound, beyond sound, a violent, silent, electrical report, which made her press her hands in pain against her ears. Across the sky, where the stars were clustered as thickly as in the Milky Way, a crack shivered, slivered, became a line of nothingness.

If this kind of thing was happening in the universe, no matter how far away from earth and the Milky Way, Meg did not wonder that her father had been summoned to Washington and Brookhaven.

"Progo, what is it? What happened?"

"The Echthroi have Xed."

"What?"

"Annihilated. Negated. Extinguished. Xed."

Meg stared in horrible fascination at the rent in the sky. This was the most terrible thing she had ever seen, more horrifying than the Mr. Jenkins-Echthros the night before. She pressed close to the cherubim, surrounding herself with wings and eyes and puffs of smoke, but she could still see the rip in the sky.

She could not bear it.

She closed her eyes to shut it out. She tried to think of the most comfortable thing possible, the safest, most reasonable, ordinary thing. What, then? The dinner table at home: winter: the red curtains drawn across the windows, and a quiet snow falling softly outdoors; an applewood fire in the fireplace and Fortinbras snoring happily on the hearth; a tape playing Holst's *The Planets*—no, maybe that wasn't too comforting; in her mind's ear she shifted to a ghastly recording of the school band, with Sandy and Dennys playing somewhere in the cacophony.

Dinner was over, and she was clearing the table and starting the dishes and only half listening to the conversation of her parents, who were lingering over their coffee.

It was almost as tangible as though she were actually there, and she thought she felt Proginoskes pushing at her mind, helping her remember.

Had she really listened that attentively to her parents while she stood running hot water over the plates? Their voices were as clear as though she were actually in the room. Her father must have mentioned the terrible thing which Proginoskes had just shown her, the terrible thing which was terrible precisely because it was not a thing, because it was nothing. She could hear, too clearly, her father's voice, calm and rational, speaking to her mother. "It isn't just in distant galaxies that strange, unreasonable things are happening. Unreason has crept up on us so insidiously that we've hardly been aware of it. But think of the things going on in our own country which you wouldn't have believed possible only a few years ago."

Mrs. Murry swirled the dregs of her coffee. "I don't think I believe all of them now, although I know they're happening." She looked up to see that the twins and Charles Wallace were out of the room, that Meg was splashing water in the sink as she scoured a pot. "Ten years ago we didn't even have a key to this house. Now we lock up when we go out. The irrational violence is even worse in the cities."

Mr. Murry absent-mindedly began working out an equation on the tablecloth. For once Mrs. Murry did not even seem to notice. He said, "They've never known a time when people drank rain water because it was pure, or could eat snow, or swim in any river or brook. The last time I drove home from Washington the traffic was so bad I could have made better time with a horse. There were huge signs proclaiming SPEED LIMIT 65 MPH, and we were crawling along at 20."

"And the children and I kept dinner hot for you for three hours, and finally ate, pretending we weren't worried that you might have been in an accident," Mrs. Murry said bitterly. "Here we are, at the height of civilization in a well-run state in a great democracy. And four ten-year-olds were picked up last week for pushing hard drugs in the school where our six-year-old is regularly given black eyes and a bloody nose."

She suddenly noticed the equation growing on the tablecloth. "What are you doing?"

"I have a hunch that there's some connection between your discoveries about the effects of farandolae on mitochondria, and that unexplained phenomenon out in space." His pencil added a fraction, some Greek characters, and squared them.

Mrs. Murry said in a low voice, "My discoveries are not very pleasant."

"I know."

"I isolated farandolae because something beyond increasing air pollution has to account for the accelerating number of deaths from respiratory failure, and this so-called flu epidemic. It was the micro-sonarscope which gave me the first clue—" She stopped abruptly, looked at her husband. "It's the same sound, isn't it? The strange 'cry' of the ailing mitochondria, and the 'cry' picked up in those distant galaxies by the new paraboloidoscope—there's a horrid similarity between them. I don't like it. I don't like the fact that we don't even see what's going on in our own back yard. L.A. is trying as honorably as a president can try in a world which has become so blunted by dishonor and violence that people casually take it for granted. We have to see a great, dramatic fissure in the sky before we begin to take danger seriously. And I have to be deathly worried about our youngest child before I regard farandolae except in a cool and academic manner."

Meg had turned from the kitchen sink at the pain in her mother's voice, and had seen her father reach across the table for her mother's hand. "My dear, this is not like you. With my intellect I see cause for nothing but pessimism and even despair. But I can't settle for what my intellect tells me. That's not all of it."

"What else is there?" Mrs. Murry's voice was low and anguished.

"There are still stars which move in ordered and beautiful rhythm. There are still people in this world who keep promises. Even little ones, like your cooking stew over your Bunsen burner. You may be in the middle of an experiment, but you still remember to feed your family. That's enough to keep my heart optimistic, no matter how pessimistic my mind. And you and I have good enough minds to know how very limited and finite they really are. The naked intellect is an extraordinarily inaccurate instrument."

Proginoskes said, "He's a wise man, your father."

"Could you hear me remembering?"

"I was remembering with you. Most of that conversation you didn't hear with your conscious mind, you know."

"I have a very good memory—" Meg started. Then she stopped herself. "Okay. I know I couldn't have remembered all that by myself. I suppose I just sort of took in the sound waves, didn't I? But how did you get it all from me?"

Proginoskes looked at her with two, ringed owl-like eyes. "You're beginning to learn how to kythe."

"To what?"

"Kythe. It's how cherubim talk. It's talking without words, just the same way that I can be myself and not be enfleshed."

"But I have to be enfleshed, and I need words."

"I know, Meg," he replied gently, "and I will keep things worded for you. But it will help if you will remember that cherubim kythe without words among each other. For a human creature you show a distinct talent for kything."

She blushed slightly at the compliment; she had a feeling that paying compliments is a habit not often indulged in by cherubim. "Progo, I wish I'd been able to see the equation Father was doodling on the tablecloth. If I'd seen it, then it might be somewhere in my mind for you to pull out."

"Think," Proginoskes said. "I'll help."

"Mother put the tablecloth in the wash."

"But you remember there were some Greek letters."

"Yes . . ."

"Let me try to find them with you."

She closed her eyes.

"That's right. Relax, now. Maybe this is the way for us to kythe.— Don't you try to think. Just let me move about."

Out of the corner of her mind's eye she seemed to see three Greek characters among the numbers in the loosely strung equation her father was scribbling on the cloth. She thought them at Proginoskes.

"$\epsilon\chi\theta$. Epsilon, chi, and theta. That's Echth," the cherubim told her.

"Echthroi—but how could Father—"

"Think of the conversation we just recalled, Meg. Your parents are very aware of the evil in the world."

"All right. Yes. I know. Okay." Meg sounded cross. "Until Charles started school I hoped maybe we could ignore it. Like ostriches or something."

The cherubim withdrew its wings from her entirely, leaving her exposed and cold on the strange hilltop. "Open your eyes and look where the sky is torn."

"I'd rather not."

"Go on. I've got all my eyes open, and you only have to open two."

Meg opened her eyes. The rent in the sky was still there. She wondered what this distant phenomenon could have to do with Charles Wallace's pallor, with mitochondritis, or whatever it was. "How—oh, Progo,
how did the Echthroi do that?"

Like Charles Wallace, he picked up her particular anxiety. "It has
to do with un-Naming. If we are Namers, the Echthroi are un-Namers,
non-Namers."

"Progo, what does that have to do with Mr. Jenkins?"

She felt a wave of apprehension roll through her. "Littleling, I think
that is what we must find out. I think that it is part of our first ordeal.
Let us go." He drew her back into himself again; again she was confronted with the single eye, was pulled through the opening, oval pupil.
Then the pupil snapped shut, and they were together on the star-
watching rock with dawn slowly lightening the east.

Progo spread his wings wide, and she moved out. "What do we do
now?" he said.

The cherubim was asking *her?* "I am only a human being, not quite
full-grown," she replied. "How would I know?"

"Megling, I've never been on your planet before. This is your home.
Charles Wallace is your brother. You are the one who knows Mr. Jenkins. You must tell me what we are to do now."

Meg stamped, loudly and angrily, against the hard, cold surface of
the rock. "This is too much responsibility! I'm still only a child! I didn't
ask for any of this!"

"Are you refusing to take the test?" Proginoskes pulled away
from her.

"But I didn't ask for it! I didn't ask for Blajeny, or you, or any
of it!"

"Didn't you? I thought you were worried about Charles Wallace."

"I am! I'm worried about everything!"

"Meg." Proginoskes was somber and stern. "Are you going to enter
into the ordeal? I must know. Now."

Meg stamped again. "Of course I'm going to. You know I have to.
Charles Wallace is in danger. I'll do anything to help him, even if it
seems silly."

"Then what do we do now?"

She shoved at her glasses as though that would help her think. "I'd
better go home now and have breakfast. Then I'll get on my school
bus—it stops at the bottom of the hill and maybe you'd better wait for
me there. Fortinbras might bark at you; I'm sure he'd know you were
in the house even if you dematerialize, or whatever you call it."

"Whatever you think best," Proginoskes said meekly.

"I'll be down at the foot of the road at seven o'clock. The high-school bus covers so much distance and makes so many stops it takes an hour and a half, and I get on at one of the first stops."

She felt an acquiescing response from the cherubim, and then he disappeared; she could not see even a shimmer, or feel a flicker of him in her mind. She headed back to the house. She kept the flashlight on, not for the known turnings of the path, but for whatever new, unknown surprises might be waiting for her.

When Meg got to the stone wall Louise the Larger was there. Waiting. Neither greeting nor attacking. Waiting. Meg approached her cautiously. Louise watched her through eyes which shone in the flashlight like the water of a very deep well.

"May I go by, please, Louise?" Meg asked timidly.

Louise uncoiled, waving slightly in greeting, still looking intently at Meg. Then she bowed her head, and slithered off into the rocks. Meg felt that Louise had been waiting for her to give her a warning for whatever lay ahead, and to wish her well. It was strangely comforting to know that Louise's well-wishing was going with her.

There was sausage as well as hot porridge for breakfast. Meg felt that she ought to eat heartily, because who knew what lay ahead? But she could manage only a few mouthfuls.

"Are you all right, Meg?" her mother asked.

"Fine. Thanks."

"You look a little pale. Sure you aren't coming down with something?"

—She's worried about all of us with this mitochondritis stuff. "Just the normal throes of adolescence," she smiled at her mother.

Sandy said, "If you don't want your sausage, I'll eat it."

Dennys said, "Half for me, okay?"

Charles Wallace slowly and deliberately ate a full bowl of porridge, but gave the twins his sausage.

"Well, then"—Meg washed her dishes and put them in the rack—"I'm off."

"Wait for us," Sandy said.

She did not want to wait for the twins, to listen to their chatter on the walk down to the bus. On the other hand, it would keep her from thinking about what lay ahead. She had thought of Mr. Jenkins for as far back as she could remember with distaste, annoyance, and occasionally outrage, but never before with fear.

When she left the house she had a horrid, premonitory feeling that it would be a long time before she returned. Again she wished that

Fortinbras were walking to the bus with them, as he often did, and then returning to make the walk again with Charles Wallace. But this morning he showed no inclination to leave the warmth of the kitchen.

"What do you suppose will happen today?" Sandy asked as they started down the hill in the chill of early morning.

Dennys shrugged. "Nothing. As usual. Race you to the foot of the hill."

5 The First Test

Meg and the cherubim reached the deserted schoolyard in safety.

"We've got a while to wait," Meg told him, "and it's okay for you, you're invisible. But I've got to find a place to hide." She could not see Proginoskes, but she talked at the faint shimmer in the air where she knew he was.

"You're too late," the cherubim said, and Meg swung around to see Mr. Jenkins coming across the schoolyard from the faculty parking lot. Mr. Jenkins. The ordinary, everyday, usual Mr. Jenkins. There was no snake hissing and clacking at him, and he himself did nothing but continue his way across the schoolyard. He looked just as he always looked. He wore his usual dark business suit, and no matter how often it was brushed there was always a small snowfall of dandruff on his shoulders. His salt-and-pepper hair was cut short, and his eyes were muddy behind his bifocals. He was neither short nor tall, fat nor thin, and whenever Meg saw him her feet seemed to grow larger and she couldn't find a resting place for her hands.

"All right, Margaret, what is this? What are you doing here?" He had every right to sound annoyed.

She had nothing to reply. She felt Proginoskes close to her, felt his mind within hers, but he had nothing to suggest.

"My dear child," Mr. Jenkins said, and his voice was unwontedly compassionate. "If you have come again about your little brother, I can now tell you that we are reviewing his case. It is not my policy of education to have one child intimidated by his peers. But our initial testing shows that Charles Wallace's talents are so unusual that unusual measures must be taken. I've had several consultations with the State Board, and we are considering getting a special tutor for him."

Meg looked warily at the principal. This sounded too good to be true.

And Louise had been trying to warn her of something. Of what?

The cherubim, too, was uneasy. She felt him moving lightly in her mind, feeling her response to this unexpectedly reasonable Mr. Jenkins.

"That is nonsense," Mr. Jenkins said to Mr. Jenkins. "We cannot make an exception for any one child. Charles Wallace Murry must learn to manage."

A second Mr. Jenkins was standing beside Mr. Jenkins.

It was impossible. It was just as impossible as—

But there *were* two identical, dour Mr. Jenkinses standing in front of her.

Proginoskes shimmered, but did not materialize. Meg backed into the shimmer; she felt that the cherubim was opening an invisible wing and pulling her close to him. She could feel his tremendous, wild heartbeat, a frightened heartbeat, thundering in her ears.

"We're Namers," she heard through the racing of the heart. "We're Namers. What is their Name?"

"Mr. Jenkins."

"No, no. This is the test, Meg, it must be. One of those Mr. Jenkinses is an Echthros. We have to know which is the *real* Mr. Jenkins."

Meg looked at the two men who stood glaring at each other. "Progo, you can feel into me. Can't you feel into them? Can't you kythe?"

"Not when I don't know who they are. You're the one who knows the prototype."

"The what?"

"The real one. The only Mr. Jenkins who is Mr. Jenkins. Look—"

Suddenly beside the two Mr. Jenkinses stood a third Mr. Jenkins. He raised one hand in greeting, not to Meg, but to the other two men as he drew level with them. "Leave the poor girl alone for a few minutes," Mr. Jenkins Three said.

The three men wheeled, stiffly, like marionettes, and walked across the schoolyard and into the building.

"We must think. We must think." Proginoskes's kythe almost became opaque for a second, and Meg felt that he was restraining himself from spouting fire.

Meg said, "Progo, if you really are a cherubim—"

There was a great and surging invisible wave of indignation all around her.

She hit the clenched fist of one hand against the palm of the other. "Wait. You told me to think, and I'm thinking."

"You don't have to think out loud. You don't have to talk to think, after all. You're deafening me. Try to kythe with me, Meg."

"I still don't understand kything. Is it like mental telepathy?"

Proginoskes hesitated. "You might say that mental telepathy is the very beginning of learning to kythe. But the cherubic language is entirely kything—with you, with stars, with galaxies, with the salt in the ocean, the leaves of the trees."

"But I'm not a cherubim. How do I do it?"

"Meg, your brain stores all the sensory impressions it receives, but your conscious mind doesn't have a key to the storehouse. All I want you to do is to open yourself up to me so that I can open the door to your mind's storehouse."

"All right. I'll try." To open herself entirely to the cherubim, to make herself completely vulnerable, was not going to be easy. But she trusted Proginoskes implicitly. "Listen," she said, "cherubim have come to my planet before."

"I know that. Where do you think I got my information?"

"What do you know about us?"

"I have heard that your host planet is shadowed, that it is troubled."

"It's beautiful," Meg said defensively.

She felt a rippling of his wings. "In the middle of your cities?"

"Well—no—but I don't live in a city."

"And is your planet peaceful?"

"Well, no—it isn't very peaceful."

"I had the idea," Proginoskes moved reluctantly within her mind, "that there are wars on your planet. People fighting and killing each other."

"Yes, that's so, but—"

"And children go hungry."

"Yes."

"And people don't understand each other."

"Not always."

"And there's—there's hate?"

"Yes."

She felt Proginoskes pulling away. "All I want to do," he was murmuring to himself, "is go some place quiet and recite the names of the stars . . ."

"Progo! You said we were Namers. I still don't *know*: what *is* a Namer?"

"I've *told* you. A Namer has to know who people are, and who they are meant to be. I don't know why I should have been shocked at finding Echthroi on your planet."

"Why are they here?"

"Echthroi are always about when there's war. They start all war."

"Progo, I saw all that awfulness you took me to see, that tearing of the sky, and all, but you still haven't told me exactly what Echthroi are."

Proginoskes probed into her mind, searching for words she could understand. "I think your mythology would call them fallen angels. War and hate are their business, and one of their chief weapons is un-Naming—making people not know who they are. If someone knows who he is, really knows, then he doesn't need to hate. That's why we still need Namers, because there are places throughout the universe like your planet Earth. When everyone is really and truly Named, then the Echthroi will be vanquished."

"But what—"

"Oh, earthling, earthling, why do you think Blajeny called for you? There is war in heaven, and we need all the help we can get. The Echthroi are spreading through the universe. Every time a star goes out another Echthros has won a battle. A star or a child or a farandola—size doesn't matter, Meg. The Echthroi are after Charles Wallace and the balance of the entire universe can be altered by the outcome."

"But Progo, what does this have to do with our test—and with three Mr. Jenkinses—it's insane."

Proginoskes responded coldly and quietly. "Precisely."

Into the cold and quiet came the sound of the school buses arriving, doors opening, children rushing out and into the school building.

Charles Wallace was one of those children.

Proginoskes moved quietly in her mind through the roar. "Don't misunderstand me, Meg. It is the ways of the Echthroi which are insane. The ways of the Teachers are often strange, but they are never haphazard. I know that Mr. Jenkins has to have something to do with it, something important, or we wouldn't be here."

Meg said, unhappily, "If I hate Mr. Jenkins whenever I think of him, am I Naming him?"

Proginoskes shifted his wings. "You're Xing him, just like the Echthroi."

"Progo!"

"Meg, when people don't know who they are, they are open either to being Xed, or Named."

"And you think I'm supposed to Name Mr. Jenkins?" It was a ridiculous idea; no matter how many Mr. Jenkinses there were, he was Mr. Jenkins. That's all.

But Proginoskes was most definite. "Yes."

Meg cried rebelliously, "Well, I think it's a silly kind of test."

"What you think is not the point. What you do is what's going to count."

"How can it possibly help Charles?"

"I don't know. We don't have to know everything at once. We just do one thing at a time, as it is given us to do."

"But how do I do it? How do I Name Mr. Jenkins when all I think of when I see him is how awful he is?"

Proginoskes sighed and flung several wings heavenwards so violently that he lifted several feet, materialized, and came down with a thud. "There's a word—but if I say it you'll just misunderstand."

"You have to say it."

"It's a four-letter word. Aren't four-letter words considered the bad ones on your planet?"

"Come on. I've seen all the four-letter words on the walls of the washroom at school."

Proginoskes let out a small puff. "Luff."

"What?"

"Love. That's what makes persons know who they are. You're full of love, Meg, but you don't know how to stay within it when it's not easy."

"What do you mean?"

"Oh—you love your family. That's easy. Sometimes when you feel awful about somebody, you get back into rightness by thinking about— well, you seem to be telling me that you got back into love once by thinking about Charles Wallace."

"Yes—"

"But this time it can't be easy. You have to go on to the next step."

"If you mean you think I have to love Mr. Jenkins, you've got another think coming," Meg snapped.

Proginoskes gave a mighty sigh. "If we pass the test, you'll go on and be taught—oh, some of the things I was taught my first billennium with the Teachers. I had to pass a galaxy of tests before I could qualify as a Star Namer. But you're a human being, and it's all quite different with you. I keep forgetting that. Am I lovable? To you?"

All about Meg, eyes opened and shut; wings shifted; a small flame burned her hand and was rapidly withdrawn. She coughed and then sucked the burned place on her hand. But all she wanted was to put her arms around Proginoskes as she would around Charles Wallace. "Very lovable," she said.

"But you don't love me the way you love that skinny Calvin?"

"That's different."

"I thought so. That's the confusing kind. Not the kind you have to have in order to Name Mr. Jenkins."

"I hate Mr. Jenkins."

"Meg, it's the test. You have to Name the real Mr. Jenkins, and I have to help you. If you fail, I fail too."

"Then what would happen?"

"It's your first time with a Teacher. And it would be your last."

"And you?"

"When one has been with the Teachers as often as I have, one is given a choice. I could throw in my lot with the Echthroi—"

"What!"

"Quite a few of those who fail do."

"But the Echthroi are—"

"You know what they are. Sky tearers. Light snuffers. Planet darkeners. The dragons. The worms. Those who hate."

"Progo, you couldn't."

"I hope I couldn't. But others have. It's not an easy choice."

"If you don't go to the Echthroi—"

All Proginoskes's eyes were shielded by his wings. "I am a Namer. The Echthroi would un-Name. If I do not go with them, then I must X myself."

"What!?"

"I'll ask you a riddle. What do you have the more of, the more of it you give away?"

"Oh, love, I suppose."

"So, if I care more about Naming than anything else, then maybe I have to give myself away, if it's the only way to show my love. All the way away. To X myself."

"If you do it—X yourself—does it last forever?" Meg asked apprehensively.

"Nobody knows. Nobody will know till the end of time."

"Do I have that choice, too, if—if we fail?" She turned away from the school building, towards the early-morning shouts and whistles, and pressed her face against the soft feathers of one great pinion.

"It is not an option given to mortals, earthling."

"All that happens to me is that I go home?"

"If you can call it *all*. There would be rejoicing in hell. But perhaps you don't believe in hell?"

Meg pushed this aside. "But if we fail, then you—"

"I must choose. It's better to X myself than to be Xed by the Echthroi."

"What you took me to see—it was what Mother talked about at the dinner table, what Father's gone to Brookhaven about—it doesn't seem to have much to do with Mr. Jenkins. It's all so cosmic, so big—"

"It isn't size that matters, Meg. Right now it's Charles Wallace. The Echthroi would annihilate Charles Wallace."

"A little boy!"

"You've said yourself that he's a special little boy."

"He is, oh, he is." She gave a startled jump as the first bell went off inside the school building, strident, demanding. "Progo, I don't understand any of it, but if you think Naming Mr. Jenkins is going to help Charles Wallace, I'll do my best. You *will* help me?"

"I'll try." But Proginoskes did not sound confident.

From all around them came the usual schoolday din. Then the door to the cafeteria/gym opened, and a Mr. Jenkins came out. Which Mr. Jenkins? There was no telling them apart. Meg looked to the cherubim, but he had dematerialized again, leaving only a shimmer to show where he was.

Mr. Jenkins came to her. She checked his shoulders. There was the dandruff. She went closer: smelled: yes, he had the Mr. Jenkins smell of old hair cream and what she always thought of as rancid deodorant. But all three of the Mr. Jenkinses could manage that much, she was sure. It was not going to be that easy.

He looked at her coldly in the usual way, down one side of his slightly crooked nose. "I assume that you are as confused by all this as I am, Margaret. Why two strange men should wish to impersonate me I have no idea. It is most inconvenient, just at the beginning of school, when I am already overworked. I am told that it has something to do with you as well as your unfortunate little brother. I had hoped that this year you, at least, would not be one of my problems. It seems to me I have had to spend more time with you than with any other student in school. It is certainly my misfortune. And now not only do I have to cope with your little brother, who is equally difficult, but here you are again."

This was Mr. Jenkins. He had played upon the theme of this speech with infinite variations almost every time she was sent to his office.

"For some reason obscure to me, you are supposed to choose between the impostors and me. It is certainly in my interests to have you pass this absurd test. Then perhaps I can keep you out of my school."

"And then," said Mr. Jenkins Two, appearing beside Mr. Jenkins One, "I will have time to concentrate on present problems instead of those which ought to be past. Now, Meg, if you will just for once in your life do it my way, not yours . . . I understand you're basically quite bright in mathematics. If you would simply stop approaching each problem in your life as though you were Einstein and had to solve the problems of the universe, and would deign to follow one or two basic rules, you—and I—would have a great deal less trouble."

This, too, was authentic Jenkins.

The shimmer of the cherubim wavered uneasily.

"Meg," Mr. Jenkins Two said, "I urge you to resolve this nonsense and tell the impostors that I am Mr. Jenkins. This whole farce is wasting a great deal of time. I am Mr. Jenkins, as you have cause to know."

She felt Proginoskes probing wildly. "Meg, when have you been most *you*, the very most *you?*"

She closed her eyes. She remembered the first afternoon Calvin had come to the Murrys'. Calvin was an honor student, but he was far better with words than with numbers, and Meg had helped him with a trigonometry problem. Since trig was not taught in Meg's grade, her easy competence was one of her first surprises for Calvin. But at the time she had not thought of surprising him. She had concentrated wholly on Calvin, on what he was doing, and she had felt wholly alive and herself.

"How is that going to help?" she asked the cherubim.

"Think. You didn't know Calvin very well then, did you?"

"No."

"But you loved him, didn't you?"

"Then? I wasn't thinking about love. I was just thinking about trig."

"Well, then," Proginoskes said, as though that explained the entire nature of love.

"But I can't think about trig with Mr. Jenkins. And I can't love him."

"You love me."

"But, Progo, you're so awful you're lovable."

"So is he. And you have to Name him."

A third Mr. Jenkins joined the other two. "Meg. Stop panicking and listen to me."

The three men stood side by side, identical, grey, dour, unperceptive, overworked: unlovable.

"Meg," Mr. Jenkins Two said, "if you will Name me, and quickly, I will see to it that Charles Wallace gets into competent medical hands immediately."

"It's hardly that easy," Mr. Jenkins Three said. "After all, her parents—"

"—do not know how to handle the situation, nor do they understand how serious it is," Mr. Jenkins Two snapped.

Mr. Jenkins Three waved this aside. "Meg, does it not seem extraordinary to you that you should be confronted with three of me?"

There seemed to be no answer to this question.

Mr. Jenkins One shrugged in annoyance.

Mr. Jenkins Two said, "It is imperative that we stick to essentials at this point. Our number is peripheral." The real Mr. Jenkins was very fond of discarding peripherals and sticking to essentials.

Mr. Jenkins Three said, "That there is only one of me, and that I am he, is the main point."

Mr. Jenkins Two snorted. "Except for the small but important fact that I am he. This trial that has been brought on us is an extraordinary one. None of us—that is, you and I, Margaret—will ever be the same again. Being confronted with these two mirror visions of myself has made me see myself differently. None of us likes to see himself as he must appear to others. I understand your point of view much better than I did before. You were quite right to come to me about your little brother. He is indeed special, and I have come to the conclusion that I have made a mistake in not realizing this, and treating him accordingly."

"Don't trust him," Mr. Jenkins Three said.

Mr. Jenkins Two swept on. "I believe that you and I had a—shall we call it a run-in?—over the imports and exports of Nicaragua, which you were supposed to learn for one of your social-studies classes. You were quite right when you insisted that it was unnecessary for you to learn the imports and exports of Nicaragua. I shall try not to make the same kind of mistake with Charles Wallace. If Charles Wallace's interests are different from those of our usual first-grader, we will try to understand that he has been taught by an eminent physicist father. I am sorry for all the needless pain you have been caused. And I can assure you that if you Name me, Charles Wallace will find school a pleasanter place, and I have no doubt his health will improve."

Meg looked warily at Mr. Jenkins Two. This was, indeed, a changed Mr. Jenkins, and she did not trust the change. On the other hand, she remembered vividly the battle they had had over the imports and exports of Nicaragua.

Mr. Jenkins Three murmured, "Methinks the gentleman doth protest too much."

Mr. Jenkins Two sputtered, "What's that?" Mr. Jenkins One looked blank.

Mr. Jenkins Three cried triumphantly, "I could have told you he would not recognize Shakespeare. He is an impostor."

Meg had her doubts whether or not the real Mr. Jenkins would recognize Shakespeare.

Mr. Jenkins Two said, "Shakespeare is peripheral. If I have often been irritable in the past it is because I have been worried. Despite your

unkind opinion of me, I do not like seeing any of my children unhappy."
He sniffed.

Mr. Jenkins One looked down his nose. "If I had the cooperation
of the School Board and the P.T.A. it might untie my hands so that I
could accomplish something."

Meg looked at the three men in their identical business suits. "It's
like a game on television."

"It is not a game," Mr. Jenkins Three said sharply. "The stakes are
much too high."

Meg asked, "What happens to you—all of you—if I Name the
wrong one?"

For a moment all the atoms of air in the schoolyard seemed to
shiver; it was as though a lightning bolt of nothingness had flashed
across the schoolyard, ripping the fabric of the atmosphere, then closed
together again. Although nothing had been visible, Meg thought of a
dark and terrible vulture slashing across the sky.

Mr. Jenkins One said, "I do not believe in the supernatural. But this
entire situation is abnormal." His rabbity nose wriggled in pink distaste.

Then all three men swung around as the side door to the school
opened, and Charles Wallace, Louise the Larger twined around his arm
and shoulders, walked down the steps and across the schoolyard.

6 The Real Mr. Jenkins

"Charles!" Meg cried.

All three Mr. Jenkinses held up warning hands, said simultaneously, "Charles Wallace Murry, what is it *now?*"

Charles Wallace looked with interest at the three men. "Hello, what's this?"

Mr. Jenkins One said, "What are you doing with that—that—"

All three men were visibly fearful of Louise. There was no telling the 'real' Mr. Jenkins by a variation in response to the snake. Louise reared her head, half closed her eyes, and made the strange, clacking, warning sound which Meg had heard the night before. Charles Wallace stroked her soothingly, and looked speculatively at the three men.

"We were supposed to bring a small pet to school today, to share with the class."

Meg thought,—Good for you, Charles, to think of Louise the Larger. If you terrified Mr. Jenkins, that would send you up a notch in the other kids' estimation. If there's one thing everybody in school agrees on, it's that Mr. Jenkins is a retarded rodent.

Mr. Jenkins Three said severely, "You know perfectly well that *small* pets were meant, Charles Wallace. Turtles or tropical fish or perhaps even a hamster."

"Or a gerbil," Mr. Jenkins Two added. "A gerbil would be acceptable."

"Why have you multiplied?" Charles Wallace asked. "I found one of you quite enough."

Louise clacked again; it was a flesh-chilling sound.

Mr. Jenkins Three demanded, "Why aren't you in class, Charles?"

"Because the teacher told me to take Louise the Larger and go home. I really don't understand why. Louise is friendly and she wouldn't hurt anybody. Only the girls were scared of her. She lives in our stone wall by the twins' vegetable garden."

Meg looked at Louise, at the hooded eyes, the wary position of the head, the warning twitching of the last few inches of her black tail. Blajeny had told them that Louise was a Teacher. Louise herself had certainly shown in the past twenty-four hours that she was more than an ordinary garden snake. Louise would know—did know, Meg was sure—the real Mr. Jenkins. Swallowing her own shyness of all snakes, she reached out towards Charles Wallace. "Let me have Louise for a little while, please, Charles."

But Proginoskes spoke in her mind. "No, Meg. You have to do it yourself. You can't let Louise do it for you."

All right. She accepted that. But perhaps Louise could still help.

Charles Wallace regarded his sister thoughtfully. Then he held out the arm around which Louise's lower half was coiled. The snake slithered sinuously to Meg. Her body felt cold, and tingled with electricity. Meg tried not to flinch.

"Mr. Jenkins," Meg said. "Each of you. One at a time. What are you going to do about Charles Wallace and Louise? Charles Wallace can't possibly walk home alone. It's too far. What are you going to do about Charles Wallace and school in general?"

Nobody volunteered an answer. All three folded their arms impassively across their chests.

"Mr. Jenkins Three," Meg said.

"Are you Naming me, Meg? That's right."

"I'm not Naming anybody yet. I want to know what you're going to do."

"I thought I had already told you. It is a situation which I shall have to guide carefully. It was foolish of Charlie to bring a snake to school. Snakes are quite frightening to some people, you know."

Louise hissed slowly. Mr. Jenkins Three turned visibly paler.

He said, "I shall have a long, quiet session with Charles Wallace's teacher. Then I will speak to each child in the first-grade room, separately. I shall see to it that each one has an understanding of the problem. If any of them group together and try bullying, I shall use strong disciplinary methods. This school has been run in far too lax and permissive a manner. From now on, I intend to hold the reins. And now, Charles Wallace, I shall drive you home. Your sister will bring your pet."

Meg turned away from him. "Mr. Jenkins Two?"

Mr. Jenkins Two detached himself by one pace from the others.

"Force, that's what that impostor is advocating. Dictatorship. I will never put up with a dictatorship. But you should not have brought the snake to school, Charlie. You should have known better. But I think I understand. You thought it would enhance your social prestige, and make you more of an equal in the eyes of your peers. There's where happiness lies, in success with your peer group. I want all my children to be like each other, so we must help you to be more normal, even if it means that you must go to school elsewhere for a while. I understand there's someone from another galaxy who's interested in helping you. Perhaps that's our answer for the time being."

Meg turned to Mr. Jenkins One. He gave a small, annoyed, Mr. Jenkins shrug. "I really do not foresee much change in my relationship with Charles Wallace in the future. Why interplanetary travel should be thought of as a solution to all earth's problems I do not understand. We have sent men to the moon and to Mars and we are none the better for it. Why sending Charles Wallace a few billion light-years across space should improve him any, I fail to see. Unless, of course, it helps his physical condition, about which nobody except myself appears concerned." He looked at his wristwatch. "How much longer does this farce continue?"

Meg could feel sharp, painful little flickers as the cherubim thought at her. She did not want to listen.

"It's all a waste of time!" she cried. "Why do I have to bother with all these Mr. Jenkinses? What can it possibly have to do with Charles?"

Louise the Larger's breath was cool and gentle against her ear. "It doess, it doess," the snake hissed.

Proginoskes said, "You don't need to know why. Just get on with it."

Charles Wallace spoke wearily. "Give me Louise, please, Meg. I want to go home."

"It's too far for you to walk."

"We'll take it slowly."

Mr. Jenkins Three said sharply, "I have already said I will drive you home. You may take the snake as long as it stays in the back seat."

Mr. Jenkins One and Two said simultaneously, "*I* will drive Charles Wallace. And the snake." They shuddered slightly, not quite simultaneously, but in syncopation.

Charles Wallace held out his arm and Louise slithered from Meg to the little boy. "Let's go," he said to the three men, turned away from them, and started to walk to where the faculty parked their cars. The Mr. Jenkinses followed him, walking abreast, all with the stiff, ungainly gait which was distinctively and solely Mr. Jenkins.

"But who will he go with?" Meg asked Proginoskes.

"The real one."

"But then—"

"I think that when they turn the corner there'll be only one of them. It gives us a small respite, at any rate." The cherubim materialized slowly, becoming at first a shimmer, then a transparent outline, then deepening in dimensions until he moved into complete visibility as the three Mr. Jenkinses disappeared. "Don't waste time," he thought sharply at her. "Think. What's the nicest thing you've ever heard about Mr. Jenkins?"

"Nice? Nothing nice. Listen, maybe all of them are impostors. Maybe they won't come back."

Again the sharp little pain. "That's too easy. One of them's real, and for some reason he's important. Think, Meg. You must know something good about him."

"I don't want to know anything good about him."

"Stop thinking about yourself. Think about Charles. The real Mr. Jenkins can help Charles."

"How?"

"We don't need to know how, Meg! Stop blocking me. It's our only hope. You must let me kythe with you." She felt him moving about within her mind, more gently now, but persistently. "You're still blocking me."

"I'm trying not to—"

"I know. Do some math problems in your head. Anything to shut out your un-love and let me in about Mr. Jenkins. Do some math for Calvin. You love Calvin. Good. Think about Calvin. Meg! Calvin's shoes."

"What about them?"

"What kind of shoes does he have on?"

"His regular school shoes, I suppose. How would I know? I think he has only one pair of shoes, and his sneakers."

"What are the shoes like?"

"I don't know. I didn't notice. I don't bother much about clothes."

"Think some more math and let me show them to you."

Shoes. Strong, fairly new Oxfords which Calvin wore over mismated red and purple socks, the kind of shoes Mr. O'Keefe could ill afford to buy for his family. Meg saw the shoes vividly; the image was given her by Proginoskes; she had been quite truthful when she told him that she didn't notice clothes. Nevertheless, her mind registered all that she saw and it was there, stored, available to the kything of the cherubim. She saw with a flash of intuition that her kything was like a small child's trying to pick out a melody on the piano with one finger, as against the harmony of a full orchestra, like the cherubic language.

In her mind's ear came the echo of Calvin's voice, coming back to her from an afternoon when she had been sent—unfairly, she thought—to Mr. Jenkins's office, and been dealt with—unfairly—there. Calvin's voice, quiet, calming, infuriatingly reasonable. "When I started seventh grade and went over to Regional, my mother bought me some shoes from a thrift shop. They cost her a dollar, which was more than she could spare, and they were women's Oxfords, the kind of black laced shoes old women wear, and at least three sizes too small for me. When I saw them, I cried, and then my mother cried. And my pop beat me. So I got a saw and hacked off the heels, and cut the toes out so I could jam my feet in, and went to school. The kids knew me too well to make remarks in my presence, but I could guess what they were sniggering behind my back. After a few days Mr. Jenkins called me into his office and said he'd noticed I'd outgrown my shoes, and he just happened to have an extra pair he thought would fit me. He'd gone to a lot of trouble to make them look used, as though he hadn't gone out and bought them for me. I make enough money in the summers now to buy my own shoes, but I'll never forget that he gave me the first decent pair of shoes I ever had. Sure I know all the bad things about him, and they're all true, and I've had my own run-ins with him, but on the whole we get along, maybe because my parents don't make him feel inferior, and he knows he can do things for me that they can't."

Meg muttered, "It'd have been a lot easier if I could have gone on hating him."

Now it was Proginoskes's voice in her mind's ear, not Calvin's. "What would be easier?"

"Naming him."

"Would it? Don't you know more about him now?"

"Second-hand. I've never known him to do anything else nice."

"How do you suppose he feels about you?"

"He's never seen me except when I'm snarly," she admitted. She found herself almost laughing as she remembered Mr. Jenkins saying, 'Margaret, you are the most contumacious child it has ever been my misfortune to have in this office,' and she had had to go home and look up 'contumacious.'

Proginoskes probed, "Do you think he'd believe anything good about you?"

"Not likely."

"Would you like him to see a different Meg? The real Meg?"

She shrugged.

"Well, then, how would you like to be different with him?"

Frantically, she said, "I wish I had gorgeous blond hair."

"You wouldn't, not really."

"Of course I would!"

"If you had gorgeous blond hair, you wouldn't be you."

"That might be a good idea. Ouch, Progo, you hurt!"

"This isn't any time for self-indulgence."

"When Mr. Jenkins is being nice, he's not being Mr. Jenkins. Being nice on Mr. Jenkins would be like blond hair on me."

Proginoskes sent ice-cold anger through her. "Meg, there's no more time. They'll be back any moment now."

Panic churned in her. "Progo, if I don't Name right, if I fail, what will you do?"

"I told you. I have to choose."

"That's not telling me. I want to know which way you're going to choose."

Proginoskes's feathers shivered as though a cold wind had blown through them. "Meg, there isn't much time. They're on their way back. You have to Name one of them."

"Give me a hint."

"This isn't a game. Mr. Jenkins was right."

She shot him an anguished glance, and he lowered several sets of eyelashes in apology. "Progo, even for Charles Wallace, how can I do the impossible? How can I love Mr. Jenkins?"

Proginoskes did not respond. There was no flame, no smoke; only a withdrawing of eyes behind wings.

"Progo! Help me! How can I feel love for Mr. Jenkins?"

Immediately he opened a large number of eyes very wide. "What a strange idea. Love isn't *feeling*. If it were, I wouldn't be able to love. Cherubim don't have feelings."

"But—"

"Idiot," Proginoskes said, anxiously rather than crossly. "Love isn't how you feel. It's what you do. I've never had a feeling in my life. As a matter of fact, I matter only with earth people."

"Progo, you matter to me."

Proginoskes puffed enveloping pale blue clouds. "That's not what I meant. I meant that cherubim only *matter* with earth people. You call it materializing."

"Then, if you become visible only for us, why do you have to look so terrifying?"

"Because when we matter, this is how we come out. When you got mattered, you didn't choose to look the way you do, did you?"

"I certainly did not. I'd have chosen quite differently. I'd have chosen to be beautiful—oh, I see! You mean you don't have any more choice about looking like a drive of deformed dragons than I do about my hair and glasses and everything? You aren't doing it this way just for fun?"

Proginoskes held three of its wings demurely over a great many of its eyes. "I am a cherubim, and when a cherubim takes on matter, this is how."

Meg knelt in front of the great, frightening, and strangely beautiful creature. "Progo, I'm not a wind or a flame of fire. I'm a human being. I feel. I can't think without feeling. If you matter to me, then what you decide to do if I fail matters."

"I fail to see why."

She scrambled to her feet, batting at the last wisps of pale blue smoke which stung her eyes, and shouted, "Because if you decide to turn into a worm or whatever and join the Echthroi, I don't care whether I Name right or not! It just doesn't matter to me! And Charles Wallace would feel the same way—I know he would!"

Proginoskes probed gently and thoughtfully into her mind. "I don't understand your feelings. I'm trying to, but I don't. It must be extremely unpleasant to have feelings."

"Progo! What will you do?"

Silence. No flame. No smoke. All eyes closed. Proginoskes folded the great wings completely. His words were very small as they moved into her mind. "X. If you fail, I will X myself."

He vanished.

Meg swung around and three Mr. Jenkinses were walking towards her from the direction of the parking lot. She faced them. "Mr. Jenkins."

Identical, hateful, simultaneous, they stepped towards her.

Mr. Jenkins One sniffed, the end of his pink nose wriggling distastefully. "I am back. I left Charles Wallace with your mother. Now will you please get rid of these two—uh—pranksters. I resent this intrusion on my time and privacy."

Mr. Jenkins Two pointed to One accusingly. "That impostor lost his temper and showed his true colors when your little brother brought his snake to school. The impostor forgot himself and called the child a sn—"

"Delete," Mr. Jenkins Three said sharply. "He used words unsuitable for a child. Blip it."

Mr. Jenkins Two said, "He doesn't love children."

Mr. Jenkins Three said, "He can't control children."

Mr. Jenkins Two said, "I will make Charles Wallace happy."

Mr. Jenkins Three said, "I will make him successful."

Mr. Jenkins One looked at his watch.

Meg closed her eyes. And suddenly she did not feel. She had been pushed into a dimension beyond feeling, if such a thing is possible, and if Progo was right, it is possible. There was nothing but a cold awareness which had nothing to do with what she normally would have thought of as feeling. Her voice issued from her lips almost without volition, cold, calm, emotionless. "Mr. Jenkins Three—"

He stepped forward, smiling triumphantly.

"No. You're not the real Mr. Jenkins. You're much too powerful. You'd never have to be taken away from a regional school you couldn't control and made principal of a grade school you couldn't control, either." She looked at Mr. Jenkins One and Two. Her hands were ice-cold and she had the sensation in the pit of the stomach which precedes acute nausea, but she was unaware of this because she was still in the strange realm beyond feeling. "Mr. Jenkins Two—"

He smiled.

Again she shook her head. "I wasn't quite as sure about you at first. But wanting to make everybody happy and just like everybody else is just as bad as Mr. Jenkins Three manipulating everybody. Bad as Mr. Jenkins is, he's the only one of the three of you who's human enough to make as many mistakes as he does, and that's you, Mr. Jenkins One—" Suddenly she gave a startled laugh. "And I do love you for it." Then she burst into tears of nervousness and exhaustion. But she had no doubt that she was right.

The air about the schoolyard was rent with a great howling and shrieking and then a cold nothingness which could only be the presence of Echthroi. It was as though rip after rip were being slashed in the air, and then the edges were drawn together and healed.

Silence. And quiet. And a small, ordinary, everyday wind.

Proginoskes materialized, delicately unfolding wing after wing to reveal his myriad various eyes.

Mr. Jenkins One, the real Mr. Jenkins, fainted.

7 Metron Ariston

Meg bent over Mr. Jenkins. She did not realize that Blajeny was there until she heard his voice.

"Really, Proginoskes, you ought to know better than to take anyone by surprise like that, particularly a still-limited one like Mr. Jenkins." He stood between the cherubim and Meg, almost as tall as the school building, half amused, half angry.

Proginoskes fluttered several wings in halfhearted apology. "I was very relieved."

"Quite."

"Will this—uh—Mr. Jenkins ever be anything but a limited one?"

"That is a limited and limiting thought, Proginoskes," Blajeny said sternly. "I am surprised."

Now the cherubim was truly abashed. He closed his eyes and covered them with wings, keeping only three eyes open, one each to gaze at Blajeny, Meg, and the prone Mr. Jenkins.

Blajeny turned to Meg. "My child, I am very pleased with you."

Meg blushed. "Shouldn't we do something about Mr. Jenkins?"

Blajeny knelt on the dusty ground. His dark fingers, with their vast span, pressed gently against Mr. Jenkins's temples; the principal's usually pasty face was grey; his body gave a spasmodic twitch; he opened his eyes and closed them again immediately; moaned.

Tension and relief had set Meg on the verge of hysteria; she was half laughing, half crying. "Blajeny, don't you realize you must be almost as frightening to poor Mr. Jenkins as Progo?" She, too, dropped to her knees beside the principal. "Mr. Jenkins, I'm here. Meg. I know you don't like me, but at least I'm familiar. Open your eyes. It's all right. Really it is."

Slowly, cautiously, he opened his eyes. "I must make an appointment with a psychiatrist. Immediately."

Meg spoke soothingly, as to a very small child. "You aren't hallucinating, Mr. Jenkins, honestly you aren't. It's all right. They're friends, Blajeny and Progo. And they're real."

Mr. Jenkins closed his eyes, opened them again, focused on Meg.

"Blajeny is a Teacher, Mr. Jenkins, and Progo is a—well, he's a cherubim." She could hardly blame Mr. Jenkins for looking incredulous.

His voice was thin. "Either I am in the process of a nervous breakdown, which is not unlikely, or I am dreaming. That's it. I must be asleep." He struggled to sit up, with Meg's assistance. "But why, then, are you in my dream? Why am I lying on the ground? Has somebody hit me? I wouldn't put it past the bigger boys—" He rubbed his hand over his head, searching for a bruise. "Why are you here, Margaret? I seem to remember—" He looked once more at Blajeny and Proginoskes and shuddered. "They're still here. No. I am still dreaming. Why can't I wake up? This isn't real."

Meg echoed Blajeny. "What is real?" She turned to the Teacher, but he was no longer paying attention to Mr. Jenkins. She followed Blajeny's gaze, and saw Louise slithering rapidly towards them.

A fresh shudder shook Mr. Jenkins. "Not the snake again—I have a phobia about—"

Meg soothed, "Louise is really very friendly. She won't hurt you."

"Snakes." Mr. Jenkins shook his head. "Snakes and monsters and giants . . . It's not possible, none of this is possible . . ."

Blajeny turned from his conversation with Louise the Larger, spoke urgently. "We must go at once. The Echthroi are enraged. Charles Wallace's mitochondritis is now acute."

"Oh, Blajeny, take us home quickly," Meg cried. "I must be with him!"

"There isn't time. We must go at once to Metron Ariston."

"Where?"

Without answering, Blajeny turned from Meg to Mr. Jenkins. "You, sir: do you wish to return to your school and continue your regular day's work? Or will you throw in your lot with us?"

Mr. Jenkins looked completely bewildered. "I am having a nervous breakdown."

"You don't need to have one if you don't want to. You have simply been faced with several things outside your current spheres of experience. That does not mean that they—we—do not exist."

Meg felt an unwilling sense of protectiveness towards this unattractive little man she had Named. "Mr. Jenkins, don't you think you'd better report that you're not well today, and come with us?"

Mr. Jenkins held out his hands helplessly. "Were there—there were—two other—two men who resembled me?"

"Yes, of course there were. But they've gone."

"Where?"

Meg turned to Blajeny.

The Teacher looked grave. "When an Echthros takes on a human body, it tends to keep it."

Meg caught hold of the stone grey of the Teacher's sleeve. "The first test—how did it happen? You didn't make it up, did you? You couldn't have told the Echthroi to turn into Mr. Jenkins, could you?"

"Meg," he replied quietly, "I told you I needed your help."

"You mean—you mean this was going to happen, anyhow, the Echthroi turning into Mr. Jenkins, even if—"

"Mr. Jenkins was a perfect host for their purposes."

Rather shakily, Mr. Jenkins tottered towards Blajeny, sputtering, "Now, see here, I don't know who you are and I don't care, but I demand an explanation."

Blajeny's voice was now more like an English horn than a cello. "Perhaps in your world today such a phenomenon would be called schizophrenia. I prefer the old idea of possession."

"Schiz—are you, sir, questioning my sanity?"

Louise's small voice whistled urgently.

"Mr. Jenkins," Blajeny said quietly, "we must leave. Either return to your school or come with us. Now."

To Meg's surprise she found herself urging, "Please come with us, Mr. Jenkins."

"But my duty—"

"You know you can't just go back to school again after what's happened."

Mr. Jenkins moaned again. His complexion had turned from grey to pale green.

"And after you've met the cherubim and Blajeny—"

"Cheru—"

Louise whistled again.

Blajeny asked, "Are you coming with us or not?"

"Margaret Named me," Mr. Jenkins said softly. "Yes. I will come."

Proginoskes reached out a great pinion and pulled Meg in to him. She felt the tremendous heartbeat, a beat which reverberated like a brass gong. Then she saw the ovoid eye, open, dilating . . .

She was through.

* * *

It was something of an anticlimax to find that they were no farther from home than the star-watching rock.

Wait: was it, after all, the star-watching rock?

She blinked, and when she opened her eyes Mr. Jenkins and Blajeny were there, and Calvin was there, too (oh, thank you, Blajeny!), holding his hand out to her, and she was warmed in the radiance of his big smile.

It was no longer autumn-cold. There was a light breeze, warm and summery. All about them, encircling them, was the sound of summer insects, crickets, katydids, and—less pleasantly—the shrill of a mosquito. Frogs were crunking away, and a tree toad sang its scratchy song. The sky was thick with stars, stars which always seemed closer to earth in summer than in winter.

Blajeny sat down, cross-legged, on the rock, and beckoned to them. Meg sat in front of him, and saw that Louise was coiled nearby, her head resting on one of Proginoskes's outstretched wings. Calvin sat beside Meg, and Mr. Jenkins stood awkwardly, shifting his weight from one leg to the other.

Meg moved a little closer to Calvin and looked up at the sky.

And gasped. The stars, the low, daisy-thick summer stars, were not the familiar planets and constellations she had so often watched with her parents. They were as different as had been the constellations where Proginoskes had taken her to see the terrible work of the Echthroi.

"Blajeny," Calvin asked, "where are we?"

"Metron Ariston."

"What's Metron Ariston? Is it a planet?"

"No. It's an idea, a postulatum. I find it easier to posit when I am in my home galaxy, so we are near the Mondrion solar system of the Veganuel galaxy. The stars you see are those I know, those which I see from my home planet."

"Why are we here?"

"The postulatum Metron Ariston makes it possible for all sizes to become relative. Within Metron Ariston you may be sized so that you are able to converse with a giant star or a tiny farandola."

Meg felt a moment of shock and disbelief. Farandolae were still less real to her than Charles Wallace's 'dragons.' "A farandola! Are we really going to see one?"

"Yes."

"But it's impossible. A farandola is so small that—"

"How small is it?" Blajeny asked.

"So small that it's beyond rational conceiving, my mother says."

Mr. Jenkins made a small confused noise and shifted weight again. Blajeny said, "And yet Mrs. Murry is convinced that she has proved the existence of farandolae. Now let us suppose: here we are in Veganuel galaxy, two trillion light-years away. Veganuel is just about the same size as your own Earth's galaxy. How long does it take the Milky Way to rotate once around?"

As no one else spoke, Meg answered, "Two hundred billion years, clockwise."

"So that gives us a general idea of the size of your galaxy, doesn't it?"

"Very general," Calvin said. "Our minds can't comprehend anything that huge, that macrocosmic."

"Don't try to comprehend with your mind. Your minds are very limited. Use your intuition. Think of the size of your galaxy. Now, think of your sun. It's a star, and it is a great deal smaller than the entire galaxy, isn't it?"

"Of course."

"Think of yourselves, now, in comparison with the size of your sun. Think how much smaller you are. Have you done that?"

"Sort of," Meg said.

"Now think of a mitochondrion. Think of the mitochondria which live in the cells of all living things, and how much smaller a mitochondrion is than you."

Mr. Jenkins said, to himself, "I thought Charles Wallace was making them up to show off."

Blajeny continued, "Now consider that a farandola is as much smaller than a mitochondrion as a mitochondrion is smaller than you are."

"This time," Calvin said, "the problem is that our minds can't comprehend anything that *micro*cosmic."

Blajeny said, "Another way of putting it would be to say that a farandola is as much smaller than you are as your galaxy is larger than you are."

Calvin whistled. "Then, to a farandola, any of us would be as big as a galaxy?"

"More or less. You *are* a galaxy for your farandolae."

"Then how can we possibly meet one?"

Blajeny's voice was patient. "I have just told you that in Metron Ariston we can almost do away with variations in size, which are, in reality, quite unimportant." He turned his head and looked in the direction of the great glacial rocks.

"The rocks," Meg asked, "are they really there?"

"Nothing is anywhere in Metron Ariston," Blajeny said. "I am trying to make things as easy for you as I can by giving you a familiar visual setting. You must try to understand things not only with your little human minds, which are not a great deal of use in the problems which confront us."

At last Mr. Jenkins sat, crouching uncomfortably on the rock. "With what can I understand, then? I don't have very much intuition."

"You must understand with your hearts. With the whole of yourselves, not just a fragment."

Mr. Jenkins groaned. "I am too old to be educable. You can't teach an old dog new tricks. I have lived beyond my time."

Meg cried, "Oh, no, you haven't, Mr. Jenkins, you're just beginning!"

Mr. Jenkins shook his head in mournful negation. "Maybe it would have been better if you'd never Named me. Why did I ever have to see you this way? Or your little brother? Or that frightful beast?"

Proginoskes made what seemed like a minor volcanic upheaval.

Mr. Jenkins stiffened a little, though he could hardly become paler. "Are there any more like you?"

"There are a goodly number of cherubim," Proginoskes replied, "but none exactly alike."

"That's it," Mr. Jenkins said. "That's precisely it." Absent-mindedly he brushed at the dandruff and lint on the shoulders of his dark suit.

Blajeny, listening carefully, bowed his great head courteously. "Precisely what, Mr. Jenkins?"

"Nobody should be exactly like anybody else."

"Is anybody?"

"Those—those—imitation Mr. Jenkinses—to see myself doubled and trebled—there's nothing left to hold on to."

Impulsively Meg got up and ran to the principal. "But they aren't like you, Mr. Jenkins! Nobody is! You *are* unique. I Named you, didn't I?"

Mr. Jenkins's eyes looked blurred and bewildered through the lenses of his spectacles. "Yes. Yes, you did. I suppose that's why I'm here—wherever here is." He turned to Blajeny. "Those other Mr. Jenkinses—you called them Echthroi?"

"Yes. The Echthroi are those who hate, those who would keep you from being Named, who would un-Name you. It is the nature of love to create. It is the nature of hate to destroy."

Mr. Jenkins said, heavily, "I fear I have not been a loving person."

Meg felt a flash of intuition as sharp and brilliant as the cherubim's flame; like flame, it burned. "Oh, Mr. Jenkins, don't you see? Every time I was in your office, being awful and hating you, I was really hating myself more than you. Mother was right. She told me that you underestimate yourself."

Mr. Jenkins responded in a strange voice she had never heard from him before, completely unlike his usual, nasal, shrill asperity. "We both do, don't we, Margaret? When I thought your parents were looking down on me, I was really looking down on myself. But I don't see any other way to look at myself."

Now at last Meg glimpsed the Mr. Jenkins who had bought shoes for Calvin, who had clumsily tried to make those shoes look worn.

Mr. Jenkins turned to Blajeny. "These Echth—"

"Echthroi. Singular, Echthros."

"These Echthroi who took on—who took on my likeness," Mr. Jenkins said, "can they cause more trouble?"

"Yes."

"They would harm Charles Wallace?"

"They would X—extinguish him," the cherubim said.

Meg reached out in longing and fear towards her brother. "We shouldn't have left him—" she started, then closed her mouth. She felt the cherubim moving gently within her, helping her, giving her little shoves of thought, and then she seemed to be with Charles Wallace, not in actuality, not in person, but in her heart. In her heart's sight she saw their mother carrying him up the stairs, Charles limp in his mother's arms, legs dangling. Mrs. Murry went into his room, a small, paneled room with a little fireplace, and one wall papered in a blue and white snowflake pattern, a safe, comfortable room. The window looked out onto the pine woods behind the house; the light which came in was gentle, and kind.

Mrs. Murry laid Charles Wallace down on his bed, and began to undress him. The child barely had the strength to help her; he made an effort to smile and said, "I'll be better soon. Meg will . . ."

"Meg will be home from school in a couple of hours," their mother said. "She'll be right up to see you. And Dr. Louise is on her way."

"Meg isn't—in school." Speaking was almost too great an effort.

Mrs. Murry did not contradict him, as perhaps she might have normally, but helped him into his pajamas.

"I'm cold, Mother."

She pulled the covers up over him. "I'll get another blanket."

A sound of feet pounding up the stairs, and the twins burst in:

"What's this? What's the matter?"

"Is Charles sick?"

Mrs. Murry answered quietly, "He's not feeling very well."

"Bad enough to go to bed?"

"Did he have trouble in school again?"

"School was fine. He took Louise and she made a great hit, evidently."

"Our Louise?"

"Louise the Larger?"

"Yes."

"Bully for you, Charles!"

"That's telling them!"

Charles Wallace managed a reasonably good smile.

"Sandy," Mrs. Murry said, "please bring up some wood for a fire. It's a little chilly. Dennys, if you'd please go to the cedar closet and get another blanket . . ."

"Okay. Sure. Right away."

"And Meg'll read to you or something when she gets home, Charles."

Meg thought she heard Charles Wallace saying once again that Meg was not in school, but it was as though a mist swept over the vivid scene, and Charles Wallace's room was gone, and Meg was standing, pressed close against the cherubim, who had one wing strongly about her.

Blajeny said, "Now, my children, we must have a lesson. Let us make believe that it is daytime. You can, you know. Believing takes practice, but neither you, Calvin, nor you, Meg, is old enough to have forgotten completely how to do it. You must make believe for yourselves and for Mr. Jenkins. This may seem a trivial task, in view of the gravity of the circumstances, but it is practice for what is to come. Now. Make believe. Turn night to day."

The cherubim withdrew his wing and Meg put her hand in Blajeny's. Her own hand was very small in comparison, as small as it had been when she was younger than Charles Wallace and had held her father's hand in complete love and trust. She looked up at Blajeny's grave, black face, looked into the strange amber eyes which sometimes seemed to hold the cold light of the moon, and which now glowed with the warmth of the sun. Color flooded the imaged sky of Metron Ariston, a vast, arching blue canopy, cloudless, and shimmering with warmth. About the rock the green grasses of summer rippled in the breeze; a bird sang, was joined by another, others, until melody was all around them. The grass was brightened by field flowers, daisies, black-eyed Susans, Indian paintbrushes, butter-and-eggs, purple thistles, all the summer flowers blooming abundantly and brilliantly.

Colors blazed more brightly than normal. Calvin's hair, the shade of an Indian paintbrush, burned like sunlight. His freckles seemed larger and more profuse than ever. The faded blue of his jacket had deepened to meet the gentian blue of his eyes. He had on one red sock and one purple sock.

Meg's old kilt, faded from countless washings, looked bright and new, but her hair, she thought, was probably as mouse-brown as ever; and Mr. Jenkins was still pasty and colorless. Louise the Larger, however, looked even larger than usual, and her coils shone with purple and gold.

Meg looked towards Proginoskes and the shining of the cherubim was so brilliant it almost blinded her; she had to look away.

"Now, my children," Blajeny said, and he included Mr. Jenkins in the appellation, "we will welcome the other member of this class."

From behind the smaller of the two glacial rocks a tiny creature appeared and scampered over to them. It looked rather like a small, silver-blue mouse, and yet it seemed to Meg to be a sea creature rather than a land creature. Its ears were large and velvety, the fur shading off into lavender fringes at the tips, blowing gently in the breeze like sea plants moving in the currents of the ocean. Its whiskers were unusually long; its eyes were large and milky and had no visible pupil or iris, but there was nothing dulled about them; they shone like moonstones.

It spoke, but with neither a mouse's squeak nor a human voice. The sound was like harp strings being plucked under water, and the long whiskers vibrated almost as though they were being played. It did not give forth words, and yet it was quite plain that it was saying something like "Hello, are you my classmates?"

Blajeny spoke in the mouse-creature's language; words did not issue from his mouth; his granite lips were closed; and yet the children heard the lovely rippling harp sound.

The mouse-creature did not seem pleased, and made sounds which conveyed a good deal of doubt. Meg understood it to be complaining that if it had to pass even the most preliminary of examinations with an earthling, it was dubious that it could do so. A cherubim might be of some help, but surely earthlings were nothing but—

Proginoskes said, "I, too, had misgivings about earthlings. But the girl earthling and I have just come through the first ordeal, and it was the girl who did it."

The mouse-creature's whiskers twingled. "It can't have been much of an ordeal. Can we please get going, Blajeny? We have only a parsec before I make my preliminary report. And I can see I have a great deal to teach whomever I'm unfortunate enough to have as a partner—even if it's the cherubim." Its long, lavender tail, which had a fish-like fan at the tip, switched, and its whiskers bristled in Meg's direction.

Meg bristled, too. "Perhaps when I'm as old as you are I'll have learned a few things to teach *you!*"

Mouse-creature's whiskers vibrated wildly. "Age is immaterial. In any case, it so happens that I was born only yesterday."

"Then what are you doing here?"

Mouse-creature drew itself up; now it reminded Meg not so much of a mouse as of a small shrimp with antennae waving wildly. "There's only one of us farandolae born every generation or so nowadays, and we start our schooling the moment we're born."

"You're a farandola!"

"Naturally. What did you expect me to be? What else could I possibly be? Everybody knows that the farandolae—"

She interrupted. "Everybody doesn't. The existence of farandolae wasn't even guessed at until a few years ago when we began to learn more about mitochondria, and my mother has just now isolated the effect of farandolae on mitochondria with her micro-sonarscope. And even with the micro-electron microscope, farandolae can just be proved to exist, they can't really be seen."

The mouse-creature's, the farandola's, whiskers twanged. "It's a very stupid breed of creature that doesn't know its own inhabitants. Especially if it's fortunate enough to be inhabited by farandolae. We are extremely important and getting more so."

Past the farandola, behind Proginoskes and Louise the Larger, the shape of a Mr. Jenkins blew rapidly across the horizon.

Mr. Jenkins, standing near Meg and Calvin, quivered.

Blajeny looked grim. "Echthroi at work."

The mouse-creature-farandola paid no attention. "My quercus, my tree, hasn't had an offspring for a hundred years—our years, of course. It will take me that long to become full-grown myself, and this is only my second phase."

Meg spoke in her most ungracious manner. "You're going to tell us about your first phase whether we want you to or not. So go ahead." The glimpse of Charles Wallace, followed by the sight of another Echthros-Mr. Jenkins, had forced her to realize that the successful passing of the first test did not mean that everything was going to be all right.

Mouse-shrimp-farandola reacted by an intensified trembling of feelers. "Yesterday morning I was still contained inside the single golden fruit hanging on my tree. At noon it burst and fell open, and there was I, newly hatched. In my tadpole stage I was delivered to Metron Ariston and transmogrified, and here am I. My name is Sporos, by the way, and I do not like your thinking names like mouse-creature and shrimp-thing at me. *Sporos*. When I have finished this phase of my education—if I finish—with one of you for a partner, I will root myself, and Deepen. After an aeon I'll send up a small green shoot out of my kelp bed, and start growing into an aqueous deciduous spore-reproducing fruit-bearing coniferous farandola."

Calvin looked horrified. "You're mad. I've studied biology. You're not possible."

"Neither are you," Sporos replied indignantly. "Nothing *important* is. Blajeny, is it my misfortune to be paired with one of these earthlings?"

Louise the Larger lifted her head out of her coils and looked at Sporos, her heavy lids met and closed.

Blajeny said, "You are hardly making yourself popular, Sporos."

"I'm not a mere earthling. Earthlings are important only because they are inhabited by farandolae. Popularity is immaterial to farandolae."

Blajeny turned away from Sporos in quiet rebuff. "Calvin. You and Sporos are to work together."

"Oh, well, you can't win them all," was more or less the effect of what Sporos was vibrating, and Meg thought it would have been a more appropriate response coming from Calvin.

Mr. Jenkins said, "Blajeny, if I may presume—"

"Yes?"

"That other—I did see another copy of myself just a few moments ago, did I not?"

"Yes. I am afraid you did."

"What does it mean?"

Blajeny said, "It means nothing good."

Proginoskes added, "You see, we aren't any place. We're in Metron Ariston. We're simply in an idea which Blajeny happens to be having in the middle of the Mondrion solar system in Veganuel galaxy. An Echthros-Mr. Jenkins oughtn't to be able to follow us here. It means—"

"What?" Meg demanded.

Like Blajeny, Proginoskes said, "Nothing good."

Sporos twingled his whiskers. "Need we stand around chittering? When are we going?"

"Very soon."

"Where?" Meg demanded. She felt prickles of foreboding.

"To a far place, Meg."

"But Mother and Father—Charles Wallace—the twins—we can't just go off this way with Charles Wallace so ill and—"

"That is why we are going, Meg," Blajeny said.

Sporos rippled his undulating notes, and Meg translated something like: "Can't you just call home, or just reach out and talk to each other when you want to?" and then a horrified, "Oh, my goodness, I don't see how anybody as ignorant as you three earthlings seem to be can possibly manage. Do you mean on your earth host you never communicate with each other and with other planets? You mean your planet revolves about all isolated in space? Aren't you terribly lonely? Isn't he?"

"He?"

"Or she. Your planet. Aren't you lonely?"

"Maybe we are, a little," Calvin conceded. "But it's a beautiful planet."

"That," Sporos said, "is as it may be. Since I was only born yesterday and came right into Metron Ariston and to Blajeny, I don't know the planets except the ones in the Mondrion solar system, and they talk back and forth all the time; they chatter too much, if you ask me."

"We didn't," Meg tried to interrupt, but Sporos twingled on.

"I do hope I wasn't born in some dreadful mitochondrion which lives in some horrible isolated human host on a lonely planet like yours. You *are* all from the same planet? I thought so. Oh dear, oh dear, I can see you aren't going to be the least help to me in passing any of the trials. I'd better see what time it is."

"How do you tell time?" Calvin asked curiously.

"By the leaves, of course. You mean to say you don't even know the time of day?"

"Of course I do. With my watch."

"What's a watch?"

Calvin extended his wrist. He was very proud of his watch, which had been a prize at school, and gave the date as well as the hour, had a sweep hand, and was a stop watch as well.

"What a peculiar object." Sporos regarded it with a certain contempt. "Does it work just for your time, or for time in general?"

"Just for our time, I guess."

"You mean, if you want to know what time it is anywhere here in Blajeny's galaxy, or in a distant mitochondrion, your watch thing won't tell you?"

"Well—no. It just tells the time for whatever time zone I'm in."

"Mighty Yadah! How confused everything must be on your planet. I only hope my human host isn't in your planet."

Mr. Jenkins said plaintively, "If someone would just explain to me what is going on—"

"Mr. Jenkins," Meg said. "You know what the Echthroi are—"

"But I don't. I only know that they impersonated me."

Blajeny placed both great hands on Mr. Jenkins's stooped shoulders and looked down at him gravely. "There are evil forces at work in the world."

Mr. Jenkins nodded mutely. He did not dispute that.

"They are throughout the universe."

Mr. Jenkins glanced at the cherubim, who had stretched out his wings to their fullest span as though to flex his muscles. "How—how big are they?"

"They are no size and they are every size. An Echthros can be as large as a galaxy and as small as a farandola. Or, as you have seen, a replica of yourself. They are the powers of nothingness, those who would un-Name. Their aim is total X—to extinguish all creation."

"What do they have to do with Charles Wallace?"

"The Echthroi are trying to destroy his mitochondria."

"But why would they bother with a child?"

"It is not always on the great or the important that the balance of the universe depends."

Louise the Larger whistled urgently, and Meg was almost sure that the snake was telling them that she would stay with Charles Wallace, that she would encourage him to keep on fighting to live. "Oh, Louise, please, please, you won't leave him? You *will* help him?"

"I will not leave him."

"Will he be all right?"

Louise answered with silence.

Blajeny said to Mr. Jenkins, "Charles Wallace will die if his mitochondria die. Do you understand that?"

Mr. Jenkins shook his head. "I thought he was making things up with his big words. I thought he was trying to show off. I didn't know there really were mitochondria."

Blajeny turned to Meg. "Explain."

"I'll try. But I'm not sure I really understand either, Mr. Jenkins. But I do know that we need energy to live. Okay?"

"Thus far."

She felt Blajeny kything information to her, and involuntarily her mind sorted it, simplified, put it into words which she hoped Mr. Jenkins would understand. "Well, each of our mitochondria has its own built-in system to limit the rate at which it burns fuel, okay, Mr. Jenkins?"

"Pray continue, Margaret."

"If the number of farandolae in any mitochondrion drops below a critical point, then hydrogen transport can't occur; there isn't enough fuel, and the result is death through energy lack." She felt the skin on her arms and legs prickling coldly. To put into words what might be happening within Charles Wallace was almost unendurable.

She felt Blajeny prodding her and continued. "Something's happening in Charles Wallace's mitochondria. I'm not sure what it is, because it's all words I don't know, but his farandolae are dying—maybe they're killing each other—no, that's not right. It sounds to me as though they're refusing to sing, and that doesn't make any sense. The point is that they're dying and so his mitochondria can't produce enough oxygen." She broke off, angrily. "Blajeny! This is all nonsense! How can we possibly stop them from doing whatever it is they're doing, when they're so small they aren't even visible? You've got to tell us! How can we help Charles?"

Blajeny's kything was calm and cold as steel. "You will know soon."

"Know what?"

"What you must do to overcome the Echthroi. When you get there, my children, you will know."

"When we get where?"

"To one of Charles Wallace's mitochondria."

8 Journey into the Interior

Now that Blajeny had said it, it seemed to Meg the only logical, the only possible course of action. If they were to save Charles Wallace, if farandolae were causing his illness, if the Echthroi were at work within him as well as without, then the only hope was for them to become small enough to go into one of his mitochondria and see what was happening with the farandolae.

"Metron Ariston—" Calvin spoke softly. "Size. Where sizes don't matter. But—to be as small as a galaxy is huge: can you make us that small?"

Blajeny smiled. "Size is really quite relative."

"Anyhow"—Meg looked at Sporos—"we're already talking with a farandola." If she had tried to imagine a farandola, it would not have looked like Sporos.

Mr. Jenkins rose stiffly and moved with his peculiar stork-like gait to Blajeny. "I don't know why I thought I might be of help. This is all over my head. I will only be a hindrance to the children. You had better send me back to my school. At least there are no surprises for me there."

"What about this morning?" Blajeny asked. "That was not a surprise for you? I cannot tell you why you have been sent to us, Mr. Jenkins, because I myself do not yet know. But Meg Named you—"

"The full implications of this are not yet clear to me."

"It means that you are part of whatever is going to happen."

Mr. Jenkins moaned.

Blajeny stretched out his arms, embracing them all in the gesture. "The mitochondrion to which I am sending you is known as Yadah. It is Sporos's birthplace."

Sporos danced around, twingling in outrage.

Meg shouted at him, "If you are in Charles Wallace, if he's your galaxy, you couldn't be in a more special place!"

Louise sent her sibilant song towards Meg. All anger vanished when Meg caught, from Louise's song, another projection of Charles, huddled under the blankets. His mother lifted him to prop him up on pillows to ease his labored breathing, then pulled down the blankets so that Dr. Louise could listen to his heart with her stethoscope. She looked up gravely and Meg understood that she was suggesting that perhaps they had better call Brookhaven.

"Oxygen, then!" Meg cried out to Louise the Larger and Blajeny. "Wouldn't oxygen help Charles?"

"For a while. Dr. Colubra will see to that when the time comes."

Tears rushed to Meg's eyes. "Oh, Louise, take care of him. Don't let him stop fighting."

Mr. Jenkins asked, "Would anybody in his right mind let a snake near a sick child?"

"Dr. Louise will," Meg said, "I'm sure she will, from something she said in mother's lab the other night. Blajeny! Is Dr. Louise a Teacher, too?"

Blajeny nodded.

Meg's heart gave a leap of hope.

"Snakes," Mr. Jenkins murmured. "Mitochondria. Echthroi."

Meg swallowed a hiccupy sob, took off her glasses and wiped the tear-smeared lenses.

Mr. Jenkins looked at her and spoke in his most stilted, academic voice. "Man. The mean point in the universe. And Charles Wallace— is that it? At this moment in time Charles Wallace is the point of equi-librium?"

Blajeny nodded gravely.

"So what happens with his mitochondria and farandolae—?" He looked to Meg for explanation.

She tried to pull herself together. "Remember, Mr. Jenkins, you're great on Benjamin Franklin's saying, 'We must all hang together, or assuredly we will all hang separately.' That's how it is with human beings and mitochondria and farandolae—and our planet, too, I guess, and the solar system. We have to live together in—in harmony, or we won't live at all. So if something is wrong with Charles Wallace's mi-tochondria—" Her voice trailed off.

Mr. Jenkins shook his head. "What can we do? What can we pos-sibly hope to do?" Then he cried out in horror. "Oh, no!"

The pseudo-Mr. Jenkins they had seen before was moving rapidly towards them. Louise reared her black coils upwards with a horrible hissing.

"Quickly!" Blajeny spread his arms wide, pulling Mr. Jenkins, Sporos, and Calvin into their span. Proginoskes caught Meg within the strength of his wings, the beat of his heart. She seemed to become part of the cherubim's heartbeat.

The oval pupil dilated, and she went through to—

She could not tell where they were; she could only sense the presence of the others. As through a vast, echoing tunnel she heard Blajeny: "I would show you something to encourage you before you go."

Meg looked about. Ahead of her was a tremendous rhythmic swirl of wind and flame, but it was wind and flame quite different from the cherubim's; this was a dance, a dance ordered and graceful, and yet giving an impression of complete and utter freedom, of ineffable joy. As the dance progressed, the movement accelerated, and the pattern became clearer, closer, wind and fire moving together, and there was joy, and song, melody soaring, gathering together as wind and fire united.

And then wind, flame, dance, song, cohered in a great swirling, leaping, dancing, single sphere.

Meg heard Mr. Jenkins's incredulous, "What was *that?*"

Blajeny replied, "The birth of a star."

Mr. Jenkins protested, "But it's so small I could hold it in the palm of my hand." And then an indignant snort, "How big am I?"

"You must stop thinking about size, you know. It is both relative and irrelevant."

At this point Meg could not be bothered with size. She wanted to know something else. "Progo, will the star be Named?"

"He calls them all by name," the cherubim said.

Meg looked in wonder at the star. It was indeed so small that she could have reached out and caught it in her hand, but its flaming was so intense that the song itself came out of the fire and was part of the burning. She thought in wonder,—I must be the size of a galaxy.

And then all thoughts dissolved in the glory of the melody and the dance.

Blajeny's voice came like thunder, "Now!"

She was pulled into Proginoskes again, into the beat of the great heart, into the darkness of the eye, into the—

No!

She was being consumed by flame. She sensed a violent jolt to the cosmic rhythm, a distortion of wild disharmony—

She tried to scream, but no sound came. She felt pain so intense that she could not bear it another second; another second and the pain would annihilate her entirely.

Then the pain was gone, and she felt once again the rhythm of the cherubic heart, very rapid, faintly irregular. "Did it have to hurt that much?" Shock and pain made her loud and angry. Her limbs trembled weakly.

Proginoskes seemed to be having trouble; his heart continued to race unevenly. She thought she understood him to say, "We had a brush with an Echthros."

Her own breathing was a shallow panting. She felt that she was all there, all her atoms reassembled, that she was Meg; and yet when she opened her eyes she could see nothing but a strange, deep green-blackness. She listened, listened, and through what seemed at first to be a sound somewhat like the shrilling of insects on a summer night, she thought she could hear—or perhaps it was feel—a steady, regular pulsing.

"Progo, where are we?"

"Yadah."

"You mean we are *in* Charles Wallace? In one of his mitochondria?"

"Yes."

It was not conceivable. "What's that sort of thrumming I feel? Is it Charles Wallace's heartbeat?"

Proginoskes moved in negation in her mind. "It's the rhythm of Yadah."

"It feels like a heartbeat."

"Megling, we're not in earth time now; we're within Yadah. In farandolae time, Charles Wallace's heart beats something like once a decade."

She shivered. Her arms and legs still felt trembly and useless. She blinked, trying to adjust her eyes to the darkness. "Progo, I can't see."

"Nobody in the interior can see, Meg. Eyes aren't needed."

Her heart beat in frightened counterpoint to the rhythm of the mitochondrion. She could not pay proper attention as Proginoskes said, "It's what might be called a circadian rhythm. All life needs rhythm to—"

She interrupted. "Progo! Blajeny! I can't move!"

She felt Proginoskes within her thoughts. His own thinking had calmed considerably; he was recovering from whatever it was that had frightened him and caused her so much pain. "Blajeny did not come with us."

"Why?"

"This is no time for silly questions."

"Why is it silly? Why can't I see? Why can't I move?"

"Meg, you must stop panicking or I won't be able to kythe with you. We won't be able to help each other."

She made a tremendous effort to calm down, but with each heartbeat she felt only more tense, more frightened. How could her heart be pounding so rapidly if Charles Wallace's beat only once a decade?

Proginoskes thought noisily at her, "Time isn't any more important than size. All that is required of you is to be in the Now, in this moment which has been given us."

"I don't feel like myself. I'm *not* myself! I'm part of Charles Wallace."

"Meg. You are Named forever."

"But Progo—"

"Say the multiplication table."

"Now who's being silly?"

"Megling, it will help bring you to yourself. Try."

"I can't." Her mind felt battered and numb. She could not even remember enough to count to ten.

"What's 7 times 8?"

She responded automatically. "56."

"What's the product of ⅔ and ⅝."

Her mind whirled, cleared. "10 over 21."

"What's the next prime number after 67?"

"71."

"Can we think together now?" There was considerable concern in Proginoskes's questioning.

The concentration the cherubim had thrust on Meg had calmed her panic. "I'm okay. Where's Calvin? Where's Mr. Jenkins? And that— that Sporos?"

"They're all here. You'll be able to kythe with them soon. But first we have to find out what the second test is."

"Find out?" Her mind was still blurred from pain and fright.

He was patient with her. "As we found out what the first test was."

"You guessed that," she said. "Do you know what this one is?"

"I think it has to do with Sporos."

"But what?"

"This is what we must discover."

"We have to hurry, then." She tried to check her impatience.

"Meg, I have to work with you and Mr. Jenkins together, because he isn't capable of letting me move about in his mind as you can, so you'll have to help. The grown farandolae don't talk the way people do, they kythe."

"Like cherubim?"

"Some of the Ancient Ones, yes. With the younger ones it's a little closer to what you called mental telepathy. Never mind the degree; Mr. Jenkins can't understand kything at all, and you'll have to help him."

"I'll try. But you'll have to help me, Progo."

"Stretch out your right hand—"

"I can't move."

"That doesn't matter. Move your hand in your mind. Kythe it. Kythe that Mr. Jenkins is standing by you, and that you're reaching out to hold his hand. Are you doing it?"

"I'm trying."

"Can you feel his hand?"

"I think so. At least, I'm making believe I can."

"Hold it. Tightly. So that he knows you're there."

Her hand, which was no longer her hand in any way she had known before, nevertheless moved in the remembered pattern, and she thought she felt a slight pressure in return. She tried to kythe to the principal. "Mr. Jenkins, are you there?"

"Hheere." It was like an echo of a faintly remembered voice hoarse with chalk dust; but she knew that she and Mr. Jenkins were together.

"Meg, you will have to kythe him everything I tell you. If I move into his mind I hurt him; he can't absorb my energy. Now, try to translate simultaneously for him: make him see that a grown farandola's *matter* does not move, except as a plant does, or a tree when there is no breeze to cause its motion, or as the great kelp forests move. A grown farandola moves by kything. Kything is not going to be easy for Mr. Jenkins, because it has been a great many years since he's known himself, his real self."

Meg sighed with a kind of anxious fatigue, suddenly realizing the enormous amount of energy taken by this intense kything. The cherubim moved lightly, swiftly within her, and his kything moved through and beyond her senses to an awareness she had never known before. She groped to contain it in images which were within Mr. Jenkins's comprehension.

The sea, a vast, curving, never-ending sea; it was as though they were in that sea, deep down under the water's surface, deeper than a whale can dive. The surface of the sea, and any light which might penetrate the surface, was hundreds of fathoms away. In the dark depths there was movement, movement which was part of the rhythm she had mistaken for Charles Wallace's heartbeat. The movement assumed shape and form, and images were kythed to her mind's eye, visual projections superimposed swiftly one over the other; she tried to send them to Mr. Jenkins:

a primordial fern forest;

a giant bed of kelp swaying to submarine currents;

a primeval forest of ancient trees with rough, silver bark;

underwater trees with silver-gold-green foliage which undulated regularly, rhythmically, not as though the long fronds were being blown by wind or current but of their own volition, like the undulation of those strange sea creatures halfway between plant life and animal life.

To the visual images music was added, strange, unearthly, rich, the surging song of the surrounding sea.

Farandolae.

She felt confusion and questioning from Mr. Jenkins. To him farandolae were little scampering creatures like Sporos, not like the sea trees she had been trying to show him.

Proginoskes kythed, "The sea trees, as you call them, are what Sporos will become when he Deepens. They are then called fara. Once he has Deepened he will no longer have to run about. A grown fara is far less limited than a human being is by time and place, because farae can be with each other any time in any place; distance doesn't separate them."

"They move without moving?" Meg asked.

"You might put it that way."

"Am I to learn to move without moving, too?"

"Yes, Meg. There's no other way in a mitochondrion. There's nothing for you to stand on in Yadah, and no space for you to move through. But because you're an earthling, and earthlings excel in adaptability, you can learn this motionless motion. Are you translating for Mr. Jenkins?"

"I'm trying."

"Keep on, Meg. We'll have time to rest later, unless—" She felt a small, sharp pain, which was immediately withdrawn. "Some of the Ancient Ones can kythe not only from mitochondrion to mitochondrion within their human hosts, but to farandolae on mitochondria in other human hosts. Do you remember how shocked Sporos was when Calvin told him that human beings can't do that kind of thing?"

"Yes, but Progo, Mr. Jenkins doesn't understand about Sporos running around like a toy mouse. I don't understand it either. He isn't a bit like the sort of sea things you just showed us."

"Sporos is, as he said, only a child, although he was juggling chronologies when he said he was born yesterday. A farandola well into adolescence has already passed through its early stages and taken root and is becoming a grown fara. It is nearly time for Sporos to leave childhood and Deepen. If he does not, it will be another victory for the Echthroi."

"But why wouldn't he Deepen?"

"Calvin is having trouble kything with him. Sporos is holding back. We have to help him Deepen, Meg. That's our second test, I'm sure it is."

To make an unwilling Sporos Deepen; it seemed a more impossible ordeal than Naming one of three Mr. Jenkinses. "How do we do it?"

He countered with another question. "Are you calm?"

Calm! Then, once again, she moved into that strange place which is on the other side of feeling. With one part of herself she knew that she was in Charles Wallace, actually inside her brother; that she was so small that she couldn't be seen in the most powerful micro-electron microscope, or heard in the micro-sonarscope; she knew, too, that Charles Wallace's life depended on what was going to happen now. She was beginning to get a glimmer of what Proginoskes meant when he talked about the dangers of feeling. She held herself very still, very cold, then turned towards the cherubim in quiet kything.

"Be a fara," he told her. "Make believe. Do the inhabitants of Yadah seem more limited than human beings because once they have taken root they can't move from their Deepening Place? But human beings need Deepening Places, too. And far too many never have any. Think about your Deepening Places, Meg. Open yourself into kything. Open."

She returned to the strange world which was below light, below sound, penetrated only by the rhythm of tides pulled by the moon, by the sun, by the rhythm of the earth itself. She became one with the kything, Deepened creatures moving in the intricate pattern of song, of the loveliness of rhythm, of joy.

Then a coldness came, a horrible, blood-freezing chill. Tendrils were drawn back, pulled away from her, isolating themselves, isolating Meg, Proginoskes, each other. The song jerked, out of rhythm, out of tune, rejecting her—

Something was wrong, horrifyingly wrong—

She felt Proginoskes hurling himself at her, into her. "Meg! That's enough for now. We must be with the others, Calvin, Mr. Jenkins, Sporos, before—"

"Before what?"

"Before the second test. We must all be together. Open. Kythe to Calvin."

"Where is he?"

"It doesn't matter where he is, Meg. You've got to get it through your head that *where* doesn't make any difference in a mitochondrion. It's why. And how. And who."

"Calvin—" She seemed to feel every muscle in her body straining, and protesting at the strain.

"You're trying too hard," the cherubim said. "Relax, Megling. You kythe with me without all that effort. You and Calvin often kythe without realizing it. And when Charles Wallace knows when something's upset you at school, knows it even before you come home, that's kything. Just be Meg. Open. Be. Kythe."

Through the darkness of under-sea she kythed. "Calvin—"

"Meg!"

"Where are you?"

Proginoskes flicked sharply at her. "Forget where."

"*How* are you?"

"All right. A little confused by everything. Sporos—"

"Where—no, *how* is Sporos?"

"Meg, he doesn't want to kythe or be with me. He doesn't want to share his world. He says that human beings are unworthy, and that may be so, but—"

She felt a swirling of kything all around her, as though the words and images of the kything were the drops of water which go to make up the ocean, drops of water which are not separate one from the other as human beings are separate. Within the flowing of the deep tides images flashed by, many little creatures like Sporos, scampering about, carefree, merry, always in the protection of the great kelpfern-trees, the Deepened Ones, about which they flitted and fluttered.

"Are you translating for Mr. Jenkins?"

"I'm trying, Progo, but I'm not sure I really feel him. I know that I'm with you, and with Calvin, but Mr. Jenkins—"

"Be with him, Meg. He needs you. He's frightened."

"If Blajeny wanted him along, there must be a reason for it. But it seems to me he's an awful liability."

She thought she felt a thin, distant "I am aware of that."

She stretched herself towards that faint response. "Mr. Jenkins—"

"That's right," Proginoskes said. "Remember, he hasn't much imagination. Or, rather, it's been frozen for a long while and hasn't had time to thaw. You'll have to kythe your whole self to him; you'll have to hold his hand, tightly, so that he can feel you and return your kythe. Can you feel his hand?"

"I—I imagine so."

"Can he feel you?"

"Mr. Jenkins! Mr. Jenkins?" she kythed questioningly. "Wait a minute, Progo, Cal, I'm not sure, something's wrong—" She broke off, gasped, "Calvin! Progo! Pro—" With every particle of herself she screamed, not a scream made with her voice, but with all of her, a scream of pain that was beyond terror.

It was the same pain that had torn across a galaxy when Proginoskes had shown her the Xing of the Echthroi; it was the pain which had slashed across the sky in the schoolyard when she had Named Mr. Jenkins; it was the pain which had almost annihilated her when Proginoskes took her the strange journey through his eye to Yadah.

She was being Xed.

9 Farandolae and Mitochondria

This was the end of Meg. There was to be no more anything. Ever. Exit Meg. Ex-Meg. X-Meg.

Then she realized that if she could think this, if she could think at all, then it was not happening. One who is Xed cannot think. The pain still burned like ice, but she could think through it. She still was.

With all of her she kythed away from the Xness. "Progo! Calvin! Help me!"

Through her cries she felt the cherubim. "Meg! I Name you! You are!"

And then numbers, numbers moving as strong and steady and rhythmic as tide.

Calvin. He was sending numbers to her, Calvin was sending back to her those first trigonometry problems they had done together. She held on to the strength of numbers as to a lifeline, until the Echthroi-pain was gone and she was free to move back into the realm of words again, human words which were much easier for Calvin than numbers.

"Calvin," she called. "Oh, Calvin." And then her kything was an anguished longing for her parents. Where was her father? Had Dr. Louise or her mother called Brookhaven? What had they told her father? Was he on his way home? And her mother—she wanted to retreat, reverse, revert, to climb back into her mother's lap as she had done when she was Charles Wallace's age and needed healing from some small hurt . . .

No, Meg,

She felt as though gentle fingers were pushing her down, forcing her to walk alone. She tried to kythe, to get her mind's voice into focus, sent its beam at last to Proginoskes and Calvin. "What happened?"

She felt a series of major earthquakes before Proginoskes managed words for her. Whatever it was that had happened, it had certainly upset the cherubim. He kythed at last, "As though once weren't enough, when you reached out for Mr. Jenkins's hand you got an Echthros-Mr. Jenkins. Now we know that at least one of them followed us here."

"How?"

"Not through Mr. Jenkins, though it's still using a Jenkins-body. Perhaps Sporos—"

"Sporos!"

"Pride has always been the downfall of the Deepening Ones. Sporos may have listened to an Echthros—we aren't sure."

"What did you do? How did you get me away from it? It hurt—it hurt more than I knew anything could hurt. And then I felt you Naming me, Progo, and you, Cal, you were sending numbers to me, and the pain went and I was back into myself again."

Calvin kythed, "Proginoskes got a lot of little farandolae to rush up and tickle the Echthros-Mr. Jenkins. It was so startled, it let you go."

"Where is it now—the Echthros-Mr. Jenkins?"

Proginoskes was sharp. "It doesn't matter where, Meg. It's here. It's with us in Yadah."

"Then we're still in danger from it?"

"All Yadah is in danger. Every mitochondrion in this human host is in danger."

"This human host?"

Proginoskes did not reply. This human host was Charles Wallace.

"What are we going to do?"

There was another volcanic upheaval before Proginoskes replied, "We must not give way to panic."

She kythed Calvinwards and felt him returning the kything. She asked, "Did you know what was happening to me?"

"Not at first. Then Progo told me." There was a terrible quietness to Calvin's reply. She felt that he was holding something back from her.

"The little farandolae—the ones who saved me—are they all right?"

There was silence.

"Are they all right, the little farandolae who startled the Echthros and saved me?"

"No." The kything came reluctantly from both Calvin and Proginoskes.

"What happened to them?"

"To surprise an Echthros is not a safe thing to do."

"The Echthros Xed them?"

"No, Meg. They Xed themselves. That's a very different matter."

"What will happen to them now?"

Proginoskes kythed slowly, "I've never seen it happen before. I've heard about it, but I've never seen it. Now I understand more than I used to. The farandolae are known by name just as the stars are. That's all I need to know."

"You haven't told me anything! Where are the little farandolae who saved me? If they Xed themselves, then where are they?"

She heard a faint "Where doesn't matter. Meg, you must get in touch with Mr. Jenkins. The real Mr. Jenkins."

Instinctively she withdrew her kything. "I don't dare try again. Do you have any idea how much that hurt?"

"Your scream shook the entire mitochondrion. I only hope it didn't hurt Charles Wallace."

She flinched, then held on to something, she wasn't sure what, but it felt like a lifeline. After a moment she knew that it was coming from the cherubim, an outflowing of love, love so tangible that she could hold on to it.

"Reach for Mr. Jenkins," Proginoskes urged. "Name him for himself again. See how much you've been able to kythe to him. And remember, you have to go at his speed, not your own."

"Why! He's holding us back!"

"Hush, Meg." Calvin kythed. "Adults take longer at this kind of thing than we do, particularly adults like Mr. Jenkins who hasn't tried new thoughts for a long time."

"But we don't have time! Charles Wallace—"

"I said he takes longer than we do, and that's true. But sometimes adults can go deeper than we can, if we're patient."

"We don't have time to be patient!"

"Meg, trust Blajeny. Mr. Jenkins must be with us for a reason. Help him. Do what Progo says."

Proginoskes kythed urgently, "We may need Mr. Jenkins to get Sporos to Deepen. Blajeny wouldn't have sent him unless—oh, Meg, a Teacher never does anything without reason. Try to reach Mr. Jenkins, Meg."

She pushed her terror aside and opened herself to kything
and she was with Charles Wallace,
not within him,
not without him,
but with him,
part of his exhaustion,

his terrifying energy loss,
his struggle to breathe.

Oh, fight, Charles,
don't stop struggling,
breathe,
breathe,
I'll try to help,
I'll do anything I can to help, even

then

She was with the twins. Charles Wallace, she thought, had sent her.

The twins were in the garden, digging, grimly spading up and turn-ing under the old tomato plants, the frost-blackened zinnias, the lettuce gone to seed, turning them under to enrich the earth for the next spring, the next planting, with set faces working silently, taking out their anxiety over Charles Wallace in physical labor.

Sandy broke the silence. "Where's Meg?"

Dennys paused, his foot on his pitchfork as he pressed it into the earth. "She should be getting home from school soon."

"Charles Wallace said she isn't in school. He said that Meg is *in* him. I heard him."

"Charles Wallace is delirious."

"Have you ever seen anyone die?"

"Only animals."

"I wish Meg would come home."

"So do I."

They went on with their preparation of the garden for the winter cold and snow.

—If the twins' job is simply to take care of their garden—Meg told herself,—your job is to reach Mr. Jenkins. Where? Nowhere. Just Mr. Jenkins.

"Mr. Jenkins. Mr. Jenkins. You are you and nobody else and I Named you. I'm kything, Mr. Jenkins. Here I am. Me. Meg. You know me and I know you."

She thought she heard a sniff, a Mr. Jenkins sniff. Then he seemed to recede again. This minuscule undersea world was totally beyond his comprehension. She tried to kythe to him once more all the images in earth equivalents which she had received, but he responded with nothing beyond anxious blankness.

"Name him," Proginoskes urged. "He is afraid to be. When you Named him in the schoolyard, that was kything, that was how you knew him from the two Echthroi-Mr. Jenkinses, how you must know him this time."

Mr. Jenkins. Unique, as every star in the sky is unique, every leaf on every tree, every snowflake, every farandola, every cherubim, unique: Named.

He gave Calvin shoes. And he didn't have to come with us to this danger and horribleness, but he did. He chose to throw in his lot with us when he could have gone back to school and his safe life as a failure.

Yes, but for an unimaginative man to come with them into the unimaginably infinitesimal unknown isn't the kind of thing a failure does.

Nevertheless, Mr. Jenkins had done it, was doing it.

"Mr. Jenkins, I love you!"

She did.

Without stopping to think she put her imagined hand into his. His fingers were slightly damp and chill, just as clammy as she had always thought Mr. Jenkins's hand would be.

And real.

10 Yadah

Of course Mr. Jenkins's hand would be damp. He'd be scared out of his wits. He was years away from games of Make Believe and Let's Pretend.

"Mr. Jenkins, are you all right?"

She felt a fumbling kything, a frightened inability to accept that they were actually in a mitochondrion, a mitochondrion within one of Charles Wallace's cells. "How long have we been here?"

"I'm not sure. So much has happened. Progo—you're sure we're in farandola time, not earth time?"

"Farandola time."

"Whew!" she told Mr. Jenkins in relief. "That means that time on earth is passing much more slowly than time is for us—aeons more slowly. Charles Wallace's heart beats only once every decade or so."

"Even so," Proginoskes warned, "there's no time to waste."

Another flash of Charles Wallace's face, ashen, eyes closed, breathing labored; of her mother's face, tight with pain; of Dr. Louise, watchful, waiting. She stood with her small hand lightly against Charles Wallace's wrist.

"I know," Meg answered the cherubim. A cold wind seemed to blow through the interstices of her ribs. She must be strong for Charles Wallace now, so that he could draw on that strength. She held her mind quiet and steady until it calmed.

Then she opened herself again to Mr. Jenkins. Muddied thoughts which could hardly qualify as kything moved about her like sluggish water, and yet she understood that Mr. Jenkins was being more open with her than he had ever been before, or than he ever was able to be with most people. His mind shuddered into Meg's as he tried to grasp the extraordinary fact that he was still himself, still Mr. Jenkins, at the same time that he was a minuscule part of the child who had been one of his most baffling and irritating problems at school.

Meg tried to let him know, in as unalarming a way as possible, that at least one of the Echthroid-Mr. Jenkinses was with them on Yadah. She did not want to recall her terror during her encounter with one of them, but she had to help Mr. Jenkins understand.

He sent her a response, first of bafflement, then fear, then a strange tenderness towards her. "You should not be asked to endure such things, Margaret."

"There's more," she told him. This more was hardest of all, to make him understand that some of the little farandolae, some of the playful, dancing creatures, had saved her from the Echthros-Mr. Jenkins, and had sacrificed themselves in doing so.

Mr. Jenkins groaned.

From Proginoskes Meg relayed to the principal, "It was better than letting the Echthroi X them. They're still—they're still part of Creation this way." She turned her kything to Proginoskes. "If the Echthroi X something, or if something Xs itself, is it forever?"

The cherubim surrounded her with the darkness of his unknowing. "But we don't need to know, Meg," he told her firmly, and the darkness began to blow away. "I am a cherubim. All I need to know is that all the galaxies, all the stars, all creatures, cherubic, human, farandolan, all, all, are known by Name." He seemed almost to be crooning to himself.

Meg kythed at him sharply. "You're Progo. I'm Meg. He's Mr. Jenkins. Now what are we supposed to do?"

Proginoskes came back into focus. "Mr. Jenkins does not want to understand what a farandola is."

"Evil is evil," Mr. Jenkins sent fumblingly Megwards. She felt his mind balking at the idea of communication where distance was no barrier. "Mice talk by squeaking, and shrimp by—I don't know much marine biology, but they must make *some* sound. But trees!" he expostulated. "Mice who put down roots and turn into trees—you did say trees?"

"No." Meg was impatient, not so much at Mr. Jenkins as at her own ineptitude in communicating with him. "The farae—well, they aren't unlike trees, sort of primordial ones, and they aren't unlike coral and underwater things like that."

"Trees cannot talk with each other."

"Farae can. And as for trees—don't they?"

"Nonsense."

"Mr. Jenkins, when you walk through the woods at home, and the wind moves in the trees, don't you ever have the feeling that if you knew how, you'd be able to understand what they were saying?"

"Never." It had been a long time since he had walked in the woods. He moved from his lodgings to the school, from the school to his lodgings, driving himself both ways. He did not have time to go for walks in the woods . . .

She felt a dim regret in his kything, so she tried to make him hear the sound of wind in the pine woods. "If you close your eyes it sounds like ocean waves, even though we're not anywhere near the ocean."

All she felt from Mr. Jenkins was another cold wash of incomprehension.

So she envisioned a small grove of aspens for him, each leaf shivering and shaking separately, whispering softly in the still summer air.

"I'm too old," was Mr. Jenkins's response. "I'm much too old. I'm just holding you back. You ought to return me to Earth."

Meg forgot that she had recently made exactly that suggestion. "Anyhow, Yadah is on Earth, or in Earth, sort of, since it's in Charles Wallace . . ."

"No, no," Mr. Jenkins said, "it's too much. I'm no help. I don't know why I thought I might be—" His kything trailed off.

Through his discouragement she became aware of Calvin. "Hey, Meg! Communication implies sound. Communion doesn't." He sent her a brief image of walking silently through the woods, the two of them alone together, their feet almost noiseless on the rusty carpet of pine needles. They walked without speaking, without touching, and yet they were as close as it is possible for two human beings to be. They climbed up through the woods, coming out into the brilliant sunlight at the top of the hill. A few sumac trees showed their rusty candles. Mountain laurel, shiny, so dark a green the leaves seemed black in the fierceness of sunlight, pressed towards the woods. Meg and Calvin had stretched out in the thick, late-summer grass, lying on their backs and gazing up into the shimmering blue of sky, a vault interrupted only by a few small clouds.

And she had been as happy, she remembered, as it is possible to be, and as close to Calvin as she had ever been to anybody in her life, even Charles Wallace, so close that their separate bodies, daisies and buttercups joining rather than dividing them, seemed a single enjoyment of summer and sun and each other.

That was surely the purest kind of kything.

Mr. Jenkins had never had that kind of communion with another human being, a communion so rich and full that silence speaks more powerfully than words.

Again Calvin was kything with quick, urgent words. *"The Wall Street Journal."*

"What!"

"Mr. Jenkins reads *The Wall Street Journal.* Maybe he might have read this."

"Read what?"

"You remember, just a few weeks ago I was telling you about a science project I did years ago when I was in fourth grade. Even the twins were interested."

Meg listened intently, trying to kythe simultaneously to Mr. Jenkins.

The subject of the old science project had come up because of the twins' garden. Sandy and Dennys were baffled and irritated. Some of the pepper plants had large, firm, healthy fruit. On others the peppers were wizened and wrinkled and pale. Calvin had been taken out to look at the undersized, flabby plants, which showed no visible sign of disease, and he had been reminded of his fourth-grade science project.

Meg asked, "Could the plants be having the same kind of trouble mitochondria are having? Could Echthroi bother things like gardens?"

Calvin pushed this question aside to think about later. "Not now, Meg. Listen. I think my science project will help Mr. Jenkins understand."

Meg seemed to see Mr. Jenkins's nose twitching as it always did when he was reluctant.

"Okay, then." She kythed to him, slowly, as simply as possible, Calvin's kything always a strong current under and through hers.

At nine years of age Calvin read avidly, every book that came into the small village library. The librarian, seeing his pleasure in books, encouraged him, gave him a special corner in the library as his own, and gave him all the old classics of the imagination to read. His span of concentration on these stories was infinite.

But he considered most of the work he was given at school a bore, particularly science projects. However, he was also fiercely competitive, and determined to be the top of his class in all subjects, even those he considered a waste of time.

When the week came when he must turn in the topic for his science project by Friday, he was disinterested and planless, but he knew he had to choose something. He was thinking about this with particular urgency on Thursday afternoon when he was helping old Mrs. Buncombe clean out her attic. What could he choose which would interest the teacher and class and not bore him completely? Mrs. Buncome was not paying him for the dirty and dusty job—her attic had not been

touched for years—but she had bribed him to do it by telling him that
there was an old set of china up in the attic, and he could take it as
payment. Perhaps she knew that the O'Keefes could never sit down to
a meal together, even if they had wanted to, because there weren't
enough plates and cups and saucers to go round.

The china was in a box at the back of the attic, and it was wrapped
in old newspapers. Some of it was broken; much of it was cracked; it
certainly was not a set of forgotten Wedgwood or Dresden. Who had
bothered to wrap it up as carefully as though it were a priceless heir-
loom? However, there was enough of the set left to make it worth taking
home. He unwrapped it for his mother, who complained ungraciously,
if correctly, that it was junk.

He cleared up the crumpled, yellowed newspapers, and began to
read one. It was an old *Wall Street Journal*; the date had been torn off,
but the paper was brittle and stained and he knew that it must be a good
many years old. His eye caught an article about a series of experiments
made by a biologist.

The biologist had the idea, unusual at the time, that plants were
capable of subjective reactions to stimuli, and he decided to measure
the strength of these reactions by attaching electrodes, like those used
in a lie detector, to the leaves of a large, healthy philodendron.

At that point in the account a section of paper was torn away, and
Calvin lost several sentences. He picked up a statement that electronic
needles would record the plant's responses on a graph, much as brain
waves or heart patterns are recorded by the electro-encephalogram or
electro-cardiogram machines.

The biologist spent an entire morning looking at the needles moving
in a straight line across the paper. Nothing happened. No reactions. The
needle did not quiver. The line moved slowly and steadily.

The biologist thought, "I'll make that plant react. I'll burn one of
its leaves."

The stylus made wild up and down markings of alarm.

The rest of the article was torn off.

Mr. Jenkins's thoughts came to Meg quite clearly, a little irritably.
"I read that article. I thought it was nonsense. Just some crackpot."

Calvin kythed, "Most major scientific discoveries have been made by crackpots—or at least, people who were thought to be crackpots."

"My own parents, for instance," Meg added, "until some of their discoveries were proved to be true."

Calvin continued. "Listen. There's more. I found another article among the papers."

This one described the biologist going on a cross-country lecturing tour. He asked one of his students to take care of, watch, and record the reactions of his philodendron.

The plant's alarm needles jumped nervously whenever the biologist's plane took off or landed.

"How would it know?" Meg asked.

"It did."

"But distance," she protested, "how could a plant, just an ordinary domestic philodendron, know what was happening miles and miles away?"

"Or care," came dourly from Mr. Jenkins.

"Distance doesn't seem to be any more important than size. Or time. As for caring—well, that's outside the realm of provable fact."

For his project Calvin had worked out a variation on the theme of plant response. He had no way of measuring the subjective responses of a plant, so he decided to plant three bean seeds.

Mr. Jenkins did not think much of this.

Meg kythed him a warning, "Wait! This was all Calvin's own idea. He was only nine years old then, and he didn't know that experiments of the same kind were already being made."

Calvin planted one of the seeds in a pot which he left in the kitchen at home. He put it on a windowsill where it would get sunlight, and he watered it daily. His brothers and sisters were warned that if they touched it they'd get clobbered. They knew he meant it, and they left his plant physically alone. However, the plant heard—

"Without ears?" Mr. Jenkins kythed crossly.

"Like Louise, maybe," Meg returned.

The plant heard the automatic ugly invective of daily speech in Calvin's home. Calvin himself stayed in the house as little as possible.

The other two seeds he took to the library, where the librarian gave him permission to put his pots in two sunny windows. One of these beans he watered and cared for dutifully. That was all. The third bean he talked to, encouraging it, urging it to grow. When the first green shoot appeared he lavished on it all the love which had so little outlet in his home. He sat, after school, close by his plant, doing his homework, reading aloud when nobody was around, sharing.

The first of the bean plants, the one in the O'Keefe's kitchen, was puny, and too pale a green, like the twins' sickly peppers. The second plant, in the library window, the plant given regular care but no special time or attention, grew normally. The third plant, the plant Calvin loved, grew strong and green and unusually large and healthy.

Mr. Jenkins kythed thinly but quite comprehensibly, "If philodendron and beans can react like that, it should help me to understand farandolae—is that what you're trying to tell me?"

"Sort of," Meg replied.

Calvin added, "See? Distance doesn't matter. They can know and converse with each other and distance doesn't really exist for them."

Mr. Jenkins sent out waves of disbelief. "And if they're loved, they'll grow? And if they aren't loved—"

"The Echthroi can move in."

Now she heard what could only be Sporos's twingling. "They're dull and slow, like all human beings, but you're getting through to them at last, cherub."

"My name is Proginoskes, if you please, mouse-creature."

The farandola was not amused. "My name is Sporos." A reproving twingle.

"Meg." Proginoskes kythed deeply into her. "Do you realize what has just been happening? You've been close to Mr. Jenkins, haven't you?"

"I guess so. Yes."

"And yet your bodies are not close together. And you already know that nothing can separate you from Calvin when you kythe together."

Yes. She was with Calvin. They were together. She felt the warmth of his quick smile, a smile which always had a slight quirk of sadness and acceptance unusual in a sixteen-year-old. He was not kything in words now, but in great waves of courage, of strength, flowing over and through her.

She accepted it, absorbed it. Fortitude. She was going to need a great deal. She opened herself, drank it in.

"All right," Proginoskes told them. "We are together. We can continue."

"What are we to do?" Mr. Jenkins asked.

"The second test," the cherubim urged. "We must pass the second test."

"And that is?"

"To Name Sporos. As Meg had to Name you."

"But Sporos is already Named!"

"Not until he has Deepened."

"I don't understand."

"When Sporos Deepens," Proginoskes told Mr. Jenkins, "it means that he comes of age. It means that he grows up. The temptation for farandola or for man or for star is to stay an immature pleasure-seeker. When we seek our own pleasure as the ultimate good we place ourselves as the center of the universe. A fara or a man or a star has his place in the universe, but nothing created is the center."

Meg asked, "The little farandolae who saved me—"

"They came of age, Meg."

She pondered this. "I *think* I understand—"

"I don't," Mr. Jenkins said. "I thought we came here to try to help Charles Wallace, that he is ill because of his mitochondria—"

Proginoskes pushed back impatience. "He is."

"But what does Sporos have to do with Charles Wallace?"

"The balance of life within Yadah is precarious. If Sporos and the others of his generation do not Deepen, the balance will be altered. If the farandolae refuse to Deepen, the song will be stilled, and Charles Wallace will die. The Echthroi will have won."

"But a child—" Mr. Jenkins asked. "One small child—why is he so important?"

"It is the pattern throughout Creation. One child, one man, can swing the balance of the universe. In your own Earth history what would have happened if Charlemagne had fallen at Roncesvalles? One minor skirmish?"

"It would have been an Echthroi victory?"

"And your history would have been even darker than it is."

"Mr. Jenkins!" Meg called. "Listen, I just remembered: For want of a nail the shoe was lost; for want of a shoe the horse was lost; for want of a horse the rider was lost; for want of a rider the message was lost; for want of the message the battle was lost; for want of the battle the war was lost; for want of the war the kingdom was lost; and all for the want of a horseshoe nail."

"We must save Charles Wallace!" Mr. Jenkins cried. "What can we do, Progo? What can we do?"

11 Sporos

A burst of harmony so brilliant that it almost overwhelmed them surrounded Meg, the cherubim, Calvin, and Mr. Jenkins. But after a moment of breathlessness, Meg was able to open herself to the song of the farae, these strange creatures who were Deepened, rooted, yet never separated from each other, no matter how great the distance.

We are the song of the universe. We sing with the angelic host. We are the musicians. The farae and the stars are the singers. Our song orders the rhythm of creation.

Calvin asked, "How can you sing with the *stars?*"

There was surprise at the question: it is the song. We sing it together. That is our joy. And our Being.

"But how do you know about stars—in here—inside—"

How could farae not know about stars when farae and stars sing together?

"You can't see the stars. How can you possibly know about them?"

Total incomprehension from the farae. If Meg and Calvin kythed in visual images, this was their limitation. The farae had moved beyond physical sight.

"Okay," Calvin said. "I know how little of ourselves, and of our brains, we've learned to use. We have billions of brain cells, and we use only the tiniest portion of them."

Mr. Jenkins added with his dry, ropy kythe, "I have heard that the number of cells in the brain and the number of stars in the universe is said to be exactly equal."

"Progo!" Meg asked. "You memorized the names of all the stars—how many are there?"

"How many? Great heavens, earthling, I haven't the faintest idea."

"But you said your last assignment was to memorize the names of all of them."

"I did. All the stars in all the galaxies. And that's a great many."

"But how many?"

"What difference does it make? I know their *names*. I don't know how many there are. It's their names that matter."

The strong kything of the farae joined Proginoskes. "And the song. If it were not for the support of the singing of the galaxies, we farae on Yadah would have lost the melody, so few of the farandolae are Deepening. The un-Namers are at work."

Meg felt a sudden chill, a pulling back, a fading of the Deepened farae; there was dissonance in the harmony; the rhythm faltered.

In her mind's eye an image was flashed of a troop of farandolae dancing wildly about one fara-tree, going faster and faster, until she felt dizzy.

"Sporos is with them," Proginoskes told her.

"What are they doing? Why are they spinning faster and faster?" The circle of farandolae revolved so rapidly that it became a swirling blur. The fronds of the great fara around whom they swirled began to droop.

"They are absorbing the nourishment which the fara needs. The fara is Senex, from whom Sporos came." There was chill in Proginoskes's words.

The speed of the dancing farandolae became like a scream in Meg's ears. "Stop!" she cried. "Stop it at once!" There was nothing merry or joyful in the dance. It was savage, wild, furious.

Then, through the raging of the dance came a strong, pure strain of melody, quiet, certain, noble. The dancing farandolae broke their circle and scampered about aimlessly; then, led by Sporos, they raced to another fara and began circling it.

The fronds of Senex greened, lifted.

Proginoskes said, "He is strong enough to hold out longer than any of the other farae. But even Senex cannot hold out forever." He stopped abruptly. "Feel."

"Feel?"

"The rhythm of the mitochondrion. Is it my fearfulness, or is Yadah faltering?"

"It is not you," Meg answered the cherubim. They were all very still, listening, feeling. Again there came a slight irregularity in the steady pulsing. A faltering. A missed beat. Then it steadied, continued.

Like a gash through the non-light of Yadah Meg had a brief vision of Charles Wallace lying in his small room, gasping for air. She thought she saw Dr. Louise, but the strange thing was that she could not tell whether it was Dr. Louise Colubra, or Louise the actual colubra. "Don't give up. Breathe, Charles. Breathe." And a steady voice, "It's time to try oxygen."

Then she was drawn back within the mitochondrion to Senex, the parent tree of Sporos. She tried to convey to him what she had just seen, but she received nothing from him in return. His incomprehension was even greater than Mr. Jenkins's had been. She asked Proginoskes, "Does Senex know that Charles Wallace even exists?"

"As you know that your galaxy, the Milky Way, exists."

"Does he know that Charles Wallace is ill?"

"As you know that your Earth is ill, by fish dying in the rivers, birds dying in the forests, people dying in the choked cities. You know by war and hate and chaos. Senex knows his mitochondrion is ill because the farandolae will not Deepen and many farae are dying. Listen. Kythe."

A group of farandolae whirled about a fara; fronds drooped; color drained. The dance was a scream of laughter, ugly laughter. Meg smelled the stench which was like the stench in the twins' garden when she had first encountered an Echthros.

She heard a voice. It was like a bad tape recording of Mr. Jenkins. "You need not Deepen and lose your power to move, to dance. No one can force you to. Do not listen to the farae. Listen to me."

The great central trunk of the surrounded fara began to weaken.

Meg tried to project herself into the dance, to break the vortex. "Sporos, come out! Don't listen. You were sent to the Teacher. You belong with us. Come out, Sporos, you are meant to Deepen!"

Then it was as though she were the end skater in a violent game of crack-the-whip and suddenly was flung so wildly across the ice that she crashed into the end of the rink. The force with which she had been thrown was so fierce that her kything was completely blacked out.

"Breathe, Meg, breathe." It was Proginoskes, using the same words which Louise was using with Charles Wallace. "Breathe, Meg. You're all right."

She reeled, staggered, regained her balance.

Again she heard the ugly laugh, and the false Mr. Jenkins voice urging, "Kill the fara!"

Then came Mr. Jenkins's own voice. "I see. I understand." She felt emanating from him a dry, dusty acknowledgment of unpleasant fact.

She returned sharply, still slightly breathless, "*I* don't understand."

Mr. Jenkins asked her, "Why did Hitler want to control the world? Or Napoleon? Or Tiberius?"

"I don't know. I don't know why anyone would. I think it would be awful."

"But you admit that they did, Margaret?"

"They wanted to," she conceded. "But they didn't succeed."

"They did a remarkably good job of succeeding for a period of time, and they will not lightly be forgotten. A great many people perished during the years of their rules."

"But farandolae—why would little farandolae like Sporos—"

"They appear to be not that unlike human beings."

She felt cold and quiet. Once Mr. Jenkins had accepted the situation, he understood it better than she did. She asked, "Okay, then, what have the Echthroi got to do with it? They're behind it, aren't they?"

Proginoskes answered, "The Echthroi are always behind war."

Meg turned in anguish towards Senex, calm and strong as an oak tree, but, unlike the oak, pliable, able to bend with wind and weather. "Senex, we've been sent to help, but I'm not strong enough to fight the Echthroi. I can't stop Sporos and the other farandolae from killing the fara. Oh, Senex, if they succeed, won't they kill themselves, too?"

Senex responded coldly, quietly. "Yes."

"This is insane," Mr. Jenkins said.

Proginoskes answered, "All war is insane."

"But, as I understand it," Mr. Jenkins continued, "we are a minutely immeasurable part of Charles Wallace?"

"We are."

"Therefore if, while we are on—or, rather, in—this mitochondrion, if Charles Wallace were to die, then—er—um—we—"

"Die, too."

"Then I fight not only for Charles Wallace's life but for Meg's, and Calvin's, and—"

"Your own."

Meg felt Mr. Jenkins's total indifference to his own life. She was not yet willing to accept the burden of his concern for her. "We musn't think about that! We musn't think about anything but Charles!"

Proginoskes wound around and through her thoughts: "You cannot show your concern for Charles Wallace now except in concern for Sporos. Don't you understand that we're all part of one another, and the Echthroi are trying to splinter us, in just the same way that they're trying to destroy all Creation?"

The dancing farandolae whirled and screamed, and Meg thought she could hear Sporos's voice: "We're not part of anybody! We're farandolae, and we're going to take over Yadah. After that—"

A hideous screech of laughter assailed Meg's ears. Again she flung herself at the dance, trying to pull Sporos out of it.

Senex drew her back with the power of his kythe. "Not that way, not by force."

"But Sporos has to Deepen! He has to!"

Then, around the edges of her awareness, Meg heard a twingling, and Calvin was with Sporos, trying to reach out to him, to kythe with him.

Sporos's response was jangly, but he came out of the wild circle and hovered on its periphery. "Why did Blajeny send you alien life forms to Yadah with me? How can you possibly help with my schooling? We make music by ourselves. We don't need you."

Meg felt Proginoskes's volcanic upheaving, felt a violent wind, searing tongues of flame. "Idiot, idiot," Proginoskes was sending, "we all need each other. Every atom in the universe is dependent on every other."

"I don't need you."

Suddenly Proginoskes kythed quietly and simply, "I need you, Sporos. We all of us need you. Charles Wallace needs you."

"I don't need Charles Wallace."

Calvin kythed urgently, "Don't you? What happens to you if something happens to Charles Wallace? Who have you been listening to?"

Sporos withdrew. Meg could not feel him at all.

Calvin emanated frustration. "I can't reach him. He slips away from me every time I think I'm getting close."

Sporos was pulled back into the whirling circle. The surrounded fara was limp, all life draining rapidly. Senex mourned, "His song is going out."

Proginoskes kythed, "Xed. Snuffed out like a candle."

Senex's fronds drooped in grief. "Sporos and his generation listen to those who would silence the singing. They listen to those who would put out the light of the song."

Mr. Jenkins raised shadowy arms prophetically. "To kill the song is the only salvation!"

"No!" Mr. Jenkins cried to Mr. Jenkins. "You are only a mirror vision of me. You are nothing!"

Nothing   nothing   nothing

The word echoed, hollow, empty, repeating endlessly. Everywhere Meg kythed she seemed to meet a projection of an Echthros-Mr. Jenkins.

"Don't you understand that the Echthroi are your saviors? When everything is nothing there will be no more war, no illness, no death.

There will be no more poverty, no more pain, no more slums, no more starvation—"

Senex kythed through the Echthros. "No more singing!"

Proginoskes joined Senex. "No more stars, or cherubim, or the light of the moon on the sea."

And Calvin: "There will never be another meal around table. No one will ever break bread or drink wine with his companions."

Meg kythed violently against the nearest Echthros-Mr. Jenkins, "You are nothing! You're only borrowing Mr. Jenkins in order to be something. Go away! You are nothing!"

Then she was aware that the real Mr. Jenkins was trying to reach her. "Nature abhors a vacuum."

Calvin replied, "Then we must fill the vacuum. That is the only thing to do."

"How?"

"If the Echthroi are nothingness, emptiness, then that emptiness can be filled."

"Yes, but how do we fill it?"

Senex kythed calmly, "Perhaps you don't want to fill it strongly enough. Perhaps you do not yet understand what is at stake."

"I do! A little boy, my brother—what do you know about my little brother?"

Senex conveyed considerable confusion. He had a feeling for the word 'brother' because all farae are—or had been—brothers. But 'little boy' meant nothing to him whatsoever.

"I know that my galactic host is ill, perhaps dying—"

"That's Charles Wallace! That's my little brother! He may be a galactic host to you, but to me he's just a little boy like—like Sporos." She turned her kythe from Senex and towards the wildly dancing farandolae who had surrounded another fara. This time she kythed herself towards them cautiously. How could she be sure which one was Sporos?

An Echthros-Mr. Jenkins whinnied with laughter. "It doesn't matter. Nothing matters." A harsh twang wounded the melody of the farae who were still singing.

Once again Meg felt faltering in the mitochondrion. Yadah was in pain. Suddenly she remembered the farandolae who had saved her from the Echthros when Proginoskes brought her into Yadah. Not all the farandolae had thrown in their lot with the Echthroi. Or were those who had Xed themselves that she might live the only ones who would defy the Echthroi?

She began calling urgently, "Sporos! Farandolae! Come away from the Echthroi. You will dance yourselves to death. Come to Senex and Deepen. This is what you were born to do. Come!"

Some of the farandolae faltered. Others whirled the faster, crying, "We don't need to Deepen. That's only an old superstition. It's a stupid song they sing, all this Glory, glory, glory. We are the ones who are glorious."

"The stars—" Meg called desperately.

"Another superstition. There are no stars. We are the greatest beings in the universe."

Ugliness seeped past Meg and to Sporos. "Why do you *want* to Deepen?"

Sporos's twingling was slightly dissonant. "Farandolae are born to Deepen."

"Fool. Once you Deepen and put down roots you won't be able to romp around as you do now."

"But—"

"You'll be stuck in one place forever with those fuddy-duddy farae, and you won't be able to run or move, ever again."

"But—"

The strength and calm of Senex cut through the ugliness. "It is only when we are fully rooted that we are really able to move."

Indecision quivered throughout Sporos.

Senex continued, "It is true, small offspring. Now that I am rooted I am no longer limited by motion. Now I may move anywhere in the universe. I sing with the stars. I dance with the galaxies. I share in the joy—and in the grief. We farae must have our part in the rhythm of the mitochondria, or we cannot be. If we cannot be, then we are not."

"You mean, you die?" Meg asked.

"Is that what you call it? Perhaps. I am not sure. But the song of Yadah is no longer full and rich. It is flaccid, its harmonies meager. By our arrogance we make Yadah suffer."

Meg felt Calvin beside Senex, urging, "Sporos, you are my partner. We are to work together."

"Why? You're no use to me."

"Sporos, we *are* partners, whether we like it or not."

Meg joined in. "Sporos! We need you to help save Charles Wallace."

"Why do we have to bother about this Charles Wallace? He's nothing but a stupid human child."

"He's *your* galaxy. That ought to make him special enough, even for you."

A cruel slashing cut between their kything, as though a great beak had cut a jagged wound. "Sporos! It is I, Mr. Jenkins. I am the teacher who is greater than all Teachers because I know the Echthroi."

Meg felt Proginoskes's kything clamp like steel.

The Echthros-Mr. Jenkins was holding Sporos, and speaking with honey-sweet words. "Do. not listen to the earthlings; do not listen to the farae. They are stupid and weak. Listen to me and you will be powerful like the Echthroi. You will rule the universe."

"Sporos!" The real Mr. Jenkins's kything was not strong enough to break through the stream. "He is not Mr. Jenkins. Do not listen!"

Calvin's kythe came more strongly than Mr. Jenkins's. "There are two Mr. Jenkinses by you, Sporos, two Mr. Jenkinses kything you. You know that one is not real. Deepen, Sporos, that is where your reality lies. That is how you will find your place, and how you will find your true center."

Meg's mind's-ears were assailed by a howling which was Echthroid, though it appeared to come from the pseudo-Mr. Jenkins. "Reality is meaningless. Nothing is the center. Come. Join the others in the race. Only a few more farae to surround and you will have Yadah for your own."

"Yadah will die," Meg cried. "We will all die. You will die!"

"If you come with us, you will be nothing," the Echthros-Mr. Jenkins spoke in cloying kythe, "and nothing can happen to nothing."

Sporos's long whiskers trembled painfully. "I am very young. I should not be asked to make major decisions for several centuries."

"You're old enough to listen to Senex," Meg told him. "You're old enough to listen to *me*. After all, I'm a galaxy to you. It's time for you to Deepen."

Sporos wriggled in the clasp of the Echthros-Mr. Jenkins. "Come, Sporos, fly with the Echthroi. Then you will crackle across the universe. There are too many mitochondria in creation. There are too many stars in the heavens. Come with us to naught, to nought."

"Deepen, Sporos, my child, Deepen."

"Sporos!" The Echthroid howl beat against the rhythm of Yadah. "We will make you a prince among Echthroi."

Meg felt a gust of wind, the familiar flicker of flame: Proginoskes. The cherubim flung his kything across the void of the Echthros-Mr. Jenkins, like a rope flung from cliff's edge to cliff's edge. "Sporos, all farandolae are royal. All singers of the song are princes."

"Nonsense. In Name only."

"The Name matters."

"Only to matter."

Proginoskes's kything was so gentle that it undercut the storm of

Echthroi. "You are created matter, Sporos. You are part of the great plan, an indispensable part. You are needed, Sporos; you have your own unique share in the freedom of creation."

"Do not listen to that hideous cherubim. He's nothing but a deformed emanation of energy. We will give you no name and you will have power."

Calvin pushed in again. "Sporos, you are my partner. Whatever we do, we must do it together. If you join the wild farandolae again I am coming into the dance with you."

Sporos quivered, "To help kill the farae?"

"No. To be with you."

Meg cried, "Progo, let's go, too! We can help Calvin." In her impetuous relief at having something to do, she did not feel the cherubim pulling her back, but plunged into the irrational tarantella and was immediately swept out of control. Calvin was whirling beside Sporos, unable to pull him away from the circle closing in on the dying fara.

Meg was totally in the power of the revolving, twangling farandolae. The orbital velocity sucked her in, through the circle and against the limp trunk of the fara.

Within the deathly center of the dance it was dark; she could not image the whirling farandolae; she could not kythe Calvin or Sporos. She heard only a silence which was not silence because within this vortex there was an emptiness which precluded the possibility of sound.

Caught in this anguished vacuum she was utterly powerless. She was sucked against the trunk of the fara, but the fara was now too weak to hold her up; it was she who had to hold the dying Deepened One, to give it her own life's blood. She felt it being drained from her. The fara's trunk strengthened. It was Meg who was dying.

Then arms were around her, holding her, pouring life back into her, Mr. Jenkins's arms, the real Mr. Jenkins. His strength and love filled her.

As she returned to life, the firm, rhythmic tendrils of the reviving fara caressed her. Mr. Jenkins held them both, and his power did not weaken. The murderous circle was broken. Calvin held Sporos in his arms and a tear slid down his cheek. Meg turned towards him, to comfort him.

The moment she kythed away from Mr. Jenkins and to Calvin, a new circle formed, not of farandolae, but of Mr. Jenkinses, Mr. Jenkinses swirling their deathly ring around the real Mr. Jenkins.

Meg whirled back towards him, but it was too late. Mr. Jenkins was surrounded. Meg cried, "Deepen, Sporos, it's the only hope!"

The scattered farandolae darted hither and thither in confusion. Proginoskes reached out wing after invisible wing to pull them in. There was a frightened twingle.

"Look at the Echthroi!" Proginoskes commanded. "They are killing Mr. Jenkins as they made you kill your own farae. Look. This is what it is like."

"Mr. Jenkins!" Meg called. "We have to save Mr. Jenkins. Oh, Sporos, Deepen, it's the second ordeal, you must Deepen."

"For Mr. Jenkins?"

"For yourself, for all of us."

"But why did Mr. Jenkins—didn't he know what would happen to him?"

"Of course he knew. He did it to save us."

"To save us all," Calvin added. "The Echthroi have him, Sporos. They are going to kill him. What are you going to do?"

Sporos turned towards Senex, the fara from whom he had been born. He reached out small green tendrils towards all the farandolae. "It is Deepening time," he said.

They heard a faint echo of the music which had been such joy when Blajeny took them to witness the birth of a star. The farae were singing, singing, strengthening. Sporos was joining in the song. All about them farandolae were Deepening, and adding their music to the flowing of the song.

Meg's exhaustion and relief were so great that she forgot Mr. Jenkins. She assumed blindly that now that Sporos and the other farandolae were Deepening, now that the second ordeal had been successfully accomplished, all was well; the Echthroi were vanquished; Charles Wallace would recover; she could relax.

Then she felt Proginoskes pushing through her thoughtlessness. "Meg! You forget! There are three tests!"

She turned from rejoicing. The circle of pseudo-Mr. Jenkinses was whirling wildly about the principal, closing in on him.

Proginoskes kythed so strongly that she was pulled back into painful awareness. "We cannot let the Echthroi get Mr. Jenkins. This is the third test, to rescue Mr. Jenkins. Senex, Sporos, everybody, help us!"

Meg heard a shrill, high scream, a scream that turned into a horrible laugh of triumph. It came from Mr. Jenkins. One Mr. Jenkins. There was no longer a spiral of Echthroid Jenkinses surrounding the principal. They had closed in, and entered their prey.

Proginoskes's kything cut like a knife. "The Echthroi have him. We must get him away."

12 A Wind in the Door

The Echthros-Mr. Jenkins reached towards them. The horrible, familiar stench assailed Meg. A loathsome kything came to her in Mr. Jenkins's tones superimposed on the whine of metal rubbing against metal. "Nonsense. Of course the Echthroi haven't got me. I am Mr. Jenkins, and I took the Echthroi into me because they are right. It is not the Echthroi who are empty; it was I. They have filled me with the pleasure of the abyss of nothingness. Come let me X you, come to me, come ..."

Sporos's long, tendrilly whiskers quivered. A faint twingling came from them, but now he was kything, his young greenery moving rhythmically, his delicate new needles and leaves and blades shimmering with the rhythm of Senex, of the singing farae, of Yadah. "Earthlings, forgive me. I will sing for you. The Echthroi cannot bear the song."

Mr. Jenkins kythed like a corkscrew. "Life as we have known it is meaningless, Margaret. Civilization has failed. Your parents know this. They are giving up."

"No, no," Calvin protested. "They're not like that, they'd never give up."

"Sing," Sporos called to the Deepening farandolae, "sing with us. Our galaxy is in danger; we must save him."

Mr. Jenkins overrode him. "There is no hope except extinguishment. Let us hasten it."

Meg cried through the boring of the corkscrew. "Mr. Jenkins, no! Stop it!"

Calvin joined her. "Mr. Jenkins, come back, come out of the Echthroi!"

"I am back. I am here. I am finally myself. Nothing. X-Mr. Jenkins. To be Xed is the only good."

Again Meg felt a bone-shattering wrench. Every muscle in her cried out in protest. Then she was flashed a brilliant image of Calvin tugging at Mr. Jenkins, powerful images of Calvin wrestling with a Mr. Jenkins suddenly wild and strong. Mr. Jenkins's thin, flabby arms beat at Calvin with steel-spring blows. Calvin, with his lithe wiriness, eluded most of the blows, and tried desperately to catch Mr. Jenkins by the wrists—caught him—

The wrists became talons, became nothing. Calvin was left holding nothing. Meg heard the screeching Echthroi-laugh, and Mr. Jenkins hit Calvin a thundering blow.

Meg saw red-blackness, Calvin reeling, being pulled, sucked into the vortex of the Echthros-Mr. Jenkins.

Then the images of Calvin staggering from the blow, steadying himself, readying himself, vanished. The images were gone, but Calvin was there, was with her, was part of her. She had moved beyond knowing him in sensory images to that place which is beyond images. Now she was kything *Calvin*, not red hair, or freckles, or eager blue eyes, or the glowing smile; nor was she hearing the deep voice with the occasional treble cracking; not any of this, but—

Calvin.

She was with Calvin, kything with every atom of her being, returning to him all the fortitude and endurance and hope which he had given her.

Then she felt Proginoskes trying to get her attention and turned her kythe unwillingly towards him. "Meg, I can help Calvin, but I can't help Mr. Jenkins. You may be able to. Try to go to him. Perhaps you can still reach him."

She pulled back. If she went to the Echthroid-Mr. Jenkins, would the pain of the Echthroi take her again? There were no little farandolae to save her this time. She could not do it, could not knowingly open herself to that pain—

But Mr. Jenkins had come into the whirling circle of death for her sake. If Mr. Jenkins was possessed by Echthroi now it was because of his love for her.

She gave a sigh of acceptance of what she must do. Then she turned her kythe towards Mr. Jenkins who was somewhere in the horrible Echthroid version of himself.

"Mr. Jenkins!" She flung her kythe towards him with all her might. And now she no longer saw the thinning brown hair, the same mouse-brown as her own, or the middle-aged eyes behind the lenses of the horn-rimmed spectacles, or the sloping shoulders with the light snowfall of dandruff, but something deeper, more real, beyond, past, through the senses, something which was the true person. She was with Mr. Jenkins as she had been with Calvin, Calvin who was so important to her that she didn't dare even whisper to herself how important he was—

Mr. Jenkins, too, was real, and she was with him, kything herself entirely to him—

From somewhere deep inside the Echthroid version of himself he was trying to say something, he was repeating, repeating, and finally she heard, a phrase he had used earlier, "Nature abhors a vacuum." The single phrase was all he could manage.

She held on to it. If the Echthroi are nothing, and Mr. Jenkins is now part of that nothing, if Calvin is being Xed into that nothing—

"Fill it! Fill it!" came Calvin's desperate kythe. Through it came a vivid image of Charles Wallace blue and gasping, her parents standing by his bed; Dr. Louise working the emergency oxygen tank; Fortinbras lying across the threshold as though to bar death from entering the room. "Fill it!"

She was cold with desperation. "Progo! Progo, what do I do?"

She heard only an echo of Calvin's call. "Fill the vacuum. Fill it." He was fighting desperately, not for his own life but for Meg's, for Charles Wallace's, for the singing farae, for the whole of being . . .

She kythed wildly. "Progo, we passed the first test, I Named Mr. Jenkins. And the second—Sporos has Deepened. Are we failing the third test? Calvin can't hold out any longer. Do I have to go into the Echthroi? Is that what I have to do? What will you do if I fail?"

She knew. She knew what Proginoskes would do.

Calvin was weakening rapidly, unable to counter the sledgehammer blows of the Echthros-Mr. Jenkins—

She flung herself into Mr. Jenkins, trying to hold the cruel arms, trying to pull him away from Calvin by the sheer force of her kythe.

The pain.

It came again, as she had known it would.

Agony. Red anguish pounding against her eyeballs . . .

. . . Charles Wallace was sharing in that anguish, his parents helpless as his small body convulsed in spasms of pain. They struggled to hold him, the Murrys, the Louises, to hold him during the convulsions, to give the racked frame support . . .

Fortinbras stood in the doorway growling, his hackles rising . . .

The Echthroi were—

Meg's kythe was faint, almost obliterated by pain. "Calvin—Mr. Jenkins—don't fight the Echthroi—help me fill them—"

Cold.

Cold beyond snow and ice and falling mercury.

Cold beyond the absolute zero of outer space.

Cold pulverizing her into nothingness.

Cold and pain.

She struggled.

You are not to X me, Echthroi. I fill you.

Cold.

Darkness.

Emptiness.

Nothing.

Naught.

Nought.

Echth

X

Then

Proginoskes.

A great cry. A tempest of wind. A lightning flash of fire across the cold, breaking, burning the cold and pain.

Proginoskes Xing.

Wings. All the wings. Stretched to their fullest span. Eyes. All the eyes opening and closing, opening, dimming—

Oh, no—

Going out—

No—

Flame. Smoke. Feathers flying. Proginoskes flinging his great cherubic self into the void of the Echthroi who were Xing Mr. Jenkins and Calvin and Meg—

and Charles Wallace.

Wings and flame and wind, a great howling of all the hurricanes in the world meeting and battling—

"Progo!" Her cry kythed across Yadah, and then she knew what she must do. She must do as Mr. Jenkins had done when he had broken through the mad circle of whirling farandolae and held her. She must hold the Echthroi, hold them by holding Mr. Jenkins and Calvin—by holding Charles Wallace—

Hold them, Meg. Hold them all. Put your arms around them, around the Echthroi spreading their gaping, tearing nothingness across creation.

Size does not matter. You can hold them all, Charles and Calvin and Mr. Jenkins and the burning sphere of the newborn star—

She cried out, "I hold you! I love you, I Name you. I Name you, Echthroi. You are not nothing. You are."

A small white feather which was not a feather floated through the cold.

> I Name you, Echthroi. I Name you Meg.
> I Name you Calvin.
> I Name you Mr. Jenkins.
> I Name you Proginoskes.
> I fill you with Naming.
> Be!
> Be, butterfly and behemoth,
> be galaxy and grasshopper,
> star and sparrow,
> you matter,
> you are,
> be!
> Be, caterpillar and comet,
> be porcupine and planet,
> sea sand and solar system,
> sing with us,
> dance with us,
> rejoice with us,
> for the glory of creation,
> sea gulls and seraphim,
> angle worms and angel host,
> chrysanthemum and cherubim
> (O cherubim)
> Be!
> Sing for the glory
> of the living and the loving
> the flaming of creation
> sing with us
> dance with us
> be with us
> Be!

They were not her words only.
They were the words of Senex,
of the Deepening Sporos,
of all the singing farae,
the laughter of the greening farandolae,
Yadah itself,

all the mitochondria,
all the human hosts,
the earth,
the sun,
the dance of the star whose birthing she had seen,
the galaxies,
the cherubim and seraphim,
wind and fire,
the words of the Glory.

Echthroi! You are Named! My arms surround you. You are no longer nothing. You are. You are filled. You are me.
You are
Meg.

"Meg!"
Her encircling arms were around Charles Wallace.
"Where—"
(Where doesn't matter.)
Here.
Here in Charles Wallace's familiar room. Meg. Calvin. Mr. Jenkins. One Mr. Jenkins. The real Mr. Jenkins.

The Murrys. Dr. Louise, her stethoscope swinging loosely about her neck, looking disheveled, exhausted, happy . . .

The twins, Dennys with a big smudge of garden earth across his face, both boys still grubby and tired from their labors.

And Charles Wallace. Charles Wallace sitting up in bed, breathing quite easily and normally. Fortinbras no longer guarded the door, which now stood invitingly open. The oxygen tank, no longer needed, was in the corner.

"Charles! Oh, Charles Wallace!" Meg hugged him, swallowing a large and unexpected sob. "Are you all right? Are you really all right?"

"He's much better," Dr. Louise said. "We know very little about mitochondritis, but—" Her delicate little bird's voice faded off, and she looked questioningly at Meg.

So did her father. "Whatever happened—wherever you were— Charles Wallace was talking about mitochondria and farandolae in his delirium, and something which sounded like Echthroi—"

"And about you," her mother added.

Meg explained flatly, "We were in one of Charles Wallace's mitochondria."

Mr. Murry pushed his spectacles up his nose in the same gesture which his daughter used. "So he said." He looked at his youngest son. "I am not in a doubting mood."

Mrs. Murry said, "Just when we thought—when we thought it was all over—Charles Wallace gasped, 'The Echthroi are gone!' and suddenly his breathing started to improve."

"All I can say," Dennys said, "is that when Charles Wallace goes back to school, he'd better not talk the way he was doing while he was delirious."

"I don't understand any of this," Sandy said. "I don't like things I don't understand."

"If Mother and Father hadn't been so upset about Charles Wallace," Dennys glared at Meg, "they'd have been furious with you for not coming right home from school."

"Where were you, anyhow?" Sandy asked.

"Do you really expect us to swallow this stuff about your being *inside* Charles Wallace?"

"If you'd just be *realistic* for once."

"After all, we were worried, too."

"And then some."

They looked at Meg, then wheeled and looked at Mr. Jenkins.

Mr. Jenkins said, "Meg is quite correct. And I was with her."

The twins replied with total and stunned silence.

Finally Dennys shrugged and said, "Maybe one day someone will get around to telling us what really went on."

"I suppose since Charles is all right—"

"We'll just be glad about that. All's well that ends well and all that stuff."

"Even if everybody's holding out on us as usual."

They turned to Dr. Louise: "Charles is really okay?" "Is Charles really all right?"

Dr. Louise answered them, "It's my opinion that he'll be completely recovered in a day or so."

Meg confronted Mr. Jenkins. "Okay, but what about school? Won't the trouble there go on just as miserably as ever?"

Mr. Jenkins sounded his most acid. "I think not."

"What will you *do*, Mr. Jenkins? Can you make things different?"

"I don't know. I cannot dictate Charles Wallace's safety. He must learn, himself, to adapt. But I have less fear of the situation than I did before. After our—uh—recent experiences, the old red schoolhouse is going to be easier to enter each morning. Now I think that I am going to find upgrading an elementary school a pleasant change, and at the moment it seems a quite possible challenge."

The twins again looked astonished. Sandy asked in a deflated way, "Well, then, isn't anybody hungry?"

"We were so worried about Charles, we haven't eaten for—"

"I'd like a turkey dinner," Charles Wallace said.

Mrs. Murry looked at him, and some of the strain eased from her face. "I'm afraid I can't manage that, but I can thaw some steaks from the freezer."

"Can I come down when dinner is ready?"

Dr. Louise looked at him with her sharply probing gaze. "I don't see why not. Meg, you and Calvin stay with him until then. The rest of us will go to the kitchen to be useful. Come along, Mr. Jenkins, you can help me set the table."

When the three of them were alone, Charles Wallace said to Calvin, "You didn't say a word."

"I didn't need to." Calvin sat on the foot of Charles Wallace's bed. He looked as tired as Dr. Louise, and as happy. He put one hand lightly over Meg's. "It will be good to have a feast together, and celebrate."

Meg cried, "How can we have a feast without Progo!"

"I haven't forgotten Progo, Meg."

"But where is he?"

"Meg, he Xed himself."

"But where is he?"

(Where doesn't matter.)

Calvin's hand pressed more strongly against Meg's. "As Progo might say, he is Named. And so he's all right. The Echthroi did not get Progo, Meg. He Xed of his own volition."

"But, Calvin—"

"Proginoskes is a cherubim, Meg. It was his own choice."

Meg's eyes were too bright. "I wish human beings couldn't have feelings. I am having feelings. They hurt."

Charles Wallace hugged her. "I didn't imagine my dragons, did I?"

As he had intended her to, she gave a watery smile.

Immediately after dinner Dr. Louise ordered Charles Wallace back to bed. Meg held out her arms to kiss him good night. She knew that he was aware of her feeling of incompleteness without Proginoskes, and, as he kissed her cheek, he whispered, "Why don't you and Calvin go out to the north pasture and the big rocks and look around?"

She nodded, then glanced at Calvin. Wordlessly they slipped out to the pantry and put on ski jackets. When they had left the house behind them, he said, "It's funny to talk instead of kything, isn't it? I suppose we'd better get used to it."

She walked close beside him, across the rich, newly spaded earth of the garden. "There are things we aren't going to be able to talk about in front of people except in kything."

Calvin reached for one of her mittened hands. "I have a feeling we're not supposed to talk about them too much."

Meg asked, "But Blajeny—where's Blajeny?"

Calvin's hand held hers firmly. "I don't know, Meg. I suspect that he's wherever he's been sent, Teaching."

They paused at the stone wall.

"It's a cold night, Meg. I don't think Louise will come out." He climbed the wall and moved swiftly to the two glacial rocks. The great stones loomed darkly against the sky. The grass about them was crunchy with frost. And empty.

Meg said, "Let's go to the star-watching rock."

The star-watching rock lay coldly under the brilliance of the stars. There was nothing there. A tear trickled down Meg's cheek, and she wiped it away with the back of one mitten.

Calvin put his arm around her. "I know, Meg. I want to know what's happened to Progo, too. All I know is that somehow or other, he's all right."

"I think I *know* he's all right. But my mind would like to be in on the knowing." She shivered.

"We'd better go in. I promised your parents we wouldn't stay out long."

She felt an extraordinary reluctance to leave, but she allowed Calvin to lead her away. When they reached the stone wall she stopped. "Wait a minute—"

"Louise isn't—" Calvin started, but a dark shadow slid out of the stones, uncoiled slowly and gracefully, and bowed to them.

"Oh, Louise," Meg said, "Louise—"

But Louise had dropped to the wall again and disappeared somewhere within it. Nevertheless Meg felt comforted and reassured. In silence they returned to the house. In the pantry they hung their jackets on the hooks; the door to the lab was closed. So was the door to the kitchen.

Then the kitchen door blew open with a bang.

Sandy and Dennys were at the dining table, doing homework. "Hey," Sandy said, "you don't need to be so violent."

"You could just *open* the door, you don't have to take it off its hinges."

"We didn't touch the door," Meg said. "It blew open."

Sandy slammed his Latin text shut. "That's nonsense. There's hardly any wind tonight, and what there is, is coming from the opposite direction."

Dennys looked up from his math paper. "Charles Wallace wants you to come upstairs to him, Meg. Shut the door, at any rate. It's cold."

Sandy got up and shut the door firmly. "You were gone long enough."

"Did you count the stars or something?"

"We don't have to count them," Meg said. "They just need to be known by Name."

Calvin's eyes met hers for a long moment and held her gaze, not speaking, not kything, simply being.

Then she went up to Charles Wallace.

A SWIFTLY TILTING PLANET

For Hal Vursell

Contents

1 In This Fateful Hour

The big kitchen of the Murrys' house was bright and warm, curtains drawn against the dark outside, against the rain driving past the house from the northeast. Meg Murry O'Keefe had made an arrangement of chrysanthemums for the dining table, and the yellow, bronze, and pale-gold blossoms seemed to add light to the room. A delectable smell of roasting turkey came from the oven, and her mother stood by the stove, stirring the giblet gravy.

It was good to be home for Thanksgiving, she thought, to be with the reunited family, catching up on what each one had been doing. The twins, Sandy and Dennys, home from law and medical schools, were eager to hear about Calvin, her husband, and the conference he was attending in London, where he was—perhaps at this very minute—giving a paper on the immunological system of chordates.

"It's a tremendous honor for him, isn't it, Sis?" Sandy asked.

"Enormous."

"And how about you, Mrs. O'Keefe?" Dennys smiled at her. "Still seems strange to call you Mrs. O'Keefe."

"Strange to me, too." Meg looked over at the rocker by the fireplace, where her mother-in-law was sitting, staring into the flames; she was the one who was Mrs. O'Keefe to Meg. "I'm fine," she replied to Sandy. "Absolutely fine."

Dennys, already very much the doctor, had taken his stethoscope, of which he was enormously proud, and put it against Meg's burgeoning belly, beaming with pleasure as he heard the strong heartbeat of the baby within. "You are fine, indeed."

She returned the smile, then looked across the room to her youngest brother, Charles Wallace, and to their father, who were deep in concentration, bent over the model they were building of a tesseract: the square squared, and squared again: a construction of the dimension of time. It was a beautiful and complicated creation of steel wires and ball bearings and Lucite, parts of it revolving, parts swinging like pendulums.

Charles Wallace was small for his fifteen years; a stranger might have guessed him to be no more than twelve; but the expression in his light blue eyes as he watched his father alter one small rod on the model was mature and highly intelligent. He had been silent all day, she thought. He seldom talked much, but his silence on this Thanksgiving day, as the approaching storm moaned around the house and clapped the shingles on the roof, was different from his usual lack of chatter.

Meg's mother-in-law was also silent, but that was not surprising. What was surprising was that she had agreed to come to them for Thanksgiving dinner. Mrs. O'Keefe must have been no more than a few years older than Mrs. Murry, but she looked like an old woman. She had lost most of her teeth, and her hair was yellowish and unkempt, and looked as if it had been cut with a blunt knife. Her habitual expression was one of resentment. Life had not been kind to her, and she was angry with the world, especially with the Murrys. They had not expected her to accept the invitation, particularly with Calvin in London. None of Calvin's family responded to the Murrys' friendly overtures. Calvin was, as he had explained to Meg at their first meeting, a biological sport, totally different from the rest of his family, and when he received his M.D./Ph.D. they took that as a sign that he had joined the ranks of the enemy. And Mrs. O'Keefe shared the attitude of many of the villagers that Mrs. Murry's two earned Ph.D.s, and her experiments in the stone lab which adjoined the kitchen, did not constitute proper *work*. Because she had achieved considerable recognition, her puttering was tolerated, but it was not work, in the sense that keeping a clean house was work, or having a nine-to-five job in factory or office was work.

—How could that woman have produced my husband? Meg wondered for the hundredth time, and imaged Calvin's alert expression and open smile.—Mother says there's more to her than meets the eye, but I haven't seen it yet. All I know is that she doesn't like me, or any of the family. I don't know why she came for dinner. I wish she hadn't.

The twins had automatically taken over their old job of setting the table. Sandy paused, a handful of forks in his hand, to grin at their mother. "Thanksgiving dinner is practically the only meal Mother cooks in the kitchen—"

"—instead of out in the lab on her Bunsen burner," Dennys concluded.

Sandy patted her shoulder affectionately. "Not that we're criticizing, Mother."

"After all, those Bunsen-burner stews did lead directly to the Nobel Prize. We're really very proud of you, Mother, although you and Father give us a heck of a lot to live up to."

"Keeps our standards high." Sandy took a pile of plates from the kitchen dresser, counted them, and set them in front of the big platter which would hold the turkey.

—Home, Meg thought comfortably, and regarded her parents and brothers with affectionate gratitude. They had put up with her all through her prickly adolescence, and she still did not feel very grown up. It seemed only a few months ago that she had had braces on her teeth, crooked spectacles that constantly slipped down her nose, unruly mouse-brown hair, and a wistful certainty that she would never grow up to be a beautiful and self-confident woman like her mother. Her inner vision of herself was still more the adolescent Meg than the attractive young woman she had become. The braces were gone, the spectacles replaced by contact lenses, and though her chestnut hair might not quite rival her mother's rich auburn, it was thick and lustrous and became her perfectly, pulled softly back from her face into a knot at the nape of her slender neck. When she looked at herself objectively in the mirror she knew that she was lovely, but she was not yet accustomed to the fact. It was hard to believe that her mother had once gone through the same transition.

She wondered if Charles Wallace would change physically as much as she had. All his outward development had been slow. Their parents thought he might make a sudden spurt in growth.

She missed Charles Wallace more than she missed the twins or her parents. The eldest and the youngest in the family, their rapport had always been deep, and Charles Wallace had an intuitive sense of Meg's needs which could not be accounted for logically; if something in Meg's world was wrong, he knew, and was there to be with her, to help her if only by assuring her of his love and trust. She felt a deep sense of comfort in being with him for this Thanksgiving weekend, in being home. Her parents' house was still home, because she and Calvin spent many weekends there, and their apartment near Calvin's hospital was a small, furnished one, with a large sign saying NO PETS, and an aura that indicated that children would not be welcomed, either. They hoped to be able to look for a place of their own soon. Meanwhile, she was home for Thanksgiving, and it was good to see the gathered family and to be surrounded by their love, which helped ease her loneliness at being separated from Calvin for the first time since their marriage.

"I miss Fortinbras," she said suddenly.

Her mother turned from the stove. "Yes. The house feels empty without a dog. But Fort died of honorable old age."

"Aren't you going to get another dog?"

"Eventually. The right one hasn't turned up yet."

"Couldn't you go look for a dog?"

Mr. Murry looked up from the tesseract. "Our dogs usually come to us. If one doesn't, in good time, then we'll do something about it."

"Meg," her mother suggested, "how about making the hard sauce for the plum pudding?"

"Oh—of course." She opened the refrigerator and got out half a pound of butter.

The phone rang.

"I'll get it." Dropping the butter into a small mixing bowl en route, she went to the telephone. "Father, it's for you. I think it's the White House."

Mr. Murry went quickly to the phone. "Mr. President, hello!" He was smiling, and Meg watched as the smile was wiped from his face and replaced with an expression of—what? Nothingness, she thought.

The twins stopped talking. Mrs. Murry stood, her wooden spoon resting against the lip of the saucepan. Mrs. O'Keefe continued to stare morosely into the fire. Charles Wallace appeared to be concentrating on the tesseract.

—Father is just listening, Meg thought.—The President is doing the talking.

She gave an involuntary shudder. One minute the room had been noisy with eager conversation, and suddenly they were all silent, their movements arrested. She listened, intently, while her father continued to hold the phone to his ear. His face looked grim, all the laughter lines deepening to sternness. Rain lashed against the windows.—It ought to snow at this time of year, Meg thought.—There's something wrong with the weather. There's something wrong.

Mr. Murry continued to listen silently, and his silence spread across the room. Sandy had been opening the oven door to baste the turkey and snitch a spoonful of stuffing, and he stood still, partly bent over, looking at his father. Mrs. Murry turned slightly from the stove and brushed one hand across her hair, which was beginning to be touched with silver at the temples. Meg had opened the drawer for the beater, which she held tightly.

It was not unusual for Mr. Murry to receive a call from the President. Over the years he had been consulted by the White House on matters of physics and space travel; other conversations had been serious, many disturbing, but this, Meg felt, was different, was causing the warm room to feel colder, look less bright.

"Yes, Mr. President, I understand," Mr. Murry said at last. "Thank you for calling." He put the receiver down slowly, as though it were heavy.

Dennys, his hands still full of silver for the table, asked, "What did he say?"

Their father shook his head. He did not speak.

Sandy closed the oven door. "Father?"

Meg cried, "Father, we know something's happened. You have to tell us—please."

His voice was cold and distant. "War."

Meg put her hand protectively over her belly. "Do you mean nuclear war?"

The family seemed to draw together, and Mrs. Murry reached out a hand to include Calvin's mother. But Mrs. O'Keefe closed her eyes and excluded herself.

"Is it Mad Dog Branzillo?" asked Meg.

"Yes. The President feels that this time Branzillo is going to carry out his threat, and then we'll have no choice but to use our antiballistic missiles."

"How would a country that small get a missile?" Sandy asked.

"Vespugia is no smaller than Israel, and Branzillo has powerful friends."

"He really can carry out this threat?"

Mr. Murry assented.

"Is there a red alert?" Sandy asked.

"Yes. The President says we have twenty-four hours in which to try to avert tragedy, but I have never heard him sound so hopeless. And he does not give up easily."

The blood drained from Meg's face. "That means the end of everything, the end of the world." She looked toward Charles Wallace, but he appeared almost as withdrawn as Mrs. O'Keefe. Charles Wallace, who was always there for her, was not there now. And Calvin was an ocean away. With a feeling of terror she turned back to her father.

He did not deny her words.

The old woman by the fireplace opened her eyes and twisted her thin lips scornfully. "What's all this? Why would the President of the United States call here? You playing some kind of joke on me?" The fear in her eyes belied her words.

"It's no joke, Mrs. O'Keefe," Mrs. Murry explained. "For a number of years the White House has been in the habit of consulting my husband."

"I didn't know he"—Mrs. O'Keefe darted a dark glance at Mr. Murry—"was a politician."

"He's not. He's a physicist. But the President needs scientific information and needs it from someone he can trust, someone who has no pet projects to fund or political positions to support. My husband has become especially close to the new President." She stirred the gravy, then stretched her hands out to her husband in supplication. "But why? Why? When we all know that no one can win a nuclear war."

Charles Wallace turned from the tesseract. "El Rabioso. That's his nickname. Mad Dog Branzillo."

"El Rabioso seems singularly appropriate for a man who overthrew the democratic government with a wild and bloody coup d'état. He is mad, indeed, and there is no reason in him."

"One madman in Vespugia," Dennys said bitterly, "can push a button and it will destroy civilization, and every thing Mother and Father have worked for will go up in a mushroom cloud. Why couldn't the President make him see reason?"

Sandy fed a fresh log onto the fire, as though taking hope from the warmth and light.

Dennys continued, "If Branzillo does this, sends missiles, it could destroy the entire human race—"

Sandy scowled ferociously. "—which might not be so bad—"

"—and even if a few people survive in sparsely inhabited mountains and deserts, there'd be so much fallout all over the planet that their children would be mutants. Why couldn't the President make him see? Nobody wants war at that price."

"It's not for lack of trying," Mr. Murry said, "but El Rabioso deserves his nickname. If he has to fall, he'd just as soon take the human race with him."

"So they send missiles from Vespugia, and we return ours to them, and all for what?" Sandy's voice cracked with anger.

"El Rabioso sees this as an act of punishment, of just retribution. The Western world has used up more than our share of the world's energy, the world's resources, and we must be punished," Mr. Murry said. "We are responsible for the acutely serious oil and coal shortage, the defoliation of trees, the grave damage to the atmosphere, and he is going to make us pay."

"We stand accused," Sandy said, "but if he makes us pay, Vespugia will pay just as high a price."

Mrs. O'Keefe stretched her wrinkled hands out to the flames. "At Tara in this fateful hour . . ." she mumbled.

Meg looked at her mother-in-law questioningly, but the old woman turned away. Meg said to the room at large, "I know it's selfish, but I wish Calvin weren't in London giving that paper. I wish I'd gone with him."

"I know, love," Mrs. Murry replied, "but Dr. Louise thought you should stay here."

"I wish I could at least phone him . . ."

Charles Wallace moved out of his withdrawn silence to say, "It hasn't happened yet, nuclear war. No missiles have been sent. As long as it hasn't happened, there's a chance that it may not happen."

A faint flicker of hope moved across Meg's face.—Would it be better, she wondered,—if we were like the rest of the world and didn't know the horrible possibility of our lives being snuffed out before another sun rises? How do we prepare?

". . . in this fateful hour," the old woman mumbled again, but turned her head away when the Murrys looked at her.

Charles Wallace spoke calmly to the whole family, but looked at Meg. "It's Thanksgiving, and except for Calvin, we're all together, and Calvin's mother is with us, and that's important, and we all know where Calvin's heart is; it's right here."

"England doesn't observe Thanksgiving," Sandy remarked.

"But we do." His father's voice was resolute. "Finish setting the table, please. Dennys, will you fill the glasses?"

While Mr. Murry carved, and Mrs. Murry thickened the gravy, Meg finished beating the hard sauce, and the twins and Charles Wallace carried bowls of rice, stuffing, vegetables, cranberry sauce, to the table. Mrs. O'Keefe did not move to help. She looked at her work-worn hands, then dropped them into her lap. "At Tara in this fateful hour . . ."

This time nobody heard her.

Sandy, trying to joke, said, "Remember the time Mother tried to make oatmeal cookies over the Bunsen burner, in a frying pan?"

"They were edible," Dennys said.

"Almost anything is, to your appetite."

"Which, despite everything, is enormous."

"And it's time to go to the table," Mrs. Murry said.

When they were in their places she automatically held out her hands, and then the family, with Mrs. O'Keefe between Mr. Murry and Meg, was linked around the table.

Charles Wallace suggested, "Let's sing *Dona nobis pacem*. It's what we're all praying for."

"Sandy'd better start then," Meg said. "He's got the best voice. And then Dennys and Mother, and then Father and you and I."

They raised their voices in the old round, singing over and over, *Give us peace, give us peace, give us peace.*

Meg's voice trembled, but she managed to sing through to the end.

There was silence as the plates were served, silence instead of the usual happy noise of conversation.

"Strange," Mr. Murry said, "that the ultimate threat should come from a South American dictator in an almost unknown little country. White meat for you, Meg?"

"Dark, too, please. Isn't it ironic that all this should be happening on Thanksgiving?"

Mrs. Murry said, "I remember my mother telling me about one spring, many years ago now, when relations between the United States and the Soviet Union were so tense that all the experts predicted nuclear war before the summer was over. They weren't alarmists or pessimists; it was a considered, sober judgment. And Mother said that she walked along the lane wondering if the pussy willows would ever bud again. After that, she waited each spring for the pussy willows, remembering, and never took their budding for granted again."

Her husband nodded. "There was a reprieve then. There may be again."

"But is it likely?" Sandy's brown eyes were sober.

"It wasn't likely then. The pussy willows, nevertheless, have budded for a good many springs." He passed cranberry sauce to Mrs. O'Keefe.

"In this fateful hour," she mumbled, and waved the sauce away.

He bent toward her. "What was that?"

"At Tara in this fateful hour," she said irritably. "Can't remember. Important. Don't you know it?"

"I'm afraid not. What is it?"

"Rune. Rune. Patrick's rune. Need it now."

Calvin's mother had always been taciturn. At home she had communicated largely in grunts. Her children, with the exception of Calvin, had been slow to speak, because they seldom heard a complete sentence until they went to school. "My grandmother from Ireland." Mrs. O'Keefe pointed at Charles Wallace and knocked over her glass.

Dennys fetched paper towels and mopped up the spilled liquid. "I suppose, cosmically speaking, it doesn't make much difference whether or not our second-rate little planet blows itself up."

"Dennys!" Meg cried, then turned to her mother. "Excuse me for using this as an example, but Den, remember when Mother isolated farandolae within a mitochondrion?"

He interrupted, "Of course I remember. That's what she got the Nobel Prize for."

Mrs. Murry held up her hand. "Let Meg speak."

"Okay then: farandolae are so minuscule and insignificant it doesn't seem they could possibly have any importance, and yet they live in a symbiotic relationship with mitochondria—"

"Okay, gotcha. And mitochondria provide us with our energy, so if anything affects our farandolae, that can affect our mitochondria—"

"And," Meg concluded, "if that happens, we could die from energy loss, as you well know."

"Go on," Sandy said.

"So if we blow up our planet it would certainly have some small effect on our solar system, and that could affect our galaxy, and that could . . ."

"The old chain-reaction theory?" Sandy asked.

"More than that. Interdependence. Not just one thing leading to another in a straight line, but everything and everyone everywhere interreacting."

Dennys threw out the wet paper towels, put a clean napkin over the soiled tablecloth, and refilled Mrs. O'Keefe's glass. Despite storm windows, the drawn curtains stirred and a draft moved across the room. Heavy drops of rain spattered down the chimney, making the fire hiss. "I still think," he said, "that you're overestimating the importance of this planet. We've made a mess of things. Maybe it's best we get blown up."

"Dennys, you're a doctor," Meg reprimanded.

"Not yet," Sandy said.

"But he's going to be! He's supposed to care about and guard life."

"Sorry, Sis," Dennys said swiftly.

"It's just his way of whistling in the dark." Sandy helped himself to rice and gravy, then raised his glass to his sister. "Might as well go out on a full stomach."

"I mean it and I don't mean it," Dennys said. "I do think we've got our priorities wrong, we human beings. We've forgotten what's worth saving and what's not, or we wouldn't be in this mess."

"Mean, don't mean," Mrs. O'Keefe grunted. "Never understand what you people are going on about. Even you." And again she pointed at Charles Wallace, though this time she did not overturn her glass.

Sandy glanced across the table at his baby brother, who looked pale and small. "Charles, you've eaten hardly anything, and you're not talking."

Charles Wallace replied, looking not at Sandy but at his sister, "I'm listening."

She pricked up her ears. "To what?"

He shook his head so slightly that only she saw; and stopped questioning.

"At Tara in this fateful hour I place all Heaven with its power!" Mrs. O'Keefe pointed at Charles and knocked over her glass again.

This time nobody moved to mop up.

"My grandma from Ireland. She taught me. Set great store on it. I place all Heaven with its power . . ." Her words dribbled off.

Mrs. O'Keefe's children called her Mom. From everybody except Calvin it sounded like an insult. Meg found it difficult to call her mother-in-law anything, but now she pushed her chair away from the table and knelt by the old woman. "Mom," she said gently, "what did your grandmother teach you?"

"Set great store on it to ward off the dark."

"But what?"

". . . All Heaven with its power,"

Mrs. O'Keefe said in a singsong way,

"And the sun with its brightness,
And the snow with its whiteness,
And the fire with all the strength it hath—"

At that moment it seemed as though a bucketful of water had been dumped down the chimney onto the fire. The flames flickered wildly, and gusts of smoke blew into the room.

"The fire with all the strength it hath," Charles Wallace repeated firmly.

The applewood logs sizzled but the flames gathered strength and began to burn brightly again.

Mrs. O'Keefe put a gnarled hand on Meg's shoulder and pressed down heavily as though it helped her to remember.

"And the—the lightning with its rapid wrath,
And the winds with their swiftness along their path—"

The wind gave a tremendous gust, and the house shook under the impact, but stood steady.

Mrs. O'Keefe pressed until Meg could barely stand the weight.

"And the sea with its deepness,
And the rocks with their steepness,
And the earth with its starkness—"

Using Meg's shoulder as a lever, she pushed herself up and stood facing the bright flames in the fireplace.

"All these I place
By God's almighty help and grace
Between myself and the powers of darkness."

Her voice rose triumphantly. "That'll teach Mad Dog Bran-what's-his name."

The twins looked at each other as though embarrassed. Mr. Murry carved some more turkey. Mrs. Murry's face was serene and uncommunicative. Charles Wallace looked thoughtfully at Mrs. O'Keefe. Meg rose from her knees and returned to her chair, escaping the unbelievably heavy pressure of her mother-in-law's hand. She was sure that her shoulder was going to hold black and blue finger marks.

As Meg moved away, Mrs. O'Keefe seemed to crumple. She collapsed into her chair. "Set high store on that, my grandma did. Haven't thought of it in years. Tried not to think. So why'd it come to me tonight?" She gasped, as though exhausted.

"It's something like *Patrick's Breastplate*," Sandy said. "We sang that in glee club in college. It was one of my favorites. Marvelous harmonies."

"Not a song," Mrs. O'Keefe contradicted. "A rune. Patrick's rune. To hold up against danger. In this fateful hour I place all Heaven with its power—"

Without warning, the lights went out. A gust of wind dashed across the table, blowing out the candles. The humming of the refrigerator ceased. There was no purring from the furnace in the cellar. A cold dampness clutched the room, filling their nostrils with a stench of decay. The flames in the fireplace dwindled.

"Say it, Mom!" Charles Wallace called. "Say it all!"

Mrs. O'Keefe's voice was weak. "I forget—"

The lightning outside was so brilliant that light penetrated the closed curtains. A tremendous crash of thunder followed immediately.

"I'll say it with you." Charles Wallace's voice was urgent. "But you'll have to help me. Come on. In this fateful hour I place all Heaven with its power . . ."

Lightning and thunder were almost simultaneous. Then they heard a gigantic crackling noise.

"One of the trees has been struck," Mr. Murry said.

"All Heaven with its power," Charles Wallace repeated.

The old woman's voice took up the words. "And the sun with its brightness . . ."

Dennys struck a match and lit the candles. At first the flames flickered and guttered wildly, but then steadied and burned straight and bright.

> *"And the snow with its whiteness,*
> *And the fire with all the strength it hath*
> *And the lightning with its rapid wrath . . ."*

Meg waited for the lightning to flash again, for the house itself to be struck. Instead, the power came back on as abruptly as it had gone off. The furnace began to hum. The room was filled with light and warmth.

> *". . . And the sea with its deepness,*
> *And the rocks with their steepness,*
> *And the earth with its starkness,*
> *All these I place*
> *By God's almighty help and grace*
> *Between myself and the powers of darkness."*

Charles Wallace lifted the curtains away from one corner of the window. "The rain's turned to snow. The ground's all white and beautiful."

"All right—" Sandy looked around the room. "What's this all about? I know something's happened, but what?"

For a moment no one spoke. Then Meg said, "Maybe there's hope."

Sandy waved her words away. "Really, Meg, be reasonable."

"Why? We don't live in a reasonable world. Nuclear war is not reasonable. Reason hasn't got us anywhere."

"But you can't throw it out. Branzillo is mad and there's no reason in him."

Dennys said, "Okay, Sandy, I agree with you. But what happened?"

Meg glanced at Charles Wallace, but he had his withdrawn, listening look.

Sandy replied, "Much as we'd like it to, a freak of weather here in the Northeastern United States isn't going to have anything to do with whether or not a South American madman pushes that button to start the war that very likely *will* be the war to end wars."

The baby moved within Meg, a strong affirmation of life. "Father, is the President going to call again?"

"He said he would when—when there's any news. One way or other."

"Within twenty-four hours?"

"Yes. I would not want to be in his position at the moment."

"Or in ours," Dennys said. "It strikes me the whole world is in it together."

Charles Wallace continued to look out the window. "The snow's stopping. The wind has shifted to the northwest. The clouds are moving. I see a star." He let the curtain drop.

Mrs. O'Keefe jerked her chin toward him. "You. Chuck. I come because of you."

"Why, Mom?" he asked gently.

"You know."

He shook his head.

"Stop him, Chuck. Stop Mad Dog Bran . . . Stop him." She looked old and small and Meg wondered how she could have pressed down so heavily on her shoulder. And twice Mrs. O'Keefe had called Charles Wallace *Chuck*. Nobody ever called him Chuck. Occasionally plain Charles, but never Charlie or Chuck.

Mrs. Murry asked, "Mrs. O'Keefe, would you like some tea? or coffee?"

Mrs. O'Keefe cackled without mirth. "That's right. Don't hear. Think I'm crackers. Not such a fool as all that. Chuck knows." She nodded toward Charles Wallace. "Woke up this morning, and wasn't going to come. Then something told me I was to come, like it or not, and didn't know why till I saw you with them big ancient eyes and the rune started to come back to me, and I knowed once more Chuck's no idiot. Haven't thought of the rune since my grandma and Chuck, till now. You've got it, Chuck. Use it." Her breath ran out. It was the longest speech they had ever heard her give. Panting, she finished. "I want to go home." And, as no one spoke: "Someone take me home."

"But, Mrs. O'Keefe," Dennys wheedled, "we haven't had salad, and it's got lots of avocado and tomato in it, and then there's flaming plum pudding."

"Flame yourself. I done what I come for. Someone take me home."

"Very well, Mrs. O'Keefe." Mr. Murry rose. "Den or Sandy, will you drive Mrs. O'Keefe home?"

"I will," Dennys said. "I'll get your coat, ma'am."

When the car had driven off, Sandy said, "One could almost take her seriously."

The Murry parents exchanged glances, and Mrs. Murry replied, "I do."

"Oh, come on, Mother, all that rune stuff, and Charles Wallace stopping Mad Dog Branzillo singlehanded?"

"Not necessarily that. But I take Mrs. O'Keefe seriously."

Meg looked anxiously at Charles Wallace, spoke to her mother. "You've always said there was more to her than meets the eye. I guess we've just seen some of that more."

"I rather think we have," her father said.

"All right, then, what was it all about? It was all—all unnatural."

"What's natural?" Charles Wallace asked.

Sandy raised his eyebrows. "Okay, little brother, what do you make of it, then? How do you plan to stop Branzillo?"

"I don't know," Charles Wallace replied seriously. "I'll use the rune."

"Do you remember it?" Meg asked.

"I remember it."

"Did you hear her call you Chuck?"

"I heard."

"But nobody ever calls you Chuck. Where did she get it?"

"I'm not sure. Out of the past, maybe."

The phone rang, and they all jumped. Mr. Murry hurried to the phone table, then drew back an instant before picking up the receiver.

But it was not the President. It was Calvin, calling from London. He spoke briefly to everybody, was sorry to miss his mother and Dennys; but he was delighted that his mother had come; his paper had gone extremely well; the conference was interesting. At the last he asked to speak to Meg again, and said only, "I love you," and hung up.

"I always fall apart on overseas calls," she said, "so I don't think he noticed anything. There isn't any point telling him when he can't do anything about it, and it would just make it awful for him . . ." She turned away as Dennys came in, blowing on his fingers.

"Calvin called from London." She swallowed her tears. "He sends you his best."

"Sorry to have missed him. How about some salad, now, and then that plum pudding?"

—Why are we trying to act normal? Meg wondered, but did not speak her thought aloud.

But Charles Wallace replied, "It's sort of like the string holding the package together, Meg. We'd all fall apart otherwise."

Her father said, "You know, my dears, the world has been abnormal for so long that we've forgotten what it's like to live in a peaceful and reasonable climate. If there is to be any peace or reason, we have to create it in our own hearts and homes."

"Even at a time like this?" Meg asked. The call from Calvin, the sound of her husband's voice, had nearly broken her control.

"Especially at a time like this," her mother said gently. "We don't know what the next twenty-four hours are going to bring, and if it should be what we fear, then the peace and quiet within us will come to our aid."

"Will it?" Meg's voice faltered again.

"Remember," Mr. Murry said, "your mother and I take Mrs. O'Keefe seriously."

"Father," Sandy chided, "you're a pure scientist. You can't take that old woman seriously."

"I take the response of the elements to her rune seriously."

"Coincidence," Dennys said without much assurance.

"My training in physics has taught me that there is no such thing as coincidence."

"Charles Wallace still hasn't said anything." Meg looked to her small brother.

Dennys asked, "What about it, Charles?"

He shook his head slowly. He looked bewildered. "I don't know. I think I'm supposed to do something, but I don't know what. But if I'm meant to do something, I'll be told."

"By some little men from outer space?" Sandy asked.

"Something in me will tell me. I don't think any of us wants more salad. Let's turn out the lights and let Father flame the pudding."

"I'm not sure I want the lights out," Meg said. "Maybe there isn't going to be any more electricity, ever. Let's enjoy it while we have it."

"I'd rather enjoy the light of the plum pudding," Charles Wallace said.

Mrs. Murry took the pudding from the double boiler where it had been steaming, and turned it out onto a plate. Dennys took a sprig of holly and stuck it on the top. Mr. Murry got a bottle of brandy and poured it liberally over the pudding. As he lit the match, Charles Wallace turned out the lights and Sandy blew out the candles. The brandy burned with a brilliant blue flame; it seemed brighter than Meg remembered from other Thanksgivings. It had always been their traditional holiday dessert because, as Mrs. Murry remarked, you can't make pie crust over a Bunsen burner, and her attempts at mince or pumpkin pie had not been successes.

Mr. Murry tilted the dish so that all the brandy would burn. The flames continued, bright and clear and blue, a blue that held in it the warmth of a summer sky rather than the chill of winter.

"And the fire with all the strength it hath," Charles Wallace said softly.

"But what kind of strength?" Meg asked. She looked at the logs crackling merrily in the fireplace. "It can keep you warm, but if it gets out of hand it can burn your house down. It can destroy forests. It can burn whole cities."

"Strength can always be used to destroy as well as create," Charles Wallace said. "This fire is to help and heal."

"I hope," Meg said. "Oh, I hope."

2 All Heaven with Its Power

Meg sat propped up on pillows in the old brass bed in the attic and tried to read, because thinking hurt too much, was not even thinking but projection into a fearful future. And Calvin was not beside her, to share, to strengthen . . . She let the book drop; it was one of her old volumes of fairy tales. She looked around the room, seeking comfort in familiar things. Her hair was down for the night and fell softly about her shoulders. She glanced at herself in the old, ripply mirror over the chest of drawers and despite her anxiety was pleased at the reflection. She looked like a child again, but a far lovelier child than she actually had been.

Her ears pricked up as she heard a soft, velvety tread, and a stripy kitten minced across the wide floorboards, sprang up onto the bed, and began grooming itself while purring loudly. There was always at least one kitten around, it seemed. She missed the old black dog. What would Fortinbras have made of the events of the evening? She would have been happier if the old dog had been in his usual forbidden place at the foot of the bed, because he had an unusual degree of sensitivity, even for a dog, to anything which could help or harm his human family.

Meg felt cold and pulled her battered quilt about her shoulders. She remembered Mrs. O'Keefe calling on all Heaven with its power, and thought shudderingly that she would settle for one large, loving dog. Heaven had shown considerable power that evening, and it was too wild and beyond control for comfort.

And Charles Wallace. She wanted her brother. Mrs. O'Keefe had called on Charles to stop Branzillo: he'd need all the powers Heaven could give him.

He had said good night to Meg in a brusque and preoccupied way, and then given her one quick blue glance which had made her keep the light on and the book open. Sleep, in any event, was far away, lost somewhere in that time which had been shattered by the President's phone call.

The kitten rose high on its legs, made three complete turns, and dropped, heavily for such a little creature, into the curve of her body. The purr slowly faded out and it slept. Meg wondered if she would ever again sleep in that secure way, relinquishing consciousness without fear of what might happen during the night. Her eyes felt dry with fatigue but she did not want to close them and shut out the reassurance of the student lamp with its double yellow globes, the sagging bookshelves she had made with boards and bricks, the blue print curtains at the window; the hem of the curtains had been sagging for longer than she cared to remember and she had been meaning to sew it up since well before her marriage.—Tomorrow, she thought,—if there is a tomorrow.

When she heard footsteps on the attic stairs she stiffened, then relaxed. They had all got in the habit of automatically skipping the seventh step, which not only creaked when stepped on, but often made a sound like a shot. She and Charles Wallace had learned to put one foot on the extreme left of the step so that it let out only a long, slow sigh; when either one of them did this, it was a signal for a conference.

She listened to his progress across the attic, heard the rocking of the old wooden horse as he gave it his usual affectionate slap on the rump, followed by the whing of a dart going into the cork board: all the little signals they had built up over the years.

He pushed through the long strands of patterned rice which curtained the doorway, stood at the foot of the bed, and rested his chin on the high brass rail of the footboard. He looked at her without smiling, then climbed over the footboard as he used to do when he was a little boy, and sat cross-legged on the foot of the bed. "She really does expect me to do something."

Meg nodded.

"For once I'm feeling more in sympathy with the twins than with Mother and Father. The twins think the whole thing is unreasonable and impossible."

"Well—remember, Mother always said there's more to her than meets the eye."

"What about the rune?"

Meg sighed. "She gave it to you."

"What am I supposed to do with it?"

"Stop Branzillo. And I guess I'm feeling like the twins, too. It just doesn't make sense."

"Have you ever really talked with her? Do you know her at all?"

"No. I don't think anyone does. Calvin thinks she stopped herself from being hurt long, long ago by not letting herself love anybody or anything."

"What's her maiden name?" Charles Wallace asked abruptly.

Meg frowned. "I don't remember. Why?"

"I'm not sure. I feel completely in the dark. But she said her grandmother gave her the rune . . . Do you know her first name?"

Meg closed her eyes, thinking. "Branwen. That's it. And she gave me a pair of linen sheets for a wedding present. They were filthy. I had to wash them half a dozen times, and then they turned out to be beautiful. They must have been from her hope chest, and they had embroidered initials, bMz."

"Z and M for what?"

"I don't remember . . ."

"Think, Meg. Let me try to kythe it."

Again she closed her eyes and tried to relax. It was as though too much conscious intensity of thinking made her brain rigid and closed, and if she breathed slowly and deeply it opened up, and memories and thoughts were freed to come to her consciousness where she could share them with Charles Wallace.

"The M—" she said slowly. "I think it's Maddox."

"Maddox. It's trying to tell me something, Maddox, but I'm not sure what. Meg, I want you to tell me everything about her you possibly can."

"I don't know much."

"Meg—" The pupils of his eyes enlarged so that the iris was only a pale blue ring. "Somehow or other she's got something to do with Branzillo."

"That's—that's—"

"—absurd. That's what the twins would say. And it is. But she came tonight of all nights, when she's never been willing to come before. And you heard her say that she didn't want to come but she felt impelled to. And then she began to remember a rune she hadn't thought of since she was a child, and she told me to use it to stop Branzillo."

"And she said we thought she was crackers."

"But she isn't. Mother and Father know that. And nobody can accuse them of being dimwitted daydreamers. What does the Z stand for?"

Again Meg shook her head. "I don't know. I don't even remember if I asked, though I think I must have."

"Branwen Maddox. Branwen Z. Maddox." He rubbed his fingers over his forehead. "Maddox. There's a clue there."

The kitten yawned and went *brrtt* as though they were disturbing it. Meg reached out and gently knuckled its hard little head and then scratched the soft fur under the chin until it started to purr again and slowly closed its eyes.

"Maddox—it's in a song, or a ballad, about two brothers fighting, like *Childe Harold* maybe. Or maybe a narrative poem—" He buried his head in his hands. "Why can't I remember!" he demanded in frustration.

"Is it that important?"

"Yes! I don't know why, but it is. Maddox—fighting his brother and angering the gods . . ."

"But, Charles—what does some old story have to do with anything?"

"It's a clue. But I can't get enough . . . Is it very cold out?"

Meg looked surprised. "I don't think so. Why?"

Charles Wallace gazed out the window. "The snow hasn't melted, but there isn't much wind. And I need to listen."

"The best listening place is the star-watching rock."

He nodded thoughtfully. The large, flattish glacial rock left over from the time when oceans of ice had pushed across the land, and which the family called the star-watching rock because it gave them a complete and unobstructed view of the sky, was indeed a good place to listen. When they lay on it to watch the stars they looked straight across the valleys to the hills. Behind the rock was a small woods. There was no sight of civilization, and little sound. Occasionally they heard the roar of a truck far away on the highway, or a plane tracking across the sky. But mostly it was quiet enough so that all they heard was the natural music of the seasons. Sometimes in the spring Meg thought she could hear the grass grow. In the autumn the tree toads sang back and forth as though they couldn't bear to let the joys of summer pass. In the winter when the temperature dropped swiftly she was sometimes startled by the sound of ice freezing with a sharp cracking noise like a rifle retort. This Thanksgiving night—if nothing more unusual or horrible happened—would be quiet. It was too late in the year for tree toads and locusts and crickets. They might hear a few tired leaves sighing wearily from their branches, or the swoosh of the tall grasses parting as a small nocturnal animal made its way through the night.

Charles Wallace said, "Good idea. I'll go."

"I'll go with you."

"No. Stay here."

"But—"

"You know Dr. Louise was afraid you were going to get pneumonia last week when you had that bad chest cold. You mustn't risk getting cold again, for the baby's sake."

"All right, Charles, but, oh—"

"Meg," he said gently. "Something's blocking me, and I need to get unblocked. I have to be alone. But I'll need you to kythe with me."

She looked troubled. "I'm out of practice—" Kything was being able to be with someone else, no matter how far away they might be, was talking in a language that was deeper than words. Charles Wallace was born with this gift; slowly she became able to read the thoughts he sent her, to know what he wanted her to know. Kything went far beyond ordinary ESP, and while it came to Charles Wallace as naturally as breathing, for Meg it took intense concentration. Charles Wallace and Calvin were the only two people with whom she was able to give and receive this language that went far beyond words.

Charles Wallace assured her. "It's like swimming, or riding a bike. Once you learn, you never forget."

"I know—but I want to go with you." She tried to hold back the thought,—To protect you.

"Meg." His voice was urgent. "I'm going to need you, but I'm going to need you *here*, to kythe with me, all the way."

"All the way where?"

His face was white and strained. "I don't know yet. I have a feeling it will be a long way, and yet what has to be done has to be done quickly."

"Why you?"

"It may not be me. We're not certain. But it has to be somebody."

—If it's not somebody, Meg thought,—then the world, at least the world as we know it, is likely to come to an end.

She reached out and gave her little brother a hug and a kiss. "Peace go with you."

She turned out the light and lay down to wait until she heard him in her mind. The kitten stretched and yawned and slept, and its very indifference was a comfort. Then the sharp sound of a dog barking made her sit up.

The barking continued, sharp and demanding, very much like Fortinbras when he was asking for attention. She turned on the light. The barking stopped. Silence. Why had it stopped?

She got out of bed and hurriedly slipped into a robe and slippers and went downstairs, forgetting the seventh step, which groaned loudly. In the kitchen she saw her parents and Charles Wallace all stroking a large, nondescript dog.

Mrs. Murry looked with no surprise at Meg. "I think our dog has found us."

Mr. Murry pulled gently at the dog's upright ear; the other drooped. "She's a 'yaller dog' in looks, but she appears to be gentle and intelligent."

"No collar or anything," Charles Wallace said. "She's hungry, but not overly thin."

"Will you fix her some food, Meg?" Mrs. Murry asked. "There's still some in the pantry left over from Fortinbras."

As Meg stirred up a bowl of food she thought,—We're all acting as though this dog is going to be with us for a long time.

It wasn't the coming of the dog that was strange, or their casual acceptance of it. Fortinbras had come to them in the same way, simply appearing at the door, an overgrown puppy. It was the very ordinariness of it which made tears prickle briefly against her lashes.

"What are we going to call her?" Mrs. Murry asked.

Charles Wallace spoke calmly. "Her name is Ananda."

Meg looked at him, but he only smiled slightly. She put the food down and the dog ate hungrily, but tidily.

"Ananda," Mrs. Murry said thoughtfully. "That rings some kind of bell."

"It's Sanskrit," Charles Wallace said.

Meg asked, "Does it mean anything?"

"That joy in existence without which the universe will fall apart and collapse."

"That's a mighty big name for one dog to carry," Mrs. Murry said.

"She's a large dog, and it's her name," Charles Wallace responded.

When Ananda had finished eating, licking Fortinbras's old bowl till it was clean, she went over to Meg, tail wagging, and held up one paw. Meg took it; the pads felt roughly leathery and cool. "You're beautiful, Ananda."

"She's hardly that," Mr. Murry said, smiling, "but she certainly knows how to make herself at home."

The kettle began to sing. "I'm making tea against the cold." Mrs. Murry turned off the burner and filled the waiting pot. "Then we'd better go to bed. It's very late."

"Mother," Meg asked, "do you know what Mrs. O'Keefe's first name is? Is it Branwen?"

"I think so, though I doubt if I'll ever feel free to call her that." She placed a steaming cup in front of Meg.

"You remember the sheets she gave us?"

"Yes, superb old linen sheets."

"With initials. A large M in the middle, with a smaller b and z on either side. Do you know what the Z stands for?"

"Zoe or Zillah or something unusual like that. Why?"

Meg answered with another question. "Does the name Branwen mean anything? It's sort of odd."

"It's a common enough Irish name. I think the first Branwen was a queen in Ireland, though she came from England. Perhaps she was a Pict, I'm not sure."

"When?" Charles Wallace asked.

"I don't know exactly. Long ago."

"More than two thousand years?"

"Maybe three thousand. Why?"

Charles Wallace poured milk into his tea and studied the cloudy liquid. "It just might be important. After all, it's Mom O'Keefe's name."

"She was born right here in the village, wasn't she?" Meg asked.

Her father replied, "There've been Maddoxes here as far back as anybody remembers. She's the last of the name, but they were an important family in the eighteenth and nineteenth centuries. They've known hard times since then."

"What happened?" Charles Wallace pursued.

Mr. Murry shook his head. "I keep thinking that one of these years your mother or I'll have time to do research into the early years of the village. Our roots are here, too, buried somewhere in the past. I inherited this house from a great-aunt I hardly knew, just at the time we were making up our minds to leave the pressures of the city and continue our research in peace and quiet—and getting the house swung the balance."

"As for time for other interests"—Mrs. Murry sounded rueful—"we don't have any more time than we did in the city. But at least here the pressure to work is our own, and not imposed on us."

"This Branwen—" Charles Wallace persisted, "was she an important queen?"

Mrs. Murry raised her fine brows. "Why this sudden and intense interest?"

"Branwen Maddox O'Keefe was extraordinarily interesting this evening."

Mrs. Murry sipped her tea. "I haven't thought about the mythologies of the British Isles since you all grew too old for reading aloud at bedtime. I suspect Branwen must have been important or I wouldn't remember her at all. Sorry not to be able to tell you more. I've been thinking more about cellular biology than mythology these last few years."

Charles Wallace finished his tea and put the cup in the sink. "All right if I go for a walk?"

"I'd rather not," his father said. "It's late."

"Please, Father, I need to listen." He sounded and looked very young.

"Can't you listen here?"

"Too many distractions, too many people's thoughts in the way . . ."

"Can't it wait?"

Charles Wallace looked at his father without answering.

Mr. Murry sighed. "None of us takes Mrs. O'Keefe and all that happened this evening lightly, but you've always tended to take too much on yourself."

The boy's voice strained. "This time I'm not taking it on myself. Mrs. O'Keefe put it on me."

His father looked at him gravely, then nodded. "Where are you going?"

"Not far. Just to the star-watching rock."

Mr. Murry rinsed his teacup, rinsed it, and rinsed it again. "You're still a child."

"I'm fifteen. And there's nothing to hurt me between home and the star-watching rock."

"All right. Don't stay long."

"No longer than necessary."

"Take Ananda with you."

"I need to be alone. Please, Father."

Mr. Murry took off his glasses, looked at his son through them at a distance, put them on again. "All right, Charles."

Meg looked at her mother and guessed that she was holding back from telling her youngest child not to forget to put on boots and a warm jacket.

Charles Wallace smiled toward their mother. "I'll wear the blue anorak Calvin brought me from Norway." He turned the last of his smile to his sister, then went into the pantry, shutting the kitchen door firmly behind him.

"Time for the rest of us to go to bed," Mrs. Murry said. "You particularly, Meg. You don't want to catch more cold."

"I'll take Ananda with me."

Her father objected. "We don't even know if she's housebroken."

"She ate like a well-trained dog."

"It's up to you, then."

Meg did not know why she felt such relief at the coming of the big yellow dog. After all, Ananda could not be her dog. When Calvin returned from London they would go back to their rented apartment, where pets were not allowed, and Ananda would remain with the Murrys. But that was all right; Ananda, she felt, was needed.

The dog followed Meg upstairs as though she'd been with the Murrys all her life, trotted through the cluttered attic and into Meg's room. The kitten was asleep on the bed, and the big dog sniffed the small puff of fur, tail wagging in an ecstasy of friendliness. Her tail was large and long, with a smattering of golden feathers, which might possibly indicate some kind of setter or Labrador blood in her genetic pattern, the kind of tail which could create as much havoc in a china shop as a bull. The kitten opened its eyes, gave a small, disinterested hiss, and went back to sleep. With one leap, Ananda landed on the bed, thumping heavily and happily with her mighty tail. The kitten rose and stalked to the pillow.

As she had so often said to Fortinbras, Meg announced, "Sleeping on the bed isn't allowed." Ananda's amber eyes looked at her imploringly and she whined softly. "Well—only up here. Never downstairs. If you want to be part of this household you'll have to understand that."

Ananda thumped; light from the student lamp glinted against her eyes, turning them to gold. Her coat shone with a healthy glow.

"Make way for me." Meg climbed back into bed. "Now, Ananda"— she was taking comfort in reverting to her child's habit of talking out loud to the family animals—"what we're going to do is listen, very intently, for Charles Wallace. You have to help me kythe, or you'll have to get off the bed." She rubbed her hand over Ananda's coat, which smelled of ferns and moss and autumn berries, and felt a warm and gentle tingling, which vibrated through her hand and up her arm. Into her mind's eye came a clear image of Charles Wallace walking across what had once been the twins' vegetable garden, but which was now a small grove of young Christmas trees, a project they could care for during vacations. Their magnificent vegetable garden had been plowed under when they went to college. Meg missed it, but she knew that both her parents were much too busy to tend to more than a small patch of lettuce and tomatoes.

Charles Wallace continued to walk along the familiar route.

Hand resting on Ananda, the tingling warmth flowing back and forth between them, Meg followed her brother's steps. When he reached the open space where the star-watching rock was, Ananda's breathing quickened; Meg could feel the rise and fall of the big dog's rib cage under her hand.

There was no moon, but starlight touched the winter grasses with silver. The woods behind the rock were a dark shadow. Charles Wallace looked across the valley, across the dark ridge of pines, to the shadows of the hills beyond. Then he threw back his head and called,

> *"In this fateful hour*
> *I call on all Heaven with its power!"*

The brilliance of the stars increased. Charles Wallace continued to gaze upward. He focused on one star which throbbed with peculiar intensity. A beam of light as strong as a ladder but clear as water flowed between the star and Charles Wallace, and it was impossible to tell whether the light came from the piercing silver-blue of the star or the light blue eyes of the boy. The beam became stronger and firmer and then all the light resolved itself in a flash of radiance beside the boy. Slowly the radiance took on form, until it had enfleshed itself into the body of a great white beast with flowing mane and tail. From its forehead sprang a silver horn which contained the residue of the light. It was a creature of utter and absolute perfection.

The boy put his hand against the great white flanks, which heaved as though the creature had been racing. He could feel the warm blood coursing through the veins as the light had coursed between star and boy. "Are you real?" he asked in a wondering voice.

The creature gave a silver neigh which translated itself into the boy's mind as "I am not real. And yet in a sense I am that which is the only reality."

"Why have you come?" The boy's own breath was rapid, not so much with apprehension as with excitement and anticipation.

"You called on me."

"The rune—" Charles Wallace whispered. He looked with loving appreciation at the glorious creature standing beside him on the star-watching rock. One silver-shod hoof pawed lightly, and the rock rang with clarion sound. "A unicorn. A real unicorn."

"That is what you call me. Yes."

"What are you, really?"

"What are *you*, really?" the unicorn countered. "You called me, and because there is great need, I am here."

"You know the need?"

"I have seen it in your mind."

"How is it that you speak my language?"

The unicorn neighed again, the sound translucent as silver bubbles. "I do not. I speak the ancient harmony."

"Then how is it that I understand?"

"You are very young, but you belong to the Old Music."

"Do you know my name?"

"Here, in this When and Where, you are called Charles Wallace. It is a brave name. It will do."

Charles Wallace stretched up on tiptoe to reach his arms about the beautiful beast's neck. "What am I to call you?"

"You may call me Gaudior." The words dropped on the rock like small bells.

Charles Wallace looked thoughtfully at the radiance of the horn. "Gaudior. That's Latin for *more joyful*."

The unicorn neighed in acquiescence.

"That joy in existence without which . . ."

Gaudior struck his hoof lightly on the rock, with the sound of a silver trumpet. "Do not push your understanding too far."

"But I'm not wrong about Gaudior?"

"In a sense, yes; in a sense, no."

"You're real and you're not real; I'm wrong and I'm right."

"What is real?" Gaudior's voice was as crystal as the horn.

"What am I supposed to do, now that I've called on all Heaven with its power and you've come?"

Gaudior neighed. "Heaven may have sent me, but my powers are closely defined and narrowly limited. And I've never been sent to your planet before. It's considered a hardship assignment." He looked down in apology.

Charles Wallace studied the snow-dusted rock at his feet. "We haven't done all that well by our planet, have we?"

"There are many who would like to let you wipe yourselves out, except it would affect us all; who knows what might happen? And as long as there are even a few who belong to the Old Music, you are still our brothers and sisters."

Charles Wallace stroked Gaudior's long, aristocratic nose. "What should I do, then?"

"We're in it together." Gaudior knelt delicately and indicated that Charles Wallace was to climb up onto his back. Even with the unicorn kneeling, it was with difficulty that the boy clambered up and sat astride, up toward the great neck, so that he could hold on to the silver mane. He pressed his feet in their rubber boots as tightly as he could against the unicorn's flanks.

Gaudior asked, "Have you ridden the wind before?"

"No."

"We have to be careful of Echthroi," Gaudior warned. "They try to ride the wind and throw us off course."

"Echthroi—" Charles Wallace's eyes clouded. "That means *the enemy*."

"Echthroi," Gaudior repeated. "The ancient enemy. He who distorted the harmony, and who has gathered an army of destroyers. They are everywhere in the universe."

Charles Wallace felt a ripple of cold move along his spine.

"Hold my mane," the unicorn advised. "There's always the possibility of encountering an Echthros, and if we do, it'll try to unseat you."

Charles Wallace's knuckles whitened as he clutched the heavy mane. The unicorn began to run, skimming over the tops of the grasses, up, over the hills, flinging himself onto the wind and riding with it, up, up, over the stars . . .

3 The Sun with Its Brightness

In her attic bedroom Meg regarded Ananda, who thumped her massive tail in a friendly manner. "What's this about?" Meg demanded.

Ananda merely thudded again, waking the kitten, who gave a half-hearted *brrtt* and stalked across the pillow.

Meg looked at her battered alarm clock, which stood in its familiar place on the bookcase. The hands did not seem to have moved. "Whatever's going on, I don't understand."

Ananda whined softly, an ordinary whine coming from an ordinary dog of questionable antecedents, a mongrel like many in the village.

"Gaudior," Meg murmured. "More joyful. That's a good name for a unicorn. *Gaudior, Ananda:* that joy without which the universe will fall apart and collapse. Has the world lost its joy? Is that why we're in such a mess?" She stroked Ananda thoughtfully, then held up the hand which had been pressing against the dog's flank. It glowed with radiant warmth. "I told Charles Wallace I'm out of practice in kything. Maybe I've been settling for the grownup world. How did you know we needed you, Ananda? And when I touch you I can kythe even more deeply than I've ever done before." She put her hand back on the comfortable flank and closed her eyes, shivering with the strain of concentration.

She saw neither Charles Wallace nor the unicorn. She saw neither the familiar earth with the star-watching rock, the woods, the hills, nor the night sky with its countless galaxies. She saw nothing. Nothing. There was no wind to ride or be blown by.

Nothing was. She was not. There was no dark. There was no light. No sight nor sound nor touch nor smell nor taste. No sleeping nor waking. No dreaming, no knowing.

Nothing.

And then a surge of joy.

All senses alive and awake and filled with joy.

Darkness was, and darkness was good. As was light.

Light and darkness dancing together, born together, born of each other, neither preceding, neither following, both fully being, in joyful rhythm.

The morning stars sang together and the ancient harmonies were new and it was good. It was very good.

And then a dazzling star turned its back on the dark, and it swallowed the dark, and in swallowing the dark it became the dark, and there was something wrong with the dark, as there was something wrong with the light. And it was not good. The glory of the harmony was broken by screeching, by hissing, by laughter which held no merriment but was hideous, horrendous cacophony.

With a strange certainty Meg knew that she was experiencing what Charles Wallace was experiencing. She saw neither Charles Wallace nor the unicorn, but she knew through Charles Wallace's knowing.

The breaking of the harmony was pain, was brutal anguish, but the harmony kept rising above the pain, and the joy would pulse with light, and light and dark once more knew each other, and were part of the joy.

Stars and galaxies rushed by, came closer, closer, until many galaxies were one galaxy, one galaxy was one solar system, one solar system was one planet. There was no telling which planet, for it was still being formed. Steam boiled upward from its molten surface. Nothing could live in this primordial caldron.

Then came the riders of the wind when all the riders sang the ancient harmonies and the melody was still new, and the gentle breezes cooled the burning. And the boiling, hissing, flaming, steaming, turned to rain, aeons of rain, clouds emptying themselves in continuing torrents of rain which covered the planet with healing darkness, until the clouds were nearly emptied and a dim light came through their veils and touched the water of the ocean so that it gleamed palely, like a great pearl.

Land emerged from the seas, and on the land green began to spread. Small green shoots rose to become great trees, ferns taller than the tallest oaks. The air was fresh and smelled of rain and sun, of green of tree and plant, blue of sky.

The air grew heavy with moisture. The sun burned like brass behind a thick gauze of cloud. Heat shimmered on the horizon. A towering fern was pushed aside by a small greenish head on a long, thick neck, emerging from a massive body. The neck swayed sinuously while the little eyes peered about.

Clouds covered the sun. The tropical breeze heightened, became a cold wind. The ferns drooped and withered. The dinosaurs struggled to move away from the cold, dying as their lungs collapsed from the radical change in temperature. Ice moved inexorably across the land. A great white bear padded along, snuffling, looking for food.

Ice and snow and then rain again and at last sunlight breaking through the clouds, and green again, green of grass and trees, blue of sky by day, sparkle of stars by night.

Unicorn and boy were in a gentle, green glade, surrounded by trees.

"Where are we?" Charles Wallace asked.

"We're here," the unicorn replied impatiently.

"Here?"

Gaudior snorted. "Don't you recognize it?"

Charles Wallace looked around at the unfamiliar landscape. Tree ferns spread their fronds skyward as though drinking blue. Other trees appeared to be lifting their branches to catch the breeze. The boy turned to Gaudior. "I've never been here before."

Gaudior shook his head in puzzlement. "But it's your own Where, even if it's not your own When."

"My own what?"

"Your own Where. Where you stood and called on all Heaven with its power and I was sent to you."

Again Charles Wallace scanned the unfamiliar landscape and shook his head.

"It's a very different When," Gaudior conceded. "You're not accustomed to moving through time?"

"I've moved through fifteen years' worth of time."

"But only in one direction."

"Oh—" Understanding came to the boy. "This isn't my time, is it? Do you mean that Where we are now is the same place as the star-watching rock and the woods and the house, but it's a different time?"

"For unicorns it is easier to move about in time than in space. Until we learn more what we are meant to do, I am more comfortable if we stay in the same Where."

"You know Where we are, then? I mean—When we are? Is it time gone, or time to be?"

"It is, I think, what you would call Once Upon a Time and Long Ago."

"So we're not in the present."

"Of course we are. Whenever we are is present."

"We're not in *my* present. We're not When we were when you came to me."

"When I was called to you," Gaudior corrected. "And When is not what matters. It's what happens in the When that matters. Are you ready to go?"

"But—didn't you say we're right here? Where the star-watching rock was—I mean, will be?"

"That's what I said." Gaudior's hoof pawed the lush green of the young grass. "If you are to accomplish what you have been asked to accomplish, you will have to travel in and out."

"In and out of time?"

"Time, yes. And people."

Charles Wallace looked at him in startlement. "What?"

"You have been called to find a Might-Have-Been, and in order to do this, you will have to be sent Within."

"Within—Within someone else? . . . But I don't know if I can."

"Why not?" Gaudior demanded.

"But—if I go Within someone else—what happens to my own body?"

"It will be taken care of."

"Will I get it back?"

"If all goes well."

"And if all does not go well?"

"Let us hold firmly to all going well."

Charles Wallace wrapped his arms about himself as though for warmth. "And you wonder that I'm frightened?"

"Of course you're frightened. I'm frightened, too."

"Gaudior, it's a very scary thing just to be told casually that you're going to be inside someone else's body. What happens to *me?*"

"I'm not entirely sure. But you don't get lost. You stay you. If all goes well."

"But I'm someone else, too?"

"If you're open enough."

"If I'm in another body, do I have to be strong enough for both of us?"

"Perhaps," Gaudior pointed out, "your host will be the stronger of the two. Are you willing?"

"I don't know . . ." He seemed to hear Meg warning him that it was always disastrous when he decided that he was capable of taking on, singlehanded, more than anyone should take on.

"It would appear," Gaudior said, "that you have been called. And the calling is never random, it is always according to the purpose."

"What purpose?"

Gaudior ignored him. "It appears that you are gifted in going Within."

"But I've never—"

"Are you not able to go Within your sister?"

"When we kythe, then, yes, a little. But I don't literally go Within Meg, or become Meg. I stay me."

"Do you?"

Charles Wallace pondered this. "When I'm kything with Meg, I'm wholly aware of her. And when she kythes with me, then she's more aware of me than she is of herself. I guess kything is something like your going Within—that makes it sound a little less scary."

Gaudior twitched his beard. "Now you have been called to go Within in the deepest way of all. And I have been called to help you." The light in his horn pulsed and dimmed. "You saw the beginning."

"Yes."

"And you saw how a destroyer, almost since the beginning, has tried to break the ancient harmonies?"

"Where did the destroyer come from?"

"From the good, of course. The Echthros wanted all the glory for itself, and when that happens the good becomes not good; and others have followed that first Echthros. Wherever the Echthroi go, the shadows follow, and try to ride the wind. There are places where no one has ever heard the ancient harmonies. But there is always a moment when there is a Might-Have-Been. What we must do is find the Might-Have-Beens which have led to this particular evil. I have seen many Might-Have-Beens. If such and such had been chosen, then this would not have followed. If so and so had been done, then the light would partner the dark instead of being snuffed out. It is possible that you can move into the moment of a Might-Have-Been and change it."

Charles Wallace's fingers tightened in the silver mane. "I know I can't avert disaster just because Mrs. O'Keefe told me to. I may be arrogant, but not that arrogant. But my sister is having a baby, and I can be strong enough to attempt to avert disaster for her sake. And Mrs. O'Keefe gave me the rune . . ." He looked around him at the fresh green world. Although he was still wearing boots and the warm Norwegian anorak, he was not uncomfortable. Suddenly song surrounded him, and a flock of golden birds settled in the trees. "When are we, then? How long ago?"

"Long. I took us all the way back before this planet's Might-Have-Beens, before people came and quarreled and learned to kill."

"How did we get to here—to long ago?"

"On the wind. The wind blows where it will."

"Will it take us Where—When—you want us to go?"

The light of the unicorn's horn pulsed, and the light in the horn, holding the blue of the sky, was reflected in Charles Wallace's eyes. "Before the harmonies were broken, unicorns and winds danced together with joy and no fear. Now there are Echthroi who are greedy for the wind, as for all else, so there are times when they ride the wind and turn it into a tornado, and you had better be grateful we didn't ride one of those—it's always a risk. But we did come to When I wanted, to give us a little time to catch our breaths."

The golden birds fluttered about them, and then the sky was filled with a cloud of butterflies which joined the birds in patterned flight. In the grass little jeweled lizards darted.

"Here the wind has not been troubled," Gaudior said. "Come. This glimpse is all I can give you of this golden time."

"Must we leave so soon?"

"The need is urgent."

Yes, the need was indeed urgent. Charles Wallace looked up at the unicorn. "Where do we go now?"

Gaudior pawed the lush green impatiently. "Not Where; can you not get that through your human skull? When. Until we know more than we know now, we will stay right here in your own Where. There is something to be learned here, and we have to find out what."

"You don't know?"

"I am a mere unicorn." Gaudior dropped his silver lashes modestly. "All I know is that there is something important to the future right here in this place where you watch stars. But whatever it was did not happen until the ancient music of the spheres was distorted. So now we go to a When of people."

"Do you know when that When is?"

The light in Gaudior's horn dimmed and flickered, which Charles Wallace was beginning to recognize as a sign that the unicorn was troubled or uncertain. "A far When. We can ride this wind without fear, for here the ancient harmonies are still unbroken. But it may roughen if the When we enter is a dissonant one. Hold on tight. I will be taking you Within."

"Within—who am I going Within?" Charles Wallace twined the mane through his fingers.

"I will ask the wind."

"You don't know?"

"Questions, questions." Gaudior stomped one silver hoof. "I am not some kind of computer. Only machines have glib answers for everything." The light in the horn pulsed with brilliance; sparks flew from Gaudior's hoofs, and they were off and up. The smooth flanks became fluid, and slowly great wings lifted and moved with the wind.

The boy felt the wind swoop under and about them. Riding the unicorn, riding the wind, he felt wholly in freedom and joy; wind, unicorn, boy, merged into a single swiftness.

Stars, galaxies, circled in cosmic pattern, and the joy of unity was greater than any disorder within.

And then, almost without transition, they were in a place of rocks and trees and high grasses and a large lake. What would, many centuries later, become the star-watching rock was a small mountain of stone. The woods behind the rock was a forest of towering fern trees and giant umbrageous trees he did not recognize. In front of the rock, instead of the valley of Charles Wallace's When, there was a lake stretching all the way to the hills, sparkling in the sunlight. Between the rock and the lake were strange huts of stone and hide, half house, half tent, forming a crescent at the lake's edge.

In front of and around the dwellings was activity and laughter, men and women weaving, making clay from the lake into bowls and dishes, painting the pottery with vivid colors and intricate geometrical designs. Children played at the water's edge, splashing and skipping pebbles.

A boy sat on an outcropping of rock, whittling a spear with a sharp stone. He was tanned and lean, with shining hair the color of a blackbird's wing, and dark eyes which sparkled like the water of the lake. His cheekbones were high, and his mouth warm and full. He gave the making of the spear his full concentration. He looked across the glinting waters of the lake and sniffed the scent of fish. Then he turned back to his spear, but his sensitive nostrils quivered almost imperceptibly as he smelled in turn the green of grass, the blue of sky, the red blood of an animal in the forest. He did not appear to notice the unicorn standing behind him on the hill of stone, or if he did, he took the beautiful creature completely for granted. Gaudior's wings were folded back into the flanks now, so that they were invisible; the light in the horn was steady.

Meg pressed her hand intently against Ananda. The big dog turned her head and licked her hand reassuringly with her warm, red tongue.

Meg felt her senses assailed with an awareness she had never experienced with such intensity before, even in childhood. The blue of
sky was so brilliant it dazzled her inner eye. Although it was cold in
the attic, she could feel the radiant warmth of the day; her skin drank
the loveliness of sun. She had never before smelled rock, nor the richness of the dark earth, nor the wine of the breeze, as she smelled them
now.

Why? How? She could see the unicorn, but she could not see
Charles Wallace. Where was he?

Then she understood.

Charles Wallace was Within the boy on the rock. In some strange
way, Charles Wallace *was* the boy on the rock, seeing through his eyes,
hearing through his ears (never had bird song trilled with such sparkling
clarity), smelling through his nose, and kything all that his awakened
senses received.

Gaudior neighed softly. "You must be careful," he warned. "You
are not Charles Wallace Murry. You must lose yourself as you do when
you kythe with your sister. You must become your host."

"My host—"

"Harcels, of the People of the Wind. You must not know more than
he knows. When you think thoughts outside his thoughts, you must keep
them from him. It is best if you do not even think them."

Charles Wallace stirred timidly within Harcels. How would he, himself, accept such an intrusion by another? Had he ever been so intruded?

"No," Gaudior replied, speaking only to that part of Charles Wallace
which was held back from complete unity with Harcels. "We do not
send anyone Within unless the danger is so great that—"

"That—"

The light in the horn flickered. "You know some of the possibilities
if your planet is blown up."

"A few," Charles Wallace said starkly. "It just might throw off the
balance of things, so that the sun would burst into a supernova."

"That is one of the possibilities, yes. Everything that happens within
the created Order, no matter how small, has its effect. If you are angry,
that anger is added to all the hate with which the Echthroi would distort
the melody and destroy the ancient harmonies. When you are loving,
that lovingness joins the music of the spheres."

Charles Wallace felt a ripple of unease wash over him. "Gaudior—
what am I supposed to do—Within Harcels?"

"You might start by enjoying being Within him," Gaudior suggested. "In this When, the world still knows the Old Music."

"Does he see you, as I do?"

"Yes."

"He is not surprised."

"To joy, nothing is surprising. Relax, Charles. Kythe with Harcels. *Be* Harcels. Let yourself go." He struck one hoof against rock, drawing sparks, leapt from the rock in a great arc, and galloped into the woods.

Harcels rose, stretched languorously. He, too, leapt from the rock with the gravity-defying ease of a ballet dancer, landed on the springy grass, rolled over in merriment, sprang to his feet, and ran to the water's edge, calling to the children, the weavers, the potters.

At the edge of the lake he stood very still, isolating himself from the activity around him. He pursed his lips and whistled, a long sweet summons, and then called softly, "Finna, Finna, Finna!"

Halfway across the lake there was a disturbance in the water and a large creature came swimming, leaping, flying, toward Harcels, who in turn flung himself into the water and swam swiftly to meet it.

Finna was akin to a dolphin, though not as large, and her skin was an iridescent blue-green. She had the gracious smile of a dolphin, and the same familiarity with sea and air. As she met Harcels she sent a small fountain of water through her blowhole, drenching the boy, who shouted with laughter.

For a few moments they wrestled together, and then Harcels was riding Finna, leaping through the air, holding tight as Finna dove down, down deep below the surface, gasping as she flashed again up into the sunlight, sending spray in every direction.

It was sheer joy.

What Charles Wallace had known in occasional flashes of beauty was Harcels's way of life.

In the attic bedroom Meg kept her hand on Ananda. A shudder moved like a wave over them both. "Oh, Ananda," Meg said, "why couldn't it have stayed that way? What happened?"

—When? Charles Wallace wondered.—When are we?

For Harcels, all Whens were Now. There was yesterday, which was gone, which was only a dream. There was tomorrow, which was a vision not unlike today. When was always Now, for there was little looking either backward or forward in this young world. If Now was good, yesterday, though a pleasurable dream, was not necessary. If Now was good, tomorrow would likely continue to be so.

The People of the Wind were gentle and harmonious. On the rare occasions when there was a difference of opinion, it was mediated by the Harmonizer, and his judgment was always accepted. Fish were caught, flesh shot with bow and arrow, never more than needed. Each person in the tribe knew what he was born to do, and no gift was considered greater or less than another. The Harmonizer held a position no more lofty than the youngest cook just learning to build a fire or clean a fish.

One day a wild boar of monstrous size chased a small party of hunters, and the smallest and slowest among them was gored in the side. Harcels helped carry him home, and knelt all through the night with the Healer, bringing fresh cool moss to lay against the fevered wound, singing the prayers of healing as each star moved in its own ordained dance across the sky.

In the morning there was great rejoicing, for not only was the fiery wound cooling but it was recognized that Harcels had found his gift and would be apprenticed to the Healer, and when the Healer went to dwell with those who move among the stars, Harcels would take his place.

The melody was clear and pure. The harmony was undistorted. Time was still young and the sun was bright by day and moved without fear to rest in the realm of distant stars by night.

Harcels had many friends among his people, but his heart's companions were beasts: Finna, and Eyrn, a great bird something between an eagle and a giant gull, and large enough for Harcels to ride. Eyrn's feathers were white, tipped with rose, shading to purple. She was crowned with a tuft of rosy feathers, and her eyes were ruby. With Harcels firmly astride she would fly high, high, higher, until the air was thin and the boy gasped for breath. She flew far and high, so that he could see the dwellings of distant tribes, could see the ocean that stretched, it seemed, across all the rest of the world.

Harcels asked the Teller of Tales about the other tribes.

"Leave them be," the Teller of Tales said in the sharpest voice he had ever been heard to use.

"But it might be fun to know them. They might have things to teach us."

"Harcels," the Teller of Tales said, "I, too, have ridden a creature like your Eyrn, and I have had my steed descend in a hidden place, that I might watch unseen. I saw a man kill a man."

"But why? Why ever would one man kill another?"

The Teller of Tales looked long into the clear eyes of the boy. "Let us hope you will never have to know."

It was easy for Charles Wallace to live Within Harcels, in the brightness of the young sun, where darkness was the friend of light. One day when Harcels was astride Eyrn, they flew over a cluster of dwellings and the boy started to ask Eyrn to descend, but Charles Wallace gently drew his thoughts to the pleasure of flight as Eyrn threw himself upon a stream of wind and glided with the merest motion of wings. Charles Wallace was not certain that this small interference was permissible; he knew only that if Harcels learned the ways of the tribes who knew how to kill, his joy would vanish with his innocence.

—It was the right thing to do, Meg kythed to him fiercely.—It has to be the right thing.

She looked again at the clock. The hands had barely moved. While the seasons were following each other in swift succession in that Other Time where Charles Wallace lived Within Harcels, time was arrested in her own present moment. Time was moving only in that When in which the land so familiar and dear to her was different, where the flat star-watching rock was a hill of stone, the green valley a lake, and the little woods a dark forest.

She sighed achingly for a time so full of joy that it was difficult to realize it had once been real.

Ananda whined and looked at Meg with great anxious eyes.

"What is it?" Meg asked in alarm. She heard Gaudior's neigh, and saw a pulsing of silver light, the diamond-brilliant light which lit the unicorn's horn.

Charles Wallace was astride Gaudior's great neck, looking from within his own eyes at Harcels, Within whom he had known such spontaneity and joy that his own awareness would evermore share in it. He rubbed his cheek gently against the unicorn's silver neck. "Thank you," he whispered.

"Don't thank me," Gaudior snorted. "I'm not the one to decide whom you go Within."

"Who does, then?"

"The wind."

"Does the wind tell you?"

"Not until you are Within. And don't expect it to be this way every time. I suspect that you were sent Within Harcels to help get you accustomed to Within-ing in the easiest way possible. And you must let yourself go even more deeply into your hosts if you are to recognize the right Might-Have-Beens."

"If I let myself go, how can I recognize?"

"That you will have to discover for yourself. I can only tell you that this is how it works."

"Am I to be sent Within again now?"

"Yes."

"I'm not as afraid as I was, but, Gaudior, I'm still afraid."

"That's all right," Gaudior said.

"And if I let more of myself go, how can I kythe properly with Meg?"

"If you're meant to, you will."

"I'm going to need her . . ."

"Why?"

"I don't know. I just know that I am."

Gaudior blew three iridescent bubbles. "Hold tight, tight, tight. We're off on the wind, and there may be Echthroi this time who will try to take you from my back and throw you off the rim of the world."

4 The Snow with Its Whiteness

The great unicorn flung himself into the wind and they were soaring among the stars, part of the dance, part of the harmony. As each flaming sun turned on its axis, a singing came from the friction in the way a finger moved around the rim of a crystal goblet will make a singing, and the song varies in pitch and tone from glass to glass.

But this song was exquisite as no song from crystal or wood or brass can be. The blending of melody and harmony was so perfect that it almost made Charles Wallace relax his hold on the unicorn's mane.

"No!" Meg cried aloud. "Hold on, Charles! Don't let go!"

A blast of icy cold cut across the beauty of the flight, a cold which carried a stench of death and decay.

Retching, Charles Wallace buried his face in Gaudior's mane, his fingers clenching the silver strands as the Echthroid wind tried to drag him from the unicorn's back. The stench was so abominable that it would have made him loosen his grasp had not the pungent scent of Gaudior's living flesh saved him as he pressed his face against the silver hide, breathing the strangeness of unicorn sweat. Gaudior's bright wings beat painfully against invisible wings of darkness beating at them. The unicorn neighed in anguish, his clear tones lost in the howling of the tempest.

Suddenly his hoofs struck against something solid. He whinnied with anxiety. "Hold on tightly, don't let go," he warned. "We've been blown into a Projection."

Charles Wallace could hardly be clutching the mane with more intensity. "A what?"

"We've been blown into a Projection, a possible future, a future the

Echthroi want to make real." His breath came in gasping gulps; his flanks heaved wildly under Charles Wallace's legs.

The boy shivered as he remembered those darkly flailing wings and the nauseous odor. Whatever the Echthroi wanted to make real would be something fearful.

They were on a flat plain of what appeared to be solidified lava, although it had a faint luminosity alien to lava. The sky was covered with flickering pink cloud. The air was acrid, making them cough. The heat was intense and he was perspiring profusely under the light anorak, which held in the heat like a furnace.

"Where are we?" he asked, wanting Gaudior to tell him that they were not in his own Where, that this could not possibly be the place of the star-watching rock, of the woods, only a few minutes' walk from the house.

Gaudior's words trembled with concern. "We're still here, in your own Where, although it is not yet a real When."

"Will it be?"

"It is one of the Projections we have been sent to try to prevent. The Echthroi will do everything in their power to make it real."

A shudder shook the boy's slight frame as he looked around the devastated landscape. "Gaudior—what do we do now?"

"Nothing. You mustn't loosen your hold on my mane. They want us to do something, and anything we do might be what they need to make this Projection real."

"Can't we get away?"

The unicorn's ears flicked nervously. "It's very difficult to find a wind to ride when one has been blown into a Projection."

"But what do we do?"

"There is nothing to do but wait."

"Is anybody left alive?"

"I don't know."

Around them a sulfurous wind began to rise. Both boy and unicorn were convulsed with paroxysms of coughing, but Charles Wallace did not loosen his grasp. When the seizure was over, he dried his streaming eyes on the silver mane.

When he looked up again, his heart lurched with horror. Waddling toward them over the petrified earth was a monstrous creature with a great blotched body, short stumps for legs, and long arms, with the hands brushing the ground. What was left of the face was scabrous and suppurating. It looked at the unicorn with its one eye, turned its head as though calling behind it to someone or something, and hurried toward them as fast as its stumps would take it.

"Oh, Heavenly Powers, save us!" Gaudior's neigh streaked silver. The anguished cry called Charles Wallace back to himself. He cried,

"With Gaudior in this fateful hour
I call on all Heaven with its power
And the sun with its brightness,
And the snow with its whiteness . . ."

He took a deep breath and hot air seared his lungs and again he was assailed by an unquellable fit of coughing. He buried his face in the unicorn's mane and tried to control the spasm which shook him. It was not until the racking had nearly passed that he became aware of something cool brushing his burning face.

He raised his eyes and with awed gratitude he saw snow, pure white snow drifting down from the tortured sky, covering the ruined earth. The monster had stopped its ponderous approach and was staring up at the sky, mouth open to catch the falling flakes.

With the snow came a light wind, a cool wind. "Hold!" Gaudior cried, and raised his wings to catch the wind. His four hoofs left the ground and he launched himself into the wind with a surge of power.

Charles Wallace braced, trying to tighten the grip of his legs about the unicorn's broad neck. He could feel the wild beating of Gaudior's heart as with mighty strokes he thrust along the wind through the darkness of outer space, until suddenly they burst into a fountain of stars, and the stench and the horror were gone.

The unicorn's breath came in great gulps of star-lit air; the wings beat less frantically; and they were safely riding the wind again and the song of the stars was clear and full.

"Now," said Gaudior, "we go."

"Where?" Charles Wallace asked.

"Not Where," Gaudior said. "When."

Up, up, through the stars, up to the far reaches of the universe where the galaxies swirled in their starry dance, weaving time.

Exhausted, Charles Wallace felt his eyelids drooping.

"Do not go to sleep," Gaudior warned.

Charles Wallace leaned over the unicorn's neck. "I'm not sure I can help it," he murmured.

"Sing, then," Gaudior commanded. "Sing to keep yourself awake." The unicorn opened his powerful jaws and music streamed out in full and magnificent harmony. Charles Wallace's voice was barely changing from a pure treble to a warm tenor. Now it was the treble, sweet as a flute, which joined Gaudior's mighty organ tones. He was singing a melody he did not know, and yet the notes poured from his throat with all the assurance of long familiarity.

They moved through the time-spinning reaches of a far galaxy, and he realized that the galaxy itself was part of a mighty orchestra, and each star and planet within the galaxy added its own instrument to the music of the spheres. As long as the ancient harmonies were sung, the universe would not entirely lose its joy.

He was hardly aware when Gaudior's hoofs struck ground and the melody dimmed until it was only a pervasive beauty of background. With a deep sigh Gaudior stopped his mighty song and folded his wings into his flanks.

Meg sighed as the beauty of the melody faded and all she heard was the soft movement of the wind in the bare trees. She realized that the room was cold, despite the electric heater which augmented the warm air coming up the attic stairs from the radiators below. She reached over Ananda to the foot of the bed and pulled up her old eiderdown and wrapped it around them both. A gust of wind beat at the window, which always rattled unless secured by a folded piece of cardboard or a sliver of wood stuck between window and frame.

"Ananda, Ananda," she said softly, "the music—it was more—more real than any music I've ever heard. Will we hear it again?"

The wind dropped as suddenly as it had risen, and once again she could feel the warmth coming from the little heater. "Ananda, he's really a very small boy . . . Where is Gaudior going to take him now? Whom is he going to go Within?" She closed her eyes, pressing the palm of her hand firmly against the dog.

It was the same Where as the Where of Harcels, but there were subtle differences, though it was still what Gaudior had called Once Upon a Time and Long Ago, so perhaps men still lived in peace and Charles Wallace would be in no danger. But no: time, though still young, was not as young as that, she felt.

The lake lapped close to the great rock and stretched across the valley to the horizon, a larger lake than the lake of Harcels's time. The rock itself had been flattened by wind and rain and erosion, so that it looked like an enormous, slightly tilted tabletop. The forest was dark and deep, but the trees were familiar, pine and hemlock and oak and elm.

* * *

Dawn.

The air was pure and blue and filled with the fragrance of spring. The grass around the rock looked as though it had been covered with a fall of fresh snow, but the snow was a narcissus-like flower with a spicy scent.

On the tabletop stood a young man.

She did not see Charles Wallace. She did not see the unicorn. Only the young man.

A young man older than Charles Wallace. Harcels had been younger. This young man was older, perhaps not as old as Sandy and Dennys, but more than fifteen. She saw no hint of Charles Wallace within the man, but she knew that somehow he was there. As Charles Wallace had been himself and yet had been Harcels, so Charles Wallace was Within the young man.

He had been there all night, sometimes lying on his back to watch the stars swing slowly across the sky; sometimes with his eyes closed, as he listened to the lapping of the small waves on the pale sand, the clunkings of frogs and the hoot of a night bird, the sound of an occasional fish slipping through the water. Sometimes he neither heard nor saw; he did not sleep, but abandoned his senses and lay on the rock patiently opening himself to the wind.

Perhaps it was his gift of kything practiced with Meg that helped Charles Wallace slip more and more deeply into the being of another.

Madoc, son of Owain, king of Gwynedd.

Madoc, on the dawning of his wedding day.

Meg's eyes slowly lowered; her body relaxed under the warmth of the eiderdown; but her hand remained on Ananda as she slid into sleep.

Madoc!

It was for Charles Wallace as though a shuttered window had suddenly been opened. It was not a ballad or a song he was trying to remember, it was a novel about a Welsh prince named Madoc.

He heard Gaudior's warning neigh. "You are Within Madoc. Do not disturb him with outside thoughts."

"But, Gaudior, Madoc was the key figure in the book—oh, *why* can't I remember more!"

Again Gaudior cut him off. "Stop trying to think. Your job now is to let yourself go into Madoc. Let go."

Let go.

It was almost like slipping down, deeper and deeper, into the waters of a pool, deeper and deeper.

Let go.

Fall into Madoc.
Let go.

Madoc rose from the rock and looked to the east, awaiting the sunrise with exalted anticipation. His fair skin was tanned, with a reddishness which showed that he was alien to so fierce a sun. He looked toward the indigo line of horizon between lake and sky, with eyes so blue that the sky paled in comparison. His hair, thick and gold as a lion's mane, was nearly covered with an elaborate crown of early spring flowers. A lavish chain of flowers was flung over his neck and one shoulder. He wore a kilt of ferns.

The sky lightened, and the sun sent its fiery rays over the edge of the lake, reaching up into the sky, pulling itself, dripping, from the waters of the night. As the sun seemed to make a great leap out of the dark, Madoc began to sing in a strong, joyful baritone.

> *"Lords of fire and earth and water,*
> *Lords of rain and wind and snow,*
> *When will come the Old Man's daughter?*
> *Time to come, or long ago?*
> *Born of friend or borne by foe?*

> *Lords of water, earth, and fire,*
> *Lords of wind and snow and rain,*
> *Where is found the heart's desire?*
> *Has she come? will come again?*
> *Born, as all life's born, with pain?"*

When he finished, still looking out over the water, his song was taken up as though by an echo, a strange, thin, cracked echo, and then an old man, dressed with the same abundance of flowers as Madoc, came out of the forest.

Madoc bent down and helped the old man up onto the rock. For all the Old One's age, his stringy-looking muscles were strong, and though his hair was white, his dark skin had a glow of health.

> *"Lords of snow and rain and wind,*
> *Lords of water, fire, and earth,*
> *Do you know the one you send?*
> *Does it call for tears or mirth?*
> *Shall we sing for death or birth?"*

When the strange duet was ended, the old man held up his hand in a gesture of blessing. "It is the day, my far-sent son."

"It is the day, my to-be-father. Madoc, son of Owain, king of Gwynedd, will be Madoc, son of Reschal, Old One of the Wind People."

"A year ago today, you sang the song in your delirium," Reschal said, "and it was the child of my old age who found you in the forest."

"And it is mirth that is called for," the young man affirmed, "and we shall sing today for birth, for the birth of the new One which Zyll and I will become when you join us together."

"On the night that Zyll was born," the Old One said, "I dreamed of a stranger from a distant land, across a lake far greater than ours—"

"From across the ocean"—the young man put his hand lightly on the Old One's shoulder—"from the sea which beats upon the shores of Cymru, the sea which we thought went on and on until a ship would fall off at the end of the world."

"The end of the world—" the old man started, but broke off, listening.

The young man listened, too, but heard nothing. "Is it the wind?"

"It is not the wind." Reschal looked at the young man and put a gnarled hand on the richly muscled arm. "Madoc, son of Owain, king of Gwynedd—how strange those syllables sounded to us. We did not know what is a king, nor truly do we yet."

"You have no need of a king, Old One of the People of the Wind. Owain, my father, is long buried: I am a lifetime away from Gwynedd in Cymru. When the soothsayer looked into the scrying glass and foretold my father's death, he saw also that I would live my days far from Gwynedd."

The old man again lifted his head to listen.

"Is it the wind?" Still, Madoc could hear nothing beyond the sounds of early morning, the lapping of the lake against the shore, the stirring of the wind in the hemlocks which made a distant roaring which always reminded him of the sea he had left behind him.

"It is not the wind." There was no emotion in the old man's face, only a continuing, controlled listening.

The young man could not hide the impatience in his voice. "When is Zyll coming?"

The dark Old One smiled at him with affection. "You have waited how many years?"

"I am seventeen."

"Then you can wait a while longer, while Zyll's maidens make her ready. And there are still questions I must ask you. Are you certain in your heart that you will never want to leave Zyll and this small, inland people and go back to the big water and your ship with wings?"

"My ship was broken by wind and wave when we attempted to land on the rocky shores of this land. The sails are torn beyond mending."

"Another ship could be built."

"Old One, even had I the tools to fell the trees for lumber for a new ship, even had my brother and my companions not perished, I would never wish to leave Zyll and my new brethren."

"And your brother and your companions?"

"They are dead," Madoc said bleakly.

"Yet you hold them back so that they cannot continue their journey."

"We were far from home." Madoc spoke softly. "It is a long journey for their spirits."

"Are the gods of Gwynedd so weak they cannot care for their own?"

Madoc's blue eyes were dark with grief. "When we left Gwynedd in Cymru because of the quarreling of my brethren over our father's throne, it seemed to us the gods had already abandoned us. For brothers to wish to kill each other for the sake of power is to anger the gods."

"Perhaps," the old man said, "you must let the gods of Gwynedd go, as you must free your companions from your holding."

"I brought them to their death. When my father died, and my brothers became drunk with lust for power, as no wine can make a man drunk, I felt the gods depart. In a dream I saw them turn their backs on our quarreling, saw them as clearly as anything the soothsayers see in their scrying glass. When I awoke, I took Gwydyr aside and said that I would not stay to watch brother against brother, but that I would go find the land the Wise Ones said was at the farther end of the sea. Gwydyr demurred at first."

"He thought he might become king?"

"Yes, but Gwydyr and I were the youngest. The throne was not likely to be ours while the other five remained alive."

"Yet you, Madoc, the seventh son, were the favored of the people."

"Had I let them proclaim me king, there would have been no way to avoid bloodshed. I left Gwynedd to prevent the horror of brother against brother."

"Have you"—the old man regarded Madoc keenly—"in fact left it?"

"I have left it. Gwynedd in Cymru is behind me. It will be ruled by whomever the gods choose. I do not wish to know. For now I am Madoc, son-to-be of Reschal, soon to be husband of Zyll of the People of the Wind."

"And Gwydyr? Have you let him go?"

Madoc gazed across the lake. "In many ways it seemed that I was older than he, though there were seven years between us. When we came to the tribe on the Far Side of the Lake he was afraid of their dark skins and hair and their strange singing that was full of hoots and howls, and he ran from them. They kept me as guest, yet I was a prisoner, for they would not let me go into the forest to look for my brother. They sent a party of warriors to search for him, and when they returned they carried only the belt with the jeweled buckle which marked him as the son of a king. They told me he had been killed by a snake; Gwydyr did not know what a snake is, for we have none in Gwynedd. They told me that he had called my name before he died, and that he had left me the Song of the King's Sons. And they buried him out in the forest. Without me, they buried my brother, and I do not even know the place where he is laid."

"That is the way of the People on the Far Side of the Lake," the old man said. "They fear the dead and try to escape the ancient terror."

"The ancient terror?"

Reschal looked at the tender sky of early morning. "That which went wrong. Once there were no evil spirits to blight the crops, to bring drought or flood. Once there was nothing to fear, not even death."

"And what happened to bring fear?"

"Who knows? It was so long ago. But is it not in Gwynedd, too?"

"It is in Gwynedd," Madoc replied soberly, "or brother would not have turned against brother. Yes, we too know what you call the ancient terror. Death, it is thought, or at least the fear of death, came with it. Reschal, I would that I knew where those across the lake had laid my brother, that I may say the prayers that will free his soul."

"It is their way to put the dead far from them and then to lose the place. They hide the dead, even from themselves, that their spirits may not come to the lake and keep the fish away."

"And your people?"

The old man pulled himself up proudly. "We do not fear the spirits of our dead. When there has been love during life, why should that change after death? When one of us departs we have a feast of honor, and then we send the spirit to its journey among the stars. On clear nights we feel the singing of their love. Did you not feel it last night?"

"I watched the stars—and I felt that they accepted me."

"And your brother? Did you feel his light?"

Madoc shook his head. "Perhaps if I could have found the place where they buried him . . ."

"You must let him go. For the sake of Zyll you must let him go."

"When will come the Old Man's daughter?" Madoc asked. "I left the People on the Far Side of the Lake to try to find my brother's grave, and in the forest I was quickly lost. For days I wandered, trying to make my way back, straying farther and farther from them. I was nearly dead when Zyll came hunting the healing herbs which are found only in the deepest part of the forest. *When will come the Old Man's daughter? Where is found the heart's desire?* Here, Reschal."

"You will let Gwydyr go to his place among the stars?"

"Does it call for tears or mirth? Shall we sing for death or birth?" Madoc sang softly. "I have shed my tears for the past. Today is for mirth. Why have you dragged me through tears again?"

"So that you may leave them behind you," Reschal said, and raised his withered arms to the sun. The lake, the shore, the rock, the forest behind, were bathed in golden light, and as though in response to Reschal's gesture there came a sound of singing, a strange wild song of spring and flowers and sunlight and growing grass and the beating of the heart of all of those young and in love. And Madoc's tears were dried, and thoughts of his lost companions and brother receded as the singing filled him with expectancy and joy.

The children of the tribe came first, wearing chains of flowers which flapped against their brown bellies as they danced along. Madoc, shining with delight, turned from the children to the Old One. But Reschal's eyes were focused on the unseen distance across the lake and he was listening, not to the children, but to that sound for which he had been straining before. And now Madoc thought that he, too, heard a throbbing like a distant heartbeat. "Old One, I hear it now. What is it?"

Reschal gazed across the water. "It is the People Across the Lake. It is their drums."

Madoc listened. "We have heard their drums before, when the wind blows from the south. But today the wind blows from the north."

The old man's voice was troubled. "We have always lived in peace, the People of the Wind and those Across the Lake."

"Perhaps," Madoc suggested, "they come to my wedding celebration?"

"Perhaps."

The children had gathered around the rock and were looking expectantly at Madoc and Reschal. The Old One raised his arm again, and singing drowned out the steady beating of the drums, and the men and women of the tribe, ranging from coltish girls and boys to men and women with white hair and wrinkled skin, came dancing toward the great rock. In their midst, circled by a group of young women, was Zyll. She wore a crown on her head to match Madoc's, and a short skirt made entirely of spring flowers. Her copper skin glowed as though lit by the sun from within, and her eyes met Madoc's with a sparkle of love.

Nowhere, Madoc thought, could wedding garments be more beautiful, no matter how much gold was woven into the cloth, nor with how many jewels the velvets and satins were decorated.

The flower-bedecked crowd parted to let Zyll come to the rock. Madoc stooped for her upraised hands, and gently lifted her so that she stood between him and Reschal. She bowed to her father, and then began to move in the ritual wedding dance. Madoc, during the year he had spent with the Wind People, had seen Zyll dance many times before: at the birth of each moon; at the feast of the newborn sun in winter; at the spring and autumn equinox, dance for the Lords of the lake, the sky, the rain and rainbow, the snow and the wind.

But for the Wind Dancers, as well as for all the other Wind People with their various gifts, there was only one Wedding Dance.

Madoc stood transfixed with joy as Zyll's body moved with the effortless lightness of the spring breeze. Her body leapt upward and it seemed that gravity had no power to pull her down to earth. She drifted gently from sky to rock as the petals fall from flowering trees.

Then she held out her hands to Madoc, and he joined in the dance, marveling as he felt some of Zyll's effortlessness of movement enter his own limbs.

At first, when Zyll had found Madoc half dead in the forest, and had brought him to the Wind People, they had been afraid of him. His blue eyes, his pale skin, reddened by exposure, his tawny hair, were unlike anything they had ever seen. They approached him shyly, as though he were a strange beast who might turn on them. As they became accustomed to his presence, some of the Wind People proclaimed him a god. But then his anger flashed like lightning, and though there were some who said that his very fieriness announced him the Lord of the storm, he would have none of their attempts to set him apart.

"Stay with your own wind gods," he commanded. "You have served them well, and you live in the light of their favor. I, too, will serve the Lords of this place, for it is their pleasure that I am still alive."

Gradually the Wind People began to accept him as one of themselves, to forget his outer differences. The Old One said, "It is not an easy thing to refuse to be worshipped."

"When people are worshipped, then there is anger and jealousy in the wake. I will not be worshipped, nor will I be a king. People are meant to worship the gods, not themselves."

"You are wise beyond your years, my son," Reschal said.

"My father did not want to be worshipped. But some of his sons did. That is why I am here."

Across the lake the drums were silent.

The Old One watched Madoc and Zyll as their bodies slowly ceased the motions of the dance. Then he lifted Madoc's hand and placed it over Zyll's, and then put a hand on each of their heads. And as he did so, the sound of drums came again. Loud and close. Threatening.

A ripple went through the Wind People as they saw three dugout canoes approaching swiftly, each paddled by many men. Standing in the bow of the middle and largest dugout was a tall, fair-skinned, blue-eyed man.

With a glad shout Madoc leapt from the rock and ran to the water's edge. "Gwydyr!"

5 The Fire with All the Strength It Hath

In the attic Meg lay quietly in bed, her eyes closed. Her hand continued to rub rhythmically against Ananda, receiving the tingling warmth. Behind her lids her eyes moved as though she were dreaming. The kitten stood up, stretched its small back into a high arch, yawned, and curled up at her feet, purring.

Charles Wallace-within-Madoc felt the young man's surge of joy at seeing his brother alive, the brother he had thought dead and buried in a forgotten part of the forest.

The man in the dugout jumped overboard and ran splashing to shore.

"Gwydyr! You are alive!" Madoc held out his arms to his brother.

Gwydyr did not move into the embrace. His blue eyes were cold, and set close together. It was then that Madoc noticed the circlet around his brother's head, not of flowers, but of gold.

"Gwydyr, my elder brother." The joy slowly faded from the sunny blue of Madoc's eyes. "I thought you dead."

Gwydyr's voice was as cold as his eyes. "It was my wish that you should think so."

"But why should you wish such a thing!"

At the pain in Madoc's voice, Zyll dropped lightly from the rock and came to stand close by him.

"Did you not learn in Gwynedd that there is room for one king only?"

Madoc's eyes kept returning to Gwydyr's golden crown. "We left Gwynedd for that reason, to find a place of peace."

Gwydyr gestured behind him, and the drummers began to beat

slowly on the taut skins. The paddles were rested and the men splashed into the shallow water, and pulled the dugouts onto the shore.

Gwydyr raised the corners of his lips into what was more a grimace than a smile. "I have come to claim the Old Man's daughter."

The sound of the drums was an aching pain in Madoc's ears. "My brother, I wept for your death. I thought to rejoice to see you alive."

Gwydyr spoke with grim patience as though to a dim-witted child. "There is room for no more than one king in this place, little brother, and I, who am the elder, am that king. In Gwynedd I had no hope against six brothers. But here I am king and god and I have come to let the Wind People know that I reign over the lake and all the lands around. The Old Man's daughter is mine."

Zyll pressed against Madoc, her fingers tight on his arm.

Reschal spoke in his cracked voice. "The People of the Wind are people of peace. Always we have lived in amity with those Across the Lake."

Again Gwydyr's lips distorted into a smile. "Peace will continue as long as you give us half of your fish and half of all you hunt and if I take with me across the water the princess who stands beside my brother."

Zyll did not move from Madoc's side. "You come too late, Elder Brother. Madoc of Reschal and I have been made One."

"Madoc of Reschal. Ha! My laws are stronger than your laws." Gwydyr gestured imperiously. The men with the paddles pulled the blades off the shafts, and stood holding dangerously pointed spears.

A united cry of disbelief, then anger, came from the Wind People.

"No!" Madoc cried, outrage giving his voice such volume that it drowned out the beating of the drums, the shouting of the warriors with the spears, the anger of the Wind People. "There will be no bloodshed here because of the sons of Owain." He stepped away from Zyll and Reschal and confronted Gwydyr. "Brother, this is between you and me." And now he smiled. "Unless, of course, you are afraid of Madoc and need your savages with spears to protect you."

Gwydyr made an enraged gesture. "And what of your peaceable Wind People?"

Then Madoc saw that the festive garlands were gone from the young men, flung in a heap in front of the great rock. Instead of flowers they carried spears, bows and arrows.

Reschal looked at him gravely. "I have been hearing the war drums since last sundown. I thought it better to be prepared."

Madoc flung his arms wide. There was grim command in his voice.

"Put down your arms, my brothers. I came to you in peace. I will not be the cause of war."

The young men looked first at Madoc, then at the People Across the Lake, their spears threatening.

"Brother," Madoc said to Gwydyr, "have your men put down their spears. Or do you fear to fight me in fair combat?"

Gwydyr snarled an order, and the men on the shore behind him placed their spears carefully on the sand in easy reach.

Then the Old One nodded at the young men, and they, too, put down their weapons.

Gwydyr shouted, "If we are to fight for the Old Man's daughter, little brother, I choose the weapon."

"That is fair," Madoc replied.

Zyll made a soft moan of anxiety and placed her hand on his arm.

"I choose fire," Gwydyr announced.

Madoc sang:

> "Lords of water, earth, and fire,
> Where is found the heart's desire?"

"Fire it shall be, then. But in what form?"

"You must *make* fire, little brother," Gwydyr said. "If your fire cannot overcome mine, then I will be king of the Wind People as well as those Across the Lake, and I will claim the Old Man's daughter for my own." His close-set eyes flickered greedily.

Reschal walked slowly toward him. "Gwydyr, sixth son of Owain, pride has turned the light behind your eyes to ice, so that you can no longer see clearly. You will never take my daughter."

Gwydyr gave the old man a mighty shove, so that he fell sprawling on the beach, face down. Zyll screamed, and her scream was arrested in mid-air, to hang there.

Madoc sprang to help the old man, and bent down on one knee to raise Reschal from the sand. But his eyes followed the Old One's to a small pool of water in a declivity in the sand, and his movements, like Zyll's scream, were suspended. Only the reflection in the small pool of water moved. Gwydyr's face was quivering in the wind-stirred puddle, his face so like and so unlike Madoc's. The eyes were the same blue, but there was no gold behind them, and they turned slightly in to a nose pinched with cruelty and lust. This was not, Madoc thought, the brother who had come with him to the New World. Or was it? and he had never truly seen his brother before, only Gwydyr as he hoped him to be.

Ripples moved over the shallow oval and the reflection shimmered like the reflections in the soothsayers' scrying glass in Gwynedd.

Madoc had always feared the scrying glass; so he feared the small oval of water which reflected Gwydyr's face, growing larger and larger, and darker and darker, quivering until it was no longer the face of a man but of a screaming baby. The face receded until Madoc saw a black-haired woman holding and rocking the baby. 'You shall be great, little Madog,' she said, 'and call the world your own, to keep or destroy as you will. It is an evil world, little Madog.' The baby looked at her, and his eyes were set close together, like Gwydyr's, and turned inward, just so, and his mouth pouted with discontent. Again the face grew larger and larger in the dark oval and was no longer the face of a baby, but a man with an arrogant and angry mien. 'We will destroy, then, Mother,' the man said, and the face rippled until it was a small, slightly pear-shaped sphere, and on the sphere were blotches of green and brown for land, and blue and grey for seas, and a soft darkness for clouds, and from the clouds came strange dark objects which fell upon the land and fell upon the sea, and where they fell, great clouds arose, umbrellaing over the earth and the sea; and beneath the bulbous clouds was fire, raging redly and driven wild by wind.

Gwydyr's voice rippled across the scrying oval of water. "I choose fire, little brother. Where is your fire?"

The flames vanished and the oval was only a shallow pool reflecting nothing more than the cloud that moved across the sun.

Time resumed, and Zyll's scream continued as though it had never been broken. Madoc raised Reschal from the beach, stepping into the oval as he did so, splashing the shallow water onto the sand. "Stand back, Old One," he said. "I will break the scry." And he stamped once more on the water left in the puddle, until there was not enough to hold the least reflection.

From the central dugout came one of the warriors, carrying a smoking brazier. Gwydyr took one of the spears and held the sharp end over the coals. "You must make your own fire, Madoc!" He laughed derisively.

Madoc turned to the rock where the young men had laid their chains of flowers. He gathered the flowers in his arms and placed them in a heap over the oval where the water had been. Then he took the crown of flowers from his head and added it to the garlands. As though responding to a signal, Zyll cast hers on the fragrant pile. One by one all the men, women, children of the Wind People threw their headpieces onto the heap of flowers, Reschal last of all.

"What do you think you're doing?" Gwydyr screamed, dancing about on the sand, thrusting his flaming spear at his brother.

Madoc leapt aside. "Wait, Gwydyr. You chose fire. You must let me fight fire with fire."

"You, you alone must make the fire. These are my rules."

Madoc replied quietly, "You were always one for making your own rules, Brother Gwydyr."

"I am the king, do you hear me, I am the king!" Gwydyr's voice rose hysterically.

Madoc, moving as though in a dream, pushed his brother's words aside, and focused the blue fire of his eyes on the great pyre of flowers. The scent of crushed blossoms rose like smoke. Madoc thrust his arms shoulder-deep into the garlands and pushed them aside so that once more he could see the oval. A thin film of water had bubbled up from the sand.

"No more of Gwydyr's nightmares," he commanded, staring fixedly at the water, which sparkled from the sun. The water rippled and shimmered and resolved itself once again into a mother holding a baby, but a different baby, eyes wide apart, with sunlight gleaming through the blue, a laughing, merry baby. "You will do good for your people, El Zarco, little Blue Eyes," the mother crooned. "Your eyes are an omen, a token for peace. The prayer has been answered in you, blue for birth, blue for mirth."

Then the oval broke into shimmering, and all that was reflected was the cloudy sky. Madoc looked heavenward then, and cried in a loud voice,

> "I, Madoc, in this fateful hour
> Place all Heaven with its power
> And the sun with its brightness,
> And the snow with its whiteness,
> And the fire with all the strength it hath . . ."

The sun burst from behind the clouds and shafted directly onto the garlands. The scent of roses mingled with the thin wisp of smoke which rose from the crushed petals. When the smoke was joined by a small tongue of flame, Madoc leapt toward his brother. "There is my fire, Gwydyr." He wrenched the spear from his brother and threw it with all his might into the lake. "Now we will fight in fair combat." And he clasped Gwydyr to him as though in love.

For time out of time the two brothers wrestled by the lake, both panting with exertion, but neither seeming to tire beyond the other. Their bodies swayed back and forth in a strange dance, and the People of the Wind and those Across the Lake watched in silence.

The sun completed its journey across the sky and dropped into the forest for the night's rest, and still the brothers held each other in an anguished grip and their breathing was louder than the wind in the trees.

The fire slowly consumed the garlands, and when there was nothing left but a handful of ashes, Madoc forced Gwydyr into the lake, and held him down under the water until rising bubbles told him that his brother was screaming for mercy. Then he raised him from the lake and water spewed from Gwydyr's mouth as dark as blood, and he hung limply in Madoc's arms.

Madoc gestured to the People Across the Lake. "Bring out your boats and take your king back to your own land." His voice held scorn and it held pain and his blue eyes were softened by tears.

The three boats pushed into the water. The spear-oars were returned to their blades. Madoc dumped Gwydyr like a sack of grain into the center dugout. "Go. Never let us hear the sound of the war drums again." He reached into the canoe and took the golden circlet from Gwydyr's head and tossed it far out into the lake.

Then he turned his back on his brother and splashed ashore.

Zyll was waiting for him.

Madoc looked at her and sang,

> *"Lords of water, earth, and fire*
> *Lords of rain and snow and water,*
> *Nothing more do I aspire,*
> *For I have the Old Man's daughter,*
> *For I have my heart's desire."*

And to him Zyll sang,

> *"Now we leave our tears for mirth.*
> *Now we sing, not death, but birth."*

Madoc held her close in his arms. "Tomorrow I will mourn for my brother, for this death is far worse than the other. But tonight we rejoice."

The children lifted their voices and began to sing, and then all the People of the Wind were singing, and Reschal said softly to Madoc, "That which your brother wanted us to believe from the scry is part of his nightmare. Perhaps our dreams will be stronger than his."

"Yes, Old One," Madoc said, but he thought of the things he had seen falling from the sky, and the strange mushrooming clouds and the fire, and shuddered. He looked at the water that had seeped into the oval. But all that he saw was the smiling face of the moon.

The moon slipped behind the trees to join, briefly, her brother, sun. The stars danced their intricate ritual across the sky. The People Across the Lake looked at Gwydyr, and his golden crown was gone, and so was his power.

Madoc's arms encircled Zyll and he cried out in his sleep and tears slid through his closed eyelids and wet his lashes, and while he still slept, Zyll held him and kissed the tears away.

"Come," Gaudior said.

Charles Wallace stood by the unicorn, blinking. "Was it a dream?" He looked at the dark lake lapping the shore, at the tilted rock; it was empty.

Gaudior blew silver bubbles that bounced off his beard. "You were Within Madoc, deep Within this time."

"Madoc, son of Owain, king of Gwynedd. The Madoc of the book. And hasn't there been a recurring theory that Welsh sailors came here before Leif Ericson? . . . Something about Indians with blue or grey eyes . . ."

"You should know," Gaudior chided. "You were Within Madoc."

"It can't all have been real."

"Reality was different in those days," Gaudior said. "It was real for Madoc."

"Even the fire among the garlands?"

"Roses often burn. Theirs is the most purifying flame of all."

"And the scry—what Madoc saw in the water—was that a kind of Projection?"

The light in Gaudior's horn flickered. "Gwydyr was on the side of evil, and so he was open to the Projections of the Echthroi."

"So the terrible baby was a Projection the Echthroi want to have happen?"

"I'm never entirely sure about Projections," Gaudior admitted.

"And there was the other baby . . ." Charles Wallace closed his eyes to try to visualize the scry. "The blue-eyed baby, the answer to prayer, who was going to bring peace. So he's equally possible, isn't he?"

"It's all very confusing"—Gaudior shook his mane—"because we move in different dimensions, you and I."

Charles Wallace rubbed his fingers over his forehead as he had done in Meg's room. "It's all in the book somewhere. Why am I being blocked on that book?" The unicorn did not reply. "A book against war, a book about the legend of Madoc and Gwydyr, who came from Wales to this land . . . and what else? I can't get it . . ."

"Leave it alone," Gaudior advised.

Charles Wallace leaned against the unicorn, pressing his forehead against the silver hide, thinking out loud. "All we know is that a Welsh prince named Madoc did come to the New World with his brother Gwydyr and that Madoc married Zyll of the People of the Wind. Gaudior, if, unknowing, while I was Within Madoc I gave him the rune, would that have been changing a Might-Have-Been?"

The unicorn replied unhelpfully, "It's all very complicated."

"Or—did Madoc have the rune himself? How could he, if it came from Ireland and St. Patrick?"

Gaudior raised his head and pulled back the dark silver of his lips in a ferocious grimace, baring his dangerous teeth. But all he did was open his mouth and drink wind as though quenching a terrible thirst.

Charles Wallace looked about, and as he looked, the scene rippled like the waters in the scrying oval on the beach, and the lake receded until he was looking across a wintry valley, and the rock was no longer a slightly tilted table but the flat star-watching rock, thinly crusted with snow.

Gaudior lowered his head and licked wind from his lips. "Gwydyr did not stay with the People Across the Lake."

"I wouldn't think he would, but how do you know?"

Gaudior raised tufted brows. "I have just been talking with the wind. Gwydyr left the lake in disgrace, and moved southward, ending up in South America."

Charles Wallace clapped his hand to his forehead. "That's it! It's in the book, too. Gwydyr going to Patagonia. And Vespugia is part of Patagonia. And there was a connection that was lost and had to be found, but what *was* it? I keep almost remembering, and then it's as if someone slams a door on my memory."

Gaudior sniffed. "Echthroi, probably. They'll try to block anything that might be a clue to the Might-Have-Been they don't want you to discover."

Charles Wallace nodded. "Mad Dog Branzillo was born in Vespugia. But right here, where we stand, Madoc came and married Zyll and made the roses burn for peace. What happened to the Wind People? Where are they now?"

"They were lovers of peace," Gaudior replied shortly. "Your planet does not deal gently with lovers of peace."

Charles Wallace sat on the rock, the thin rim of snow crackling beneath him. He put his head down on his knees. "I think I have to find out what the connection is between Wales and Vespugia, between Madoc and Gwydyr and Mad Dog Branzillo."

Meg stirred and opened her eyes. Her hand lay lightly on Ananda. "Such dreams, Fortinbras," she murmured, "such strange dreams." Her sleepy gaze drifted toward the clock and suddenly she was wide awake. "Ananda! For a moment I thought you were Fort. And it wasn't dreaming, was it? It was kything, but not clear and sharp, the way it was when Charles Wallace was Within Harcels. He was deeper Within Madoc, and so I have to dig deeper to find the kythe. And Charles wants me to find something out for him . . . but what?" She pushed her fingers through her hair, closed her eyes tightly, and concentrated, her hand pressing against Ananda. "Something about a lake . . . about burning roses . . . and two brothers fighting . . . yes . . . and Mad Dog Branzillo and Wales. That's it. He wants me to find a connection between Mad Dog Branzillo and Wales. And that hardly seems possible, much less likely." She listened to the sounds within the silence of the night, the sounds which were so familiar that they were part of the silence. The old house creaked comfortably. The wind brushed softly against the window.—Nobody's likely to be asleep, not tonight. And Sandy's a history buff. I'll go ask him.

She got out of bed, pushed her feet into furry slippers, and went downstairs. There was light shining under the door of the twins' room, so she knocked.

"What are you doing up, Sis?" Dennys asked. "You need your sleep."

"So do you, doc. I'm up for the same reason you are."

"I often study late," Dennys said. "What can we do for you?"

"What do you know about Vespugia?"

Dennys said, "With your hair down like that, you look about fifteen."

"I'm an old married woman. What about Vespugia?"

Sandy replied, "I was just reading about it in the encyclopedia. It's part of what used to be called Patagonia. Sort of between Argentina and Chile."

"Branzillo was born there?"

"Yes."

"Who colonized Vespugia?"

"Oh, the usual mishmash. Spaniards, a few English, and a group from Wales while it was still part of Patagonia."

Madoc was from Wales. She asked carefully, "Wales—when was that?"

"There's a legend that some Welshmen came to North America even before Leif Ericson, and that one of them went south, looking for a warm climate, and eventually settled in Vespugia—or where Vespugia is now. But that's only legend. However, it's fact that in 1865 a party left Wales for Patagonia and settled in the open wastelands near the Chubut River."

"So maybe Mad Dog Branzillo has some Welsh blood in him?"

"It's perfectly possible, although Branzillo hardly sounds Welsh."

"What year did you say the group left Wales?"

"1865."

"Are those the only times Wales is mentioned in connection with Vespugia?"

"In this encyclopedia."

She thought for a minute. "All right. What happened in 1865 that I ought to know about?"

Dennys said, "Meg, sit down if you're going to get Sandy to give you a history lesson. Is this something to do with being pregnant, like a passion for strawberries?"

"Raspberries. And I don't think it has much to do with being pregnant."

"Let me get *The Time Tables of History.*" Sandy reached for the bookcase and pulled out a large and battered volume, and began turning the pages. "Aha. 1865. Appomatox was on April 9, and Lincoln was assassinated on the fourteenth. The Civil War ended on May 26."

"Quite a year."

"Yup. In England, Lord Palmerston died, and was succeeded as Prime Minister by Lord John Russell."

"I don't know much about him."

"And back to the once-more-United States, the Thirteenth Amendment abolished slavery."

"Would there have been slavery in Vespugia?"

"Not sure. Bolivar died in 1830, and his influence would likely have filtered through to Vespugia. So I doubt if there'd have been slaves."

"Well, good."

"Okay, and also in 1865 the Atlantic cable was finally completed. Oh, and here's something for you, Den: Lister caused a scandal by insisting on antiseptic surgery and using carbolic acid on a compound wound."

Dennys applauded. "You're almost as veritable an encyclopedia as Charles Wallace."

"Charles has it in his head and I have to look it up in a reference book. My sphere of knowledge is considerably more limited. Mendel came out with his law of heredity that year"—he peered down at the book again—"and the Ku Klux Klan was founded, and Edward Whymper climbed the Matterhorn. And Lewis Carroll wrote *Alice's Adventures in Wonderland*."

"Indeed, 1865 was quite a year," Dennys said. "What have you learned, Meg?"

"I think maybe a lot. Thanks, both of you."

"Get back into bed," Dennys chided. "You don't want to get chilled wandering around this drafty old barn in the middle of the night."

"I'm warm." She indicated her heavy robe and slippers. "I'm taking care. But thanks."

"If we made you some hot chocolate, would you drink it?"

"I'm off hot chocolate."

"Some consommé or bouillon?"

"No, thanks, really, I don't want anything. I'll get back into bed."

Sandy called after her, "And also in 1865 Rudyard Kipling was born, and Verlaine wrote *Poèmes saturniens*, and John Stuart Mill wrote *Auguste Comte and Positivism*, and Purdue, Cornell, and the universities of Maine were founded."

She waved back at him, then paused as he continued, "And Matthew Maddox's first novel, *Once More United*, was published."

She turned back, asking in a carefully controlled voice, "Maddox? I don't think I've ever heard of that author."

"You stuck to math in school."

"Yeah, Calvin always helped me with my English papers. Did this Matthew Maddox write anything else?"

Sandy flipped through the pages. "Let's see. Nothing in 1866, 1867. 1868, here we are, *The Horn of Joy*."

"Oh, that," Dennys said. "I remember him now. I had to take a lit course my sophomore year in college, and I took nineteenth-century American literature. We read that, Matthew Maddox's second and last book, *The Horn of Joy*. My prof said if he hadn't died he'd have been right up there with Hawthorne and James. It was a strange book, passionately anti-war, I remember, and it went way back into the past, and there was some weird theory of the future influencing the past—not my kind of book at all."

"But you remember it," Meg remarked.

"Yeah, I remember it, for some reason. There was a Welsh prince whose brothers were fighting for the throne. And he left Wales with one of his brothers, and was shipwrecked and landed somewhere on the New England coast. There was more, but I can't think of it right now."

"Thanks," Meg said. "Thanks a lot."

Ananda greeted her joyfully at the head of the stairs. Meg fondled the dog's floppy ear. "I really would have liked something hot to drink, but I didn't want Sandy and Dennys coming up to the attic and staying to talk when we have to concentrate on kything with Charles Wallace." She got back into bed and Ananda jumped up beside her and settled down. The clock's hands had moved ahead fifteen minutes, the length of time she had spent with Sandy and Dennys. And time was of the essence. But she felt that the trip downstairs had been worth it. She had found the author and the title of the book for Charles Wallace. And she had found a connection between Wales and Vespugia in 1865. But what did the connection mean? Madoc was Welsh, but he didn't go to Vespugia, he came here, and married here.

She shook her head. Maybe Charles Wallace and Gaudior could make something out of it.

And how any of this could connect with Mrs. O'Keefe was a mystery.

6 The Lightning with Its Rapid Wrath

"Thanks, Meg," Charles Wallace whispered. "Oh, Gaudior, she really did help us, she and the twins." He leaned forward to rest his cheek against the unicorn's neck. "The book was by Matthew Maddox. I don't think I ever read it, but I remember Dennys talking about it. And Mrs. O'Keefe was a Maddox, so she's *got* to be descended from Matthew."

"Descended," Gaudior snorted. "You make it sound like a fall."

"If you look at Mrs. O'Keefe, that's what it's like," Charles Wallace admitted. "1865. Can we go there?"

"Then," the unicorn corrected. "When. We can try, if you think it's important. We'll hope for a favorable wind."

Charles Wallace looked alarmed. "You mean we might get blown into another Projection?"

"It's always a risk. We know the Echthroi are after us, to stop us. So you must hold on."

"I'll hold on for dear life. The last thing I want is to get blown into another Projection."

Gaudior blew softly through his teeth. "I find our most recent information not very helpful."

"But it could be important, a group of Welshmen going to South America in 1865. I think we should try to go to Vespugia."

"That's a long way, and unicorns do not travel well to different Wheres. And to try to move in *both* space and time—I don't like it." He flicked his tail.

"Then how about trying to move to 1865, right here, the year Matthew Maddox published his first novel? Then we could try to move from 1865 here to 1865 in Vespugia. And maybe we could learn something from Matthew Maddox."

"Very well. It's less dangerous to go elsewhen first than to try to go elsewhen and elsewhen and elsewhere simultaneously." He began to gallop, and as he flung himself onto a gust of wind, the wings lifted and they soared upward.

The attack, just as they went through a shower of stars, was completely unexpected. A freezing gust blasted the wind on which they were riding, taking away Charles Wallace's breath. His knuckles whitened as he clenched the mane, which seemed to strengthen into steel wire to help him hold his grasp. He had a horrible sense of Gaudior battling with a darkness which was like an anti-unicorn, a flailing of negative wings and iron hoofs. The silver mane was torn from his hands as he was assailed by the horrible stench which accompanied Echthroi. Dark wings beat him from the unicorn's back and he felt the burning cold of outer space. This was more horrible than any Projection. His lungs cracked for lack of air. He would become a burnt-out body, a satellite circling forever the nearest sun . . .

A powerful wrench, and air rushed into his battered lungs. He felt a sharp tug at the nape of his neck, and the blue anorak tightened against his throat. The agonizing stench was gone and he was surrounded by the scent of unicorn breath, smelling of stars and frost. Gaudior was carrying him in his mouth, great ivory teeth clamped on the strong stuff of the anorak.

Gaudior's iridescent wings beat against the dark. Charles Wallace held his breath. If Gaudior dropped him, the Echthroi would be waiting. His armpits were cut from the pulling of the anorak, but he knew that he must not struggle. Gaudior's breath gusted painfully from between clenched teeth.

Then the silver hoofs touched stone, and they were safely at the star-watching rock. Gaudior opened his teeth and dropped the boy. For the first moments Charles Wallace was so weak that he collapsed onto the rock. Then he struggled to his feet, still trembling from the near disaster. He stretched his arms to ease his sore armpits and shoulders. Gaudior was breathing in great, panting gusts, his flanks heaving.

The soft breeze around them filled and healed their seared lungs.

Gaudior rolled his lips, and took a deep draught of clear air. Then he bent down and nuzzled Charles Wallace in the first gesture of affection he had shown. "I wasn't sure we were going to get away. The Echthroi are enraged that the wind managed to send you Within Madoc, and they're trying to stop you from going Within anyone else."

Charles Wallace stroked the unicorn's muzzle. "You saved me. I'd be tumbling in outer space forever if you hadn't grabbed my anorak."

"It was one chance in a million," Gaudior admitted. "And the wind helped me."

Charles Wallace reached up to put his arms around Gaudior's curving neck. "Even with help, it wasn't easy. Thank you."

Gaudior made a unicorn shrug; his curly beard quivered. "Unicorns find it embarrassing to be thanked. Please desist."

It was a hot, midsummer's day, with thunderheads massed on the horizon. The lake was gone, and the familiar valley stretched to the hills. The woods was a forest of mighty elms and towering oaks and hemlock. In the far distance was what looked like a cluster of log cabins.

"I don't think this looks like 1865," he told Gaudior.

"You'd know more about that than I would. I didn't have much opportunity to learn earth's history. I never expected this assignment."

"But, Gaudior, we have to know When we are."

"Why?"

Charles Wallace tried to quell his impatience, which was all the sharper after the terror of the attack. "If there's a Might-Have-Been we're supposed to discover, we have to know When it is, don't we?"

Gaudior's own impatience was manifested by prancing. "Why? We don't have to know everything. We have a charge laid on us, and we have to follow where it leads. You've been so busy trying to do the leading that we almost got taken by the Echthroi."

Charles Wallace said nothing.

"Perhaps," Gaudior granted grudgingly, "it wasn't entirely your fault. But I think we should not try to control the Whens and the Wheres, but should go Where we're sent. And what with all that contretemps with the Echthroi, you're still in your own body, and you're supposed to be Within."

"Oh. What should I do?"

Gaudior blew mightily through flared nostrils. "I will have to ask the wind." And he raised his head and opened his jaws. Charles Wallace waited anxiously until the unicorn lowered his head and raised one wing, stretching it to its full span. "Step close to me," he ordered.

Charles Wallace moved under the wing and leaned against Gaudior's flank. "Did the wind say When we are?"

"You make too many demands," Gaudior chided, and folded his wing until Charles Wallace felt smothered. Gasping for breath, he tried to push his way out into the air, but the wing held him firmly, and at last his struggling ceased.

When he opened his eyes the day had vanished, and trees and rock were bathed in moonlight.

*   *   *

He was Within. Lying on the rock, looking up at the moon-bathed sky. Only the most brilliant stars could compete with the silver light. Around him the sounds of summer sang sweetly. A mourning dove complained from her place deep in the darkest shadows. A grandfather frog boomed his bull-call. A pure trilling of bird song made him sit up and call out in greeting, "Zylle!"

A young woman stepped out from the shadows of the forest. She was tall and slender, except for her belly, which was heavy with child. "Thanks for meeting me, Brandon."

Charles Wallace-within-Brandon Llawcae gave her a swift hug. "Anything I do with you is fun, Zylle."

Again, as when he was Within Harcels, he was younger than fifteen, perhaps eleven or twelve, still very much a child, an eager, intelligent, loving child.

In the moonlight she smiled at him. "The herbs I need to ease the birthing of my babe are found only when the moon is full, and only here. Ritchie fears it would offend Goody Adams, did she know."

Goody, short for Goodwife. That's what the Pilgrims said, instead of Mrs. This was definitely not 1865, then. More than a century earlier, perhaps even two centuries. Brandon Llawcae must be the son of early settlers . . .

"Let yourself go," Gaudior knelled. "Let yourself be Brandon."

"But why are we here?" Charles Wallace demurred. "What can we learn here?"

"Stop asking questions."

"But I don't want to waste time . . ." Charles Wallace said anxiously.

Gaudior whickered irritably. "You are here, and you are in Brandon. Let go."

Let go.

Be Brandon.

Be.

"So," Zylle continued, "it is best that Ritchie not know, either. I can always trust you, Brandon. You don't open your mouth and spill everything out when to do so would bring no good."

Brandon ducked his head shyly, then looked swiftly up at Zylle's eyes, which were a startling blue in her brown face. "I have learned from the People of the Wind that 'tis no harm to hold a secret in the heart."

Zylle sighed. "No, it is no harm. But it grieves me that you and I may not share our gifts with those we love."

"My pictures." Brandon nodded. "My parents want me to try not to see my pictures."

"Among my people," Zylle said, "you would be known as a Seer, and you would be having the training in prayer and trusting that would keep your gift very close to the gods, from whom the gift comes. My father had hoped that Maddok might have the gift, because it is rare to have two with blue eyes in one generation. But my little brother's gift is to know about weather, when to plant and when to harvest, and that is a good gift, and a needed one."

"I miss Maddok." Bran scowled down at the rock. "He never comes to the settlement any more."

Zylle placed her hand lightly on his shoulder. "It's different in the settlement now that there are more families. Maddok no longer feels welcome."

"I welcome him!"

"He knows that. And he misses you, too. But it isn't only that the settlement is larger. Maddok is older, and has to do more work at home. But he will always be your friend."

"And I'll always be his. Always."

"Your pictures—" Zylle looked at him intently. "Are you able to stop seeing them?"

"Not always. When I look at something that holds a reflection, sometimes the pictures come, whether I will or no. But I try not to ask them to come."

"When you see your pictures, it is all right to tell me what you see, the way you used to tell Maddok."

"Ritchie is afraid of them."

She pressed his shoulder gently. "Life has been nothing but hard work for Ritchie, with no time for seeing pictures or dreaming dreams. Your mother tells me that in Wales there are people who are gifted with the second sight, and that these people may be feared for their gift but they are not frowned on."

"Ritchie says I would be frowned on. It is different here than in Wales. Especially since Pastor Mortmain came and built the church and scowled whenever Maddok visited the settlement or I went to the Indian compound."

"Pastor Mortmain would try to separate the white people from the Indians."

"But *why?*" Brandon demanded. "We were friends."

"And still are," Zylle assured him. "When did you last see a picture?"

"Tonight," he told her. "I saw the reflection of a candle on the side of the copper kettle Mother had just polished, and I saw a picture of here, this very place, but the rock was much higher, and there"—he pointed to the valley—"it was all a lake, with the sun sparkling on the water."

She looked at him wonderingly. "My father, Zillo, says that the valley was once a lake bed."

"And I saw Maddok—at least, it wasn't Maddok, because he was older, and his skin was fair, but he looked so like Maddok, at first I thought it was."

"The legend," she murmured. "Oh, Brandon, I feel we are very close, you and I. Perhaps it is having to keep our gifts hidden that brings us added closeness." While they were talking she had been gathering a small plant that grew between the grasses. She held the blossoms out to the moonlight. "I know where to find the healing herbs, herbs that will keep babies from choking to death in the winter, or from dying of the summer sickness when the weather is hot and heavy as it is now. But your mother warns me that I must not offer these gifts; they would not be well received. But for myself, and the birthing of Ritchie's and my baby, I will not be without the herbs which will help give me a good birthing and a fine child." She began to spread the delicate blossoms on the rock. As the moonlight touched them, petals and leaf alike appeared to glow with inner silver. Zylle looked up at the moon and sang,

> "Lords of fire and earth and water,
> Lords of moon and wind and sky,
> Come now to the Old Man's daughter,
> Come from fathers long gone by.
> Bring blue from a distant eye.
>
> Lords of water, earth, and fire,
> Lords of wind and snow and rain,
> Give to me my heart's desire.
> Life as all life comes with pain,
> But blue will come to us again."

Then she knelt and breathed in the fragrance of the blossoms, took them up in her hands, and pressed them against her forehead, her lips, her breasts, against the roundness of her belly.

Brandon asked, "Do we take the flowers home with us?"

"I would not want Goody Adams to see them."

"When Ritchie and I were born, there wasn't a midwife in the settlement."

"Goody Adams is a fine midwife," Zylle assured him. "Had she been here, your mother might not have lost those little ones between you and Ritchie. But she would not approve of what I have just done. We will leave the birthing flowers here for the birds and moon and the wind. They have already given me their help."

"When—oh, Zylle, do you know when the baby will come?"

"Tomorrow." She stood. "It's time we went home. I would not want Ritchie to wake and find me not beside him."

Brandon reached for her long, cool fingers. "It was the best day in the world when Ritchie married you."

She smiled swiftly, concealing a shadow of worry in her eyes. "The people of the settlement look with suspicion on an Indian in their midst, and a blue-eyed Indian at that."

"If they'd only listen to our story that comes from Wales, and to your story—"

She pressed his fingers. "Ritchie warns me not to talk about our legend of the white man who came to us in the days when there were only Indians on this continent."

"Long ago?"

"Long, long ago. He came from across the sea, from a land at the other end of the world, and he was a brave man, and true, who lusted neither after power nor after land. My little brother is named after him."

"And the song?" Brandon asked.

"It's old, very old, the prayer for a blue-eyed baby to keep the strength of the prince from over the sea within the Wind People, and the words may have changed over the years. And I have changed, for I have made my life with the white people, as the Golden Prince made his with the Wind People. For love he stayed with the princess of a strange land, and made her ways his ways. For love I leave my people and stay with Ritchie, and my love is deep, deep, for me to be able to leave my home. I sing the prayer because it is in my blood, and must be sung; and yet I wonder if my child will be allowed to know the Indian half of himself?"

"He?"

"It will be a boy."

"How do you know?"

"The trees have told me in the turning of their leaves under the moonlight. I would like a girl baby, but Ritchie will be pleased to have a son."

The footpath through the grasses led them to a brook, which caught the light of the moon and glimmered in the shifting shadows of the leaves. The brook was spanned by a natural stone bridge, and here Zylle paused, looking down at the water.

Brandon, too, looked at their reflections shifting and shimmering as the wind stirred the leaves. While he looked at Zylle's reflection, the water stirring her mouth into a tender smile, he saw, too, a baby held close in her arms, a black-haired, blue-eyed baby with gold behind its eyes.

Then, while he gazed, the eyes changed in the child and turned sullen, and the face was no longer the face of a baby but the face of a man, and he could not see Zylle anywhere. The man wore a strange-looking uniform with many medals, and his jowls were dark, jutting pridefully. He was thinking to himself, and he was thinking cruel thoughts, vindictive thoughts, and then Brandon saw fire, raging fire.

His body gave a mighty shudder and he gasped and turned toward Zylle, then glanced fearfully at the brook. The fire was gone, and only their two faces were reflected.

She asked, "What did you see?"

Eyes lowered, gazing on the dark stone of the bridge, he told her, trying not to let the images reappear in his mind's eye.

She shook her head somberly. "I make nothing out of it. Certainly nothing good."

Still looking down, Brandon said, "Before I was made to feel afraid of my pictures, they were never frightening, only beautiful."

Zylle squeezed his hand reassuringly. "I'd like to tell my father about this one, for he is trained in the interpretation of visions."

Brandon hesitated, then: "All right, if you want to."

"I want him to give me comfort," she said in a low voice.

They turned from the brook and walked on home in silence, to the dusty clearing with its cluster of log cabins.

The Llawcaes' cabin was the first, a sizable building with a central room for sitting and eating, and a bedroom at either end. Brandon's room was a shed added to his parents' room, and was barely large enough to hold a small bed, a chest, and a chair. But it was all his, and Ritchie had promised that after the baby was born he would cut a fine window in the wall, as people were beginning to do now that the settlement was established.

Brandon's cubbyhole was dark, but he was used to his own room's night and moved in it as securely as though he had lit a candle. Without undressing, he lay down on the bed. In the distance the thunder growled, and with the thunder came an echo, a low, rhythmic rumbling which

Brandon recognized as the drums of the Wind People as they sang their prayers for rain.

In the morning when he wakened, he heard bustling in the central room, and went in to find his mother boiling water in the big black kettle suspended from a large hook in the fireplace. Goody Adams, the midwife, was bustling about, exuding importance.

"This is a first birth," she said. "We'll need many kettles of water for the Indian girl."

"Zylle is our daughter," Brandon's mother reminded the midwife.

"Once an Indian, always an Indian, Goody Llawcae. Not forgetting that we're all grateful that her presence among us causes us to live in peace with the savage heathen."

"They're not—" Brandon started fiercely.

But his mother said, "The chores are waiting, Brandon."

Biting his lip, he went out.

The morning was clear, with a small mist drifting across the ground and hazing the outline of the hills. When the sun was full, the mist would go. The settlers were grateful for the mist and the heavy dews, which were all that kept the crops from drying up and withering completely, for there had been no rain for more than a moon.

Brandon went to the small barn behind the cabin to let their cow out into the daylight. She would graze with the other cattle all day, and at dusk Brandon would ride out on his pony to bring her home for milking. He gave the pony some oats, then fed the horse. In the distance he could hear hammering. Goodman Llawcae and his son Ritchie were the finest carpenters for many miles around, and were always busy with orders.

—I'm glad Ritchie didn't hear Goody Adams call Zylle's people savage heathens, he thought.—It's a good thing he was in with Zylle. Then he started back to the house. The picture he had seen in the brook the night before troubled him. He was afraid of the dark man with cruel thoughts, and he was afraid of the fire. Since he had tried to repress the pictures, they had become more and more frightening.

When he reached the cabin and went in through the door, which was propped open to allow all the fresh air possible to enter, his mother came out of the bedroom and spoke to Ritchie, who was pacing up and down in front of the fireplace.

"Your father needs you, Ritchie. Zylle is resting now, between pains. I will call you at once should she need you."

Goody Adams muttered, "The Indian girl does not cry. It is an omen."

Ritchie flung back his head. "It is the mark of the Indian, Goody. Zylle will shed no tears in front of you."

"Heathen—" Goody Adams started.

But Goody Llawcae cut her short. "Ritchie. Brandon. Go to your father."

Ritchie flung out the door, not deigning to look at the midwife. Brandon followed him, calling, "Ritchie—"

Ritchie paused, but did not turn around.

"I hate Goody Adams!" Brandon exploded.

Now Ritchie looked at his young brother. "Hate never did any good. Everyone in the settlement feels the lash of Goody Adams's tongue. But her hands bring out living babies, and there's been no childbed fever since she's been here."

"I liked it better when I was little and there was only us Llawcaes, and the Higginses, and Davey and I used to play with Maddok."

"It was simpler then," Ritchie agreed, "but change is the way of the world."

"Is change always good?"

Ritchie shook his head. "There was more joy when there were just the two families of us, and no Pastor Mortmain to put his dead hand on our songs and stories. I cannot find it in me to believe that God enjoys long faces and scowls at merriment. Get along with you now, Bran. I have work to do, and so do you."

When Brandon finished his chores and hurried back to the cabin, walking silently, one foot directly in front of the other, as Maddok had taught him, Ritchie, too, had returned, and was standing in the doorway. The sun was high in the sky and beat fiercely on the cabins and the dusty compound. The grass was turning brown, and the green leaves had lost their sheen.

Ritchie shook his head. "Not yet. It's fiercely hot. Look at those thunderheads."

"They've been there every day." Brandon looked at the heavy clouds massed on the horizon. "And not a drop of rain."

A low, nearly inaudible moan came from the cabin, and Ritchie hurried indoors. From the bedroom came a sharp cry, and Brandon's skin prickled with gooseflesh, despite the heat. "Oh God, God, make Zylle be all right." He focused on one small cloud in the dry blue, and there he saw a picture of Zylle and the black-haired, blue-eyed baby. And as he watched, both mother and child changed, and the mother was still black-haired, but creamy of skin, and the baby was bronze-skinned and blue-eyed, and the joy in the face of the mother was the same as in the picture of Zylle. But the fair-skinned mother was not in the familiar landscape but in a wild, hot country, and her clothes were not like the homespun or leather he was accustomed to, but different, finer than clothes he had seen before.

The baby began to cry, but the cry came not from the baby in the picture but from the cabin, a real cry, the healthy squall of an infant.

Goody Llawcae came to the door, her face alight. "It's a nephew you have, Brandon, a bonny boy, and Zylle beaming like the sun. Though sorrow endure for a night, joy cometh in the morning."

"It's afternoon."

"Don't be so literal, lad. Run to let your father know. Now!"

"But when may I see Zylle and the baby?"

"After his grandfather has had the privilege. Run!"

When Goody Adams had at last taken herself off, the Llawcaes gathered about the mother and child. Zylle lay on the big carved bed which Richard Llawcae had made for her and Ritchie as a wedding present. Light from the door to the kitchen-living room fell across her as she held the newborn child in her arms. Its eyes were tightly closed, and it waved tiny fists in searching gestures, and its little mouth opened and closed as though it were sipping its strange new element, air.

"Oh, taste and see," Zylle murmured, and touched her lips softly to the dark fuzz on the baby's head. His copper skin was still moist from the effort of birth and the humidity of the day. In the distance, thunder growled.

"His eyes?" Brandon whispered.

"Blue. Goody Adams says the color of the eyes often changes, but Bran's won't. No baby could ask for a better uncle. May we name him after you?"

Brandon nodded, blushing with pleasure, and reached out with one finger to touch the baby's cheek.

Richard Llawcae opened the big, much-used Bible, and read aloud, "I love the Lord, because he hath heard my voice and my supplications. The sorrows of death compassed me, and the pains of hell gat hold upon me: I found trouble and sorrow. Then called I upon the name of the Lord. Gracious is the Lord, and righteous. I was brought low, and he helped me. Return unto thy rest, O my soul; for the Lord hath dealt bountifully with thee."

"Amen," Zylle said.

Richard Llawcae closed the Book. "You are my beloved daughter, Zylle. When Ritchie chose you for his betrothed, his mother and I were uncertain at first, as were your own people. But it seemed to your father,

Zillo, and to me that two legends were coming together in this union. And time has taught us that it was a blessed inevitability."

"Thank you, Father." She reached out to his leathery hand. "Goody Adams did not like it that I shed no tears."

Goody Llawcae ran her hand gently over Zylle's shining black hair. "She knows that it is the way of your people."

—Savages, heathen savages, Brandon thought.—That's what Goody Adams thinks of Zylle's people.

When Bran went to do his evening chores a shadow materialized from behind the great trunk of a pine tree. Maddok.

Brandon greeted him with joy. "I'm glad, glad to see you! Father was going to send me to the Indian compound after chores, but now I can tell you: the baby's come! A boy, and all is well."

The shadow of a smile moved across Maddok's face, in which the blue eyes were as startling as they were in Zylle. "My father will be glad. Your family will allow us to come tonight, to see the baby?"

"Of course."

Maddok's eyes clouded. "It's not 'of course.' Not any more."

"It is with us Llawcaes. Maddok—how did you know to come, just now?"

"I saw Zylle yesterday. She told me it would be today."

"I didn't see you."

"You weren't alone. Davey Higgins was with you."

"But you and Davey and I always played together. It was the three of us."

"Not any more. Davey has been forbidden to leave the settlement and come to the compound. Your medicine man's gods do not respect our gods."

Brandon let his breath out in a sigh that was nearly a groan. "Pastor Mortmain. It's not our gods that don't respect your gods. It's Pastor Mortmain."

Maddok nodded. "And his son is courting Davey's sister."

Brandon giggled. "I'd love to see Pastor Mortmain's face if he heard himself referred to as a medicine man."

"He is not a good medicine man," Maddok said. "He will cause trouble."

"He already has. It's his fault Davey can't see you."

Maddok looked intently into Brandon's eyes. "My father also sent me to warn you."

"Warn? Of what?"

"We have had runners out. In the town there is much talk of witch-craft."

Witchcraft. It was an ugly word. "But not here," Brandon said.

"Not yet. But there is talk among your people."

"What kind of talk?" Brandon asked sharply.

"My sister shed no tears during the birth."

"They know that it is the way of the Indian."

"It is also the mark of a witch. They say that a cat ran screaming through the street at the time of the birth, and that Zylle put her pain into the cat."

"That is nonsense." But Brandon's eyes were troubled.

"My father says there are evil spirits abroad, hardening men's hearts. He says there is lust to see evil in innocence. Brandon, my friend and brother, take care of Zylle and the baby."

"Zylle and I picked herbs for the birthing," Brandon said in a low voice.

"Zylle was taught all the ways of a good delivery, and she has the healing gifts. But that, too, would be looked upon as magic. Black magic."

"But it's not magic—"

"No. It is understanding the healing qualities of certain plants and roots. People are afraid of knowledge that is not yet theirs. My father is concerned for Zylle, and for you."

Brandon protested. "But we are known as God-loving people. Surely they couldn't think—"

"Because you are known as such, they will wish to think," Maddok said. "My father says you should go more with the other children of the settlement, where you can see and hear. It's better to be prepared. I, too, will keep my ears open." Without saying goodbye, he disappeared into the forest.

Late in the evening, when most of the settlement was sleeping, Zylle's people came through the woods, silently, in single file, approaching the cabin from behind, as Maddok had done in the afternoon.

They clustered around Zylle and the baby, were served Goody Llawcae's special cold herb tea, and freshly baked bread, fragrant with golden cheese and sweet butter.

Zillo took his grandson into his arms, and a shadow of tenderness moved across his impassive face. "Brandon, son of Zylle of the Wind People and son of Ritchie of Llawcae, son of a prince from the distant land of Wales; Brandon, bearer of the blue," he murmured over the sleeping baby, rocking him gently in his arms.

Out of the corner of his eye, Brandon saw one of the Indian women go to his mother, talking to her softly. His mother put her hand to her head in a worried gesture.

And before the Indians left, he saw Zillo take his father aside.

Despite his joy in his namesake, there was heaviness in his heart when he went to bed, and it was that, as much as the heat, which kept him from sleeping. He could hear his parents talking with Ritchie in the next room, and he shifted position so that he could hear better.

Goody Llawcae was saying, "People do not like other people to be different. It is hard enough for Zylle, being an Indian, without being part of a family marked as different, too."

"Different?" Ritchie asked sharply. "We were the first settlers here."

"We come from Wales. And Brandon's gift is feared."

Richard asked his wife, "Did one of the Indians give you a warning?"

"One of the women. I had hoped this disease of witch-hunting would not touch our settlement."

"We must try not to let it start with us," Goodman Llawcae said. "At least the Higginses will stand by us."

"Will they?" Ritchie asked. "Goodman Higgins seems much taken with Pastor Mortmain. And Davey Higgins hasn't come to do chores with Brandon in a long time."

Richard said, "Zillo warned me of Brandon, too."

"Brandon—" Goody Llawcae drew in her breath.

"He saw one of his pictures last night."

On hearing this, Brandon hurried into the big room. "Zylle told you!"

"She did not, Brandon," his father said, "and eavesdroppers seldom hear anything pleasant. You did give Zylle permission to speak to her father, and it was he who told me. Are you ashamed to tell us?"

"Ashamed? No, Father, not ashamed. I try not to ask for the pictures, because you don't want me to see them, and I know it disturbs you when they come to me anyhow. That is why I don't tell you. I thought you would prefer me not to."

His father lowered his head. "It is understandable that you should feel this way. Perhaps we have been wrong to ask you not to see your pictures if they are God's gift to you."

Brandon looked surprised. "Who else would send them?"

"In Wales it is believed that such gifts come from God. There is not as much fear of devils there as here."

"Zylle and Maddok say my pictures come from the gods."

"And Zillo warned me," his father said, "that you must not talk about your pictures in front of anybody, especially Pastor Mortmain."

"What about Davey?"

"Not anybody."

"But Davey knows about my pictures. When we were little, I used to describe them to Davey and Maddok."

The parents looked at each other. "That was long ago. Let's hope Davey has forgotten."

Ritchie banged his fist against the hard wood of the bedstead. Richard held up a warning hand. "Hush. You will wake your wife and son. Once the heat breaks, people's temperaments will be easier. Brandon, go back to bed."

Back in his room, Brandon tossed hotly on his straw pallet. Even after the rest of the household was quiet, he could not sleep. In the distance he heard the drums. But no rain came.

The next evening when he was bringing the cow home from the day's grazing, Davey Higgins came up to him. "Bran, Pastor Mortmain says I am not to speak to you."

"You're speaking."

"We've known each other all our lives. I will speak as long as I can. But people are saying that Zylle is preventing the rain. The crops are withering. We do not want to offend the Indians, but Pastor Mortmain says that Zylle's blue eyes prove her to be not a true Indian, and that the Indians were afraid of her and wished her onto us."

"You know that's not true!" Brandon said hotly. "The Indians are proud of the blue eyes."

"I know it," Davey said, "and you know it, but we are still children, and people do not listen to children. Pastor Mortmain has forbidden us to go to the Indian compound, and Maddok is no longer welcome here. My father believes everything Pastor Mortmain says, and my sister is being courted by his son, that pasty-faced Duthbert. Bran, what do your pictures tell you of all this?" Davey gave Brandon a sidewise glance.

Brandon looked at him directly. "I'm twelve years old now, Davey. I'm no longer a child with a child's pictures." He left Davey and took the cow to the shed, feeling that denying the pictures had been an act of betrayal.

Maddok came around the corner of the shed. "My father has sent me to you, in case there is danger. I am to follow you, but not be seen. But you know Indian ways, and you will see me. So I wanted you to know, so that you won't be afraid."

"I am afraid," Brandon said flatly.

"If only it would rain," Maddok said.

"You know about weather. Will it rain?"

Maddok shook his head. "The air smells of thunder, but there will be no rain this moon. There is lightning in the air, and it turns people's minds. How is Zylle? and the baby?"

Now Brandon smiled. "Beautiful."

At family prayers that evening the Llawcae faces were sober. Richard asked for wisdom, for prudence, for rain. He asked for faithfulness in friendship, and for courage. And again for rain.

The thunder continued to grumble. The heavy night was sullen with heat lightning. And no drop fell.

The children would not talk with Brandon. Even Davey shamefacedly turned away. Mr. Mortmain, confronting Brandon, said, "There is evil under your roof. You had better see to it that it is removed."

When Brandon reported this, Ritchie exploded. "The evil is in Mr. Mortmain's own heart."

The evil was as pervasive as the brassy heat.

Pastor Mortmain came in the evening to the Llawcaes' cabin, bringing with him his son, Duthbert, and Goodman Higgins. "We would speak with the Indian woman."

"My wife—" Ritchie started, but his father silenced him.

"It is late for this visit, Pastor Mortmain," Richard said. "My daughter-in-law and the baby have retired."

"Then they must be wakened. It is our intention to discover if the Indian woman is a Christian, or—"

Zylle walked into the room, carrying her child. "Or what, Pastor Mortmain?"

Duthbert looked at her, and his eyes were greedy.

Goodman Higgins questioned her gently. "We believe you to be a Christian, Zylle. That is true, is it not?"

"Yes, Goodman Higgins. When I married Ritchie I accepted his beliefs."

"Even though they were contrary to the beliefs of your people?" Pastor Mortmain asked.

"But they are not contrary."

"The Indians are pagans," Duthbert said.

Zylle looked at the pasty young man over the baby's head. "I do not know what pagan means. I only know that Jesus of Nazareth sings the true song. He knows the ancient harmonies."

Pastor Mortmain drew in his breath in horror. "You say that our Lord and Saviour sings! What more do we need to hear?"

"But why should he not sing?" Zylle asked. "The very stars sing as they turn in their heavenly dance, sing praise of the One who created them. In the meeting house do we not sing hymns?"

Pastor Mortmain scowled at Zylle, at the Llawcaes, at his son, who could not keep his eyes off Zylle's loveliness, at Goodman Higgins. "That is different. You are a heathen and you do not understand."

Zylle raised her head proudly. "Scripture says that God loves every man. That is in the Psalms. He loves my people as he loves you, or he is not God."

Higgins warned, "You must not blaspheme, child."

"Why," demanded Pastor Mortmain, "are you holding back the rain?"

"Why ever should I wish to hold back the rain? Our corn suffers as does yours. We pray for rain, twice daily, at morning and at evening prayer."

"The cat," Duthbert said. "What about the cat?"

"The cat is to keep rodents away from house and barn, like all the cats in the settlement."

Pastor Mortmain said, "Goody Adams tells us the cat is to help you fly through the air."

Duthbert's mouth dropped slightly, and Ritchie shouted with outrage. But Zylle silenced him with a gesture, asking, "Does your cat help you to fly through the air, Pastor Mortmain? No more does mine. The gift of flying through the air is given to only the most holy of people, and I am only a woman like other women."

"Stop, child," Goodman Higgins ordered, "before you condemn yourself."

"Are you a true Indian?" Pastor Mortmain demanded.

She nodded. "I am of the People of the Wind."

"Indians do not have blue eyes."

"You have heard our legend."

"Legend?"

"Yes. Though we believe it to be true. My father has the blue eyes, too, as does my little brother."

"Lies!" Pastor Mortmain cried. "Storytelling is of the devil."

Richard Llawcae took a step toward the small, dark figure of the minister. "How strange that you should say that, Pastor Mortmain. Scripture says that Jesus taught by telling stories. *And he spake many things unto them in parables . . . and without a parable spake he not unto them.* That is in the thirteenth chapter of the Gospel according to Matthew."

Pastor Mortmain's face was hard. "I believe this Indian woman to be a witch. And if she is, she must die like a witch. That, too, is in Scripture." He gestured to Goodman Higgins and Duthbert. "We will meet in church and make our decision."

"Who will make the decision?" Ritchie demanded, not heeding his father's warning hand. "All the men of the settlement, in fair discussion, or you, Pastor Mortmain?"

"Be careful," Goodman Higgins urged. "Ritchie, take care."

"David Higgins," Richard Llawcae said, "our two cabins were the first in this settlement. You have known us longer than anyone else here. Do you believe that my son would marry a witch?"

"Not knowingly, Richard."

"You were here with us during the evenings when the Indians came to listen to our stories, and we heard their own legend that matched ours. You saw how the Indian legend and the Welsh one insured peace between us and the People of the Wind, did you not, now, David?"

"Yes, that is so."

Pastor Mortmain intervened. "Goodman Higgins has told me of the storytelling which preceded the sop of reading from Scripture."

"Scripture was never a sop for us, Pastor. Those early years were hard. Goody Higgins died birthing Davey, and after her death in one week three of David's children died of diphtheria, and another only a year later coughed his life away. My wife lost four little ones between Richard and Brandon, one at birth, the other three as children. We were sustained and strengthened by Scripture then, as we are still. As for the stories, the winter evenings were long, and it was a pleasant way to while away the time as we worked with our hands."

Goodman Higgins shuffled his feet. "There was no harm in the stories, Pastor Mortmain. I have assured you of that."

"Perhaps not for you," Pastor Mortmain said. "Come."

Goodman Higgins did not look up as he followed Pastor Mortmain and Duthbert out of the cabin.

Nightmare. Brandon wanted to scream, to make himself wake up, but he was not asleep, and the nightmare was happening. When he did his chores he was aware that Maddok was invisibly there, watching over him. Sometimes he heard him rustling up in the branches of a tree. Sometimes Maddok let Brandon have a glimpse of him behind a tree trunk, behind the corner of a barn or cabin. But wherever he went, Maddok was there, and that meant that the Indians knew all that was happening.

* * *

A baby in the settlement died of the summer sickness, which had always been the chief cause of infant mortality during the hot months, but it was all that was needed to convict Zylle.

Pastor Mortmain sent to the town for a man who was said to be an expert in the detection of witches. He had sent many people to the gallows.

"And that's supposed to make him an expert?" Ritchie demanded.

The settlement crackled with excitement. It seemed to Brandon that people were enjoying it. The Higgins daughter walked along the dusty street with Duthbert, and did not raise her eyes, but Pastor Mortmain's son smiled, and it was not a pleasant smile. People lingered in their doorways, staring at Pastor Mortmain and the expert on witches as they stood in front of the church. Davey Higgins stayed in his cabin and did not come out, though the other children were as eager as their parents to join in the witch hunt.

It was part of the nightmare when the man from the city who had hanged many people gave Pastor Mortmain and the elders of the village his verdict: there was no doubt in his mind that Zylle was a witch.

A sigh of excitement, of horror, of pleasure, went along the street.

That evening when Brandon went to the common pasture to bring the cow home, one of the other boys spat on the ground and turned away. Davey Higgins, tying the halter on the Higgins cow, said, "It is the Lord's will that the witch should die."

"Zylle is not a witch."

"She's a heathen."

"She's a Christian. A better one than you are."

"She's a condemned witch, and tomorrow they take her to the jail in town, though she'll be brought back here to be hanged—"

"So we can all see." One of the boys licked his lips in anticipation.

"No!" Brandon cried. "No!"

Davey interrupted him. "You'd better hold your tongue, or I could tell things about you to make Pastor Mortmain condemn you as a witch, too."

Brandon looked levelly at Davey while the others teased him to tell. Davey flushed. "No. I didn't mean anything. Brandon is my friend. It's not his fault his brother married a witch."

"How could you let them take Zylle and the baby away?" Brandon demanded of Ritchie and his parents. "How could you!"

"Son," Richard Llawcae said, "Zylle is not safe here, not now with feelings running high. There are those who would hang her immediately.

Your brother and I are going to town tomorrow to speak to people we know there. We think they will help us."

But the witch-hunting fever was too high. There was no help. There was no reason. There was only nightmare.

Goody Llawcae stayed in the town to tend Zylle and the baby; that much was allowed, but it was not through kindness; there were those who feared that Zylle might try to take her own life, or that something might happen to prevent them seeing a public hanging.

Richard and Ritchie refused to erect the gallows.

Avoiding their eyes, Goodman Higgins pleaded, "You must not refuse to do this, or you, too, will be accused. In the town they have convicted entire families."

Richard said, "There was another carpenter, once, and he would have refused to do this thing. Him I will follow."

There were others more than willing to erect a crude gallows. A gallows is more easily built than a house, or a bed, or a table.

The date for the hanging was set.

On the eve, Brandon went late to bring the cow in from the pasture, in order to avoid the others. When he got to the barn, Maddok was waiting there in the shadows.

"My father wants to see you."

"When?" Bran asked.

"Tonight. After the others are asleep, can you slip away without being seen?"

Bran nodded. "You have taught me how to do that. I will come. It has meant much to me to know that you have been with me."

"We are friends," Maddok said without a smile.

"Is it going to rain soon?" Brandon asked.

"No. Not unless prayer changes things."

"You pray every night. So do we."

"Yes. We pray," Maddok said, and slipped silently into the woods.

In the small hours of the morning, before dawn, when he was sure everybody in the settlement would be asleep, Brandon left the cabin and ran swiftly as a young deer into the protecting shadows of the woods.

Maddok was standing at the edge of the forest, waiting. "Come. I know the way in the dark more easily than you."

"Zillo knows everything? You've told him?"

"Yes. But he wants to meet with you."

"Why? I'm still only a child."

"You have the gift of seeing."

Brandon shivered.

"Come," Maddok urged. "My father is waiting."

They traveled swiftly, Brandon following Maddok as he led the way, over the brook, through the dark shadows of the forest.

At the edge of the Indian clearing, Zillo stood. Maddok nodded at his father, then vanished into the shadows.

"You won't let it happen?" Brandon begged. "If Zylle is harmed, Ritchie will kill."

"We will not let it happen."

"The men of the settlement expect the Indians to come. They have guns. They are out of their right minds, and they will not hesitate to shoot."

"They must be prevented. Have you seen anything in a vision lately?"

"I have tried not to. I am afraid."

"No one knows you are here?"

"Only Maddok."

Zillo pulled a polished metal sphere from a small pouch and held it out to catch the light of the late moon. "What do you see?"

Brandon hesitantly looked into it. "This is right for me to do, when my father . . . ?"

Zillo's eyes were expressionless. "I have held this action in prayer all day. It is not your father's wish to deny a gift of the gods, and at this time we have no one in the tribe with the gift of seeing."

As Brandon looked, the light in the metal sphere shifted, and he saw clouds moving swiftly across the sky, clouds reflected in water. Not taking his eyes from the scrying metal he said, "I see a lake where the valley should be, a lake I have seen before in a picture. It is beautiful."

Zillo nodded. "It is said there was a lake here in long-gone days. In the valley people have found stones with the bones of fish in them."

"The sky is clouding up," Brandon reported. "Rain is starting to fall, spattering into the water of the lake."

"You see no fire?"

"Before, I saw fire, and I was afraid. Now there is only rain."

The severity of Zillo's face lifted barely perceptibly. "That is good, that picture. Now I will teach you some words. You must learn them very carefully, and you must make sure that you do not use them too soon. Only the blue-eyed children of the Wind People are taught these words, and never before have they been given to one not of the tribe. But I give them to you for Zylle's saving."

On the morning of the execution Zylle was returned to the settlement. Infant Brandon was taken from her and given to Goody Llawcae.

"He is too young to be weaned," Goody Llawcae objected. "He will die of the summer sickness."

"The witch will not harm her own child," Pastor Mortmain said.

It took six of the strongest men in the settlement to restrain Ritchie and Richard.

"Tie the witch's hands," the man from the city ordered.

"I will do it," Goodman Higgins said. "Hold out your hands, child."

"Show her no gentleness, Higgins," Pastor Mortmain warned, "unless you would have us think you tainted, too. After all, you have listened to their tales."

Goody Llawcae, holding the crying baby, said, "Babies have died of the summer sickness for years, long before Zylle came to dwell among us, and no one thought of witchcraft."

Angry murmurs came from the gathered people. "The witch made another baby die. Let her brat die as well."

Ritchie, struggling compulsively, nearly broke away.

Pastor Mortmain said, "When the witch is dead, you will come back to your senses. We are saving you from the evil."

The people of the settlement crowded about the gallows in ugly anticipation of what was to come. Davey Higgins stayed in the doorway of his cabin.

Goodman Higgins and Pastor Mortmain led Zylle across the dusty compound and up the steps to the gallows.

Brandon thought his heart would beat its way out of his body. He felt a presence beside him, and there was Maddok, and he knew that the rest of the tribe was close by.

"Now," Maddok whispered.

And then Brandon cried aloud the words which Zillo had taught him.

> *"With Zylle in this fateful hour*
> *I call on all Heaven with its power*
> *And the sun with its brightness,*
> *And the snow with its whiteness,*
> *And the fire with all the strength it hath,*
> *And the lightning with its rapid wrath—"*

Thunderstorms seldom came till late afternoon. But suddenly the sky was cleft by a fiery bolt, and the church bore the power of its might. The crash of thunder was almost simultaneous. The sky darkened from a humid blue to a sulfurous dimness. Flame flickered about the doorway of the church.

The Indians stepped forward until the entire settlement was aware of their presence, silent and menacing. Several men raised guns. As Duthbert fired, lightning flashed again and sent Duthbert sprawling, a long burn down his arm, his bullet going harmlessly into the air. Flames wreathed the belfry of the church.

Zillo sprang across the compound and up the steps to the gallows. "No guns," he commanded, "or the lightning will strike again. And this time it will kill."

Duthbert was moaning with pain. "Put down the guns—don't shoot—"

Pastor Mortmain's face was distorted. "You are witches, all of you, witches! The Llawcae boy has the Indian girl's devil with him that he can call lightning! He must die!"

The Indians drew in closer. Maddok remained by Brandon. And then Davey Higgins came from the door of his cabin and stood on Brandon's other side.

Ritchie broke away from the men who were holding him, and sprang up onto the gallows. "People of the settlement!" he cried. "Do you think all power is of the devil? What we have just seen is the wrath of God!" He turned his back on the crowd and began to untie Zylle.

The mood of the people was changing. Richard was let loose and he crossed the dusty compound to Pastor Mortmain. "Your church is burning because you tried to kill an innocent woman. Our friends and neighbors would never have consented to this madness had you not terrified them with your fire and brimstone."

Goodman Higgins moved away from Pastor Mortmain. "That is right. The Llawcaes have always been God-fearing people."

The Indians drew closer.

Ritchie had one arm about Zylle. He called out again:

"The Indians have always been our friends. Is this how we return their friendship?"

"Stop them—" Pastor Mortmain choked out. "Stop the Indians! They will massacre us—stop them—"

Ritchie shouted, "Why should we? Do you want us to show you more compassion than you have shown us?"

"Ritchie!" Zylle faced him. "You are not like Pastor Mortmain. You have a heart in you. Show them your compassion!"

Zillo raised a commanding hand. "This evil has been stopped. As long as nothing like this ever happens again, you need not fear us. But it must never happen again."

Murmurs of "Never, never, we are sorry, never, never," came from the crowd.

Pastor Mortmain moaned, "The fire, the fire, my God, the church, the church is burning."

Ritchie led Zylle down the steps and to his mother, who put the baby into her daughter-in-law's waiting arms. Brandon, standing between Maddok and Davey, watched as his mother and Zylle, his father and brother, turned their backs on the burning church and walked across the compound, past their chastened neighbors, past the watchful Indians, and went into their cabin. He stayed, his feet rooted to the ground as though he could not move, while the people of the settlement brought ineffectual buckets of water to try to control the flames and keep the fire from spreading to the cabins around the church. He watched the belfry collapse, a belfry erected more to the glory of Pastor Mortmain than to the glory of God.

And then he felt the rain, a gentle rain which would fall all day and sink into the thirsty ground, a rain which would continue until the deepest roots of plant and tree had their chance to drink. A rain which put out the fire before it spread to any of the dwellings.

Behind the three boys the People of the Wind stood silently, watching, as the people went slowly into their cabins. When there was no one left by the empty gallows except the three children, Zillo barked a sharp command and the Indians quickly dismantled the ill-built platform and gallows, threw the wood on the smoking remains of the church, and left, silently.

The horror was over, but nothing would ever be the same again.

When Brandon and Maddok went into the Llawcae cabin, Zillo was there, holding the baby. The kettle was simmering, and Goody Llawcae was serving herb tea, "to quieten us."

"I am angry." Ritchie looked past Brandon to his mother. "Your herbs will not stop my anger."

"You have cause to be angry," his father said. "Anger is not bitterness. Bitterness can go on eating at a man's heart and mind forever. Anger spends itself in its own time. Small Brandon will help to ease the anger."

Zillo handed the baby to Ritchie, who took his son and held him against his strong shoulder. Ritchie looked, then, at his brother. "Where did you get those words you called out just before the storm?"

"From Zillo."

"When?"

"Last night. He sent for me."

Zillo looked at Richard and Ritchie, his eyes fathomless. "He is a good lad, your young one."

Richard Llawcae returned Zillo's gaze, and put his arm lightly around Brandon's shoulders. "The ways of the Lord are mysterious, and we do not need to understand them. His ways are not our ways—though we would like them to be. We do not need to understand Brandon's gifts, only to know that they are given to him by God." He turned to the Bible and leafed through the pages until he had found the passage he wanted. "The Lord is faithful, who shall establish you, and keep you from evil. And the Lord direct your hearts into the love of God. Now the Lord of peace himself give you peace always by all means . . ."

Brandon, worn out by lack of sleep, by terror and tension, put his head down on his arms and slid into sleep, only half hearing as Ritchie said that he could not continue to live in the settlement. He would take Zylle and the baby and return to Wales, where they could start a new life . . .

The world was bleak for Brandon when Ritchie and Zylle and the baby left.

One day as he was doing his chores, Maddok appeared, helped him silently, and then together they went through the woods toward the Indian compound.

Under the great shadowing branches of an oak, Maddok paused. He looked long at Brandon. "It is right that Zylle should have gone with Ritchie."

Brandon looked at Maddok, then at the ground.

"And it is right that you and I should become brothers. My father will perform the ceremony tonight, and you will be made one of the People of the Wind."

A spark of the old light appeared in Brandon's face. "Then no one can keep us apart."

"No one. And perhaps you will marry one of the People of the Wind. And perhaps our children will marry, so that our families will be united until eternity."

Brandon reached for Maddok's hands. "Until eternity," he said.

7 The Winds with Their Swiftness

And Charles Wallace was on Gaudior's back.

"I've read about the Salem trials, of course," he mused aloud. "Is there—oh, Gaudior, do other planets have the same kind of horror as ours?"

"There are horrors wherever the Echthroi go."

"Brandon: he's younger than I. And yet—am I like Brandon? Or is he like me?"

"I do not think you would be accepted by a host who is alien to what you are—Gwydyr, for instance."

"I hate to think I caused Brandon so much pain—"

"Do not take too much on yourself," Gaudior warned. "We don't know what would have happened had you not been Within Brandon."

"What did we learn Within? It's a strange triangle: Wales and here; Wales and Vespugia; Vespugia and here. It's all interconnected, and we have to find the connections—oh!" He stepped back from Gaudior with a startled flash of comprehension.

"What now?" Gaudior asked.

Charles Wallace's voice rose with excitement. "When Madoc is spelled the Welsh way, it's Madog! Get it?"

Gaudior blew a small bubble.

"Madog. Mad Dog. It's a play on words. Mad Dog Branzillo may really be Madog. El Rabioso. Mad Dog. It's a ghastly sort of pun. Madoc: Madog: Mad Dog."

The unicorn looked down his long nose. "You may have something there."

"So there's another connection! Gaudior, we have to go to Patagonia, to Vespugia. I understand that it isn't easy for unicorns to move in both time and space, but you've got to try."

Gaudior raised his wings and stretched them up toward the sky. "The last time we gave explicit directions to the wind, look what happened."

"We didn't get to 1865. But we did learn important things about Madoc's descendants."

"Is that all you remember?" The unicorn folded his wings.

"It's in the book, Matthew Maddox's—"

"Somehow or other," Gaudior said, "we are blundering closer and closer to the Might-Have-Been which the Echthroi don't want us to get to, and the closer we get, the more they will try to prevent us. Already you have changed small things, and they are angry."

"What have I changed?"

"Don't you know?"

Charles Wallace bowed his head. "I tried to stop Harcels from seeing the ways of other men."

"And . . ."

"Zylle—I tried to stop them from hanging her. Would she have been hanged—without the rune?"

"There are many things unicorns do not feel they need to know."

"And there are some things we do need to know if we're to succeed in doing what Mrs. O'Keefe asked me to do." For a moment he looked startled, remembering Calvin's mother. "How strange that it should have come from Mrs. O'Keefe—the charge. And the rune."

"That should teach you something."

"It does. It teaches me that we have to go to Vespugia to find the connection between Mom O'Keefe and Mad Dog Branzillo."

The light in Gaudior's horn flickered rapidly.

"I know—" Charles Wallace stroked the unicorn's neck. "The Echthroi nearly got us when we were aiming for 1865 in our own Where. Perhaps we have to leave the star-watching rock and aim for 1865 in Patagonia, when the Welsh group arrived there. Perhaps they met Gwydyr's descendants. I think we have no choice now except to go to Patagonia."

"They may attack us again." Gaudior's anxious neigh broke into silver shards. "It might be a good idea for you to tie yourself to me. If the Echthroi tear you from my back again, it isn't likely that I'd be able to catch you a second time."

Charles Wallace looked all around him, carefully, and saw nothing but the woods, the rock, the valley, the mountains beyond. Then: "I know!" He slid off Gaudior's back to the rock. "I forgot to bring in the hammock this autumn. Meg usually does it. It's just a few yards along the path, between two old apple trees. It's a woven rope one, and it's hung on good stout laundry rope, from Mortmain's General Store— Mortmain! Gaudior, do you suppose—"

"We don't have time for suppositions," Gaudior warned. "Bind yourself to me."

Charles Wallace hurried along the path, with the unicorn following, prancing delicately as bare blackberry canes reached across the path and tore at his silver hide.

"Here we are. Mother likes the hammock to be far away from the house so that she can't possibly hear the telephone." He started untying one end of the hammock. The branches of the apple trees were bare of leaves, but a few withered apples still clung palely to the topmost branches. The earth around the trees and under the hammock smelled of cider vinegar and mulching leaves.

"Make haste slowly," Gaudior advised, as Charles Wallace's trembling fingers fumbled with the knots. The air was cold, and the unicorn bent his neck so that he could breathe on Charles Wallace's fingers to warm them. "Think only about untying the knots. The Echthroi are near."

Warmed by the unicorn's breath, the boy's fingers began to lose their stiffness, and he managed to untie the first knot. Two more knots, and one end of the hammock dropped to the leafy ground, and Charles Wallace moved to the second tree, where the hammock seemed even more firmly secured to the gnarled trunk. He worked in silence until the hammock was freed. "Kneel," he told the unicorn.

Charles Wallace dragged one end of the hammock under the unicorn, so that the heavy webbing was under Gaudior's great abdomen. With difficulty he managed to fling the rope up over Gaudior's flanks. He clambered up and bound the rope securely around his waist. "It's a good thing Mother always uses enough rope for five hammocks."

Gaudior whickered. "Are you tied on securely?"

"I think so. The twins taught me to make knots."

"Hold on to my mane, too."

"I am."

"I don't like this," Gaudior objected. "Are you sure you think we ought to try to go to Patagonia?"

"I think it's what we have to do."

"I'm worried." But Gaudior began to run, until he had gathered enough speed to launch himself.

*   *   *

The attack came almost immediately, Echthroi surrounding boy and unicorn. Charles Wallace's hands were torn from Gaudior's mane, but the rope held firm. The breath was buffeted out of him, and his eyelids were sealed tight against his eyes by the blasting wind, but the Echthroi did not succeed in pulling him off Gaudior's back. The rope strained and groaned, but the knots held.

Gaudior's breath came in silver streamers. He had folded his wings into his flanks to prevent the Echthroid wind from breaking them. Boy and unicorn were flung through endless time and space.

A cold, stenching wind picked them up and they were flung downward with a violence over which the unicorn had no control. Helplessly they descended toward a vast darkness.

They crashed.

They hit with such impact that Charles Wallace thought fleetingly, just before he lost consciousness, that the Echthroi had flung them onto rock and this was the end.

But the descent continued. Down down into blackness and cold. No breath. A feeling of strangling, a wild ringing in the ears. Then he seemed to be rising, up, up, and light hit his closed eyes with the force of a blow, and clear cold air rushed into his lungs. He opened his eyes.

It was water and not rock they had been thrown against.

"Gaudior!" he cried, but the unicorn floated limply on the surface of the darkness, half on his side, so that one of Charles Wallace's legs was still in the water. The boy bent over the great neck. No breath came from the silver nostrils. There was no rise and fall of chest, no beat of heart. "Gaudior!" he cried in anguish. "Don't be dead! Gaudior!"

Still, the unicorn floated limply, and small waves plashed over his face.

"Gaudior!" With all his strength Charles Wallace beat against the motionless body.—The rune, he thought wildly,—the rune . . .

But no words came, except the unicorn's name. "Gaudior! Gaudior!"

A trembling stirred the silver body, and then Gaudior's breath came roaring out of him like an organ with all the stops pulled out. Charles Wallace sobbed with relief. The unicorn opened eyes which at first were glazed, then cleared and shone like diamonds. He began to tread water. "Where are we?"

Charles Wallace bent over the beautiful body, stroking neck and mane in an ecstasy of relief. "In the middle of an ocean."

"Which ocean?" Gaudior asked testily.

"I don't know."

"It's your planet. You're supposed to know."

"Is it my planet?" Charles Wallace asked. "The Echthroi had us. Are you sure we aren't in a Projection?"

Unicorn and boy looked around. The water stretched to the horizon on all sides. Above them the sky was clear, with a few small clouds.

"It's not a Projection." Gaudior whickered. "But we could be anywhere in Creation, on any planet in any galaxy which has air with oxygen and plenty of water. Does this seem to you like an ordinary earth ocean?" He shook his head, and water sprayed out from his mane. "I am not thinking clearly yet . . ." He gulped air, then regurgitated a large quantity of salt water. "I have drunk half this ocean."

"It looks like a regular ocean," Charles Wallace said tentatively, "and it feels like winter." His drenched anorak clung to his body in wet folds. His boots were full of water, which sloshed icily against his feet. "Look!" He pointed ahead of them to a large crag of ice protruding from the water. "An iceberg."

"Which direction is land?"

"Gaudior, if we don't even know what galaxy or planet we're on, how do you expect me to know where land is?"

With difficulty Gaudior stretched his wings to their fullest extent, so that they shed water in great falls that splashed noisily against the waves. His legs churned with a mighty effort to keep afloat.

"Can you fly?" Charles Wallace asked.

"My wings are waterlogged."

"Can't you ask the wind where we are?"

A shudder rippled along the unicorn's flanks. "I'm still half winded—the wind—the wind—we hit water so hard it's a wonder all our bones aren't broken. The wind must have cushioned our fall. Are you still tied on?"

"Yes, or I wouldn't be here. Ask the wind, please."

"Winded—the wind—the wind—" Again Gaudior shook water from his wings. He opened his mouth in his characteristic gesture of drinking, gulped in the cold, clear breeze, his lips pulled back to reveal the dangerous-looking teeth. He closed his eyes and his long lashes were dark against his skin, which had paled to the color of moonlight. He opened his eyes and spat out a great fountain of water. "Thank the galaxies."

"Where are we?"

"Your own galaxy, your own solar system, your own planet. Your own Where."

"You mean this is the place of the star-watching rock? Only it's covered by an ocean?"

"Yes. And the wind says it's midsummer."

Charles Wallace looked at the iceberg. "It's a good thing it's summer, or we'd be dead from cold. And summer or no, we'll die of cold if we don't get out of water and onto land, and soon."

Gaudior sighed. "My wings are still heavy with water and my legs are tiring."

A wave dashed over them. Charles Wallace swallowed a mouthful of salty water and choked, coughing painfully. His lungs ached from the battering of the Echthroid wind and the cold of the sea. He was desperately sleepy. He thought of travelers lost in a blizzard, and how in the end all they wanted was to lie down in the snow and go to sleep, and if they gave in to sleep they would never wake up again. He struggled to keep his eyes open, but it hardly seemed worth the effort.

Gaudior's legs moved more and more slowly. When the next wave went over them, the unicorn did not kick back up to the surface.

As water and darkness joined to blot out Charles Wallace's consciousness, he heard a ringing in his ears, and through the ringing a voice calling, "The rune, Chuck! Say it! Say the rune!"

But the weight of the icy water bore him down.

Ananda's frantic whining roused Meg.

"Say it, Charles!" she cried, sitting bolt-upright.

Ananda whined again, then gave a sharp bark.

"I'm not sure I remember the words—" Meg pressed both hands against the dog, and called out,

> "With Ananda in this fateful hour
> I place all Heaven with its power
> And the sun with its brightness,
> And the snow with its whiteness,
> And the fire with all the strength it hath,
> And the lightning with its rapid wrath,
> And the winds with their swiftness along their path..."

The wind lifted and the whitecaps were churned into rolling breakers, and unicorn and boy were raised to the surface of the water and caught in a great curling comber and swept along with it across the icy sea until they were flung onto the white sands of dry land.

8 The Sea with Its Deepness

Unicorn and boy vomited sea water and struggled to breathe, their lungs paining them as though they were being slashed by knives. They were sheltered from the wind by a cliff of ice onto which the sun was pouring, so that water was streaming down in little rivulets. The warmth of the sun which was melting the ice also melted the chill from their sodden bodies, and began to dry the unicorn's waterlogged wings. Gradually their blood began to flow normally and they breathed without choking on salt water.

Because he was smaller and lighter (and billions of years younger, Gaudior pointed out later), Charles Wallace recovered first. He managed to wriggle out of the still-soaking anorak and drop it down onto the wet sand. Then with difficulty he kicked off the boots. He looked at the ropes which still bound him to the unicorn; the knots were pulled so tight and the cord was by now so sodden that it was impossible to untie himself. Exhausted, he bent over Gaudior's neck and felt the healing sun send its rays deep into his body. Warmed and soothed, his nose pressed against wet unicorn mane, he fell into sleep, a deep, life-renewing sleep.

When he awoke, Gaudior was stretching his wings out to the sun. A few drops of water still clung to them, but the unicorn could flex them with ease.

"Gaudior," Charles Wallace started, and yawned.

"While you were sleeping," the unicorn reproved gently, "I have been consulting the wind. Praise the Music that we're in the When of the melting of the ice or we could not have survived." He, too, yawned.

"Do unicorns sleep?" Charles Wallace asked.

"I haven't needed to sleep in aeons."

"I feel all the better for a nap. Gaudior, I'm sorry."

"For what?"

"For making you try to get us to Patagonia. If I hadn't, we might not have been nearly killed by the Echthroi."

"Apology accepted," Gaudior said briskly. "Have you learned?"

"I've learned that every time I've tried to control things we've had trouble. I don't know what we ought to do now, or Where or When we ought to go from here. I just don't know . . ."

"I think"—Gaudior turned his great head to look at the boy—"that our next step is to get all these knots untied."

Charles Wallace ran his fingers along the rope. "The knots are all sort of welded together from wind and water and sun. I can't possibly untie them."

Gaudior wriggled against the pressure of the ropes. "They appear to have shrunk. I am very uncomfortable."

After a futile attempt at what looked like the most pliable of the knots, Charles Wallace gave up. "I've got to find something to cut the rope."

Gaudior trotted slowly up and down the beach. There were shells, but none sharp enough. They saw a few pieces of rotting driftwood, and some iridescent jellyfish and clumps of seaweed. There were no broken bottles or tin cans or other signs of mankind, and while Charles Wallace was usually horrified at human waste and abuse of nature, he would gladly have found a broken beer bottle.

Gaudior turned inland around the edge of the ice cliff, moving up on slipping sand runneled by melting ice. "This is absurd. After all we've been through, who would have thought I'd end up like a centaur with you permanently affixed to my back?" But he continued to struggle up until he was standing on the great shoulder of ice.

"Look!" Charles Wallace pointed to a cluster of silvery plants with long spikes which had jagged teeth along the sides. "Do you think you could bite one of those off, so I can saw the rope with it?"

Gaudior splashed through puddles of melted ice, lowered his head, and bit off one of the spikes as close to the root as his large teeth permitted. Holding it between his teeth he twisted his head around until Charles Wallace, straining until the rope nearly cut off his breath, managed to take it from him.

Gaudior wrinkled his lips in distaste. "It's repellent. Careful, now. Unicorn's hide is not as strong as it looks."

"Stop fidgeting."

"It itches." Gaudior flung his head about with uncontrollable and agonized laughter. "Hurry."

"If I hurry I'll cut you. It's coming now." He moved the plant-saw back and forth with careful concentration, and finally one of the ropes parted. "I'll have to cut one more, on the other side. The worst is over now."

But when a second rope was severed, Charles Wallace was still bound to the unicorn, and the plant was limp and useless. "Can you bite off another spike?"

Gaudior bit and grimaced. "Nothing really has to taste that disagreeable. But then, I am not accustomed to any food except starlight and moonlight."

At last the ropes were off boy and beast, and Charles Wallace slid to the surface of the ice cliff. Gaudior was attacked by a fit of sneezing, and the last of the sea water flooded from his nose and mouth. Charles Wallace looked at the unicorn and drew in his breath in horror. Where the lines of rope had crossed the flanks there were red welts, shocking against the silver hide. The entire abdominal area, where the webbed hammock had rubbed, was raw and oozing blood. The water which had flooded from Gaudior's nostrils was pinkish.

The unicorn in turn inspected the boy. "You're a mess," he stated flatly. "You can't possibly go Within in this condition. You'd only hurt your host."

"You're a mess, too," Charles Wallace replied. He looked at his hands, and the palms were as raw as Gaudior's belly. Where the anorak and his shirt had slipped, the rope had cut into his waist as it had cut Gaudior's flanks.

"And you have two black eyes," the unicorn informed him. "It's a wonder you can see at all."

Charles Wallace squinted, first with one eye, then the other. "Things are a little blurry," he confessed.

Gaudior shook a few last drops from his wings. "We can't stay here, and you can't go Within now, that's obvious."

Charles Wallace looked at the sun, which was moving toward the west. "It's going to be cold when the sun goes down. And there doesn't seem to be any sign of life. And nothing to eat."

Gaudior folded his wings across his eyes and appeared to contemplate. Then he returned the wings to the bleeding flanks. "I don't understand earth time."

"What's that got to do with it?"

"Time is of the essence, we both know that. And yet it will take weeks, if not months, for us to heal."

When the unicorn stared at him as though expecting a response,

Charles Wallace looked down at a puddle in the ice. "I don't have any suggestions."

"We're both exhausted. The one place I can take you without fear of Echthroi is my home. No mortal has ever been there, and I am not sure I should bring you, but it's the only way I see open to us." The unicorn flung back his mane so that it brushed against the boy's bruised face with a silver coolness. "I have become very fond of you, in spite of all your foolishness."

Charles Wallace hugged the unicorn. "I have become fond of you, too."

Joints creaking painfully, Gaudior knelt. The boy clambered up, wincing as he inevitably touched the red welts which marred the flanks. "I'm sorry. I don't want to hurt you."

Gaudior neighed softly. "I know you don't."

The boy was so exhausted that he was scarcely aware of their flight. Stars and time swirled about him, and his lids began to droop.

"Wake up!" Gaudior ordered, and he opened his eyes to a world of starlit loveliness. The blurring of his vision had cleared, and he looked in awe at a land of snow and ice; he felt no cold, only the tenderness of a soft breeze which touched his cuts and bruises with healing gentleness. In the violet sky hung a sickle moon, and a smaller, higher moon, nearly full. Mountains heaved snow-clad shoulders skyward. Between the ribs of one of the foothills he saw what appeared to be a pile of enormous eggs.

Gaudior followed his gaze. "The hatching grounds. It has been seen by no other human eyes."

"I didn't know unicorns came from eggs," the boy said wonderingly.

"Not all of us do," Gaudior replied casually. "Only the time travelers." He took in great draughts of moonlight, then asked, "Aren't you thirsty?"

Charles Wallace's lips were cracked and sore. His mouth was parched. He looked longingly at the moonlight and tentatively opened his mouth to it. He felt a cool and healing touch on his lips, but when he tried to swallow he choked.

"I forgot," Gaudior said. "You're human. In my excitement at being home it slipped my mind." He cantered off to one of the foothills and returned with a long blue-green icicle held carefully in his teeth. "Suck it slowly. It may sting at first, but it has healing properties."

The cool drops trickled gently down the boy's parched throat, like rays of moonlight, and at the same time that they cooled the burning, they warmed his cold body. He gave his entire concentration to the moonsicle, and when he had finished the last healing drops he turned to thank Gaudior.

The unicorn was rolling in the snow, his legs up in the air, rolling and rolling, a humming of sheer pleasure coming from his throat. Then he stood up and shook himself, flinging splashes of snow in all directions. The red welts were gone; his hide was smooth and glistening perfection. He looked at the sore places on Charles Wallace's waist and hands. "Roll, the way I did," he ordered.

Charles Wallace threw himself into the snow, which was like no other snow he had ever felt; each flake was separate and tingly; it was cool but not chilling, and he felt healing move not only over the rope burns but deep within his sore muscles. He rolled over and over, laughing with delight. Then came a moment when he knew that he was completely healed, and he jumped up. "Gaudior, where is everybody? all the other unicorns?"

"Only the time travelers come to the hatching grounds, and during the passage of the small moon they can be about other business, for the small moon casts its warmth on the eggs. I brought you here, to this place, and at this moon, so we'd be alone."

"But why should we be alone?"

"If the others saw you they'd fear for their eggs."

Charles Wallace's head came barely halfway up the unicorn's haunches. "Creatures your size would be afraid of me?"

"Size is immaterial. There are tiny viruses which are deadly."

"Couldn't you tell them I'm not a virus and I'm not deadly?"

Gaudior blew out a gust of air. "Some of them think mankind *is* deadly."

Charles Wallace, too, sighed, and did not reply.

Gaudior nuzzled his shoulder. "Those of us who have been around the galaxies know that such thinking is foolish. It's always easy to blame others. And I have learned, being with you, that many of my preconceptions about mortals were wrong. Are you ready?"

Charles Wallace held out his hands to the unicorn. "Couldn't I see one of the eggs hatch?"

"They won't be ready until the rising of the third moon, unless . . ." Gaudior moved closer to the clutch, each egg almost as long as the boy was tall. "Wait—" The unicorn trotted to the great globular heap, which shone with inner luminosity, like giant moonstones. Gaudior bent his curved neck so that his mane brushed softly over the surface of the shells. With his upper teeth he tapped gently on one, listening, ears cocked, the short ear-hairs standing up and quivering like antennae. After a moment he moved on to another shell, and then another, with unhurried patience, until he tapped on one shell twice, thrice, then drew back and nodded at the boy.

This egg appeared to have rolled slightly apart from the others, and as Charles Wallace watched, it quivered, and rolled even farther away. From inside the shell came a sound of tapping, and the egg began to glow. The tapping accelerated and the shell grew so bright the boy could scarcely look at it. A sharp cracking, and a flash of brilliance as the horn thrust up and out into the pearly air, followed by a head with the silver mane clinging damply to neck and forehead. Dark silver-lashed eyes opened slowly, and the baby unicorn looked around, its eyes reflecting the light of the moons as it gazed on its fresh new environment. Then it wriggled and cracked the rest of the shell. As fragments of shell fell onto the snowy ground they broke into thousands of flakes, and the shell became one with the snow.

The baby unicorn stood on new and wobbly legs, neighing a soft moonbeam sound until it gained its balance. It stood barely as tall as Charles Wallace, testing one forehoof, then the other, and kicking out its hind legs. As Charles Wallace watched, lost in delight, the baby unicorn danced under the light of the two moons.

Then it saw Gaudior, and came prancing over to the big unicorn; by slightly lowering the horn it could have run right under the full-grown beast.

Gaudior nuzzled the little one's head just below the horn. Again the baby pranced with pleasure, and Gaudior began to dance with it, leading the fledgling in steps ever more and more intricate. When the baby began to tire, Gaudior slowed the steps of the dance and raised his head to the sickle moon, drew back his lips in an exaggerated gesture, and gulped moonlight.

As the baby had been following Gaudior in the steps of the dance, so it imitated him now, eagerly trying to drink moonlight, the rays dribbling from its young and inexperienced lips and breaking like crystal on the snow. Again it tried, looking at Gaudior, until it was thirstily and tidily swallowing the light as it was tipped out from the curve of the moon.

Gaudior turned to the nearly full moon, and again with exaggerated gestures taught the little one to drink. When its flanks were quivering with fullness, Gaudior turned to the nearest star, and showed it the pleasures of finishing a meal by quenching its thirst with starlight. The little one sipped contentedly, then closed its mouth with its tiny, diamond-like teeth, and, replete, leaned against Gaudior.

Only then did it notice Charles Wallace. With a leap of startlement, it landed on all four spindly legs, squealed in terror and galloped away, tail streaming silver behind it.

Charles Wallace watched the little creature disappear over the horizon. "I'm sorry I frightened it. Will it be all right?"

Gaudior nodded reassuringly. "It's gone in the direction of the Mothers. They'll tell it you're only a bad dream it had coming out of the shell, and it'll forget all about you." He knelt.

Reluctantly Charles Wallace mounted and sat astride the great neck. Holding on to a handful of mane, he looked about at the wild and peaceful landscape. "I don't want to leave."

"You human beings tend to want good things to last forever. They don't. Not while we're in time. Do you have any instructions for me?"

"I'm through with instructions. I don't even have any suggestions."

"We'll go Where and When the wind decides to take us, then?"

"What about Echthroi?" Charles Wallace asked fearfully.

"Because we're journeying from the home place the wind should be unmolested, as it was when we came here. After that we'll see. We've been in a very deep sea, and I never thought we'd get out of it. Try not to be afraid. The wind will give us all the help it can." The wings stretched to their full span and Gaudior flew up between the two moons, and away from the unicorn hatching grounds.

Meg sighed with delight.

"Oh, Ananda, Ananda, that was the most beautiful kythe! How I wish Charles Wallace could have stayed there longer, where he's safe . . ."

Ananda whined softly.

"I know. He has to leave. But the Echthroi are after him, and I feel so helpless . . ."

Ananda looked up at Meg, and the tufts of darker fur above the eyes lifted.

Meg scratched the dog between the ears. "We did send him the rune when he was in the Ice Age sea, and the wind came to help." Anxiously she placed her hand on Ananda, and closed her eyes, concentrating.

She saw the star-watching rock, and two children, a girl and a boy, perhaps thirteen and eleven, the girl the elder. The boy looked very much like a modern Brandon Llawcae, a Brandon in blue jeans and T-shirt—so it was definitely not 1865.

Charles Wallace was Within the boy, whose name was not Brandon. Chuck.

Mrs. O'Keefe had called Charles Wallace *Chuck*.

Chuck was someone Mrs. O'Keefe knew. Someone Mrs. O'Keefe had said was not an idiot.

Now he was with a girl, yes, and someone else, an old woman. Chuck Maddox, and his sister, Beezie, and their grandmother. They were laughing, and blowing dandelion clocks, counting the breaths it took for the lacy white spores to leave the green stem.

Beezie Maddox had golden hair and bright blue eyes and a merry laugh. Chuck was more muted, his hair a soft brown, his eyes blue-grey. He smiled more often than laughed. He was so much like Brandon that Meg was sure he must be a direct descendant.

"Ananda, why am I so terribly frightened for him?" Meg asked.

"Lets blow dandelion clocks," Beezie had suggested.

"Not around the store you don't," their father had said. "I'll not have my patch of lawn seeded with more dandelion spore than blows here on its own."

So Chuck and Beezie and the grandmother came on a Sunday afternoon, across the brook, along to the flat rock. In the distance they could hear the sound of trucks on the highway, although they could not see them. Occasionally a plane tracked across the sky. Otherwise, there was nothing to remind them of civilization, and this was one of the things Chuck liked best about crossing the brook and walking through the woods to the rock.

Beezie handed him a dandelion. "Blow."

Chuck did not much like the smell of the spore; it was heavy and rank, and he wrinkled his nose with distaste.

"It doesn't smell all that bad to me," Beezie said. "When I squish the stem it smells green, that's all."

The grandmother held the snowy fronds to her nose. "When you're old, nothing smells the way it used to." She blew, and the white snow-flakes of her dandelion flew in all directions, drifting on the wind.

Chuck and his sister had to blow several times before the clock told its time. The grandmother, who was quickly out of breath, and who had pressed her hand against her heart as she struggled up the fern-bordered path from the brook, blew lightly, and all the spores flew from the stem, danced in the sunny air, and slowly settled.

Chuck looked at Beezie, and Beezie looked at Chuck.

"Grandma, Beezie and I huff and puff and you blow no stronger than a whisper and it all blows away."

"Maybe you blow too hard. And when you ask the time, you mustn't fear the answer."

Chuck looked at the bare green stem in his grandmother's fingers.

"I blew four times, and it isn't nearly four yet. What time does your dandelion tell, Grandma?"

The spring sun went briefly behind a small cloud, veiling the old woman's eyes. "It tells me of time past, when the valley was a lake, your pa says, and a different people roamed the land. Do you remember the arrowhead you found when we were digging to plant tulip bulbs?" Deftly she changed the subject.

"Beezie and I've found lots of arrowheads. I always carry one. It's better'n a knife." He pulled the flat chipped triangle from his jeans pocket.

Beezie wore jeans, too, thin where her sharp knees were starting to push through the cloth. Her blue-and-white-checked shirt was just beginning to stretch tightly across her chest. She dug into her pockets like her brother, pulling out an old Scout knife and a bent spoon. "Grandma, blowing the dandelion clocks—that's just superstition, isn't it?"

"And what else would it be? Better ways there are of telling the time, like the set of the sun in the sky and the shadows of the trees. I make it out to be nigh three in the afternoon, and near time to go home for a cup of tea."

Beezie lay back on the warm ledge of rock, the same kind of rock from which the arrowhead had been chipped. "And Ma and Pa'll have tea with us because it's Sunday, and the store's closed, and nobody in it but Pansy. Grandma, I think she's going to have kittens again."

"Are you after being surprised? What else has Pansy to do except frighten the field mice away."

Despite the mention of tea, Chuck too lay back, putting his head in his grandmother's lap so she could ruffle his hair. Around them the spring breeze was gentle; the leaves whispered together; and in the distance a phoebe called wistfully. The roaring of a truck on the distant highway was a jarring note.

The grandmother said, "When we leave the village and cross the brook it's almost as though we crossed out of time, too. And then there comes the sound of the present"—she gestured toward the invisible highway—"to remind us."

"What of, Grandma?" Beezie asked.

The old woman looked into an unseen distance. "The world of trucks isn't as real to me as the world on the other side of time."

"Which side?" Chuck asked.

"Either side, though at the present I know more about the past than the future."

Beezie's eyes lit up. "You mean like in the stories you tell us?"

The grandmother nodded, her eyes still distant.

"Tell us one of the stories, Grandma. Tell us how Queen Branwen was taken from Britain by an Irish king."

The old woman's focus returned to the children. "I may have been born in Ireland, but we never forgot we came from Branwen of Britain."

"And I'm named after her."

"That you are, wee Beezie, and after me, for I'm Branwen, too."

"And Zillah? I'm Branwen Zillah Maddox." Beezie and Chuck knew the stories of their names backwards and forwards but never lost pleasure in hearing them.

Meg opened her eyes in amazement.
Branwen Zillah Maddox. B.Z. Beezie.
Mrs. O'Keefe.
That golden child was Mrs. O'Keefe.
And Chuck was her brother.

"Zillah comes from your Maddox forebears," the grandmother told the children, "and a proud name it is, too. She was an Indian princess, according to your pa, from the tribe which used to dwell right here where we be now, though the Indians are long gone."

"But you don't know as much about Zillah as you do about Branwen."

"Only that she was an Indian and beautiful. There are too many men on your father's side of the family, and stories come down, nowadays, through women. But in Branwen's day there were men who were bards."

"What's bards?" Chuck asked.

"Singers of songs and tellers of tales. Both my grandma and my grandpa told me the story of Branwen, but mostly my grandma, over and over, and her grandma told her before that, and the telling goes back beyond memory. Britain and Ireland have long misunderstood each other, and this misunderstanding goes back beyond memory, too. And in the once upon a time and long ago when the Irish king wooed the English princess, 'twas thought there might at last be peace between the two green and pleasant lands. There was feasting for many moons at the time of the nuptials, and then the Irish king sailed for Ireland with his wife."

"Wouldn't Branwen have been homesick?" Beezie asked.

"And of course she'd have been homesick. But she was born a princess and now she was a queen, and queens know how to mind their manners—or did in those days."

"And the king? What was he like?"

"Oh, and handsome he was, as the Irish can be, as was my own sweet Pat, who bore well the name of the blessed saint, with black hair and blue eyes. Branwen knew not that he was using her to vent his spleen against her land and her brethren, knew it not until he trumped up some silly story of her sitting in the refectory and casting her eye on one of his men. So, to punish her—"

"For what?" Chuck asked.

"For what, indeed? For his own jealous fantasies. So, to punish her, he sent her to tend the swine and barred her from the palace. So she knew he had never loved her, and her heart burned within her with anguish. Then she thought to call on her brother in England, and she used the rune, and whether she and hers gave the rune to Patrick, or whether their guardian angels gave it to each of them, she called on all Heaven with its power—"

The children chanted the rune with her.

> "And the sun with its brightness,
> And the snow with its whiteness,
> And the fire with all the strength it hath,
> And the lightning with its rapid wrath,
> And the winds with their swiftness along their path,
> And the sea with its deepness,
> And the rocks with their steepness,
> And the earth with its starkness,
> All these I place
> By God's almighty help and grace
> Between myself and the powers of darkness!"

The grandmother continued, "And the sun shone on her fair hair and warmed her, and the gentle snow fell and made all clean the sty in which the Irish king had set her, and the fire burst from the fireplace of his wooden palace and the lightning struck it and it burned with mighty rage and all within fled the fury. And the wind blew from Britain and the sails of her brother Bran's ship billowed as it sped over the deep sea and landed where the rocks were steep and the earth stark. And Bran's men scaled the rock and rescued their beloved Branwen."

"Is it a true story, Grandma," Beezie asked, "really?"

"To those with the listening ear and the believing heart."

"Chuck has the believing heart," Beezie said.

The grandmother patted his knee. "One day maybe you will be the writer your father wanted to be. He was not cut out for a storekeeper."

"I love the store," Beezie said defensively. "It smells good, of cinnamon and fresh bread and apples."

"I'm hungry," Chuck said.

"And wasn't I after saying before we got into storytelling that we should get along home for tea? Pull me up, both of you."

Chuck and Beezie scrambled to their feet and heaved the old woman upright. "We'll pick a bouquet for Ma and Pa on the way," Beezie said.

The narrow path was rough with rocks and hummocks of grass, and walking was not easy. The grandmother leaned on a staff which Chuck had cut for her from a grove of young maples which needed thinning. He went ahead, slowing down when he saw Beezie and his grandmother lagging behind him. A bouquet of field flowers was growing in Beezie's hands, for she paused whenever she saw that the old woman was out of breath. "Look, Chuck! Look, Grandma! Three more jacks-in-the-pulpit!"

Chuck was hacking away with his arrowhead at a strand of bittersweet snaking around a young fir tree, strangling it with coils strong as a boa constrictor's. "Ma used to have us looking for bittersweet a year or so ago, and now it's taking over. It'll kill this tree unless I cut through it. You two go along and I'll catch up."

"Want my knife?" Beezie offered.

"No. My arrowhead's sharp."

For a moment he stared after his sister and grandmother as they wended their slow way. He sniffed the fragrance of the air. Although the apple trees were green, the pink and white blossoms were still on the ground. The scent of lilac mingled with the mock orange. He might be able to hear the trucks on the road and see the planes in the sky, but at least here he couldn't smell them.

Chuck liked neither the trucks nor the planes. They all left their fumes behind them, blunting the smell of sunlight, of rain, of green and growing things, and Chuck 'saw' with his nose almost more than with his eyes. Without looking he could easily tell his parents, his grandmother, his sister. And he judged people almost entirely by his reaction to their odor.

'I don't smell a thing,' his father had said after Chuck had wrinkled his nose at a departing customer.

Chuck had said calmly, 'He smells unreliable.'

His father gave a small, surprised laugh. 'He *is* unreliable. He owes me more than I can afford to be owed, for all his expensive clothes.'

When the strand of bittersweet was severed, Chuck stood leaning against the rough bark of the tree, breathing in its resiny smell. In the distance he could see his grandmother and Beezie. The old woman smelled to him of distance, of the sea, which was fifty or more miles away, but perhaps it was a farther sea which clung to her. 'And you smell green,' he had told her. 'Ah, and that's because I come from a far green country and the scent of it will be with me always.'

'What color do I smell?' Beezie had asked.

'Yellow, like buttercups and sunlight and butterfly wings.'

Green and gold. Good smells. Home smells. His mother was the blue of sky in early morning. His father was the rich mahogany of the highboy in the living room, with the firelight flickering over the polished wood. Comfortable, safe smells.

And suddenly the thought of the odor of cookies and freshly baked bread called to him, and he ran to catch up.

The family lived over the store in a long, rambling apartment. The front room, overlooking the street, was a storeroom, filled with cartons and barrels. Behind it were three bedrooms: his parents', his own little cubbyhole, and the bigger room Beezie shared with the grandmother. Beyond these were the kitchen and the large long room which served as living and dining room.

There was a fire crackling in the fireplace, for the spring evenings were apt to be chilly. The family was seated about a large round table set for tea, with cookies and bread still warm from the oven, a pitcher of milk, and a big pot of tea covered with the cozy the grandmother had brought with her from Ireland.

Chuck took his place, and his mother poured his tea. "Did you save another tree?"

"Yes. I really should take Pa's big clippers with me next time."

Beezie pushed the plate of bread and butter to him. "Take your share quickly or I'll eat it all up."

Chuck's sensitive nostrils twitched. There was a smell in the room which was completely unfamiliar to him, and of which he was afraid.

The father helped himself to a cookie. "This is one of the times I wish Sunday afternoons came more than once a week."

"You've been acting tired lately." His wife looked at him anxiously.

"Being tired is the natural state of a country storekeeper who doesn't have much business sense."

The grandmother moved creakily from her chair at the table to her rocker. "Hard work's not easy. You need more help."

"Can't afford it, Grandma. How about telling us a story?"

"You've heard them all as many times as there are stars in the sky."

"I never tire of them."

"I'm told out for today."

"Oh, come on, Grandma," Mr. Maddox cajoled. "You never tire of storytelling, and you know you make most of it up as you go along."

"Stories are like children. They grow in their own way." She closed her eyes. "I will just take a small snooze."

"You tell me about the Indian princess, then, Pa," Beezie ordered.

"I don't know much about her as far as provable facts are concerned. My illustrious forebear, Matthew Maddox, from whom I may have inherited an iota of talent, wrote about her in his second novel. It was a best-seller in its day. Sad he couldn't have known about its success, but it was published posthumously. It was a strange sort of fantasy, with qualities which make some critics call it the first American science-fiction novel, because it played with time, and he'd obviously heard of Mendel's theories of genetics. Anyhow, Beezie love, it's a fictional account of the two brothers from ancient Wales who came to this country after their father's death, the first Europeans to set foot on these uncharted shores. And, as the brothers had quarreled in Wales, so they quarreled in the New World, and the elder of the two made his way to South America. Madoc, the younger brother, stayed with the Indians in a place which is nameless but which Matthew Maddox implies is right around here, and he married the Indian princess Zyll, or Zillah, and in the novel it is his strain which is lost, and must be found again."

"Sounds interesting," Chuck said.

Beezie wrinkled her nose. "I don't much like science fiction. I like fairy tales better."

"*The Horn of Joy* has elements of both. The idea that the proud elder brother must be defeated by the inconsequential but honest younger brother is certainly a fairy-tale theme. There was also a unicorn in the story, who was a time traveler."

"Whyn't you tell us about it before?" Beezie asked.

"Thought you'd be too young to be interested. Anyhow, I sold my copy when I was offered an outrageously large sum for it when I . . . it was too large an amount to turn down. Matthew Maddox, for a nineteenth-century writer, had an uncanny intuition about the theories of space, time, and relativity that Einstein was to postulate generations later."

"But that's not possible," Beezie protested.

"Precisely. But it's all in Matthew's book, nevertheless. It's an evocative, haunting novel, and since Matthew Maddox assumed that he was descended from the younger Welshman, the one who stayed here, and the Indian princess, I've followed his fancy that the name Maddox comes from Madoc." A shadow moved across his face. "When my father had a stroke and I had to leave my poet's garret in the city and come help out with the store, I had to give up my dream of following in Matthew's footsteps."

"Oh, Pa—" Chuck said.

"I'm mainly sorry for you children. I never had a chance to prove whether or not I could be a writer, but I'm a failure as a merchant." He rose. "I'd better go down to the store for an hour or so and work on accounts."

When he left, holding on to the banister as he went down the steep stairs, the smell that made Chuck afraid went with him.

Chuck told no one, not even Beezie, about the smell which was in his father but was not of his father.

Twice that week, Chuck had nightmares. When he cried out in terror his mother came hurrying, but he told her only that he had had a bad dream.

Beezie wasn't put off so easily. "You're worried about something, Chuck."

"There's always something to worry about. Lots of people owe Pa money, and he's worried about bills. I heard a salesman say he couldn't give Pa any more credit."

Beezie said, "You're too young to worry about things like that. Anyhow, it isn't the kind of thing you worry about."

"I'm getting older."

"Not that old."

"Pa's giving me more to do. I know more about the business now."

"But that's not what you're worried about."

He tried another tack. "I don't like the way Paddy O'Keefe's always after you in school."

"Paddy O'Keefe's repeated sixth grade three times. He may be good at baseball, but I'm not one of the girls who thinks the sun rises and sets on him."

"Maybe that's why he's after you." He had succeeded in deflecting her attention.

"I don't let him near me. He never washes. What does he smell like, Chuck?"

"Like a dandruffy woodchuck."

One evening after supper Beezie said, "Let's go see if the fireflies are back." It was Friday, and no school in the morning, so they could go to bed when they chose.

Chuck felt an overwhelming desire to get out of the house, away from the smell, which nearly made him retch. "Let's go."

It was still twilight when they reached the flat rock. They sat, and the stone still held the warmth of the day's sun. At first there were only occasional sparkles, but as it got darker Chuck was lost in a daze of delight as a galaxy of fireflies twinkled on and off, flinging upward in a blaze of light, dropping earthward like falling stars, moving in continuous effervescent dance.

"Oh, Beezie!" he cried. "I'm dazzled with gorgeousness."

Behind them the woods were dark with shadows. There was no moon, and a thin veil of clouds hid the stars. "If it were a clear night," Beezie remarked, "the fireflies wouldn't be as bright. I've never seen them this beautiful." She lay back on the rock, looking up at the shadowed sky, then closing her eyes. Chuck followed suit.

"Let's feel the twirling of the earth," Beezie said. "That's part of the dance the fireflies are dancing, too. Can you feel it?"

Chuck squeezed his eyelids tightly closed. He gave a little gasp. "Oh, Beezie! I felt as though the earth had tilted!" He sat up, clutching at the rock. "It made me dizzy."

She gave her bubbling little giggle. "It can be a bit scary, being part of earth and stars and fireflies and clouds and rocks. Lie down again. You won't fall off, I promise."

He leaned back, feeling the radiance soak into his body. "The rock's still warm."

"It's warm all summer, because the trees don't shade it. And there's a rock in the woods that's always cool, even on the hottest day, because the leaves are so close together that the sun's fingers never touch it."

Chuck felt a cold shadow move over him and shuddered.

"Someone walk over your grave?" Beezie asked lightly.

He jumped up. "Let's go home."

"Why? What's wrong? It's so beautiful."

"I know—but let's go home."

When they got back, everything was in confusion. Mr. Maddox had collapsed from pain, and been rushed to the hospital. The grandmother was waiting for the children.

The frightening smell had exploded over Chuck with the violence of a mighty wave as he entered.

The grandmother pulled the children to her and held them.

"But what is it? What's wrong with Pa?" Beezie asked.

"The ambulance attendant thought it was his appendix."

"But he will be all right?" she pleaded.

"Dear my love, we'll have to wait and pray."

Chuck pressed against her, quivering, not speaking. Slowly the smell was dissipating, leaving a strange emptiness in its wake.

Time seemed to stand still. Chuck would glance at the clock, thinking an hour had passed, only to find it barely a minute. After a long while Beezie fell asleep, her head in her grandmother's lap. Chuck was watchful, looking from the clock to the telephone to the door. But at length he, too, slept.

In his sleep he dreamed that he was lying on the flat rock, and feeling the swing of the earth around the sun, and suddenly the rock tilted steeply, and he was sliding off, and he scrabbled in terror to keep from falling off the precipice into a sea of darkness. He cried out, "Rocks—steep—" and the grandmother put her hand on the rock and steadied it and he stopped dreaming.

But when he woke up he knew that his father was dead.

9 The Rocks with Their Steepness

The sudden shrilling of the telephone woke Meg with a jolt of terror. Her heart began to thud, and she pushed out of bed, hardly aware of Ananda. Her feet half in and half out of her slippers, one arm shoved into her robe, she stumbled downstairs and into her parents' bedroom, but they were not there, so she hurried on down to the kitchen.

Her father was on the phone, and she heard him saying, "Very well, Mrs. O'Keefe. One of us will be right over for you."

It was not the President.

But Mrs. O'Keefe? In the middle of the night?

The twins, too, were in the doorway.

"What was that about?" Mrs. Murry asked.

"As you gathered, it was Mrs. O'Keefe."

"At this time of night!" Sandy exclaimed.

"She's never called us before," Dennys said, "at any time."

Meg breathed a sigh of relief. "At least it wasn't the President. What did she want?"

"She said she's found something she wants me to see, and ordered me to go for her at once."

"I'll go," Sandy said. "You can't leave the phone, Dad."

"You've got the weirdest mother-in-law in the world," Dennys told Meg.

Mrs. Murry opened the oven door and the fragrance of hot bread wafted out. "How about some bread and butter?"

"Meg, put your bathrobe on properly," Dennys ordered.

"Yes, doc." She put her left arm into the sleeve and tied the belt. If she stayed in the kitchen with the family, then time would pass with its normal inevitability. The kythe which had been broken by the jangling of the telephone was lost somewhere in her unconscious mind. She hated alarm clocks, because they woke her so abruptly out of sleep that she forgot her dreams.

In the kything was something to do with Mrs. O'Keefe. But what? She searched her mind. Fireflies. Something to do with fireflies. And a girl and a boy, and the smell of fear. She shook her head.

"What's the matter, Meg?" her mother asked.

"Nothing. I'm trying to remember something."

"Sit down. A warm drink won't hurt you."

It was important that she see Mrs. O'Keefe, but she couldn't remember why, because the kythe was gone.

"I'll be right back," Sandy assured them, and went out the pantry door.

"What on earth . . ." Dennys said. "Mrs. O'Keefe is beyond me. I'm glad I'm not going in for psychiatry."

Their mother set a plateful of fragrant bread on the table, then turned to put the kettle on. "Look!"

Meg followed her gaze. Coming into the kitchen were the kitten and Ananda, single file, the kitten with its tail straight up in the air, mincing along as though leading the big dog, whose massive tail was wagging wildly. They all laughed, and the laughter froze as the two creatures came past the table with the telephone. Twice since the President's call the phone had rung, first Calvin, then his mother. When would it ring again, and who would call?

It surprised Meg that the warm bread tasted marvelous, and the tea warmed her, and she was able, at least for the moment, to relax. Ananda whined beseechingly, and Meg gave her a small piece of toast.

Outside came the sound of a car, the slamming of a door, and then Sandy came in with Mrs. O'Keefe. The old woman had cobwebs in her hair, and smudges of dirt on her face. In her hand she held some scraps of paper.

"Something in me told me to go to the attic," she announced triumphantly. "That name—Mad Dog Branzillo—it rang a bell in me."

Meg looked at her mother-in-law and suddenly the kythe flooded back. "Beezie!" She cried.

Mrs. O'Keefe lunged toward her as though to strike her. "What's that?"

Meg caught the old woman's hands. "Beezie, Mom. You used to be called Beezie."

"How'd you know?" the old woman demanded fiercely. "You couldn't know! Nobody's called me Beezie since Chuck."

Tears filled Meg's eyes. "Oh, Beezie, Beezie, I'm so sorry."

The family looked at her in astonishment. Mr. Murry asked, "What is this, Meg?"

Still holding her mother-in-law's hands, Meg replied, "Mrs. O'Keefe used to be called Beezie when she was a girl. Didn't you, Mom?"

"It's best forgotten," the old woman said heavily.

"And you called Charles Wallace *Chuck*," Meg persisted, "and Chuck was your little brother and you loved him very much."

"I want to sit down," Mrs. O'Keefe said. "Leave the past be. I want to show you something." She handed a yellowed envelope to Mr. Murry. "Look at that."

Mr. Murry pushed his glasses up his nose. "It's a letter from a Bran Maddox in Vespugia to a Matthew Maddox right here."

The twins looked at each other. Sandy said, "We were just talking about Matthew Maddox tonight when we were looking something up for Meg. He was a nineteenth-century novelist. Is there a date on the letter?"

Mr. Murry carefully drew a yellowed sheet of paper from the old envelope. "November 1865."

"So the Matthew Maddox could be the one whose book Dennys studied in college!"

"Let Father read the letter," Dennys stopped his twin.

My beloved brother, Matthew, greetings, on this warm November day in Vespugia. Is there snow at home? I am settling in well with the group from Wales, and feel that I have known most of them all our lives. What an adventure this is, to start a colony in this arid country where the children can be taught Welsh in school, and where we can sing together as we work.

The strangest thing of all is that our family legend was here to meet me. Papa and Dr. Llawcae will be wild with excitement. We grew up on the legend of Madoc leaving Wales and coming to the New World, the way other children grew up on George Washington and the cherry tree. Believe it or not—but I know you'll believe it, because it's absolutely true—there is an Indian here with blue eyes who says he is descended from a Welsh prince who came to America long before any other white men. He does not know how his forebears got to South America, but he swears that his mother sang songs to him about being the blue-eyed descendant of a Welsh prince. He is called Gedder, though that is not his real name. His mother died when he and his sister were small, and they were brought up by an English sheep rancher who couldn't pronounce his Welsh name, and called him Gedder. And his sister's name—that is perhaps the most amazing of all: Zillie. She does not have the blue eyes, but she is quite beautiful, with very fine features, and shining straight black hair, which she wears in a long braid. She reminds me of my beloved Zillah.

Gedder has been extraordinarily helpful in many ways, though he has a good deal of arrogance and a tendency to want to be the leader which has already caused trouble in this community where no man is expected to set himself above his brothers.

But how wonderful that the old legend should be here to greet me! As for our sister Gwen, she shrugs and says, "What difference does a silly old story make?" She is determined not to like it here, though she's obviously pleased when all the young men follow her around.

Has Dr. Llawcae decided to let Zillah come and join me in the spring? The other women would welcome her, and she would be a touch of home for Gwen. I'm happy here, Matthew, and I know that Zillah would be happy with me, as my wife and life's companion. Women are not looked down on here— Gwen has to admit that much. Perhaps you could come, and bring Zillah with you? The community is settled enough so that I think we could take care of you, and this dry climate would be better for you than the dampness at home. Please come, I need you both.

Your affectionate brother,
Bran

Mr. Murry stopped. "It's very interesting, Mrs. O'Keefe, but why is it so important for me to see it?"—that you called in the middle of the night, he seemed to be adding silently.

"Don't you see?"

"No, sorry."

"Thought you was supposed to be so brilliant."

Mrs. Murry said, "The letter was mailed from Vespugia. That's strange enough, that you should have a letter which was mailed from Vespugia."

"Right," the old woman said triumphantly.

Mr. Murry asked, "Where did you find this letter, Mrs. O'Keefe?"

"Told you. In the attic."

"And your maiden name was Maddox." Meg smiled at the old

woman. "So they were forebears of yours, this Bran Maddox, and his brother, Matthew, and his sister, Gwen."

She nodded. "Yes, and likely his girlfriend, Zillah, too. Maddoxes and Llawcaes in my family all the way back."

Dennys looked at his sister's mother-in-law with new respect. "Sandy was looking up about Vespugia tonight, and he told us about a Welsh colony in Vespugia in 1865. So one of your ancestors went to join it?"

"Looks like it, don't it? And that Branzillo, he's from Vespugia."

Mr. Murry said, "It's a remarkable coincidence—" He stopped as his wife glanced at him. "I still don't see how it can have any connection with Branzillo, or what it would mean if it did."

"Don't you?" Mrs. O'Keefe demanded.

"Please tell us," Mrs. Murry suggested gently.

"The names. Bran. Zillah. Zillie. Put them together and they aren't far from Branzillo."

Mrs. Murry looked at her with surprised admiration. "How amazing!"

Mr. Murry asked, "Are there other letters?"

"Were. Once."

"Where are they?"

"Gone. Went to look. Began thinking about this Branzillo when I went home. Remembered Chuck and me—"

"Chuck and you what, Mom?" Meg probed.

Mrs. O'Keefe pushed her cobwebby hair away from her eyes. "We used to read the letters. Made up stories about Bran and Zillah and all. Played games of Let's Pretend. Then, when Chuck—didn't have the heart for Let's Pretend any more, forgot it all. Made myself forget. But that name, Branzillo, struck me. Bran. Zillah. Peculiar."

Mr. Murry looked bemusedly at the yellowed paper. "Peculiar, indeed."

"Where's your little boy?" Mrs. O'Keefe demanded.

Mr. Murry looked at his watch. "He went for a walk."

"When?"

"About an hour ago."

"In the middle of the night, and at his age?"

"He's fifteen."

"No. Twelve. Chuck was twelve."

"Charles Wallace is fifteen, Mrs. O'Keefe."

"A runt, then."

"Give him time."

"And you don't take care of him. Chuck needs special care. And people criticize me for not taking care of my kids!"

Dennys, too, looked at his watch. "Want me to go after him, Dad?"

Mr. Murry shook his head. "No. I think we have to trust Charles Wallace tonight. Mrs. O'Keefe, you'll stay awhile?"

"Yes. Need to see Chuck."

Meg said, "Please excuse me, everybody. I want to go back to bed." She tried to keep the urgency from her voice. She felt a panicky need to get back to the attic with Ananda. "Chuck *was* twelve," Mrs. O'Keefe had said. Chuck was twelve when what? Anything that happened to Chuck was happening to Charles Wallace.

Mrs. Murry suggested, "Would you like to take a cup of tea with you?"

"No, thanks, I'm fine. Someone call me when Charles gets in?"

Ananda followed her upstairs, contentedly licking her lips for the last buttery crumbs.

The attic felt cold and she got quickly into bed and wrapped the quilt around herself and the dog.—Charles Wallace wanted me to find a connection between Wales and Vespugia, and Dennys found one in his reference books. But it's a much closer connection than that. The letter Mrs. O'Keefe brought was from 1865, and from Vespugia, so the connection is as close as her attic.

Despite the warm glow of the electric heater, she shivered.

—Those people in the letter must be important, she thought,—and the Bran who wrote the letter, and his sister Gwen. Certainly the name Zillie must have some connection with Madoc's Zyll, and Ritchie Llawcae's Zylle, who was nearly burned for witchcraft.

—And then, the Matthew he wrote to must be the Matthew Maddox who wrote the books. There's something in that second book that matters, and the Echthroi don't want us to know about it. It's all interconnected, and we still don't know what the connections mean.

—And what happened to Beezie, that she should end up as Mom O'Keefe? Oh, Ananda, Ananda, whatever happened?

She lay back against the pillows and rubbed her hand slowly back and forth over the dog's soft fur, until the tingling warmth moved up her arm and all through her.

"But why Pa?" Beezie demanded over and over again. "Why did Pa have to die?"

"There's never an answer to that question, my Beezie," the grandmother replied patiently. "It's not a question to be asking."

"But I do ask it!"

The grandmother looked tired, and old. Chuck had never before thought of her as old, as being any age at all. She was simply Grandma, always there for them. Now she asked, not the children, but the heavens, "And why my Patrick, and him even younger than your father. Why anything?" A tear slid down her cheek, and Beezie and Chuck put their arms around her to comfort her.

Mrs. Maddox went over the ledgers so patiently kept up to date by her husband. The more she looked, the more slowly her hands turned the pages. "I knew it was bad, but I didn't know it was this bad. I should have realized when he sold Matthew Maddox's book . . ."

Chuck crawled up into the dark storage spaces under the eaves, looking for treasure. He found a bottle full of pennies, but no gold or jewels to give his mother. He found an old *Encyclopaedia Britannica*, the pages yellow, the bindings cracked, but still useful. He found a set of china wrapped in old newspapers dated long before he and Beezie were born, which he hoped they might be able to sell. He found a strongbox, locked.

He brought his findings to the living room. His mother was in the store, but Beezie and the grandmother were there, doing the week's baking.

"The pennies are old. They may be worth something. The china's good. It may pay for our fuel for a month or so. What's in the box?"

"There isn't a key. I'm going to break it." He took hammer and screwdriver and wrench, and the old lock gave way and he was able to lift the lid. In the box was a sheaf of letters and a large notebook with a crumbling blue leather binding. He opened the book to the first page, and there was a watercolor sketch, faded only slightly, of the spring countryside.

"Grandma! It's our rock, our picnic rock!"

The old woman clucked. "And so it is."

The rock was shaded in soft blues and lavenders merging into grey. Behind it the trees were lush with spring green. Above it flew a flock of butterflies, the soft blues of the spring azures complemented by the gold and black of the tiger swallowtails. Around the rock were the familiar spring flowers, dappling the grass like the background of a tapestry.

Chuck exclaimed in delight, "Oh, Beezie, oh, Grandma!" Reverently he turned the page. In beautiful script was written, *Madrun, 1864, Zillah Llawcae.*

The grandmother wiped her floury hands carefully and put on her spectacles, bending over the book. Together they read the first page.

Madrun.

Past ten o'clock. Through my bedroom window I can look down the hill to the Maddoxes' house. Mr. and Mrs. Maddox will be asleep. They get up at five in the morning. Gwen Maddox— who knows? Gwen has always considered herself a grownup and me a child, though we're separated by only two years.

The twins, my dear twins, Bran and Matthew. Are they awake? When Bran lied about his age, so afraid was he he'd miss the war, and went to join the cavalry, I feared he might be killed in battle. When I dreamed of his homecoming, as I did each night when I looked at his diamond on my finger and prayed for his safety, I never thought it could be like this, with Bran withdrawn and refusing to communicate with anyone, even his twin. If I try to speak to him about our marriage, he cuts me short, or turns away without a word. Matthew says there have been others who have suffered this sickness of spirit because of the horrors of war.

I am, and have been for nearly seventeen years, Zillah Llawcae. Will I ever be Zillah Maddox?

They continued to turn the pages, more quickly now, not pausing to read the journal entries, but looking at the delicate paintings of birds and butterflies, flowers and trees, squirrels and wood mice and tree toads, all meticulously observed and accurately reproduced.

A shiver ran up and down Chuck's spine. "Pa's mother was a Llawcae. This Zillah could be one of our ancestors . . . and she was alive when she painted all this, and it's just the way it is now, just exactly the same."

He turned another page; his eye was caught, and he read:

This is my seventeenth birthday, and a sorry one it has been, though Father and I were invited to the Maddoxes' for dinner. But Bran was there and yet he wasn't there. He sat at the table, but he hardly ate the delicious dishes which had been especially prepared, to tempt him as much as in honor of me, and if anyone asked him a question he answered in monosyllables.

He turned the page and paused again.

Matthew says Bran almost had a conversation with him last night, and he is hopeful that the ghastly war wounds of his mind and spirit are beginning to heal. I wear his ring with its circle of hope, and I will not give up hoping. What would I do without Matthew's friendship to comfort and sustain me? Had it not been for Matthew's accident, I wonder which twin would have asked for my hand? A question better not raised, since I love them both so tenderly.

The grandmother took the top letter from the packet. "It's from Bran Maddox, the one Zillah's talking about, but it's from some foreign place, Vespugia? Now where would that be?"

"It's part of what used to be Patagonia."

"Pata—?"

"In South America."

"Oh, then." She drew the letter out of its envelope.

My beloved brother, Matthew, greetings, on this warm November day in Vespugia. It there snow at home? I am settling in well with the group from Wales, and feel that I have known most of them all our lives . . .

When she finished reading the letter, she said, "Your poor pa would have been thrilled at all this."

Chuck, nodding, continued to turn the pages, reading a line here and there. As well as the nature pictures, the young Zillah Llawcae had many sketches of people, some in ink, some in watercolor. There was an ink drawing of a tall man in a stovepipe hat, carrying a black bag and looking not unlike Lincoln, standing by a horse and buggy. Underneath was written, "Father, about to drive off to deliver a baby."

There were many sketches of a young man, just beyond boyhood, with fair hair, a clear, beardless complexion, and wide-apart, far-seeing eyes. These were labeled, "My beloved Bran," "My dearest Bran," "My heart's love." And there were sketches of someone who looked like Bran and yet not like Bran, for the face was etched with lines of pain. "My dear Matthew," Zillah had written.

"It's so beautiful," Beezie said. "I wish I could paint like that."

But the old woman's thoughts had shifted to practicality. "I wonder, would this notebook bring a few dollars?"

"Grandma, you wouldn't sell it!" Chuck was horrified.

"We need money, lad, if we're to keep a roof over our heads. Your ma'll sell anything she can sell."

The antiques dealer who bought the pennies and the set of china

for what seemed to Chuck and Beezie a staggering sum was not interested in Zillah's notebook.

Mrs. Maddox looked at it sadly. "I know it's worth something. Your
father would know where I should take it. If only I could remember the
name of the person who bought Matthew Maddox's book."

But Chuck could not feel it in his heart to wish the beautiful journal
sold. His grandmother took an old linen pillowcase and made a cover
to protect the crumbling leather binding, and on it Beezie embroidered
two butterflies, in blue and gold. She was as entranced with the journal
as was Chuck.

They shared the notebook and the letters with the grandmother,
reading aloud to her while she did the ironing or mending, until they
had her as involved as they were. The present was so bleak that all three
found relief in living the long past.

Beezie and Chuck looked at the old foundation behind the store.
"That's where the Maddoxes' house must have been. They didn't live
above the store, the way we do."

"Our apartment was all part of the store."

"I wonder what happened to the house?"

"We'll never know," Beezie said drearily.

"I tried to check one of Matthew Maddox's books out of the library," Chuck said. "But the librarian said they haven't been around in
a long time. She thinks somebody must have lifted them. But I did get
some books on Vespugia. Let's go upstairs and look at them."

They compared the photographs in the books with the watercolors
in the final pages of the journal, where Zillah had tried to reproduce in
ink and paint what Bran had described in his letters. Zillah's painting
of vast plains rising terrace-fashion up to the foot of the Andes gave
them a feeling of a world so different it might have been another planet.

Beezie had turned back to Zillah's notebook, to a painting of a tall
and handsome Indian, with strange blue eyes set rather too close to his
aquiline nose. The caption read: "This is how I think Gedder must look,
the Indian who Bran writes is descended from Madoc's brother."

Chuck reached for one of Bran's letters and read:

I wish I was more drawn to Gedder, who is so obviously drawn
to Gwen. I feel an ingrate when I think of all he has done for
us. Building is completely different in Vespugian weather than
at home—or in Wales, and I shudder to think what kind of
houses we might have built had Gedder not shown us how to
construct dwellings to let the wind in, rather than to keep it out.

And he showed us what crops to plant, hardy things like cabbage and carrots, and how to make windbreaks for them. All the Indians have helped us, but Gedder more than the others, and more visibly. But he never laughs.

"I don't trust people who don't laugh." He put the letter down.

Beezie got a baby-sitting job that began right after school, so Chuck took her place at the cash register, pretending that he was Matthew Maddox and that the store was big and flourishing. The grandmother took in ironing and sewing, and her old hands were constantly busy. There was no time for leisurely cups of tea and the telling of tales. Chuck moved more and more deeply into his games of Let's Pretend. Matthew and Zillah, Bran and Gwen, Gedder and Zillie, all were more alive for him than anyone except Beezie and the grandmother.

One evening Mrs. Maddox stayed late downstairs in the store. When Chuck came home from chopping wood for one of their neighbors, he found Beezie and his grandmother drinking herb tea. "Grandma, I'm hungry." He could feel his belly growling. Supper had been soup and dry toast.

Seeming to ignore his words, the old woman looked at him. "Duthbert Mortmain's been calling on your ma. He's downstairs now."

"I don't like him," Beezie said.

"You may have to," the grandmother told her.

"Why?" Chuck asked. He remembered Duthbert Mortmain as a lumbering, scowling man who did small plumbing jobs. How did he smell? Not a pleasant smell. Hard, like a lump of coal.

"He's offered to marry your ma and take over the store."

"But Pa—"

"The funeral baked meats are long cold. Duthbert Mortmain's got a shrewd business head, and no one's bought the store, nor likely to. Your ma's not got much choice. And for all her hard work and heavy heart, she's still a pretty woman. Not surprising Duthbert Mortmain should fall for her."

"But she's our *mother*," Beezie protested.

"Not to Duthbert Mortmain. To him she's a desirable woman. And to your mother, he's a way out."

"Out of what?" Chuck asked.

"Your mother's about to lose the store and the roof over our heads. Another few weeks and we'll be out on the street."

Chuck's face lit up. "We could go to Vespugia!"

"Going anywhere takes money, Chuck, and money's what we don't have. You and Beezie'd be put in foster homes, and as to your ma and me . . ."

"Grandma!" Beezie clutched the old woman's sleeve. "You don't want Ma to marry him, do you?"

"I don't know what I want. I'd like to know that she was taken care of, and you and Chuck, before I die."

Beezie flung her arms about the old woman. "You're not going to die, Grandma, not ever!"

Chuck's nostrils twitched slightly. The scent of dandelion spore was strong.

The old woman untangled herself. "You've seen how death takes the ready and unready, my Beezie. Except for my concern about your future, and your mother's, I'm ready to go home. It's been a long time I've been separated from my Patrick. He's waiting for me. The last few days I've kept looking over my shoulder, expecting to see him."

"Grandma"—Beezie pushed her fingers through her curls—"Ma doesn't *love* Duthbert Mortmain. She can't! I hate him!"

"Hate hurts the hater more'n the hated."

"Didn't Branwen?"

"Branwen hated not. Branwen loved, and was betrayed, and cried the rune for help, and not for hate or revenge. And the sun melted the white snow so that she could sleep warm at night, and the fire in her little stove did not burn out but flickered merrily to keep her toasty, and the lightning carried her message to her brother, Bran, and her Irish king fled to his ship and the wind blew him across the sea and his ship sank in its depths and Bran came to his sister Branwen and blessed the stark earth so that it turned green and flowering once more."

Beezie asked, "Did she ever love anybody again, after the Irish king?"

"I've forgotten," the old woman said.

"Grandma! Why don't we use the rune? Then maybe Ma won't have to marry Duthbert Mortmain."

"The rune is not to be used lightly."

"This wouldn't be lightly."

"I don't know, my Beezie. Patterns have to be worked out, and only the very brash tamper with them. The rune is only for the most dire emergency."

"Isn't this an emergency?"

"Perhaps not the right one." The old woman closed her eyes and rocked back and forth in silence, and when she spoke it was in a rhythmic singsong, much as when she intoned the words of the rune. "You will use the rune, my lamb, you will use the rune, but not before the time is ripe." She opened her eyes and fixed Beezie with a piercing gaze which seemed to go right through her.

"But how will I know when the time is ripe? Why isn't it ripe now?"

The old woman shook her head and closed her eyes and rocked again. "This moment is not the moment. The night is coming and the clouds are gathering. We can do nothing before they are all assembled. When the time is ripe, Chuck will let you know. From the other side of darkness, Chuck will let you know, will let you know, will let . . ." Her words trailed off, and she opened her eyes and spoke in her natural voice. "To bed with both of you. It's late."

"Horrid old Duthbert Mortmain," Beezie said to Chuck one fine summer's day. "I won't call him Pa."

"Nor I."

Duthbert Mortmain seemed quite content to have them call him Mr. Mortmain.

He ran the store with stern efficiency. With their mother he was gentle, occasionally caressing her soft hair. People remarked on how he doted on her.

A sign over the cash register read NO CREDIT. Beezie and Chuck helped out in the afternoons and on Saturdays as usual. And their mother still did not smile, not even when Duthbert Mortmain brought her a box of chocolates tied with a lavender ribbon.

She no longer smelled of fear, Chuck thought, but neither did she smell of the blue sky of early morning. Now it was the evening sky, with a thin covering of cloud dimming the blue.

Duthbert Mortmain saved his pleasantries for the customers. He laughed and made jokes and gave every appearance of being a hearty, kindly fellow. But upstairs in the evenings his face was sour.

"Don't be noisy, children," their mother warned. "Your—my husband is tired."

Beezie whispered to Chuck, "Pa was tired, too, but he liked to hear us laugh."

"We were his own children," Chuck replied. "We don't belong to Duthbert Mortmain, and he doesn't like what doesn't belong to him."

Duthbert Mortmain did not show his vicious temper until the following spring. There was never a sign of it in the store, even with the most difficult customers or salesmen, but upstairs he began to let it have its way. One morning his wife ("I hate it when people call her Mrs. Mortmain!" Beezie exploded) came to breakfast with a black eye, explaining that she had bumped into a door in the dark. The grandmother, Beezie, and Chuck looked at her, but said nothing.

And it became very clear that Duthbert Mortmain did not like children, even when they were quiet. Whenever Chuck did anything which displeased his stepfather, which was at least once a day, Mortmain boxed his ears, so that at last they rang constantly.

When Beezie sat at the cash register, her stepfather pinched her arm every time he passed, as though in affection. But her arms were so full of black and blue marks that she kept her sweater on all the time to hide the bruises.

One day at recess in the schoolyard, Chuck saw Paddy O'Keefe come up to Beezie, and hurried over to them to hear Paddy asking, "Old Mortmain after you?"

"What do you mean?"

"You know what I mean."

"No. I don't." But she shivered.

Chuck intervened, "You leave my sister alone."

"Better tell old Mortmain to leave her alone, runt. You ever need any help, Beezie, you just let me know. Li'l ole Paddy'll take care of you."

That night Duthbert Mortmain's temper flared totally out of control.

They had finished the evening meal, and when Beezie was clearing the table, her stepfather reached out and pinched her bottom, and Chuck saw the look of cold hatred she turned on him.

"Duthbert—" their mother protested.

"Duthbert Mortmain, take care." The grandmother gave him a long, level gaze. She spoke not another word, but warning was clear in her eyes. She put cups and glasses on a tray, and started for the sink.

Mortmain, too, left the table, and as the old woman neared the stairway he raised his arm to strike her.

"No!" Beezie screamed.

Chuck thrust himself between his grandmother and stepfather and took the full force of Mortmain's blow.

Again Beezie screamed, as Chuck fell, fell down the steep stairs in a shower of broken china and glass. Then she rushed after him.

Chuck lay in a distorted position at the foot of the stairs, looking up at her with eyes that did not see. "Gedder pushed me. He pushed me. Don't let him marry Gwen. Zillah, don't let Gedder, don't let . . ."

10 The Earth with Its Starkness

A field of dandelions. Yellow. Yellow. Exploding into white, into a blizzard of white, a terror of white. Green stems, sickly trickling ooze.
Grandma.
Grandma.

Grandma, you're not going to die. Not ever.

Gedder.
Smell. Bad smell.
Gun. Gedder's gun. Stop him
terrible fall
Gwen   Zillah
head hurts
hurts

crystal horn heals
Matthew's unicorn comes
tip touches head with light heals

Beezie! Grandma! Ma! Pa!

Two stones in the cemetery.
A fight at the edge of the cliff, like Gwydyr and Madoc at the edge of the lake. Bad. Bad.
Breeze, never let him touch you.

* * *

From inside himself Charles Wallace watched as the unicorn lowered his head and the blazing tip of the horn touched Chuck's head, pouring light into it. He kept the horn there until the light had poured itself out, and the spasms of pain subsided and the boy stopped babbling and slept.

"Charles Wallace!"

He listened. The voice sounded like Gaudior, and yet it was not Gaudior, and he no longer saw the silver beauty of the unicorn nor the light of the horn. Nothing was visible, not even darkness. Something was happening, and he did not know what. He was still Within Chuck, and yet he was intensely conscious of himself as Charles Wallace, and something was pulling him.

Meg sat up, blinking and rubbing her hand against Ananda's fur. The kitten had returned and was sleeping on the pillow. At first Meg did not know why there were tears on her cheeks, or why she was frightened.

She closed her eyes in sadness and saw the unicorn standing motionless by the star-watching rock. A pear-shaped drop of crystal slid from Gaudior's eye and shattered into a thousand fragments on the stone. The unicorn looked up at the sky. The stars were sparkling brilliantly. Small wisps of starlit cloud moved in the rapid north wind. She thought she heard Gaudior saying, 'The Old Music was in them once. That was a victory for the Echthroi.'

Meg thought of Mrs. O'Keefe waiting downstairs. Yes. That was a victory for the enemy, indeed. That Beezie, the golden child, should have become the old hag with missing teeth and resentful eyes was unbearable.

There's more to her than meets the eye.

Infinitely more.

And what now? What's going to happen?

To Chuck?

To Charles Wallace?

"Charles Wallace!"

He listened. Was it Gaudior? He could hear, but he could not see, and the voice echoed as though coming from a great distance.

"Charles Wallace." The voice was compassionate. "You don't have to stay Within Chuck now that this has happened. We did not expect this."

Charles Wallace felt cold and confused and therefore cross. "But I *am* Within Chuck."

"Yes. And Chuck is unconscious, and when he comes to, he will not be the same. His skull has been fractured. Although the healing of the horn has taken away the worst of the pain it could not repair the brain damage. And so there have been instructions that you are to be released now if you so desire."

Charles Wallace felt weighed down by darkness and pain.

The almost-Gaudior voice continued. "Within Chuck as he is now, you will have no control over his actions. His brain is short-circuited. If there is a Might-Have-Been which you should alter in order to avert disaster, you will have no ability either to recognize it or to change it."

"If you release me from Within Chuck, then what?"

"You will be sent Within someone else, and then you will be better able to accomplish your mission. Time is of the essence, as you understand. And we do not know what may happen while you are trapped Within this injured child."

"Who are you?" Charles Wallace asked the invisible voice. "You sound like Gaudior, but you aren't Gaudior."

The voice laughed gently. "No, I am not Gaudior. All the healing light went from his horn, but he could not cure Chuck, though he kept him from dying—and that may not have been a kindness. He has gone home to dip his horn in the pools of healing to replenish it."

"Then who are you?"

Again the voice laughed. "You saw me when Gaudior took you home after you nearly drowned in the Ice Age sea. I am the unicorn you saw come forth from the shell."

"Why can't I see you? Why can't I see anything?" The words of the voice had reassured him, and yet he still felt foreboding.

"While you are in Chuck, you see only what Chuck sees, and he is unconscious, and will be for several days. Come, Charles Wallace, there's no time to be lost. Let us help you out of Chuck. If Mad Dog Branzillo is to be prevented from starting a holocaust you must not dally."

"I have to think—" Something was wrong, and he did not know what.

"Charles Wallace. Gaudior will corroborate what I have told you. Chuck's brain has been damaged. He's little better than an idiot. Come out."

"If I come out, will I see you?" There was something about the voice which was inconsistent with the visual image of the baby unicorn; but of course it would no longer be a baby.

"Of course you'll see me. Hurry. There's a terrible urgency about what you are to accomplish."

"I?"

"Of course, you. You were selected, weren't you?"

"No. Beezie—Mrs. O'Keefe—laid a charge on me."

"Because you're the only one who can prevent Branzillo."

"But I can't—"

"Of course you can." The voice was tenderly patient. "Why do you think you were chosen?"

"Well—Gaudior seemed to think it was that I might be able to go Within people, because of the way Meg and I kythe."

"Exactly. You were chosen because of your special gifts, and your unusual intelligence. You know that yourself, don't you?"

"Well—I can kythe. And I know my I.Q.'s high, as far as that goes. But that's not enough—"

"Of course it is. And you have the ability to see the difference between right and wrong, and to make the correct decisions. You were selected because you are an extraordinary young man and your gifts and your brains qualify you. You are the only one who can control the Might-Have-Been."

Charles Wallace's stomach was churning.

"Come, Charles Wallace. You have been chosen. You are in control of what is going to happen. You are needed. We must go."

Charles Wallace began to throw up. Was it in reaction to the tempting words, or because Chuck, with his bashed-in skull, was vomiting? But he knew that whatever the voice looked like, it was not a unicorn. When he had stopped retching he said, "I don't know who you are, but you're not like Gaudior. Gaudior would never say what you've just said. It was trying to use my high I.Q. and trying to control things that got us into trouble in the first place. I don't know what I'm supposed to use, but it's not my intellect or strength. For better or worse, I'm Within Chuck. And I've never come out of Within on my own. It's always happened to me. I'm staying Within."

Meg let out a long sigh. "He made the right choice, didn't he?"

Ananda's warm tongue gently touched Meg's hand.

Meg closed her eyes, listening. She thought she heard a howl of defeat, and she whiffed the ugly stench of Echthroi.

So they had been trying to get at Charles Wallace in a much more subtle way than by trying to snatch him from Gaudior's back or throw him into Projections.

Duthbert Mortmain had nearly killed Chuck. Nothing went in straight lines for him any more, not time, not distance. His mind was like the unstable earth, full of faults, so that layers shifted and slid. It was like being in a nightmare from which there was no possibility of waking. She ached for him, and for Charles Wallace Within him.

Pain and panic
the world tilting
twirling on its axis, out of control
spinning off   away from the sun   into the dark
light bursting against his eyes, an explosion of light
a kaleidoscope of brilliant colors   assailing his nostrils
"Chuck!" The voice came echoing from a vast distance, echoing along the unseen walls of a dark tunnel.

"Chuck! It's Beezie, your sister. Chuck, can you hear me?"

He was weighted down by the vast heaviness of the atmosphere, but he managed to lift one finger in response to Beezie's calling, afraid, as he did so, that if the weight lifted he would fall off the wildly tilting earth . . .

"He hears me! Ma, Chuck moved his finger!"

Slowly the rampant, out-of-control speed lessened, and the planet resumed its normal pace. Colors stopped their kaleidoscopic dance and stayed in place. Smells became identifiable once more: coffee; bread; apples. Beezie: the gold was not as brilliant as it had been, but it was still Beezie. And their mother: the blue was cloudy now, hardly blue at all, closer to the grey of rain clouds. Grandma: where is Grandma's smell? Why is there emptiness? Where is the green?

"Grandma!"

"She's dead, Chuck. Her heart gave out."

"Gedder pushed her. He killed her."

"No, Chuck." Beezie's voice was bitter, and the bitterness further muted the gold. "Duthbert Mortmain. He was furious with her, and he was going to strike her, but you saved her, and he hit you instead, and you fell all the way down the stairs and fractured your skull. And Grandma—she just . . ."

"What? Did Gedder—"

"No, no, not Gedder, Chuck, Duthbert Mortmain. He felt as awful as he's capable of feeling. He and Ma drove you to the hospital, and I stayed home with Grandma, and she looked at me and said, 'I'm sorry, Beezie, I can't wait any longer. My Patrick's come for me.' And she gave a little gasp, and that was all."

He heard her, but between the stark words came other sounds and the smell of a hot and alien wind. Time's layers slipped and slid under him. "But Gwen shouldn't marry Gedder. Gwydyr's children shouldn't marry Madoc's."

There was panic in Beezie's voice. "What are you talking about? Chuck, please don't. You scare me. I want you to get all the way well."

"Not Let's Pretend. Real. Gwen and Gedder—it would be bad, bad . . ."

The cliff loomed high over him, dark, shadowing. Gedder was at the top of the cliff, waiting, waiting . . . who was he waiting for?

Chuck slowly improved, until he could put cans and boxes on the store shelves. Even though he could not manage school, he recovered enough to mark the prices on the store's stock. He seldom made a mistake, and when he did, Duthbert Mortmain did not box his ears.

Sometimes Chuck saw him as Mortmain, sometimes as Gedder, when his worlds warped. "Gedder is nicer than he used to be," he reported to Beezie. "He's nicer to Ma. And to Grandma and me."

"Grandma—" A sob choked Beezie's voice. "Chuck, how can you! How can you play Let's Pretend about that?" Her voice rose with outrage. "How can you go away from me like this when I need you? Don't leave me!"

He heard and he did not hear. He was caught between the layers and he could not get into the right layer so that he could be with Beezie. "Grandma says I'm not to let him hear me call him Gedder, because that's not his real name, so I won't." He had intended to say, he thought he was saying, 'I'll never leave you, Beezie,' but the words of the other layer came out of his mouth. "Where's Matthew? I want to talk to him. He has to get Zillah to Vespugia."

Sometimes the earth started to tilt again and he could not stand upright against the velocity. Then he had to stay in bed until the tilting steadied.

He climbed the attic stairs one day when the earth was firm under his feet, and crawled into all the dimmest and most cobwebby corners, until his hands felt a packet. At first he thought it was an old tobacco pouch, but then he saw that it was oilskin wrapped about some papers. Letters. And newspaper clippings.

Letters from Bran to Zillah, to Matthew. Urgent letters.

He looked at them and the words danced and flickered. Sometimes they seemed to say one thing, sometimes another. He could not read the small print. He pushed the heels of his hands against his eyeballs and everything sparkled like fireworks. He sobbed with frustration, and took the letters and clippings downstairs and put them under his pillow.

—I'll tell Grandma. She'll help me read them.

The kythe came to Meg in distorting waves.

One minute she understood, and the next she was caught up in Chuck's shifting universe. She pulled herself away from the kythe to try to think.

—What's coming clear, she thought,—is that it's important to know whether Mad Dog Branzillo is from Madoc's or Gwydyr's line. Somehow or other, it's between the two babies in the scry, the scry which both Madoc and Brandon Llawcae saw.

We don't know much about Gwydyr's line. He was disgraced, and he went to Vespugia eventually, and we think Gedder is his descendant.

We know a little more about Madoc's line. From each time Charles Wallace has gone Within, we know that most of Madoc's ancestors stayed around here.

So Branzillo's ancestors matter. And it's all in Matthew Maddox's book that Charles Wallace can't get at because the Echthroi are blocking him. But what can Charles Wallace do about it, even if he and Gaudior ever do get to Patagonia?

Slowly, she moved back into the kythe.

"Chuck." It was Beezie's voice.

"Here I am."

"How do you feel?"

"Dizzy. The earth's spinning, like the night we saw the fireflies."

"The night Pa died."

"Yes. Like then."

"You remember?" she asked in surprise.

"Of course."

"Lots of things you don't remember. That's why you can't go to school any more. Chuck—"

"What?"

"Ma's going to have a baby."

"She can't. Pa's dead."

"She's married again."

"She and Gedder can't have a baby. It would be bad."

"I thought you were talking the way you used to. I thought you were all right!" Her voice rose in frustration and outrage. "Not Gedder! Mortmain!"

He tried to come back to her, but he could not. "Same difference. Same smell. The baby has to come from Madoc. Bran and Zillah have to have the baby because of the prayer."

"What prayer?" she shouted.

> *"Lords of blue and Lords of gold,*
> *Lords of winds and waters wild,*
> *Lords of time that's growing old,*
> *When will come the season mild?*
> *When will come blue Madoc's child?"*

"Where'd you learn that?"

"The letters."

"What letters?"

He became impatient. "Bran's letters, of course."

"But we've read them all. There wasn't anything like that in them."

"Found some more."

"When? Where?"

"In the attic. Grandma helps me read them."

"Where are they?" she demanded.

He fumbled under his pillow. "Here."

Chuck walked through a spring evening, smelling of growing grass, and blossoms drifting from the trees. He walked over the fields, over the brook, drinking the water rushing with melting snow, lifting his head, clambering to his feet, going on to the flat rock. Pain walked with him, and there was a dark veil of cloud between his eyes and the world. If a chair was pulled out of place he walked into it. Trees and rocks did not move; he felt safer at the rock than anywhere else.

He did not tell anybody about the veil.

He began to make mistakes in stamping the prices on the stock, but Duthbert Mortmain assumed it was because the fall had made him half-witted.

The baby came, a boy, and the mother no longer worked in the store. Paddy O'Keefe had dropped out of school and came in to help. Chuck followed Paddy's instructions, marking the cans with the stamp which Paddy set for him. He heard Paddy say, "He's more trouble than he's worth. Whyn't you send him to the nuthouse?"

Mortmain muttered something about his wife.

"Aren't you afraid he'll hurt the baby?" Paddy asked.

After that, Chuck stayed out of the way as much as possible, spending the warm days at the flat rock, the cold ones curled up in the attic. He saw Beezie to talk to only in the evenings, and Sunday afternoons.

"Chuck, what's wrong with your eyes?"

"Nothing."

"You're not seeing properly."

"It's all right."

"Ma—"

"Don't tell Ma!"

"But you ought to see a doctor."

"No! All they want is any excuse to put me away. You must have heard them, Paddy and Duthbert. They want to put me in an institution. For my own good, Mortmain said to Ma. He said I'm an idiot and I might hurt the baby."

Beezie burst into tears and flung her arms around her brother. "You wouldn't!"

"I know I wouldn't. But it's the one thing Ma might listen to."

"And you're not an idiot!"

His cheeks were wet with Beezie's tears. "If you tell them about my eyes they'll put me in an insane asylum for my own good and the baby's. I'm trying to keep out of the way."

"I'll help you, oh, Chuck, I'll help you," Beezie promised.

"I have to stay long enough to make sure Matthew sends Zillah to Vespugia. He's saving the money."

"Oh, Chuck," Beezie groaned. "Don't let them hear you talk like this."

As the veil deepened and darkened, his inner vision lightened. When the weather was fine he lay out on the flat rock all day, looking up toward the sky and seeing pictures, pictures more vivid than anything he had seen with unveiled eyes. His concentration was so intense that he became part of all that was happening in the pictures. Sometimes in the evenings he told Beezie about them, pretending they were dreams, in order not to upset her.

"I dreamed about riding a unicorn. He was like moonlight, and so tall I had to climb a tree to get on his back, and we flew among the fireflies, and the unicorn and I sang together."

"That's a lovely dream. Tell me more."

"I dreamed that the valley was a lake, and I rode a beautiful fish sort of like a porpoise."

"Pa said the valley was a lake, way back in prehistory. Archaeologists have found fish fossils in the glacial rocks. Maybe that's why you dreamed it."

"Grandma told us about the lake, the day we blew dandelion clocks."

"Oh, Chuck, you're so strange, the way you remember some things . . ."

"And I dreamed about a fire of roses, and-" He reached gropingly for her hand. "I can move in and out of time."

"Oh, Chuck!"

"I can, Beezie."

"Please—please stop."

"It's only dreams," he comforted.

"Well, then. But don't tell Ma."

"Only you and Grandma."

"Oh, Chuck."

He knew the route to the rock so well that it was easier for him to go in the dark, when he could see nothing, than in sunlight when shafts of brilliance penetrated the veil like spears and hurt his eyes and confused his sense of direction.

Time. Time. There wasn't much time.

Time. Time was as fluid as water.

He stood by Matthew's couch. "You can't wait any longer. You have to get Zillah to Vespugia now, or it will be too late."

Matthew is writing, writing against time. It's all in the book Pa talked about. They don't want me to see the book.

Ritchie is cutting a window in Brandon's room, before leaving for Wales . . .

But Zillah isn't there . . . Why is there an Indian girl instead?

Because it isn't Zillah's time. She comes later, in Matthew's time

Unicorns can move in time

and idiots

space is more difficult

Paddy wants me out of the way. Paddy and Mortmain. Not much time

> *Lords of space and Lords of time,*
> *Lords of blessing, Lords of grace,*
> *Who is in the warmer clime?*
> *Who will follow Madoc's rhyme?*
> *Blue will alter time and space*

Did you not learn in Gwynedd that there is room for one king only?

You will be great, little Madog, and call the world your own, to keep or destroy as you will. It is an evil world, little Madog.

You will do good for your people, El Zarco, little Blue Eyes. The prayer has been answered in you, blue for birth, blue for mirth

Which blue will it be

They are fighting
up on the cliff
on the steep rock

the world
it's tilting
it's going too fast
I'm going to fall

11 All These I Place

The light came back slowly. There had been shadows, nothing but deepening shadows, and pain, and slowly the pain began to leave and healing light touched his closed lids. He opened them. He was on the star-watching rock with Gaudior.

"The wind brought you out of Chuck."

"What happened to him?"

"Mortmain had him institutionalized. Are you ready? It's time—" A ripple of tension moved along the unicorn's flanks.

Charles Wallace felt the wind all about them, cold, and yet strengthening. "What Chuck saw—two men fighting—was it real?"

"What is real?" Gaudior replied infuriatingly.

"It's important!"

"We do not always know what is important and what is not. The wind sends a warning to hurry, hurry. Climb up, and hold very tight."

"Should I bind myself to you again?"

"The wind says there's no time. We'll fly out of time and through galaxies the Echthroi do not know. But the wind says it may be difficult to send you Within, even so. Hold on, and try not to be afraid."

Charles Wallace felt the wind beneath them as Gaudior spread his wings. The flight at first was serene. Then he began to feel cold, a deep, penetrating cold far worse than the cold of the Ice Age sea. This was a cold of the spirit as well as the body. He did not fall off the unicorn because he was frozen to him; his hands were congealed in their clenched grasp on the frozen mane.

Gaudior's hoofs touched something solid, and the cold lifted just enough so that the boy was able to unclench his hands and open his frozen lids. They were in an open square in a frozen city of tall, windowless buildings. There was no sign of tree, of grass. The blind cement was cracked, and there were great chunks of fallen masonry on the street.

"Where—" Charles Wallace started, and stopped.

The unicorn turned his head slowly. "A Projection—"

Charles Wallace followed his gaze and saw two men in gas masks patrolling the square with machine guns. "Do they see us?"

The question was answered by the two men pausing, turning, looking through the round black eyes of their gas masks directly at unicorn and boy, and raising their guns.

With a tremendous leap Gaudior launched upward, wings straining. Charles Wallace pressed close to the neck, hands twined in the mane. But for the moment they had escaped the Echthroi, and when Gaudior's hoofs touched the ground, the Projection was gone.

"Those men with guns—" Charles Wallace started. "In a Projection, could they have killed us?"

"I don't know," Gaudior said, "and I didn't want to wait to find out."

Charles Wallace looked around in relief. When he had left Chuck, it was autumn, the cold wind stripping the trees. Now it was high spring, the old apple and pear trees in full blossom, and the smell of lilac on the breeze. All about them, the birds were in full song.

"What should we do now?" Charles Wallace asked.

"At least you're asking, not telling." Gaudior sounded unusually cross, so the boy knew he was unusually anxious.

Meg shivered. Within the kythe she saw the star-watching rock and a golden summer's day. There were two people on the rock, a young woman, and a young man—or a boy? She was not sure, because there was something wrong with the boy. But from their dress she was positive that it was the time of the Civil War—around 1865.

The Within-ing was long and agonizing, instead of immediate, as it had always been before. Charles Wallace felt intolerable pain in his back, and a crushing of his legs. He could hear himself screaming. His body was being forced into another body, and at the same time something was struggling to pull him out. He was being torn apart in a battle between two opposing forces. Sun blazed, followed by a blizzard of snow, snow melted by raging fire, and violent flashings of lightning, driven by a mighty wind, which whipped across sea and land . . .

His body was gone and he was Within, Within a crippled body, the body of a young man with useless legs like a shriveled child's . . . Matthew Maddox.

From the waist up he looked not unlike Madoc, and about the same age, with a proud head and a lion's mane of fair hair. But the body was nothing like Madoc's strong and virile one. And the eyes were grey, grey as the ocean before rain.

Matthew was looking somberly at the girl, who appeared to be about his age, though her eyes were far younger than his. "Croeso f'annwyl, Zillah." He spoke the Welsh words of endearment lovingly. "Thank you for coming."

"You knew I would. As soon as Jack O'Keefe brought your note, I set off. How did you get here?"

He indicated a low wagon which stood a little way from the rock.

She looked at the powerful torso, and deeply muscled shoulders and arms. "By yourself, all the way?"

"No. I can do it, but it takes me a long time, and I had to go over the store ledgers this morning. When I went to the stables to find Jack to deliver the note, I swallowed my pride and asked him to bring me."

Zillah spread her billowing white skirts about her on the rock. She wore a wide-brimmed leghorn hat with blue ribbons, which brought out the highlights in her straight, shining black hair, and a locket on a blue ribbon at her throat. To Matthew Maddox she was the most beautiful, and desirable, and—to him—the most unattainable woman in the world.

"Matt, what's wrong?" she asked.

"Something's happened to Bran."

She paled. "How do you know? Are you sure?"

"Last night I woke out of a sound sleep with an incredibly sharp pain in my leg. Not my own familiar pain, Bran's pain. And he was calling out to me to help him."

"O dear Lord. Is he going to be all right?"

"He's alive. He's been reaching out to me all day."

She buried her face in her hands, so that her words were muffled. "Thank you for telling me. You and Bran—you've always been so close, even closer than most twins."

He acknowledged this with a nod. "We were always close, but it was after my accident that—it was Bran who brought me back into life, Zillah, you know that."

She dropped her hand lightly on his shoulder. "If Bran is badly wounded, we're going to need you. As once you needed Bran."

After the accident, five years earlier, when his horse had crashed into a fence and rolled over on him, crushing his pelvis and legs and fracturing his spine, Bran had shown him no pity; instead, had fiercely tried to push his twin brother into as much independence as possible, and refused to allow him to feel sorry for himself.

'But Rollo jumps fences twice as high with ease.'

'He didn't jump that one.'

'Bran, just before he crashed, there was a horrible, putrid stink—'

'Stop going back over things. Get on with it.'

They continued to go everywhere together—until the war. Unlike Bran, Matthew could not lie about his age and join the cavalry.

"I lived my life through Bran, vicariously," Matthew told Zillah. "When he went to war, it was the first time he ever left me out." Then: "When you and Bran fell in love, I knew that I had to start letting him go, to try to find some kind of life of my own, so that he'd be free. And it was easier to let go with you than with anyone else in the world, because you've always treated me like a complete human being, and I knew that the two of you would not exclude me from your lives."

"Dear Matt. Never. And you are making your own life. You're selling your stories and poems, and I think they're as good as anything by Mark Twain."

Matthew laughed, a warm laugh that lightened the pain lines in his face. "They're only a beginner's work."

"But editors think they're good, too, and so does my father."

"I'm glad. I value Dr. Llawcae's opinion as much as anybody's in the world."

"And he loves you and Bran and Gwen as though you were my brothers and sister. And your mother has been a second mother to me since my own dear mama died. As for our fathers—they may be only distant kin, but they're like as two peas in a pod with their passion for Wales. Matt—have you said anything about Bran to Gwen or your parents?"

"No. They don't like the idea that Bran and I can communicate without speech or letters the way we do. They pretend it's some kind of trick we've worked out, the way we used to change places with each other when we were little, to fool people. They think what we do isn't real."

"It's real, I don't doubt that." Zillah smiled. "Dear Matt, I think I love you nearly as much as Bran does."

A week later, Mr. Maddox received official news that his son had been wounded in battle and would be invalided home. He called the family into the dark, booklined library to inform them.

Mrs. Maddox fanned herself with her black lace fan. "Thank God."

"You're glad Bran's been wounded!" Gwen cried indignantly.

Mrs. Maddox continued to fan herself. "Of course not, child. But I'm grateful to God that he's alive, and that he's coming home before something worse than a bullet in the leg happens to him."

—It *is* worse, Mama, Matthew thought silently.—Bran has been shutting me out of his thoughts and he's never done that before. All I get from him is a dull, deadening pain. Gwen is more right than she knows, not to be glad.

He looked thoughtfully at his sister. She was dark of hair and blue of eye like Zillah, making them appear more like sisters than distant cousins. But her face did not have Zillah's openness, and her eyes were a colder blue and glittered when she was angry. After Matthew's accident she had pitied him, but had not translated her pity into compassion. Matthew did not want pity.

Gwen returned his gaze. "And how do you feel about your twin's coming home, Matthew?"

"He's been badly hurt, Gwen," he said. "He's not going to be the same debonair Bran who left us."

"He's still only a child." Mrs. Maddox turned toward her husband, who was sitting behind the long oak library table.

"He's a man, and when he comes home the store will become Maddox and Son," her husband said.

—Maddox and Son, Matthew thought without bitterness—not Maddox and Sons.

He turned his wheelchair slightly away. He was totally committed to his writing; he had no wish to be a partner in Maddox's General Store, which was a large and prosperous establishment in the center of the village, and had the trade of the surrounding countryside for many miles. The first story of the rambling frame building was filled with all the foodstuffs needed for the village. Upstairs were saddles and harnesses, guns, plows, and even a large quantity of oars, as though Mr. Maddox remembered a time when nearly all of the valley had been a great lake. A few ponds were all that remained of the original body of water. Matthew spent most mornings in the store, taking care of the ledgers and all the accounts.

Behind the store was the house, named Merioneth. The Llawcae home, Madrun, stood beyond Merioneth, slightly more ostentatious, with white pillars and pink-brick façade. Merioneth was the typical three-storied white frame farmhouse with dark shutters which had replaced the original log cabins.

'People think we're putting on airs, giving our houses names,' Bran had complained one day, before the accident, as he and Matthew were walking home from school.

Matthew did a cartwheel. 'I like it,' he said as he came right side up. 'Merioneth is named in honor of a distant cousin of ours in Wales.'

'Yah, I know, Michael Jones, a congregational minister of Bala in Merioneth.'

'Cousin Michael's pleased that we've given the house that name. He mentions it almost every time he writes to Papa. Weren't you listening yesterday when he was telling us about Love Jones Parry, the squire of Madrun, and his plan to take a trip to Patagonia to inspect the land and see if it might be suitable for a colony from Wales?'

'That's the only interesting bit,' Bran had said. 'I love to travel, even just to go with Papa to get supplies. Maybe if the squire of Madrun really does take that trip, we could go with him.'

It was not long after this that the accident happened, and Matthew remembered how Bran had tried to rouse him from despair by telling him that Love Jones Parry had actually gone to Patagonia, and reported that although the land was wild and desolate, he thought that the formation of a Welsh colony where the colonists would be allowed to teach their native tongue in school might be possible. The Spanish government paid scant attention to that section of Patagonia, where there were only a few Indians and a handful of Spaniards.

But Matthew refused to be roused. 'Exciting for you. I'm not going to get very far from Merioneth ever again.'

Bran had scowled at him ferociously. 'You cannot afford the luxury of self-pity.'

—It is still an expensive luxury, Matthew thought,—and one I can ill afford.

"Matt!" It was Gwen. "A penny for your thoughts."

He had been writing when his father had summoned them, and still had his note pad on his lap. "Just thinking out the plot for another story."

She smiled at him brightly. "You're going to make the name of Maddox famous!"

"My brave baby," Mrs. Maddox said. "How proud I am of you! That was the third story you've sold to *Harper's Monthly*, wasn't it?"

"The fourth—Mama, Papa, Gwen: I think I must warn you that Bran is going to need all our love and help when he comes home."

"Well, of course—" Gwen started indignantly.

"No, Gwen," he said quietly. "Bran is hurt much more than just the leg wound."

"What are you talking about?" his father demanded.

"You might call it Bran's soul. It's sick."

* * *

Bran returned, limping and withdrawn. He shut Matthew out as effectively as though he had slammed a door in his twin's face.

Once again Matthew sent a note to Zillah to meet him at the flat rock. This time he did not ask Jack O'Keefe for help, but lying on the wagon, he pulled himself over the rough ground. It was arduous work, even with his powerful arms, and he was exhausted when he arrived. But he had allowed more than enough time. He heaved himself off the wagon and dragged over to the rock, stretched out, and slept under the warm autumn sun.

"Matt—"

He woke up. Zillah was smiling down at him. "F'annwyl." He pushed the fair hair back from his eyes and sat up. "Thanks for coming."

"How is he today?"

Matthew shook his head. "No change. It's hard on Papa to have another crippled son."

"Hush. Bran's not a cripple!"

"He'll limp from that leg wound for the rest of his life. And whether or not his spirit will heal is anybody's guess."

"Give him time, Matt . . ."

"Time!" Matthew pushed the word away impatiently. "That's what Mama keeps saying. But we've given him time. It's three months since he came home. He sleeps half the day and reads half the night. And he's still keeping himself closed to me. If he'd talk about his experiences it might help him, but he won't."

"Not even to you?"

"He seems to feel he has to protect me," Matthew said bitterly, "and one of the things I've always loved most in Bran was his refusal to protect or mollycoddle me in any way."

"Bran, Bran," Zillah murmured, "the knight in shining armor who went so bravely to join the cavalry and save the country and free the slaves . . ." She glanced at the ring on her finger. "He asked me to return his ring. To set me free, he said."

Matthew stretched out his hand to her, then drew it back.

"There has to be time for me as well as for Bran. When he gave me this ring I promised I'd be here for him when he returned, no matter what, and I intend to keep that promise. What can we do to bring him out of the slough of despond?"

Matthew ached to reach out to touch her fair skin, to stroke her hair as black as the night and as beautiful. He spread his hand on the warm rock. "I tried to get him to take me riding. I haven't ridden since he went away."

"And?"

"He said it was too dangerous."

"For you? Or for him?"

"That's what I asked him. And he just said, 'Leave me alone. My leg pains me.' And I said, 'You never used to let me talk about it when my legs and back hurt.' And he just looked at me and said, 'I didn't understand pain then.' And I said, 'I think you understood it better then than you do now.' And we stopped talking because we weren't getting anywhere, and he wouldn't open an inch to let me near him."

"Father says his pain should be tolerable by now, and the physical wound is not the problem."

"That's right. We've got to get him out of himself somehow. And Zillah, something else happened that I need to talk to you about. Yesterday when I hoped I could get Bran to take me riding I wheeled out to the stable to check on my saddle, and when I pushed open the stable door there were Jack and—and—"

"Gwen?"

"How did you guess?"

"I've noticed him looking at her. And she's looked right back."

"They were doing more than looking. They were kissing."

"Merchant's daughter and hired hand. Your parents would not approve. How about you?"

"Zillah, that's not what I mind about Jack O'Keefe. He's a big and powerful man and he has nothing but scorn for me—or anything with a physical imperfection. I saw him take a homeless puppy and kill it by flinging it against the wall of the barn."

She put her hands over her eyes. "Matt! Stop!"

"I think it's his enormous physical healthiness that attracts Gwen. I'm a total cripple, and Bran's half a one, at least for now. And Jack is life. She doesn't see the cruelty behind the wide smile and loud laugh."

"What are you going to do about it?"

"Nothing. For now. Mama and Papa have enough on their minds, worrying their hearts out over Bran. And if I warn Gwen, she'll just think I'm jealous of all that Jack can do and all that I cannot. I'll try to talk to Bran, but I doubt he'll hear."

"Dear Matt. It comforts me that you and I can talk like this." Her voice was compassionate, but it held none of the pity he loathed. "My true and good friend."

One night after dinner, while the men lingered over the port, Mr. Maddox looked at Bran over the ruby liquid in his glass. "Matthew and Zillah would like you to join them in their Welsh lesson this week."

"Not yet, Papa."

"Not yet, not yet, that's all you've been saying for the past three months. Will Llawcae says your wound is healed now, and there's no reason for your malingering."

To try to stop his father, Matthew said, "I was remarking today that Gwen looks more Indian than Welsh, with her high cheekbones."

Mr. Maddox poured himself a second glass of port, then stoppered the cut-glass decanter. "Your mother does not like to be reminded that I have Indian blood, though it's generations back. The Llawcaes have it, too, through our common forebears, Brandon Llawcae and Maddok of the People of the Wind, whose children intermarried. Maddok was so named because he had the blue eyes of Welsh Madoc—but then, I don't need to repeat the story."

"True," Bran agreed.

"I like it." Matthew sipped his wine.

"You're a romanticizer," Bran said. "Keep it for your writing."

Mr. Maddox said stiffly, "As your mother has frequently pointed out, black hair and blue eyes are far more common in people of Welsh descent than Indian, and Welsh we indubitably are. And hard-working." He looked pointedly at Bran.

Later in the evening Matthew wheeled himself into Bran's room. His twin was standing by the window, holding the velveteen curtains aside to look across the lawn to the woods. He turned on Matthew with a growl. "Go away."

"No, Bran. When I was hurt I told you to go away, and you wouldn't. Nor will I." Matthew wheeled closer to his brother. "Gwen's in love with Jack O'Keefe."

"Not surprised. Jack's a handsome brute."

"He's not the right man for Gwen."

"Because he's our hired hand? Don't be such a snob."

"No. Because he is, as you said, a brute."

"Gwen can take care of herself. She always has. Anyhow, Papa would put his foot down."

There was an empty silence which Matthew broke. "Don't cut Zillah out of your life."

"If I love Zillah, that's the only thing to do. Free her."

"She doesn't want to be free. She loves you."

Bran walked over to his bed with the high oak bedstead and flung himself down. "I'm out of love with everything and everybody. Out of love with life."

"Why?"

"Do you have to ask me?"

"Yes, I do. Because you aren't telling me."

"You used to know without my having to tell you."

"I still would, if you weren't shutting me out."

Bran moved his head restlessly back and forth on the pillow. "Don't you be impatient with me, twin. Papa's bad enough."

Matthew wheeled over to the bed. "You know Papa."

"I'm no more cut out to be a storekeeper than you are. Gwen's the one who has Papa's hard business sense. But I don't have a talent like yours to offer Papa as an alternative. And he's always counted on me to take over the business. And I don't want to. I never did."

"What, then?" Matthew asked.

"I'm not sure. The only positive thing the war did for me was confirm my enjoyment of travel. I like adventure—but not killing. And it seems the two are seldom separated."

It was the nearest they had come to a conversation since Bran's return, and Matthew felt hopeful.

Matthew was writing on his lap desk in a sunny corner of the seldom-used parlor.

There Bran found him. "Twin, I need you."

"I'm here," Matthew said.

Bran straddled a small gilt chair and leaned his arms on the back. "Matt, nothing is the way I thought it was. I went to war thinking of myself as Galahad, out to free fellow human beings from the intolerable bondage of slavery. But it wasn't as simple as that. There were other, less pure issues being fought over, with little concern for the souls which would perish for nothing more grand than political greed, corruption, and conniving for power. Matt, I saw a man with his face blown off and no mouth to scream with, and yet he screamed and could not die. I saw two brothers, and one was in blue and one was in grey, and I will not tell you which one took his saber and ran it through the other. Oh God, it was brother against brother, Cain and Abel all over again. And I was turned into Cain. What would God have to do with a nation where brothers can turn against each other with such brutality?" Bran stopped speaking as his voice broke on a sob.

Matthew put down his lap desk and drew his twin to him, and together they wept, as Bran poured out all the anguish and terror and nightmare he had lived through. And Matthew held him and drew the pain out and into his own heart.

When the torrent was spent, Bran looked at his twin. "Thank you."

Matthew held him close. "You're back, Bran. We're together again."

"Yes. Forever."

"It's good to have you coming back to life."

"Coming back to life hurts. I need to take my pain away."

Matthew asked, startled, "What?"

"Matt, twin, I'm going away."

"What!" Matthew looked at Bran standing straight and strong before him. The yellow satin curtains warmed the light and brightened Bran's hair. "Where?"

"You'll never guess."

Matthew waited.

"Papa had a letter from Wales, from Cousin Michael. A group left for Patagonia to start a colony. They're there by now. I'm going to join them. How's that for an old dream come true?"

"We were going together . . ."

"Dear my twin, you're making a name for yourself here with your pen. I know that the creation of a story is work, even if Papa doesn't. But you couldn't manage a life of physical hardship such as I'll be having in the Welsh colony."

"You're right," Matthew acknowledged. "I'd be a burden."

"I won't be far from you, ever again," Bran assured him, "even in Patagonia. I promise to share it with you, and you'll be able to write stories about it as vividly as though you'd been there in body. Cousin Michael writes that the colony is settling in well, in a small section known as Vespugia, and I'll tell you everything about it, and describe a grand cast of characters for you."

"Have you told Zillah?"

Bran shook his head.

"Twin, this affects Zillah too, you know. She wears your ring."

"I'll tell everyone tonight at dinner. I'll get Mama to ask the Llawcaes."

Dinner was served in the dining room, a large, dark, oak-paneled chamber that seemed to drink in the light from the crystal chandelier. Heavy brown curtains like the ones in the library were drawn against the cold night. The fire burning brightly did little to warm the vast cavern.

During the meal, conversation was largely about the Welsh expedition to Patagonia, with both Mr. Maddox and Dr. Llawcae getting vicarious excitement out of the adventure.

"What fun," Gwen said. "Why don't you go, Papa? If I were a man, I would."

Matthew and Bran looked at each other across the table, but Bran shook his head slightly.

After dessert, when Mrs. Maddox pushed back her chair, nodding to Gwen and Zillah to follow her, Bran stopped them. "Wait, please, Mama. I have something to tell everybody. We've all enjoyed discussing the Patagonian expedition, and the founding of the colony in Vespugia. Years ago, before Matt's accident, we dreamed of joining the squire of Madrun when he made his journey to see if it would be a suitable place for a colony. So perhaps it won't surprise you that I have decided to join the colonists and make a new life for myself in Vespugia. Today I've written Cousin Michael and Mr. Parry in Wales, and sent letters to Vespugia."

For a moment there was stunned silence.

Bran broke it, smiling. "Dr. Llawcae says a warmer climate will be better for me."

Mr. Maddox asked, "Isn't going to Patagonia rather an excessive way to find a warmer climate? You could go south, to South Carolina or Georgia."

Bran's lips shut in a rigid expression of pain. "Papa, do you forget where I've come from and what I've been doing?"

Mrs. Maddox said, "No, son, your father does not forget. But the war is over, and you must put it behind you."

"In the South? I doubt I would be welcome in the Confederate states."

"But Vespugia—so far away—" Tears filled Mrs. Maddox's eyes. Zillah, her face pale but resolute, drew a fresh handkerchief from her reticule and handed it to her. "If you'd just continue to regain your strength, and go on studying Welsh with Matthew, and come into the business with your father—"

Bran shook his head. "Mama, you know that I cannot go into the business with Papa. And I have no talent, like Matthew's, which I could use here. It seems that the best way to pull myself together is to get out, and what better way to learn Welsh than to be with people who speak it all the time?"

Mr. Maddox spoke slowly, "You took me by surprise, son, but it does seem to be a reasonable solution for you, eh, Will?" He looked at the doctor, who was tamping his pipe.

"In a way, I identify with Madoc, Papa," Bran said. "Matt and I were rereading T. Gwynn Jones's poem about him this evening." He looked at Gwen. "Remember it?"

She sniffled. "I never read Welsh unless Papa forces me."

"Madoc left Wales in deep despair because brother was fighting against brother, just as we did in this ghastly war, 'until it seemed as if God himself had withdrawn his care from the sons of men.' . . . *ymdroi gyda diflastod as anobaith Madog wrth ystried cyflwr gwlad ei ededigaeth, lle'r oedd brawd un ymladd yn erbyn brawd hyd nes yr oedd petal Duw ei hun wedi peidio â gofalu am feibion dynion.*"

Mr. Maddox drew on his pipe. "You do remember."

"Good lad," Dr. Llawcae approved.

"I remember, and too well I understand, for there were many nights during the war when God withdrew from our battlefields. When the sons of men fight against each other in hardness of heart, why should God not withdraw? Slavery is evil, God knows, but war is evil, too, evil, evil."

Zillah pushed her empty dessert plate away and went to kneel by Bran, impulsively taking his hand and pressing it against her cheek.

He took her hand in his. "I went to war thinking that mankind is reasonable, and found that it is not. But it has always been so, and at last I am growing up, as Matthew grew up long before me. I know that he would give a great deal to come to Vespugia with me, and I to have him, but we both know that it cannot be."

Mrs. Maddox was still weeping into the handkerchief Zillah had given her. "Never again can there be a war that can do such terrible things to people."

Mr. Maddox said, "My dear, it is not good for us to keep reminding Bran of the war. Perhaps getting away from Merioneth and going to Vespugia will be the best way for him to forget."

Matthew looked at his father and saw him letting his dream of *Maddox and Son* disappear into the wilderness of Vespugia.

"Bran." Zillah rose and looked down at him.

"Little Zillah."

"I'm not little Zillah any more, Bran. You changed that the night before you went to war when you put this ring on my finger."

"Child," Dr. Llawcae remonstrated, "it is the dearest wish of my heart that Llawcaes and Maddoxes be once more united in marriage. I gave Bran my blessing when he came to me to ask for your hand. But not yet. You're only seventeen."

"Many women are married and mothers at seventeen. I want to go to Vespugia with Bran, as his wife."

"Zillah," Dr. Llawcae said, "you will wait. When Bran is settled, in a year or two, he can send for you."

Bran pressed Zillah's hand. "It needn't all be decided tonight."

* * *

In the end, Bran went with Gwen, not with Zillah. Mr. Maddox caught Gwen and Jack O'Keefe kissing behind the stable door, and announced flatly that she was to accompany her brother to Vespugia. No amount of tears, of hysterics from Gwen, of pleading from Mrs. Maddox, could change his stand.

Gwen and Zillah wept together. "It's not fair," Gwen sobbed. "A woman has no say in her own life. I hate men!"

Matthew tried to intercede with Dr. Llawcae for Zillah, but the doctor was adamant that she should wait at least until she was eighteen, and until Bran had suitable living arrangements.

Store and house were empty after they left. Matthew spent the morning working on accounts, and in the afternoon and evenings he stayed in his corner of the empty parlor, writing. His first novel was published and well received and he was hard at work on his second. It was this, and conversations with Zillah, who came frequently to Merioneth from Madrun, which kept him going.

"Bran's all right," he assured Zillah. "He sends love."

"They can't even have reached Vespugia yet," Zillah protested. "And there's certainly been no chance for him to send a letter."

"You know Bran and I don't need letters."

She sighed. "I know. Will Bran and I ever be like that?"

"Yours will be a different kind of unity. Better, maybe, but different."

"Will he send for me?"

"You must give him time, Zillah—time once again. Time to settle into a new world and a new way of life. And time for your father to get used to the idea of having his only child go half the way across the world from him."

"How's Gwen?"

"Part sulking and feeling sorry for herself, and part enjoying all the sailors on the ship making cow's eyes at her and running to do her bidding. But she's not going to be happy in Vespugia. She's always hated hot weather, and she's never liked roughing it."

"No, she wasn't a tomboy, like me. She thought Father was terrible to let me run wild and play rough games with you and Bran. Will your father relent and let her come home?"

"Not while Jack's around. There's no second-guessing Papa, though, when he latches on to an unreasonable notion." He paused. "Remember the old Indian verses, Zillah?"

"About black hair and blue eyes?"

"Yes. They've been singing around in my head, and I can't get them out, especially one verse:

"Lords of spirit, Lords of breath,
Lords of fireflies, stars, and light,
Who will keep the world from death?
Who will stop the coming night?
Blue eyes, blue eyes, have the sight."

"It's beautiful," Zillah said, "but I don't really know what it means."

"It's not to be taken literally. The Indians believed that as long as there was one blue-eyed child in each generation, all would be well."

"But it wasn't, was it? They've been long gone from around here."

"I think it was a bigger all-rightness than just for their tribe. Anyhow, both you and Gwen have at least a drop of Indian blood, and you both have the blue eyes of the song."

"So, in a way," Zillah said dreamily, "we're the last of the People of the Wind. Unless—"

Matthew smiled at her. "I think you're meant to have a black-haired, blue-eyed baby."

"When?" Zillah demanded. "Bran's a world away from me. And I'll be old and white-haired and wrinkled before Papa realizes I'm grown up and lets me go." She looked at him anxiously.

Matthew's work began to receive more and more critical acclaim, and Mr. Maddox began thinking of it as something 'real,' rather than fanciful scribbling not to be taken seriously. One of the unused downstairs rooms was fixed up as a study, and Dr. Llawcae designed a larger and more efficient lap desk.

The study was at the back of the house and looked across the lawn to the woods, and in the autumn Matthew feasted on the glory of the foilage. The room was sparsely furnished, at his request, with a black leather couch on which he could rest when sitting became too painful. As the cold weather set in, he began more and more often to spend the nights there. In front of the fireplace was a butler's table and a comfortable lady chair upholstered in blue, the color of Zillah's eyes: Zillah's chair, he thought of it.

It was midsummer before letters began to arrive on a regular basis. True to his promise, Bran sent Matthew vivid descriptions:

How amazingly interconnected everything is, at least to us who have Welsh blood in our veins. My closest friends here are Richard Llawcae, his wife, and his son Rich. They must be at least distant kin to all of us, for Llawcae is not a common name, even in Wales. Richard says they have forebears who emigrated to the New World in the very early days, and then went back to Wales, for nothing there was as bad as the witch-hunting in the Pilgrim villages and towns. One of their ancestors was burned, they think, or nearly so. They don't know exactly where they came from, but probably around Salem.

Rich has eyes for no one but Gwen, and I wish she would see and return his love, for I can think of no one I'd rather have as a brother-in-law. But Gwen sees Gedder before Rich. Gedder is taller and bigger and stronger—perhaps—and certainly more flamboyant. He worries me. Zillie has told me of his fierce ambitions, and his manner toward all of us becomes a little more lordly every day. God knows he is helpful—if it weren't for the Indians, I'm not sure the colony would have survived, for everything is different from at home—times for planting, what to plant, how to irrigate, etc. We are grateful indeed that the Indians not only have been friendly but have given us all the help they could. Yet I could wish Gedder had been more like his brethren and not so pushy and bossy. None of us likes the way Gedder treats his sister, as though she were his slave and inferior.

It is astounding how Zillie has the same features as Gwen and Zillah, the wide-apart eyes with the faintest suggestion of a tilt—though hers are a warm brown, and not blue—and the high cheekbones and delicate nose. And, of course, the straight, shining black hair. People have remarked on the likeness between Gwen and Zillie. I haven't talked with anyone except the Llawcaes about the Madoc legend following us to Vespugia, and they don't laugh it away. Truly, truth is stranger than fiction. Put it into a story for me, Matt.

—I will, Matthew promised silently.—I will. But you must tell me more.

My house is nearly finished, large and airy, with verandas. Everyone knows that it is being built for my bride, and for our children. Zillie often comes and stands, just out of the way, and looks, and that makes me uncomfortable. I don't think she comes of her own volition. I think Gedder sends her. I talk much about my Zillah, and how I long for the day when she will arrive. Matthew, twin, use your influence on Dr. Llawcae to let her come soon. Why is he keeping her with him? I need her, now.

As winter closed in and Matthew could not go out of doors, Zillah began to come from Madrun to Merioneth nearly every day at teatime, and Matthew missed her more than he liked to admit when she did not appear. He was hurrying to finish his second novel, considerably more ambitious than the first, but he tired quickly, and lay on the black couch, reaching out to Bran and Vespugia, all through the winter, the summer, and into a second winter. He felt closer to his twin than ever, and when he neared the shallows of sleep he felt that he actually was in arid Vespugia, part of all that was happening in the tight-knit colony.

In the mornings, when he worked with his soft, dark pencil and large note pad, it was as though he were setting down what he had seen and heard the night before.

"You're pale, Matt," Zillah said one afternoon as she sat in the lady chair and poured his tea.

"It's this bitter cold. Even with the fire going constantly, the damp seeps into my bones."

He turned away from her concern and looked out the window at the night drawing in. "I have to get my book finished, and there's not much time. I have a large canvas, going all the way back to the Welsh brothers who fought over Owain of Gwynedd's throne. Madoc and his brother, Gwydyr, left Wales, and came to a place which I figure to have been somewhere near here, when the valley was still a lake left from the melting of the ice. And once again brothers fought. Gwydyr wanted power, wanted adulation. Over and over again we get caught in fratricide, as Bran was in that ghastly war. We're still bleeding from the wounds. It's a primordial pattern, left us from Cain and Abel, a net we can't seem to break out of. And unless it is checked it will destroy us entirely."

She clasped her hands. "Will it be checked?"

He turned back toward her. "I don't know, Zillah. When I sleep I have dreams, and I see dark and evil things, children being killed by hundreds and thousands in terrible wars which sweep over them." He reached for her hand. "I do not croak doom casually, f'annwyl. I do not know what is going to happen. And irrationally, perhaps, I am positive that what happens in Vespugia is going to make a difference. Read me the letter from Bran that came today once more, please."

She took the letter from the tea table and held it to the lamp.

Dear my twin, and dear my Zillah, when are you coming? Matthew, if you cannot bring Zillah to me, then Zillah must bring you. She writes that the winter is hard on you, and she is worried. There would be much to hold your attention here. Llewellyn Pugh languishes for love of Zillie, and I think she would turn to him did Gedder not keep forcing her on me, no matter how loudly I say that I am betrothed, and that my Zillah is coming to join us any day now. Do not make me a liar!

We have had our first death, and a sad one it was, too. The children are forbidden to climb up onto the cliff which protects the colony from the winds, but somehow or other, one of them managed the steep climb, and fell. We all grieve. It may be a good thing that there is so much work for everybody that there is little idle time, and this helps us all, particularly the parents of the little one. Rich has been a tower of strength. He was the one of us who was able to bring tears from the mother, partly because he was not ashamed to weep himself.

"He is a good man, that Rich," Matthew said. "He'd do anything in the world for Gwen."

"You talk as though you know him."

Matthew smiled at her. "I do. I know him through Bran. And through my novel. What happens with Rich, with Bran, with Gwen, with Zillie—it matters to my story. It could even change it." She looked at him questioningly. "This book is pushing me, Zillah, making me write it. It excites me, and it drives me. In its pages, myth and matter merge. What happens in one time can make a difference in what happens in another time, far more than we realize. What Gedder does is going to make a difference, to the book, perhaps to the world. Nothing, no one, is too small to matter. What *you* do is going to make a difference."

In the early winter Matthew caught a heavy chest cold, which weakened him, and Dr. Llawcae came daily. Matthew spent the days on the black leather couch, wrapped in blankets. He continued to work on his novel and sold several more stories. He kept his earnings, which were considerable, in a small safe in his study. And now he left the study not at all.

When he was too exhausted to write, he slid into a shallow sleep, filled with vivid dreams in which Bran and the Vespugian colony were more real than chilly Merioneth.

He was at the flat rock in his dream, the rock where he used to meet Zillah when he sought privacy. But instead of Zillah there was a boy, perhaps twelve years old, dressed in strange, shabby clothes. The boy was lying on the rock, and he, too, was dreaming, and his dream and Matthew's merged.

Gedder is after Gwen. Stop him. The baby must come from Madoc.

Gwydyr's line is tainted. There is nothing left but pride and greed for power and revenge. Stop him, Matthew.

He saw his twin, but this was not Bran in Vespugia . . . Was it Bran? It was a young man, about their age, standing by a lake. Behind him stood another, a little older, who looked like Bran and yet not like Bran, for there was resentment behind the eyes. Like Gedder. The two began to wrestle, to engage in mortal combat.

At the edge of the lake a huge pile of flowers smoldered, with little red tongues of flame licking the petals of the roses—

"Matthew!"

He opened his eyes and his mother was hovering over him with a cup of camomile tea.

Beside the growing pages of the manuscript lay a genealogy which he had carefully worked out, a genealogy which could go in two different directions, like a double helix. In one direction there was hope; in the other, disaster. And the book and Bran and the Vespugian colony were intertwined in his mind and heart.

The winter was bitter cold.

"As the days begin to lengthen, the cold begins to strengthen," Matthew said to Dr. Llawcae, who listened gravely to Matthew's heart and his chest.

He leaned back and looked at the young man. "Matthew, you are encouraging Zillah."

Matthew smiled. "I've always encouraged Zillah, from the days when we were all children and she wanted to climb trees as high as Bran and I did."

"That's not what I mean. You're encouraging her in this wild-goose chase to go to Vespugia and join Bran."

"When Bran asked you for Zillah's hand, you gave him your blessing," Matthew reminded the doctor.

"That was with the understanding that Bran would stay here and become his father's partner."

"Once a blessing is given, Dr. Llawcae, it cannot be withdrawn." Matthew urged, "Zillah's heart is in Vespugia with Bran. I understand how she has taken her mother's place in your house and at your table. But she is your daughter, Dr. Llawcae, and not your wife, and you must not keep her tied to you."

The doctor's face flushed darkly with anger. "How dare you!"

"Because I love Zillah with all my heart, and I always have. I will miss her as much as you. Without Zillah, without Bran, I would be bereft of all that makes life worthwhile. But I will not hold them back out of selfishness."

The doctor's face grew darker. "You are accusing me of selfishness?"

"Inadvertent, perhaps, but selfishness, nonetheless."

"You—you—if you weren't a cripple, I'd—" Dr. Llawcae dropped his raised hand, turned, and left the room.

One afternoon in March, with occasional splatters of rain coming down the chimney and hissing out in the fire, Matthew looked intensely at Zillah, presiding over the tea tray. "Zillah. It's time. You must go to Vespugia."

"You know I want to." She reached out to hold his thin fingers. "Father says maybe next year."

"Next year's too late. Bran needs you now. What are you going to do about your father? Next year will always be next year. He'll not let you go."

She stared into the fire. "I'd rather go with Father's blessing, but I'm afraid you're right, and he's not going to give it. The problem is money, and finding a ship, and booking passage—all the things that are difficult, if not impossible, for a girl."

"You must go, this spring as soon as the ice breaks and ships can sail."

"Why, Matt, such urgency, all of a sudden?"

"Bran reached out to me last night—"

"Is something wrong?"

"Not with Bran. But Gedder—Rich—" He was seized with a fit of coughing, and when he leaned back he was too weak to talk.

Zillah continued to come daily to sit in the lady chair by the fire, to preside over the tea tray, and warm him with her smile. For the next few weeks he did not mention her going to Vespugia. Then one day, when the bare outlines of the trees were softened with coming buds, he greeted her impatiently.

He could hardly wait for her to sit down behind the tea tray. "Zillah, open the safe." Carefully, he gave her the combination, watching her fingers twirl the dial as she listened. "All right. Good. Bring out that big manila envelope. It's for you."

She looked at him in surprise. "For me?"

"I've been busy these last weeks."

"Father says you're pushing yourself too hard. Is the book done?"

"To all intents and purposes. There's some deepening to do, and a certain amount of revision. But I've been busy in other ways. Open the envelope."

She did so. "Money, and—what's this, Matt?"

"A ticket. There's a ship sailing for South America in four days. You must be on it."

"But, Matthew, I can't let you—"

"I've earned the money by my writing. It's mine to do with what I will. Zillah, Bran needs you. You must go. You will swing the balance."

"What balance?"

"The line must be Madoc's and not Gwydyr's—"

"I don't understand. You're flushed. Are you—"

"I'm not feverish. It's part of the book . . . You do love Bran?"

"With all my heart."

"Enough to leave Madrun without your father's blessing, and secretly?"

She held the manila envelope to her breast.

"You'll go?"

"I'll go?" She took his cold hand and held it to her cheek.

"All will be well," he promised. "When thou passest through the waters, I will be with thee; and through the rivers, they shall not overflow thee: when thou walkest through the fire, thou shalt not be burned; neither shall the flame kindle upon thee. For the fire is roses, roses . . ."

He did not see her again. Neither could bear the pain of parting.

Dr. Llawcae came storming over to Merioneth. Matthew could hear him shouting, "Where did she get the money? How did she get the passage?"

Matthew smiled, fleetingly grateful that Dr. Llawcae considered him such a cripple that he could not possibly have made the necessary arrangements.

When the doctor came into the study to check Matthew's heart, his temper had cooled enough so that he was no longer shouting. "I suppose you're pleased about this?"

"Zillah and Bran love each other," Matthew replied quietly. "It is right that they be together. And you have always been so interested in your Welsh heritage, and in this colony, that you will end up feeling differently. You can visit them—"

"Easy enough to say. What about my practice?"

"You haven't taken a vacation in years. You've earned a few weeks away."

Dr. Llawcae gave him only a cursory examination, saying, "You'll feel better when warmer weather comes."

* * *

Summer was slow in coming.

Matthew sent the book off to his publisher. The pain in his back was worse each day, and his heart skipped and galloped out of control. In his dreams he was with Bran, waiting for Zillah. He was with Gwen, still resentful, but beginning to laugh again with Rich, to respond to his steadfast love, his outgoing ways. At the same time she was still intrigued by Gedder, by his fierce dark looks and the hiddenness behind his eyes, so unlike Rich's candid ones. She knew that Rich loved her, but Gedder's strangeness fascinated her.

She's playing with Rich and Gedder and it will make trouble, the boy on the rock told Matthew as he slipped deeper into the dream.

Gedder and Bran. Standing on the cliff and looking down at the houses of the settlement. Gedder urging Bran to marry Zillie, to give Gwen in marriage to him, in order to secure the future.

"What future?" Bran asked.

Gedder looked appraisingly down at the prospering colony. "Ours."

And Zillie came and looked adoringly at Bran, Zillie so like and so unlike Zillah.

Wait, twin! Wait for Zillah! Do not trust Gedder—

Matthew was jolted out of the dream as his supper tray was brought. He ate a few bites, then pushed the tray away and slid back into the dream.

Felt the Vespugian heat, warming his chilled bones.

Bran, if only I could have come with Zillah.

Gedder again. Gedder in his favorite place up on the cliff's lip, looking down on the colony, the colony he wants for his own.

Someone's with him. Not Bran. Rich.

Quarreling. Quarreling over Gwen, over the colony. Quarreling at the cliff's edge.

Danger.

Matthew stirred restlessly on the couch, his eyes tightly closed. The boy was there, the child from another time, urging him. "Matthew, you must help Rich. Please . . ."

Once upon a time and long ago, men did not quarrel in this way, when the morning stars sang together and the children of men shouted for joy

But dissonance came

Madoc and Gwydyr fought

Gedder and Rich

Rich, watch out! Gedder has a knife—

Rich sees, sees in time, grasps the knife hand, twists it, so that the knife drops. Gedder reaches after it, snarling with anger, reaching for the knife so that he loses his balance and falls—falls after the knife, over the edge of the cliff, falls, falls . . .

Zillie screams and cannot stop screaming.

Matthew waited for the next letter from Bran, but it did not come until the lilac bushes were in full bloom.

My very dear twin,

Zillah is here, at last she is here, but my dearest heart has arrived to a community in confusion and desolation. Gwen weeps and will not stop. Zillie's tears no longer flow, but her eyes hold anguish. Gedder is dead, and—inadvertently—by Rich's hand. Gedder provoked a quarrel, and drew a knife. Rich took the knife from him, and Gedder, lunging after it, lost his balance and fell from the cliff to his death. It was an accident; nobody blames Rich, even Zillie. But Rich feels he cannot stay here with us, not with blood on his hands.

Will it ever cease, the turning of brother against brother? Gedder wanted power, and I cannot grieve for his death, only for his life, with its inordinate lust and pride. Why does Gwen weep? I do not think she knows. 'I am homesick,' she cries, 'I want to go home.' So Rich will take her home. And what will happen then, who knows?

Gwydyr fought Madoc and lost and the battle continued through to Gedder, brother against brother.

And the ship which brought Zillah carried Gwen and Rich to the Northern continent, to lilies of the valley and lilacs in the dooryard, to Merioneth and the store, and Papa will at last have his partner, and the store will be Maddox and Llawcae.

Oh, Zillah, my Zillah

> Lords of melody and song,
> Lords of roses burning bright,
> Blue will right the ancient wrong,
> Though the way is dark and long,
> Blue will shine with loving light.

A coughing fit jerked Matthew awake, away from Vespugia, from Bran and Zillah.

"Gwen—" he gasped, "Rich—Can't wait—sorry—"

Then the coughing took him, and when the racking had passed, there was nothing but agony. His back was an explosion of pain and the room began to get dark, and a rank stink like spoiling flowers choked him. There was no longer any light or warmth in the crackling flames . . .

"Matthew!" Meg opened her eyes, and she was calling the name aloud. The kitten, disturbed, jumped down from the bed. Ananda did not move.

—What happened? What happened to Matthew? to Charles Wallace? Is Charles Wallace all right?

—Strange, she thought,—the kythe with Matthew was clearer than any since Harcels. Maybe because Matthew and Bran were kythers.

She reached out to Charles Wallace, and felt only absence. Nor did she sense Gaudior. Always, when Charles Wallace was brought out of Within, she could see him, could see the unicorn.

"I'm going downstairs," she said aloud, and pushed her feet into her slippers.

Ananda followed her downstairs, stepping on the seventh step so that it let out a loud groan, and the dog yelped in surprise. Behind them the kitten padded softly, so light that the seventh step made the merest sigh.

The kitchen fire was blazing, the kettle humming. Everything looked warm and comfortable and normal, except for Mrs. O'Keefe in the rocking chair. The kitten padded across to her and jumped up on her lap, purring, and flexing its sharp little claws.

Meg asked, "Charles Wallace isn't back yet?"

"Not yet. Are you all right, Meg?" her mother asked.

"I'm fine."

"You look pale."

"Maybe I'll take Sandy and Dennys up on their offer of bouillon, if it's still good."

"Sure, Sis," Sandy said. "I'll make it. Chicken or beef?"

"Half a spoon of each, please, and a slosh of lemon juice." She looked at the twins with fresh comprehension. Was she closer to Charles Wallace than to the twins because they were twins, sufficient unto themselves? She glanced at the phone, then at her mother-in-law. "Mom— Beezie, do you remember Zillah?"

Mrs. O'Keefe looked at Meg, nodded her head, shook it, closed her eyes.

"Mom, Zillah really did get to Vespugia, didn't she?" Meg looked at the old woman, needing reassurance.

Mrs. O'Keefe huddled her arms about herself and rocked. "I forget. I forget."

Mrs. Murry looked anxiously at her daughter. "Meg, what is this?"

"It makes all the difference who Branzillo's forebears were."

Sandy handed Meg a steaming cup. "Sis, the past has happened. Knowing who Branzillo's ancestors were can't change anything."

"There was a time when it hadn't happened yet," Meg tried to explain, realizing how strange she sounded. "It's the Might-Have-Been Charles Wallace was to change, and I think he's changed it. It's the charge Mom O'Keefe laid on him when she gave him the rune."

"Stop talking!" Mrs. O'Keefe pushed herself up out of the rocking chair. "Take me to Chuck. Quickly. Before it's too late."

12 Between Myself and the Powers of Darkness

They ran, pelting across the frozen ground, which crunched under their feet, Meg and the twins and Mrs. O'Keefe. They ran across the rimed lawn and through the aisles of the twins' Christmas trees to the stone wall.

Meg held her hand out to Mrs. O'Keefe and helped her over the low wall. Then, still holding her mother-in-law's hand, pulling her along, she ran down the path, past the two large glacial rocks, to the star-watching rock.

Charles Wallace was lying there, eyes closed, white as death.

"Beezie!" Meg cried. "The rune! Quickly!"

Mrs. O'Keefe was panting, her hand pressed to her side. "With me . . ." She gasped. "Grandma . . ."

Dennys knelt on the rock, bending over Charles Wallace, feeling for his pulse.

"With Chuck in this fateful hour," Mrs. O'Keefe gasped, and Meg joined in, her voice clear and strong:

> *"I place all Heaven with its power*
> *And the sun with its brightness,*
> *And the snow with its whiteness,*
> *And the fire with all the strength it hath,*
> *And the lightning with its rapid wrath,*
> *And the winds with their swiftness along their path,*
> *And the sea with its deepness,*
> *And the rocks with their steepness,*
> *And the earth with its starkness,*
> *All these I place*

By God's almighty help and grace
Between myself and the powers of darkness!"

Light returned slowly. There had been pain, and darkness, and all at once the pain was relieved, and light touched his lids. He opened them, to the sharpness of starlight. He was lying on the star-watching rock, with Gaudior anxiously bending over him, tickling his cheek with the curly silver beard.

"Gaudior, what happened?"

"We barely got you out in time."

"Did Matthew—"

"He died. We didn't expect it quite so soon. The Echthroi—"

"I guess we got to 1865 after all." Charles Wallace looked up at the stars.

"Stand up." Gaudior sounded cross. "I don't like to see you lying there. I thought you were never going to open your eyes."

Charles Wallace scrambled to his feet, lifted one leg, then the other. "How strange to be able to use my legs again—how wonderful."

Gaudior knelt beside him. "Climb."

Charles Wallace, legs shaky as though from long disuse, clambered onto the great back.

He rode a Gaudior who had become as tiny as a dragonfly, rode among the fireflies, joining their brilliant dance, twinkling, blinking, shooting over the star-watching rock, over the valley, singing their song, and he was singing, too, and he was himself, and yet he was all he had learned, he carried within himself Brandon and Chuck and their song and the song was glory . . .

And he rode a Gaudior who had become as large as a constellation, rode among the galaxies, and he was himself, and he was also Madoc, and he was Matthew, Matthew flying through showers of stars, caught up in the joy of the music of the spheres . . .

part of the harmony, part of the joy

The silver neigh of the unicorn sounded all about the star-watching rock, rippling over Meg and the twins, Mrs. O'Keefe and Charles, and the night was illumined by the flash of the horn, blinding them with oblivion as it pointed at each of them in turn.

Meg thought she heard Charles Wallace call, "Gaudior, goodbye— oh, Gaudior, goodbye . . ."

Who was Gaudior?

She knew once who Gaudior was.

Again she heard his silver knell ringing in farewell.

Sandy asked, "Hey, did you see lightning?"

Dennys looked bewildered. "It's too cold. And look at all the stars."

"What was that flash, then?"

"Beats me. Like everything else tonight. Charles, what was with you? I couldn't find a pulse and then suddenly it throbbed under my fingers."

Slowly, color was returning to the boy's cheeks. "You came just in time." He looked at Mrs. O'Keefe, who still had her hand to her side and was breathing with painful gasps. "Beezie. Thank you." There was infinite sadness in his voice.

"That's what Meg called her," Sandy said. "What is all this?"

"Mom O'Keefe laid a charge on me . . ."

Dennys said, "We told you it was nuts for you to think you could stop Branzillo single-handed. Did you fall asleep or something? You could have got frostbite." He sounded concerned and uncertain.

"Come on in, now," Sandy added, "and no more of this nonsense."

"After the President's call, you call it nonsense?" Meg demanded fiercely.

"Meg, you shouldn't be out in the cold," Dennys objected.

"I'm all right."

Charles Wallace took Mrs. O'Keefe's hands in his. "Thank you."

"Chuck's no idiot." Mrs. O'Keefe thumped Charles Wallace on the shoulder.

"Come on," Sandy urged. "Let's get moving."

Dennys held Mrs. O'Keefe's arm. "We'll help you."

They returned to the house, Sandy and Dennys supporting Mrs. O'Keefe; Meg holding Charles Wallace's hand as though they were both small children once more.

Ananda greeted them ecstatically.

Mrs. Murry hurried to her youngest son, but refrained from touching him. "She's really adopted us, hasn't she? You'd think she'd been with us forever."

"Watch out for that tail." Mr. Murry moved between the dog and the model of the tesseract. "A couple of indiscriminate wags and you could undo years of work." He turned to his daughter. "Meg, you shouldn't have gone out in this weather with your cold."

"It's all right, Father. My cold's better and I didn't get chilled. Did the President—"

"No. Nothing yet."

Meg tried to think. What did she remember? The President's call, of course. Mrs. O'Keefe's rune, and the response of the weather. The coming of Ananda. Kything with Charles Wallace in the attic, kything through aeons of time, kything which had faded to dreams because the unicorn—

A unicorn. That was absurd.

There was Mrs. O'Keefe's phone call in the middle of the night. Sandy went for her and brought her back to the house, and she had an old letter—who was it from? What did it say?

"Well, Charles." Mr. Murry regarded his son gravely. "How about the charge?"

Charles Wallace did not reply immediately. He was studying the model of the tesseract, and he touched one of the Lucite rods carefully, so that the entire model began to vibrate, to hum softly, throwing off sparkles of brilliance. "We still don't know much about time, do we? I think—" He looked bewildered. "Father, I think it's going to be all right. But not because I was intelligent, or brave, or in control. Meg was right, earlier this evening, when she talked about everything, everywhere, interreacting."

"You were gone longer than we expected."

"I was gone a long time. An incredibly long time."

"But what did you do?" Sandy asked.

"And where did you go?" Dennys added.

"Mostly I stayed right by the star-watching rock—"

"Father!" Meg exclaimed. "The letter Mom O'Keefe brought. Charles hasn't seen it."

Mrs. O'Keefe held out the yellowed paper to Mr. Murry.

"Please read it to me, Father." Charles Wallace looked pale and exhausted.

"My dear Gwen and Rich," Mr. Murry read,

Thank you for writing us so promptly of Papa's death. Zillah and I are grateful that he died peacefully in his sleep, with none of the suffering he feared. I know that you both, and little Zillah, are a consolation for Mama. And Papa had the satisfaction of having Rich for his partner, and of knowing that the name of Maddox and Llawcae will not be lost, for our young Rich talks with great enthusiasm about going to Merioneth when he is old enough.

Our little Matthew is a rapidly growing boy. I had hoped that as he grew out of babyhood he would be called Matthew, but he keeps the nickname given him by the Indian children, Branzillo, a combination of my name and Zillah's. Little Rich tries to keep up with his big brother in every way . . .

Mr. Murry looked up. "The letter breaks off there. Strange—it seems diff—is that what I read before?"

Mrs. Murry frowned slightly. "I'm not sure. It didn't sound quite— but we're all exhausted with strain and lack of sleep. Memory plays queer tricks at times like this."

"It has to be what Father read before," Sandy said flatly. "It offends my reasonable mind, but it really does seem possible that Branzillo's forebears came from around here."

"The letter did come from Mrs. O'Keefe's attic," Dennys said. "So it's even likely that he's distantly descended from her forebears, and that would make them umpteenth cousins."

Sandy protested, "But what effect could that have on his starting a nuclear war? Or—we hope—on not starting one?"

Charles Wallace turned away from the argument, looked once more at the tesseract, then went to Mrs. O'Keefe, who was once again huddled in the rocking chair in front of the fire. Meg left the twins and followed Charles Wallace.

"Beezie," he asked softly, "what happened to Chuck?"

—Beezie, Chuck. They were in the vanishing kythe. Meg stepped closer to the rocker to hear Mrs. O'Keefe's reply.

"He died," she said bleakly.

"How?"

"They took him away and put him in an institution. He died there, six months later."

Charles Wallace expelled a long, sad breath. "Oh, Beezie, Beezie. And the baby?"

"Took after Duthbert Mortmain. Died in the State Penitentiary. Embezzlement. Let it be. What's done's done. What's gone's gone."

Ananda pressed against Meg, and she stroked the raised head. Beezie. Chuck. Paddy O'Keefe. The kythe flickered briefly in Meg's mind. Beezie must have married Paddy for more or less the same reasons that her mother had married Duthbert Mortmain. And she learned not to feel, not to love, not even her children, not even Calvin. Not to be hurt. But she gave Charles Wallace the rune, and told him to use it to stop Mad Dog Branzillo. So there must be a little of the Old Music left in her.

"Matthew's book," Charles Wallace said. "It's happening, all that he wrote."

The phone rang.

Mrs. Murry looked toward her husband, but did not speak.

They waited tensely.

"Yes, Mr. President?" Mr. Murry listened, and as he listened, he smiled. "El Zarco is setting up a Congress for the working out of peace plans and the equitable distribution and preservation of the earth's resources. What's that, Mr. President? He wants me to come as an advisor on the use of space for peace? Well, yes, of course, for a few weeks ... This is splendid news. Thank you for calling." He put down the receiver and turned to his family.

"El Zarco—" Meg whispered.

"Madog Branzillo's favorite nickname, you know that," her father said. "The Blue-eyed."

"But his threats—"

Her father looked at her in surprise. "Threats?"

"Of war—"

Everybody except Charles Wallace and Mrs. O'Keefe was looking at her.

"The phone call before dinner—" she said. "Wasn't the President afraid of war?"

"El Zarco has put down the militant members of his cabinet. He's always been known as a man of peace."

Charles Wallace spoke softly, so only Meg could hear. "They haven't traveled with a unicorn, Meg. There was no El Rabioso for them. When Matthew sent Zillah to marry Bran, and when Gedder was killed, that was the Might-Have-Been. El Rabioso was never born. It's always been El Zarco." He held her hand so tightly that it hurt.

Mrs. O'Keefe looked at Meg, nodding. "Baby will be born."

"Oh, Mom," Meg cried. "Will you be glad to be a grandmother?"

"Too late," the old woman said. "Take me home. Chuck and Grandma are waiting for me."

"What's that?" Mr. Murry asked.

"Chuck and Grandma—never mind. Just take me home."

"I'll drive you," Mr. Murry said.

Meg kissed her mother-in-law good night. It was the first time she had ever kissed her. "See you, Mom. See you soon."

When the car drove off, Dennys turned to his sister. "I'm not sure she'll make it to be a grandmother, Meg. I think her heart's running out."

"Why?"

"Badly swollen ankles. Blue tinge to her fingernails and lips. Shortness of breath."

"She ran all the way to the star-watching rock."

"She was short of breath before then. It's a wonder it didn't kill her. And what all that was about I'll never know."

"This whole evening's confusing," Sandy agreed. "I suggest we just forget it and go to bed. And Mrs. O'Keefe would never have made it back without Dennys and me, Meg. But you're right, Mother, she's quite an old girl."

"She is, indeed," Mrs. Murry agreed. "And I agree with you, Sandy, about getting to bed. Meg, you need your sleep."

The baby within Meg stirred. "You're more than right about Mom O'Keefe, Mother, more right than any of us could possibly have imagined. There's much much more to her than meets the eye. I hate the thought of losing her, just as we're discovering her."

Charles Wallace had once again been contemplating the intricate model of the tesseract. He spoke softly to his sister. "Meg, no matter what happens, even if Dennys is right about her heart, remember that it was herself she placed, for the baby's sake, and yours, and Calvin's, and all of us—"

Meg looked at him questioningly.

Charles Wallace's eyes as he returned her gaze were the blue of light as it glances off a unicorn's horn, pure and clear and infinitely deep. "In this fateful hour, it was herself she placed between us and the powers of darkness."

MANY WATERS

For Stephen Roxburgh

Contents

1 Virtual Particles and Virtual Unicorns

A sudden snow shower put an end to hockey practice.

"We can't even see the puck," Sandy Murry shouted across the wind. "Let's go home." He skated over to the side of the frozen pond, sitting on an already snow-covered rock to take off his skates.

There were calls of agreement from the other skaters. Dennys, Sandy's twin brother, followed him, snow gathering in his lashes, so that he had to blink in order to see the rock. "Why do we have to live in the highest, coldest, windiest spot in the state?"

Hoots of laughter and shouted goodbyes came from the other boys. "Where else would you want to live?" Dennys was asked.

Snow was sliding icily down the inside of his collar. "Baki. Fiji. Someplace warm."

One of the boys knotted his skate laces and slung his skates around his neck. "Would you really? With all those tourists?"

"Yeah, and jet-setters crowding the beach."

"And beautiful people."

"And litterbugs."

One by one the other boys drifted off, leaving the twins. "I thought you liked winter," Sandy said.

"By mid-March, I'm getting tired of it."

"But you wouldn't really want to go to some tourists' paradise, would you?"

"Oh, probably not. Maybe I would have, in the olden days, before the population explosion. I'm famished. Race you home."

By the time they reached their house, an old white farmhouse about a mile from the village, the snow was beginning to let up, though the wind was still strong. They went in through the garage, past their mother's lab. Pulling off their windbreakers, they threw them at hooks, and burst into the kitchen.

"Where's everybody?" Sandy called.

Dennys pointed to a piece of paper held by magnets to the refrigerator door. They both went up to it, to read:

DEAR TWINS, AM OFF TO TOWN WITH MEG AND CHARLES WAL-
LACE FOR OUR DENTAL CHECKUPS. YOUR TURN IS NEXT WEEK.
DON'T THINK YOU CAN GET OUT OF IT. YOU'VE BOTH GROWN
SO MUCH THIS YEAR THAT IT IS ESSENTIAL YOU HAVE YOUR
TEETH CHECKED.

LOVE, MOTHER

Sandy bared his teeth ferociously. "We've never had a cavity."

Dennys made a similar grimace. "But we *have* grown. We're just under six feet."

"Bet if we were measured today we'd be over."

Dennys opened the door to the refrigerator. There was half a chicken in an earthenware dish, with a sign:

VERBOTEN. THIS IS FOR DINNER.

Sandy pulled out the meat keeper. "Ham all right?"

"Sure. With cheese."

"And mustard."

"And sliced olives."

"And ketchup."

"And pickles."

"No tomatoes here. Bet you Meg made herself a BLT."

"There's lots of liverwurst. Mother likes that."

"Yuck."

"It's okay with cream cheese and onion."

They put their various ingredients on the kitchen counter and cut thick slices of bread fresh from the oven. Dennys peered in to sniff apples slowly baking. Sandy looked over to the kitchen table, where Meg had spread out her books and papers. "She's taken more than her fair share of the table."

"She's in college," Dennys defended. "We don't have as much homework as she does."

"Yeah, and I'd hate that long commute every day."

"She likes to drive. And at least she gets home early." Dennys plunked his own books down on the big table.

Sandy stood looking at one of Meg's open notebooks. "Hey, listen to this. Do you suppose we'll have this kind of junk when we're in college? *It seems quite evident that there was definite prebiotic existence of protein ancestors of polymers, and that therefore the primary beings were not a–amino acids.* I suppose she knows what she's writing about. I haven't the foggiest."

Dennys flipped back a page. "Look at her title. *The Million Doller question: the chicken or the egg, amino acids or their polymers.* She may be a mathematical genius, but she still can't spell."

"You mean, you know what she's writing about?" Sandy demanded.

"I have a pretty good idea. It's the kind of thing Mother and Dad argue about at dinner—polymers, virtual particles, quasars, all that stuff."

Sandy looked at his twin. "You mean, you *listen?*"

"Sure. Why not? You never know when a little useless knowledge is going to come in handy. Hey, what's this book? It's about bubonic plague. I'm the one who wants to be a doctor."

Sandy glanced over. "It's history, not medicine, stupe."

"Hey, why are lawyers never bitten by snakes?" Dennys asked.

"I don't know. And don't care."

"Well, you're the one who wants to be the lawyer. Come on. Why do lawyers never get bitten by snakes?"

"I give up. Why do lawyers never get bitten by snakes?"

"Professional courtesy."

Sandy groaned. "Very funny. Ha. Ha."

Dennys slathered mustard over a thick slice of ham. "When I think about the amount of schooling still ahead of us, I almost lose my appetite."

"Almost."

"Well, not quite."

Sandy opened the refrigerator door, looking for something else to pile on his sandwich. "We seem to eat more than the rest of the family put together. Charles Wallace eats like a bird. Well, judging by the amount we spend on bird feed, birds are terrible gluttons. But you know what I mean."

"At least he's settling down in school, and the other kids aren't picking on him the way they used to."

"He still doesn't look more than six, but half the time I think he knows more than we do. We're certainly the ordinary, run-of-the-mill ones in the family."

"The family can do with some ordinary, run-of-the-mill people. And we're not exactly dumb. If I'm going to be a doctor and you're going to be a lawyer, we've got to be bright enough for all that education. I'm thirsty."

Sandy opened the cupboard above the kitchen door. Only a year before, they had been too short to reach it without climbing on a stool. "Where's the Dutch cocoa? That's what I want." Sandy moved various boxes of lentils, barley, kidney beans, cans of tuna and salmon.

"Bet Mother's got it out in the lab. Let's go look." Dennys sliced more ham.

Sandy put a large dill pickle in his mouth. "Let's finish making the sandwiches first."

"Food first. Fine."

With sandwiches an inch or more thick in their hands, and full mouths, they went back out to the pantry and turned into the lab. In the early years of the century, when the house had been part of a working dairy farm, the lab had been used to keep milk, butter, eggs, and there was still a large churn in one corner, which now served to hold a lamp. The work counter with the stone sink functioned as well for holding lab equipment as it had for milk and eggs. There was now a formidable-looking microscope, some strange equipment only their mother understood, and an old-fashioned Bunsen burner, over which, on a homemade tripod, a black kettle was simmering.

Sandy sniffed appreciatively. "Stew."

"I think we're supposed to call it *boeuf bourguignon*." Dennys reached up to the shelf over the sink and pulled down a square red tin. "Here's the cocoa. Mother and Dad like it at bedtime."

"When's Dad coming home?" Dennys wanted to know.

"Tomorrow night, I think Mother said."

Sandy, his mouth full, held his hands out to the wood stove. "If we had our driver's licenses, we could go to the airport to meet him."

"We're good drivers already," Dennys agreed.

Sandy stuffed another large bite of sandwich into his mouth, and left the warmth of the stove to wander to the far corner of the lab, where there was a not-quite-ordinary-looking computer. "How long has Dad had this gizmo here?"

"He put it in last week. Mother wasn't particularly pleased."

"Well, it *is* supposed to be her lab," Sandy said.

"What's he programming?" Dennys asked.

"He's usually pretty good about explaining. Even though I don't understand most of it. Tessering and red-shifting and space/time continuum and stuff." Sandy stared at the keyboard, which had eight rather than the usual four ranks of keys. "Half of these symbols are Greek. I mean, literally Greek."

Dennys, ramming the last of his sandwich into his mouth, peered over his twin's shoulder. "Well, I more or less get the usual science signs. That looks like Hebrew, there, and that's Cyrillic. I haven't the faintest idea what these keys are for."

Sandy looked down at the lab floor, which consisted of large slabs of stone. There was a thick rug by the sink, and another in front of the shabby leather chair and reading lamp. "I don't know how Mother stands this place in winter."

"She dresses like an Eskimo." Dennys shivered, then put out one finger and tapped on the standard keys of the computer: "TAKE ME SOMEPLACE WARM."

"Hey, I don't think we ought to mess with that," Sandy warned.

"What do you expect? A genie to pop up, like the one in Aladdin and the magic lamp? This is just a computer, for heaven's sake. It can't do anything it isn't programmed to do."

"Okay, then." Sandy held his fingers over the keyboard. "A lot of people think computers are alive—I mean, really, sort of like Aladdin's genie." He tapped out on the standard keys: "SOMEPLACE WARM AND SPARSELY POPULATED."

Dennys shouldered him aside, adding: "LOW HUMIDITY."

Sandy turned away from the odd computer. "Let's make the cocoa."

"Sure." Dennys picked up the red tin, which he had set down on the counter. "Since Mother's using the Bunsen burner, we'd better go back to the kitchen to make the cocoa."

"Okay. It's warmer there, anyhow."

"I could do with another sandwich. If they've gone all the way into town, supper'll probably be late."

They left the lab, closing the door behind them. "Hey." Sandy pointed. "We didn't see this." There was a small note taped to the door: EXPERIMENT IN PROGRESS. PLEASE KEEP OUT.

"Uh-oh. Hope we didn't upset anything."

"We'd better tell Mother when she gets back."

"Why didn't we *see* that note?"

"We were busy stuffing our faces."

Dennys crossed the hall and opened the kitchen door and was met with a blast of heat. *"Hey!"* He tried to step back, but Sandy was on his heels.

"Fire!" Sandy yelled. "Get the fire extinguisher!"

"Too late! We'd better get out and—" Dennys heard the kitchen door slam behind them. "We've got to get out—"

Sandy yelled, "I can't find the fire extinguisher!"

"I can't find the walls—" Dennys groped through a pervasive mist, his hands touching nothing.

Came a great sonic boom.

Then absolute silence.

Slowly the mist began to clear away, to dissipate.

"Hey!" Sandy's changing voice cracked and soared. "What's going on?"

Dennys's equally cracking voice followed. "Where on earth . . . What's happened . . ."

"What was that explosion?"

"Hey!"

They looked around to see nothing familiar. No kitchen door. No kitchen. No fireplace with its fragrant logs. No table, with its pot of brightly blooming geraniums. No ceiling strung with rows of red peppers and white garlic. No floor with the colorful, braided rugs. They were standing on sand, burning white sand. Above them, the sun was in a sky so hot that it was no longer blue but had a bronze cast. There was nothing but sand and sky from horizon to horizon.

"Is the house all right?" Sandy's voice shook.

"I don't think we went into the house at all . . ."

"You don't think it was on fire?"

"No. I think we opened the door and we were here."

"What about the mist?"

"And the sonic boom?"

"And what about Dad's computer?"

"Uh-oh. What're we going to *do*?" Dennys's voice started out in the bass, soared, and cracked to a piercing treble.

"Don't panic," Sandy warned, but his voice trembled.

Both boys looked around wildly. The brazen sunlight beat down on them. After the cold of snow and ice, the sudden heat was shocking. Small particles of mica in the sand caught the light and blazed up at them. "Hey." Dennys's voice cracked again. "What're we going to *do*?"

Sandy tried to speak calmly. "We're the ones who do things, remember?"

"We just did something." Dennys was bitter. "We just blew ourselves here, wherever here is."

Sandy agreed. "Stupid. We were stupid, mucking around with an experiment-in-progress."

"Only we didn't know it was in progress."

"We should have stopped to think."

Dennys looked around at sky and sand, both shimmering with heat. "What do you suppose Dad was up to? If we knew that—"

"Space travel. Tessering. Getting past the speed of light. You know that." Anxiety made Dennys sharp.

The sun beat down on Sandy's head, so that he reached up and wiped sweat from around his eyes. "I wish we'd never thought of that Dutch cocoa."

Dennys pulled off his heavy cable-knit sweater. Licked his dry lips. Moaned. "Lemonade."

Sandy, too, stripped off his sweater. "We got what we asked for, didn't we? Heat. Low humidity. Sparse population."

Dennys looked around, squinting against the glare. "Sparse wasn't meant to mean *no*body."

Sandy unbuttoned his plaid flannel shirt. "I thought we asked for a beach."

"Not on Dad's gizmo we didn't. Just sparse population. Do you suppose we've blown ourselves onto a dead planet? One where the sun is going into its red-giant phase before it blows up?"

Despite the intense heat, Sandy shivered, glanced at the sun, then quickly away. "I think the sun in its red-giant phase would be bigger. This sun doesn't look any larger than our own sun in movies set in deserts."

"Do you suppose it is our own sun?" Dennys asked hopefully.

Sandy shrugged. "We could be anywhere. Anywhere in the universe. If we were going to play with that doggone keyboard, we should have been more specific. I wish we'd just settled for Baki or Fiji, beautiful people or no."

"I'd just as soon see a beautiful person. Right now. I wish we hadn't done whatever it is we've done." Dennys pulled off his cotton turtleneck, stripping down to his white briefs and tank top.

Sandy stood on one leg to start pulling off his warmly lined pants, glanced again at the fierce sun, then quickly closed his eyes. "They'll miss us when they get back from the dentist."

"But they won't know where to look. Mother has more sense than we have. She'd never mess around with anything of Dad's unless he was right there."

"Mother's not interested in astrophysics. She's into virtual particles and things like that."

"She'll still miss us."

"Dad'll be home tomorrow," Sandy said hopefully. He was now stripped to his underclothes.

Dennys picked up his things and made a tidy bundle. "Unless we find some shade, we're going to have to put our clothes back on in half an hour, or at least some of them, or we'll get a vicious sunburn."

"Shade." Sandy groaned, and scanned the horizon. "Den! Do I see a palm tree?"

Dennys held his hand to shade his eyes. "Where?"

"There. All the way over there."

"Yes. No. Yes."

"Let's head toward it."

"Good. At least it's something to *do*." Dennys trudged off. "If it's the same time of day it was when we left home——"

"It was winter at home." Sandy's eyes were almost closed against the glare. "The sun was already setting."

Dennys pointed to their shadows, as long and skinny as they were. "The sun's slightly behind us . . . We might be heading east, if it's our own kind of sun."

Sandy asked, "Are you scared? I am. We've really got ourselves into a mess."

Dennys made no reply. They trudged along. They had left on their shoes and socks, and Dennys suggested, "It might be easier walking barefooted."

Sandy bent down and touched the sand with the palm of his hand, then shook his head. "Feel it. It would burn our feet."

"Do you still see that palm tree?"

"I think so."

They moved across the sand in silence. After a few minutes it seemed firmer under their feet, and they saw that there was rock under the sand.

"That's better," Sandy said.

"Hey!"

The ground seemed to shudder under their feet. Dennys flailed his arms to try to keep his balance, but was flung to the ground. "Is this an earthquake or something?"

Sandy, too, was thrown down. Around them they could hear a noisy grating of rock, and a deep, thunderous roaring beneath them. Then there was silence, abrupt and complete. The rock steadied under them. The earthquake, or whatever it was, had lasted less than a minute, but it had been of sufficient force to push up a large section of rock, making a small cliff about six feet high. It was striated and raw-looking, but it provided a shadow that stretched across the sand.

Both boys climbed to their feet and headed into the welcome shade. Sandy touched the sheared-off rock, and it felt cool. "Maybe we could sit here for a minute . . ."

The sun was still fiercely hot, but the slab of rock they sat on was cool. The relief of the shade was so great that for a few minutes they sat in silence. Their bodies were slippery with sweat; it trickled into their eyes. They sat without moving, trying to take every advantage of the shade.

"I don't know what's going to happen next, but whatever it is, I'm not likely to be surprised," Sandy said at last. "Are you sure it was Dad's experiment we weren't supposed to interrupt? Couldn't it have been Mother's?"

"Mother's doing something with sub-atomic particles again," Dennys said. "Last night at dinner, she spent most of the time talking about virtual particles."

"It sounded crazy to me," Sandy said. "Particles which have a tendency to life."

"That's right." Dennys nodded. "Virtual particles. Almost-particles. What you said. Particles which tend to be."

Sandy shook his head. "Most of Mother's sub-atomic experiments are so, oh, so sort of infinitesimal, it hasn't mattered if we've come into the lab."

"But maybe if she's looking for a virtual particle—" Dennys sounded hopeful.

"No. It sounds to me more like something of Dad's. It was just sort of wishful thinking when I asked if it could be something of Mother's. Why didn't we see that notice on the door?"

"Yeah. Why?"

"*And* I wish our parents did ordinary things," Sandy complained. "If Dad was a plumber or an electrician, and if Mother was somebody's secretary, it would be a lot easier for us."

"And we wouldn't have to be such great athletes and good guys at school," Dennys agreed. "And—" He broke off as the earth started to tremble again. It was a brief tremor, with no heaving of stones, but both boys sprang to their feet.

"Hey!" Sandy jumped, almost knocking Dennys over.

From behind the rock cliff came a very small person, perhaps four feet tall. Not a child. He was firmly muscled, darkly tanned, and there was a down of hair across his upper lip and on his chin. He wore a loincloth, with a small pouch at the waist. As he saw them, he reached for the pouch in a swift, alarmed gesture.

"Hey, wait." Sandy held up his open hands, palm forward.

Dennys repeated the gesture. "We won't hurt you."

"Who are you?" Sandy asked.

"Where are we?" Dennys added.

The small man looked at them in mingled curiosity and fear. "Gi-

ants!" he cried. He had a man's voice, a young man's voice, deeper
than Sandy's or Dennys's.

Sandy shook his head. "We're not giants."

"We're boys," Dennys augmented. "Who are you?"

The young man touched himself lightly on the forehead. "Japheth."

"That's your name?" Sandy asked.

He touched his forehead again. "Japheth."

Perhaps this was the custom of the country, wherever in the universe
it was. Sandy touched his own forehead. "Alexander. Sandy."

Dennys made the same gesture. "Dennys."

"Giants," the young man stated.

"No," Sandy corrected. "Boys."

The young man rubbed his head where a purplish egg was forming.
"Stone hit me. Must be seeing double."

"Japheth?" Sandy asked.

The young man nodded. "Are you two? Or one?" He rubbed his
eyes perplexedly.

"Two," Sandy said. "We're twins. I'm Sandy. He's Dennys."

"Twins?" Japheth asked, his fingers once more reaching for the
pouch at his side, which appeared to be filled with tiny arrows, about
two inches long.

Dennys opened his hands wide. "Twins are when"—he had started
to give a scientific explanation, stopped himself—"when a mother has
a litter of two babies instead of one." His voice was soothing.

"You're animals, then?"

Sandy shook his head. "We're boys." He was ready to ask "What
are you?" when he noticed a tiny bow near the pouch of arrows.

"No. No." The young man looked at them doubtfully. "Only giants
are as tall as you. And the seraphim and nephilim. But you have no
wings."

What was this about wings? Dennys asked, "Please, J—Jay—where
are we? Where is this place?"

"The desert, about an hour from my oasis. I came out, dowsing for
water." He bent down and picked up a wand of pliable wood. "Gopher
wood is the best for dowsing, and I had my grandfather's—" He stopped
in midsentence. "Higgaion! Hig! Where are you?" he called, as the twins
might have called for their dog at home. "Hig!" He looked, wide-eyed,
at the twins. "If anything has happened to him, my grandfather will—
there are so few of them left—" He called again urgently, "Higgaion!"

From behind the outcropping of rock came something grey and
sinuous which the twins at first thought was a snake. But it was followed
by a head with small, bright, black eyes, and great fans of ears, and a

chunky body covered with shaggy grey hair, and a thin little rope of a tail.

"Higgaion!" The young man was joyful. "Why didn't you come when I called you?"

With its supple trunk, the little animal, the size of a small dog or a large cat, indicated the twins.

The young man patted its head. He was so small that he did not have to bend down. "Thank El you're all right." He gestured toward the twins. "They seem friendly. They say they aren't giants, and while they are as tall as seraphim or nephilim, they don't seem to be of their kind."

Cautiously, the little animal approached Sandy, who dropped to one knee, holding out his hand for the creature to sniff. Then, tentatively, he began to scratch the hairy chest, as he would have scratched their dog at home. When the little animal relaxed under his touch, he asked Japheth, "What's seraphim?"

"And nephilim," Dennys added. If they could find out what these people were who were as tall as they, it might give them some kind of a clue as to where they had landed.

"Oh, very tall," Japheth said. "Like you, but different. Great wings. Much long hair. And their bodies—like you, not hairy. The seraphim are golden and the nephilim are white, whiter than sand. Your skin—it is different. Pale, and smooth, and as though you never saw sun."

"At home, it's still winter," Sandy explained. "We get very tan in the summer when we work outdoors."

"Your little animal," Dennys questioned, "looks sort of like an elephant, but what is it?"

"It's a mammoth." Japheth slapped the creature affectionately.

Sandy withdrew his hand from petting Higgaion. "But mammoths are supposed to be huge!"

Dennys saw in his mind's eye a picture of a mammoth in a nature book at home, very like Japheth's animal. Japheth himself was a miniature version of a strong and handsome young man, not a great deal older than themselves, perhaps as old as their sister's friend Calvin, who was in graduate school. Perhaps in this place, wherever it was, everything was in miniature.

"There aren't many mammoths left," Japheth explained. "I'm a good dowser, but mammoths are very fine for scenting water, and Higgaion is the best of all." He patted the little animal's head. "So I borrowed him from Grandfather Lamech, and together we found a good source of water, but I'm afraid it's too far from the oasis to be much use."

"Thank you for explaining," Sandy said, then turned to Dennys. "Do you think we're dreaming?"

"No. We came home from hockey practice. We made sandwiches. We went into the lab to find the Dutch cocoa. We messed around with Dad's experiment-in-progress. We were stupid beyond belief. But it isn't a dream."

"I'm glad to hear you say that," Japheth said. "I was beginning to wonder, myself. I thought I might be dreaming, because of the stone hitting my head in the earthquake."

"It was an earthquake?" Sandy asked.

Japheth nodded. "They come quite often. The seraphim tell us that things aren't settled yet."

"So maybe this is a young planet." Dennys sounded hopeful.

Japheth asked, "Where have you come from, and where are you going?"

"Take me to your leader," Sandy murmured.

Dennys nudged him. "Shut up."

Sandy said, "We're from planet earth, late twentieth century. We got here by accident, and we don't know where we're going."

"We'd like to go home," Dennys added, "but we don't know how."

"Where is home?" Japheth asked.

Sandy sighed. "A long way away, I'm afraid."

Japheth looked at them. "You are flushed. And wet." He himself did not seem to feel the intense heat.

Dennys said, "We're perspiring. Profusely. I'm afraid we'll get sun-stroke if we don't find shade soon."

Japheth nodded. "Grandfather Lamech's tent is closest. My wife and I"—he flushed with pleasure as he said *my wife*—"live halfway across the oasis, by my father's tent. And I have to return Higgaion to Grandfather, anyhow. And he's very hospitable. I'll take you to him, if you like."

"Thank you," Sandy said.

"We'd like to come with you," Dennys added.

"At this point, we don't have much choice," Sandy murmured.

Dennys nudged him, then took his turtleneck from the bundle of clothes and pulled it back on, his head emerging from the rolled cotton neck, which had mussed up his light brown hair so that a tuft stuck out like a parakeet's. "We'd better cover ourselves. I think I'm sunburned already."

"Let's go, then," Japheth said. "I'd like to be home before dark."

"Hey—" Sandy said suddenly. "At least we speak the same lan-guage. Everything's been so wild and weird I hadn't realized it till—"

Japheth looked at him in a puzzled manner. "You sound very strange to me. But I *can* understand you, if I listen with my under-hearing. You talk a little like the seraphim and the nephilim. You can understand me?"

The twins looked at each other. Sandy said, "I hadn't really thought about it till now. If I think about it, you do sound, well, different, but I can understand you. Right, Den?"

"Right," Dennys agreed. "Except it was easier when we weren't thinking about it."

"Come on," Japheth urged. "Let's go." He looked at Sandy. "You'd better cover yourself, too."

Sandy followed Dennys's example and pulled on his turtleneck.

Dennys unrolled his flannel shirt and draped it over his head. "Sort of like a burnoose to keep us from getting sunstroke."

"Good idea." Sandy did the same.

"If," Dennys added morosely, "it isn't already too late." Then he said, "Hey, Japh—" stumbled over the name. "Hey, Jay, what's that?"

On the horizon to the far left, moving toward them, appeared a creature which shimmered in and out of their vision, silvery in color, as large as a goat or a pony, with light flickering out from its forehead.

Sandy also shortened Japheth's name. "What's that, Jay?" The mammoth pushed its head under Sandy's hand, and he began to scratch between the great fan-like ears.

Japheth looked toward the barely visible creature, smiling in recognition. "Oh, that's a unicorn. They're very odd. Sometimes they are, and sometimes they aren't. If we want one, we call and it'll usually appear."

"Did you call on one?" Sandy asked.

"Higgaion may have thought about one, but he didn't really call it. That's why it isn't all the way solid. Unicorns are even better about scenting for water than mammoths, except that you can't always count on them. But probably Higgaion thought one might be able to confirm where we thought there was a spring." He smiled ruefully. "Grandfather always knows what Hig is thinking, and I make guesses."

The twins stopped and looked at each other, but the mammoth had left Sandy and was trotting after Japheth, who was walking toward the oasis again, so they followed. In the intensity of the desert heat, their limbs felt heavy and uncooperative. When they looked to where the unicorn had been, it was no longer there, though there was left in its place a mirage-like shimmering.

Sandy panted. "I don't believe this."

Dennys, jogging beside him, agreed. "We've never had very willing suspensions of disbelief. We're the pragmatists of the family."

"I *still* don't believe it," Sandy said. "If I blink often enough, we'll be back in the kitchen at home."

Dennys took one of the flapping sleeves of his shirt and wiped his eyes. "What I believe right now is that I'm hot. Hot. Hot."

Japheth turned his head and looked back. "Giants! Come on. Stop talking."

With their long legs, it was easy enough for the twins to catch up with Japheth. "We're not giants," Dennys reiterated. "My name is Dennys."

"Dennysim."

Dennys touched his forehead, as Japheth had done. "One Dennys. Me."

Sandy, too, touched his forehead. "I'm Sandy."

"Sand." Japheth looked around. "We have plenty of Sand."

"No, Jay," Sandy corrected. "It's short for Alexander. Sandy."

Japheth shook his head. "You call me Jay. I call you Sand. Sand is something I understand."

"Talking of strange names"—Dennys looked at the mammoth, who was again butting at Sandy, to be petted—"Hig—"

"Hig-gai-on." Japheth sounded it out.

"Are all mammoths his size? Or are there some really big ones?"

Japheth looked puzzled. "Those that are left are like Higgaion."

Sandy looked at his brother. "Didn't horses start out very little, back in pre-history?"

But Dennys was looking at the horizon. "Look. Now you can see that there are lots of palm trees."

Although they could now see that there were many trees, the oasis was still far away. Despite their much longer legs, the boys began to lag behind Japheth and the mammoth, who were moving across the sand at an easy run.

"I'm not sure I can make it," Dennys said, grunting.

Sandy's steps, too, lagged. "I thought we were the great athletes," he said, panting.

"We've never been exposed to heat like this before."

Japheth, evidently realizing that they were no longer behind him, turned around and jogged back toward them, seemingly cool and unwinded. "What's the matter? You're both all red. The same red. You truly are two people?"

"We're twins." Sandy's voice was an exhausted croak.

Dennys panted. "I think—we're getting—heat—heat prostration."

Japheth looked at them anxiously. "Sun-sickness can be dangerous." He reached up and touched Dennys's cheek. Shook his head. "You're cold and clammy. Bad sign." He put his hand against his forehead. Appeared to be thinking deeply. Then: "What about a unicorn?"

"What about it?" Sandy asked. He felt tired and irritable.

"If we could get a couple of unicorns to become real and solid for us, they could carry you to the oasis."

The twins looked at each other, each seeing a red, sweating mirror version of himself. "We've never gone in for mythical beasts," Dennys said.

Sandy added, "Meg says unicorns have been ruined by over-popularity."

Japheth frowned. "I don't understand what you're saying."

Dennys, too, frowned. Thinking. Then: "Jay's unicorns sound more like Mother's virtual particles than like mythical beasts."

Sandy was exasperated. "Virtual particles aren't mythical. They're theoretical."

Dennys shot back, "If Mother can believe in her way-out theories, we ought to be able to believe in virtual unicorns."

"What kind of unicorns?" Japheth looked puzzled. "Is it because you're some strange kind of giant that there's all this confusion?"

"Unicorns have never been a matter of particular importance before." Sandy wiped his hands across his face and was surprised to find that the beads of sweat were indeed cold.

"They're important now." Dennys groaned. "Mother believes in virtual particles, so there's no reason there can't be virtual unicorns."

"Hig—" Japheth urged.

The mammoth turned and faced the horizon. A faint shimmering glimmered on the sand in front of him. Slowly it took the shape of a unicorn, transparent but recognizable. Beside it, another unicorn began to shimmer.

"Please, unicorns," Dennys begged. "Be real."

Slowly the transparency of both creatures began to solidify, until there were two unicorns standing on the sand, with silvery-grey flanks, silver manes and beards. Silver hooves, and horns of brilliant light. They looked at the twins and docilely folded their legs under to lie down.

"Oh!" Japheth exclaimed. "It's a good thing you're both so young. For the moment, I'd forgotten that unicorns will not let themselves be touched by anyone who is not a virgin."

The twins glanced at each other. "Well, we don't even have our driver's licenses yet," Dennys said.

"Get up on them before they decide they aren't needed," Japheth ordered.

The twins climbed each onto the back of one of the silver creatures, both feeling that this was a dream from which they could not wake up. But, without the unicorns, they would never make it to the oasis.

The unicorns flew across the desert, their hooves barely touching the surface. Occasionally, where the sand had been blown clear and there was rock, a silver hoof struck with a clang like a bell, and sparks flew upward. Small desert creatures watched them fly by. Sandy noticed, but did not mention, some scattered bones bleached by sun and wind.

"Hold on!" Japheth cried in warning. "Don't fall off!"

But there was a sense, in riding the unicorns, of unreality. If this was no stranger than their mother's world of particle physics, it was at least equally as strange.

"Hold on!" Japheth shouted again.

But Dennys felt himself sliding off the smooth flanks. He tried to grasp the mane, but it sifted through his fingers like sand. Was the unicorn becoming less real, or was the still-blazing sun affecting him?

"Dennys! Don't fall off!" Sandy shouted.

But Dennys felt himself slipping. He did not know whether it was himself or the unicorn who kept flickering in and out of being.

Then he felt something solid, Sandy on his unicorn pressing against him. Sandy's strong arms shoving him back onto the unicorn, the virtual particle suddenly real, not just something in the lab. His head hurt.

Japheth and the mammoth were running beside them, amazingly swift for such small creatures. "Hurry," Japheth urged the unicorns. "Hurry."

Sandy, his flannel shirt still draped over his head, was hardly aware that he was supporting his brother. His arms felt as fluid as water. He was breathing in great searing gulps which burned his throat. His head began to swell, to be filled with hot air like a balloon, so that he was afraid he was going to float off into the sky.

The mammoth passed Japheth and the unicorns, leading the way to the oasis, so that his stocky legs were no more than a blur of motion, like hummingbirds' wings. Occasionally he would raise his trunk and make a trumpeting noise, urging the unicorns along. Japheth ran alongside, beginning to breathe, open-mouthed, with effort.

But they were not fast enough for Dennys, who was slipping into unconsciousness, and as the world blackened before his eyes, his unicorn's horn became dim and the silver creature began to dissolve as Dennys lost sight and hearing and thought. And Dennys flickered in and out of being with his mount.

Sandy, barely holding on to consciousness, was not aware that the arm he had held Dennys with was now holding nothing. He felt himself drop to the ground. He did not land on searing sand but on soft green. His burning body was shaded and cooled by the great fans of a palm tree.

His unicorn had made it to the oasis.

2 Pelican in the Wilderness

Sandy slid slowly into consciousness, eyes tightly closed. No alarm clock jangling, so it must be Saturday. He listened to hear if Dennys was stirring in the upper bunk. Felt something cool and wet sprayed across his body. It felt good. He did not want to wake up. On Saturday they had heavy chores. They washed the floor of their mother's lab, of the bathrooms. If it was snowing again, there would be snow to shovel.

"Sand—"

He did not recognize the odd, slightly foreign voice. He did not recognize the smell that surrounded him, pungent and gamy. Again his body was sprayed with cool wetness.

"Sand?"

Slowly, he opened his eyes. In the light which came from directly above him, he saw two brown faces peering anxiously into his. One face was young, barely covered with deep amber down. The other face was crisscrossed with countless wrinkles, a face with ancient, leathered skin and a long beard of curling white.

Unwilling to believe that he was not waking from a dream, he reached up to touch Dennys's mattress above him. Nothing. He opened his eyes more widely.

He was in a tent, a sizable tent made of goatskins, judging by the smell. Light came in from the roof hole, a rosy, sunset light. A funny little animal crossed the tent to him and sprayed his body with water, and he realized that he was hot with sunburn. The animal was bringing water from a large clay pot and cooling him with it.

"Sand?" the young man asked again. "Are you awake?"

"Jay?" He struggled to sit up, and his burned skin was scratched by the skins on which he was lying.

"Sand, are you all right?" Japheth's voice trembled with anxiety.

"I'm okay. Just sunburned."

The old man put his hand against Sandy's forehead. "You have much fever. The sun-sickness is hard on those unaccustomed to the desert. Are you from beyond the mountains?"

Sandy looked at the ancient man, who was even smaller than Japheth but had the same brightly blue eyes, startling against the sun-darkened skin. Sandy touched his forehead as Japheth had done. "I'm Sandy."

"Sand. Yes. Japheth has told me." The old man touched his forehead, tipped with softly curling white hair. "Lamech. Grandfather Lamech. Japheth carried you to my tent."

Sandy looked around in alarm. "But Dennys—where's Dennys?" He was now fully awake, aware that he was not in the bunk bed at home but in this strange desert place which might be on any planet in any solar system in any galaxy anywhere in the universe. He shuddered. "Dennys?"

"He went out with the unicorn."

"What!"

"Sand," Japheth explained patiently, "Dennys must have fainted. I told you about unicorns. Sometimes they are, sometimes they aren't. When Den fainted, the unicorn went out, and took Den with him."

"But we've got to find him, bring him back!" Sandy tried to struggle to his feet.

Grandfather Lamech pushed him back down onto the skins with amazing strength for so small a person. "Hush, Sand. Do not worry. Your brother will be all right."

"But—"

"Unicorns are very responsible," Lamech explained.

"But—"

"It is true that they are unreliable in that we cannot rely on them to be, but they are very responsible."

"You're crazy," Sandy said.

"Hush, Sand," Grandfather Lamech repeated. "We do not know where the unicorns go when they go out, but when somebody calls the unicorn again and it appears, Den will appear, too."

"You're sure?"

"Yes. I am sure," the old man said, and for a moment Sandy relaxed at the authority in his voice.

Then: "Well, call a unicorn, call him now!"

The old man and Japheth looked at Higgaion. Higgaion raised his trunk toward the roof hole of the tent. The rosy glow had faded, and the old man and Japheth and Higgaion were barely visible shadows in the tent. There was a sudden flash, and Sandy could see the shimmering silver body of a unicorn. But no Dennys.

"Dennys!" he cried.

And heard Japheth echo, "Den!"

Higgaion appeared to be consulting with the unicorn. Then he looked toward Japheth and the old man. Trumpeted.

There was another flash of light, and then a faint glimmering and the unicorn was gone.

Grandfather Lamech said, "It would appear that someone has already called the unicorn on which the Den was riding."

Sandy jumped to his feet, but was so weak that he sank back onto the skins. "But he could be anywhere, anywhere!" he cried wildly.

"Hush," the old man repeated. "He is on the oasis. We will find him."

"How?" Sandy's voice was a frightened small boy's squeak.

Japheth said, "I will look for him. When I find him, I will bring him to you."

"Oh, Jay—I want to come with you."

"No." Grandfather Lamech was firm. "You have the sun-sickness. You must stay here until you are well." He looked up at the roof hole. The fading sunset was gone, and the moon, not full, but beaming bright, shone down on them. The old man touched Sandy's arm, his thigh. "Tomorrow you will be all blisters."

Sandy's head felt strangely buzzing and he knew that it was from fever and that Grandfather Lamech was right. "But Dennys—"

"I will find him and bring him to you," Japheth promised.

"Oh, Jay, thank you."

The young man turned to his grandfather. "One of the women—my wife, or one of my sisters—will bring you a night-light, Grandfather."

The old man looked at the moonlight which brightened the tent. "Thank you, my dear grandson. My grandchildren are kind to me, so kind . . ." His voice faltered. "My son . . ."

Japheth sounded embarrassed. "You know I can't do anything with Father. I don't even tell him when I've come to your tent."

"Better that way." The old man was sorrowful. "Better that way. But one day—"

"Of course, Grandfather. One day. I'll be back with the Den as soon as I can." He pushed out of the tent, and the flap slapped closed behind him.

Higgaion dribbled cool water from the jar onto the cloth on Sandy's burning forehead.

"Giant"—the little old man leaned over him—"where do you come from?"

"I'm not a giant," Sandy said. "Really. I'm just a boy. Dennys and I are still growing, but we're not giants, we're just ordinary tall."

The old grandfather shook his head. "In our country you are giants. Can you tell me where you come from?"

"Home." Sandy felt hot and feverish. Home might be galaxies away. "New England. The United States. Planet earth."

The wrinkles in the old man's forehead crisscrossed each other as he frowned. "You don't come from around here. Nor from Nod. The people there are no taller than we are." He put his hand on Sandy's forehead. The hand felt cool, and dry as an autumn leaf crumbling to dust. "Your fever will go down, but you must stay here, in my tent, out of the sun, until the burning is healed. I will ask one of the seraphim to come tend to you. Seraphim do not burn in the sun. They are better healers than I." Sandy relaxed into Grandfather Lamech's kindness.

The mammoth started toward the water jar, then dropped to its haunches, whimpering in terror, as something screeched past the tent like an out-of-control jet plane. But on this planet, wherever it was, there were no planes.

The old man leaped to his feet with amazing agility and grabbed a wooden staff.

The hideous screech, not bird, not human, came again, closer, and then the tent flap was pushed aside and a large face peered in. It was the largest face Sandy had ever seen, a man's face with filthy hair and a matted beard, tangled eyebrows over small, suspicious eyes, and a bulbous nose. From the mat of hair came two horns, curved downward, with sharp points like boar's teeth. The mouth opened and shouted, *"Hungry!"*

The rest of the creature pushed into the tent. The head did not belong to a man's body but to a lion's, and as it came all the way into the tent, Sandy saw that the lion did not have a lion's tail but a scorpion's. Sandy was terrified.

The old man beat at it futilely with his staff. The man / lion / scorpion knocked the staff out of his hand and sent him flying across the tent. Grandfather Lamech fell onto a pile of skins. The mammoth lay flat on the skins by Sandy, trembling.

"Hungry!" The roar made the skins of the tent tremble. Instinctively, Sandy thrust the mammoth behind him and, exerting the last remnant of his strength, rose, tottering, to his full height and took a step toward the monster.

"Giant!" the man's head screeched. "Giant!" And scorpion's tail, lion's body, and man's head backed out of the tent, so that the flap snapped back into place.

The old man pulled himself out of the corner where he had been flung. "Ridiculous manticore," he grumbled, "wanting to eat my mammoth."

Higgaion got unsteadily to his feet, raised his trunk, and trumpeted, but it was more of a whiffle than a call of triumph. He rubbed up against Sandy.

The old man retrieved his staff. "Thank you. You saved my mammoth from being eaten."

"I didn't do anything." Sandy's legs crumpled under him as he fell back onto the skins. "It's the first time I've ever scared anybody, just by being tall and sunburned."

"A gentle giant," the old man said.

Sandy felt too weak to contradict him. "Anyhow, the manticore is a mythical beast."

Grandfather Lamech shook his head. "I don't know what you mean."

"Things like manticores are mythical," Sandy stated. "They aren't supposed to be real."

Grandfather Lamech's smile crinkled. "You will have to ask the seraphim to explain. In this time many things are real, you see." He looked around. "Where's the scarab beetle?"

The mammoth, too, looked around, but they both stopped, and the old man's face lit up as a soft scratching was heard on the outside of the tent flap. It was obviously some kind of signal, because he called out gladly, "Come in, Granddaughter." Then he turned courteously to Sandy. "Yalith, my youngest granddaughter."

The tent flap opened enough to let a girl through, a girl about the size of the old man, barely four feet tall. She carried a shallow stone bowl which contained oil and a softly burning wick. By its light, which was brighter than the moonlight, which had moved beyond the roof hole, Sandy could see that the girl, who wore only a loincloth, like Japheth and Grandfather Lamech, was gently curved, with small rosy breasts. Her skin was the color of a ripe apricot. Her softly curling hair was a deep bronze, which glimmered in the lamplight and fell against her shoulders. She looked, Sandy thought, about his age, and suddenly his burning skin was not as painful as it had been, and he felt energy returning to his limbs. He got to his knees and stood to greet her, bowing clumsily.

She saw him and almost dropped the stone lamp. "A giant!"

The mammoth reached up with his trunk to Sandy, and Grandfather

Lamech said, "He says that he is not a giant, dear Yalith. Japheth carried him here, and they tell me that there is another one just like him, but he went out with a unicorn. Japheth is looking for him. This one"—he beamed at Sandy—"appears to be human, and he just saved Higgaion from the manticore."

Yalith shuddered. "I heard it screeching and going off with a rat." She put her stone lamp on a wooden keg. "I've brought your night-light, Grandfather Lamech."

"Thank you, my dear." There was a deep tenderness in the old man's voice.

Sandy bowed again. "Hello. My name's Sandy Murry." He could not keep a foolish grin off his face.

She looked at him dubiously, backing away slightly. "You do not speak like one of us. Are you sure you're not a giant?"

"I'm a boy. I'm sorry I look so awful. I have a fierce sunburn."

Now she looked at him without flinching. "Oh, yes, you do. How do we help you?"

Higgaion dipped his trunk into the water pot again and showered Sandy with it.

Grandfather Lamech said, "Higgaion is keeping his skin wet. But I think we ought to get one of the seraphim to look at him."

"Yes. That would be good. Where did you say you were from, giant—Sand?"

"The United States," Sandy said, though he knew it would mean nothing to this beautiful, strange girl.

The girl smiled at Sandy, and the warmth of her smile enveloped him.

"The United States is—are—a place," he tried to explain. "You might say that my brother and I are representatives."—Even if inadvertent ones.

"And you have a brother, who is out with a unicorn?"

Her question made it sound as though Dennys and the unicorn had gone off cavorting someplace together.

"My brother Dennys. We're twins. Identical twins. We do look a lot alike to people who don't know us well. Your brother Japheth is trying to find him."

"Well, he will find him, then. Do you need anything more, Grand-father Lamech?"

"No, my dear Yalith."

"I'd better go home, then. My brothers' wives are all there, and our mother likes to have me around to help keep everybody from fighting."

She smiled, turning from the old man to Sandy, who was dizzy with fever, but also with Yalith. He gazed at her as she said good night to them. For the first time in his life, Sandy had a flash of gratitude that Dennys was not with him.

Then anxiety surfaced. "Dennys—"

"Japheth will find him," the old man said. "Meanwhile—Higgaion, see if you can find our scarab friend."

Higgaion trumpeted softly and left the tent.

After Yalith and Higgaion had gone, Sandy was assailed by a wave of feverish sleep. It was dark now, with no moonlight coming through the tent's roof hole, and the oil lamp burned low. He closed his eyes, curled on his side to sleep, and felt an emptiness.

Dennys. He was just as happy that Dennys had not seen Yalith. Nevertheless, he had never before gone to sleep without Dennys. At home he could just reach up and punch the mattress above his to get his twin's attention. At Scout camp they had always been in the same cabin. Despite their parents' efforts to allow the twins to develop as individuals, never dressing them alike, the fact remained that they were twins. He did not know what it was like to go to sleep without Dennys.

Higgaion came in and went to Grandfather Lamech, plucking something from his ear with his trunk and holding it out to the old man. Grandfather Lamech took it on his palm, a scarab beetle, glinting bronze in the lamplight. The old man stroked it gently with a trembling forefinger, and closed his palm.

Then came a vivid flash of light, similar to that of the unicorn's horn, and a tall presence stood in the tent, smiling at the old man, then looking quietly at Sandy. The personage had skin the same glowing apricot color as Yalith's. Hair the color of wheat with the sun on it, brightly gold, long, and tied back, falling so that it almost concealed tightly furled wings, the light-filled gold of the hair. The eyes were an incredibly bright blue, like the sea with sunlight touching the waves.

Lamech greeted him respectfully. "Adnarel, we thank you." Then he said to Sandy, "The seraph will be able to help you. Seraphim know much about healing."

So this was a seraph. Tall, even taller than the twins. But the only resemblance was in height. Otherwise, it was totally different, beautiful, but alien. The seraph turned to Lamech. "What have we here?"

Lamech bowed, seeming more than ever like a small brown nut in comparison with the great winged one. If all the ordinary people in this strange place were as little as Japheth and Lamech and Yalith, it was small wonder that Sandy and Dennys were confused with giants. Lamech said, "We have with us a stranger—"

Adnarel touched Sandy's shoulder, pressing him back down on the skins as he started to struggle to his feet.

Lamech continued, "He is, as you can see, almost as tall as you are, but not as—not as completely formed."

"He is very young," Adnarel the seraph said, "barely hatched, as it were. But you are correct. He is not one of us. Nor of the nephilim."

"Nor of us," Lamech said. "But we think he is not to be feared."

Adnarel reached out to touch Sandy gently on the back, the long fingers delicately exploring the shoulder blades. "No wings, not even rudimentary ones."

Higgaion approached the seraph, butting him to get his attention, then indicated the water pitcher.

Adnarel reached down to scratch between the mammoth's ears. "Call the pelican," he ordered.

Higgaion left the tent. Lamech looked up, up, to meet Adnarel's startling blue eyes. "Are we doing the right thing, keeping him cool and wet to bring down the fever and heal the burning?"

Adnarel nodded, as the tent flap opened and Higgaion returned, followed by a pelican, large and white and surprising. It waddled over to the clay water pitcher, opened its great beak, and filled the pitcher.

Lamech asked anxiously, "The pelican will see to it that we have plenty of water? It will take many trips to the well, too many for me now that I am old and—"

"Fear not. Alarid will see to it," Adnarel reassured.

"A pelican in the desert?" Sandy asked, feeling that the great bird was part of a fevered dream.

"A pelican in the wilderness," Adnarel agreed. He dropped to one knee and put his hand against Sandy's reddened cheeks. Through the fingers flowed a healing warmth, a warmth which had nothing to do with the stifling heat in the tent. Sandy had almost grown accustomed to the strong, gamy smell of the skins, but the seraph seemed to bring a lightness and a freshness to the air.

"Where, young one, are you from?" Adnarel asked.

Sandy sighed. "Planet earth, where I hope I still am?"

The seraph smiled again, not answering the question. He touched Sandy's forehead gently, and the touch helped him to clarify his thoughts, which seemed to lose their focus. "And from where on planet earth do you come?"

"From the United States. The Northeast. New England."

"How did you get here?"

"I'm not sure, uh, sir." There was something about Adnarel's presence which brought out the old-fashioned forms of respect. "Our father is working with a theory about the fifth dimension and the tesseract . . ."

"Ah." Adnarel nodded. "Did he send you?"

"No, uh, no, we—"

"We?"

"Dennys, my twin brother, and I. It was our fault. I mean, we have never before done anything so incredibly stupid as to mess with anything of Dad's when an experiment was in progress, except we didn't realize that an experiment was in progress."

"Where is Dennys?"

"Oh, please—" Sandy implored.

Grandfather Lamech explained, "The brother, the Dennys, went out with a unicorn, and has evidently been called back elsewhere. Japheth is looking for him."

The seraph listened gravely, nodding at what Sandy felt was an insufficient and unclear explanation. "Fear not," Adnarel said to Sandy. "Your brother will be returned. Meanwhile, Grandfather Lamech and Higgaion are doing the best thing for you, in keeping your skin moistened." From a pocket deep in his gown he took out what looked like a handful of herbs and dropped them into the water jar. "This will help the healing." He smiled. "It is good that you have at least some knowledge of the Old Language."

"But I don't—" Sandy started.

"You have been able to understand, and talk with, first Japheth, and now Grandfather Lamech, have you not?"

"Well. Yes. I guess so."

"Perhaps the gift has been awakened because you have not had time to think." The seraph's smile illumined the tent. Adnarel turned from Sandy to Lamech. "When the cool of night comes, wrap him in this." And the seraph took off his own creamy robe. His wings were visible now, as golden and shining as his long hair. He gave an effect of sunniness in the dark tent, lit only by the oil lamp. "The animal skins are too rough for his burned flesh. I will come by in the morning to see how he is doing. Meanwhile, I will check on Japheth and see if he has found the brother."

As Adnarel talked, Sandy felt his eyes close. Japheth was looking for Dennys. Adnarel was going to help him. Surely, if the seraph was involved, then everything would be all right.

His thoughts drifted off into soft darkness.

3 Japheth's Sister Yalith

When Yalith left her grandfather's tent, she hurried toward home, near the center of the oasis. At her side she had a small pouch of darts, similar to Japheth's, but instead of the miniature bow she carried a small blowpipe. The arrows were tipped with a solution which would temporarily stun but not kill a predator, even one as large as the manticore. The manticores were strong and bad-tempered, but not intelligent or brave. She feared the manticores less than she feared some of the young men in the town, and she kept a dart in her hand in case she needed it.

After leaving the grazing grounds around Lamech's tent, she walked through one of his groves that led her onto the desert of white sand lapping against brown grasses. Wherever there were not enough wells to provide for irrigation, the desert took over. But she preferred walking across the desert to the dusty, dirty paths of the oasis. Stars were bright against the velvet black of sky. At her feet, a late beetle hustled to burrow itself under the sand until morning. To her right, high in the trees of Lamech's groves, the baboons were chittering sleepily.

She looked toward the horizon, and on an outcropping of rock similar to the one the earthquake had made when Sandy and Dennys met Japheth and the mammoth Higgaion, she saw the shadow of a supine form. She looked to make sure it was a lion, then called softly, "Aariel!"

The creature rose slowly, languidly, and then leapt down from the rock and loped toward her, and she saw that she had been deceived in the starlight, for it was not a lion but one of the great desert lizards, called dragons by most people, although its wings were atrophied and it could not fly.

She stood frozen with anxiety on the starlit sand, her hand holding one of the tiny arrows. As the lizard neared her, it rose straight upward to a height of at least six feet, and suddenly arms were outstretched above the head; the tail forked into two legs, and a man came running toward her, a man of extraordinary beauty, with alabaster-white skin and wings of brilliant purple. His long hair was black with purple glints, and his eyes were the color of amethysts.

"You called me, lovely one?" He bent down toward her tenderly, a questioning smile on his lips, which were deeply rosy in his white face.

"No, no," she stammered. "Not you. I thought—I thought you were Aariel."

"No. I am Eblis, not Aariel. And you called, and here I am," his voice soothed, "at your service. Is there anything you want?"

"Oh, no, thank you, no."

"No baubles for your ears, your lovely little neck?"

"Oh, no, thank you, no," she repeated. Her sisters would think her stupid for refusing his offer. The nephilim were generous. This nephil could give her everything he had offered, and more.

"And all of a sudden you have changed," he said. "You were a child, and now you are not a child any longer."

Instinctively, she folded her hands across her breasts, stammering. "B-but, I am a child. I'm not nearly a hundred years old yet . . ."

He reached out one long, pale hand and softly pushed her starlit hair back from her forehead. "Do not be afraid of growing up. There are many pleasures ahead for you to taste, and I would help you to enjoy them all."

"You?" She looked, startled, at the glorious creature by her, light shimmering like water from the purple wings.

"I, sweet little one, I, Eblis, of the nephilim."

No nephil had paid attention to her before. She was too young. Then she saw, in her mind's eye, the strange young giant in her grandfather's tent. She was no longer a child. She did not react to the young giant as a child.

"There are many changes to come," Eblis said, "and you will need help."

Her eyes widened. "Changes? What kind of changes?"

"People are living too long. El is going to cut the life span back. How old is your father?"

"He must be, oh, close to six hundred years. Middle-aged." She looked at her fingers. Ten. That was really as far as she could count accurately.

"And your Grandfather Lamech?"

"Let's see. He was very young when he had my father, not quite two hundred years old. He, too, has lived for very long. His father,

Methuselah, my great-grandfather, lived for nine hundred and sixty-nine years. And his father was Enoch, who walked with El, and lived three hundred and sixty and five years, and then El took him—" Involved in the great chronologies of her fathers, she was not prepared for him to unfurl his great wings and gather her in, enveloping her in great swirls of purple touched with brilliance as with stars. She gasped in surprise.

He laughed softly. "Oh, little one, little innocent one, how much you have to learn, about men's ways, and about El's ways, which are not men's ways. Will you let me teach you?"

To be taught by a nephil was an honor she had never expected. She was not sure why she was hesitant. She breathed in the strange odor of his wings, smelling of stone, of the cold, dark winds which came during the few brief weeks of winter.

Enveloped in Eblis's wings, she did not hear the rhythmic thud as a great lion galloped toward them across the desert, roaring as it neared them. Then both Yalith and Eblis turned and saw the lion rising to its hind legs, as the lizard had done, leaping up into the sky, a great, tawny body with creamy wings, gilt-tipped, unfurling and stretching to a vast span. The great amber eyes blazed.

Eblis removed his wings from around Yalith, hunched them behind his back. "Why this untoward interruption, Aariel?"

"I ask you to leave Yalith alone."

"What's it to you? The daughters of men mean nothing to the seraphim." Eblis smiled down at Yalith, stroking his long fingers delicately across her burnished hair.

"No?" Aariel's voice was low.

"No, seraph. A nephil may go to a daughter of man. A nephil understands pleasure." He touched a fingertip to Yalith's lips. "I would teach you, sweeting. I think you would like what I can give you. I will leave you now to Aariel's tender ministries. But I will see you again." He turned away from them, toward the desert, and his nephil form dropped into that of the great dragon/lizard. He loped away into the shadows.

Yalith said, "Aariel, I don't understand. I thought I saw you on the rock. I was sure it was you, and I called, and then it wasn't you, it was Eblis."

"The nephilim are masters of mimicry. He wanted you to think it was I. I beg you, little one, be cautious."

Her eyes were troubled. "He was very kind to me."

Aariel put his hand under her chin and looked into her eyes, clear and still childlike. "Who would not be kind to you? Are you on your way somewhere?"

"Home. I took Grandfather Lamech his night-light. But, oh, Aariel, there is a strange young giant in Grandfather Lamech's tent. Japheth carried him there. He has a terrible sunburn. He can't be from anywhere around here. He says he is not a giant, and I have never seen anyone like him. He is as tall as you are, and his body is not hairy, it is smooth like yours, like the nephilim, and his skin, where it wasn't burned red, was pale. Not white, like the skin of the nephilim, but pale and tender, like a baby's."

"You seem to have observed him carefully," Aariel said.

"There's never been anyone like him on the oasis before." She flushed, turned slightly away.

Aariel asked, "What is being done for his burn? Does he have fever?"

"Yes. Higgaion is keeping him sprayed with cool water, and they are going to ask a seraph what to do for him."

"Adnarel?"

"Yes. The scarab beetle."

"Good."

"He is not one of you, this young giant, and he is not one of the nephilim. Their skin burns white and whiter in the sun, like white ash when the fire has burned fiercely in the winter weeks."

The creamy wings trembled, the golden tips shimmering in the starlight. "If his skin burns, he is not of the nephilim."

"Nor of you."

"Does he have wings?"

"No. In that, he is like a human. He seemed very young, though he is as long as you, and thin."

"Did you observe his eyes?"

She did not notice the twinkle in his own. "Grey. Nice eyes, Aariel. Steady. Not burning, like—not giving out light, like yours. More like human eyes, mine, and my parents' and brothers' and sisters'."

Aariel touched her gently on the shoulder. "Go on home, child. Do not fear to cross the oasis. I will see that you are not harmed."

"You and Eblis. Thank you." Like a child, she held her face up for a kiss, and Aariel leaned down and pressed his lips gently against hers. "You will not be a child much longer."

"I know . . ."

He touched her lips again, lightly, and a moment later a large lion was running lightly across the desert.

Yalith turned onto a sandy path through a field of barley. At the end of the path was a stone road cutting through white buildings of sun-baked clay, low buildings, built to withstand the frequent earth tremors.

Some of these low buildings contained small shops for baked goods, for stone lamps, for oil; there were shops with hanging meat, shops with bows and arrows, shops with spears of gopher wood. Some entryways were curtained with strands of bright beads, which tinkled in the evening breeze.

Out of one of these came a nephil, his arm around a young woman who was gazing up at him adoringly, leaning against him so that her rosy breasts touched his pale flesh. Her glossy black hair fell down her back, past her hips; and the eyes with which she regarded him were the deep blue of lapis lazuli.

Yalith stopped in her tracks. The girl was Mahlah, Yalith's sister, the only girl besides Yalith to be in the home tent. Their two older sisters were married and lived in another part of the oasis with their husbands. Mahlah had been away from the home tent a great deal lately. Now Yalith knew where she had been.

Mahlah saw her younger sister and smiled.

The nephil smiled, too, graciously acknowledging Yalith.

Before they came out of the shadows, Yalith thought he was Eblis, with a sense of shock and betrayal. But in the full starlight she could see that his wings were much lighter, a delicate lavender. She could not tell what color his long hair was, but it, too, was lighter, and seemed to have an orange glow. He had a sinuous, snake-like curve to his neck, and hooded eyes.

He smiled again, tenderly. "Mahlah will stay with me this night. You will let your mother know."

Yalith blurted out, "Oh, but she will worry. We are not allowed to stay out at night . . ."

Mahlah laughed joyously. "Ugiel has chosen me! I am his betrothed!"

Yalith gasped. "But does Mother know?"

"Not yet. You tell her, little sister."

"But shouldn't you tell her yourself? You and—"

"Ugiel."

"But shouldn't you—"

Mahlah's laugh pealed again, like little bells. "The old ways are changing, little sister. This night I meet Ugiel's brethren."

The nephil stretched a soft wing about Mahlah. "Yes, little sister. The old ways are changing. Go and tell your mother."

Yalith turned, and they watched her go, fingers waving at her in farewell. At the end of the street she heard footsteps and turned to see a young man following her. She reached for a dart and put it in her blowpipe, but he disappeared around the corner of a building.

The low white buildings gave way to tents, each tent surrounded by the land of the dweller, at first the small plots of the shopkeepers, then groves and fields, sometimes many acres. Along the path she saw sheep, goats, camels grazing. Grapes were ripe on the vines.

Her father's tent was a large one, flanked by several smaller tents. She hurried into the main tent, calling out to her mother.

It was the smell that brought Dennys back to consciousness. His nostrils twitched. His stomach heaved. There was a smell of cooking, smoky, rancid. A smell worse than the rotten-cheese smell of silage which clung to the farm-hands near home. A smell far stronger than that of the manure spread on the fields in the spring; that was a fresh, growing smell. This was old manure, rotting. A smell that made the urinals in the lavatories at school seem sweet. And over it all, but not covering it, a cloying smell of perfume and sweat, body sweat which had never been near a shower.

He opened his eyes.

He was in an enclosed space, lit by the moonlight pouring in through a hole in what seemed to be some kind of curved roof, and by the equally brilliant light which poured from a unicorn's horn. The silver creature looked around, sniffing, pawing the dirty earthen floor. At its feet, a mammoth cringed.

Dennys almost cried out, "Higgaion!" But this mammoth was not the one who had accompanied Japheth. This mammoth had matted fur on its flanks, and it was so thin that the skeleton showed through. Its eyes were dulled, and it seemed to be apologizing to the unicorn.

Staring at the unicorn, still unaware of Dennys, were several small people. But, just as the mammoth was unlike Higgaion, so these people were unlike Japheth. They smelled. The men's bodies were hairy, giving them a simian look. Their goatskin loincloths were not clean. There were two full-bearded men, and two women, naked except for the loin-cloths. Both the women had red hair, and the younger woman's hair was so vivid it almost seemed like flame, and some care had been taken with it. The older woman was wrinkled and discontented-looking.

The unicorn's light flashed against the younger woman's green eyes, making them sparkle like emeralds. "You see!" she cried triumphantly. "I knew our mammoth could call us a unicorn!"

The light in the horn dimmed.

The younger of the two men, who had matted brown hair and a red beard unkempt and spotted with food, snarled at the girl. "And now, dear sister Tiglah, that we have a unicorn in the tent, what do you want of it?"

The girl approached the unicorn, her hand held out as though to pet it. The horn blazed with blinding brilliance, and then the tent was dark so suddenly that it took several seconds for Dennys's eyes to adjust to the moonlight coming through the hole in the roof.

The men roared with laughter. "Ho, Tiglah, you thought you could fool us, didn't you?"

Even the older woman was laughing. Then she saw Dennys, who was struggling to his knees. "Great auk, what have we here?"

The redheaded girl gasped. "A giant!"

The older, bowlegged man approached Dennys. He held a spear, and Dennys, gagging from the stench in the tent, felt an overriding surge of fear. The man nudged him with the spear, so that he fell back onto a pile of filthy skins. The man flipped him over, using the spear, which scratched but did not cut him. He felt the tip of the spear as it was drawn lightly along his shoulder blades.

"Is this one yours, Tiglah?" the younger man asked. "I thought you were seeing a nephil."

Tiglah looked curiously at Dennys. "He's no nephil."

The older woman stared. "If he's a giant, he's a baby giant. He can't hurt us."

"What will we do with him?" Tiglah asked.

The brown, hairy man withdrew his spear. "Throw him out." His voice held no particular malice. Dennys was just a thing, to be disposed of. He felt two pairs of hands lifting him, as the younger man helped his father. The mammoth whimpered, and the older woman kicked at him. Certainly, Dennys thought, anything would be better than this horrible-smelling place full of horrible little people.

There was a brief whiff of fresh air. A glimpse of a night sky crusted with stars. A smoky redness on the horizon, like the light from some enormous industrial city. Then he felt himself being flung, thrown, like offal. He felt himself rolling down a steep incline. He gagged. Vomited. He had been thrown into what was evidently a garbage dump. It was even worse than wherever he had been before.

He managed to pull himself up onto his knees. He was in some kind of pit. There was an overwhelming stench of feces, of rotting flesh. He did not know what else was in the pit with him, and he did not want to know. Frantically he scrambled up the side, climbing, slipping on bones, on ooze, on decaying filth, sliding back, climbing, sliding, slipping, scrabbling, until at last he pulled himself out and up onto his feet and stood there tottering, filthy and terrified.

There was no sign of Sandy. No sign of the unicorn. Or of Japheth and Higgaion. He had no idea where he was. He looked around. He was standing on a dirt path which bordered the pit. Beside it was his rolled-up bundle of clothes. On the other side of the path were a number of tents. He had seen pictures of bedouin tents in his social studies books at school. These were similar, though they seemed smaller and more closely clustered. It was probably from one of these tents that he had been thrown. Beyond the tents were palm trees, and he staggered toward these.

He needed to shower. Did he ever need to shower! He carried with him the smell of the pit. He ran, barely keeping himself upright, to the grove of palms. Beyond these he could see white. White sand. The desert. If he could only reach the desert, he could roll in the moon-washed sand and get clean.

"Sandy!" he called, but there was no Sandy. "Jay! Jay!" But no small, kind young man appeared. "Higgaion!" He shuddered. If he never saw any human being again, he would not go back to the tent where he had been poked at with a spear, and from which he had been thrown, like garbage.

Racing, he was suddenly out of the grove of palms and sliding in sand. He fell down, rolled and rolled, then picked up handsful of sand and rubbed it over himself, wiping off the slime and filth of the pit. He pulled off his turtleneck and flung it away. Rolled again in sand. His underclothes were filthy from the pit and he tore them off, flinging them after the turtleneck. He did not even realize that he was scraping off his own sunburned skin, so eager was he to get clean. The sand was cool under the daisy field of stars, and he took off his sneakers and socks, flinging them after his clothes. They would never be clean again. He rubbed more sand on his feet, his ankles, his legs, not even realizing that he was sobbing like a small child.

After a while, from sheer exhaustion, he calmed down. Began to assess his situation. He was badly sunburned. He had made it worse by scouring himself with sand. He was shivering, but it was not from cold; it was from fever.

He sat there, naked as Adam, on the white desert, his back to the oasis. The not yet full moon was sliding down toward the horizon. Above him, there were more stars than he had ever seen before. Ahead of him was that strange reddish glow, and then he saw that it came from a mountain, the tallest in a range of mountains on the far horizon. Of course. If he and Sandy had somehow or other blown themselves onto a young planet in some galaxy or other, naturally volcanoes would still be active.

How active? He hoped he wouldn't find out. At home the hills were low; old hills, worn down by wind and rain, by the passing of the glaciers, by eons of time. Home. He began to sob again.

With a great effort, he calmed himself. He and Sandy were the practical ones of the family, the ones who found solutions to problems. They could do minor repairs when the plumbing misbehaved. They could rewire an old lamp and make it work again. Their mother's reading lamp in the lab was one they had bought at a church bazaar and made over for her. Their large vegetable garden in the summer was their pride and joy, and they sold enough of their produce to augment their allowances considerably. They could do anything. Anything.

Even believe in unicorns. He thought of the unicorn, the unicorn he had come to think of as a virtual unicorn, and who had, somehow or other, brought him to that tent of horrible, primitive little people who had thrown him into the pit. The sad, undernourished mammoth evidently had called the unicorn, and Dennys had been called back into being, too. But the unicorn had gone out in a blaze of light. A unicorn, even a virtual one, evidently could not stand the smell.

All right. If he thought that a unicorn couldn't stand the ugliness of the smell, it must mean that he believed in unicorns. Virtually.

Of course there were no unicorns. But neither was it possible that he and Sandy, tapping into their father's partly programmed experiment, could have been flung to wherever in the universe they were, on a backward planet of primitive life forms. Again he looked around. The stars were so clear that he seemed to hear a chiming of crystal. From the mountain came a wisp of smoke, a small tongue of fire.

"Oh, virtual unicorn!" he cried. "I want to believe in you, and if you don't come, I will die." He felt something cool and soft nudging his bare body, and there was the scraggly little mammoth, touching him tentatively with the pink tip of its long grey trunk. And then a burst of silver blazed in front of him, and was reduced to a shimmer. A unicorn knelt before him on the sand. Dennys did not have the strength to mount the unicorn and sit astride. He gave the mammoth a look of mute gratitude, then draped himself over the unicorn's back. He closed his eyes. He was burning with fever. He would burn the unicorn. He felt that they were exploding like the volcano.

Mahlah, Yalith's sister, betrothed to Ugiel the nephil, lay on a small rock ledge, ten minutes' walk into the desert. Her heart beat rapidly with excitement. Ugiel had brought her to the rock, covered her with kisses, and then told her to wait until he returned with his brethren to seal their betrothal.

She heard the beating of wings and looked up, catching her breath.

Above her a pelican, white against the night sky, flew in circles which grew smaller as it descended. It touched the ground and raised its great wings until they seemed to brush the stars, and there was no longer a pelican in front of Mahlah but a seraph, with wings and hair streaming silver in the desert wind, and eyes as bright as stars.

Mahlah scrambled to her feet, letting her long black hair swirl about her. "Alarid—"

The seraph took her hand, looking down into her eyes. "Are we really losing you?"

She withdrew her hands, dropping her gaze, laughing a small, self-conscious laugh. "Losing me? What do you mean?"

"Is it true that you and Ugiel—"

"Yes, it is true," she said proudly. "Be happy for me, Alarid. Ugiel is still your brother, is he not?"

Alarid dropped to one knee, so that he no longer towered over her. "Yes, we are still brothers, though we have chosen very different ways."

"And you're sure yours is the better way?" There was scorn in Mahlah's voice.

Alarid shook his head sadly. "We do not judge. The seraphim have chosen to stay close to the Presence."

"But you're too close to be able to see it! The nephilim have distance and objectivity." He looked at her, and her glance wavered for a moment. "Yes. Ugiel told me that."

Alarid rose slowly to his full height. With one silver wing he drew her briefly to him, and she smelled starlight. Then he let her go. "You will not forget us?"

"How could I forget you!" she exclaimed. "You have been my friend since Yalith took me out to greet the dawn and I met you and Aariel."

"You have not greeted the dawn lately."

"Oh—I am learning about the night."

Alarid bent down and kissed the top of her dark head. Then he walked slowly across the desert. Tears fell silently onto the sand.

Mahlah looked down. When she raised her head, she saw a pelican flying up, up, to be lost among the stars.

Yalith hurried into her family tent. "Mahlah is betrothed to one of the nephilim!"

No one heeded her. Her parents, brothers, and sisters-in-law were lying around on goatskins, eating, and drinking wine her father had made from the early grapes. Several stone lamps lit the tent with a warm glow; too warm, Yalith thought. Almost no breeze came through the open tent flap, or the roof hole. The moon was descending, and only stars were visible. She looked around for Japheth, her favorite brother, but did not see him. Probably he was still out looking for the brother of the young giant in her grandfather's tent.

Her mother was stirring something in a wooden bowl, intent on what she was doing. A mammoth, well fed, with lustrous long hair on its flanks, lay sleeping at her feet.

Someone had been sick, probably Ham, who had a weak stomach, and the smell of Ham's sickness mingled with the smell of wine, of meat from the stewpot, of the skins of the tent. Yalith was accustomed to all these odors, and noticed only that Ham was lying back on a pile of skins, looking pale. Ham was, in any event, the lightest-skinned in the family, and the smallest, having been, according to Matred, born a full moon early. Anah, his red-haired wife, knelt by him, offering him wine. Languidly he pushed it away, then pulled Anah down to him, kissing her full, sensual mouth.

Yalith went up to Matred, her mother. Repeated: "Mahlah is betrothed."

Matred looked up briefly. "She's not old enough."

"Oh, Mother, of course she is. And she is."

"Old enough?" Matred was preoccupied with what she was doing. "Betrothed."

"Who is it this time?"

"It's not one of us. It's one of the nephilim."

Matred shivered, but went on stirring, without focus. "Mahlah has changed. She is no longer my merry little girl who was satisfied to see a butterfly, or a drop of dew on a spider's web. She is no longer satisfied to be with us in the home tent." A tear dropped into the bowl.

Yalith patted her mother's arm. "She's grown up, Mother."

"So have you. But you don't go chasing about the oasis at night. You don't run after nephilim."

"Maybe the nephil ran after her?"

"She's pretty enough. But it is not right for me to hear something like this at secondhand. That is not how things are done. That is not how my daughter behaves."

"I'm sorry," Yalith said uncomfortably. "I was walking home from Grandfather Lamech's, and I saw them, Mahlah and a nephil. His name is Ugiel. He asked me to tell you, so that you would not be worried."

"Worried!" Matred exclaimed. "Just don't tell your father, that's all. What's to prevent this Ugh—"

"Ugiel."

"This nephil from coming himself, with Mahlah, to tell me and your father, according to the custom."

Yalith frowned worriedly. "He said that times are changing." Eblis had said that, too. She felt a jolt of insecurity in the pit of her stomach. She did not tell her mother about Eblis.

Matred put down her wooden spoon with a bang. "There are many who think it an honor to be noticed by a nephil and accept their ways. Anah"—Matred looked across at her son Ham's wife, redheaded, still luscious, but beginning to be overblown—"Anah tells me that her younger sister, Tiglah, is being singled out by a nephil for marriage. Anah is thrilled."

"But you're not."

"Tiglah is not my daughter. Mahlah is." Matred turned away. "Child, I am not star-dazzled by the nephilim. They are very different from us."

"They are beautiful—"

"Beautiful, yes. But they will make changes, and not all changes are good."

—I don't want things to change, Yalith thought. And then, in her mind's eye, she saw again the young giant who had bowed to her in Grandfather Lamech's tent, and who was unlike anybody she had ever seen.

Matred continued: "Change is, I suppose, inevitable, and sometimes it brings good things." She looked across the tent to her oldest son, Shem, who was sitting with his wife, Elisheba, eating some of the grapes from the vineyard which were not pressed for wine but kept for the table. Shem was pulling one grape at a time from the bunch, and throwing it to Elisheba. She would catch each grape in her open mouth and they would both laugh with pleasure at this simple, sensual game. It seemed amazingly young and romantic for this stocky, solid couple. "Elisheba is a great help to me. And then, Japheth's wife—"

Yalith looked to where a young woman with softly curling black hair against creamy skin was scouring a wooden bowl with sand. The young woman looked up and waved in greeting.

Matred said, "She comes to us from another oasis, and with a strange name."

"O-holi-bamah." Yalith sounded it out.

"Look at her," Matred commanded.

Yalith looked again at her sister-in-law. Oholibamah was fairer of complexion than Yalith or the other women, even fairer than Ham. Her hair and brows were blacker than the night sky, a rippling, purply black. When Oholibamah stood, she was nearly a head taller than the other women. And beautiful. She always seemed lit by moonlight, Yalith thought. "What about her?" she asked her mother.

"Look at her, child. Look at her."

Yalith was shocked. "You mean you think she—"

Matred shrugged slightly. "She is the youngest daughter of a very old man." She held up the fingers of both hands. "More than ten years younger than her brothers and sisters. I love Oholibamah as though she were my own. And if Oholibamah was indeed sired by a nephil, then great good has been brought into our lives."

Yalith looked at Oholibamah as though seeing her for the first time. After Yalith and Mahlah, Oholibamah was the youngest woman in the tent, younger by several years than Elisheba, Shem's wife, or Anah, Ham's wife. All three of Yalith's brothers had married at unusually young ages, and all three had grumbled at having to take on domestic duties so soon. Shem had protested, "But we are too young to marry. I'm the oldest, and I've barely reached my first hundred years."

His father had replied, "There is a certain urgency, my son."

"Why? And how will you find wives for us when we are so young?"

"You are fine-looking men," the patriarch assured him.

Ham had joined in. "But why the rush, Father? What is this urgency you speak of?"

The patriarch pulled at his long beard, which was beginning to show white. "Yesterday, when I was working in the vineyard, the Voice spoke to me. El told me that I must find wives for you."

"But why?" Ham protested. "We're young, and we need time."

"There are changes, great changes coming," the patriarch said.

"Is the volcano going to erupt?" Shem asked.

"If the volcano erupts," Ham said, "wives won't do us any good."

Their father told them only that the word of El had come to him in the vineyard, and that El had given no explanation.

Elisheba and Anah were easily found for Shem and Ham. The patriarch had a reputation as an honest man. He had the largest and best vineyards on the oasis, and fine flocks of goats and sheep. The fame of his wine had spread to many other oases round about. Matred was a woman of unquestionable virtue and beauty, and her girth attested to her skills as a cook. It was a privilege to marry into her tent.

Japheth was young enough so that no one stepped forward. His face was still smooth and beardless. His body hair was no more than soft down. His eyes were friendly and guileless. But he was on the threshold of manhood. His father went off on his camel one day, and came back with Oholibamah.

Japheth had been at the well, getting water for the animals, when he saw a young girl on a white camel, a young girl of fair complexion, with dark hair tumbling richly against her ivory shoulders. His eyes met Oholibamah's eyes, dark as the night sky between stars, and his knees became fluid. She slid off the white camel's back and came toward him, slender hands outstretched. Their love was a bright flower, youthful, and radiantly beautiful.

Oholibamah. O-holy-bamah. A name as strange as her moonlit beauty. But soon it flowed easily from their lips.

Oholibamah was Yalith's first real friend. They were not far apart in age, both of them barely out of childhood and into womanhood. They were alike, too, in their unlikeness to the others. They saw and rejoiced in what most people of the oasis never noticed. Both liked to leave the tent at first dawn to watch and wait for the sun to rise over the desert, delighting in the calling of the stars just before daylight. It was during one of her dawn walks that Yalith had met the great lion who was the seraph Aariel, and on another walk, when she had persuaded Mahlah to join her, that she had introduced Aariel and Alarid the pelican to her sister. But once Oholibamah came, Mahlah preferred to sleep in the morning.

So Yalith and her youngest sister-in-law would slip out quietly. When the great red disk of day pulled above the white sand, and the stars dimmed and their songs faded out, scarab beetles who had slept under the sand during the hours of the dark came scuttling up into the light. At the edge of the oasis, the baboons leapt from the trees, clapping their hands and shrieking for joy at the rising of the sun. Behind them on the oasis the cocks crowed, and in the desert the lions roared their early-morning roar before retreating to their caves to sleep during the heat of the day. Yalith and Oholibamah shared a silent and joyful companionship.

Now, in the warm and noisy tent, Oholibamah beckoned to Yalith. "Have you eaten?"

"No." Yalith shook her head. "I meant to eat with Grandfather, but I forgot all about food because there was a strange young—"

Ham interrupted her, calling out from the pile of skins on which he was reclining. "I have a headache, Oholi. I need you."

Oholibamah said sharply, "Let Anah rub your head. She is your wife."

"Her fingers do not have the touch that yours do." And, indeed, Oholibamah had a reputation for having healing in her fingers.

She was still sharp. "If you don't want a headache, don't eat and drink too much." She turned away and went to the cook pot, ladled some stew into a wooden bowl, and handed it to Yalith. The mammoth left Matred and came and nudged Yalith's knee.

"No, Selah," Yalith scolded. "You know I won't give you anything more to eat. You're getting fat." She deftly picked pieces of meat and vegetable from the bowl and ate them, then raised it to her lips to drink the broth. It tasted wonderful, and she realized that she was very hungry.

Beside her, Oholibamah sighed.

"What's the matter?" Yalith asked.

The mammoth moved to the older girl, who scratched its grey head. "I was walking through the town this morning. We needed some provisions. One of the nephilim came out of one of the bathhouses, smelling of oil and spices, and stood in my path." She paused.

"And?" Yalith prodded.

"He said that I was one of them, one of their daughters."

Yalith glanced at her mother, then back at Oholibamah. Thought of Eblis and his glorious purple wings. "Would that be so terrible?"

"It is absurd. I love my parents. I love my father."

Yalith had never seen Oholibamah's parents. And how would she herself feel if someone suggested that her father was not, in fact, her father? But now that Matred had put the thought in her mind, it was easy to believe that Oholibamah had been sired by a nephil. She had gifts of healing. Ham was right about that. Her voice when she sang was beautiful as a bird's. She saw things no one else saw.

But then, Yalith reminded herself, she, too, was different, the seventh child of her parents, and she knew quite well who her parents were, and that they had been disappointed when they had had a fourth daughter instead of a fourth son.

"Did you hear me saying that Mahlah is betrothed to a nephil?" she asked Oholibamah.

"Yes, I heard. Mahlah likes pretty things. The wives of the nephilim live in houses of stone and clay, not in tents. I'm sure Mahlah feels proud to have been chosen."

"What do you think about it?" Yalith asked.

"I'm not sure. I'm not sure what I think about the nephilim. Especially if—" She broke off.

"And the seraphim?" Yalith asked.

"I'm not sure what I think about them, either." Oholibamah pressed her fingers against her ears as Ham started to shout.

For a small man, he had a powerful voice. "Selah, come here! If Oholibamah won't help me, then I need a unicorn!"

Anah said crossly, "You know a unicorn can't come near you."

"It doesn't have to come near," Ham grunted. "They can cast their light from any distance. It's only the light I need."

Anah muttered, "You need more than that."

"Yalith! You can call a unicorn. Or Selah! Call me a unicorn!"

A sudden flash of light made them all blink. It was as though lightning had somehow managed to get inside the heavy hides of the tent, perhaps flashing down through the roof hole.

"Get away!" Ham cried. "Who are you!"

He was not referring to the unicorn, which stood glimmering in the tent. On the skins right by Ham lay a very young man, with raw, sunburned skin, and eyes glazed with fever.

Matred peered down at the boy. "How did he get here? Ham, is he a friend of yours?"

Ham looked totally bewildered. "I've never seen him before."

"What is he?" Shem demanded.

The patriarch, who had been chewing on a mutton bone, looked at the boy. "Another kind of giant," he said disgustedly.

Oholibamah said, "Whoever he is, give him air. Don't crowd around. Look, he has sun fever. Oh my, he looks terrible."

Elisheba, Shem's wife, peered at the boy. "If he's a giant, he's a very young one."

Yalith managed to push between Matred and Oholibamah so that she could see. She shrieked, "It's my young giant!"

"What's that, daughter?" Matred asked. "You've seen him before?"

"In Grandfather's tent, when I took him his night-light."

The patriarch scowled. "If my father, Lamech, doesn't want a giant in his tent, why should I have him in mine?"

"Oh, please, Father," Yalith begged.

"You've really seen him before?" Oholibamah asked.

"When I brought Grandfather Lamech his night-light," Yalith repeated, "there was this young, sunburned giant in his tent." She looked at the fevered young man. "I'm not sure this is . . . Where's Japheth?"

The tent flap was pushed aside, and Japheth came in. "Why, here I am, looking for a unicorn and—"

Selah raised her trunk and trumpeted.

"Why!" Japheth exclaimed. "I've been looking all over the oasis and there's one right here! And—so is the Den, the one I've been looking for!" He dropped to his knees. "Great auk. Is he alive?"

Oholibamah ordered, "Move back, all of you." She put her hand against Dennys's bare chest. "He's alive, but he's burning with fever."

Anah moved back slightly, pushing her red hair away from her face with a dirty hand. "Is he a seraph or a nephil?"

Yalith shook her head. "He doesn't have wings. Oh, Japheth, I'm glad you're back. He is the other one, isn't he, the one you were looking for?"

"Yes," Japheth said. "But he looks burned nearly to death."

Oholibamah pressed her hand against the reddened forehead, wincing at the heat of it, turning to look for the unicorn, who had almost dimmed out of being. "Unicorn, can you help?"

The unicorn's outline sharpened, and it bent toward the flushed boy, and light flowed from its forehead, cooling the burning skin.

Ham pushed up from his pelts and blundered toward the unicorn. "Me. I need help. I feel sick. Help *me*." His fair hair was stringy with sweat. The even lighter hair on his chest held drops of moisture.

Again there was a flash of light, and when they could see again, the unicorn had disappeared.

"Idiot." Anah's green eyes sparked. "You know you can't get near a unicorn."

"Meanwhile," the patriarch said, "how are we going to get rid of this half-baked giant?"

"My dear," Matred protested, "surely we should show him some hospitality."

"My good father, Lamech, evidently threw him out of *his* tent," her husband retorted.

"No, Father!" Yalith protested. "You don't understand! There are *two* giants, and Grandfather has the other one in his tent and is taking care of him."

"I don't know what you're talking about," her father said. "How can there be two of these peculiar giants?"

"Oh, Father, if only you'd go to *see* Grandfather Lamech!"

"I will have nothing to do with coddling the old man. Or his strange giants. We have enough troubles without sick giants being added to them."

Yalith knelt beside Oholibamah and looked at the boy, who lay breathing shallowly, eyelids twitching slightly. Yalith reached out a tentative finger and touched the boy's flushed cheek. "You're not Sand? You're his brother?"

The reddened eyelids opened slightly. "Dennys. Dennys." Then the boy flung his arm over his face, as though to ward off a blow. His limbs began to shake convulsively.

"What's happened?" Japheth demanded. "Somebody's hurt him. And he doesn't recognize me."

"He's afraid!" Elisheba's voice was shocked.

Shem protested, "Surely Grandfather Lamech couldn't have hit him!"

"Never," Japheth defended swiftly.

"Not Grandfather!" Yalith spoke at the same time.

"El! His skin is rubbed raw!" Oholibamah exclaimed. "Someone between Grandfather Lamech's tent and here has hurt him."

Matred bent close, asking softly, "Who could have done this? Even to a deformed giant?"

Japheth asked, "Dennys?"

"Dennys," the boy moaned.

"Where have you been? Did someone call you and the unicorn back into being? Who was it?"

Oholibamah touched her husband's hand. "Selah called a unicorn, and suddenly this wounded giant was here."

"But he's been somewhere else on the oasis." Japheth took his wife's hand and pressed it against his cheek. "And he has been abused. He's barely conscious. This is terrible."

Anah peered over Yalith's shoulder. "Are you sure he's human?"

Japheth frowned. "They said they are twins, but I think twins is human."

The patriarch murmured, "What with the wingèd creatures around, sleeping with the daughters of men, it is hard to know anymore who is human and who is not." He looked at Oholibamah, but not unkindly.

Oholibamah touched Dennys's forehead again, and he opened his eyes and flinched. "Shh. I will not hurt you." She looked at Yalith and Japheth. "The unicorn's horn has taken away some of his fever, but he is still very hot. Was it this bad when you saw him, Japheth?"

Japheth shook his head. "He was sun-sick, worse than the Sand, but not like this."

The patriarch asked, "You say there are two of these giants?"

"Two. Exactly alike. I left the one called Sand in Grandfather Lamech's tent"—he looked rather defensively at his father—"to go look for this one. And then, to my surprise, when I'd given up for the night, he was here, right in our own home tent."

Ham suggested, "We've never seen two look-alikes. We should send someone to Grandfather Lamech's tent to make sure there's another one."

"You doubt me?" Japheth demanded.

"Just want to make sure," Ham said.

Less hotly, Japheth said, "I found it difficult to believe at first, myself."

Cutting across their conversation, Oholibamah said, "We should bathe him with water, to try to keep him cool and moist."

"Water!" Matred exclaimed. "Even the mammoths are having difficulty scenting for water. But there is plenty of wine."

"Not my wine!" the patriarch roared. "Woman! You have no idea how hard I work in the vineyard."

"I do," Japheth commented mildly. "I work with you."

Oholibamah frowned slightly. "I don't think wine will do."

Japheth said, "Higgaion sprayed water from Grandfather Lamech's water pot on the Sand, and I think it helped." He looked toward Selah, who again was at Matred's feet.

Anah glanced out of the corner of her green eyes at pasty Ham, then at Dennys's recumbent form. "If his skin didn't look like raw meat, he'd be quite gorgeous."

Elisheba, Shem's wife, stocky and sensible-looking, with thickly curling black hair and dark, placid eyes, snorted. "Keep away from him, Anah. You saw that the unicorn went right to him. For all his giant's size, he's barely more than a baby. And he's trembling. He's frightened."

Matred said fiercely, "Whatever, he shall not be ill-treated again."

Yalith looked gratefully at her mother.

Her father snorted. "Women. I'm always being bullied by women and their good works. Matred feeds any lazy beggar who comes to the tent, and Elisheba helps her keep the soup pot full."

"People do not choose to be poor and hungry," Matred said calmly. "We have enough, and to spare. Husband, I will not have this young giant abused."

"Do what you want with him," the patriarch said. "It makes no difference to me, as long as I'm not bothered about it."

Oholibamah looked at her husband. "We shouldn't leave him here. It's too hot and crowded. He was near death when the unicorn's light touched him, and I think he's still very ill."

"Listen to Oholi," Ham said. "She knows what she's talking about."

For Yalith, no matter what Japheth had said, Dennys was the same young man she had seen in her grandfather's tent. She had been afraid of him when she had first seen him, and now, this time, it was the young giant who seemed terrified. "Where can we take him?"

"He's just a child," Oholibamah suggested. "What about the women's tent?"

In Yalith's eyes, Sandy/Dennys was not a child.

Elisheba asked, "How near to the time of the moon is it for any of us?"

Matred, who was the one to keep track of such things, drew her brows together in thought, and touched her fingers, counting. "Not for a while. Soon he will be well enough to sleep here in the big tent. Or he will be dead."

Yalith shuddered. "Don't say that. He is our guest. We don't let our guests die."

"My dear," Matred said. "He is badly burned. His skin is raw, as though someone has been scraping him, like a carrot."

"Perhaps we should call on one of the seraphim?" Japheth suggested.

His mother nodded. Looked at Yalith. "Your friend Aariel would come, would he not?"

"I think so, yes." If she had to call Aariel, Yalith would make very certain that it was Aariel, not Eblis, though she was not sure why she felt that making sick calls was not part of the business of the nephilim.

"Elisheba," Matred continued, "if you will look into the chest by my sleeping skins, you will find some soft linen for him to lie on. The animal skins are too rough."

Anah simpered, "Mother always knows best, eh, Ham?" and moved away.

"I will crush some figs and make juice for him to drink." Matred always felt better when there was something to do.

Oholibamah pressed her palm against Dennys's forehead again. "He is so hot." She frowned, as he flinched and moaned, eyes tightly closed.

The patriarch said, "If he's going to die on us, get him out of the tent, quickly."

Yalith protested, "Father!"

Japheth reached comfortingly for her hand.

The patriarch said, "You will have to learn, daughter, that you cannot nurse every broken-winged bird or wounded salamander back to health."

"I can try!"

"Perhaps you make them suffer more that way," her father suggested, "than if you let them die?"

"Oh, Father—"

"Now." Matred bustled back. "Enough talk. Japheth will help us carry our strange little giant to the women's tent. Quick, now!"

4 Grandfather Lamech and Grandfather Enoch

When Dennys opened his eyes and found himself surrounded by little brown people, he was terrified. How had he got back into that terrible tent? Surely the unicorn wouldn't have returned him to the people who had tossed him out into the dung heap. Where was the unicorn?

Brilliant light flared against his closed eyelids, then darkness. He began to shiver, uncontrollably, and he felt a hand against his forehead. Cool. Gentle. It might almost have been his mother's hand. When he had had flu, only his mother's touch could cool him. "Mother," he moaned. Then, like a small child, "Mommy . . ."

A small woman leaned over him, looked at him with twinkly eyes surrounded by a crisscrossing of wrinkles. She did not look as though she would throw him into a garbage pit.

She moved away, and then two pairs of younger eyes were looking at him. One pair was a deep amber, with golden flecks, and belonged to a girl with hair as amber as the eyes. Beautiful eyes. Pure. The other girl's eyes were black, but a black which held light, and wisdom. Wherever he was, it could not be the tent from which he had been thrown by the men while the girl with flaming-red hair looked on.

Men. He looked around fearfully. There were men there. Spears were stacked against the side of the tent. One of the men held a wine-skin. They did not seem to be threatening.

Then one of the small men came over to him, and smiled down at him, and he felt a great wave of relief. It was Japheth.

"Jay—" he whispered through parched lips.

"Den!" Japheth exclaimed gladly. "Oholi, he's coming back to consciousness!"

"Jay—" Dennys's teeth were chattering.

"Who's hurt you?" Japheth asked. "Can you tell us?"

Dennys closed his eyes again.

"Don't bother him with questions now," Oholibamah said.

"Don't be afraid, Den," Japheth encouraged. "We're not going to let anybody hurt you." Japheth bent down to him. "I'm going to carry you to some place where it's cool and quiet. Don't be afraid." Japheth picked Dennys up as carefully as possible and slung him over his shoulder.

Japheth was the tallest man in the tent; even so, he was so much smaller than Dennys that the boy's feet dragged on the ground, and he curled his fingers to keep them from scraping, too. No wonder in this place he and Sandy were thought of as giants. Dennys had a feverish vision of a trip his class had taken to a museum, where everybody had been amazed at the exhibition of knights' armor. How small those knights must have been! The people on this planet where he and Sandy had been flung were even smaller than the medieval knights.

His thoughts misted off, as tenuous as the virtual unicorns. The remembrance of the field trip to the museum was no more of a dream than his being carried by Japheth, who was amazingly strong for so small a man, a short young shepherd carrying a lamb. A very small shepherd. Dennys's toes scraped over a rock, and he cried out. If he could wake up, if he could shake off the heat of this feverish dream, he and Sandy would be in their bunk bed at home.

He opened his eyes, and the stars were brilliant, and he took a gulp of fresh air. Then his head brushed against a tent flap, and he felt himself being lowered onto something soft but so delicate that he could feel the rough skins underneath. He licked his cracked lips and realized that he had a raging thirst. "Water, Jay," he managed to croak, but could not summon the energy to add, *please.*

The black-eyed girl bent over him and held a wineskin to his lips, and he tasted something bitter and sweet at the same time. It stung his throat as he swallowed, but at least it was wet.

The black-eyed girl withdrew the skin. "We shouldn't give him too much wine."

"I forgot the fig juice," the plump, nut-like woman exclaimed. "I'll be right back."

Dennys heard the pad of bare feet, and the thud of a leather tent flap falling.

"He recognizes me now." Japheth's voice was troubled.

"I don't think he's afraid of us anymore," the younger girl said, the one with amber eyes.

"Water—" Dennys begged.

The amber-eyed girl said, wistfully, "Grandfather Lamech's wells still have water to spare."

The other girl agreed. "I wouldn't mind going to get a pitcherful, but I wish Grandfather Lamech did not live at the bottom of the oasis."

Japheth put his arm lovingly about the girl. "I'll take one of the camels and go. I don't want either of you crossing the oasis at this time of night. Every moon, there are more bandits and thieves."

"Oh, but be careful," the younger girl begged.

"Take my camel, love," the black-haired woman offered. "She's the swiftest, and you'll be safe on her."

"Thank you, Oholibamah, my wife." Japheth leaned to her and kissed her on the lips. Dennys, watching through the confusion of headache and fever, thought that it was a nice kiss. It was the kind of kiss he had seen his father give his mother. A real kiss. If he lived through this, he would like to kiss someone like that.

He heard Japheth leave, and closed his eyes, sliding into a fevered sleep. Like his virtual unicorn, he seemed to flicker in and out of being. He retreated deep within himself in order to retreat from the flaming pain of his scraped skin. He did not know how long he had been unconscious before he became aware of the two women speaking softly.

"Why won't my father reconcile with Grandfather Lamech?" the lighter voice asked. "I had to beg him for the oil for Grandfather's night-light."

The older girl, the one Japheth had kissed, with an odd name, Oholi something, had a voice like velvet. "Your father was hurt when Grandfather Lamech insisted on staying in his own tent."

"But as long as Grandfather can care for himself—"

"It's complicated," the dark voice said. "People don't revere old people the way they used to. They don't want to listen to their stories."

"I love Grandfather's stories!"

"I, too, Yalith."

Yalith, that was the name of the amber-eyed one. Yalith and Oholi. Dennys was vaguely aware of something cool touching his skin, something that numbed the pain.

The one called Oholi continued. "I always enjoy it when it's my turn to take him the night-light. And at least your mother feels as we do. She'll always manage to get the oil for us to take to him."

"When did it change?" Yalith asked. "People need to sit at the feet of the old people and listen. But now—I heard Anah say that her grandfather was put out in the desert to die, and his bones were picked clean by vultures."

"Oh, El, what are we coming to!"

At the trouble in the dark voice, Dennys opened his eyes.

"He is still so hot, so hot," Oholi said. "I wish we knew who had hurt him."

"But what could we do?" Yalith asked. "What in El's name could we do? People are ugly to one another today. Were we this cruel before the nephilim and the seraphim came?"

"I don't know."

"And who came first?"

"I don't know," the dark-eyed one repeated. "There is much we don't know. Where did this young wounded giant come from, for instance?"

"The other one," Yalith said, "the one in Grandfather Lamech's tent, said that they came from some kind of Nighted Place."

"United States," Dennys corrected automatically. Then Yalith's words registered. "Where is my brother?"

"Oh, good, he's coming to!" Yalith cried. Then said, kindly, to Dennys, "He's in my Grandfather Lamech's tent, being cared for by Grandfather and Higgaion. He's sun-struck, too, but not nearly as badly as you are."

The words began to buzz into meaninglessness as Dennys slid back into unconsciousness. He knew that the combination of too much sun, of being thrown into the pit, of scraping himself with sand, had made him ill. Very ill, indeed. This was far worse than when he had flu and a temperature of over 105°. Then he had antibiotics to fight the fever. Heaven knew what had been in that garbage pit. Heaven knew what horrible infection might follow. He thought that he was probably dying from overexposure to the sun, and he didn't much mind, except that he wished he was at home, on his own planet, rather than here, wherever in the universe here was, with these strange small people. He wished he was young enough to call out and wake his mother, so that she would come in to him and she would wake him from the nightmare and take off the knight's helmet that was pinching his skull and giving him a terrible headache.

He drifted into darkness.

For the first few days in Grandfather Lamech's tent, Sandy was miserable. His reddened skin bubbled into blisters. Where he didn't sting, he itched. But as his fever abated he began to look for Yalith in the evening. She did not come, and he felt only a weary indifference to the older women who brought the light, often staying to chat with the old man so that they would have an excuse to stare at Sandy.

He knew now that Dennys was safe in a tent near Japheth's, and

that he was being well cared for. He knew that he and Dennys were
objects of intense curiosity to the women who came each evening.

"I've never seen anything like it!" the oldest one, called Matred,
exclaimed. "Except that our giant is burned so much more badly, I
would not believe that they are two."

Anah and Elisheba took their turns taking the night-light to Grandfather Lamech, whispering over Sandy and his likeness to their own
twin, still burning with fever in the women's tent. But they shyly held
back from talking with Sandy, speaking softly so that he could not hear
what they were saying.

Adnarel came each day, at least long enough to drip fresh herbs or
powders into the water with which Higgaion continued to bathe the
burned skin. The pelican kept the water jar filled, and when Grandfather
Lamech thanked the great bird, he treated it as more than a pelican,
causing Sandy to wonder. The old man spent hours cooking concoctions
to tempt Sandy's appetite, and the ones that tasted best were the ones
which reminded him of his mother's Bunsen-burner stews. Sandy
wanted to ask the old man about the women who came in the evening
and, most importantly, to ask him why Yalith was not one of them, but
he was embarrassed and held his peace. And slept, and slept, healing.

On the first night when it was apparent that Sandy's fever had left
him and he was weak but recuperating, Lamech suggested that they go
out of the tent and sit under the stars. "Their light cannot harm your
healing skin. Your skin is so fair, so fair. No wonder you had the sun
fever." He held out his hand and Sandy took it, letting the old man pull
him to his feet. His legs felt weak and unused. Lamech pushed through
the tent flap, holding it aside for Sandy, who had to bend over to go
through. Not far from the tent was a large and ancient fig tree, too old
to bear fruit any longer. One root had pulled up from the ground and
formed a low seat, before it dipped down into the earth again. Lamech
sat on it, and beckoned to Sandy to sit beside him.

"Look." Lamech pointed to the sky.

Sandy had already been staggered by the glory of the night sky on
his nocturnal visits to the grove which served as outhouse. He had tried
to question the old man as to where he was, what planet, what galaxy.
But Lamech had been bewildered. Sun, moon, and stars revolved around
the oasis and the desert, put there by El for their benefit. So Sandy still
had no idea where he and Dennys had ended up with their foolishness.

Now he simply looked up at the sky in awe. At home, even in
winter when the air was clearest, even deep in the countryside where
they lived, the stars were not like these desert stars. It seemed that he

could almost see the arms of spiral galaxies moving in their great circular dance. Between the radiance of the stars, the blackness of the firmament was deeper and darker than velvet.

Except at the far horizon. "Hey," Sandy asked. "Why is it so light over there? Is there a big city, or something?"

"It is the mountain," Lamech said.

Sandy squinted and could just make out a range of mountains against the sky, with one peak higher than the others, a long way off, much farther off than the palm tree which had led them to Japheth and Higgaion and the oasis. "A volcano?" he asked.

Lamech nodded.

"Does it erupt often?"

Lamech shrugged. "Perhaps once in every man's lifetime. It is far away. When it goes off, we do not get the fire, but we get a rain of black dust that kills our crops."

The light tingeing the horizon was indeed so far away that it did not even dim the magnificence of the stars. Sandy asked, "Is it always this clear?"

"Except during a sandstorm. Do you have sandstorms on the other side of the mountain?" Lamech had set it in his mind that the twins came from beyond the mountains. That was as far away as he understood.

"No. We're nowhere near a desert. Everything is green where we live, except in winter, when the trees lose their leaves and the ground has a good cover of snow."

"Snow?"

Sandy reached down and picked up a handful of the clean white sand. "It is even whiter than this, and it is softer, and it—in winter it falls from the sky and covers the ground, and it's called poor man's fertilizer, and we need it to make sure we'll have good crops in summer. Dennys and I have a big vegetable garden."

The old man's face brightened. "When you are better and can go out in the daylight, I will show you my garden. What do you grow in yours?"

"Oh, tomatoes and sweet corn and broccoli and brussels sprouts and carrots and onions and beans, and almost anything you want to eat. We eat what we can, and what we can't, we can." Then he realized that the old joke would mean nothing to Lamech. He amended, "We can some of our produce, or freeze it."

"Can? Freeze?"

"Well, uh, putting by food that we've grown in the summer so that we'll have it to eat in the winter."

"Do you grow rice?" Lamech asked.

"No."

"You don't have good enough wells for it?"

"We have wells," Sandy said, "but I don't think we have the right kind of growing conditions for rice." He was going to have to look up rice cultivation when they got home.

"Lentils?" Lamech pursued.

"No."

"Dates?"

"It's too cold where we live for palm trees."

"I've never been on the other side of the mountains. It must be a very strange place."

Sandy did not know how to correct him. "Well, where we live, it's very different."

The old man murmured. "You are the beginning of change. We are living in end times. It can be very lonely."

Sandy, looking at the stars, did not hear. "Grandfather Lamech, is my brother really getting better?"

"Yes. That is what I am told."

"Who tells you?"

"The women, when they bring the night-light."

"Do the men never come? I haven't seen your son."

"It is only the women who care." Lamech's voice was bitter.

"Japheth—"

"Ah, Japheth. Japheth comes when he can, my youngest grandson, my dear boy." He sighed, wearily. "When my son, my only son, was born, I predicted that he would bring us relief from our work, from the hard labor that has come upon us because of the curse upon the ground."

Sandy felt an uncomfortable prickling. "What curse?"

"When our forebears had to leave the Garden, they were told, *Accursed shall the ground be on your account. It will grow thorns and thistles for you. You shall gain your bread by the sweat of your brow*." He sighed again, then all his many wrinkles wreathed upward in a smile. "It is as I predicted. My son has brought us relief. The vines flourish. The herds and flocks increase. But he has grown proud in his prosperity. I am lonely in my old age. I am glad that you have come."

The mammoth came out of the tent and came to them, putting his head on Lamech's knee. "The women keep telling me that I am welcome in my son's tent. But I will stay here, where my son was born, where his mother died. That is no reason for my son to refuse to come see me, because I choose to remain in my own tent. He is stiff-necked. What will he do in his turn when his sons want his tent?"

"Does he want your tent?"

"I have the deepest and best wells on the oasis. I have always given him all the water he needs for his vineyards, but he complains about having to fetch it. Too bad. I will stay in my own tent."

"Maybe," Sandy suggested, "your son is stubborn because his father is stubborn?"

The old man smiled reluctantly. "It could be so."

"If he doesn't come to see you, why don't you go see him?"

"It is too far for an old man to walk. I have given my camels and all my animals to my son. I keep only my groves and garden." Lamech reached out and patted Sandy's knee with his gnarled hand. "I hope you won't be wanting to leave right away, now that you are getting well. It is pleasurable having someone to share my tent."

Higgaion nudged the old man.

Lamech laughed. "You're a mammoth, my dear Higgaion. And while I have deep devotion for you, I am feeling the need of a human companion, especially during my last days."

"Your last days?" Sandy asked. "What do you mean?"

"I am not as old as my father, Methuselah, but I am older than *his* father, Enoch. Now, there was a strange man, my grandfather. He walked with El and then he was not. And he was younger than I. El has told me to number my days."

Sandy felt distinctly uncomfortable. "How many numbers?"

Lamech laughed. "Dear young giant, you know that numbers are merely many or few. The voice of El said few. Few can mean one turn of the moon, or several."

"Hey, wait a minute," Sandy said. "Grandfather Lamech, are you telling me that someone said you're going to die?"

Lamech nodded. "El."

"El what?"

"El. These are troubled times. Men's hearts are turning to evil. It is good that I will be able to go quietly. My years are seven hundred and seventy and seven—"

"Hey! Wait!" Sandy said. "Nobody lives that long. Where I come from."

Lamech pursed his lips. "We have not used our long years well."

Suddenly the starlight seemed cold. Sandy shivered. Lamech's fingers again touched his knee. "Don't worry. I won't leave you until you are all well, and reunited with your brother, and are both able to take care of yourselves and return home."

"Home," Sandy said wistfully, looking up at the stars. "I don't even know where home is, from here. I'm not sure how we got here, and I'm a lot less sure about how we're going to get home."

Higgaion raised his trunk to touch his ear, and Sandy noticed that the scarab beetle was there, bright as an earring. Sandy understood that the glorious seraph Adnarel sometimes took the form of a scarab beetle—but of course that was impossible. Now he looked at the bronze glitter, suddenly wondering.

Lamech mused, "Japheth asked me where I would go when I die." He smiled. Even in the starlight, the skin of his skull showed through the thin wisps of hair. "I thought my Grandfather Enoch might come back, or send some kind of message. I hope my son will put aside his stubbornness long enough to come and plant me in the ground."

Higgaion nudged him again, and the old man laughed. "Who knows? Perhaps I will come up again in the spring, like the desert flowers. Perhaps not. Very little is known about such things. After living for so many hundreds of years, I look forward to a rest."

The mammoth moved over to Sandy, standing on his stocky hind legs and putting his big forepaws on Sandy's knees, like a dog. Sandy picked him up, holding him tightly for comfort, and the pink tip of the trunk delicately patted his cheek. "Grandfather Lamech, I think I'd better go back to the tent. I'm cold."

Lamech looked first at Sandy, then at the mammoth. "Yes. This is enough for a first excursion."

Sandy went gratefully to his sleeping skins, and Higgaion lay down at Sandy's feet. Sandy tried not to scratch. The pink skin under the paper-like flakes was tender. He closed his eyes. He wanted to see Yalith. He wanted to talk to Dennys. How were they going to be able to get home from this strange desert land into which they had been cast and which was heaven knew where in all the countless solar systems in all the countless galaxies?

5 The Nephilim

Dennys was sleeping fitfully when he heard the tent flap move. He opened his eyes and could see only the small light of a stone lamp coming toward him. He called out in alarm. "Who is it?" Yalith or Oholibamah would not have needed the light.

He felt a gentle pressure, something soft touching his arm, and realized that it was a mammoth. He vaguely remembered seeing a mammoth when he had been in the big tent.

A bearded man squatted beside him. "We thought you might like Selah, our mammoth, for company, now that you are getting better."

"Thank you," Dennys said. "Who are you?"

"Yalith's father, Noah."

It was not always easy for Dennys to remember where he was. When his fever rose, he thought he was at home, and dreaming. When the fever dropped, he understood dimly that somehow or other he and Sandy had precipitated themselves into a primitive desert world inhabited by small brown people. He remembered Yalith, the beautiful, tiny person with amber hair and eyes who tended him gently. He remembered the slightly older person, and at least part of her name, Oholi, who poured first water and then unguents and oils onto his skin, and who seemed to know what to do to make him feel better. He remembered Japheth, Oholi's husband, who, like a shepherd, had carried Dennys to this tent, which he thought of as a strange kind of hospital.

He had not seen Yalith's father since he had been taken, half dead, from the big smelly tent to this smaller, quieter one. The piece of linen he had been given to lie on helped protect his raw, healing skin. Even so, it hurt to move. He shifted position carefully. "My brother Sandy, how is he?"

"Almost all well, I am told." Noah's deep voice was kind. The name had a familiar ring in this unfamiliar world, but Dennys could not place it in his fever-muddled mind. The man continued, "The women tell me he has made new skin. You, too, will be well soon."

Dennys sighed. That was still hard to believe, with the remains of his skin coming off in painful patches, leaving oozing misery until dark scabs formed. "When can I see my brother?"

"As soon as you are well. Not long."

"Where is he?"

"As you have been told. In my father Lamech's tent."

"I keep forgetting."

"That is from the sun fever."

"Yes. Brain fever, I think it used to be called in India."

"India?"

"Oh. Well. That's a place on our planet where the British—people with skin like mine—used to go to, oh, muck around with white men's burdens and stuff, and built an enormous empire. Anyhow, they couldn't take the sun. And their empire's gone. Thank you for taking such good care of me. How did you know the right things to do for burns?"

"It was mostly common sense," the man said. "Oholibamah can tell with her fingers how much fever you have, and we try to cool you accordingly. And she consulted with the seraphim about the use of herbs."

"Who are the seraphim?" Dennys asked.

The stocky brown man smiled. "You are better. This is the first time you have asked questions."

"You have been to see me before?"

"Several times."

Selah snuggled up against him, and he put his arm around her, and his skin was healed enough so that her fur did not scratch and hurt. "And seraphim?"

"They are sons of El. We do not know where they came from, or why they are here."

"Are they angels?"

"You have angels where you come from?"

"No," Dennys said. "But we don't have mammoths or virtual unicorns, either. I am not as much of a skeptic as I used to be."

"Skeptic?"

"Someone who doesn't believe in anything that can't be seen and touched and proved one hundred percent. Someone who has to have laboratory proof."

"Lab what?"

"Oh. Well. I guess you can't prove virtual particles any more easily than you can prove virtual unicorns."

"What kind of unicorns?"

"Oh. Just what I call them."

The man interrupted. "Are you feverish again?"

"No." Dennys touched the back of his hand to his cheek, which felt quite cool. "Sorry. Your name is—what?"

"Noah. How many times do I have to tell you?"

Noah. Noah and the flood. So they were on their own earth after all, and not in some far-flung galaxy. Somehow or other, he and Sandy had been flung through time into the pre-flood desert. That was a lot better than being in some unknown corner of the universe. Or was it? "I wish I had a Bible," he said.

"A—Perhaps you need a drink of something cool?"

"I'm all right. I'm sorry." There would not have been a Bible in Noah's time. Probably not even a written language. Not yet. Neither Dennys nor Sandy had given much of their concentration to Sunday school. They didn't go in for stories.

No? He remembered their mother reading to them every night until too much homework got in the way. What did she read? Stories. Greek and Roman myths. Indian tales, Chinese tales, African tales. Fairy tales. Bible stories.

Who was Noah? Noah and the flood. Noah built an ark and took his wife, and their sons and their sons' wives, and many animals, onto the ark. What about Yalith? He couldn't remember anything about Yalith. Or Oholi—Oholibamah. Japheth. Maybe that had a familiar ring.

Shem. Yes. Maybe. But not Elisheba. Elisheba was all right. She had rubbed ointment all over him one day, matter-of-factly, when something had taken Yalith and Oholi away, not flinching at the suppurating sores, the crusting scabs. She had talked through, at, and around him the day she had attended him in the hospital tent, and he remembered her muttering something about it being a shame to leave the old grandfather all alone in his tent with only a mammoth to take care of him.

Selah snuggled against Dennys's shoulder. He continued to try to think. There was Shem. And there was Ham. He barely remembered a small, pale man and a redheaded woman in the big tent that first night. "Is Higgaion all right?" he asked suddenly.

"Higgaion?" Noah sounded surprised. "He's helping take care of your brother."

"Are there many mammoths around?" Dennys asked.

"Very few. Many have been eaten by manticores, and most of the rest have fled to where they feel safer." Noah shook his head. "It is a hard time for mammoths. Hard times are coming for us all. El has told me that."

Dennis frowned. This pre-flood world was weird. Mammoths. Manticores. Virtual unicorns. Seraphim and—

"Who are the nephilim?" he asked.

Noah pulled at his beard. "Who knows? They are tall, and they have wings, though we seldom see them fly. They tell us that they come from El, and that they wish us well. We do not know. There is a rumor that they are like falling stars, that they may be falling stars, flung out of heaven."

"Seraphim, too?"

"We do not know. We do not know how it is that their skin is young and not yet shriveled from the sun, though they are ageless, it would seem—older, even, than my Grandfather Methuselah."

—Old as Methuselah. It had a familiar ring. Vaguely.

Dennys shifted on Matred's linen cloth. The remnant of his bundle of clothes had been found, and taken by Japheth and Oholibamah, to be aired and put away. In this hot land he would not need flannel shirts or cable-knit sweaters. He had been given a soft kid loincloth, and Yalith had told him that Sandy had been given one, too.

In this tent where he was recovering, the stench was less disturbing than in the big tent. Yalith had bathed him with water scented with herbs and flowers. Oholibamah had rubbed him with fragrant ointment. Both young women were reticent about where they came by the perfumes, and Dennys thought he had heard Yalith saying something about Anah and Mahlah. Anah: Ham's redheaded wife, he reminded himself. Mahlah was Yalith's sister, who, it appeared, seldom came home. Who were all these people he did not remember as being part of the story? He needed Sandy. Sandy might be able to suggest some way for them to get home before the flood. How much had this El told Noah?

Noah said, "El has told me that these are end times for us all. Perhaps we will have a great earthquake."

"An earthquake?"

Noah shrugged. "The mind of El is a great mystery."

"Is he good, this El?"

"Good and kind. Slow to anger, quick to turn again and forgive."

"But you still think he's going to nuke everybody?"

"What's that?"

"You think he's going to send some big disaster and wipe everybody out?"

Noah shook his head. "It is true, as El says, that people's hearts are turned to wickedness."

"Yalith's isn't," Dennys said. "Oholibamah's and Japheth's aren't. I'd be dead if it wasn't for them."

"And for my wife, Matred," Noah added. "I might not have let you stay in my tents had it not been for Matred." He looked thoughtfully at Dennys. "Sometimes I have wondered why I let the women insist on keeping you. But I think you mean us no harm."

"I don't. We don't. Listen, what about my brother? When can I see Sandy?"

"As you have been told, he is in my father's tent." Noah's voice indicated that the subject was now closed.

"Have you seen him? Sandy?" Dennys asked.

"I do not go to my father's tent."

"Why not?"

"He is a stiff-necked old man, insisting on staying alone in his own tent, with his wells, the best in the oasis."

"But why don't you go see him?" Dennys was baffled.

"He is old. It is nearly time for him to die. He can no longer tend to his crops."

"But don't you help him?"

"I have all I can do, taking care of my herds and my vineyards."

"But he's your father!"

"He should not be so stubborn."

"Listen, he's taking care of Sandy all by himself. He doesn't have Yalith or Oholibamah to do the nursing. Only the mammoth."

"One of the women takes him a light every night."

"But he's your father," Dennys protested. "Wouldn't he appreciate it if you took him the night-light?"

Before Noah's growl became audible, the tent flap shifted and a pelican waddled in, followed by Yalith. A pelican seemed a strange creature to appear in this desert place. The bird approached Dennys, then opened its enormous bill, and from it flowed a stream of cool, fresh water, filling the large bowl from which the women bathed him.

Dennys asked, "Hey, you've been here before, haven't you?"

Yalith spoke delightedly. "He is truly better! He's remembering things."

The water felt healing as Yalith dipped a cloth in it and cooled his skin. She knelt beside him and with the wet cloth touched some of the loosened scabs. "They will soon be off."

Dennys regarded the pelican. "Where did the water come from?"

"From Grandfather Lamech's. And the pelican has been kind enough to bring it to us, flying across the oasis."

The pelican nodded gravely to Dennys.

"Do you have a name?"

The pelican blinked.

Yalith said, "When he is a pelican, we usually call him pelican."

"When he is a pelican! What else is he?"

"Don't confuse the young giant," Noah said.

"I can't be much more confused than I am," Dennys expostulated. It was a relief to know that he was still on his own planet; even so, he felt lost, and far from anything familiar.

The pelican stretched its angled wings toward the roof hole, raised its beak, seemed to thin out and stretch upward, and suddenly a tall and radiant personage was looking down at Dennys.

"What—" he gasped.

"A seraph," Yalith said.

The glowing skin of the seraph was the color of Yalith's, and there were great silvery wings, and hair the color of the wings. Was it a man? A woman? Did it matter? Yet, with Yalith and Oholibamah, and even more with Anah, Dennys was very well aware that he was male and they were female.

The seraph raised its wings, then dropped them loosely. "Fear not. I am Alarid, and I have been helping with your healing. At last you are getting better. No. Don't try to stand. You are still too weak." Strong arms enfolded Dennys, and he was taken out of the tent and lowered onto a soft bed of moss. In the starlight, the moss shimmered like water.

"There," the seraph said. "So. I am Alarid. And you are the Den."

"Dennys."

"Den is simpler."

"And your name is Alarid? And what about Oholibamah?"

Alarid smiled gravely. "I take your point, Dennys. Forgive me. Now, I have conferred with my companion, Adnarel, who has been helping to take care of the Sand."

"Sandy. Alexander."

"Alexander? Is there not an Alexander who wants to conquer the world?"

"Not in our time," Dennys said. "Way back in history. Not as far back as now. But back."

"Ah," Alarid said. "I tend to see time in pleats. Now, Dennys, there seems to be considerable confusion over who and what you are, and why you are here."

In his weakness, Dennys could not hold back the tears which sprang to his eyes. "We are fifteen-year-old boys who come from a long time away."

"You come from a far time, and yet you speak the Old Language?"

"The what?"

"The Old Language, the language of creation, of the time when the stars were made, and the heavens and the waters and all creatures. It was the language which was spoken in the Garden—"

"What garden?"

"The Garden of Eden, before the story was bent. It is the language which is still, and will be, spoken by all the stars which carry the light."

"Then," Dennys said flatly, "I don't know why I speak it."

"And speak it with ease," Alarid said.

"Does Sandy speak it, too?" Dennys asked.

Alarid nodded. "You were both speaking it when you met Japheth and Higgaion in the desert, were you not?"

"We certainly didn't realize it," Dennys said. "We thought we were speaking our own language."

Alarid smiled. "It *is* your own language, so perhaps it is best that you didn't realize it. Do others of your time and place speak the Old Language?"

"I don't know. Sandy and I aren't any good at languages."

"How can you say that," Alarid demanded, "when you have the gift of the original tongue?"

"Hey. I don't know. Sandy and I are the squares of the family. Our older sister and our little brother are the special ones. We're just the ordinary—"

Alarid interrupted him. "Because that is how you are, or because that is how you choose to be?"

Dennys looked at the seraph, his eyes widening. "What happened to the Old Language?"

"It was broken at Babel."

"Babel?"

"The tower of human pride and arrogance. It has not happened yet, in this time you are in now. You do not know the story?"

Dennys blinked. "I think I remember something. People built a big tower, and for some reason they all began to speak in different languages, and couldn't understand each other anymore. It was in, oh, prehistory, and it's a story to, sort of, explain why there are so many different languages in the world."

"But underneath them all," Alarid said, "is the original language, the old tongue, still in communion with the ancient harmonies. It is a privilege to meet one who still has the under-hearing."

"Hey," Dennys said. "Listen. I guess because we got here so unexpectedly and everything was so strange, and we didn't have time to think, and when we met Japheth it just seemed natural to speak to him—"

"It is a special gift," Alarid told him.

"We're not special, neither Sandy nor I. We're just the sort of ordinary kid who gets along without making waves."

"Where in the future," Alarid asked him abruptly, "do you come from?"

"A long, long way," Dennys said. "We live at the end of the twentieth century."

Alarid closed his eyes. "A time of many wars."

"Yes."

"And the heart of the atom has been revealed."

"Yes."

"You have soiled your waters and your air."

"Yes."

"Because you speak the Old Language there must be some reason for you to be here. But for the future to touch the past can be dangerous. It could cause a paradox. How did you get here?"

"I'm not sure." Dennys frowned, then added, "Our father is a physicist who specializes in space travel, in the tesseract."

"Ah, yes. But space travel is supposed to deal with space, not time."

Dennys said, "But you can't separate space and time. I mean, space/time is a continuum, and . . ."

Yalith and Noah came out of the tent, and Yalith put her hand lightly against Alarid's. "Look, he is very pale. You are tiring him."

"Be careful of our young giant," Noah warned.

Alarid regarded Dennys. "You are right. This is enough for tonight." The seraph's eyes were compassionate, and their silver-green seemed to darken. "I am glad that you are better, and that you are coming back to yourself. Please, be very careful what you say, what you do. Be careful that you do not change anything."

"Listen," Dennys said. "All I want is to go home. To my own time. I'm just grateful to be on my own planet, and I'm not a bit interested in rewriting the Bible." Did Alarid know that there was going to be a Bible? That there was going to be a flood? He looked at the seraph, whose face, serene and severe at the same time, did not change expression. Dennys was willing to accept that Alarid and the pelican who brought the water were somehow one and the same, but he was not willing to accept that his presence in this time and place might have an effect on anyone except himself. And, of course, Sandy.

"Sleep well, Dennys," Alarid said. "Yalith and Oholibamah will continue to take good care of you."

—Yalith, Dennys thought. For Yalith he might be willing to change history.

Sandy could not sleep. Not only was the tent hot, but Higgaion was snoring. Grandfather Lamech was not. Grandfather Lamech was tossing. Turning. Grunting. Sighing.

At last, Sandy could not stand it any longer. He crawled over to Grandfather Lamech's sleeping skins. "Grandfather, are you awake?"

"Um."

"What's the matter?"

The old man grunted.

Sandy spoke to him as he would have to Dennys. "Come on. I know something's bothering you. What is it?"

"El spoke to me."

Sandy tried to peer at him through the dark. Did this mean that the old man was about to die? Right then? That night?

But the old man said, "Great troubles are coming after I die. Terrible things are going to happen."

"What kind of terrible things?"

Lamech moved restlessly. "El did not say. Only that men's hearts are evil and hard, and it repents El that he has made human creatures."

"So what's he going to do about it?"

"I don't know," Lamech said. "But I fear for my son and his family. El plans to spare no one. I fear for Yalith. I fear for you, Sand, so far from your home."

"Oh, I can take care of myself," Sandy said automatically. But his words sounded hollow.

Yalith and Oholibamah came to Dennys in the deep dark just before dawn.

"You need to get out of the tent into some air," Oholibamah told him. "You need to exercise. You will not recover until you walk about under the sky."

"Starlight is healing." Yalith's voice was as gentle, he thought, as a small brook. But there were no brooks in this arid land.

He followed them out of the tent. Each took one of his hands, and their hands were small as children's. They walked past the grove which served as outhouse, which was as far from the tents as he had ventured. Beyond them, the large tent was a dark shadow, with the smaller tents clustered about it.

His bare feet were still tender, and he walked gingerly. The girls guided him to the smoothest ways, until the sharp dry grasses and pebbles gave way to sand, and they were in the desert. The sand felt cool to the burning soles of his feet.

They paused at a low slab of white rock, which cast a silvery shadow on the sand. "Japheth and I agreed that this is as far as you should go," Oholibamah said. "Let's sit here and rest for a while. We'll take you back to the tent before dawn."

He sat between them on the rock, leaning back on his elbows so that he could look up at the sky. "I've never seen so many stars."

"You don't have stars where you come from?" Yalith asked.

"Oh, yes, we have stars. But our atmosphere is not as clear as yours, and not nearly as many stars are visible."

Yalith clasped Dennys's arm tightly. "It is frightening when the stars are hidden by the swirling sand. Their song is distorted, and I can't hear what they say."

"What the stars say?" Dennys asked.

"Listen," Yalith suggested. "Alarid says you are able to understand."

At first, Dennys heard only the desert silence. Then, in the distance, he heard the roar of a lion. Behind them, on the oasis, the birds chirred sleepily, not yet ready for their dawn concert. A few baboons called back and forth. He listened, listened, focusing on one bright pattern of stars. Closed his eyes. Listened. Seemed to hear a delicate, crystal chiming. Words. *Hush. Heal. Rest. Make peace. Fear not.* He laughed in excitement. Opened his eyes to twinkling diamonds.

Yalith laughed, too. "What did they say?"

"They told me—I think—to get well, and—and to make peace. And not to be afraid. At least, I think I heard them, and I don't think it was just my imagination." Suddenly he was glad that Sandy was not there. Sandy was pragmatic. Sandy would likely think Dennys was hallucinating from sunstroke. At school, if Dennys got lost in a daydream, Sandy always managed to cover for him.

"Yes, that is what the stars told you." Yalith turned toward him with a delighted smile, very visible in the starlight. "You see!" she said to Oholibamah. "It is not everybody who can listen to the night. If the stars told you to make peace, Den, perhaps you will be the one to make peace between my father and my grandfather."

"A big perhaps," Oholibamah said.

"But maybe, maybe he can." She turned back to Dennys. "What else do you hear?"

Dennys listened again. Heard the wind rattling the palm leaves like sheafs of paper. There seemed to be words in the wind, but he could not make any sense out of them. "I can't understand anything clearly—"

Yalith withdrew her fingers and clasped her hands together. Shook her head. Opened her eyes. "The wind seems to be talking of a time when she will blow very hard, over the water. That's strange. The nearest water is many days away from here. I cannot understand what she is trying to say."

"The wind blows where she wills," Oholibamah said. "Sometimes she is gentle and cooling. Sometimes she is fierce and blows in our eyes and stings our skin like insects and we have to hide in the tents until she is at peace again. It is good, dear Den, that you have not come at a time when the wind blows hot against the sand. You will heal better now, at the time when she is more gentle, and the grapes and gardens grow."

They were silent then, listening to the dawn noises becoming louder, as birds and baboons began to get ready to greet the day. Tentatively, Dennys reached for Yalith's hand. She gave his fingers a little squeeze, then freed herself and jumped up. "It is time we took you back to the tent. This is more than enough for a first excursion. How do you feel?"

"Wonderful." Then, acknowledging: "A little tired." It would be good to lie down on the soft linen spread over the skins. To sleep a little. To have something cool to drink. He stifled a yawn.

"Come." Oholibamah held out her strong hands. To his surprise, he needed her help in getting up.

When Yalith and Oholibamah needed ointments and unguents for Dennys's burned skin, Anah, or Mahlah, if she happened to be home, would take them across the oasis to the close cluster of houses and shops to meet Tiglah, Anah's sister.

"I don't like it," Japheth said to his wife. "I don't like your going to such places."

She bent toward him to kiss him. "We don't go in. I wouldn't take Yalith into such a place even if Mahlah—"

Japheth gave a shout of anger and anguish. "What has happened to Mahlah!"

Oholibamah said, softly, "We all have choices to make, dear one, and we do not all choose the same way."

"Why can't I get what you need for you?"

"Oh, love, it is a house for women. You would not be welcome."

"I have seen men coming out. And nephilim."

"Japheth. My own. Please don't argue. We'll be all right. Anah is tough."

"And Mahlah?"

Oholibamah put her arms around her husband, pressed her cheek against his. Did not answer.

Mahlah went with Oholibamah and Yalith less and less frequently, because she was less and less often in the home tent. And when she was there, she came in late, after everybody else was asleep, then slept late herself, and managed to avoid confrontation with Matred.

Matred, herself, allowed Mahlah to avoid her. She was waiting for her daughter to come to her and her husband with Ugiel, according to custom, but Ugiel did not come, and Mahlah did not speak, and Matred said nothing to Noah of Mahlah's betrothal to a nephil. Until the betrothal was made formal, and recognized by Mahlah's family, there would be no talk of marriage.

Marriages were often casual affairs, no more than an agreement between the two sets of parents, with the bride's mother and father bringing her to the tent of the groom. Matred liked to have things done properly, not overdone, but well done. Yalith and Mahlah's two older sisters, Seerah and Hoglah, had been taken to their husbands' tents after Matred and Noah had prepared a feast, with plenty of Noah's good wine.

Elisheba, Shem's wife, had come quietly to Noah's compound and Shem's tent, accompanied by her widowed father, and bearing several gold rings, and her teraphim, the small figures of her household gods. Anah, Matred said, had had a vulgar wedding, with crowds of people, many uninvited. There were musicians, dancers, and far too much wine, inferior, at that—who would dare compete with Noah's wine?—for far too many days. Such excesses were not only unnecessary, they were unseemly.

Cleaning out the big tent with Yalith's help, Matred said, "I do not understand Mahlah."

Yalith shook out a sleeping skin. "Neither do I. I wish she would come speak to you and Father, instead of avoiding you."

Matred fiercely beat the dust out of one of the floor skins. "If your father knew what she's up to, he'd be furious. There's something on his mind, something he's not telling me about, or he'd have noticed her strange behavior. You think that this Ugh—"

"Ugiel."

"That nephil—you think he means to marry her?"

"I don't know." Yalith scrubbed out one of the stone lamps with sand. "Mahlah thinks so."

"Speak to her," Matred begged. "Try to make her see reason. All she needs is to come to us with her nephil and tell us that they are betrothed, and we will make all the arrangements for a wedding feast."

"I'll try," Yalith said, "but I'm not sure she'll listen." Mahlah had always been closer to and more like the older sisters than Yalith, the youngest, the different one. "I'll try," she reassured her mother.

The next day she went with Oholibamah and Anah to get a fresh supply of the ointment that softened Dennys's scabs. Perhaps Mahlah would be with the redheaded Tiglah, and Yalith could talk with her then.

Anah walked slowly, with her usual undulating of hips. Yalith and Oholibamah walked on ahead.

"Tiglah frightens me," Yalith whispered to Oholibamah. "I know she's Anah's sister, and she is probably the most beautiful woman on the oasis, but—"

"Her beauty is for sale," Oholibamah stated flatly. "But there is no reason to be afraid of her."

They turned onto the narrow path which ran between low white stone buildings. "I don't like coming here," Yalith murmured.

"I don't like it, either," Oholibamah said, "but there is no other way to get the salves for the Den. The last of his scabs will be off in a few days. Then we can forget the ointment. The herbal water the pelican brings will be enough."

"Den is getting better," Yalith said. "That's one good thing."

"Only one?" Oholibamah laughed.

Yalith shuddered. "Everything seems to be changing. Mahlah avoids our parents. And my father keeps hearing the Voice in the vineyards, and whatever it says is upsetting him, but he won't tell us what El says."

"What El says is good." Oholibamah smiled. "El said that Japheth was to marry. That is why I am here."

"You wouldn't rather have waited?"

"I love Japheth." Oholibamah's voice was tender. "I know we were both very young and unready for marriage. But we love each other. When the time comes, we will have children together."

Yalith sighed. "I would like to love someone the way you love Japheth."

"Be patient, little sister. Your time will come."

They had reached the white house with the brightly beaded curtains at the entry, the house where Tiglah got the ointments they needed, and they stopped to wait for Anah, who made it very clear that she was doing them a great favor in being the go-between. The beads glittered and jangled, and Tiglah came out, followed by Mahlah—Tiglah with her head of radiant red hair, Mahlah with her cascade of black hair, the two girls startling foils for each other.

"Where's Anah?" Tiglah asked.

"She's coming." Oholibamah looked back down the path to where Anah was slowly following them.

"Mahlah!" Yalith exclaimed. "I'm glad to see you. I need to talk to you."

Mahlah raised her hands and pushed back a thick fall of black hair. "That's funny. I want to talk to you, too. Shall we go inside?"

"No." Yalith drew back. "Please—"

"I could have your hair brushed," Mahlah coaxed, "the way Tiglah's and mine is, so it would look more beautiful."

"No," Yalith repeated.

Mahlah shrugged. "We can sit over here then, while Anah and Oholibamah go with Tiglah to get the ointment." She led Yalith a little way down the path to a low wall. Yalith, with sudden and unexpected shock, saw that Mahlah's usually flat belly was softly rounding.

"Mahlah," she urged. "Please, please, you and Ugiel please come to our parents and tell them that you're betrothed."

Mahlah's little hands proudly touched the small roundness. "And will be married soon."

"Then please come and tell them. Mother will need time to prepare a wedding feast."

"No, she won't," Mahlah said. "That is not how things are done with the nephilim. I will have a nephil wedding."

"But Mother—"

Again Mahlah's little hands stroked her stomach. "I'm sorry, really, I'm sorry. But she had it her own way with our sisters. She'll probably have it her own way with you. So she'll just have to let me do it my way."

"But why? Isn't the old way good enough for you?"

Mahlah laughed. "Customs change. We have to move with the times." There was a slight hiss to her speech which Yalith had never heard before. She sounded more like Ugiel than like Mahlah. The sisters sat side by side on the wall, the silence between them becoming more and more uncomfortable, until at last Yalith broke it.

"What did you want to see me about?"

"Can't you guess?"

"No."

"Eblis."

Yalith looked at her in surprise. "But why—"

"He likes you," Mahlah said. "He says he has offered to teach you."

"No—"

"Why not?"

"I'm taking care of the Den. That's why we're here, to get salve for him."

Again Mahlah sounded more like Ugiel than like Yalith's sister.

"That's all very noble. But it needn't stop you from going out with Eblis. Don't you realize what an honor that is, to have Eblis interested in you?" She sounded strangely sibilant.

"I know he does me much honor." Yalith's voice was low.

"What's wrong, then?"

"I have to stay with the Den," Yalith whispered.

"I know you're taking good care of him. But Oholi is there, too, isn't she?"

"She—she is Japheth's wife. She has to be in her own tent. She tells me what to do, but—"

"Little sister," Mahlah said. "Don't be foolish."

Yalith looked down at her long, straight toes. Blurted out, "I don't care about Eblis as much as I do about the Den and the Sand."

"What!" Mahlah was scandalized.

"You heard me."

"But we don't know if they're even human!"

"We know that the nephilim are not," Yalith retorted.

"They're more than human," Mahlah said proudly. "The two—what are they? twins?—they seem subhuman."

"No," Yalith protested. "They're human, I know they are."

"Giants human?"

"Yes."

"And you think if you start going out with giants, human or no, our parents wouldn't be upset?"

"Everybody loves them . . ."

"Yes? Anyhow, they're too young, much too young."

"I know that." Yalith hung her head even lower. "But I think that, where they come from, years are counted differently than here. And I would be willing to wait."

"For which one?" Mahlah demanded.

A slow flush spread across Yalith's cheeks. She still thought of the twins as one person divided into two places. "I saw the Sand first, in Grandfather Lamech's tent, and I have helped bring the Den back to life when he was nearly dead."

"That is not enough reason for this stupidity. Eblis can give you anything you want."

"Even if I want the twins?"

"Don't be a fool," Mahlah snapped, and jumped down from the wall as Anah and Oholibamah came toward them, Oholibamah carrying a small jar.

"Well, Mahlah." Anah looked at her pointedly. "Are you getting ready to move into your own tent?"

Mahlah smiled a secret smile and tossed her head so that the dark hair glinted in the light. "I will not have a tent. I will have a house, a house of white stones." She drew back as a snake uncoiled at her feet, spreading a jeweled hood. "Ugiel—" she gasped.

For a moment of mirage, the snake seemed to uncoil upward, to raise great lavender wings, to quiver with white skin and amethyst eyes. Then the mirage was gone, and the snake undulated across the path and disappeared into a clump of scrubby palmettos.

Yalith reached for Oholibamah's hand.

Anah gave Mahlah a malicious smile. "Is he playing tricks with you?"

Mahlah raised her head proudly. "Ugiel comes to me only when I am alone." She turned back to Yalith, asking in such a low voice that she excluded the others, "If it were not for the young giants, would you go with Eblis?"

"I don't know," Yalith said. "I don't know."

Mahlah spoke in a louder voice. "Tell our parents I'll be sure to let them know when I'm married."

"Couldn't you bring yourself to tell them, beforehand?" Yalith begged.

Mahlah shrugged. "We'll see. I have to go now." And she turned back to the low white house and shouldered her way through the tinkling curtain of beads.

"Let's go," Anah said. "I have other things to do." And instead of dawdling as she had done on the way in, she strode off impatiently.

Oholibamah spoke calmly. "It's really very good of Anah, and of Tiglah, too, to get the ointments for us."

"They aren't doing it for nothing," Yalith said. "I gave them all my share of the figs, and the crop was good this year. And you gave them all your almonds."

Oholibamah stated a known fact. "Anah and Tiglah don't know how to do something for nothing. That's how they are."

"But Mahlah wasn't like that," Yalith protested. "She's changed. I don't know her anymore."

She jumped as a rat scuttled across her toes. Again there was a flickering of height, of wings and brilliant eyes, and then there was only the sleek body of the rat. Yalith thought of the dragon/lizard Eblis, who could offer her more than she could dream. And then she thought of the twins, of Sandy bowing to her in her grandfather's tent, of Dennys sitting with her at night—Dennys, who was able to understand the language of the stars.

And she knew she would never go with Eblis.

She turned, to see tears in Oholibamah's eyes. "Oholi," she started in surprise.

Oholibamah reached up to wipe away her tears, smiled her quick smile. "This morning I saw my face reflected in the water jar. Oh, Yalith, little Yalith, I love my father, and now I don't know if he is my father, after all."

Yalith took her sister-in-law's hand. "If you love him, he is your father, no matter what."

Oholibamah nodded gratefully. "Thank you, little sister. I needed to hear that."

"You are my brother's wife," Yalith continued, "and my friend. And if—well, if the nephilim are related to the seraphim, which my father believes, then you are like the seraphim."

"Hurry up," Anah called, and beckoned to them imperiously.

"We're coming," Oholibamah said. And they hurried toward the central section of the oasis, where Noah's vineyards were, and his grazing grounds, and his tents. And where Dennys was waiting for them.

The moon set, its path whiter than the desert sands dwindling into shadow. The stars moved in their joyous dance across the sky. The horizon was dark with that deep darkness which comes just before the dawn.

A vulture flew down, seemingly out of nowhere, stretching its naked neck, settling its dark feathers.

—Vultures are underestimated. Without us, disease would wipe out all life. We clean up garbage, feces, dead bodies of man and beast. We are not appreciated.

No sound was heard and yet the words seemed scratched upon the air.

A scarab beetle burrowed up out of the sand and blinked at the vulture.—It is true. You help keep the world clean. I appreciate you.

And it disappeared beneath the sand.

A crocodile crawled across the desert, lumbering along clumsily, far from its native waters. It was followed by the dragon/lizard, who stretched his leather wings, showing off. A dark, hooded snake slithered past them both.

A small, brown, armored creature, not much bigger than the scarab beetle, skittered along beside the snake.—We are invulnerable. We have survived the fire of the volcanoes, the earthquakes that pushed the continents apart and raised the mountain ranges. We are immortal. We cover the planet.

A bat, brighter than gold, swooped low over the cockroach.—You are proud, and you can survive fire and ice, but I could eat you if I had to. I hope I never have to.

And the golden bat soared high, a bright flash against the dark.

A tiny mimicry of a crocodile, with a blunt nose, a skink scrabbled along beside the crocodile and the dragon/lizard.—I am small, and swift, and my flesh is not edible and causes damage to the brain. I am the way that I am. That is how I am made.

On the skink's back, a flea tried to dig through the armored flesh.— I, too, am the way that I am.

A shrill whine cut across the clear air. A mosquito droned.—I, too. I, too. I will feast on your blood.

A small, slimy worm wriggled across the sand, leaving a thin trail. A slug's viscous path followed.—I am not like the snail, needing a house. I am sufficient unto myself.

A red ant crawled along the dragon/lizard's wing, and held tight as it tried to shake the biting insect off. A rat, sleek and well filled, wriggled its nose and whiskers and looked at the vulture's naked neck.—I, too, eat the filth off the streets. I eat flesh. I prefer living flesh, but I will take what I can get. I, too, help keep the world clean.

No sound was heard. Like negative light, the words cracked the desert night.

The twelve oddly assorted creatures began to position themselves into a circle.

The nephilim.

Oholibamah lay in Japheth's arms on a large, flat stone a short walk into the desert. So intent were they in each other that they did not notice the lion pacing past them, the pelican flying high in the sky, the scarab beetle coming out of the sand.

"My beloved," Japheth whispered into the pearly shell of Oholibamah's ear. "My mother spoke to me about it long ago. If you have nephil blood, it explains some of your healing power."

"But I don't know—it isn't certain—"

Japheth covered her mouth with his. Then pulled back just enough to say, "You are my wife, and we are one, and that is all that matters."

And they were one. And it was good.

Yalith left the tent and went outside to wait for dawn. She had spent over an hour working at Dennys's scabs, carefully pulling off those which were loose enough. Most of the oozing sores had healed. More and more of Dennys's care was given over to her, as Oholibamah could trust her to do what the boy needed. Oholibamah, after all, had duties in her own tent.

Matred prepared meals for the boy, soups, and mashed fruits which were soft enough for him to swallow.

"But what do we do with him when he is well?" Noah asked his wife.

"He is our guest," Matred said. "We ask him what we can do to help him."

"He wants to go home," Yalith said.

"Yes, but where is home?" her mother asked.

Now Yalith crossed one of her father's vineyards, went to the small grove that the women used, and relieved herself, then walked on until she came to where the desert lapped whitely against the oasis. She picked up a handful of the fine sand and rubbed it against her palms, between her fingers, to clean them.

The moon had set, and the dawn stars were low on the horizon. She would take a long nap the next day during the heat of the sun. Often, the best sleeping was done then.

In the coolness just before morning she liked to go sit on one of the great exposed rocks and rest, and listen to the slow song of the setting stars. Lamech, her grandfather, had taught her how to listen to the stars. Only Yalith and Japheth, of Noah and Matred's children, could understand the celestial language.

Matred tended to think it a waste of time. "I have too much to do, keeping tent. How else would I keep the soup pot full for the poor who come to us for food? Who would keep the manticore from eating Selah if I didn't have boiling wine to throw in its ugly face? Who would see to it that the great auk's eggs aren't stolen? Who else dares to speak to the gorgons and griffins? And what with everybody's appetite, I never have a chance to get away from the hearth."

Yalith did her fair share of the work, and now she was doing most of Mahlah's, too, but she needed time to herself, to listen to what the stars might have to say. Her father heard a Voice in the vineyards, but it seemed to Yalith that in the quiet dawn there were voices all around her, waiting to speak, waiting for her to hear. When the birds woke and started their orchestra, the other voices would be quiet. She was filled with a vague sense of foreboding, but she had to come and listen.

When she was not listening for whatever it was that was going to be spoken, she found her mind sliding to thoughts of the twins. As she spent more time with Dennys, nursing him through the chills and fever of his delirium, she saw that the twins might look alike but they were definitely not one boy in two skins.

The twins were often the topic of conversation in the big tent in the evenings—how they were alike, and how they were different. It was generally accepted that they must be some strange breed of giant, from the other side of the mountains. Although they were immensely tall, they were also unbelievably young.

"Fifteen, he told me," Matred said one evening when it was she who had taken the lamp to Grandfather Lamech, and some of her special broth to Sandy. "Fifteen," she repeated to the others in the big tent. "At fifteen, our men are still children. The Sand and the Den are not babies. I simply do not understand."

"The Den is certainly not a baby," Yalith replied. "Now that he is getting better, he is full of questions. He wants to know what the herbs are that the pelican puts in the water, and what the salves are made of."

"The Sand," Elisheba said, "wants to know where the salves come from. They are certainly full of questions." She laughed her hearty laugh and told them that Sandy had wanted to know who ran the oasis. Was there a mayor? Or a selectman?

The words had no meaning. Elisheba had told Sandy that those who sought power were greedy, wanting gifts, and bribes, and willing to steal from the poor. "Shem hunts for us all, and I help with the wine-making," she said contentedly. "That is enough for us. We have plenty to eat, and to give to those in need. Matred is a good mother to us all, with her fine sons and daughters."

"Mahlah and Yalith are not married yet," Matred prodded.

"They are still young," Noah said.

"I thought the Voice told you—"

"Not about Mahlah and Yalith. They should have time to grow up."

"I think," Matred said pointedly, "that Mahlah is grown up."

Yalith sat on the cool, starlit stone, the echoes of the evening's conversation still in her ears. She wondered if Matred had noticed the swelling of Mahlah's belly—Mahlah, whose betrothal to the nephil was not yet acknowledged by her mother.

Yalith was so deep in thought that the stars had to hiss at her to get her attention.

6 Adnarel and the Quantum Leap

Yalith looked up and saw a circle of strange animals. In the center of the circle stood Mahlah, looking pale and frightened. Her dark hair covered her breasts, her body. Yalith started to cry out, to leap up and go to her sister, but it seemed that a firm hand came across her mouth, held her down on the rock.

The cobra uncoiled, hood spreading, swaying as though to unheard music, then stretched up and up into the loveliness of lavender wings, and amethyst eyes that reflected the starlight. "I, Ugiel, call my brothers. Naamah!"

The vulture stretched its naked neck, until great black wings and coal-black eyes in a white face were revealed.

"Rofocale!"

A shrill drone, a mosquito whine, and then there stood on the desert a nephil with wings of flaming red and eyes like garnets.

"Eisheth!"

The crocodile opened its mouth, showing its terrible teeth. It appeared to swallow itself, and vomit forth a tall, green-winged, emerald-eyed nephil.

Yalith trembled as she saw the dragon/lizard.

"Eblis!"

He burst from his scales, beautiful; awe-inspiring.

"Estael!"

The cockroach scuttled a few inches and then burst open and dust rose, and dissipated to reveal another of the nephilim.

"Ezequen!" The skink.

"Negarsanel!" The flea.

"Rugziel!" The worm.

"Rumael!" The slug.

"Rumjal!" The red ant.

"Ertrael!" The rat.

One by one, the creatures transformed themselves into the nephilim with their white skin and brilliant, multi-colored wings.

Ugiel raised his arms. "I, Ugiel, in the presence of my brother nephilim, take to wife Mahlah, penultimate daughter of Noah and Matred."

Mahlah slowly moved toward him, was folded in the great wings.

Yalith fought for breath. Her chest felt constricted, and she gasped for air.

Then she saw that there was another circle, outside the circle of the nephilim.

The pelican who daily brought water for her pitcher stretched himself into the tall, bright personage with silvery hair and wings. "Alarid!"

Light seemed to flash against the bronze shell of the scarab beetle, who rose up in a rush of golden wings and burnished skin. "Adnarel!"

A tawny lion with a great ruff of fur about its neck rose on its hind legs and stretched into its seraphic form. "Aariel!" The golden tips of his wings glimmered in the starlight.

A golden snake, as large as the cobra, but as bright as the cobra was dark, called out as it was transformed, "Abasdarhon!"

One by one, the seraphim called out their names as they changed form. A golden bat shot up into the air. "Abdiel!"

A ruffled white owl widened its round silver eyes, and the eyes were suddenly the silver eyes in a seraphim's face, and moon-blue wings seemed to touch the sky. "Akatriel!"

A white leopard, swift as the wind, called, "Abuzohar!"

A soft, furred mouse rose, crying, "Achsah!"

By the mouse a tiger moved, stood, stretched. "Adabiel!"

A white camel and a giraffe rose moments apart.

"Admael!"

"Adnachiel!"

Lastly, a white goose flew skyward, its wings changing to snow-white. "Aalbiel!"

There seemed a healing in the calling of their names.

Although the circle of seraphim was outside that of the nephilim, when they spread their great wings to the fullest span the wing tips touched.

Likewise, the nephilim raised their wings, turning so that they faced the seraphim, and the glory of their wings brushed.

"Brothers," Alarid said. "You are still our brothers."

Ugiel touched his lavender wings to Alarid's silver ones. "No. We have renounced you and all that you stand for. This planet is ours. Its people are ours. We do not know why you stay."

Alarid replied firmly, "Because, no matter how loudly you renounce us, we are still brothers, and that can never be changed."

For a fragment of a second, Ugiel seemed more cobra than nephil. Yalith choked back a scream. Mahlah, small and frail, still stood in the center of the circle, protected only by her dark hair.

Eblis, shimmering in and out of his dragon/lizard form, touched wings with Aariel. "We have made our choice. We have forsworn heaven."

"Then the earth will never be yours." Aariel was once more a lion, and with a great roar he galloped away, vanishing into the far horizon.

The two circles broke up with a great flurry of brilliant wings. Yalith blinked, and when she opened her eyes, she saw only a tall, lavender-winged nephil, with his arm tenderly about Mahlah—Mahlah, who was no smaller than any other woman of the oasis, but who came barely to Ugiel's waist.

Yalith sat on the rock, as though frozen into motionlessness. Ugiel's wings spread, wrapped gracefully, protectingly, about Mahlah. Yalith thought she caught a whiff of stone. Then there was a flash, not bright like the unicorns', but a flash of darkness even darker than the night, and then the desert in front of her was empty. Mahlah and Ugiel were gone.

She cried out in fear.

"Little one," a gentle voice spoke behind her. "Why are you afraid?"

She turned to see Eblis, his purple wings lifted so that they seemed to mingle with the night sky.

"Mahlah—" she said. "I am afraid for Mahlah."

"Why fear, my precious? Ugiel will take care of her. As I will take care of you. There are rumors on the oasis of fearful things to come, the volcano erupting, the mountain falling, earthquakes such as have never been felt before, terrible heavings unlike the silly little tremors you hardly notice."

She nodded. "I think my father is afraid. But what can we do? If the volcano is going to erupt, there is no way we can stop it."

"No. Nor can you run from it. But I will protect you."

"How?"

"Nephilim have powers. If you will come with me, I will keep you safe."

"Come with you? Where?"

"I will make a home for you full of lovely things. You will no longer have to sleep on rough skins, still smelling of animals. I will give you food and wine such as you have never tasted. Come, my lovely little jewel, come with me."

"When—" She faltered.

"Now. Tonight."

She thought of the two circles, the seraphim and the nephilim. It was Eblis who was offering her protection, not Aariel. Mahlah had gone with Ugiel, not with Alarid. "What about my family?" she asked. "What about my twins?"

"Only you," Eblis said. "That is as far as my powers extend."

She looked up at the stars. Shook her head. "Twin Den still needs me."

"Love is patient," Eblis said. "I will wait. But I think that in the end you will come to me." His hand soothed her soft, burnished hair, and there was pleasure in his touch.

She blinked, looked at the brilliant pattern of stars, and it seemed that she could see Sandy bowing to her in her grandfather's tent, could see Dennys holding her hand as the pain of his burns made him cry out.

Eblis touched her hair again. "I will wait."

Japheth came to visit Dennys, examined him carefully, touching the remaining scabs, gently pulling off a flaking strip of paper-thin skin. "You are better."

"Much better." Dennys smiled at him, and the smile no longer seemed to crack the burned skin of his face. "I go out at night with Yalith and Oholibamah, and we listen to the stars."

"It is good that you can hear the stars." Japheth sat beside Dennys on a pile of skins, putting his hands, stained purple from winemaking, on his brown knees.

Dennys looked troubled. "They keep telling me to make peace. At least, I think that is what I hear the stars saying to me."

Japheth nodded. "Oholi told me. Peace between my father and grandfather. Have you talked to my father about his quarrel with Grandfather Lamech?"

"Yes, once when he came to visit me. But I didn't really understand what their quarrel is about."

"Water," Japheth said flatly. "That is what most quarrels on the oasis are about. Grandfather has the best and deepest wells on the oasis, and he's letting his own gardens and groves go to seed in his old age."

"But he lets you take all the water you need from his wells, doesn't he?"

Japheth sighed, then laughed. "Oh, Den, the quarrel is so old and stupid I think that both my father and grandfather have forgotten what it is about. They are both stiff-necked and stubborn."

"Your grandfather—what is he like? I mean, if he's so old, is he able to take proper care of Sandy?"

"Oh, I'm sure he is. Grandfather Lamech is as hospitable as our mother, and kind, and gentle. It was he who taught Yalith and me to listen to the stars, and to understand the wind, and to love El." He sighed again. "Oh, Den, I'm sorry to involve you in our family quarrel."

Dennys sighed, too. He did not reply. He looked up at the brazen sky, behind which were the stars. And they had already involved him. He shivered.

Grandfather Lamech and Higgaion began taking Sandy out in the daylight, not into the direct and brutal sunlight, but in the shade of a thick grove. Like Dennys, Sandy wore only a loinskin. His underclothes were folded with the rest of his things, in case they were ever needed again. The loinskin, unlike his own clothes, could be scrubbed clean with sand, and eventually discarded and replaced. He liked the freedom of the loinskin, liked the way his own skin had healed and was slowly turning a rosy tan.

Adnarel came by Grandfather Lamech's tent almost every day, and as Sandy grew stronger and more willing to accept that he was not going to wake up in his own bed at home, he grew more aware of his surroundings and of the tender care given him by the tiny ancient man.

"Hey, Grandfather Lamech," he said one morning after breakfast, "now that I'm better, it's time I stopped free-loading."

The old man looked at him questioningly. "What's that?"

"What can I do to help?" Sandy asked. "I've never done any cooking, but isn't there stuff outdoors I could do to be useful? At home, Dennys and I chop wood and mow the lawn and we have this huge vegetable garden."

At the mention of the garden, Lamech's eyes brightened. "I have a vegetable garden, and lately I have much neglected it. Higgaion helps with the watering, but I am too old for the long hours of work, and now there are great weeds choking the plants."

"Let me at it!" Sandy cried. "Dennys and I are terrific gardeners."

Grandfather Lamech's face creased into a broad smile. "Not so fast, my son. The time for work in the garden is in the earliest morning, and just as the sun is setting in the evening."

"Oh."

The old man laughed. "Truly, you do not want to go out in the garden during the day, or you will be felled by the sun all over again.

But as soon as the sun drops behind the palms I will show you the garden. I thank you, dear my Sand. You have been sent to me by El— this I believe."

"Hey, it's the least I can do," Sandy protested.

In the late afternoon, when the sun's rays were slanted, Lamech and Higgaion led him past a small grove to the garden, which was indeed in need of helping hands. Great weeds of varieties Sandy had never before seen grew higher than many of the vegetables. This was going to be a full-time job. The weeds had deep roots, he discovered as he tried to pull one up. He found a sharp stone and would have started digging had Lamech not stopped him.

"You are not quite ready for such hard work, and it is still hot. Tomorrow morning you can try coming out for an hour."

"All right. It'll make me feel at home, working in a garden again." Sandy knew that he did not have to win Grandfather Lamech's approval, but he had a deep sense of happiness that he could do something for the old man who had been so kind to him. Despite the profusion of weeds, the garden was lush with more vegetables than he had ever seen before.—Too bad there was no way to can or freeze them.

"We sun-dry some of these." Lamech pointed to a long row of red ovals on tall, leafy stalks, and another of something purple that looked like eggplant but was twice the height of the plants at home. If these people of the desert were smaller than anyone Sandy had ever seen, their plants were larger. "That way," the old man continued, "we can eat them in the winter in soups and stews. I have groves of fruit trees, too, that need pruning and harvesting. Japheth and Oholibamah come when they can, to help me out, but they have more than enough to do in my son's vineyards. It must have been ordered in the stars that you should come just as I have to accept that I can no longer manage on my own." His face was joyful.

Sandy felt bathed in the old man's joy. There was certainly going to be no time for boredom. And if there was plenty to do, there would be less time in which to worry about getting home.

One morning Adnarel said, "The Den is much improved."

Sandy nodded. "Good. But why do you call us the Sand and the Den, as though Sands and Dens were some kind of rare species?"

Adnarel's bright laugh pealed. "We picked it up from Japheth. And to Japheth the Sand and the Den are indeed rare species, of a kind never before seen on the oasis, or indeed on any oasis roundabout. It is good that your head is covered." Adnarel nodded approvingly at the woven

straw hat Matred had brought over one night with the night-light. "Lamech tells me you are doing valiant work in the garden."

Sandy pulled the hat firmly down on his head. "The weeds are
something else. We have weeds at home, but not like these. But I'm
getting rid of them, little by little. Hey. Does your name, Adnarel, mean
anything?"

"That I am in the service of the Maker of the Universe."

"Why are you sometimes Adnarel, the way you are now, and sometimes you seem to be a scarab beetle?" Sandy started to scratch his
shoulder where skin still flaked, stopped himself.

"I am not sure you will understand," Adnarel said. "The scarab
beetle is my earthly host."

"What on earth do you need an earthly host for?"

Adnarel sighed. "I said you might not understand."

"Hey." Sandy was indignant. "Dennys and I may not be the geniuses
of the family, but we're nobody's idiots."

"True," Adnarel agreed. "And I suspect that you also understand
that energy and matter are interchangeable."

"Well, sure. Our parents are scientists."

"On the other hand, you live in a time and place where those like
myself are either forgotten or denied. It was not easy to get you to
believe in a unicorn until the need was desperate."

Unthinkingly, Sandy scratched his forearm, and shreds of skin blew
across the ground. "When you're in the scarab beetle, can you understand everything we say?"

"Certainly."

"Then why do you bother to come out?"

"When I am in the scarab beetle, I must accept its limitations."

Sandy grunted. "I think better when I have Dennys around to
bounce ideas off. When am I going to be able to see him again?"

"As soon as he is able to be moved. Grandfather Lamech has offered
his hospitality. It is less noisy and crowded here than in the big tent."

Sandy sighed. "People have been very kind to us. You, too."

Adnarel smiled a smile so grave that it was not far from a frown.
"We do not yet know why you are here. There must be a purpose to
your presence. But we do not know what it is." His eyes seemed to
shoot golden sparks at Sandy. "Do you?"

"I wish I did," Sandy said. "It all seems to have been some kind of
silly accident."

"I doubt that," Adnarel said.

* * *

Noah came again to visit Dennys. "I am told that you are nearly well."

"Yes. Thank you."

"Oholibamah says that you will soon be ready to be moved."

Dennys felt a surge of panic. "Moved? Where?"

"To my father Lamech's tent. To be reunited with your brother."

The panic subsided. "I would like that. Is it far?"

"Half the oasis."

The tent flap had been pegged open, and through it and through the roof hole Dennys could hear the stars. Could hear their chiming at him. "Will you take me?"

Noah pulled at his beard. "I do not go to my father's tent."

"I don't understand."

"It is his place to come to me."

"Why? Aren't you the son?"

"He is old. He cannot care for his land as it should be cared for."

"I'm sorry, Father Noah, but I still don't see why you won't help him."

"I told you." Noah's voice was gruff. "I work long hours in the vineyard. There is not time for coddling the old man."

"Is speaking to your father coddling, or whatever you call it? Sandy and I get mad at our father. He pays more attention to our sister and our little brother than he does to us, because they're the geniuses and we're only—but even when we're mad at him, he's still our father."

"So?"

"When we get home, we're going to have a lot of explaining to do to our father. He will probably be very angry with us."

"Why?"

"Well, we sort of got in the middle of something he was working on."

"I don't know what you're talking about," Noah said.

"Neither do I, exactly," Dennys admitted. "The thing is, we're going to have to talk to our father when we get home. It would be a stupid thing if we tried to avoid him."

"So why are you telling me this?"

"Well—I really do think you should talk with your father."

"Umph."

"I don't mean to be rude or anything, but it sounds to me as though all this argument about wells and stuff has gone on for so long it doesn't make sense anymore. And he's an old man, and you're much younger, and you should be strong enough to back down."

"Backing down is being strong?"

"It takes a lot of courage to say 'I'm sorry.' That's what Sandy and I are going to have to say to our father when we get home."

"Then why say it?" Noah growled.

"Because things won't be right between us till we do."

"You're too young to be telling me what to do." Noah was testy. "You would not even be alive now if we hadn't taken you in."

"That's true, and I am more grateful than words can say." The stars chimed at him again. "Father Noah, please go see your father, and make peace with him before he dies."

Noah grunted. Rose. Walked out of the tent.

Dennys looked at the patch of velvet sky he could see through the open flap. The stars were brilliant. And silent.

Tiglah, the red-haired, rubbed the juice of some red berries on her lips, over her cheekbones. Took a stick of wood which she had shredded at one end to make a brush, and used it on her abundant curls. She had taken the worst of the tangles out with her fingers, and the brush was only to add sheen.

—I am beautiful, truly beautiful, she thought.—My hair is as red as my nephil's wings. We are beautiful together.

A mosquito shrilled near her ear, lit on her neck, and bit.

"Ouch!" she protested. "Why did you do that?"

The mosquito was gone, and a nephil, with wings like flame, stood before her. "Because you are indeed truly beautiful. You are so beautiful I could eat you up."

She burst into tears. "Rofocale, don't bite me!"

The nephil laughed. "It was just a tiny bite. Tell me, little Tiglah, have you seen again the young giant your father and brother threw out of your tent?"

"No. I think the women from Noah's tent are nursing him."

"Your sister?"

Tiglah laughed. "I wouldn't want to depend on Anah if I needed nursing. The younger ones. Oholibamah and Yalith. Anah is helpful when they need ointments, and—"

"How did he get into your tent in the first place?"

She pouted. "How would I know? I called for a unicorn, and suddenly this pale young giant was there, too. I was sorry they threw him out. I'd like to have had a chance to talk with him."

"Tiglah, my beauty, you'll do anything I ask, won't you?"

"As long as you don't ask me to do anything I don't want to do."

"I want you to get to know this young giant. Find out where he comes from, why he is here. Will you do that for me?"

"With pleasure."

"Not too much pleasure," Rofocale chided. "I want him to be at-tracted to you. I do not want you to be attracted to him. You are mine. Are you not?"

She raised her lips to his. His lips were as red as hers, although no berry juice had been rubbed on them.

"Mine," Rofocale purred. "Mine, mine, mine."

In the cool of the evening, Sandy sat on the low bench made by the root of the old fig tree. Higgaion was curled up at his feet, making little bubbles as he slept and dreamed.

A man with a full brown beard flecked with white, and with springing brown hair, strode toward him, turning in from the public path and toward Grandfather Lamech's tent. He went up to boy and mam-moth. Stared. "You are the Sand."

"I am Sandy. Yes."

"They told me that you look like one boy in two bodies. Now I believe them."

"Who are you?" Sandy asked curiously.

"I am Noah. Your brother is in one of my tents, and my wife and daughters are taking good care of him."

"Thank you," Sandy said. "We're very grateful."

Noah continued to stare at him. "If I did not know that the Den is in one of my tents, I would think that you were he. How can this be?"

"We're twins," Sandy explained wearily.

"Twins. We have known nothing of twins before." He paused and looked at Sandy, then at the tent. "Is my father in his tent?"

Sandy nodded. "He's resting." Then he added, "But I know he'd be happy to see you." He wished he felt as certain as he sounded. Grand-father Lamech struck him as being a very stubborn person, with his natural stubbornness augmented by age.

Without speaking further, Noah went into the tent.

Noah!

Suddenly the name registered. Sandy had not heard Noah called by name. Lamech referred to him, when he spoke of him, as 'my son.' The women who came with the night-light called him Father.

Noah.

The galaxies seemed to swirl. Sandy had been convinced that he and Dennys had blown themselves somewhere far from home, at least out of their own solar system, and probably out of their own galaxy. If this Noah was the Noah of the story of Noah and the flood, they were still on their own planet. They had blown themselves in time, rather

than in space. And to get home from time might be far more difficult
than getting home from space, no matter how distant.

But it seemed to fit. Desert people. Nomads, with tents. Cattle. Camels. People used to be smaller than end-of-twentieth-century people.
Way back in pre-flood days it was logical that they would be a great
deal smaller. Higgaion was small for a mammoth.

He put his head in his hands, suddenly dizzy.

Dennys sat with Japheth and Oholibamah, and with Yalith, on one
of the desert rocks. The sky was still flushed with light. The first stars
were trembling into being.

Japheth looked at Dennys in the last light. "You talked with my
father."

"Yes."

"Oh, I'm so glad!" Yalith cried.

"Father has gone off somewhere," Japheth said. "In the direction of
Grandfather Lamech's tent."

Oholibamah looked up at the sky. "He will be happier now. All of
us will be happier. Where there is an unreconciled quarrel, everybody
suffers."

Dennys looked troubled. "I'm not sure he really listened to me."

"But you heard the stars," Oholibamah said, "and you were obedient
to their command."

Japheth added, "That is all anybody can do. Now it is in El's hands."

Briefly, Dennys closed his eyes.—I hope Sandy doesn't think I'm
crazy. I hope *I* don't think I'm crazy. Obeying stars, yet.

"I feel like running," Oholibamah said, and jumped down and ran
fleetly across the desert, Japheth following her.

"Come!" Yalith called, and leapt from the rock. Dennys, with his
long legs, caught up with them easily, and suddenly he was holding
hands with Yalith and Oholibamah, and the four of them twirled in a
joyous dance. Moonlight and starlight bathed them. Dennys, leaping in
the night, felt more alive than he had ever felt before.

Sandy and Higgaion sat up, startled, as they heard a roar from the
tent. At first it seemed to be a roar of anger. Then laughter. Then there
was absolute silence. Sandy could feel his heart beating faster. Higgaion's ears were lifted in alarm. He raised his trunk.

"They wouldn't hurt each other, would they—" Sandy spoke aloud.
Higgaion stared at him out of bright, beady eyes.

Then the tent flap was shoved aside, and Lamech and Noah pushed through with difficulty, because they had their arms about each other, and tears were streaming down their cheeks.

Lamech's voice was so choked with emotion that the words were muffled. "This my son was dead and is alive again, was lost and is found."

Noah hugged the old man roughly. "This is my father, my stubborn old father. We are two peas in a pod for stubbornness." He looked at Sandy. "As you and the Den are two peas in a pod."

"Hey," Sandy said, "I'm glad you two have made up."

"It was the Den," Noah said. "He just kept at me and at me."

Sandy looked surprised. At home, at school, Dennys seldom talked first. He followed Sandy's lead, but seldom initiated anything. "Well. That's good."

"He is nearly healed now, too. Soon he will be able to come to you. My father—" He paused. "I would be happy to have the Den stay, but my tent is crowded, and noisy. And my father has invited you to stay with him."

"That's terrific," Sandy said. "Thanks, Grandfather, thanks a lot. And Dennys can help me with the garden."

"So we should celebrate," Noah said, and handed his father a small wineskin. "There is not much of this, but it is my very best."

"A little will suffice." The old man held the wineskin to his lips, then smacked them in appreciation. "Indeed, your very best." He handed the skin to Sandy, who took a small sip, barely managed to swallow it without making a face.

"El has talked with you, too?" Lamech asked his son.

"He has. When El spoke, I used to understand what was being said. Now it is all confusion. What does El say to you?"

Grandfather Lamech put his arm about his son's shoulders. "El tells me these are end days."

"End of what?" Noah asked.

"Of all that we know, I think," the old man said. "It is not just a question of moving our tents to where there is more water and better pasture for your beasts. Sometimes I, too, feel that the words are all confusion. El talks of many waters, but there is no water anywhere around, except in the wells."

Sandy, sitting next to the old man, with the mammoth lying nearby, shuddered. Grandfather Lamech, if he did not die first, and Noah and his family, and a good many animals, would be the only ones to escape drowning in the great flood.

—I already know the story, he thought, and was glad that the night hid his deep flush of embarrassment. It did not seem right that he should know something that Grandfather Lamech and Noah did not know.

But what did he know? Vague memories of Sunday school. God, angry at the wickedness of the world, and sending a flood, but telling Noah to build an ark and bring the animals on. And then there were terrible rains, and finally a dove brought Noah a sprig of green, and the ark landed on Mount Ararat. Not much of a story unless you were part of it.

Was Grandfather Lamech in the story? He did not remember. Grandfather patted Sandy gently, his usual way of expressing affection, and went on talking. In his concern about the flood, Sandy lost track of the conversation. He heard Grandfather Lamech saying, "My grandfather, Enoch, was three hundred and sixty-five years, and then he was not."

Sandy's ears pricked up. "What do you mean, he was not?"

Grandfather Lamech said, "He walked with El. He was a man of warm heart. And El took him."

It was a weird story. "El took him? How?"

"I was only a boy," Grandfather Lamech said. "He—my Grandfather Enoch was walking through the lemon grove—the same lemon grove I will show you tomorrow—he was walking through the lemon grove with El, and then they were not there."

If this was part of the story of Noah and the flood, Sandy did not remember it. "Is it customary," he asked, "for someone just to be not?"

Grandfather Lamech laughed. "Oh, dear, not at all customary. But my Grandfather Enoch was not an ordinary man. He went away from us to be with El at a very young age. He was only three hundred and sixty-five years old."

"That's exactly a solar year," Sandy said.

"A what?"

"A solar year. For starters, it takes our planet three hundred and sixty-five days to go around the sun."

"Nonsense," Noah said. "We don't go around the sun. It goes around us."

"Oh," Sandy said. "Well. Never mind."

Grandfather Lamech patted his knee. "It is all right. Things may be different where you come from. Do you know El?"

"Well, yes, sort of, though we say God."

Grandfather Lamech appeared not to have heard. "My Grandfather Enoch—how I do miss him. El talks with me, and sometimes I am able to understand, but I have never been able to walk with El in the cool of the evening, like two friends."

"What do you think happened to him, then, to Grandfather Enoch?"

Lamech nodded and nodded, as though answering. Finally he said, "El took him, and that is all I need to know."

"Father," Noah said, "you talk with El more than anyone I know."

"Because my years are long, my son. It was not always so. I am glad indeed that you have come to me before I die."

"You're not going to die for a long time yet!" Noah cried. "You will live as long as our forefather Methuselah."

"No, my son." Grandfather Lamech's arm about Noah's shoulders tightened again. "My time is near."

"Perhaps El will take you, as he took Grandfather Enoch."

Grandfather Lamech laughed again. "Oh, my son, I am full of years, and now that you have come to me, I am ready to die. El does not need to take me in the same way he took Grandfather Enoch."

Sandy looked at the two small men, hugging and laughing and crying all at the same time. It seemed likely that Grandfather Lamech would die before the flood. How soon? And how soon was the flood? He had come to love Grandfather Lamech, who, with Higgaion, had nursed him so tenderly.

—And what about Yalith? he wondered suddenly. He did not remember her name in the story.

—And what about us, Sandy and Dennys? What would happen to us if there was a flood?

7 The Seraphim

Sandy slept that night as usual on Adnarel's cloak. He wondered if Adnarel knew about the coming flood and the destruction of almost all life on earth. His arms tightened about Higgaion, with whom he slept much as, when he was a small boy, he had slept with his arms around a small brown plush triceratops. His fingers moved through Higgaion's shaggy hair, stroked a great fan of an ear. Felt something hard. The scarab beetle.

It gave him a feeling of comfort, although he found it difficult to associate the bronze beetle with the great seraph. Well. Thinking about this could wait till morning. Dennys was the thinker, Sandy the doer. The gentle tip of Higgaion's trunk stroked the back of Sandy's neck, and he relaxed into sleep.

Adnarel came in the morning, in his seraphic form.

Sandy said, "I've been thinking." After all, not only Dennys could think.

Adnarel smiled. "Sometimes that is a good idea. Sometimes not."

"Dennys and I are in the middle of the story of Noah and the flood, aren't we?"

Adnarel's azure eyes regarded him. "So it would seem."

"How are we going to get home?"

Adnarel shrugged his golden wings. "The way you arrived, perhaps?"

"Somehow, I don't think that's going to be possible. In the meanwhile, Dennys is in one of Noah's tents, halfway across the oasis."

"That is true. But he is nearly ready to come to you."

"It's a long way. Is he strong enough to walk it?"

"Possibly."

"I was thinking maybe you could call a unicorn for him."

"Certainly. That is a possibility."

"But then I thought"—Sandy's forehead wrinkled anxiously—"when we were riding the unicorns to the oasis, he went out with the unicorn."

"That is no problem," Adnarel reassured him. "If we should call a unicorn to bring him from Noah's tents to Lamech's, and if, for some reason, they were both to go out, then we would recall the unicorn to Grandfather Lamech's tent, and Dennys would be here, too."

Sandy asked curiously, "If Dennys fell off the unicorn right away, and if the unicorn went out of being with him, could you call them to Grandfather Lamech's tent faster than it would take them in, sort of, the ordinary way."

"Oh, certainly. Fear not."

"Wow. Wait till I tell our father. That's what he's working on, traveling without the restrictions of time. Tessering."

Adnarel nodded. "That is indeed one way of thinking about it. Your father is on the right track."

Sandy wrinkled his brow in concentration. "Okay, then. If Dennys and the unicorn went out, and then you called them back into being, and they appeared here, that would be a quantum leap, wouldn't it?"

"Tell me what you mean." Adnarel's azure eyes probed Sandy.

"Well, it's like, oh, in particle physics—well, you can measure a quantum where it is, but not on its journey from there to here. At least—you can't measure a quantum in both its speed and its place in space, not at the same time. A quantum can be measured where it is, and then it can be measured where it's got to. So—" He paused for breath.

"So?" Adnarel asked, smiling.

"Oh, I wish Dennys was here. He could explain it better than I can. But . . . when you call a unicorn into being, you can see it, maybe measure it. But you can't measure it when it's gone out. Not until you call it back into being. So maybe that's what space and time travel is going to have to be like. A quantum leap. Or what my father would call a tesseract."

"You are an intelligent young man," Adnarel said. "This is not easy to understand."

Sandy realized that he had closed his eyes, almost stopped breathing, in order better to concentrate. He opened his eyes, took in a deep gulp of air. "Can *you* do it?"

"Do what?"

"Tesser. Take a quantum leap."

Adnarel smiled again. "When I am in the scarab beetle, as I have told you, I am limited by what limits the beetle. When I am in my seraphic form, I have fewer limits."

"Can you get off this planet if you want to?" Sandy asked. "I mean, can you travel to other solar systems or other galaxies?"

"Oh, certainly. We are here because there is need. Our brothers, the nephilim, cannot leave this planet. They have lost some of their freedoms."

"Why?" Sandy asked.

But Adnarel was examining Sandy's healed skin. "You are beginning to get a nice protective tan. When your twin comes, each of you must spend a little time, and then a little more, in the sun, until your skin can bear the rays without burning. You must always remember to stay in the tent during the noon hours. Even in the shade, you can burn from the sun's reflection."

"I've been sunburned before," Sandy said. "Once when our Scout troop went to the beach for the day, and we all got burned. But it was nothing like this."

"I think you come from a more northerly part of the planet," Adnarel said, "and this sun is younger than it is in your time."

"And not so much pollution now between earth and sun. Does anybody here ever have allergies?"

Adnarel smiled. "Allergies do not come until later."

"Hey," Sandy said. "Grandfather Lamech's granddaughter Yalith, the one with hair the color of you when you're in the scarab beetle—why has she never come back with the night-light? Why is it always somebody else?"

"Yalith has been busy, taking care of your brother."

For a moment Sandy was washed over with a sick wave of jealousy. He shook himself. If he and Dennys were not interested in mythical beasts, neither were they interested in girls. They went to the regional school dances, but usually stuck with the other members of the hockey and basketball teams. There was going to be plenty of time for girls later. Sometime after they had their driver's licenses and weren't dependent on parents to drive them. Sometime when they met girls who were not silly and giggly and showing off.

But Yalith was not silly or giggly and she did not show off and she was not at all like any of the girls at school. Even though he had been dizzy with fever that first night in Grandfather Lamech's tent, his memory of Yalith was as vivid as though she had come with the stone lamp the night before. Her bronze hair had held sunlight even in the dark shadows of the tent. Her body was tiny and perfect. Her eyes, like her hair, held sunlight. Trying to keep his voice level and not succeeding, for it cracked immediately, he said, "Well, I wish Yalith would bring the night-light tonight."

Adnarel looked at him, and Sandy blushed. He understood why he was feeling the way he was feeling, and at the same time he did not at all understand the way he was feeling, and this conflicting mixture of emotion confused him. His cheeks were as hot as they had been from fever and sunburn. He wondered how much Adnarel saw. But the seraph looked at him calmly. "Now I have business elsewhere. You worked very hard in the garden this morning during the dawn hours. Good work. You may stay out for fifteen more minutes. I will send my griffin friend to tell you when it is time to go inside."

"What's a griffin?"

"Ah, yes, I forget again," Adnarel said. "A griffin is a mythical beast."

"Not like the manticore, I hope." Sandy was not likely to forget the manticore.

"Griffins have a larger vocabulary than the manticore. Some of them can be fierce, but my friend is as gentle as a lamb."

"What does he look like?"

"*She* is half lion, half eagle."

"Which half is which?" Sandy's mind for the moment was off Yalith.

"Her front half is that of an eagle, her rear half that of a lion. She can fly like an eagle, and she has the strength of a lion." Adnarel turned and strode through Grandfather Lamech's grove of royal palms, date palms, coconut palms, scrub palms, all of which blocked the hot wind and provided such a thick shade that Sandy felt comfortably cool. He lay back and looked at the vast expanse of sky, then quickly shut his eyes against the glare.

At home the summer sky was blue, and the blue was made brighter by the white cumulus clouds. Except for an occasional grey day, the sky was constantly in motion, protected by the encircling hills. Here the sky stretched naked from horizon to horizon, licked by volcanic flames, burning in the sun.

A shadow deeper than the shadow of the trees fell across his face. He opened his eyes, expecting to see the griffin.

Instead, a young woman was looking down at him. He caught his breath. She was the most spectacularly beautiful girl he had ever seen. Tiny, like all the people of the oasis. She wore a white goatskin which covered one shoulder. Her hair was a sunburst of red. Her eyes were almond-shaped and as green as the spring grass at home. Her body was perfect, her skin the color of a peach.

"Hello!" she said, looking at him with a radiant smile. "I'm really glad to see you again."

Sandy looked at her in astonishment.

"You haven't forgotten me, have you? I'm really sorry for what happened, when my father and brother . . ."

"I don't know what you're talking about." Sandy could not keep his eyes off her.

"About when you suddenly appeared in our tent, and my father and brother . . ." Again her words trailed off, as though she didn't want to finish the sentence.

"I've never been in your tent." Sandy was confused. "I've only been out of Grandfather Lamech's tent to work in the garden.—Oh. Maybe you mean my brother."

She opened her eyes wide. Her lashes were long and dark and beautiful. "Your brother?"

"My twin brother," Sandy said. "We do look very much alike."

"You haven't been staying in one of Noah's tents?"

"No. That's my brother Dennys."

"Oh. Who are you, then?"

"I'm Sandy."

"Well, then, Sandy, I'm very happy to meet you, and I'm glad you're being nicely cared for."

"What's your name?" Sandy asked.

"I'm Tiglah. I'm Anah's sister."

"Anah?"

"Ham's wife. Noah's daughter-in-law. And I'm Mahlah's friend. Do you know Mahlah?"

"No."

"Mahlah is Noah's daughter, the next-to-the-youngest. Yalith is the youngest. Mahlah is the beauty of that family. We've been giving Yalith and Oholibamah salves to help heal your brother. Oh, dear, this is confusing. I mean, I was really startled to find you here, instead of at Noah's, and then you aren't you at all, I mean you're not the one who appeared in my father's tent that night and who . . . Giants who look alike! And have no wings . . ."

Sandy sighed. "In our time and place we're not anywhere near as tall as giants. We're just tall, and we probably haven't even finished growing."

"You aren't as white of skin as the nephilim, and you don't have wings, but you're as tall as they are. And as handsome, in a different sort of way." She reached out and stroked his face. Then she bent closer, and he was half-fascinated, half-repelled by the strong odor of perspiration mingled with heavy perfume. She had rubbed something red onto her lips and over her cheekbones. It looked like the juice of some kind of berry. She bent closer and brushed her lips against his.

"Hey!" Sandy protested.

"You're sweet, you know," she said. "You're really sweet. You're young, aren't you?"

Sandy said, stiffly, "We're adolescents."

"What's that?"

"Teenagers."

She shook her head. "The nephilim don't have any age at all. They just are. But they've been around. There isn't anything they don't know."

Sandy sighed. "Well, I'm not like the nephilim."

Her lips touched his again, warm and fruit-smelling.

A bird's scream cut across the sky. Above them was the shadow of two dark, flapping wings, then a thud, and a flailing of a long, ropy tail, as the griffin landed. Out of the beak came a negative squawk which was quite evidently "No, no, no." And another squawk which sounded very like "Tiglah."

Tiglah leaned against the trunk of a tall palm, stretching her arm up to reveal her figure to perfection. "Go away, griffin. I like this young giant, and I think he likes me."

The griffin cried an eagle cry, and pushed herself between Tiglah and Sandy. Her beak opened. "Go, go, go."

"No, no, no," Tiglah mimicked. "He's just fine right here with me to tend him. The other one that looks like him has Yalith and all those other women hovering over him. It's only fair that he should have some female care, too, isn't it, Sandy?"

Before he could answer, the griffin had gently but firmly pushed Tiglah toward the path.

"You'd better not hurt me!" she shouted indignantly. "Rofocale is my friend."

From the griffin's beak came a sound very much like a mosquito shrilling. Tiglah kicked at it, hitting just where eagle and lion joined. Her toenails were long and sharp. The lion's tail flicked back and forth in irritation. Then the griffin pushed at Sandy, urging him toward the tent.

"I don't want to go in yet." Sandy looked at Tiglah's smiling green eyes.

Tiglah's voice was cajoling. "Wouldn't you like to come with me to one of the bathhouses?"

"Bathhouses with *water*?" Sandy asked eagerly. Dirt from the garden was deep in his nails, and he could not clean it all off with sand.

"Water? Whatever for?" she asked.

"To bathe in."

"Goodness no!" She sounded shocked. "What an unhealthy idea! We bathe by being rubbed with oil, and we have lovely perfumes that cover all the bad smells." She giggled. "Whoever heard of bathing with water?"

Sandy felt himself being propelled toward the tent by the griffin. He was not sure how he felt about bathhouses with no water, and where perfume covered the bad smells, any more than he was sure about Tiglah. There was nobody remotely like her in school or in the village. She gave him a pleasurable prickly feeling. And, as she had pointed out, Dennys was being tended by Yalith.

The griffin pushed him into the tent.

Grandfather Lamech was waiting for him with a bowl of soup. He looked smaller than ever, and incredibly ancient. His hand, holding the bowl, shook slightly. Sandy looked at him anxiously.

He said, "Sand dear, you're late."

"Sorry, Grandfather Lamech. I was talking to a girl."

Grandfather Lamech asked, suspiciously, "What girl?"

"Her name is Tiglah, and she's the sister of one of Noah's daughters-in-law."

"Anah's sister," the old man said. "Be careful, Sand."

"She's beautiful," Sandy said. "I mean, she is absolutely gorgeous."

"That may be," Grandfather Lamech said. "But it is not enough."

Sandy thought the subject had better be changed. "I'm thirsty. The soup was great, Grandfather, but is there anything cool to drink? Water?"

The old man shook his head. "I can give you some fruit juice. Water is too precious to waste it in drinking. You do not have wells where you come from?"

"Sure we do," Sandy said. "There isn't any town water where we live, and we have an artesian well."

"And your water just keeps on coming?"

"Well, in the autumn when it hasn't rained for a while, we aren't allowed to take long showers, and our parents warn us not to flush the toilet every time we use it—"

"The what?"

"Sorry," Sandy apologized. "I keep forgetting." Grandfather Lamech was tidier about his body's needs than many of the people on the pathways near his compound. Sandy had been requested courteously to go to a small grove which drained onto the desert, whenever he needed. But many people used no special place at all. When Sandy had wandered away from Grandfather Lamech's, and onto the public path, he had seen that the streets were full of human dung as well as camel dung, goat dung, cow dung. Perhaps the fierceness of the sun burned away things that would cause disease. He'd have to ask Dennys. Dennys knew more about sanitation and viruses and germs than Sandy did. Although, if he went into environmental law when he grew up, he'd have to learn about such things.

Grandfather Lamech gave him a bowl of still-unfermented grape juice, and Sandy drank it thirstily. He sniffed at the pot sitting in the banked embers of the fire. Grandfather Lamech cooked in the cool of the night, then set the pot in the ashes, where it kept comfortably warm.

"Smells good, Grandfather Lamech. What is it?"

"Pottage," the old man said.

"What's that?"

"Lentils, onions, and rice, well seasoned."

"Hey, I'm going to have to tell my mother how to make that when I get home." A brief wave of homesickness enveloped him as his mind's eye saw the lab, and a casserole of pottage cooking over the Bunsen burner.

Higgaion, too, sniffed. He had his own bowl, and he ate the same food as Sandy and the old man.

Grandfather Lamech seemed daily more tottery. If Dennys came to the tent, would it be too much for him?

But now that Noah and Lamech were reconciled, Noah not only came to Lamech's tent to talk, he brought great kettles of food, skins of wine, bunches of grapes. And the two men laughed and cried, and Noah hugged his father. "Oh, my father, you must live forever!"

And Lamech did not answer.

In the end, Dennys was to cross the oasis on a camel, a white camel with a long, supercilious nose, sneering rubbery lips, and extraordinary gentian eyes, shaded by long lashes.

Noah had cut his foot on a sharp stone, and Matred forbade him to accompany Dennys. "Now that you and your father are reconciled, do you want to spoil everything with an infected foot? It is healing well, but the public paths are full of filth. You are not to leave the tent until it has healed."

"Women," Noah grunted. But he obeyed Matred.

"Our Den will be all right," she reassured him. "If he is in the care of the seraphim, he will reach Grandfather Lamech safely."

Alarid, the seraph whose host was the pelican, and who brought water to the tent for Dennys; Alarid, who had warned him not to change anything, came with another seraph. This one had wings of pale blue, and eyes like moonstones, a deeper, brighter blue.

"So," Alarid said to Dennys, not quite accusingly, "you have already made changes."

"But I haven't!" Dennys expostulated.

"You persuaded Noah to go to his father, when he would listen to no one else."

"I didn't really say all that much," Dennys said. "I sort of just listened to the stars. So I wasn't really the one—"

"I am not here to accuse you," Alarid said. "We are full of joy that Lamech and Noah are speaking again, and it may well be that it was necessary for your brother to prepare the old man for reconciliation." He indicated the other seraph, who had been standing quietly listening. "This is Admael."

The seraph did not extend his hand. Seraphim evidently did not shake hands. Admael bowed, and Dennys returned the bow.

Together, the two seraphim carefully examined Dennys. "Yalith and Oholibamah have taken excellent care of you," Alarid said.

Admael nodded in quiet approval.

"They've been marvelous," Dennys agreed. "I think I'd be dead if they hadn't." The scabs were long gone from his skin. He could run across the desert without tiring. He knew that it was time.

He looked at Alarid. "And you, too. Thank you." He bowed to the seraph.

"Admael will carry you to Grandfather Lamech's tent," Alarid said.

Admael's moonstone eyes beamed toward Dennys. "I will wait outside." With a grave look, the seraph left.

"I should thank everybody." Dennys hesitated. He was eager to be with Sandy again, yes, and yet he was not at all eager to leave Yalith. And, of course, Oholibamah and Japheth. If he went to Grandfather Lamech's tent, would he ever see Yalith again? Would her delicate fingers slide confidingly into his hand the way they did when she took him out at night to listen to the stars, or when they danced under the desert sky?

"Fear not," Alarid said. "I have thanked them for you, all of them, Noah and Matred, Shem and Elisheba, Ham and Anah, Japheth and Oholibamah, and oh, yes, Yalith, too. In any event, you will be seeing them frequently. Now that Grandfather Lamech and Noah are reconciled, there will be much coming and going between the two tents. Are you ready?"

"Ready." He would see Yalith again. Surely she would come to Grandfather Lamech's tent to visit him. Surely he would feel the touch of her delicate fingers.

He followed Alarid out of the tent. Night had fallen, and the sky was crusted with stars. He was getting used to the pattern of early rising, the long afternoon nap, and going late to sleep when the fiery sands had cooled down and the very air had lost its burning quality.

He looked for Admael, but there was no seraph. Instead, a white camel stood in the dim shadow of the tent.

Noah was waiting for him, standing by the camel, leaning on a stick, his foot bound in a clean skin. "This is not goodbye, my son. We are all eager to see you and the Sand together. Then maybe we will believe that you really are two. The seraphim has looked at my foot and says that I will be able to walk on it safely in a couple of days." He held out his hand, palm up. "Put your foot there, and I will help you up onto the camel's back. Even for a young giant like you, a camel's back is a long way up."

The camel had no real saddle, but heavy skins were spread on its back. Dennys was not at all sure how easy it was going to be for him to stay seated. There was nothing for him to hold on to, no reins, no pommel. But Admael in his camel form seemed to be a real flesh-and-blood camel, not nebulous, like the virtual unicorns. He did not think the camel would lose its tendency to life.

Matred came hurrying out of the tent, carrying a bundle, tears streaming down her cheeks. "Here are your clothes. Perhaps, sometime, you will need them. Goodbye, our dear twin. We will miss you."

And suddenly he was surrounded by the entire family, weeping, laughing, reaching up to the camel's flanks to hug Dennys's feet, which was as close to him as they could reach, even on tiptoe.

Japheth had his arm around Oholibamah, and Yalith was standing with them. They blew him kisses, which he blew back, and then, without warning, the camel took off, and everybody called after them, "Goodbye, twin Den, goodbye, and we'll see you soon!"

"Goodbye!" he called in return, trying to wave at them without falling off.

The camel turned off the oasis onto the desert as the calls faded into the distance. Dennys clutched the bundle of clothes Matred had given him—what remained of his clothes after he had thrown away the ones fouled in the garbage pit. He could not imagine ever needing winter clothes again. He could not imagine going farther than Lamech's tent, where he and Sandy would be reunited.

He remembered reading somewhere that to ride a camel was like being on a small ship rolling in rough seas, and that seemed to him to be a very good description. He bent over and clutched the white hair on the camel's neck, trying to let his body swing with the camel's odd rhythm. A soft night breeze only faintly gritty with sand touched his cheeks. Above them, the desert stars gave out a cooling light. In the distance the mountain smoked, and the horizon burned red. Dennys was glad the oasis was as far away as it was from the still active volcano.

The camel lurched swiftly across the desert. Dennys found that the more he leaned into the animal's syncopated rhythm the less tendency he had to slither off. The camel was going with such speed that it would be halfway across the desert before it realized that Dennys had fallen, so he'd better hang on.

He tried to breathe in time with the arhythmic ride. He would be incredibly sore in the morning. This was far harder on the muscles than riding a horse. He noticed a shift in pace, a quickening of rhythm. He clutched at the camel's neck, barely managing to hold on. Barely. He began to slip to one side, with the skins under him sliding with him.

The white camel was racing across the desert. Suddenly Dennys realized that the sound of camel's hooves on sand, on stone under sand, was echoed by another sound.

A voice from close behind them roared, *"Hungry!"* and Dennys felt a breath so hot that it seared. He felt himself slipping farther and farther off the camel, until he was clinging to the side, and then he realized that the camel had turned, so that it was between Dennys and whatever it was that was roaring. He found himself sliding so that he was head down, peering under the camel's belly.

Something was peering at him from the other side of the camel. A face. Whiskers. A bulbous nose. Bleary eyes. Horns which curved down, with sharp, wicked points. Dennys looked for the body that belonged to the face and saw, instead, a lion's body. Looked along the lion's body to where the tail should be and saw, instead, a scorpion's tail, its sting rattling. He had never seen anything like it before. He did not want to see it now. Clutching the camel's white hair, he tried to struggle up onto its back again.

The camel whickered, and continued to race across the desert.

"Hungry!" the creature roared.

Dennys felt very small. Very young. Very afraid. "Is it going to eat me?"

The camel glanced back at Dennys, the gentian eyes enigmatic.

"Hey!" he protested. "Aren't you going to stop *it*?"

The huge face loomed over the camel's back. *"Hungry!"* it roared again. The enormous lips opened, to reveal a double set of ugly, stumpy teeth, which looked as though they had been worn down from gnawing. The purplish lips opened.

Dennys pulled at the camel's hair. "Hey. Help." The ugly creature's breath came closer. The bloodshot eyes were looking directly at Dennys's grey ones. He tried to stare it down. The tongue, thick but long as a snake's, flicked toward him. He drew back, shielding himself with the camel, but the man/lion/scorpion bounded over the camel's back, landing on the sand beside Dennys.

"Camel!" he shouted. "Please be Admael!" He sidestepped away from the monster.

Again the camel agilely placed itself between Dennys and the creature. Gave Dennys a glance. Dennys remembered that seraphim did not like to interfere or change things.

"Hey!" he shouted. "If he eats me, won't that change the course of things?"

With a flash of lightning almost like the unicorn's, the camel stretched its whiteness up to the sky, seeming to brush against the stars, to catch blue fire, and then Admael stood beside Dennys. "Go, manticore, go quickly. And don't go to any of the tents. And don't even think of eating any of the mammoths. Do your hunting in the desert."

Tears began to trickle down the manticore's cheeks, dampening its scraggly beard.

"And don't try to make me feel sorry for you." Admael paused. "Though I am sorry for you. You appear to be one of nature's more peculiar efforts."

The manticore turned, head drooping, and with its lion's body it padded across the desert, scorpion sting clacking as it went.

"Wow!" Dennys said. "That was a close call."

"Not really. Manticore's courage is as skimpy as its vocabulary." Admael picked up the skins which had served as saddle. "Let's go." Dennys looked at him questioningly. "It isn't far. I've been running parallel to the oasis. Can you walk a little?"

"Sure." He'd just as soon walk as be bounced around on the camel's back. But he asked, curiously, "You're not going to be a camel?"

Admael had slung the skins over one shoulder. "Not now. It takes considerable energy to transfer. We do not like to waste power when it is not necessary. The manticore is basically a coward, but there may be other dangers in the night desert. It's best that we keep moving."

Admael glanced upward, and when Dennys looked skyward, he saw the dark wings of a vulture blotting out the stars in swift circles.

The circle of the nephilim was dark against the desert, a dark shot with flames brighter than those from the mountain as they flickered in and out of their animal hosts in a show of power. They spoke from their nephil forms in bursts of primal energy, reverting in negative lightning to their animal hosts, and bursting with bright wings again in order to speak.

The crocodile opened its enormous jaws, then lifted green wings as it stretched skyward. "What are they doing here?"

"What *are* they?" Pewter wings faded like smoke and a rat's tail swished back and forth over the sand.

There was a sulfurous smell as the nephilim flickered in and out, charging the air. "Not true giants." Red wings and hair flamed in the hot wind and then a mosquito whined shrilly.

"Not one of us." Purple wings misted and the dragon/lizard stretched its useless wings.

"Though they speak the ancient tongue."

"They burn in the sun."

"They can't change form."

"Young. Infants."

"Almost men, though."

"They don't belong here."

"What to do with them?" Bronze wings dissolved and shrank with a tearing sound as the cockroach lifted its armored wings.

"Do we let them live?" Great garnet wings dimmed the clouds, dropped with a sharp crack, and the red ant's small body cast a dark shadow in the starlight.

Flicker. Flame. Shadow. In and out in prideful bursts of energy.

"Ummm," moaned the nephil who was the cobra. "Maybe we promise them that they will live."

"Ummm, kkk." The vulture appeared briefly and clicked its beak. Then dark wings shadowed the stars. "Power. Put them in our power."

Yellow wings puffed into sulfur and the flea leapt from the dragon/lizard to the vulture, then raised wings high. "Power. That's right."

"Temptation," the dragon/lizard nephil suggested.

"Temptation. Good." And the mosquito droned.

"Lust," suggested the cobra, and the nephil's face was whiter than the sand.

"Ummm. Lust," agreed the vulture. "Kkk. Lust."

*   *   *

"We'll sleep tomorrow in the heat of the day." The reunited Sandy and Dennys sat outside Grandfather Lamech's tent as the stars wheeled across the sky. The old man had gone in, after having sat outside with them to eat a fresh mess of pottage, and to prepare bowls of fig juice.

Higgaion was curled in the star shade of the tree, his flanks heaving in and out as he slept, occasionally twitching in dreams.

"Noah and Matred have a mammoth called Selah," Dennys said. "Usually she sleeps by Yalith's sleeping skins, but sometimes she came into my tent and slept with me. It was weird being without you." Dennys wriggled his bare toes in the sand.

"Yeah," Sandy agreed. "It was weird for me, too. Higgy and Grandfather Lamech have been very good to me." He wanted to ask about Yalith. But something stayed his tongue. He said, instead, "I love Grandfather Lamech. You will, too."

"He seems okay," Dennys agreed. "I'm glad Japheth was the first person we saw. Otherwise, I'd suspect everybody of being like those awful people who threw me out of their tent into the town dump."

"It sounds rough."

"Well, everybody in Noah's tenthold was wonderful to me."

"Dennys." Sandy was suddenly somber. "Do you remember the story? The story of Noah and the ark?"

Dennys shifted uncomfortably. "The story we got blown into. At first I thought we were in some way-out solar system."

"It might be easier if we were," Sandy said. "Grandfather Lamech sent me into town today to trade fruit for lentils. I passed a lot of people. They're all going to be drowned."

Dennys looked at the glow of the volcano on the horizon. "I know. Everybody except Noah and Matred, Shem and Elisheba, Ham and Anah, Japheth and Oholibamah."

Now Sandy's voice cracked. "What about Yalith?"

Dennys managed to keep his voice from soaring. "I don't know. But I don't think Oholibamah, Elisheba, or Anah are called by name in the story. Matred isn't, either." His voice jumped an octave. "Nor Yalith. At least as far as I can remember. I wish we had a Bible."

"It was a very patriarchal society," Sandy said. "I do remember that."

"Meg would call it chauvinistic," Dennys said. "Whoever wrote the Bible was a man. Men."

"I thought it was supposed to be God. Wasn't that what we were taught in Sunday school?"

"When we were little maybe. The thing is, the Bible was set down by lots of people over lots of years. Centuries. It's supposed to be the Word of God, not written by God."

"Okay," Sandy said, "but nobody ever mentioned that there were twins named Sandy and Dennys Murry with Noah and his family."

"Do you have any idea," Dennys ventured, "when the rains are supposed to start?"

Sandy shook his head. "No, I don't. And I don't know how we're going to get out of here and go home. Do you?"

"I thought you might have thought of something to do," Dennys said.

"I don't have a clue. You pay more attention than I do when everybody goes on at the dinner table about tessering and red shifts and mitochondria and farandolae and stuff."

"Mitochondria." Dennys looked at his twin. "Do you remember when something was wrong with Charles Wallace's mitochondria, and we thought he was going to die?"

"We went out to the vegetable garden," Sandy said.

"Because we had to *do* something."

"Even though we knew it didn't have anything to do with helping Charles Wallace get well."

"But it was something to do."

They were silent for a dark space. Then Sandy said, "Well, we can do it again, work in a garden. Grandfather Lamech has this huge vegetable garden—I mean, you've never seen such gigantic plants. And weeds. I've pulled up a mountain of weeds, wait and see, and I've hardly made a dent. And then there are his groves to prune and water. There's plenty to do. Whether it helps anything or not."

Under them the ground trembled slightly, but by now they were both so used to the shifting and sliding of the young planet that they hardly noticed. "Well. That's good. The garden, I mean. As long as we don't get sunstroke again."

"Oh, we work only in the early morning and the evening. Grandfather Lamech is very careful about that."

"Good, then."

"Yes, but none of that gets us home. What do we do now?" Sandy was asking himself, rather than his twin.

"I think," Dennys spoke slowly, "that we don't do anything. I mean, this is way outside our experience."

"Outside anybody's experience," Sandy added. "I think you're right. We wait. With our eyes and ears open." He looked over to where Higgaion was sleeping. The scarab was not in its usual place on Higgaion's ear. Therefore, he thought, Adnarel must be somewhere else. Doing what?

"We wait," Adnarel said. "To do anything is to make changes, to cause a paradox."

"Does not their very being here in itself constitute a paradox?" Alarid, who was sometimes a pelican, asked.

Admael, who had carried Dennys across the desert, said, "They have already made changes. The boy, Dennys, caused Noah to reconcile with his father, when it seemed that nothing would ever make that come about."

Adnachiel, his wings as sunny as the hide of his giraffe host, said, "Perhaps the boy Sandy played a part."

Aalbiel, with wings as white as those of a snow goose, asked, "Could they have been sent for this?"

Aariel, tawny as a lion, said softly, "We do not know. Perhaps they are part of the pattern."

Abdiel, sometimes a golden bat, spoke equally softly. "There are many things that even the angels in heaven do not know. And we have chosen—"

"Been chosen," Abasdarhon, whose host was the golden snake, corrected.

"Accepted being chosen," Akatriel, whose eyes were as round and wise and fierce as an owl's, corrected further.

"—to stay with the children of humankind," Abdiel continued. "Therefore, we have relinquished some of our powers and there is much that we do not know."

Abuzohar, who was sometimes a white leopard, inclined his head, his face luminous as the moon. "As long as the One knows, there is no need for us to know."

Achsah, with wings and hair the soft grey velvet of his mouse host, nodded. "They are innocent boys, for the children of men. Likable. And they speak the Old Language."

Adabiel, orange wings vivid as the tiger, agreed. "Good in their hearts. And they brought out Noah's goodness. Could that be part of the plan?"

Admael said, "We still have no real idea why they are here, or how they are to be returned to wherever it is they come from."

Adnachiel, sometimes a giraffe, looked up at the stars. "We willingly gave up some of our powers when we chose to stay on this planet."

"We do not *have* to stay." Abdiel's seraphim wings were as bright a gold as his bat ones. "We are free to leave at any time and to resume our full powers."

Adnarel threw off light like the sun flashing against the scarab beetle. "It was our free choice. And now—I would not leave while they—the twins—are still here."

"We may not be able to save them," Alarid warned.

"Then I will stay with them," Admael said, for a fraction of a second looking more like a white camel than like a seraphim.

Eleven luminous heads slowly nodded in agreement with Admael.

8 Oholibamah, Japheth's Wife

Mahlah and Tiglah were waiting near Grandfather Lamech's ancient fig tree. Mahlah's belly was softly rounded. Tiglah was round by nature, all soft curves and delicate plumpness that had not yet run to softness, as Anah's was doing.

The twins came from the garden, where they had weeded two long rows of plants which might have been forebears of tomatoes, and pulled off the suckers. Higgaion was in the tent with Grandfather Lamech. The twins did not see Mahlah and Tiglah until the two girls came to meet them. Tiglah walked slowly toward Sandy. She tossed her head so that her red hair flew about her face. She lowered the heavy fringes of her lashes. "I'm sorry my father and brother didn't treat you better when you appeared in our tent that time." She paused, and added virtuously, "They have to be very careful that strange men don't take advantage of me." Then she stopped. "Am I speaking to the right one?"

"No," Dennys said.

Mahlah fluttered her small hands like birds. Her dark hair concealed her swollen belly. "But which one of you was guest in my father's tent?"

Sandy stepped forward. "My brother Dennys. You're Yalith's sister?"

"Yes. Mahlah. But I am Ugiel's bride and no longer live in the home tent."

Sandy looked at her, thinking that although Mahlah was beautiful, it was in an obvious way; she had none of the subtle loveliness he associated with Yalith. Tiglah's flashy beauty was almost an assault. He still didn't know what to make of her. "Tiglah?"

She giggled, so that dimples came and went on either side of her reddened lips. "Don't you remember me?"

"You were talking to me the other day, before the griffin came."

"Yes, and the silly griffin interrupted us. I think she was jealous. But she's not here now. Would you like to come with us?" She turned from Sandy, to include Dennys in the invitation.

"Where?" Dennys asked suspiciously. His first encounter with Tiglah's family had made him far more cautious than Sandy had cause to be. He did not trust her, nor, indeed, any of the small people who did not come from Noah's tenthold.

Mahlah, unlike Tiglah, was not a giggler. She smiled. "We'd like to get to know you better. My father thinks the world of you. So let's go for a little walk."

Dennys looked at the sky, which was already beginning to shimmer with heat. "It's too hot. Thank you, anyhow."

Tiglah pushed her fingers through her curls, so that they glinted with gold in the sunlight. She, too, looked at the sky. "It's not going to be really hot until the sun is above the palm trees." She turned her dimpled smile toward Sandy. "We'd really love to show you around a little. You haven't seen much of the oasis."

Sandy stepped forward. He had not enjoyed his brief excursions onto the public path, but if Tiglah and Mahlah were there to show them where to go, it might be fun. It was time to go farther than Grandfather Lamech's compound and the nearby shops. "Well—"

"You go, if you like." Dennys was firm. "I nearly died of sunstroke, and I'm keeping out of the sun."

Sandy looked at his brother, noticing the still pinkly mottled skin. "I'm sorry. My skin's all healed. I forgot—"

"You go, if you like," Dennys repeated.

Sandy shook his head. "No. Grandfather Lamech wanted us to bring him some onions for his stew, and we were too busy weeding. We'd better go pull them before the sun gets too high."

A great whirring of wings shook the sky above them, and the griffin landed between the two boys and Mahlah and Tiglah.

"Go away, spoilsport." Tiglah kicked at the griffin, and her green eyes sparked with resentment.

Dennys backed away in fear. The griffin looked to him as fierce as the manticore.

"It's all right," Sandy reassured him. "It's a griffin, and she's a friend."

The griffin spread her eagle wings so that the two girls were screened. Opened her bill and squawked something like "On-yons."

"Okay, okay," Sandy said. "We won't forget."

The griffin folded her wings. Her lion's tail swished back and forth.

Tiglah walked cautiously around her, and put her small hand on Sandy's arm. "Later, then? You would like to come for a walk, wouldn't you?"

Would he? Tiglah made Sandy feel very peculiar. She was both alluring and unsettling. And she was very different from Yalith, of the bronze hair and eyes and luminous smile. He would go anywhere with Yalith. But Tiglah? "I don't know," he said cautiously. "Dennys and I have a lot to talk about."

Mahlah, too, skirted the griffin, asking, "Are you sure you are two separate people? My husband, Ugiel, can take different forms, yet it is always he."

"We are twins," Dennys stated. "Aren't there any twins around here?"

Tiglah moved her fingers slowly up and down Sandy's arm, and it prickled, so that the freckles he had acquired in the sun seemed to stand up. "Two look-exactly-alikes? No. Of course, we can tell you apart right now, because *your* skin"—her fingers caressed Sandy's forearm—"is strong, and you are getting quite tanned, and you both have freckles across your nose. Whereas *his*"—she indicated Dennys—"still looks raw and uncooked."

"But handsome," Mahlah purred. "We don't have any men on the oasis who are as tall and like gods as you are."

The griffin cried again, "On-yons."

Sandy had already turned in the direction of the vegetable garden when he noticed Dennys looking past the clump of trees to the public path. Yalith and Oholibamah were coming toward them, carrying a large kettle between them.

Mahlah drew her lips up in what was more a grimace than a smile. "Well, sisters dear, are you pursuing the twin giants?"

Oholibamah's low voice was pleasant. "Good morning. Matred sent us with a meal. Grandfather Lamech is too old to cook for so many."

Unheeding, Yalith looked at the twins, from Dennys to Sandy, and back to Dennys. "It is not just the difference in your skins that tells you apart." She looked troubled.

"Let's put the kettle on the fire," Oholibamah suggested.

"You don't have to go with them." Tiglah wrinkled her nose in distaste as Yalith and Oholibamah started into the tent.

"Stay and talk with us," Mahlah wheedled.

But the twins had turned their backs on the two girls and were looking after Yalith as she disappeared into the tent.

The griffin shrieked with pleasure and flew off, spiraling higher and higher into the sky.

*   *   *

Dennys had picked half a basketful of onions before he began to recount for Sandy, in detail this time, his experience in Tiglah's tent.

"But it was her father and brother who threw you out, wasn't it?"

"She was there."

"But it wasn't really her fault."

"She didn't even try to stop them," Dennys said. "And even if it wasn't her fault, I wouldn't trust anybody who came from that tent."

"Well." Sandy picked up his basket of onions and hefted it to one shoulder. "I can't say I blame you for feeling the way you do." He did not add that, nevertheless, Tiglah was still the most absolutely gorgeous girl he had ever seen. Except Yalith. Who wasn't gorgeous at all. Whatever Yalith had, it was better than gorgeousness.

And were Yalith and Mahlah and Tiglah going to be drowned?

Dennys, picking up at least part of Sandy's thoughts, said, "Still—I wouldn't want Tiglah to be drowned. And I guess she's going to be."

Sandy felt a chill move over his skin, despite the sun, which was rising higher and hotter. "And Yalith?"

Dennys picked up his basket. "Oholibamah is Japheth's wife. Ham, Shem, and Japheth, with their wives, go on the ark. That's the story. Oholibamah loves Yalith. I mean, they're really friends. I don't think Oholibamah would let Yalith drown."

"If she doesn't have any say about who goes on the ark, can she prevent it?"

Dennys said, "Hey, we're talking as if that old ark story is true. But Noah doesn't seem to have any inkling of it, and he talks with this El of theirs."

"God." Sandy shifted his basket of onions from one shoulder to the other. "Isn't there some kind of flood story in all cultures?"

"I think so," Dennys replied. "I mean, even in our day the planet is still shifting its plates and causing earthquakes. We've had an awful lot of weird weather, volcanoes erupting all over the planet, and tornadoes and hurricanes."

"Well, about those flood stories," Sandy continued. "There must have been some kind of major weather cataclysm."

"Yeah, but there've been wild weather patterns all through history. Ice ages. Whatever it was that finished off the dinosaurs, a comet, or that Nemesis star. Or the earth shifting slightly on its axis and altering climate and seasons. So a big flood isn't all that impossible."

Sandy said in a flat voice, "Maybe we'll get drowned, too. Maybe it would be better than being nuked."

"More inevitable than nuking. Nothing that hasn't happened yet has to happen." Dennys pushed into the tent and wearily set his basket of onions down near Grandfather Lamech's cooking stones. Sandy followed suit. They looked over to where the old man lay napping on his pile of skins, eyes closed, breathing shallowly. Higgaion was curled at his feet, and little bubbling sounds came rhythmically from his trunk.

Sandy said, thoughtfully, "If we get nuked, it will be because of people. Power and greed and corruption. It wouldn't be a natural disaster. But a flood is a natural disaster."

Dennys nodded. "Nuking would be something completely different. Not natural."

"Yeah, but remember, Dad says it doesn't have to happen. People *can* restrain themselves. We've had the power for half a century, and we've refrained. But if the plates of the earth slide, that can't be stopped. If a comet should hit us, we couldn't stop it. And storms and blizzards. Those are inevitable."

"When we had the hurricane, and the big oak was ripped out by the roots, nobody could have stopped that. It *is* different—things that can be stopped and things that can't, like tornadoes and earthquakes and—"

"And floods," Sandy said flatly.

Grandfather Lamech startled them with a loud snore.

"It doesn't do any good to talk about it," Dennys said. "Any of it. If there's going to be a flood, we can't do anything about it. But we *can* work in Grandfather Lamech's garden."

The old man snored again.

"Right now, we'd better nap, too," Sandy suggested.

Dennys dropped onto the clean sleeping skins which had been provided for him. "Hey, it's good to be back with you again."

But he missed Yalith's gentle fingers against his burned skin.

Every day, someone from Noah's tenthold came to Grandfather Lamech's tent with the main meal. When Yalith and Oholibamah came, they often stayed to eat with the old man and the twins. Yalith was equally gracious with each of them, but sometimes she sat looking at them in bemusement, letting Oholibamah do the work. The twins, in their turn, looked at Yalith and did not look at each other.

Occasionally, one of the men brought the meal. Japheth, like his wife and Yalith, would stay to eat, to talk.

Shem, who was the hunter, was cordial, but not chatty. He would stand, leaning on his spear, until he was certain that Grandfather Lamech had everything he needed. Then he would leave.

Japheth had told the twins that when Shem went hunting, he would always stop to thank the animal he had killed, thank it for giving them the food necessary for life.

"Do all the hunters give thanks?" Sandy asked.

"Not anymore. I think they used to, long ago. But now most of the hunters just kill, and often more than they need. Some kill just for the sake of killing."

Dennys said, "That is true in our time, too. At home, our land is posted against hunters and trappers, but that doesn't stop the jacklighters."

"The what?" Japheth asked.

Dennys tried to explain. "Hunters who shine a bright light into the eyes of the deer. It blinds them and they freeze and can't move, and then the hunters shoot. Jack-lighting is illegal, but that doesn't stop a lot of people."

"A lot?" Japheth asked.

Dennys stated, "A few can seem like a lot."

Sandy nodded. The twins liked what Japheth had told them about Shem.

One morning Anah and Elisheba came with the food for the day. Anah, Ham's wife, was obviously Tiglah's sister, but her hair did not have the brilliance of Tiglah's, and her eyes were not as rich a green. She was becoming flabby, with dimples all over, in her cheeks, her chin, her elbows, her knees. She was softer than Tiglah.

Elisheba was like Shem, solid, muscled, kind. At home, in the twins' part of the world, she would have looked comfortable in a flowered housedress, and she would scrub her kitchen floor every day, and shift all the furniture to sweep under it. There was something more familiar about Elisheba than about many of the other women, who had an Oriental strangeness. Anah's and Tiglah's eyes were almond-shaped, their cheekbones high.

After the pot had been set on the stones, Anah put her hands on her rounded hips, looking in open admiration at Sandy and Dennys. "Another hundred years and you'll be the most handsome men on the desert."

Dennys looked at Grandfather Lamech's wrinkled face and trembling hands, thinking that the old man, at any rate, was not going to live for another hundred years. And even if the flood held off, he and Sandy did not have the life span of these tiny desert people. But he said nothing. He did not like Anah; Anah was Tiglah's sister.

Elisheba picked up the empty pot from the day before, which the twins had scoured clean with sand. "I wonder if they'll grow wings?" She tended to speak of Sandy and Dennys as though they could not hear.

"I think they're a new breed," Anah said, "not seraph or nephil, but a completely different kind of giant." Her gaze slid from one twin to the other, then back to Elisheba. "What," she suggested, "would you think of having two husbands?"

Elisheba laughed. "One is all I can manage."

"Thank you for the dinner." Sandy turned away from Anah's gaze, which was uncomfortably reminiscent of Tiglah's. "It smells good."

"And please thank Matred for us."

Anah put her fingers lightly against Sandy's wrist. "You're welcome to come eat in Noah's tent at any time, you know that."

Sandy was glad when she was gone.

The big tent was dark and quiet. Matred poked her elbow against Noah's ribs. "What about Mahlah?"

"Humph?" Noah mumbled sleepily.

"Husband. It cannot have escaped your notice that Mahlah is with child."

Noah rolled over. "I have been very busy."

"*Noah.*"

"It is time Mahlah brought her young man to our tent," Noah said. "We will prepare a feast."

"It is not a young man," Matred said. "At least, it is not one of our young men, and I don't think they're young, I think they are old, far older than any of us, even Grandfather Methuselah."

"Woman, what—or who—are you talking about?"

"Mahlah," Matred said impatiently, "and her nephil."

Noah sat up. "What are you trying to tell me?"

"I am telling you"—Matred kept her voice low—"that Mahlah is with child by a nephil, and that she has had some kind of nephil wedding." Quickly she put her hand over Noah's mouth to stifle his roar of outrage.

"This is not how things are done." He pushed her hand away, but kept his voice under control. "There has been no wedding feast. No nephil has come to our tent."

"The nephilim do not do things the way we do. Their customs are not our customs."

"This is Mahlah's will? She loves this nephil?"

"So it would seem. She sends messages by Yalith. She does not want to tell us these things herself."

Noah growled. "It is the way of things to lose a daughter to another man's tent, but not without the proper formalities."

"When Mahlah does speak to me"—Matred's voice was heavy—
"she keeps reminding me that times have changed."

Noah sighed. "It is not what we would have chosen for our daughter, but after all, Oholibamah—"

Matred leaned against her husband, and he put his arm around her.
"I would rather have it one of our young giants. At least they are truly
young, and I think they are good."

"They fit in with us," Noah agreed, "and the nephilim do not. It
seems now as though our twins have been with us always."

"The moons have slipped by," Matred said. "Seven or eight of them,
at least."

"They have worked wonders in my father's gardens and groves. It
is hard work, and yet they never complain."

"Perhaps Yalith—" Matred started, then said, "It is time we asked
them to take another evening off and come to our tent. I wish Mahlah
had not been lured by the nephilim. They glitter, but I do not think they
are loving."

"I will speak to Mahlah." Noah pulled Matred down onto the sleeping skins.

"If she will speak with you," Matred said.

The twins enjoyed their visits to the big tent, the noise and singing
and laughter. Once, at the time of the full moon, Noah's married daughters were there with their husbands and children, and there was dancing
and music and loud quarreling and reconciling.

"I wish Mahlah were here," Matred said.

Less than a moon later, Anah and Elisheba, bringing a big pot of
vegetable stew to Grandfather Lamech's tent, again invited the twins to
the big tent. "But you should feel free to come more often," Anah said.
"You don't have to wait for an invitation."

Sandy felt her eyes inviting him. He turned away. "We don't like
to leave Grandfather Lamech too often."

Higgaion, lying stretched out by the embers, swished his stringy
little tail, raised his head, and put it back down with a thump.

Again Anah lavished her smile on Sandy. "You're getting nearly as
brown as one of us, and you have freckles all across your nose."

"The Den, too." Elisheba's smile was friendly. "I never believed
he'd make it. Matred thought he was going to die. But Oholibamah is
a healer. And Yalith was marvelous with him."

Sandy felt a sharp twinge of jealousy. When Yalith came with the
night-light or with the evening meal, she was careful, overcareful, he

thought, to smile no more at one twin than at the other. "All that was a long time ago." He was surprised at how cross his voice sounded. "We've both been well for months now."

"For what?"

"Oh. Many moons." *Moon* and *month* did come from the same root, after all, but the people of the oasis thought of time in moons and crops and the movement of the stars.

"Yalith will be looking for a husband one of these years." Anah's voice was suggestive.

Elisheba was brusque. "Yalith will make a good wife. But not yet."

Anah's eyes strayed from twin to twin. "Hmm." She pursed her lips.

Elisheba jiggled Anah's arm. "We'd better be getting back, or Matred will be after us."

"She doesn't scare me," Anah said.

"Who said anything about being scared? There's a lot of work to do, and she's getting too old to do it all herself."

"Too fat," Anah muttered.

"Who's talking?"

Still bickering, the two women left, taking the empty pot with them.

The twins went out to the vegetable garden, putting on Matred's straw-woven hats. The sun was not yet high, the shadows still long. "We'll stay just a little while," Sandy said.

They worked hard. The weeds, it seemed, grew up as fast as they could clear them. Weeding was a never-ending job. They did not mention Yalith. They had more than enough to do to keep them busy.

Grandfather Lamech no longer came out to the garden with them, but spent most of the day in the tent, drowsing. After the long afternoon sleep he would sometimes accompany them to the well, where they drew water, filling large clay jars, one for use in the tent. The others were for the garden, which Higgaion helped them water, spraying with his trunk, which was almost as good as a hose.

"It's good to be working in a garden," Sandy said, "even if it's not the garden at home."

"Who do you suppose is tending to the garden at home?" Dennys asked. "It's got to be at least harvest time by now. That is, if time there is passing like time here."

"Everything is different here," Sandy said. "People living longer, for instance."

"So maybe time is different, too. At home we had alarm clocks and those electronic bells at school, and here time just slides by and I hardly even notice it."

"I don't want to think about it, about time," Sandy said. He looked at his twin. "We're browner than we ever got at home. Anah's right about that."

"And our hair is bleached. At least, if mine is like yours, it is."

Sandy looked at his twin. "Well, your hair is lots lighter than it used to be."

"I wonder what it would feel like to wear clothes again?" They were used to wearing loincloths. They were even used to no showers, no water for bathing. The smells of the tent were hardly noticeable.

With a strong green vine, Sandy was tying up tall, green-leafed bushes, giant versions of the basil they planted between the tomatoes in the garden at home. Grandfather Lamech often chopped up the leaves to season his stews. "I'm not homesick anymore. At least, I'm not home*sick*."

"I try not to think about it too often," Dennys said, "except to remind myself that since I didn't die of sunstroke, then somehow or other we ought to be able to get home."

"We won't be the same," Sandy said.

Sandy made a face. "Hey, I don't like the way Tiglah keeps coming around. I don't think I'm ready for Tiglah."

"Tiglah," Dennys said, "is what the kids at school would call an easy lay."

"Except," Sandy said, "there isn't *any*body remotely like Tiglah at school."

"She's older." Still, neither of them mentioned Yalith.

"Yeah," Sandy said.

"The thing is—" Dennys paused. "Something's happened. We're not just kids anymore."

"I know." Sandy bent over one of the plants.

Dennys pulled up a resisting weed with such force that he sat down. "We haven't seen Adnarel lately. Or any of the other seraphim."

Sandy finished tying the plant to a bamboo stalk. Images of scarab beetle and pelican, camel and lion, flashed before him. He always felt better if Adnarel was with them. When the seraph was in his scarab-beetle form, he was usually near Grandfather Lamech's sleeping skins, or on Higgaion's ear. He gave Sandy a sense of security. "I think the seraphim like us."

"But the others don't," Dennys said. "I mean, the other ones, the nephilim. I've seen them looking at us when they thought we weren't noticing. And a mosquito kept buzzing around me the other day after Tiglah had been around. I don't think it was just a mosquito."

"Rofocale," Sandy said. "I heard her call one of the nephilim Ro-focale."

"They don't like us," Dennys said.

* * *

When supplies were needed, the twins left Grandfather Lamech's and went to the nearby shops, carrying figs, dates, and the produce of their garden to barter for rice or lentils. On the dusty paths they passed many of the people of the oasis, who always paused to look up at Sandy and Dennys, surreptitiously if not openly.

When they passed nephilim, with whom they could look eye-to-eye, brilliant wings quivered, but the nephilim did not acknowledge their presence, except in sudden reversion to the animal host, so that a tall, bright-winged man would vanish, and there would be a skink scuttling across the path, or a red ant, or a slug leaving its slimy trail.

The women, at least the young ones, let Sandy and Dennys know that they were admired. Small hands reached up to touch them. They were bathed in lavish smiles. Tiglah seemed to know when they needed rice or beans or lentils, and would be waiting at whichever stall they were headed for.

The men and the older women were different. Sometimes the twins were cursed at, spat at. They did not tell Grandfather Lamech, who would have been distressed. They learned to go to the few venders who treated them kindly and did not try to cheat.

Dennys said, one day, "Hey, Sand. If you want to go for a walk with Tiglah, don't let me stop you."

"I don't want to." Sandy turned his gaze from the side of the path, where a vulture was picking the flesh from a small carcass.

"I mean, just because it was her father and brother who threw me into the garbage pit—I mean, I'm not stopping you, or anything."

"No problem," Sandy agreed.

They were careful with each other as they had never been careful before.

And still they did not mention Yalith.

Yalith and Oholibamah were helping Matred to clean the big tent when they were disturbed by the flap being pushed open, and a lavender-winged nephil came in. He spoke without greeting. "It is nearly Mahlah's time. She will need you to help with the birthing of the baby."

Matred held the broken palm branch which she was using as a broom. "Do you not have one of your own kind to help?"

Ugiel looked at Oholibamah with hooded eyes. Flicked a long finger in her direction. "She will be of use. And Mahlah will need her mother and sister."

Oholibamah took a step away from the nephil. "How will we know when to come?"

"Tonight. At the time of the moonrise. I, Ugiel of the nephilim, tell you so."

"We will come," Matred pronounced. "I will not have my daughter labor alone."

"Good. I will expect you."

"We will come," Matred repeated, "but you will wait outside."

Ugiel shrugged. "Have it your own way. It is a woman's job to see to all the blood and mess of a birth." He started out, then turned his burning gaze on Yalith.

She did not drop her eyes. Biting her lower lip, she met his stare.

"You cannot have them both, you know," Ugiel said.

Then he was gone.

Yalith and Oholibamah spread skins over some low scrub palms. Some skins they would discard, if they were too soiled. Others they would scrape and beat clean.

"What did he mean?" Oholibamah asked.

"Who?"

"Ugiel."

"About what?"

"About not having them both."

Yalith picked up a skin foul with spills and put it in the dump pile. "Who ever knows what a nephil means?"

"You do, and I do," Oholibamah said. "He meant our young twins."

Yalith picked up another skin, appearing to examine it closely. "The Sand was the first one I met. The Den is the one we saved from the sun death."

"And they are two people, not one," Oholibamah reminded her.

"I know. Oh, yes, Oholi, I know that. They are very different when you get to know them."

"And you do not love one more than the other?"

Yalith shook her head. "Anyhow, they are too young."

"Are they that young in their own time?"

"We don't know anything about their own time."

Oholibamah sat on a stump, a pile of cleaned skins across her knees. "I love my Japheth. I am very happy with him. I want you to be happy, too."

Yalith shivered. "Mahlah seems to be happy, married to a nephil."

"Our twins are not nephilim."

"But they are different. They are not like us."

"And you love them."

"Yes."

"You love them both."

Yalith picked up a pile of skins to be discarded. "I'm going to throw these away. Then we'd better stop. The sun's getting high and it's too hot for this kind of work."

Matred said to Elisheba, "You have not been to the women's tent for two moons."

Elisheba nodded, put her hands to flushed cheeks in an unwontedly girlish gesture.

Matred embraced her. "Is it true?"

"Yes. You will have yet another grandchild." Hugging each other, they danced with joy.

Eblis the dragon/lizard was waiting for Yalith when she went to the well for water. He was not in his animal host, but was leaning against the trunk of a royal palm, purple wings wrapped around him, so that he was almost lost in shadows.

When he stepped forward, Yalith was so startled that she almost dropped the clay pitcher which she carried on one shoulder.

Eblis rescued the pitcher and put it down. "Every day you grow lovelier." He touched her gently on one cheek.

Yalith blushed and reached for the pitcher.

"Let me help you," Eblis said. When the pitcher was full, he touched her again, tracing her brows with one pale finger. "Ugiel is right, you know."

"I don't know what you're talking about."

"Oh, yes, you do, my sweet one, yes, you do. And I am the only answer to your problem."

She looked at him questioningly.

"I want you, lovely little one. You know that I want you. I can give you all that Ugiel gives your sister Mahlah, and you know how happy she is."

"I know . . ."

"Those stupid young giants who dazzle you with their youth can give you nothing except grief. You cannot choose between them, and if you should choose one, what would happen to the other?"

"They have not asked me—" She faltered.

"But I have. I do. I want you."

He bent toward her, and suddenly she felt nothing but fear. It was as he said: he wanted her. He did not love her. She picked up the water pitcher and fled, heedless of the water splashing on the ground.

9 Mahlah's Time, Lamech's Time

The afternoon was the hottest the twins had ever experienced. Sandy woke from unpleasant dreams of erupting volcanoes, to see Dennys sitting up on his sleeping skins, shiny with sweat.

Higgaion spent the midday sleeping hours with Lamech. At night he dutifully took turns with the twins, but Sandy suspected that the past few nights had been spent at Grandfather Lamech's feet. The old man's extremities tended to get cold from lack of circulation.

"Is anything wrong?" Sandy asked.

"It's terribly hot."

Thunder rumbled in the distance.

"That might mean rain," Sandy said. For the moment he had forgotten that rain might mean flood.

So had Dennys. "Oh, good, for the orchards and the garden. Even with all our watering—"

The thunder came again, with a crackling, electrical sound.

Higgaion padded over to them, whimpering, looking across the tent to Grandfather Lamech.

The two boys hurried to the old man. The flap had been pegged open to let in as much breeze as possible, and the air outside was sulfurous, the sky a greenish-yellow.

Sandy squatted at one side of Grandfather Lamech, Dennys at the other. The old man was propped high on folded skins. Dennys took one of his hands and was shocked at how cold it was. He began to massage it, trying to get some circulation into the withered fingers.

Lamech opened his eyes and smiled, first at one twin, then the other. When he spoke, his voice was so faint that they had to strain to hear. "In your time and place—over the mountain—is it better?"

Sandy and Dennys looked at each other.

Sandy said, "It's very different."

"How?" the voice whispered.

"Well. People are taller. And we don't live as long."

"How long?"

Dennys answered in words which seemed to him an echo of something long lost. "Threescore years and ten."

"Sometimes fourscore," Dennys amended.

Dennys looked at Sandy, at his tan, healthy skin, muscled arms and legs, clear eyes. "We have big hospitals—places to take care of sick people. But I'm not sure I'd have had any better care for my sunstroke there than I got from Yalith and Oholibamah."

Sandy said, "We have showers and washing machines. And radios and rockets and television. And jet planes."

Dennys smiled. "But I came to your tent on a white camel. Almost all the way."

Lamech whispered, and both boys bent down to hear. "People's hearts—are they kinder?"

Sandy thought of the first vender who had tried to give him half the amount of lentils Grandfather Lamech had requested, and who had snarled and cursed when Sandy protested.

Dennys wondered how much real difference there was between terrorists who hijacked a plane and Tiglah's father and brother, who had thrown him into the garbage pit.

"People are people—" Sandy started.

Simultaneously, Dennys said, "I guess human nature is human nature."

Lamech reached out a trembling hand to each boy. "But you have been to me as my own."

Dennys gently squeezed the cold hand.

Sandy mumbled, "We love you, Grandfather Lamech."

"And I you, my sons."

"El's words are strange words. I don't understand," Lamech said. "I don't understand the thoughts of El."

Neither did the twins.

Lightning and thunder came simultaneously. Light splashed through the roof hole and the open tent flap. The walls of the tent shook from the violence of the thunder and a long earth tremor.

But no rain fell.

The twins sat on the root bench to watch the stars come out. Higgaion stayed in the tent with Grandfather Lamech. The sky still had a yellow tinge, though there was no further lightning or thunder. Tongues of flame licked up from the volcano. High in the trees, the baboons chittered nervously.

Sandy curled his toes on the soft moss under the tree root. "We've never been to a deathbed."

"No."

"I thought *that* was going to be one, this afternoon with Grandfather Lamech."

Dennys shook his head. "I think he wanted to ask us those questions."

"Does he know there's going to be a great flood?"

"I think his El that he talks to has told him."

Sandy picked up a fallen frond of palm and looked at it in the last light. "But the flood was a natural phenomenon."

Dennys shook his head slightly. "Primitive peoples have always tended to believe that what we call natural disasters are sent by an angry god. Or gods."

"What do you think?" Sandy asked.

Again Dennys shook his head. "I don't know. I know a lot less than I did before we came to the oasis."

"Anyhow"—Sandy's voice was flat—"it didn't work."

"What didn't work?"

"The flood. Wiping out all those people, and then starting all over again. People are taller, and we do even worse things to one another because we know more."

Dennys took the palm frond out of Sandy's hand. "I wouldn't choose Ham and Anah to repopulate the world, if I were doing the choosing."

"Oh, they're not that bad," Sandy said. "And Shem and Elisheba are all right. Not terribly exciting. But solid. And Japheth and Oholibamah are terrific."

"Well. What you said. It didn't work."

"Maybe nobody should've been saved." Sandy's voice was hoarse.

Yet again, Dennys shook his head. "Human beings—people have done terrible things, but we're not all that bad, not all of us."

"Like who?"

"There've been people like—oh, Euclid and Pasteur and Tycho Brahe."

Sandy nodded. His voice came out more normally. "I like the way Tycho Brahe was so in awe of the maker of the heavens that he put on his court robes before going to his telescope."

"Who told you that?"

"Meg."

"I like that, I really do. Hey, and I think Meg would like us to mention Maria Mitchell. Wasn't she the first famous woman astronomer?"

"I miss Meg. And Charles Wallace. And our parents."

But Dennys was still involved in his list. "And the wise men who followed the star. They were astronomers. Hey!"

"What?"

"If the flood had drowned everybody, if the earth hadn't been repopulated, then Jesus would never have been born."

Sandy, his nostrils assailed by a now familiar but still disturbing odor, hardly heard. "Shh."

"What?"

"Look."

A small, shadowy form left the public path and came toward them. "Tiglah."

"She doesn't give up," Dennys mumbled.

Tiglah had learned that Dennys was not to be touched, not by her fingers, at any rate. She approached the twins demurely, eyes cast down, giving her eyelashes the full benefit of their lustrous length. She reached out and put her hand lightly against Sandy, as though to steady herself. "It's a fine evening, after all," she said.

Dennys pulled back from the mingled odor of sweat and perfume.

"It's okay." Sandy looked dubiously at the yellow light pulsing on the horizon.

Tiglah said, "I thought you might like to know that Mahlah is going to have her baby tonight."

"How do you know?" Dennys demanded.

"Rofocale told me."

"How does *he* know?" Sandy asked.

"He and Ugiel are friends. Yalith and Oholibamah are going to help."

The twins had seen kittens and puppies being born, and once a calf, and they had played with baby lambs and piglets on a neighboring farm. They looked at each other. "I'll bet Oholibamah's a good midwife," Dennys said.

Tiglah continued, "They tell me that Oholibamah's mother had a hard time birthing her. Nephil babies tend to be large." She sounded anxious.

Dennys looked at her sharply. "Does that worry you?"

"It might, one day. I hope it won't be too hard on Mahlah. She's such a little thing. Like me."

"Well," Dennys said. "Thanks for telling us." His tone was dismissive.

"It's going to be a beautiful night." Tiglah's fingers strayed toward Sandy's arm.

Dennys turned his face away and looked toward the tent. The flap was still pegged open. Higgaion was sitting in the opening, waving his trunk slightly, as though to catch the breeze.

Sandy looked at Tiglah, hesitated.

Swiftly, Tiglah coaxed. "It's such a nice night for a walk. After Mahlah's baby is born, Yalith and Oholibamah will be walking home and we might meet them . . ."

Sandy rose to the bait. "Well . . . but not far . . . or for long . . ."

"Of course not," Tiglah reassured. "Just a little walk."

Sandy became aware of Dennys carefully not looking at him. "Are you coming?"

"No."

"Do you mind if I go?"

"Of course not."

"I won't be long."

"Feel free."

They were not communicating. Sandy did not like the feeling. But he stood. Tiglah reached up and put her small hand in his much larger one. When they reached the public path, he looked back. Higgaion had left the tent and was standing by Dennys.

The night was heavier than usual. The stars looked blurred, and almost close enough to touch. The rainless storm had increased rather than decreased the heat. The mountain smoked.

"Let's go by the desert," Tiglah suggested, "and watch the moonrise."

To step off the oasis onto the desert was like stepping off a ship onto the sea. The desert sand felt cool to Sandy's feet, which were now accustomed to the hot sands by day, to walking on stones, on sharp, dry grasses.

Tiglah led the way to a ledge of rock. "Let's sit."

Moonrise over this early desert was very different from moonrise at home. At home, as the moon lifted above the horizon, it was a deep yellow, sometimes almost red. Here, in a time when the sea of air above the planet was still clear and clean, the moon rose with a great blaze of diamonds.

Sandy's eyes were focused on the brilliant light of the rising moon, and he was not prepared to have the light suddenly darkened by Tiglah's face as she pressed her lips against his. She was up on her knees in order to reach him, and her lips smelled of berries. Then he was surrounded by her particular odor of scented oils and her own unwashed body.

He knew what she wanted, and he wanted it, too; he was ready, but not, despite her gorgeousness, with Tiglah. Tiglah was not worth losing his ability to touch a unicorn.

But Yalith—

He knew that he and Dennys should do nothing to change the story, to alter history. Even with Yalith . . .

He was getting ahead of himself. Yalith was not Tiglah. Yalith smiled on both of them with equal loveliness.

Tiglah's red hair, turned silver-gold in the moonlight, tumbled about his face, drowning him in its scent. She massaged the back of his head, his neck. Her breathing mingled with his. He knew that if he did not break this off, he would not be able to. With a deep inward sigh, he pulled away. Stood.

Tiglah scrambled to her feet, stared up at him reproachfully. "Don't you like it? Don't you like what I was doing?"

"Yes, I like it." His voice was hoarse. "I like it too much."

"Too much? How can anything be too much? What is there in life except pleasure, and the more the better! How can you talk of too much?"

"You're too much." He tried to laugh. "I think I'd better go now. Grandfather Lamech isn't well."

"He's dying," Tiglah said bluntly. "Rofocale told me."

"Rofocale doesn't know everything."

"He knows more than we do, more than any mortal."

Sandy stood still. He thought he heard the shrill whine of a mosquito. Then silence. He turned and started walking back to the oasis. Tiglah slid down from the rock, ran to catch up with him, and reached for his hand.

"You, too," she said. "You must be of the same breed as Rofocale, so tall, so strong. You could pick me up, and throw me over your shoulder. Where do you come from?"

He was tired of answering the old questions. "Another part of the planet. Another time."

"Why have you come?"

"It was a mistake," he said shortly.

"But why was it a mistake to come? It's wonderful that you're here! How long are you going to stay?"

"I don't know."

"But you do have plans? What are you going to *do*?"

"Take care of Grandfather Lamech's garden and groves."

"Is that all? You didn't come all this way just for that! You must have come for some reason."

"No," he said. He removed his arm from her hand.

"No," Tiglah said. "I didn't find out anything. I asked him all the questions you told me to, but he didn't tell me anything."

Rofocale towered over her, his wings flaming like the sun even in the moonlight. "He must have said something."

"He said he came from far away, and that it was a mistake to come."

"Mistake?" Rofocale queried. The garnet pool of his eyes looked opaque. "Could El have made another mistake?"

"You think your El sent them?"

"Who else? They are certainly not native. They may be as much of a threat to us as the seraphim. At least the seraphim are careful not to manipulate or change things."

"You think the young giants will?"

"Who knows? And you couldn't get anything out of him?"

The dimple in Tiglah's chin deepened. "At least he came with me this time."

"So he did. And did you kiss him?"

She nodded. "He tasted so young. Young as the morning."

"Did he like it?"

"He liked it. But just as I thought he was ready to go further, he pulled back. But give me time, Rofocale. This is, after all, the first time he's been willing to go with me."

Rofocale in a movement of swift grace knelt so that their eyes were level. "You must work fast, my little Tiglah."

"Why? What's the hurry?"

Rofocale rubbed the back of his hand against his forehead. "Some of our powers have been weakened. We can no longer tell—but Noah knows something. His sons married abnormally young, and hurriedly. Noah still speaks with the One on whom I have turned my back. There may not be another hundred years."

"But why do you want me to—to seduce him?"

"Wouldn't that put him in your—and my—power?" He drew her to him. "What you do with the naked giant will not make you any less mine, little lovely one. I like my women to be experienced in the ways of lust."

"Will I make a baby for you?"

He spread his wings so that she was wrapped in a cloud of flame. "Soon."

* * *

"Soon," Oholibamah said. "Soon. Press down, Mahlah, press down. Hard."

"Soon," Yalith echoed reassuringly. "It will come soon."

Matred said nothing.

Mahlah, lying on her back on a pile of skins, screamed. Her hands groped frantically, and Matred took them in a firm grasp, while Mahlah clutched.

"It's gone on so long," Yalith whispered. "How much more can she take?"

"Get up," Matred ordered Mahlah.

Mahlah wailed, "I can't. I can't. Oh, let it come, let it come soon—"

"Get up," Matred repeated. "Squat."

"I did, I did, until I was so tired I couldn't—"

"You've rested enough." Matred's voice was rough. "Help her up," she ordered Yalith and Oholibamah.

The two girls had to use all their strength to pull the resisting Mahlah off the skins.

"Squat," Matred said. "Bear down. Now. Now. Push."

"The moon is setting," Yalith said.

Oholibamah looked at Matred. "My mother went through this. She is still alive."

"Yes, my dear," Matred said. "Thank you." It was Oholibamah's first open acknowledgment that she had been sired by one of the nephilim, and Matred pressed her shoulder in gratitude.

The moon set. The sun rose. It was stifling in the small white clay house. The four women streamed sweat. Mahlah's hair was as wet as though it had been dipped in the water jar. Her eyes were wide open in agony. She moaned, screamed, shrieked. Occasionally, between contractions, her mouth would fall open laxly and her lids would droop shut as she dropped into an exhausted sleep, only to be wakened as she was assailed by a fresh pain.

The sun slid low in the sky.

"Squat," Matred ordered. "You must squat again."

Three nights and three days. Squatting, lying, screaming.

—She will die, Yalith thought.—This cannot go on.

"Soon," Oholibamah continued to reassure the tortured Mahlah. "It will come soon. Press down. Harder."

Matred's voice was sharp with anxiety. "Work, Mahlah, work. We cannot have this baby for you. Work. Push."

For the fourth night, the moon rose.

"*Push,*" Matred commanded.

A long, grunting groan came from Mahlah, more terrible than her screams.

"Now. *Now*."

The groan seemed as though it would tear Mahlah apart.

"Now." And at last Matred reached between Mahlah's legs to help draw the baby out of her body. The baby's head was so large that Yalith could hear Mahlah's flesh rip as the child came out. Matred shook it, patted its buttocks, and the air rushed into its lungs and it howled.

While Sandy was with Tiglah, Dennys went in to Grandfather Lamech, uneasy about him. He walked to where the old man was lying.

"Son?"

"It's Dennys, Grandfather."

An old hand groped for his. Dennys held it, and it was cold, deathly cold. "Can I do something for you, Grandfather?"

A serene smile wreathed the old man's face. "El has spoken."

Dennys waited.

The old man seemed to be trying to suck in enough air to speak. Finally he said, "All will not be lost. Oh, my son, Den, El has repented. While you were in the garden, El spoke to me here in the tent. I have never heard him here before. Oh, my son, Den, my son, my son, Noah will be spared. Noah and his family. El has spoken."

"From what, Grandfather Lamech?"

"Eh?"

"From what will they be spared?"

The old fingers trembled in Dennys's hand. "El spoke of many waters. This I do not understand. But no matter. What is of concern is that my son will be spared." The fingers pressed against Dennys's. "But you, my son? What will happen to you? I do not know."

"I don't know either, Grandfather." Dennys massaged the withered old hand until a little warmth returned.

Ugiel stood looking down at the baby lying between Mahlah's breasts. The young mother looked pale and exhausted, but radiant.

The three women who had shared her labor were nearly as exhausted as Mahlah. Oholibamah had deep circles under her eyes, and her cheeks were ashen. It was she who had somehow or other stanched the blood that poured out, nearly taking Mahlah's life with it; she who had brought the afterbirth out safely. Her hands and arms were stained red from holding Mahlah's torn flesh together until the rush of blood slowed to a trickle and the danger of hemorrhaging was over.

Ugiel paid no attention to the others. He gazed at his baby. It had a full head of hair, black, like Mahlah's. He flipped it over and fingered the soft down outlining the shoulder blades. "I am pleased," he said.

Matred was sharp. "And well you might be. It almost killed her. Without Oholibamah, it would have." She turned away from Ugiel and fed Mahlah some of the strengthening broth Elisheba had sent over.

"Go home," she said to Yalith and Oholibamah. "Go and get something to eat, and rest. I will stay with Mahlah. Elisheba will be by later."

Oholibamah, also ignoring Ugiel, looked at mother and child. "She will need much care for the next several days. Be sure to call me if the bleeding starts again."

"I will," Matred promised.

Ugiel bent over Mahlah and with one long finger touched the baby on its eyelids, its nose. "I am pleased," Ugiel said again.

Oholibamah sat in the big tent, letting Elisheba feed them lentil soup.

Oholibamah said, "He didn't care whether she lived or not, as long as she had the baby."

Yalith paused in the act of raising her bowl to her lips. "Do you really think that?"

"You heard him, didn't you? 'Why doesn't she get on with it?' he said. 'Why is it taking so long?' And then he would go away and not come back for hours and hours."

"Mother said she didn't want him around—" Then Yalith stopped. Matred had been with her older daughters when they gave birth, shooing their husbands away but giving a running account of the delivery. Nor had the husbands gone far away. They had, in fact, been maddeningly underfoot. They had not simply vanished, like Ugiel, leaving everything to the women. She finished her soup in silence.

Oholibamah, too, drank. Her dark brows drew together. Her raven-black hair had come loose from its thong and fallen about her shoulders.

"Oholibamah—" Yalith said softly.

"What is it?"

"The nephilim marry our women, give them babies. But the seraphim—"

"They do not marry. Or give babies."

"But in many ways they are like the nephilim."

Oholibamah pushed her dark hair back in a weary gesture. "No. I think that once the nephilim were like the seraphim."

"What happened to change them?"

"I don't know."

Yalith thought of Aariel, with the bright amber eyes and leonine grace, and then of Eblis, and she was glad she had run from the purple-winged nephil. She wanted nothing to do with Eblis, if he was like Ugiel, who did not care whether his wife lived or died. Could Ugiel once have been like Aariel? Could Eblis?

Oholibamah said, "I think that the seraphim are free to leave us for the stars at any time if they want to. I don't think the nephilim can. Not anymore. They stay with us, not because they have chosen to, but because they have to."

Noah and Japheth came into the tent, their arms and hands as stained with grape juice as Oholibamah's had been with blood. Japheth embraced his wife. Yalith ran to her father. "Mahlah has had her baby! It is all right!"

Noah put his arms around his youngest child, but he seemed strangely disinterested.

"Did you hear, Father?" Yalith demanded. "Mahlah's long travail is over at last!"

"That is good to hear," Noah said heavily. "We were worried."

"What is it?" Oholibamah asked. "Is something wrong?"

Japheth's arm tightened about his wife.

Noah drew Yalith close. "El has spoken. Strange words."

"Good words?" Yalith asked.

Oholibamah looked at Japheth questioningly, but he shook his head.

"Strange words," Noah repeated. "I do not know what to make of them."

"Be happy for Mahlah, Father," Yalith said. "It was such a hard birth, so long. If it had not been for Oholi—"

"Mahlah will be all right," Oholibamah said. "She is young and strong and will heal quickly."

"It is a big baby, Father," Yalith continued. "It is the biggest baby I have ever seen, with dark hair, like Mahlah's, and a button of a nose."

"At least it is a baby." Noah's voice was bitter.

"You are upset," Oholibamah said.

"Yes, I suppose I am upset. El has asked me to do strange things. I do not understand. Great changes are coming. Terrible changes."

"Japheth—" Oholibamah whispered.

"Hush. Later."

Within the comfort of her father's arms, Yalith shivered. "But now we can rejoice, Father, because Mahlah has had a safe delivery."

Noah continued to hold his daughter, pressing his lips against her bright hair. "We did not have a wedding feast for Mahlah. That hurt Matred. I had hoped that we could have a wedding feast for you."

"Oh, but I hope you will!" Yalith exclaimed. She thought of Mahlah's strange wedding, and she did not want one like that, isolated from her family and friends. Then she thought of the twins. In their own way, they were as alien as the nephilim and the seraphim, and yet they were human, totally human. And she loved them. She pressed her cheek against her father's chest, so that she did not see the expression on his face.

Oholibamah did, but before she could speak, Japheth had pulled her to him again in a loving embrace.

A soft whimpering woke the twins. Higgaion had come over to their sleeping skins to summon them.

Sandy opened his eyes. "Higgy, what's the matter?"

Dennys sat up, abruptly wide awake. "Is it Grandfather Lamech?" He looked at Higgaion, asking, "Should we get Noah?"

"Is Grandfather—" Sandy could not finish the sentence.

The two boys scrambled across the tent to the old man's sleeping skins. Grandfather Lamech was breathing in strange, shallow pants. Dennys reached to touch him, and saw the scarab beetle. He felt a surge of relief. Spoke urgently. "Adnarel, we need Admael. If he could be his camel self, he could carry one of us to Noah's tent far more quickly than either Sandy or I could run." Dennys gently touched the bronze armor of the scarab beetle, which thinned out and disappeared under his finger, so that he was touching only a corner of the old man's sleeping skin. Adnarel stood by them, a golden glimmer in the gloom of the tent. "I will get Admael. Wait with Grandfather Lamech." With one of his swift, graceful gestures, he bowed and went out.

Sandy and Dennys each took one of Grandfather Lamech's hands, which felt as cold and lifeless as marble. Sandy said, "Adnarel is calling Admael for us. We'll get Noah for you, as quickly as we can."

The old man breathed softly. "My good boys."

Dennys watched Grandfather Lamech's straining effort to breathe. Gently he put his arm under the small, frail body, easing it into a sitting position. The old man leaned against the boy, and his breathing lightened. "I'll stay with you, Grandfather." Dennys looked at Sandy and nodded.

Sandy nodded back.

"I can wait," the old man whispered, "until the last star goes out."

Adnarel returned. He knelt by Grandfather Lamech, examining him gently. He turned to the twins. "Admael is waiting outside. You don't need to rush, Sand. There will be time."

Grandfather Lamech gasped. "Until the baboons—"

Adnarel smiled. "Until the baboons clap their hands and shout for joy to welcome the dawn."

Dennys said, "I'll stay with Grandfather."

Adnarel nodded, touching Dennys's shoulder lightly. "Good. I will be here if you need me." His bright form misted, swirled softly like fog, and the scarab beetle shone against Higgaion's ear.

When Dennys had ridden the white camel across the desert, coming from Noah's tent, he had still been weak from his sunstroke. Sandy was well and strong, and had little difficulty keeping his seat, his body quickly becoming accustomed to the erratically rolling rhythm. They crossed the desert without trouble. On a high outcropping of white rock, a lion stood majestically to watch their progress.

There was no sound around Noah's tenthold beyond contented snores. Sandy pulled back the flap to the big tent, calling, "Noah!"

It was Matred's sleepy voice that answered, "Who is it?"

"It's Sandy. Grandfather Lamech sent me to get Noah."

"El." Noah's voice was deep. "I'll be right out."

Sandy stood outside, listening to the sound of night insects mingling with snores from Ham and Elisheba's tent. He looked up at the sky and the low, blurred stars seemed to be calling him, but he could not understand what they were trying to say.

Noah came out, wearing a fresh loincloth.

"Dennys is with Grandfather," Sandy said, "and Higgaion."

Noah nodded.

"Adnarel said there would be time, but you'll get there faster if you ride the camel alone. I'll walk back."

Again Noah nodded, accepting the offer. The camel's legs were folded under it so that Noah could climb up easily. He sat astride, his work-gnarled fingers gripping the hair at the camel's neck. The white beast rose slowly, leaned its head on the long, arched neck low enough so that it could nuzzle Sandy softly, then took off, heading for the desert.

Sandy followed slowly. He knew that as soon as Noah reached the tent, Dennys would leave Grandfather Lamech, to allow the old man his last minutes with his son. Dennys would be waiting for him, probably sitting out on the root bench, perhaps with Higgaion to wait with him. But Sandy could not make his feet hurry. He jumped down onto the desert, and sand lapped at his feet. He let it run like water through his toes.

When Grandfather Lamech died, what then? Would it be near time for the flood? Would Sandy and Dennys be allowed to stay in the old man's tent and take care of his garden and groves?

Asking these questions of the silent stars did nothing to ease the lump of sorrow in his throat. He moved slowly over the sand, stubbed his toe on a hidden rock. Said "Ouch" in a loud voice. Walked on.

On his rock, the lion now lay still, watchful, its ears pricking as Sandy plodded by.

The horizon was touched with a faint rose color. The stars were dimming. The birds were waking in the trees. He thought he heard a sleepy jabbering from the baboons. He turned in toward the oasis. He could not delay his return any longer.

His head was down; he was looking at his feet moving across the sand. He did not notice sounds behind him. Suddenly something noxious was thrown over his head, blinding him. He was picked up roughly, his feet jerked out from under him. Two people were carrying him. The foul-smelling skin over his head was pressed hard against his mouth so that he could not scream. He tried to wriggle out of the clutch of whoever was carrying him, and a fist crashed into his belly, winding him, and something sharp pricked his arm.

10 The Song of the Stars

Yalith left the tent and slipped away, to the desert, to the rock where the great lion lay. He jumped down from the rock as she approached, and she ran to him, flinging her arms around his great ruffed neck, and sobbing, so that her words were barely coherent. "Grandfather Lamech is dying." Her tears spotted his fur. When her weeping was spent, the great cat's tongue gently licked her tears away, and then they sat, Yalith between the front paws, in silent communion.

The stars moved in their slow dance, dimmed. Neither lion nor girl moved. But Yalith, leaning against the great tawny chest, hearing the thudding of the lion's heart in time with the soft singing of the stars, moved into peace.

Outside Grandfather Lamech's tent, Dennys sat on the old root of the fig tree, Higgaion at his feet. Neither moved. Above them, the stars were quiet.

Within the tent, Noah held his father up so that the old man could breathe.

"My son," Lamech whispered. "You have been a blessing to me and to the land . . ."

Noah's tears rolled quietly down his cheeks, into his beard. "I have been stubborn and stupid—"

A faint laugh came from his father. "I did not say that you are not human. But you listen to El?"

"I try, Father. I try."

"El has told me that through you shall blessing . . ." The old man's breath failed.

"Hush, Father. Don't try to talk."

"It is . . . it is our last . . ."

"I listen, Father. To you. To El."

"You will do what—"

"Yes, Father. I will do what El tells me."

"No matter . . ."

"No matter how strange it seems."

"Yalith—"

Noah's tears flowed more freely. "Oh, Father, I don't know."

"Never fear." For a moment Lamech's voice was strong, and he sounded almost like one of the seraphim. Then the strength faded, and he spoke in a thin whisper. "El will take care of . . ."

"Father. Father. Don't go."

"Don't hold me back, my son . . . my son . . ."

Noah's tears fell like rain.

"Our dear twins—"

"What, Father?"

The old man gasped, and then smiled a surprised smile of joy, so radiant that it seemed to light the darkened tent. Had lightning flashed to make the smile visible?

"Father!" Noah cried. And then, "Father!" And then his sobs broke like waves across the dry sands of the desert.

The stars did not sing. The sky was silent. Higgaion sat up, ears alert. Dennys raised his head, and it seemed that the stars were holding their light.

And suddenly the bright presence of a seraphim stood before him, and the starlight again fell onto his upturned face.

Japheth and Oholibamah held vigil for Grandfather Lamech in their own way. They went to the desert, to their particular resting rock, and sat quietly, holding hands.

At last Japheth spoke: "Thank El that my father and grandfather are reconciled. It would be much harder to bear this if—"

Oholibamah smiled. "Two stubborn old men. Yes, it is better this way. We have the Den to thank for this."

"It was a happy day when I first found them in the desert, our young giants. They have taken good care of Grandfather."

Oholibamah sighed. "We are going to miss him. Yalith, especially; she was the closest to him of us all."

"True." Japheth cradled her dark head with his hand. "But Father says it is best that death has come to get him now. He is too old and frail to stand the trip."

"What trip?" Oholibamah asked.

Japheth's eyes were darkly unhappy. "Oh, my dear one, it is what I promised to tell you. Father says that El has told him strange things. And that he has been given very specific instructions."

"What instructions?"

Japheth sounded uncomfortable. "Oh, my wife, it is very strange indeed. El has told my father to build a boat, an ark."

Oholibamah, who had been leaning against her husband, sat up abruptly. "An ark? In the middle of the desert?"

"I said it was strange."

"Could he have made a mistake?"

"El?"

"Not El. Your father. Could he have misunderstood what El was telling him?"

Japheth shook his head. "He sounded very certain. He said that El had also told Grandfather Lamech the things which are to come."

"An ark." Oholibamah's dark brows drew together. "An ark, in a desert land. It makes no sense. Has your father told the others?"

"Not yet." Japheth pulled Oholibamah back against him. "He says they will laugh."

"They will," Oholibamah agreed. But she did not laugh.

"I have never seen him more serious," Japheth said.

"What's the ark to be built of?" Oholibamah asked.

"Gopher wood. At least we have plenty of that. And then he is to put pitch inside and outside to make it watertight."

"From what water?" Japheth was silent. She turned so that she could look at him. "This does not sound like your father."

Japheth spoke in a low voice. "Nor does it sound like El."

Oholibamah stroked his face. "We do not know what El does or does not sound like. El is a great mystery."

Japheth laughed. "So is a big boat in the desert."

"How big?" Oholibamah asked.

Japheth flung out his hands. "Three hundred cubits long, fifty cubits wide, and thirty cubits high."

Oholibamah asked curiously, "El gave these precise measurements?"

"According to Father."

"I don't understand," Oholibamah said. "I wish you'd had a chance to talk to Grandfather."

Japheth shook his head, wiping the tears from his eyes.

"And our twins," Oholibamah said. "What will happen to our twins now?"

"It is possible they might go on taking care of Grandfather's garden and groves. But I'm not sure. Grandfather's death is the beginning of a big change."

Oholibamah nodded. "There are dissonances in the song of the stars."

"Have you heard it?" Japheth asked.

Oholibamah nodded. "The song has changed. Yes, I have heard it. But why should Grandfather Lamech's death be the beginning of change? He is a very old man."

Japheth agreed. "It is not at all strange that he should die."

Oholibamah mused, "Perhaps it is strange that Grandfather Lamech should die just as El gives extraordinary commands to Lamech's son."

"Oh, my beloved," Japheth said. "You are wise. Sometimes I wish you were not quite so wise."

They twined their arms about each other. Japheth put his lips against hers, and they took comfort in their love.

When it became apparent that Sandy had not returned to Lamech's tent, nor had he stayed in Noah's, there was great consternation.

Noah's sons and their wives had come with Matred across the desert, and stood sadly outside Grandfather Lamech's tent.

"We haven't seen him," Japheth said anxiously to his father. "We thought he was following you."

Yalith reached for her brother. "We were so busy with our grief, we didn't even think . . ."

Noah pulled at his beard. "He said he would follow me."

Ham said, not unkindly, "Whatever's happened, we can't look for him now, not with the morning sun rising."

Shem explained to Dennys, "In our country, in this heat, the dead must be buried quickly."

Dennys tried to hide his panic at Sandy's inexplicable absence. Sandy was reliable. If there was a reason for his not having followed Noah to Grandfather Lamech's tent, he would somehow or other send word.

How? There were no telephones. But wouldn't he have tried to find one of the seraphim? He wouldn't just have gone off somewhere, without telling anybody.

Matred put a motherly arm about Dennys. "Now we must anoint Grandfather Lamech's body and prepare it for burial at sundown. Then we will leave our grief and look for the Sand. There is some reasonable explanation for his absence, I'm sure."

Anah suggested, "Perhaps he's somewhere with my sister. I think they're very taken with each other."

Dennys shook his head. He did not believe it. Sandy would not go off with Tiglah, knowing that Grandfather Lamech was dying.

Yalith slipped her hand into his and squeezed it comfortingly. She kissed him lightly on the cheek, like a butterfly, and then went with her mother and the other women into the tent. The men stayed outside while Lamech's body was rubbed with oil and spices and wrapped in clean white skins.

The sun rose high in the sky, beat down on them with the fierceness of a brass gong.

Japheth said, "Do not even think of going off to look for him in this heat, Den. The sun would strike you down, and that would not help your brother."

Had it not been for Japheth, Dennys would have put on one of Matred's woven hats and gone to look for Sandy. But Dennys knew that Japheth was right.

"Surely he's somewhere in the shade," Shem said. The palm grove where they were sitting shielded them with its dense shade. "Don't worry, Den. The Sand is a sensible lad."

"Yes, but—" Dennys started. And stopped himself. The people of Noah's tenthold were grieving for Lamech. Higgaion was in the tent with the women and the old men, and Dennys knew that it was irrational of him to feel abandoned by the mammoth. He was, after all, Lamech's mammoth.

The tent flap was pushed open slightly and Higgaion trudged out, and toward Dennys, raising his trunk in sorrowful greeting and asking to be picked up, much as a small child will raise its arms to be lifted.

Dennys gathered up the little creature and held it against him, letting his tears drop onto the mammoth's shaggy head.

At sunset, Noah and his sons carried Grandfather Lamech's body to a shallow cave not far across the desert. The women followed. Dennys stood between Yalith and Oholibamah, as Noah and Shem, Ham and Japheth dug a grave in the sand just inside the cave. Dennys had offered to help with the difficult digging, not only out of love for the old man, but also to take his mind off his near-terror over Sandy.

Noah told him, gently, that it was the custom that only the sons should do this final act of love, but that Dennys should stay with the women and the sons-in-law, because he had become a child of the family.

The sun slid below the horizon. The sky was a deep crimson. As the sun vanished, there was a faint glow on the far horizon, and the young moon began to peer over the edge of the planet. The moon's diamond crescent seemed strangely subdued as it rose, and Dennys, standing to one side, thought that he could hear a soft and mournful dirge. A star trembled into being, then another, and another. They joined the singing of the moon, singing for Lamech, whose years had been long, whose life had been full, and who, at the end, had been reconciled with his son.

Noah and Matred's older daughters, Seerah and Hoglah, and their husbands and children, stood in a cluster, wailing loudly. Mahlah stood to one side with her baby. Ugiel, she apologized, was not able to come. She looked curiously at Dennys.

Sandy, Noah told Mahlah in the same words she had used of Ugiel, was not able to come.

"Why?" Mahlah asked. No one answered.

Oholibamah spoke in a low voice, for Japheth, Dennys, and Yalith alone. "Mahlah will ask Ugiel about Sandy when she goes back."

Yalith whispered, "Will he know?"

Oholibamah shook her head. "If he does, he won't tell. I suspect the nephilim have something to do with this."

Japheth frowned. "I hope you aren't right about that."

Dennys looked at them with fresh fear.

The grave was dug.

As the son and grandsons picked the old man up to place him in the grave, Dennys sensed, rather than heard, presences behind them, and turned to see the golden bodies of seraphim standing in a half circle. Once again, he could hear clearly the singing of the moon and the stars.

Aariel called, "Yalith!"

Startled, she let out a small cry.

Aariel raised arms and wings skyward, and the song increased in intensity. "Sing for Grandfather Lamech."

Obediently, Yalith raised her head and sang, a wordless melody, achingly lovely. Above her, the stars and the moon sang with her, and behind her the seraphim joined in great organ tones of harmony.

Japheth took Oholibamah's hands and drew her out onto the clear sands, and they began to dance in rhythm with the song. They were joined by Ham and Anah, and the four of them wove patterns under the stars, touching hands, moving apart, twirling, touching, leaping. Shem and Elisheba joined in, then Noah and Matred and the older daughters and their husbands, and then Yalith took Dennys's hands and drew him into the kaleidoscope of moving bodies, an alleluia of joy and grief and wonder, until Dennys forgot Sandy, forgot that Grandfather Lamech would never be in his tent again, forgot his longing to go home. The crimson flush at the horizon turned a soft ash-rose, then mauve, then blue, as more and more stars brightened, and the harmony of the spheres and the dance of the galaxies interwove in radiance. Slowly the dancers moved apart, stopped. Dennys closed his eyes in a combination of joy and fierce grief, opening them only when the requiem was over. The sky was brilliant with the light of the moon and the stars. The seraphim were gone. Yalith stood beside him, tears streaming down her cheeks.

Noah and his sons tamped down the earth over Grandfather La-mech's grave.

Sandy opened his eyes and could see nothing. His limbs felt numb. Whatever had pricked him had temporarily paralyzed him. There was a strange tingling in his limbs as feeling began to return. He knew about the tiny darts that Japheth and Yalith and some of the others in Noah's tenthold used, and guessed that something similar had been used on him.

Why?

He smelled goat, urine, sweat. As his eyes adjusted to the darkness, he could see that he was in a small tent. The smoke hole was covered, so that very little light came through. It was a much smaller tent than Noah's or Grandfather Lamech's. He tried to move his arms and found that his hands were tied, bound firmly with thong. So were his feet.

As sensation returned to him, he wriggled around and finally managed to sit up, his back against the rough skins of the tent, his bound hands in front of him. He raised them and tried to bite at the thongs. The taste made him gag. The thongs had been wound about his wrists so many times that it was futile to try to chew through them, nor could he find a knot to try to bite.

He stopped his useless reflexive efforts and tried to think.

He had been kidnapped on his way from Noah's tent to Lamech's. Why? When terrorists hijacked a plane, they wanted something. What use would he be to anybody as a hostage? This was a world still without money, without political prisoners. As far as he knew, nobody held anything against Lamech or Noah.

So, why?

His stomach growled. How long had the poisoned dart kept him asleep? What time was it? He could not see even a line of light to indicate where the tent flap was. The light from the covered smoke hole was so faint that it might even have come from stars.

There had to be a tent flap. He wriggled around so that his feet touched the tent wall, and kept wriggling, feeling with his toes. Wriggled until he was exhausted and had found no way out. Rested. Wriggled again. Again. At last his feet felt a line of roughness. He pushed, and the flap moved slightly, enough so that he could tell that it was indeed night outside. Stars. A single palm tree silhouetted against them. He had no idea where he was, or even if he was still on his own oasis.

Worn out from his efforts, he fell asleep, his head just out of the tent. Sunlight blazing against his lids woke him, and he managed to slither back into the tent and sat leaning against the taut skins by the entrance. His stomach made loud, hungry noises. What wouldn't he give for a mess of Grandfather Lamech's pottage.

Grandfather.

When he got out of this tent and back where he belonged, there would no longer be the tiny, shriveled old man tending the hearth fire.

Come on, Sandy. He's *old*. Seven hundred seventy-seven years. And Noah was pushing six hundred years old. It didn't make any sense. Except, he believed them. And after the flood people weren't going to live that long. At least, he thought that was how it was going to be.

"Twin!"

It was a girl's soft voice. His heart leaped. Yalith.

Then smell followed sound. Not Yalith. Tiglah.

"Twin?" she repeated.

"Hello, Tiglah." He did not sound welcoming. He remembered what Dennys had told him about the people in Tiglah's tent. So it was they who were the terrorists. Terrorism was not just a twentieth-century phenomenon. It was evidently part of human nature, and it didn't get wiped out by the flood. There seemed less and less point to the flood.

"You recognized my voice!" she chortled.

—No, your smell, you slut, he wanted to say.

She pushed in through the flap and pegged it back to let in the light. She had taken unusual pains with her hair, so that it glistened brightly. Her loincloth was of white goat-skin. "Dennys?" She was tentative.

"Sandy."

"Oh, I'm so glad it's you! Dennys doesn't seem to like me, and I think you do, don't you?"

"Why would I like anybody who's kidnapped me and tied me up and starved me?"

"But *I* didn't do that!"

"You obviously knew about it."

"But I didn't do it! My father and brother did. I wouldn't hurt you for anything!"

"But you don't mind if your father or brother hurt me?"

"Oh, beloved Sand, I can't stop them! I've come to bring you food and comfort."

He sniffed. There was a nourishing smell of stew beyond the odor of the tent, as well of Tiglah's perfumed and unwashed body. If they'd already used some kind of poisoned dart on him, was it safe to eat the stew?

Tiglah said, "I made it myself, so I know it's all right, and it's good, too."

"I can't eat with my hands tied up."

She paused. Appeared to be thinking. "I'll feed you!" Her dimples came and went with her lavish smile.

"No. I'm not a baby. Untie my hands." He did not say please. How could he ever have been attracted by this girl?

She paused again. "All right. I'll untie your hands and stay with you while you eat."

"My feet, too," Sandy ordered. "I need to go to the bathroom."

"What?"

"I need to urinate."

"Oh, for auk's sakes. Can't you just do it in the tent?"

"No. You can come with me if you want. I don't care, but I need to go."

She knelt by him and began working at the thongs, first on his wrists, then his ankles. When he was freed, he stood up, feeling very wobbly. This tent was not nearly as high as Grandfather Lamech's or Noah's, and he bumped his head on the roof skins.

She took his hands and rubbed his wrists where the thongs had chafed them.

"Let's go," he said.

"Where?"

"I told you. I need to relieve myself."

"Come along, then." She pulled him out of the tent and to a small, grassy hummock a few feet away. There was no grove to provide privacy or a modicum of sanitation. "Go ahead."

"Turn around."

"You'll run away."

He looked about. He did not recognize the part of the oasis where this solitary tent was. A few yards away were some palms, and a rocky field dotted with black-and-white goats grazing under the high brassy sky. He had no idea in which direction to go. "I won't run. Turn around."

"Promise?"

"I promise." He suspected that his promise meant more than would Tiglah's. When he was through, he said, "All right."

She whirled around and caught his hand again. "Now come and have some of my good goat-meat stew."

They ducked back into the tent, and she brought him a wooden bowl full of meat and vegetables. He had learned to eat with his fingers, if not as delicately as Yalith, at least tidily enough so that he did not slop food on himself. Tiglah's concoction was not bad. The goat meat was a little strong, but she had cooked it until it was tender. When he finished, cleaning the bowl with his fingers, he felt better.

"I'll have to tie you up again," Tiglah apologized. "They won't like it that I let you loose at all."

"Who're *they*?"

"Oh, the men of my father's tent."

"What's it all about?"

"What?"

"Kidnapping me. Keeping me tied in this stinking tent."

She shrugged and giggled. "How would I know? They're always up to things."

"And you're not?"

"I'm only a girl." She was full of righteous indignation. "I like you! Why would I want to tie you up?"

"Then don't."

She had the thongs in her hands. "But I have to."

"Why?"

"They'd be furious. They'd hit me. They might kill me."

Would they? He wasn't sure. But he understood Dennys's refusal to have anything to do with Tiglah. Never again.

"How long are they going to keep me here? What do they think they're going to get out of it?"

"Noah's vineyards," she said.

"What!"

"Noah's vineyards. They're the best on any oasis."

"That's idiotic. Noah wouldn't give up his vineyards. They're his livelihood."

"He'd better give them up," Tiglah said, "or they'll kill you."

Sandy stood up, outraged, hitting his head against the roof skins. "Do they know Grandfather Lamech is dying—is dead?"

"Of course."

"They're monstrous."

"They're clever. They knew everybody would be paying attention to silly old Lamech and wouldn't miss you. They're *very* clever."

"Oh, no, they're not," Sandy said. "No one gives in to terrorists. Noah won't give anybody his vineyards."

"Then they'll kill you."

"And what good will that do? They still won't have the vineyards, and they'll have murder on their hands."

"Oh, Sand. Sit down. This tent wasn't made for giants. I hate to tie you up again, but I have to. Unless—"

"Unless what?"

"Come with me."

"What would your family think of that?"

"They'd hate it. But I care more about you than I do about them."

Sandy did not believe her. There was a trap here. This had something to do with the nephilim, with that mosquito Rofocale. What, he did not know. Tiglah did not love him enough to anger her family. She did not love him at all. But she would obey Rofocale.

He felt a sharp sting and slapped, but missed the mosquito, who buzzed out of the tent. Furious, he scratched at the bite. "Tie me up and go away."

She pressed her face close to his. "You won't come with me?"

"No."

"You'll risk being killed?"

His mouth twisted into a half grin. "There are fates worse than death," and he laughed, because Tiglah did not have the faintest idea what he was talking about.

"I haven't bound you yet . . ." she whispered.

"No."

"You're a giant. You could grab me and run off with me, and you could tell them you'll kill me if they try to capture you again."

It was tempting. He shook his head, and a great wave of sadness washed over him. Tiglah had never heard of the great heroes of lance and spear, of longbow and sword. But this was what she was tempting him to be. What he could be if he wanted to be.

What in him was urging him to reject this attractive role? What was telling him to say no? It was more than his suspicion that all this was some kind of nephil trap.

The sadness washed over him again. Violence was no longer an option. The splitting of the atom had put an end to that, though the world was slow to realize it.

Yes, he could overcome Tiglah with ease. She was inviting him. But even if there was no trick in it, he would not do it. Violence met with violence produced only more violence. His stomach knotted.

"Are you sure?" Tiglah's voice had a little whine in it.

"Of what?"

"That you won't come with me."

He smiled without mirth. There was poison in Tiglah's offer, of that he was certain. "No, Tiglah, I won't come with you. Yes, to you I'm a giant. I'm young and strong. But then what? I couldn't survive in the desert. I've seen bones there, and not all of them are animal."

She pouted. "I thought you liked me."

"You're a delicious dish, Tiglah. Now please bind me again, but perhaps you don't need to do it as tightly as before."

She was offended. She tied the thongs as tightly as she could, with vicious little jerks, but Sandy used enough strength so that she did not succeed. Then she flounced out, slapping the tent flap closed behind her.

He didn't mind the darkness. Enough light came in through the edges of the closed roof hole. He needed to think. He was extremely confused at his own reactions. He and Dennys had had their fair share of fistfights when they were younger, though perhaps not as many as their sister, Meg. They played mostly team games and did not go in for boxing or wrestling. Was he being a coward? He knew that Tiglah's father and brother would not hesitate to use bow and arrow, stone knives, or spears. He knew they were quite capable of killing him, just as much if he ran away as if he stayed. In fact, he thought he had more chance of surviving if he stayed and figured out some way and route of escape than if he rushed out to the desert, unthinking. He was not so much afraid as outraged. He did not think he was a coward.

So. What to do? Violence was not going to work. Violence was what these little men turned to, and he did not want to be like them.

He wondered if they had gone to Noah with their wild demand for his vineyards. He did not know Noah as well as Dennys did, but he did not think Noah would give in. Sandy's rejection of violence had nothing to do with giving in. Anything but.

After Grandfather Lamech was buried in the grave in the small cave, and the singing had died out, and the seraphim were gone, Noah and his family walked slowly toward the big tent. Wherever there was an outcropping or rock or a cave, Japheth, holding his tiny bow and darts, would hurry to look, Dennys on his heels.

"I do not like this," Noah said.

Dennys and Japheth returned from peering into the deep shadows of a little cave. The starlight was so bright that the shadows seemed to increase in darkness. "Is Sandy lost in the desert?" Dennys's voice cracked more than usual in his anxiety.

In the distance they heard a howl: *"Hungry!"*

Yalith reached for Dennys's hand and squeezed it.

Shem said, "If the manticore is hungry, then he hasn't found anything to eat."

Oholibamah said, "Don't worry about the manticore. Sandy scared it away from Grandfather Lamech's tent."

Could Sandy scare the manticore again, if they met out on the desert? Dennys was not certain, not after his own encounter with the ugly creature.

Elisheba said, "Sandy would never have just wandered off on his own."

Yalith nodded. "He was following you to Grandfather Lamech's tent."

Noah rubbed his beard. "Yes, yes, that's what we thought. But when he didn't come, then we thought he must have stayed in the big tent."

Anah said, "Well, he didn't, and that's that. I think he's off with my sister, Tiglah, that's what I think."

Nobody replied. The stars moved slowly across the sky. Dennys tried to listen for their singing, but he could hear nothing. After the glorious requiem for Grandfather Lamech, they were silent.

The moon was dipping behind the horizon when they reached Noah's tents, tired, sorrowful, anxious.

"Now, before anything else, all of us must eat," Matred said.

Noah said, "She is right. Come, Den."

Dennys accepted the bowl of broth Matred gave him. He knew that he needed all his strength for whatever lay ahead.

With his strong teeth, Shem pulled the meat off a mutton bone. Elisheba handed him a bowl of broth. "Will you go look for the Sand?" Shem, the hunter, was the one who knew the oasis and the desert best. Japheth and Ham worked in the vineyards, close to home. Shem was the one who should go, and Dennys flashed Elisheba a glance of gratitude. Absently, he patted Selah, who was leaning against him, putting her trunk on his knee.

Shem saw that Dennys had finished his broth, and nodded. He reached for one of the tall spears leaning against the inner wall of the tent. Hefted it. Offered it to Dennys. Dennys took it, though he had never used a spear. Shem checked his small quiver of blow darts, then reached for a second spear, and nodded at Dennys, not speaking. The boy followed the short, stocky man out of the tent, feeling a little hope. There was something about Shem that gave him confidence.

Noah said, "Japheth and I will search the paths of the oasis."

Ham said, "Anah and I will go to the marketplaces."

Matred spoke too cheerfully. "If the Sand returns to the tent, which seems likely, we will let everybody know."

Shem and Dennys pushed out of the tent flap. The stars were dimming. Light tinged the eastern horizon. Heat was already beginning to shimmer in watery mirages on the desert. Dennys had on one of Matred's woven hats and hoped it would be adequate once day broke.

Shem looked at him. "Once the sun is high, you must go back to the tent."

Dennys nodded. Shem, like Japheth, was right about that. Already his skin was prickling from heat as well as anxiety. He tried to keep himself from imagining what might have happened to his twin. He followed Shem. Followed. The heat bore down. The futile searching seemed interminable. After what must have been several hours he asked, "Where's Higgaion?"

Shem said, "He will spend the day mourning at Grandfather Lamech's grave. Then he will come to us. Selah will help lighten his grief."

"Higgaion scents for water," Dennys said with sudden hope. "Do you think he could scent for Sandy?"

Shem leaned on his spear, thinking. "Mammoths are strange creatures. They can do strange things. Let us try."

Shem strode off. He walked at a rapid pace, but Dennys, with his much longer legs, could easily have outstripped him and had to hold himself back. Grandfather Lamech's burial cave was about halfway between his tent and Noah's, and the sun was rising by the time they reached it. Higgaion was stretched out on the sand. His fan-like ears lifted at the approaching footsteps.

Dennys hurried to him. "Higgy, do you think you could scent for Sandy, the way you scent for water?"

The mammoth's little eyes had been shadowed with grief. Now they brightened. Shem dropped to his knees by Higgaion, bending down toward him in intimate communication, speaking softly.

The mammoth raised his trunk in a small, hopeful trumpet.

Dennys's eyes, too, were hopeful. "Oh, Shem, what could have happened to him?"

Shem's voice was heavy. "Some people are wicked, and the imagination of their hearts is only to do evil."

"What about Grandfather?" Dennys asked.

Shem stroked his beard in a gesture much like Noah's. "Grandfather knew. There is much wickedness. It, too, smells. You do not smell wicked, Den, nor does the Sand. Grandfather said that there is a great warmth in your hearts, and that is a pleasing smell." It was the longest speech Shem had ever made.

"Thank you," Dennys said. Then: "Let's go."

Shem shook his head, glancing up at the sun. "I thought we would have found him by now."

"Come *on*," Dennys urged.

"Den, I have hunting to do if we are to eat tonight."

"But—"

"My sisters and their families ate hugely, did you notice?"

—Funeral baked meats, Dennys thought angrily.

"Den, we must eat if we are to have strength for whatever—"

Dennys turned to Higgaion. "Come on, Higgy."

"Den. I hunt best alone. But I will continue to search for the Sand. Find Japheth."

"But he's—"

"He and Father will be searching near the tent. Do not go off with Higgaion alone. It is not safe."

Dennys looked at Shem's anxious face. Not safe. Not safe, because whatever had happened to Sandy might happen to Dennys . . .

"We will not stop until we find him," Shem said. "Go find Japheth. You and Higgaion."

Noah sat in the big tent, cross-legged, his elbows on his knees, his head bent down to his hands. Matred came and sat beside him.

"I don't know where he is," Noah said. "Where he could be."

"Rest, husband," Matred urged. "He will be found."

Noah nodded. "My heart is heavy. I grieve for my father."

"He was an old man, full of years," Matred consoled him.

"The Sand is not."

"You think something has happened to him?"

"Why else would he not have joined me at my father's tent? He is not like the young men of the oasis, thinking of nobody but themselves."

"He and the Den are not like anybody else," Matred said. "We do not know that something terrible has happened."

Noah did not reply, nor did he look at her. "And I must begin to build the ark."

Matred said, "El has never before asked you to do anything wild."

"Is it so wild? If the rains cover the earth, as he says they will, it will not be a wild thing to have an ark."

"The rains had better not cover the earth for a while," Matred said. "You have to build the ark, find all the animals."

"I will begin right away."

"And you will be laughed at. You will be the big joke of the oasis."

"I do not find it amusing," Noah said. "My father is dead. The Sand is El knows where."

"Why don't you ask El?"

"I have. El says only that I must begin to build the ark. El says nothing about the Sand."

"Or the Den?"

Noah grunted in agreement.

"Will you bring them onto the ark?"

"Of people, only you, and our sons, and their wives. No more."

"Yalith—" Matred started, but stopped as two men came, unannounced, through the open tent flap.

Tiglah's father and brother.

11 Many Waters Cannot Quench Love

Yalith went out into the desert. She was anxious, and anything but sleepy. She wanted to fling herself into Matred's lap and sob, as though she were still a little girl. She wanted to cry herself to sleep.

But she was no longer a little girl, and her eyes felt dry and burning. She was not used to being out at this time of day. She was not sure what drew her to the desert, because there was no hope that she might see Aariel. He would be in his cave, sleeping.

Nevertheless, she walked in that direction, and as she approached she was amazed to see him lying in the shadows at the mouth of the cave. Although she was certain it was Aariel, she was cautious. She had been certain that it was Aariel when the lion turned into the dragon/lizard Eblis.

She whispered, "Aariel—"

The lion rose, stretched, yawned, then paced toward her.

"Oh, Aariel!" She flung her arms about the tawny neck, though her tears were spent. "We don't know where the Sand is! Grandfather Lamech sent him to get my father. The Sand knew that Grandfather was dying, so he gave the camel to my father so that he could get back to Grandfather Lamech in time, and the Sand said that he would walk back. And Grandfather died, and everybody was thinking about him, and we didn't even notice, at first, that the Sand was not with any of us, and then we had to bury Grandfather, and—oh, oh, Aariel, we don't know what has happened—"

Aariel let her talk. When her voice faded and she pressed her face once again into his fur, he transformed slowly, gently, until she was enfolded in his wings. "Higgaion has gone to scent for him."

"He left Grandfather's grave?"

"For the living, yes. The Den and Japheth will go with him."

"Oh, that's good, I'm glad, I'm glad! Higgaion will be sure to find him, and Japheth will know what to do, and the Den, too."

Aariel drew her into the shade of the entrance to his cave.

"Aariel—my father is going to build a boat, an enormous boat."

"That is wise," Aariel said gravely.

"For my brothers and their wives. For animals of every kind."

"Yes, to preserve the species."

"But not for my sisters, Seerah and Hoglah, and their husbands and children. Not for Mahlah and her nephil baby. Not for—not for me."

Aariel drew her close. "Many waters cannot quench love, neither can the floods drown it." His voice was calm, gentle.

"What about the twins?" Again her eyes filled.

The seraph's arm was strong as it held her. "I do not know."

"But you know that El told my father to build an ark?"

"Yes. That I know."

"But you don't know about the twins?"

"We do not have to know everything."

"But you could ask—"

"We have asked."

"Are the stars silent, too?"

"The stars are silent."

"Aariel, I'm afraid."

"Fear not. I will hold you," he promised.

"I am more afraid for the Sand and the Den than I am for myself. I love them."

"And they love you."

"I don't want them to die. Will they die?"

Aariel folded his wings about her. He did not look at her. "I do not know."

Sandy slept. He still did not understand his reaction to Tiglah and her proposals for escape, but after a while he stopped questioning himself. When the time came for him to do something, he would know what to do.

Daylight was not a good time for escape. Perhaps in the cover of the night . . .

"Twin!"

It was Tiglah's voice, Tiglah's smell.

She pegged open the flap. "You have a visitor," she said.

He sat up, instantly alert. So her father and brother had come to kill him.

But it was Rofocale who came into the tent, bowing low to enter, so that his flaming wings dragged in the dust. Like Sandy, he was too tall to stand upright in this small tent. With swift grace he sat, facing Sandy, staring at him with garnet eyes. His bright hair was tied back, his cheeks white as snow.

He thrust out one hand and touched Sandy on the knee. The touch was that cold which is so cold that it burns. Sandy flinched, but did not cry out. "Why are you still here?" Rofocale demanded.

Sandy replied in his calmest voice. "I have been kidnapped and am being held hostage. If I escape and leave this tent, I will be easily seen. There is no way I can lose myself in a crowd. I am as tall as you are. I'd make an easy target."

"Why have you come?"

"Come? I didn't come. Tiglah's father and brother kidnapped me, and I suspect you put them up to it."

Rofocale said, "I am not asking why you are here, in this tent. I am asking why you and your brother chose to come to this oasis."

"It was a mistake," Sandy said, as he had said to Tiglah.

Rofocale again stretched out his hand, again touched Sandy on the knee. Sandy had had frostbite one winter, and this was how it had felt. "If it was a mistake for you to come, why do you not leave?"

Sandy said, slowly, deliberately, "We will leave when it is time to leave."

"And how, then, do you plan to leave?"

How, indeed? "We will know that when the time comes."

"You do not belong here."

"No. I belong with Noah and his family."

Rofocale made a noise like a mosquito shrill. "You do not belong here on this oasis. There are no giants like you in this time and place. Why do you not have wings?"

"We fly in planes and spaceships."

"What?"

The nephilim did not know everything. Sandy said, "We have machines that fly."

"Can you leave the planet?"

"We have gone to the moon. We fly among the stars."

"You?"

"I am too young," Sandy said. "My father has made several space flights."

"Did El send you to torment us?"

"What do you think?" Sandy asked.

"You are not of us, the nephilim. Neither are you, I think, of the seraphim."

"No. We are human beings."

"Mortals?"

"Yes."

"Then why have you come?"

"It was a mistake," Sandy said again.

"Would you like me to take you out of this place, this little tent?"

"No."

"They will come and kill you."

"Perhaps."

"Noah is unwilling to give up his vineyards."

"He is quite right. One does not give in to terrorists."

"You are foolish. I could give him a message, if you like. If you ask him, I think he will give up the vineyards."

"I wouldn't ask him."

"Then you will die."

"You'd like that, wouldn't you?" Sandy asked. "Perhaps you'd like to kill me yourself?"

"I will leave you. You are insolent."

"Why don't you like us, my brother and me?"

"You do not belong to our world. You will cause trouble. I think you have been sent to cause trouble to the nephilim." Rofocale rose. Energy crackled in the air, so that Sandy's skin prickled, and a mosquito flew away.

In a few minutes, Tiglah came in. "Did he tell you?" She was giggling. In the light slanting from outside, the dimple in her chin seemed a cleft.

"That your father and brother plan to kill me, yes, he told me."

"Not that." She was consumed with laughter.

He saw nothing funny. "What, then?"

"About Noah."

"He said that Noah is unwilling to give up his vineyards."

"No, no, not that, either."

"What, then?" He was irritated at her giggles.

"Noah is building a boat. A boat!" Her laughter peeled out.

Sandy sat up. Asked, carefully. "Why is he building a boat?"

"An ark, he says." Her laughter was derisive. "The nearest sea or river is moons away."

"Then why is he doing it?" Sandy asked.

"Who knows."

"Is he building it by himself?"

"Oh, no, it's a very big boat. I mean, hugely big. His sons are helping him. He says it is going to rain!" Her laughter jarred against Sandy's ears. "We have rain only in the spring, and then not much. He is the laughingstock of the oasis."

Sandy sat, alert, watching her.

"Rofocale thinks he may be building it to get rid of you. A boat where there is no water is silly."

"I'm hungry," Sandy said.

"Oh, I've brought you more food."

"Then just leave it with me."

She pouted. "You don't want me to sit and talk with you while you eat? I'll unbind your hands and feet."

"I'll manage." Sandy flexed his muscles so that the thongs looked tight. "I need to think."

"About the silly ark?"

"About a lot of things."

"Well . . . all right." She left the tent, returned with a bowl of stew. "You're sure you don't want me to stay?"

Sandy was firm. "Quite sure. Give up, Tiglah. Go."

Pouting, she went.

He sniffed at the stew. Ugh. It was spoiling. He pushed it aside, worked his hands out of the thongs, unbound his feet. If Noah was already building the ark, there was no time to wait. Dangerous or not, as soon as it got dark, Sandy would leave the tent, head for the desert, try to find out where on the oasis he was being held, and head for whichever was nearer, Grandfather Lamech's tent or Noah's.

Then he lay down to rest and wait for nightfall.

"They have gone too far," Noah said, "taking our Sand."

The family was gathered back in the tent, retreating from the heat of the sun.

Ham said, "You're certainly not going to give them the vineyards!"

Noah shook his head. "I told them that I would not. But now—I have already turned one of the older vineyards that needed replanting into a lumberyard. What difference will the vineyards make if they are all covered with water?"

Ham said, "We are helping you with this idiocy, Father, because you have asked us to. But surely you don't believe that there will be that much rain?"

"That is what I have been told."

Shem had returned from hunting, and was sitting on a pile of skins with Selah next to him. "You're sure it was the voice of El?"

"I am sure."

Elisheba suggested, "It couldn't, maybe, have been the voice of a nephil?"

"I know the voice of El from that of a nephil."

"They mimic very cleverly."

"El is El. If one of the nephilim tried to sound like El, then El would tell me that."

Matred looked up from her stewpot. "When will the rain start?"

"When the ark is ready."

Shem said, "What about our sisters and their husbands and their children?"

Noah wiped his hands across his beard. "I am to make a window in the ark, and set a door in the side, with lower, second, and third stories. El told me that I am to bring in animals of every kind, and my wife, my sons, and their wives."

Oholibamah's voice was sharp. "What about Yalith?"

Noah shook his head sorrowfully.

Shem protested, "But it's going to be a big boat, Father! Surely there's room for more than just the eight of us."

"Animals," Noah repeated, "of every kind, so that, when the flood waters abate, there will be both animal and human beings to repopulate the earth."

"I don't believe any of this," Ham said. "But if it should come to pass, I will give my place on the ark to Yalith."

Oholibamah looked at him in grateful surprise.

"Nonsense," Anah said. "When you build this ark, and nothing happens, how are you going to face everybody?"

Noah stroked his beard. "I obey El."

"And our twins?" Oholibamah asked. "What about them?"

"And where is the Sand?" Elisheba asked.

"Japheth and the Den will surely find him," Noah said. Selah raised her trunk and bugled. "And if they do not return with the Sand by sunrise, I will change my mind. I will give them the vineyards. When the flood waters abate, I will plant new vines."

Ham said, wonderingly, "You really believe that there is going to be a flood! We don't have enough rain, even in the spring, to be any use. If it weren't for our wells, there would be no oasis."

Shem asked, "Has our father ever made a fool of himself before?"

"No," Anah replied. "But there's always a first time."

Admael the white camel crossed the length of the oasis to where Sandy was imprisoned. It was at the farthest end of the oasis, as far from Noah's tent in one direction as was Grandfather Lamech's in the other. Admael did not go up to the tent, but folded himself down on the ground a few yards away, to wait.

Adnachiel the giraffe grazed on some tender leaves, stretching his long, golden neck. High up in the tree, sleeping during the daylight hours, sat Akatriel the owl, his head hunched into his feathers.

Together they waited.

Japheth and Dennys followed Higgaion, who trotted, zigzagging back and forth, from the outlying edges of the oasis to the desert, scenting, shaking his head so that the heightening sun glinted against his curved tusks, scenting. Back and forth. Into the oasis. Onto the desert.

"The sun is high," Japheth said. "You must find shade, Den."

Dennys shook his head, stubbornly. His body gleamed with sweat.

Japheth looked at him with concern. "We're not far from Grandfather Lamech's tent. Perhaps we'll find Adnarel there, and we could ask him for help."

Relieved, Dennys panted, "Fine." Higgaion was staggering with exhaustion. There had been no sign of Sandy.

Higgaion led the way back to the oasis, his energy renewed now that they had a destination. Japheth was untired, jogging along, breathing easily. Dennys was grateful for his own long legs; without them, he would not have been able to keep up.

As they approached Grandfather Lamech's groves and could see the dark shadow of his tent, Higgaion trumpeted and quickened his pace, so that Japheth was running. When they reached the tent, the heat seemed to intensify, and their shadows were dark and squat. Higgaion paused, pointing with his trunk to light flashing off something half buried in the sand by the tent flap.

"Adnarel!" Dennys cried. "Oh, Adnarel!"

Japheth bent down and lifted the scarab beetle out of the sand, stroked it gently with one finger, and it seemed to burst from his hand, and Adnarel stood before them, blazing gold.

"Oh, Adnarel," Dennys cried, "Sandy never came home after he gave Noah the camel! We don't know what's happened to him!"

Adnarel bowed gravely, listening, saying nothing.

Japheth said, "I worry that he may not have gone wherever it is of his own free will."

Adnarel turned to Japheth. "Explain what you are thinking."

"Since he didn't follow my father to Grandfather's tent as he said he would do, then I am afraid that perhaps someone . . ." His voice trailed off.

Adnarel's wings glittered. "You are thinking of Tiglah?"

"It was Anah's suggestion . . ."

"No," Dennys contradicted.

"We know she's a seductress," Japheth said.

"No," Dennys repeated. "Sandy would never have gone off with Tiglah, with Grandfather dying. Never."

Adnarel nodded. "Of course. He would not have disappeared of his own volition."

"Then where is he?" Dennys demanded.

Adnarel raised his wings, slowly lowered them. "What are you doing to try to find him?"

Japheth did not know of the visit of Tiglah's father and brother to Noah's tenthold. "We are all searching, but we have found no trace anywhere."

Adnarel looked at the two young men, eye to eye with Dennys, down for Japheth, small and lean and strong.

Japheth continued: "Sandy cares about Grandfather Lamech. He cares about his brother. It is not in his character to go off at such a time."

"Nephilim," Adnarel said softly.

A ripple of concern rolled across Higgaion's flanks. Japheth said, "That's what we were afraid of. But even they couldn't make him vanish completely, could they?"

"They are masters of illusion," Adnarel said. "They can make any part of the oasis look like someplace else. They can disguise odors. That is why Higgaion's scenting was to no avail."

"But where do you think he is?" Dennys's voice soared with anxiety.

"I think the nephilim have used human greed. I suspect that some of the less pleasant people of the oasis, perhaps the men of Tiglah's tent, have taken him and put him in some little-used tent and are asking some kind of ransom for him. They are acquisitive, but they don't like to work for what they get, and they would be easy to tempt into doing whatever the nephilim want."

Dennys raised his head as he heard the strong beating of wings, and a pelican plummeted out of the sky, and then Alarid stood beside them. "The nephilim are afraid of the twins." His wings shook silver.

"But why?" Japheth asked. "The twins are good."

Adnarel and Alarid touched wing tips. Adnarel said, "The nephilim fear what they do not understand. Did Higgaion go all the way across the oasis with his scenting?"

Japheth nodded.

"To the far end?" Alarid asked.

"Yes."

"Try once more. This time, go straight across the length of the oasis and concentrate at the farthest point. They will have taken him as far away from Noah's tents as possible."

"And they're not likely to have gone in the direction of Grandfather Lamech's tent," Alarid added.

Higgaion's stringy little tail flicked.

Japheth said, "The sun is high. The Den cannot cross the oasis at full noon without getting the sun sickness again."

Both seraphim looked at Dennys, already red and sweating. "You are right. The Den will stay here, in Grandfather Lamech's tent, for the afternoon rest. One of us will stay with him, in case . . ." Adnarel did not finish.

Alarid said, "And we will see to it that he gets to Noah's tenthold before sundown. Whether you find the Sand or not, you must be home by then."

Higgaion raised his trunk in an impatient trumpet.

"We'll go," Japheth said. He looked up at the seraphim, asking in a low voice, "Are you worried?"

Gravely they acknowledged the question.

In the dark heat of the prison tent, Sandy slept fitfully, dreaming a confusion of meaningless dreams. Tiglah was tying his thongs tightly and shoving a bowl of spoiled meat at him. His nostrils twitched.

It was not Tiglah's smell. It was not even the smell of rancid goat meat. He opened his eyes and saw only a small dark shadow, felt something soft nudging him. He reached out his hand and touched something firm and curved. Moved his hand along whatever it was, until his fingers felt a roughness. It was a tusk, broken off at the point. His eyes adjusted to the dim light and he saw that he was touching a mammoth, not Higgaion or Selah, both of whom were sleek and well fed, with polished tusks, but an underfed mammoth with stringy hair, and one tusk broken off just at the point, the other slightly farther up. It was nudging him with the tip of its trunk.

What the mammoth wanted of him he was not sure. But it was apparent that it meant him no harm, and that its overtures were friendly. Sandy began to stroke the shaggy head, then ran his fingers over the ivory tusks. This little beast had obviously been abused, so it was likely that it came from Tiglah's tent. He was grateful for the company. Perhaps a mammoth, even a mangy mammoth, would be helpful when night came, not so much helpful in the actual escape as in finding Noah's tenthold.

"Now," he said to the mammoth, fondling the fanshaped ears, "if I only had a unicorn, then I could get out of here." He stopped. Then: "Hey. I didn't think of a unicorn before, because basically I still don't believe in unicorns."

Dennys, he remembered, had summoned a unicorn after Tiglah's father and brother had nearly killed him, dumping him into the garbage pit. It wasn't easy for Dennys to believe in unicorns either, but when he had to, he did.

If Sandy could believe something as outrageous as that he and Dennys had actually landed in the pre-flood desert, and that they had become so close to Noah's tenthold, especially Yalith, that they were like family, and if he could believe that he was now petting a mammoth, why should it be hard to believe in a unicorn, even if it was what Dennys called a virtual unicorn? His mother believed in virtual particles, and his mother was a scientist who had won the Nobel Prize for discovering particles so small they were scarcely conceivable even with a wild leap of the imagination.

"What'll I do?" he asked the mammoth, who responded by cuddling closer to him.

If Sandy left the tent on his own, they would be lying in wait for him—Rofocale, if not Tiglah's father and brother—and they would not hesitate to kill him. Even night would not provide enough cover, with the brilliance of the stars illuminating the oasis.

"The problem is," he said to the mammoth, "that I always have to see things to believe in them. But, after all, I have seen unicorns, two of them. I have seen them, therefore I can believe in them."

The mammoth reached with its trunk to touch, softly, the boy's cheek. In his mind's ear Sandy seemed to hear, "Some things have to be believed to be seen."

"Unicorn!" he whispered, and the mammoth slipped its trunk into the palm of his hand. "Unicorn, please tend to life. Please tend to be."

Against the darkness of the tent came a starburst of light, and a unicorn stood, trembling, beside him.

"Oh, you *are*!" Sandy cried. "Oh, thank you!" He held out his hand. The unicorn came to him with silver steps, folded its delicate legs, and lay down, putting its head in Sandy's lap, so that the light of the horn flowed over the scraggly little mammoth, who lifted its head gratefully. Sandy fondled the silvery mane, soft as moonbeams. "Now what?" he asked the two disparate creatures.

The light of the horn glittered, but neither unicorn nor mammoth answered him.

"If I could fall asleep," Sandy mused, "or stop believing in unicorns, then you would lose your tendency to life and go out, and take me with you, the way you took Dennys. The problem is that now I believe in you. And as long as I believe in you, you'll continue to be, won't you?"

The unicorn nuzzled him, as affectionate as the mammoth.

"As long as I stay with you," Sandy whispered, "I think I'm safe, because I'm absolutely certain that Tiglah couldn't come near you, or her father or brother. But if they try to, and you go out of being, will you take the mammoth and me out of being with you? If we don't take the mammoth, they'll hurt him again. So will you take us?"

It was a rather intimidating thought. He had asked Dennys how it had felt the two times he had gone out with the unicorn, and Dennys had answered that it hadn't felt at all. But perhaps, Sandy thought, that might have been because Dennys had sunstroke and a high fever. Then he remembered Grandfather Lamech—or was it Japheth?—telling him that unicorns never lost anybody.

He put one arm about the unicorn, the other about the mammoth, and waited. This was a far better plan than going with Tiglah, or trying to cross the desert alone.

"You see," he said to the two creatures, who pressed confidingly against him. "When the time came for me to do something, I knew what to do, and I did it."

He held unicorn and mammoth close.

The nephilim gathered. Proud. Arrogant. Flickering in and out of their hosts as they spoke.

Rofocale the mosquito said, "I have put an illusion around the tent. It is on the edge of the desert at the farthest end of the oasis, but the illusion makes it look as though it is surrounded by flocks and groves."

Eblis the dragon/lizard asked, "Are giant twins worth this much trouble?"

Rofocale answered, "I think they know something we do not know. When I questioned the one that Tiglah caught for me, he gave evasive answers."

Ugiel the cobra said, "There is danger in the air. The stars are drawing back. I am concerned for my baby."

Naamah the vulture went "Kkk. We chose to be silent with El. We chose never to hear the Voice again, never to speak with the Presence."

Ertrael the rat said, "We could ask the seraphim."

"Never," said Estael the cockroach.

"But they still speak with El," Ertrael said. "The stars still talk with them."

"I do not care to listen to the stars," Eisheth the crocodile pronounced.

"They might tell us," said Rumjal the red ant, "whether or not we are in danger."

"How can we be in danger?" Eblis asked. "We are immortal."

"And the one we caught," said Rofocale, "told me that he is mortal. If he is to be believed."

Naamah the vulture clacked his beak. "I smell that there will soon be much for us to eat."

"How?" Rofocale demanded. "What is going to happen?"

Eblis the dragon/lizard asked, "Will someone tell me what Noah is building?"

"A good question," said Rumael the slug.

Rofocale gave his screeching laugh. "A boat! That is what my Tiglah tells me. He is building a boat!"

"A boat?" Eisheth the crocodile demanded. "Why on earth would he build a boat?"

Rugziel the worm asked, "Could the twin giants have told him something that we do not know?"

Rofocale said, "We need to get rid of the twin giants. Everything has been different since they came."

"Noah reconciled with his father. Kkk," said Naamah the vulture.

"And Lamech has died," Estael the cockroach agreed.

"My lovely Yalith prefers the young giants to me," Eblis said. "They must have some strange power, to make her turn from me to such soft-skinned, wingless creatures."

"And Noah is building a boat," Rofocale added.

"And Matred weeps," said Rumjal the red ant.

"We should find out," Ugiel suggested, "whether or not they—the young giants—are truly mortal or not."

Rofocale screeched again. "Tiglah's father and brother will find that out for us."

Higgaion finally found the tent where Sandy was imprisoned, because the unicorn was there. Rofocale's power of illusion had indeed made the tent seem to be in the middle of the oasis, had indeed altered Sandy's scent. But the unicorn had come to the tent after the illusion was set. Higgaion sniffed. He smelled silver, and he smelled light. He nudged Japheth excitedly.

Tentatively, Japheth pushed open the tent flap. Enough of the late-afternoon light came through the tent hole so that he could see Sandy and the unicorn, their heads together in affection. The abused mammoth was only a dark shadow under Sandy's arm.

"Sand!"

Sandy opened his eyes. "Jay!"

The young man started to rush forward to embrace him, then stopped short as though held by some invisible barrier. The unicorn's light brightened.

Higgaion followed Japheth into the tent, sitting back on his haunches in surprise as he saw the mammoth who pressed closely against Sandy, blinking fearfully.

Sandy's protective arm tightened. "It's all right. Nobody's going to hurt you." Then: "Jay, how did you find me?"

"Are you all right?" Japheth asked anxiously.

"Oh, I'm fine, but Tiglah's father and brother want to kill me . . ."

"No." Japheth touched his fingers to his tiny bow. "No, Sand."

"And look what they've done to their mammoth," Sandy said indignantly. "They've nearly starved him, and they've broken his tusks."

"All right," Japheth said hurriedly. "We'll take him with us. But we'd better get out of here before they come back."

"I think I'm safe as long as I'm with the unicorn," Sandy said, "because they won't be able to come near."

Japheth smiled. "I can't, either." He stared at boy and unicorn. "Sand. Do you remember when I first met you and the Den in the desert, and we called unicorns, and the Den went out?"

"Of course I remember."

"Can't you go out with the unicorn now?"

Sandy sighed. "The problem is, Jay, that I *believe* in the unicorn."

The mangy mammoth suddenly pricked up its ears and started to whimper. Higgaion pushed himself up onto his feet, and Japheth swung around to see the tent flap open violently. Two small, chunky men came in, carrying spears. Tiglah's father and brother.

"Auk! What have we here?" the older man demanded.

"A *unicorn*," the younger man exclaimed. "And one of Noah's sons. Well, well." He moved toward Sandy and the unicorn, then drew back with a sharp intake of breath. "You, young giant!" he shouted. "Come along! We want you."

"Sorry," Sandy said. "You can't have me." He looked at Japheth and the two men from Tiglah's tent and wondered anew at how small they were. Tiglah's father was made even shorter by his bowed legs. No wonder they had used the poisoned dart on him. In a fair struggle, they would never have captured him.

Japheth's pleasant features were distorted by anger. "You've done enough harm. Get out of here."

The tent was so small that the three little men were close together, with Sandy, his arms still about unicorn and mammoth, near enough to draw back at the odor of the men from Tiglah's tent.

"Auk's nuts to you," Tiglah's brother said.

Japheth glanced swiftly at Sandy, then in a reflex so swift it hardly seemed motion, he drew one of the darts from his quiver and jabbed it into Sandy's arm.

The two men from Tiglah's tent shouted in surprise and anger. Tiglah's father roared, "What happened?"

Where Sandy and the unicorn and mammoth had been there was only a pile of filthy skins.

Japheth replied calmly, "They went out with the unicorn."

Both men roared in frustration. "Call him back," the bowlegged man said.

"Or we'll kill you," the younger man threatened.

"And what good will that do you?" Japheth demanded. "You'll never get the Sand back without me."

Tiglah's brother snarled, deep in his throat, and lunged at Japheth with his spear, but Higgaion jumped between them, tripping the red-bearded man so that he sprawled on the floor of the tent. He snarled up at his father, "Why didn't you stop him?"

"Me? What could I do?"

"You let him go out with the unicorn, and our mammoth, too."

Tiglah's brother scrambled clumsily to his feet, hefting his spear. "Give us your father's vineyards, then."

"No," Japheth said, and reached for his darts.

But the older man swooped on him with the spear, and despite Japheth's quick reflex, the spear cut across his ribs, and a trickle of blood slid down his side.

Higgaion lunged at the man, trumpeting in outrage.

But the two men with their spears were too much for Japheth and the mammoth. Japheth clutched his wounded side as the mammoth lunged again and was viciously kicked by Tiglah's brother.

Suddenly a roar burst over them. *"Hungry!"* And the manticore stuck his hideous face into the tent. *"Hungry!"*

"Go away," Tiglah's father yelled.

In terror, Higgaion backed up, hitting the skins of the tent, which gave slightly. Japheth, trying to reach for the mammoth, saw that the skins were not pegged securely to the ground. Not many people bothered to set up their tents as well as Noah and Grandfather Lamech.

"Run, Hig, run!" Japheth commanded, and Higgaion backed out of the tent.

"*Hungry!*" The manticore's ugly face was followed by his lion's body and scorpion's tail.

Japheth was the farthest of the three men from the tent flap. He reached for a dart and his tiny bow, and let a dart fly, to strike the manticore in the forehead.

"*Hung—*" the manticore started, and fell, unconscious, on Tiglah's father and brother.

Swiftly, Japheth dropped to his knees and pushed out the opening in the rear of the tent through which Higgaion had left.

The mammoth was waiting outside, whimpering in terror but not willing to leave Japheth completely.

"Run!" Japheth shouted as he stood upright; and they ran. Ran without looking behind them. Onto the desert. And then the illusion that Rofocale had set was broken and Japheth knew exactly where they were. They were at the far end of the oasis, the opposite end from Grandfather Lamech's tenthold. He hardly realized that blood was streaming down his side as he hurried toward home.

Admael the camel, Adnachiel the giraffe, and Akatriel the owl left their posts and followed Japheth and the mammoth into the desert.

Japheth, running faster than he had ever run before, suddenly felt dizzy. Everything paled. He slumped slowly onto the sand. Higgaion pushed his feet against rock to slow himself down.

Akatriel flew down to the sand beside the young man, and resumed his seraph form. "He has lost much blood. He is still bleeding."

Adnachiel the giraffe bent his neck to look at Japheth's wound, then lowered himself so that he could reach the torn skin with his tongue. Carefully, thoroughly, he licked the wound.

Admael the camel galloped off.

Higgaion hunkered down beside Japheth and the giraffe, whimpering. Adnachiel continued to lick, cleaning the jagged cut the spear had made.

When it was clean, Admael returned with a furry-looking, cactus-type leaf, which he gently pressed against the wound, holding it until the bleeding slowed and stopped.

Japheth, quivering, opened his eyes, to see the seraphim reaching up out of their hosts and into their seraphic forms.

Akatriel, with eyes as wise as those of the owl he had just left, affirmed, "You are all right. You have lost much blood, and that spearhead cannot have been too clean. But Adnachiel has washed the wound and Admael has stopped the bleeding."

"And you ran much too quickly." Adnachiel nodded.

"Hig—"

Higgaion touched Japheth's hand gently with his trunk tip.

"Sand?"

Adnachiel asked, "What happened?"

"I sent him out with the unicorn," Japheth said, struggling to sit up.

Admael nodded approval. "That was good."

"Should we call the Sand back?" Japheth asked.

"Better," Adnachiel said.

Admael asked courteously of the mammoth, "Will you? Or shall I?"

"Both." Adnachiel was peremptory.

With a light briefly bright as the sun, making them all blink, the unicorn appeared. Sandy's arm slid from around its neck and he slipped onto the sand. A mangy mammoth tumbled beside him.

Japheth explained, "I used one of my darts on him, but it's a very short-lasting—"

Sandy's eyes blinked open, and he sat up.

The three seraphim stood looking at Japheth, Sandy, and the two mammoths.

"Thank you," Sandy gasped. "Oh, Jay, thank you."

Embarrassed, Japheth shrugged.

"What's happened to you?" Sandy demanded. "You're hurt."

"I'll be all right," Japheth reassured him. "The seraphim have cleaned my wound."

"Go home," Admael ordered. "Sandy, you can help Japheth. He is weaker than he realizes."

"But what happened?" Sandy demanded.

Japheth laughed. "I never thought I'd be grateful to a manticore, but I am now. They'd have killed me if a manticore hadn't pushed his way into the tent and stopped them."

The mangy little mammoth pressed against Sandy. "It's all right," Sandy reassured. "We'll never send you back. What happened to them?"

Japheth shrugged.

"Nothing, I suspect," Akatriel said. "I saw the manticore running away, weeping, a dart falling from his forehead, calling out that he was hungry."

Japheth laughed again. "I could almost feel sorry for the manticore."

"Go, now," Admael urged. "Japheth needs food and rest."

"Unicorn?" Sandy asked. "What about you?"

As he looked, the unicorn began to flicker, to fade.

Japheth said, "The unicorn knows we don't need it anymore."

Where the unicorn had been, there was only a shimmer in the air, and the scent of moonbeams and silver.

They were united in the big tent that evening. Japheth, hovered over by Matred, lay on a pile of soft skins, pale but smiling, and sipped at the strengthening broth Matred kept offering him.

The starved mammoth had been fed and lay curled up with Higgaion and Selah.

Sandy and Dennys kept grinning at each other in relief, with Sandy repeating over and over his praise of Japheth and Higgaion. "It was a wonderful idea to have Higgy scent for me. I don't know what would have happened, otherwise."

Anah looked subdued. "I am so ashamed. That my father and my brother—that my sister should have tried—I thought she *liked* the Sand—I don't know what got into any of them! Can you forgive me?"

"It was not your doing, daughter," Noah said gently.

"But to think they tried to force you to give up your vineyards! To threaten to kill the Sand and Japheth—"

"Don't dwell on it," Matred said, rubbing ointment Oholibamah had given her onto the healing wound on Japheth's side.

"Is it over?" Elisheba asked. "Or will they try something else? I don't mean your father and brother, Anah. The nephilim."

Nobody answered.

Sandy held his bowl out for a refill. "It is so much better than what Tiglah cooked for me—I wonder how I could eat the other stuff, even when it was fresh." Then he said, "Rofocale the nephil *used* Tiglah and her father and brother. They are not nice people—sorry, Anah—but I don't think they'd ever have thought of kidnapping me on their own. If the nephilim are after Dennys and me, they'll try something else."

"But why are they after you?" Japheth demanded.

Sandy finished licking his bowl clean. "They know we don't belong here."

Noah's fingers moved against his beard. "But you do. Both of you. The Den made me see that being stubborn was not brave."

Matred added, "And you both made Grandfather Lamech's last moons happy ones."

Noah had tears in his eyes. "You were to him as his own grandsons. He could not have stayed in his own tent without your help. You have become our beloved twins."

Matred wiped her eyes with the back of her hand. "And yet, husband, you have said that there is no room for them in the ark."

Dennys said quickly, "Don't worry. We know we don't belong on the ark. The nephilim aren't entirely wrong about us."

Sandy said, "But we'll be glad to help you build it. We would like to do at least that much for you, because you've been very kind to us."

Yalith and Oholibamah sat close together, hands clasped. Oholibamah said, "We still have time to be together. It will take at least two moons before the ark is finished and ready to stock. And because we have known each other, we can never be entirely separated."

Japheth said, "As we can never be completely separated from Grandfather Lamech."

Yalith nodded. Pushed back tears. Sandy was safely back with them. Japheth was wounded, but was going to be all right. This was no time for tears.

Dennys looked at Japheth and nodded. "The night that Grandfather Lamech died—how long ago it seems—Higgaion and I sat out under the stars while Noah was in the tent, waiting for Sandy." He hesitated, then plunged on. "At the moment that Grandfather Lamech died, the stars held their breaths. And so I knew. And then, because he understood Higgaion and I needed him, Adnarel was with us, saying *Fear not*, and then he was back in the scarab beetle, on Higgaion's ear, instead of off with the other seraphim, as he's been so often lately."

There was a moment of silence. Then Noah opened a fresh skin of wine. "My love for all of you is too deep for words. Dear twins, we are glad that you have come to us. And now it is time for you to leave, isn't it?"

Sandy said, firmly, "Not until we've helped you build the ark."

Sandy and Dennys stayed in the big tent, having been given sleeping skins and a place to themselves across from Noah and Matred. Higgaion and Selah slept with the little mammoth, whose ribs were beginning to fill out, and whose coat was beginning to shine.

Dennys woke up and the darkness of the tent was heavy. Around him he heard gentle snores, and the night sounds of the desert. He nudged Sandy. "Are you awake?"

"Almost."

"Now what?"

Sandy wriggled into a more comfortable position. "We'll keep on helping Noah with the ark."

"And then?"

Fully awake now, Sandy moved so that he could whisper directly into Dennys's ear. "We'll take a quantum leap."

"And how will we manage that?"

"It came to me when the mammoth and I called the unicorn to *be* in that nasty little tent where I was in prison. The nephilim cannot leave this earth. But the seraphim can."

"More to the point," Dennys asked, "can we? Or, rather, can we leave this time and get back to our own? I wouldn't want to miscalculate and land in the Middle Ages, or the year 3003."

"I'll have to speak to Adnarel about it again."

"You already have?"

"Some. When we first got here. What I think would work for us would be to call unicorns, and ride them, and for Adnarel, or any of the seraphim, to go forward to our time, and then call for the unicorns to come back."

"Wild." Dennys whistled.

"Yes, but it worked when the three seraphim called me back onto the desert sands after Japheth and Higgaion came to rescue me."

"That was space, not time, and a small distance in space, at that," Dennys pointed out.

"True. But experiments with photons, for instance, seem to show that they can communicate with each other instantaneously, and that means faster than the speed of light. And distance doesn't seem to be a problem for them."

"But it's time we have to worry about," Dennys whispered. Noah snored a very loud snore, and they could hear him turn over on his skins. Dennys continued, "If I understand Mother's experiments, an observer is essential in the world of quantum mechanics. I mean, an observer seems to be necessary to make quanta real."

Sandy moved impatiently. "I don't understand it. But Mother seems to, and so do a lot of other particle physicists. That's enough for me. I'll talk to Adnarel."

There was a heavy silence. Then Dennys said, "Anything seems to be possible. I hope this is."

Another silence. Then Sandy asked, "Do you think we could take Yalith with us?"

Dennys did not answer for a while. Then: "No. I don't think so. We're not supposed to change history."

"But she'll drown."

"I know. I love her, too." At last. It had been said.

"But if we love her—"

Dennys's voice was bleak. "I don't think we can take her with us."

Sandy reached for his twin's hand and grasped it. "A lot of people are going to drown. Would you mind changing history if it would save Yalith?"

Dennys said, "I wouldn't mind. I'd be willing to try. To try absolutely anything. But I have a feeling that we can't."

"I hate it!"

"Shh. I hate it, too."

Sandy whispered, "It's going to be dangerous, taking a quantum leap."

"Dad obviously thinks such things are possible. After all, wasn't he programming some kind of quantum leap, or tesser, when we messed around with his experiment?"

"So, if he believes in it, it's not that wild."

"Sure it's that wild. It's got to be that wild in order to work."

Sandy gave a slightly hysterical laugh. "Our father was not programming unicorns into his experiment."

Higgaion jerked in a sleeping dream, whimpered. Selah made little murmuring noises, and Tiglah's mammoth moved closer to the others.

Sandy asked, "What about the mammoths?"

Dennys stretched his arm out so that he could touch, gently, Higgaion's shaggy fur. "I wonder if they can swim?"

"It wouldn't do any good. Not for forty days and forty nights."

Dennys closed his eyes. Listened. Heard the wind high in the sky above the tent, but the words would not come clear. He whispered, "Does—does Yalith know she's not going on the ark?"

"I think so. I think Noah has told her."

"I understand that floods and other disasters happen. But if this flood is really being sent by El—"

Sandy said, "If it's being sent by El, then I don't like El, not if Yalith is going to drown."

The wind murmured. "We aren't sure yet, are we?" Dennys asked. "I mean, it hasn't happened yet. Yalith isn't in the story, so we don't know what happened to her. Grandfather Lamech truly loved his El. So we can't be sure. Grandfather loved Yalith. She was his very favorite."

"Grandfather is dead," Sandy said flatly. "If we're going to be any use building the ark, we'd better sleep now."

The wind wrapped itself about the tent. Sandy slipped quickly into sleep. Dennys lay on his back, listening, listening. The wind's song was gentle, unalarming. Although he could not make out the words, he felt the wind calming him. Slept.

* * *

"Stupid. Stupid," Ugiel, husband of Mahlah, hissed.

Rofocale's contempt came out with a mosquito shrill. "The idiots almost let the manticore get them."

"Tiglah would have done better by herself," said Eblis, who wanted Yalith.

Ertrael, sometimes a rat, demanded, "What do we do now?"

The nephilim were gathered in the darkness of the desert, for once conserving their energies. Naamah, still sounding like a vulture, went, "Kkk. Tiglah did not, in fact, do better than her father or her brother. She got no answers. The young giant did not listen to her."

Elisheth, of the crocodile-green wings, shimmered them in the starlight. "She tried. I would have thought the Sand would find her irresistible. Why did he reject her?"

"Yalith." Eblis's beautiful red lips lifted in a sneer.

Ugiel wove his neck in a rhythmic dance, as much cobra as nephil. "You are right. Because of Yalith."

"But she has no experience," Rofocale shrilled. "She is still a child. Whereas Tiglah—"

"No," Eblis contradicted, purple eyes glittering. "Yalith is not a child any longer." He wrapped purple wings about himself.

"Could we have used her?" Estael, sometimes a cockroach, asked doubtfully.

"If Ugiel hadn't married her, we might have been able to use Mahlah, Yalith's sister," said Ezequen, whose host was the skink.

Ugiel hissed, "We all know she's Yalith's sister. And my wife. And the mother of my child."

Eblis wrapped himself in wings the color of the sunset. "It is time for us to act. Us. Ourselves."

Rugziel agreed. "It is time we stopped using deputies."

Rumjal grimaced. "What do you suggest?"

Naamah stretched his neck, naked as a vulture's, and raised his wings to their full span, standing in whiteness of skin, darkness of wing, his feathers the indigo of the bird who was his host. "The circle of extinction. Whoever we completely surround we control. Kkk. Let us surround the twin giants."

Ugiel hissed in agreement.

Rofocale shrilled in anticipation.

Eblis suggested, "And let us surround Yalith, since she has foiled our plans."

"Kkk," Naamah reproved. "The giants first."

12 Neither Can the Floods Drown It

Yalith slept at the far end of the tent from the twins, but she heard them whispering, and when they stopped, she could hear the mammoths' triple snores. And she was wide awake.

She slipped out of bed and went to the desert. She saw neither lion nor dragon/lizard masquerading as lion, on the great rock. She chose a smaller rock and sat, wrapping her arms about her knees. She raised her face to the stars.

She heard them chiming, and there was no anxiety in their song.

Nevertheless, she shivered. She believed her father, believed that the rains were going to come. She was willing to die, if that was truly what El wanted.

But what about the twins?

What was going to happen?

The crystal chime of stars sang in her ears, "Fear not, Yalith."

The stars never gave false comfort.

She was less afraid.

They worked on the ark all day, taking time out in the heat to sleep. Then they worked again until it was too dark to see.

Every evening Matred prepared a festive meal. Therefore, Shem was often out hunting, rather than busy with the ark. Sandy and Dennys worked along with Noah, Ham, and Japheth. There were no hammers or nails or any of the modern tools to which they were accustomed. The boards had to be joined and pegged. At night they were tired and hungry, ate well, slept well. They were building an ark, but they did not talk of the rain.

Dennys looked at Elisheba, Anah, and Oholibamah. They were in the story, even if not by name. They would go with Noah and Matred and all the animals onto the ark. He looked at Yalith, her hair amber in the lamplight.

He slipped out of the tent, feeling a little strange. He was the follower, Sandy the leader. And now he was off, without even consulting his twin.

He walked swiftly toward Noah's well. His skin prickled as he saw the vulture, huddled on the tall trunk of a long-dead palm, then looking up as Dennys approached, peering this way and that, stretching its naked neck, staring at Dennys with hooded, suspicious eyes.

At first, Dennys saw only the dark bird. Then his eye caught a glimpse of white, and on a young fig tree near the well sat a pelican, its head tucked under its wing, so that it seemed no more than a bundle of white. Dennys heaved a sigh of relief. He had left the big tent to find one of the seraphim, and it didn't really matter which one, but he was more familiar with Alarid than with many of the others. He went up to the sleeping bird. "Hsst."

The pelican did not move.

"Alarid!" Dennys shouted. "I need to talk to you!"

The feathers quivered as the bird shoved its head farther under its wing.

"Alarid!"

The feathers ruffled, hunched, indicating, "Go away. I have nothing to say."

"But I have to speak to you. About Yalith."

At last the head emerged from the fluff of feathers, and the dark bead of eye blinked.

"Please." Dennys indicated the vulture. "Please, Alarid."

The white bird hopped down from its perch, clumsy and cumbersome.

The vulture was an ink blob of immobile darkness.

"Please," Dennys pleaded.

The pelican stretched its wings up, up, until the seraph appeared. Without speaking, Alarid turned from the well and walked toward the desert. Dennys followed. When they had left the oasis far enough behind so that the vulture was no longer visible, Alarid turned to the boy. "What is it?"

"You can't let Yalith drown in the flood."

"Why not?"

"Yalith is good. I mean, she is really *good*."

Alarid bowed his head. "Goodness has never been a guarantee of safety."

"But you can't let her drown."

"I have nothing to say in the matter."

"I should have spoken to Aariel," Dennys said in frustration. "Aariel loves her."

"He has no more say than I." The seraph turned his head away.

Dennys realized that he had hurt Alarid, but he plunged ahead. "You're seraphim. You have powers."

"True. But, as I told you, it is dangerous to change things. We do not meddle with the pattern."

"But Yalith isn't *in* the pattern." Dennys's voice rose and cracked. "There's no Yalith in the story. Only Noah and his wife and his sons and their wives."

Alarid's wings quivered slightly.

"So, since she isn't in the story, it won't change anything if you prevent her from being drowned in the flood."

"What do you want me to do?" Alarid asked.

"You aren't going to be drowned, are you?" Dennys demanded. "You, and the other seraphim?"

"No."

"Then take her wherever it is you're going to escape the flood."

"We cannot do that," Alarid said sadly.

"Why not?"

"We cannot." Again, the seraph turned his face away.

"Where are you going, then?"

Alarid turned back to Dennys and smiled, but not in amusement. "We go to the sun."

No. Yalith could not go to the sun. Nor to the moon, which Dennys had been about to suggest. Yalith could not live where there was no atmosphere. But surely there was something to be done! He made a strangled noise of outrage. "We're not in the story, either, Sandy and I. But we're here. And Yalith is here."

"That is so."

"And if we drown, that is, if Sandy and I drown, that's going to change the story, isn't it? I mean, we're not going to be born in our own time if we get drowned now, and even if that makes only a tiny difference, it will make a difference to our family. If Sandy and I don't get born, maybe Charles Wallace won't get born. Maybe Meg will be an only child."

"Who?"

"Our older sister and our little brother. I mean, the story would be *changed*."

Alarid said, "You must go back to your own time."

"That's easier said than done. Anyhow, what I wanted to talk to you about is Yalith. Listen, it's a stupid story. Only the males have names. It's a chauvinist story. I mean, Matred has a name. She's a mother. And Elisheba and Anah and Oholibamah. They're real people, with names."

"That is true," Alarid agreed.

"The nephilim," Dennys went on. "They're like whoever wrote the silly ark story, seeing things only from their own point of view, *using* people. They don't give a hoot for Tiglah or Mahlah, for instance. They're just women, so they don't matter. They don't care if Yalith gets drowned. But you ought to care!"

Alarid asked gently, "Do you think I don't care?"

Dennys sighed. "Okay. I know you care. But are you just going to stand by and do nothing and then fly off to the sun?"

Again Alarid's wings quivered. "Part of doing something is listening. We are listening. To the sun. To the stars. To the wind."

Dennys felt chastened. He had not paused to listen, not for days. "They don't tell you anything?"

"To continue to listen."

The breeze lifted, washed over Dennys in a wave of sadness. "I don't like this story," he said. "I don't like it at all."

He left Alarid. Before he reached the oasis he paused, sat on a small rock. Tried to quiet himself so that he could listen. To the wind. How could he unscramble the words of the wind which came to him in overlapping wavelets?

He closed his eyes. Visioned stars exploding into life. Planets being birthed. Yalith had spoken of the violence of Mahlah's baby's birth. The birth of planets was no gentler. Violent swirlings of winds and waters. Land masses as fluid as water. Volcanoes spouting flame so high that it seemed to meet the outward flaming of the sun.

The earth was still in the process of being created. The stability of rock was no more than an illusion. Earthquake, hurricane, volcano, flood, all part of the continuing creation of the cosmos, groaning in travail.

The song of the wind softened, gentled. Behind the violence of the birthing of galaxies and stars and planets came a quiet and tender melody, a gentle love song. All the raging of creation, the continuing hydrogen explosions on the countless suns, the heaving of planetary bodies, all was enfolded in a patient, waiting love.

Dennys opened his eyes as the wind dropped, was silent. He raised his face to the stars, and their light fell against his cheeks like dew.

They chimed at him softly. *Do not seek to comprehend. All shall be well. Wait. Patience. Wait. You do not always have to do something. Wait.*

Dennys put his head down on his knees, and a strange quiet flowed through him.

Above his head, the white wings of a pelican beat gently through the flowing streams of stars.

Work on the ark progressed slowly. In the heat of the sun, his body glistening with sweat, Dennys found it hard to remember his vision of understanding and hope. But it was still there, waiting for him, surfacing during the afternoon rest time, or at night when the sun set and the stars blossomed.

Hammer. Peg. Measure for stress.

Noah insisted on following exactly the directions which were given him.

"This El," Sandy said to Dennys, "I don't understand."

"El knows about shipbuilding," Dennys said. "The instructions and measurements are pretty much the basic proportions for modern ships. The ark's not designed for speed, but then, that's not the purpose."

"All those animals—Noah's surely going to have to shovel out a load of manure."

"I bet nobody around here has ever seen a boat this big. Maybe they've never even seen a boat."

Sandy sought out Yalith, feeling a little disloyal to be going to find her without Dennys, but going, nevertheless. Dennys had vetoed it when Sandy had suggested taking Yalith with them.

He waited for her, not far from the tentholds, in the quiet that precedes dawn. Saw her coming, pale and wraithlike, from the direction of the desert.

"Yalith."

She stopped, startled, head up.

"Yalith, it's Sandy."

"Oh. Twin Sand." Relief was in her voice. "What is it?"

He took her hand. "Yalith, what are you going to do?"

"When?"

"When the floods come."

She spoke in a low voice. "We don't know for sure that the floods are going to come. It is only what my father says."

"Yes, but what do you think? Do you believe your father?"

She was barely audible. "Yes."

"Then what are you going to do?"

"Nothing. This has already given my father and mother much grief. My mother doesn't understand why El has not called me to be in the ark with the others."

"I don't understand it either," Sandy said flatly.

"But the stars have told me not to be afraid."

"And you believe the stars?"

"Yes."

"Well, somebody's wrong, either your father or the stars."

"I trust my father. And I trust the stars."

"Well. Somebody has to *do* something. I mean, we can't just sit back and let you get drowned. Would you consider coming home with us?"

She looked at him, startled. "But where is your home? Is it on the other side of the mountains?"

"On the other side of time," Sandy said.

Her fingers tightened in his. "You and the Den are leaving?" She answered her own question. "Of course. You have to. As soon as the ark is built. As soon as the rains start."

"Will you come with us?"

"With you both?"

"Well—yes." He would love to go off to the end of the world, alone with Yalith. But he knew that he would not try to leave her world without Dennys.

"Is it many days of travel?"

"We got here sort of instantaneously. I have an idea how we might be able to get home, but first I want to know if you'll come with us."

"Oh, twin Sand." She sighed, long and deeply. "Everything is so strange. Ever since you came, nothing has been the same. Grandfather Lamech is dead. The ark is being built. I don't want to drown, but—is it very different, where you come from?"

Sandy acknowledged, "Very different. It isn't nearly as hot, and we have lots of water, so that we can take showers, and drink as much as we want. What I wouldn't give for a long glass of cold water when we're hammering away on the ark! And we wear different kinds of clothes." He looked at Yalith's small and perfect body, barely covered by the loincloth, her breasts delicate and rosy, and had a moment's absurd vision of her in one of the classrooms at the regional high school. But wouldn't anything be better than drowning? "You'll consider it, won't you? Coming with us?"

She was solemn. "Of course. It is very hard for me to imagine what it would be like without you and the Den. You are part of me. Both of you."

Sandy slipped back into the tent. Dennys was awake, waiting for him.

"Where have you been?"

"I asked Yalith to come home with us."

There was a heavy silence. At last Dennys said. "No. No, Sandy. We can't take her back with us. I mean, even if we could, we can't."

"Why not?"

"She doesn't have any immunities. Haven't you noticed, there aren't any diseases here? Don't you remember that all the natives at the bottom part of South America got killed by German measles, because they didn't have any immunities?"

"Couldn't we give her vaccinations?"

"Not for everything. Even if she caught a cold, an ordinary head cold, it would probably kill her. She doesn't have any protective antibodies. She couldn't adjust to our climate. It's too cold, too damp. It would be murder to try to take her back with us."

"Then what's going to happen?"

"I don't know."

"If she stays here, she'll drown. Wouldn't it be worth the risk to try to take her home with us?"

Dennys shook his head. "How do you think she'd get on with the kids at school?"

"She wouldn't have to go to school. She's nearly a hundred years old."

"And she doesn't look any older than we do. How would we prove her age to the school authorities? And if she *is* a hundred years old, and we bring her back to our time, what would happen? Would she shrivel all up and be ancient and die of old age?"

"Why are you thinking of all the bad things that could happen?"

"We have to think of them. If we love Yalith."

"Maybe it would be all right."

"And maybe it wouldn't. Maybe what we should do is stay here with Yalith and wait for the flood."

"I'm not willing to give up that easily."

"It's not easily."

"But we have to do something!"

—Maybe, for once, we don't, Dennys thought. "There's time yet," he said. "Maybe something will come to us, but it will have to be something real."

"Hey," Sandy said. "I'm not sure anymore what's real and what isn't. I mean, nephilim and seraphim!"

"I believe in a lot more than I used to," Dennys said. "Even if we're not supposed to change the story, we're changed, you and I."

"We are, oh, we are. And what about Yalith?"

"Wait," Dennys said. He did not tell Sandy about his talk with Alarid. Or what the wind had shown him. Or that the stars had told him to have patience, and wait. Wait.

The new moon was once again a crescent in the sky. Ripened, filled out to a sphere. Dwindled and diminished. Was born again.

Noah sent Japheth and Oholibamah to warn the people of the oasis of the impending flood.

Ham asked, "What's the point? They all know you're building this big boat. They all know you're expecting rain out of season."

Noah was stubborn. "They have a right to be warned. To prepare. And who knows—if they repent, then perhaps El will not send the flood."

"If there's no flood," Ham said, "people will laugh at us even more than they're laughing now."

Anah looked troubled. "I do not think the people of my tent will repent. They are very angry."

Noah said, "They must be given the chance."

When Japheth and Oholibamah returned from their trip about the oasis, they had been laughed at, spat at. Japheth had an ugly bruise on his cheek where an angrily thrown stone had hit him.

Even Noah and Matred's older daughters and their husbands had met them with scorn. They laughed at Japheth's earnest warning, and complained of being made to look like fools because of Noah's folly. Seerah had thrown a bowl of mash at them and screamed at Oholibamah to leave her alone. "And don't you come near my babies, you nephil woman."

Japheth had put his arm protectingly about his wife and taken her away.

Hoglah's husband had threatened to strangle them if they kept on spreading stories of flood and doom throughout the oasis. "It reflects on us," he said. "Don't you see how you're making *us* look with this idiocy? Can't you just keep quiet about Noah's delusions?"

Japheth and Oholibamah left the oasis, to go home by the desert. Oholibamah began weeping, strangely, quietly.

Japheth stopped, putting his arms around her. "My wife. What is it?"

Oholibamah struggled to stifle her silent tears. Said, "If it is all true, what El has told your father, if there is to be a great flood, then our baby will be born after—" She choked on her tears.

Japheth's face lit with delight. "Our—"

Oholibamah leaned her head against his strong shoulder. "Our baby, Japheth." Suddenly her tears turned to laughter. "Our baby!"

The result of the attempt to warn the people of the oasis was that now they gathered about the perimeter of Noah's land.

The desert wind rose hotly. Noah's eyes were fixed on the ark. He tried to ignore the catcalls and hoots of the mob.

Grimly, Matred heated wine to the boiling point. "I prefer to use it on manticores, but if they try to hurt my husband, I will make them sorry."

Ham slunk into the tent.

"What are you doing here?" his mother demanded.

"I'm tired of being laughed at."

Matred spoke fiercely. "You go right back out and help your father."

"He's insane."

"Whatever he is, it's your place to be with him. And with your wife. She's not too proud to work, and carrying your child, too." Matred smiled. There would be three babies coming. She brimmed with joy.

"Can't you stop him, Mother? He's a wild man, his eyes blazing, his beard whipped by the wind, his—Can't you speak to him."

"I have spoken," Matred said. "Go out to him. Now."

Reluctantly, Ham went out into the glaring sunlight, the burning wind. The muttering, jeering crowd was larger, as the people of the oasis gathered to stare.

Noah's hands were black with the pitch with which he was coating the ark.

A stone was thrown. It missed its mark and glanced harmlessly against the dark wood.

Sandy and Dennys left the ark and walked with deliberate steps toward the mob of little people. Dennys did not put down the plank he was sanding. Sandy still held the stone he used for a hammer. Neither boy threatened in any way; nevertheless, the people drew back slightly.

Sandy spoke in a commanding voice. "No stone throwing."

Dennys stood as tall as possible, looming over the small men in the foreground of the crowd. "Go home. Back to your tents. Now." His voice was a deep, man's voice.

There were advantages in being taken for giants. Slowly, the crowd dispersed.

Yalith sat on her favorite starlit rock, huddled over as though for warmth. She was not aware that Oholibamah had joined her until the other woman put her arm about Yalith's shoulders.

Tears sprang to Yalith's eyes. "Twin Sand and twin Den—" Her voice trailed off.

Oholibamah finished for her. "As soon as the ark is built, they will have to leave. To go to wherever it is they came from."

Yalith choked down a sob. "Twin Sand has asked me to go with them."

Oholibamah drew back in surprise. Said, "It is a solution I had not thought of."

"Then—what do you think?"

Oholibamah looked at the sky, intently, listening. Then she shook her head.

Yalith, too, looked heavenward. "The stars have never told me wrong."

Oholibamah spoke thoughtfully. "I do not know why it is not the right solution for you to go with our twins. I know only that I hear the stars, and I agree. There is something here that we do not understand. But do you hear the stars? They are telling you not to be afraid."

A soft wind brushed past their cheeks, murmuring, "Fear not. Fear not. The pattern will be perfected."

"I wish—" Yalith whispered. "I wish Grandfather Lamech was still alive. I wish that El had not told my father to build an ark, or that the rains were going to come."

"And—our twins?"

Tears slid down Yalith's cheeks. "I cannot wish that they had never come to us. Or that I had not become a woman."

Oholibamah held Yalith, rocking her like a child. "I, too, am afraid, little sister. I am carrying my Japheth's child, and I am afraid for the future. I am afraid of the terrible flood, and all the death and anguish it will bring. Sometimes I am even afraid of Noah, he seems so wild. But I trust Japheth. I trust the stars. I trust El. I trust that all this will be for good."

As the stars slid slowly toward the horizon, the sky paled, flushed with soft colors. A burst of joyous birdsong filled the air around them, and the baboons began to clap their hands.

* * *

The ark was nearly finished.

The twins talked at night in the tent, whispering in the dark. During the day they were never alone, and not everybody slept at the same time in the afternoon.

"We haven't seen any of the seraphim," Sandy said. "Not for days."

"Nor the nephilim," Dennys added.

"I'd just as soon not see the nephilim. Particularly Rofocale."

Dennys said, "Every once in a while I think I see one. Or at any rate, when I see an ant, or a worm, I get flickers of color behind my eyes, reds and oranges and blues and purples. But they don't materialize."

"I need to see one of the seraphim," Sandy said. "I need to see Adnarel. I thought maybe the scarab beetle would come with Higgaion, but I haven't seen him."

Dennys said thoughtfully, "I don't think it means that he's stayed at Grandfather Lamech's. The only time I've seen a seraph when there were a lot of people around was when Grandfather was buried, and they all came. Otherwise, it's been only when there are one or two people. And what with building the ark, and staying in Noah's tent, we're always with a gang. Maybe somehow we should slip away for a little while tomorrow and go out to the desert, just the two of us."

"Good thinking," Sandy said. "But why wait for tomorrow? We don't want to go in the heat of the day, and we'd be missed any other time. Noah and Matred are always checking on us. They're afraid one of us might be kidnapped again. So why not go now?"

"Right now?"

"Why not? We're both awake."

"Let's go."

"Don't wake Higgaion."

"Or Selah."

"Or—"

"Shh."

They slipped out quietly.

But not so quietly that Yalith did not hear them. She felt a vague disquiet. Rose from her sleeping skins and followed them.

"Kkk. They come."

"Hsss. This is what we've been waiting for."

"Szzz. At last."

The nephilim slid out of their animal hosts, raising wings turned dark by night, so that the stars were hidden.

* * *

The little mammoth woke with a jerk from a dream of being beaten by Tiglah's brother. Nudged Selah, who nudged Higgaion, who reached toward the twins, and felt only sleeping skins. Snorting in alarm, he padded across the tent toward Yalith's sleeping skins. She, too, was gone. He glanced toward Noah and Matred, both sleeping quietly.

Selah trumpeted, softly, so that only the mammoths heard, and pointed her trunk toward Higgaion's ear. The scarab beetle was there, a small, bright jewel against the grey earflap.

"What should we do?" Higgaion's eyes queried. Cocked his head as though listening. Then he gestured to the other two mammoths with his trunk, and they followed him as he hurried out of the tent and ran toward the desert.

The twins were nearly surrounded before they realized what was happening. The circle of nephilim was closing in on them, slowly, deliberately. The sharp odor of stone and cold filled their nostrils.

Sandy felt as though a hand was pressing hard on his chest. He shouted at Dennys, "Quick!" and flung himself out of the not-quite-closed circle.

Dennys followed, pushing through purple-dark wings that nearly stifled him. "Run!"

The twins' reflexes were swift, but the nephilim were swifter.

Again the circle started to form around them, and it was as though the breath was being squeezed out of them. Sandy ran, head down, like a battering ram, between Rofocale and Ugiel. Dennys rammed Eblis.

But the twins were only two, and the nephilim were many, and sure enough of their powers to proceed with deliberation and without haste. In their rush to get free of the circle, the twins had run in the opposite direction from the oasis. Now they were too far away to think of making a dash back to Noah's tenthold.

The circle of nephilim drew closer.

Yalith saw.

"Aariel!" she screamed. "Aariel!"

The golden lion bounded across the sand, past Yalith, until it was between two of the nephilim, keeping the circle from closing completely.

Came a strange pounding, and then Admael the camel galloped white as moonlight across the desert, inserting himself into the circle. A flutter of wings overhead became visible as a pelican, diving down, broke the circle again.

And three small grey bodies hurtled into the circle, blowing sand and water into the faces of the nephilim, who burst out of their formation in a rush of brilliant wings.

The lion, camel, pelican, with an upward leaping of light, became the radiant beauty of seraphim.

Sandy and Dennys ran to them, ran faster than they had ever run before. Alarid caught Sandy, and Admael held Dennys.

The nephilim sprang angrily into the sky, saw Yalith.

"Her!" Eblis cried. "I want her!"

But Aariel reached her before the nephil. Swift as Eblis was, the seraph was swifter. He enfolded Yalith in gilded wings.

The three mammoths, trumpeting joyfully, bounded around them.

Bronze flashed against Higgaion's ear, and then Adnarel stood before them. "Go!" he commanded the nephilim in a bugling voice.

"Kkk. You have no right to take them from us," Naamah said.

"And you have no right to them whatsoever." Adnarel was fierce. "Go."

From the four corners of the desert the other seraphim came, to stand with Adnarel, Alarid, Admael, and Aariel.

Then Ertrael, whose host was the rat, whined, "Tell us what is about to happen."

"Do you not know?" Alarid asked.

"I assume," Ugiel hissed, "that since Noah is building a boat, he must be planning to find some water."

"Your assumption is correct." Admael had his arm lightly across Dennys's shoulder.

"Kkk. And then what?" Naamah asked.

"Rain," Alarid said. "Much rain." The seraph raised his hand skyward, seeming to touch a bright star. A flash of lightning split the sky, bolted to earth with a great crash of thunder.

"Now," Alarid ordered the nephilim.

As the nephilim slipped, one by one, into their animal hosts, Sandy felt a drop of rain.

The seraphim gravely led the twins and Yalith deeper into the desert, not explaining where they were going.

Sandy started to ask, "Where—" then closed his mouth.

When they reached a single monolith of silvery rock, the seraphim encircled it. Aariel drew Yalith into the center of the circle.

Adnarel took Sandy by the hand, and Admael reached for Dennys, so that they were part of the circle around the monolith, Aariel, and Yalith, who looked at the seraph questioningly but without fear.

Alarid said, "Yalith, child, you did not know your Great-great-grandfather Enoch."

Mutely, she shook her head.

"But you know of him?" Aariel asked.

"I know that he did not die like ordinary men. He walked with El, and then, according to Grandfather Lamech, he was not. That is, he was not with the people of the oasis. He was with El."

With a rush of hope, Sandy remembered his conversation with Noah and Grandfather Lamech and their recounting of this strange happening.

Aariel smiled down on Yalith. "El has told us to bring you, and in the same way."

She shrank back. "I don't understand."

Dennys moved as though to go to her, but Higgaion nudged him to stay still.

Aariel said, "There is no need to understand, little one. I will take you, and it will be all right. Do not fear."

She looked very small, very young. She asked, timidly, "Will it hurt?"

"No, little one. I think you will find it a rapturous experience."

She looked up at him, trustingly.

"Enoch, your forebear, will explain everything you need to know."

Adnarel's fingers held Sandy back. "You will tell Noah and Matred?"

"I will tell them," Sandy said. "I think they will be very happy."

Dennys, who had not heard the extraordinary story of Enoch, looked confused but hopeful. If Aariel was taking Yalith somewhere, she would not be drowned after all. The seraphim were to be trusted. He was certain of that. Aariel would not take Yalith to the sun, or to the moon, or anywhere that was not possible for her with her human limitations.

Aariel said, "It is time."

Yalith remembered the words Aariel had said to her when she had gone out to the desert in the heat of the day. "Many waters cannot quench love," she whispered. "Neither can the floods drown it. Oh, twins, dear twins, I love you."

Sandy and Dennys spoke together, their voices cracking. "Yalith. Oh, Yalith. I love you."

"Will you go back now, to where you came from?"

The twins glanced at each other.

"We will try," Sandy said.

"We think the seraphim will help us," Dennys added.

"If we had been older—" Sandy started.

Dennys laughed. "If we had been older, it would have been very complicated, wouldn't it?"

Yalith, too, laughed. "Oh, I love you both! I love you both!"

Aariel urged, gently, "Come, Yalith."

"I can't say goodbye to my parents? To Japheth and Oholibamah?"

"It is best this way," Aariel said, "without goodbyes, as it was for your forebear Enoch."

Yalith nodded, then reached up to Sandy and kissed him on the lips. Then Dennys. Full, long kisses.

Aariel wrapped her in his creamy wings, glittering with gold at their tips. Then he held her only with his arms, lifted and spread the wings, beat with them softly, and then rose into the air, up, up.

They watched until all they saw was a speck of light in the sky, as though from a new star.

Sandy spoke to Noah, "Do you remember the night when you and Grandfather Lamech were talking and I was there?"

"I remember," Noah said.

"And Grandfather Lamech talked about dying."

"I remember."

"And about his Grandfather Enoch, who walked with El and then he was not, for El took him?"

"I remember that, too. Why?"

"Yalith is not."

"What are you saying?" Noah's eyes widened.

Matred put her hand to her mouth, focusing intently.

Sandy continued, "Aariel, the seraph who loves Yalith, said that she was to be taken up, like her forebear Enoch. And he held her and flew straight up into the sky. We watched."

Dennys nodded.

A light of great joy came into Noah's eyes.

Matred burst into tears.

"I felt a drop of rain," Sandy said.

Noah turned away. "The ark will be finished tomorrow."

That night, the twins sat outside the big tent. The three mammoths curled up together, near them. The rest of the family was within, asleep. Except for Yalith. Yalith's sleeping skins had been folded and put away.

"I didn't have a chance to talk with Adnarel about getting home," Sandy said.

"But Yalith is all right. At the moment, that's all that matters." A drop of rain fell on Dennys's nose.

"The rain is beginning." Sandy reached down to pet Higgaion, who was pressing against his feet. "What was it that she said about many waters?"

"Many waters cannot quench love. I think that's what she said."

Higgaion reached up with his trunk to touch Sandy's arm. "It's time for us to be going home, Higgy. I have to speak to Adnarel."

Higgaion reached with his trunk to touch his ear. The scarab beetle was not there.

Another drop of rain fell. It was a quiet, beginning rain, with occasional droplets. No thunder or lightning.

Sandy asked the sky, "Is God really doing this? Causing a flood to wipe everybody out?"

Dennys raised his face to the sky. The stars were not visible, hidden by thick veils of clouds, but it seemed that he could still hear their chiming, dim but reassuring. "Whenever there's an earthquake, or a terrible fire, or a typhoon, or whatever, everybody gets it. Good people get killed as well as bad."

Sandy was wriggling his toes against Higgaion's shaggy grey flank. "Well. Everybody dies. Sooner or later."

"Even stars die," Dennys added.

"I don't like entropy," Sandy said. "The universe winding down."

"I don't think it is winding down," Dennys contradicted. "I think it's still being birthed. Even the flood is part of the birthing."

"I don't understand." Sandy's voice was flat. "Everybody knows that entropy—"

"Everybody doesn't. And entropy is in question, anyhow. Remember, we had that in science last year. There's no such thing as an unbreakable scientific rule, because, sooner or later, they all seem to get broken. Or to change."

"Grandfather Lamech said that these are last days." The occasional slow drops of rain made Sandy on edge, and argumentative.

Another splash of rain touched Dennys's face, muting the stars. "There have been many times of last days," he said, "and they mark not only endings but beginnings."

"Is there a pattern to it all?" Sandy demanded. "Or is it all chaos and chance?"

"What do you think?" Dennys asked.

Selah had come to lie beside Higgaion, and Sandy reached to scratch her with the toes of his other foot. "Did we come here, to Yalith, to Noah, by chance?"

Dennys wiped his face with the palm of his hand. "No. I don't think so."

Sandy said, "The ark is finished. Yalith is with Grandfather Enoch. And perhaps with Grandfather Lamech. What was it Grandfather said? We know little about such things . . ."

There was a radiance in the air, and Adnarel stood before them.

"Oh, Adnarel." Sandy leapt up. "I need to talk to you about particle physics and quantum leaps."

Adnarel sat beside them, listening.

"So," Sandy concluded, "if you could go to our time and place and call the unicorns to you there, you could tesser us home."

"It does not sound impossible," Adnarel said. "It is consistent with our knowledge of energy and matter. I will talk with the other seraphim." As he turned to go, he said, "Do not stray far from the tent."

"The nephilim," Dennys agreed. Then, in a louder voice, "We will not stray. It is just that somehow we are not sleepy."

Adnarel paused. "Your love for Yalith, and hers for you, *is*, and therefore it always will be." And then he was gone.

They smelled Tiglah before they saw her. Quickly they sprang to their feet and ran to the tent flap, which was half open.

"Oh, don't go, please don't go!" Tiglah cried. "I'm alone, I promise you."

Tiglah's promises meant little. They stood warily by the tent flap, watching her as she approached. But there was nobody with her, neither father and brother, nor nephilim.

"It's starting to rain," she said. "We never have rain except in the spring. Did Noah really build this big boat because he thinks there's going to be more rain than we've ever seen before?"

Sandy nodded.

"Anah is my sister. Would there be room for me on the ark?"

"There is not room for Sandy and me," Dennys said.

"Then what are you going to do?"

"We're not sure." Sandy was cautious. "We hope to go home."

"I don't like this rain." Tiglah sniffled. "It's cold and wet."

"Rofocale will take care of you," Sandy said.

"Oh, he will, won't he! I'd better go find him. It's very nice to have known you."

"Thanks for nothing," Sandy said rudely.

"Ditto," Dennys echoed.

"You're not blaming *me* for my father and brother, are you?"

"Perhaps not for your father and brother," Sandy said, "but for doing whatever Rofocale tells you, yes."

"So go to him," Dennys urged, although he did not have much faith that the nephilim cared enough about any human being to be willing to help unless it was convenient.

"I still think it's nice to have known you," Tiglah said. "I wish I could have known you better. I mean, really *known* you."

"Sorry, Tiglah," Sandy said. "You are a great deal older and a great deal more experienced than we are."

"I could teach you—"

"No, Tiglah. The timing isn't right."

"Goodbye, then," she said.

"Goodbye," the twins echoed.

Japheth came to them. "I'm worried about you."

Sandy was still looking after Tiglah's retreating form. "Don't worry, Jay. We'll be all right."

"How?" Japheth demanded. "You know we can't take you on the ark."

"We know," Dennys agreed. He looked up at the clouds, which occasionally let a drop of rain fall. Tried to listen for the hidden stars.

"Can you get home?" Japheth asked. "To wherever you came from?" He, too, looked at the sky, shook his head as though baffled by silence.

"We're going to try," Sandy said. "Don't worry about us. You have enough to do, collecting all the animals and food and fodder and grain and everything."

Japheth nodded. "Perhaps—"

"Perhaps what?" Sandy asked.

Japheth rubbed his broad hand across his face, wiping away tears. "Oh, twins—" He rushed at them, and they flung their arms about him and the three of them rocked back and forth, holding one another.

Oholibamah went, just before dawn, to Mahlah's low white dwelling.

Mahlah was alone, nursing the baby. It was indeed a large baby, drinking greedily, and Mahlah looked pale and fragile, but she crooned over the child while she fed it.

She looked up at Oholibamah and smiled in welcome. "It's good to see you, Oholi. Come in."

Oholibamah stood, looking down at Mahlah and the child. "Is Ugiel good to you?"

"He is very good." There was deep love in Mahlah's shadowed eyes.

"You're happy with him? Truly happy, as I am with Japheth?"

"Truly happy. Though Ugiel is Ugiel and Japheth is Japheth."

"He doesn't ever hurt you?"

"Never."

"He takes care of you?"

"Very good care. And he loves our baby."

"Good," Oholibamah said. "That's all I wanted to know." And she left Mahlah and went back to the tent she shared with Japheth.

The seraphim were gathered together as dawn suffused the desert with a soft pearly light. The clouds were thickening, and in the trees the birds sang more softly than usual, and the baboons' chatter was muted.

"It does look possible, I think," Adnarel said.

Alarid nodded. "We are not bound to this place and time. Two of us should go to the twins' world and call them back."

Admael asked, "Does it really need to be unicorns? I would feel safer if I could carry them."

Adnarel's eyes widened for a moment, then nearly closed in thought. "I do not think they could take the transition from matter to energy and then back again to matter. Even we find it tiring."

"But what about the unicorns?" Adnachiel, sometimes a giraffe, asked. "What happens when they go out?"

Adnarel said, "They *are* only when they are here. Or when they are there. But not in between. It is not quite the same thing as a transfer of matter and energy."

Alarid nodded. "They have to be observed in order to be."

"Believed in," Adnachiel agreed.

"It is a long distance," Admael said, "both in time and space."

"It is a risk," Adnarel agreed, "but one I think we must take."

"Why are they here at all?" asked Achsah, with wings the same soft gray as his mouse fur.

"Do you think El sent them?" Admael suggested.

Adnarel spoke slowly. "I do not think El sent them. But neither did El prevent their coming."

"Are they part of the pattern?" Admael asked. "Is it right and proper for them to be here?"

Alarid looked up at the veiled sky. "Perhaps Aariel will have word when he returns from taking Yalith to the Presence. But I think, yes, that they are part of the pattern."

"The pattern is not set," Adnarel said. "It is fluid, and constantly changing."

"But it will be worked out in beauty in the end," Admael affirmed.

"Then you agree?" Adnarel asked. "We will try to help them to return to their own time and place in the way in which they have suggested?"

"We agree," affirmed the seraphim.

The air lightened slightly as the hidden sun lifted above the horizon. There was a faint spattering of applause from the baboons, who were confused by the clouds and the occasional drops of rain.

Despite the clouds which obscured the light of the last dim stars, the seraphims' ears were attuned to the song, although it was far away.

"Let us sing with them," Alarid suggested.

And the singing of the seraphim joined with the singing of the hidden stars, and the call of the invisible sun.

Sandy and Dennys slept fitfully. The rain had not really begun in earnest. But there was an occasional patter on the roof skins as a drop fell here, there. The three mammoths were curled into a ball at the foot of the twins' sleeping skins.

The morning songs of the oasis were softer than usual, but both boys roused from sleep and looked at each other. Nodded.

Quietly, they dressed in their clothes from home. Dennys was without the garments he had discarded after the garbage pit, but he pulled on his sweater and his lined jeans, feeling strange and constrained in clothes. The twins had become used to the freedom of being naked except for loincloths. Their winter clothes were hampering as well as hot.

They were careful not to disturb the sleeping mammoths. They looked across the tent to where Noah and Matred were still asleep. To the place which had been Yalith's and which was now empty.

Then they tiptoed out.

Adnarel was waiting for them. "It's best without goodbyes."

Dennys asked, "But you will say goodbye for us? And to Oholibamah and Japheth? And the others?"

"We will say goodbye," Adnarel said, and looked toward a clump of palms and palmettos. Admael and Alarid came out of the shadows and moved toward them, followed by Aariel, who had returned from his journey with Yalith.

"Now," Adnarel said, "we will call the unicorns."

"One more thing." Sandy held back. "You will take care of the mammoths?"

"We will take care of them. Unicorns!"

With a glimmer of silver, two unicorns solidified before them.

"Now," Adnarel said.

The two boys mounted the unicorns, sitting astride the silver backs, bathed in light from the horns.

"We leave you now," Adnarel said, "Admael and I. When we are in your time and place, we will call for the unicorns, and for you."

"You'll recognize it when you get there?" Sandy asked anxiously.

"You have given us very good parameters."

Alarid and Aariel each stood by one of the unicorns. When a drop of rain touched the light of their brilliant horns, it hissed slightly.

The unicorns crossed the oasis and moved onto the desert, Alarid and Aariel running along with them.

When they reached Aariel's great rock, the two seraphim stopped and looked at the unicorns, then at the twins.

"Are you ready?" Alarid asked.

"Ready," Dennys said.

Aariel slapped the two silver rumps, and the unicorns took off across white sand and rock. In his golden voice he cried, "Unicorns! Go home!"

Dennys felt a wave of sleep wash over him, as the rain and the unicorns quickened. Sandy, too, felt his mind softly closing. The rain was a curtain of silver.

"Alar—" Sandy murmured.

"Aar—" Dennys started.

The unicorns and the twins flickered like candles and went out.

Two unicorns in an old stone lab connected to a white clapboard farmhouse were a strange sight. So were two tall, bright-winged seraphim.

The twins looked around. Aside from the unicorns and the seraphim, everything was as usual. Wood still burned brightly in the stove. The smell of stew—of *boeuf bourguignon*—was fragrant over the Bunsen burner. The odd-looking computer was where it had been when they punched into it.

Adnarel was sitting in their mother's reading chair, his golden wings drooping behind it. Admael was peering into one of her complex microscopes, hunching his pale blue wings.

"Do you believe in unicorns?" Adnarel's azure eyes were smiling.

"How was the ride?" Admael, too, smiled, though both seraphim seemed very relieved.

The outside door banged.

Adnarel rose swiftly from the chair. Admael turned from the microscope. The twins stiffened.

Their mother's voice called, "Twins! Are you home?"

"Oh, oh," Sandy said. "We'd better get the unicorns out of here."

"They'll go as soon as they aren't believed in," Adnarel said.

Dennys exclaimed, "But Meg and Charles Wallace believe in unicorns!"

Admael asked, "And in seraphim?"

"And we're not supposed to be in the lab anyhow, with an experiment in progress." Sandy looked anxiously at Adnarel.

"Never fear," the seraph said. "You are all right?"

"Until Mother finds us in here."

Dennys added, "Looking the way we do, all sunburned."

"Compared with some of your other problems—" Admael started.

Their mother's voice called out again. "Twins! Where are you?"

"No farewells," Adnarel said. He glanced at Admael, then put both strong, long hands on Dennys's head. Admael followed suit with Sandy. Both boys felt, rather than a sense of pressure, a sense of the tops of their heads lifting, almost as the animal hosts lifted to become seraphim. And then each twin was staring at a normal winter twin, skins not darkened by the desert sun, hair not bleached almost white.

Sandy glanced briefly at Dennys's still bare feet, started to speak, then stopped as Adnarel held up his hand.

"Many waters—" The seraph reached out and clasped a unicorn horn. The light from the horn flooded back into the seraph's hand, through his body, his wings, until he was streaming with light. Admael, too, was filled with flowing light.

"Cannot quench—" he seemed to be saying. Light blazed fiercely, blinding the twins. Then the brilliance faded.

Unicorns and seraphim were gone.

Brown-haired, winter-skinned twins stared at each other.

Mrs. Murry opened the door to the lab. Behind her, Meg and Charles Wallace peered in, curiously.

"Sandy. Dennys. What are you doing here? Didn't you see the sign on the door?" She sounded extremely displeased.

"We didn't actually see it," Sandy started.

"We just came to get the Dutch cocoa," Sandy explained.

"Look," Meg said, "it's out here on the floor, by the kitchen door. Lucky it didn't spill."

"We were just going to make some," Sandy said. "Shall we make enough for you three?"

"Please," their mother said. "It's turning bitter cold. But, Sandy, Dennys, I beg you, don't go into the lab when you're asked not to. I hope you didn't touch anything you shouldn't have."

Sandy said, slowly, "It all depends. But I don't think we touched anything we shouldn't have, do you, Dennys?"

"Under the circumstances, no," Dennys said.

"Why are your feet bare, Den?" Charles Wallace asked.

"Good heavens!" Mrs. Murry exclaimed. "Put something on your feet this second, Dennys Murry, before you catch cold."

Meg opened the kitchen door, and there was the familiar odor of fresh bread, apples baking in the oven, and warmth, and brightness, and all the reassurance of home.

As they followed the others in, Sandy whispered to Dennys, "I'm very glad the kitchen is all here. But you know what—I'm homesick."

"We probably always will be, a little," Dennys agreed.

"Well." Sandy straightened up. "As soon as we have our birthdays, we can get our driver's licenses."

"And about time," Dennys said. "Now let's make that cocoa."